Memory's Fire

Memory's Fire

a novel by E. A. Gray

Summerwood Press
Santa Fe, New Mexico

For more information, contact Summerwood Press at:
2013 Calle Lejano, Santa Fe, NM 87501-8747

Library of Congress Control Number: 2020914870

ISBN 978-0-99653-833-6 (softcover : alk. paper)

ISBN 978-0-99653-834-3 (ebook)

summerwoodpress.com

To my beloved family, with special thanks to my son Eliot,
who was an excellent, essential partner on this journey

Our life goes by in changing.
—RAINER MARIA RILKE, *Duino Elegies* (#7)
(translated by GARY MIRANDA)

CONTENTS

I

"The Way Forward Is the Way Back"

The mind is a spacious country through which we are granted free passage by way of memory and desire. Past mingles with future, and present is hardly distinguishable from either, shifting with the angle of approach. We cross a long valley to greet one moment, run the river to visit another. Some we scrupulously avoid, though occasionally our inner eyes graze them and we recoil at the power they still hold. A few we return to daily, yearning to dwell on their plateaus. Others lie forgotten in pastures. We take from our domain what we want and need to gratify ourselves without diminishing it; the more we excavate from the landscape of memory, the deeper its cache.

The dead, too, have memories, though they are no longer plagued by the same desires we are. They remember all the metamorphoses of mortality so that, over time, the boundaries of their country widen. Reconciled to being dead in one form, they find solace in another. The only yen that trails the dead from their time among us is to be remembered. To that end they compel us to write histories, raise statues, mark graves, tell stories, compose epic poems, dream, conjure signs, which though they be apocryphal, still serve to memorialize them. Conversing in thought with the dead gives them a stronghold in the topography of our recall, and to that end they choose an evocative occasion to waylay us, as Hersch did me today.

I was on a ladder trimming the withered blooms from my climbing Tess of the d'Urbervilles rosebush when he appeared in the garden. His visits were rare, as he was increasingly dead and our score was settled.

Magnificent roses, my friend. They have the look of flowers accustomed to being looked at. Using T. S. Eliot as the hook.

The long skirts of shadow rippled afternoon's end. Mid-August, twelve years to the day since Hersch had died in the fire. Unlike that season, this one the adamant green of a wet summer. Alpine sun hot, air cool. Wind soughing duskily in the ponderosas, sibilancing the cottonwoods. I'd been drawn to work outdoors by the radiance of this Colorado morning and had gone on till, weary now, I was ready to finish up and reminisce with Hersch.

In the flesh of his youth, he was a man of great integrity but little ambition. Managed a sandwich shop with a college degree in philosophy. Not that I had eclipsed him, waiting tables at El Oro a few blocks from where we'd gone to elementary school in the small town of Vista Grande, New Mexico. Even beyond adolescence, we'd cultivated sloth, assuming it as a right for those years of dally. Shared a house in college, traveled through Latin America, and returned to slide into the bountiful future awaiting us. There our vision diverged, he seeking security in sandwiches, I serving chile while covertly planning my spectacular entrance into the literary world. We remained friends, Hersch and I, at ease in our lives before the fire.

The presence of good fortune is much harder to discern than its absence, as I had yet to learn.

Hersch, divining my thoughts, pulled me further into reverie. Our salad days, Bug.

Standing on my toes to reach a spent bloom, I laughed. No one has called me that since high school.

Bug was a nickname I earned for a pathetic blunder in senior English. Up till then, I was Alex, beloved son of Papito and Mamia—Harvey and Michelle Mann—raised in the faith that I would amount to something great.

A hummingbird, seeking nectar from the withered bloom in my hand, fluttered close. I halted, let the iridescent creature explore the possibilities I offered. To discover myself through hummingbird eyes, which see forward, sideways, and backward equally, would whirl me off my axis, dependent as it is on a linear perception of where I am.

My earliest memory is awaking in the dark at the age of four with the realization that I existed, as an entity distinct from others: that I was me. It was a first conception of self without any sense of meaning in being.

I am here. The impulse to create a world, in, of, and for myself. Bred of the will to say, this is my day and that my night, this my land and that my water, these my people. To do whatever necessary to efface any doubt that here I am, in my own image, engendering a realm.

Bred in each of us who has the good fortune to be sated when we hunger, safe in slumber, sheltered, cherished.

When I grew beyond the suckle and looked about, I was pleased with all I beheld. My mother and father, los parentitos, endeavored to clear impediments from my path to greatness, and to align my expectations of myself with theirs. I walked anointed by their love into the fire.

A breeze grabbed the petals from a faded bloom and wafted them onto me.

Rosed! said Hersch. You still are.

I locked the shears and descended the ladder, hung for a moment on the bottom step, recollecting Rose, in whose honor this prolific climber was planted.

She had been my King Arthur, I her Lancelot, in our years-long jousts. An Edenic childhood kinship, both of us nakedly honest, lolloping knights in the garden, hand-holding partners on school field trips. Divided in our tweens when I chose the low road of intellectual atrophy, Rose the high one of academic excellence. Between us the earth rifted, our intimacy entombed in a crevasse of her scorn. We stopped speaking outside of class, and any reasonable heart would have boxed its memories, stored them with juvenile relics in the spare closet. Mine, however, nurtured the wound, allowed it to ripen into love. All the better for being unrequited, which freed me to suffer and thereby heighten our eventual bliss.

I added the spent blooms to my bag of cuttings and walked them around back of the house to shake them onto the compost pile. It needed pitchforking, tomorrow. First thing. Then I'd get back to my writing.

By sophomore year of high school, I had decided that I would become a writer. A brilliant one. It was an untested ambition, since I wrote no more than mediocre papers for English, but I assured myself I was gestating and would break free of this seeming indifference when the time came for my novel to be born. How I would achieve such a feat was not part of my inner narrative, wherein my writings emerged miraculously from the stable of a humble mind to inspire a vision of unsurpassed grandeur.

In this clandestine assurance…Hersch prompted me.

In this clandestine assurance I entered Justine Lake's senior English class. She, a hot young teacher new to the school, whom I vowed to impress with my slacker wiles. How to appear to have read a book I hadn't. The first time it succeeded. And the second time it failed utterly.

I folded up the ladder, pushed it into the shed, stuck my gloves in a back pocket.

Go on.

But you know all this. You were there.

It's my deathday, Bug. I came to hear stories. We charnel legions are fantastic listeners. Stories of the living are the sustenance of the dead since we cannot tell you our own. Cake and icing. I want to hear them all.

The moon had waxed and waned thrice since I had last spoken with Hersch. Nor did I expect him to visit soon again. He, ageless and unbound, had vast interstellar spheres to traverse.

The stories that most attracted him were of our charmed teen years when we squandered time and counted it not lost but won. Tales I'd told him before, in words that had become ritual. I walked into the kitchen for a beer, came back out, tossed my cap on a post, and dropped heavily into a chair.

He chuckled. The unbearable weight of being.

Still a joker, Hersch in the afterlife.

I took a long swig of beer. The unbeatable draught of brew.

Then I was sorry for the comeback, imagining how much he would have enjoyed a cool one.

By senior year I had perfected several tricks for fake-reading a book. I'd check the Cliff or Spark or whatever Notes online first, of course—for plot summary, maybe some character descriptions. Then read the back cover, memorize the author's name, and get the copyright date down—

Masterful, the way you'd point out, "Well, since it was written in 1946, things were really different."

Next, I'd loosen up the spine by bending the book open; get it creased. Then I'd go through the pages, underline random sentences, dog-ear some corners, and write a bunch of numbers on the inside front cover. Of course I'd never put my name on the book so none of that stuff could be traced to me. The most important part: I'd pick out a couple of pages and actually read them. Find a beefy sentence or two and star those and add a question mark in the margin. During discussion, I'd say, "I was kind of wondering what everyone thinks about this part." Read it aloud. Add, "I mean, what's [the author] getting at?"

Teachers were knocked out by your intense reading skills, Bug; we used to say that it was the kind of thing they'd tell their friends about.

My best success with this trick happened at the beginning of senior year, when, like I said, I was trying to impress Justine. She'd assigned us Solzhenitsyn's *One Day in the Life of Ivan Denisovich*, which is such a small book I figured I could barrel through it the night before it was due and be really crisp on the details. I would have done it if you hadn't come over to play *Bloodgutters 5* and things got fierce and suddenly it was 3:00 a.m. and I was screwed. So I went with the usual strategy and just happened to pick the part where Ivan's building this wall—crucial part, it turns out. Did my thing and then added—and this was truly inspired, especially on two hours of sleep— "I mean, is this *a metaphorical* wall?" Stunned the whole class and Justine, too.

Here's the other awesome thing that happened and it's another trick that you'll recall I perfected: Sitting next to the smartest girl, which made me look, act, and sound smarter. Being wasted and ignorant coming into class, I'd grabbed a seat next to Rose.

Double score, Rose being brilliant and you in love with her.

Exactly. She was superior in every way, the kind of girl who knew what a metaphor is, and I was sure she'd be all over that question, which she was. "In one sense, yes, it is, I think," she said, giving me her extremely-smart-girl-who-deems-you-worthy-for-once look. "It's the wall inside himself, the wall of discipline he's erected to keep himself alive and sane." To which I added, "Yeah, that's what I got, too."

I was doing all right till that big-mouth nerd Vincent, who also read books and liked metaphors, said, "What about when he gives the biscuit to Alyosha? A walled-in man wouldn't do that." I shook my head, baffled (truly), and turned to Rose. Like, I mean, it was her thing. She frowned, and in her ice-cube voice shot back at Vince, "I think he wants something from Alyosha." I couldn't add, "Yeah, right," because then it would have been on me to say what he wanted, so I just raised my eyebrows and wrote "What?" in the margin. Then Vincent started arguing with Rose and I was off the hook. Justine smiled at me: King of the Hill for a day.

Hersch undulated, his waves of pleasure breaking over me. Even long gone he was child-like, osmosing his favorite tales told exactly as they should be. And dead, he didn't need to hear them but once to know the correct rendering.

A triumph, dude! We celebrated with a HubbaBurger, double meat, cheese, green chile, and fries. But the second time, when you crashed, when you got the name Bug: tell me that one.

Four months later, I decided to try the metaphorical thing again. Justine had assigned Kafka's *The Metamorphosis*, and I'd gotten through the first two pages when you and Joey talked me into checking out the scene at Bayhouse.

Sock Monsters were playing; it was kind of a random event and really amazing, not to be missed.

Right, but naturally we got home way late, so all I could do was skim the first two pages again and the last couple (that's another trick I'd learned). Being the fool I was back then,

I thought there wasn't much to the Kafka story: guy turns into a gigantic bug and dies. Creepy.

So I strolled into class early and scanned for Rose, who was always early: the smart kids get there first. Things were heating up, and at what seemed like the perfect moment, an awkward pause after two kids had said something pretty inane, I threw in, "What if this is a *metaphorical* bug?" I was feeling so damn confident I think I even smiled, waiting for the stun to kick in. Rose whipped an exasperated stare at me, Vince giggled, and Justine shook her head. "Of course it is," she said real slow with what sounded like pity. "But what's the metaphor?"

You were shredded, man, metaphorically trashed worse than ever.

I considered lying down on the floor, rolling onto my back, and waving my arms and legs in the air like bug boy did in the story, but before I could clown my way out of this disaster, George—Spanky—piped up. Spanky, you remember, was one of those kids who almost never talked and it was pretty much a good thing because he almost never had anything to add. Which was true this time, too. "Well, I think he really does turn into a bug. Like, why would he say he does and write all that wack stuff about his body if he wasn't a real bug?" The thing that didn't usually happen after a Spanky comment is that a bunch of kids backed him up: he got a whole lot of yeah right's and that what I think's and how do you know he doesn't's. The class actually got into a debate about it.

"The title threw me at first, see, *Metamorphosis*. I thought it was going to be about a caterpillar turning into a butterfly, like we learned in bio," Roanna (aka Blip) whined.

Blip was kind of a distance-learner that semester, showing up no more than a couple of times a week.

Rose came right back at her. "We learned about caterpillars in fourth grade. Metamorphosis is just another word for change or transformation."

But Blip wouldn't quit. "And then it started out with all those feeble legs squiggling around, so I was pretty sure I was right except no cocoon got spun and he died. I guess some of them don't make it."

"When his sister stretches her arms out at the end, the gesture could be interpreted as her being the butterfly. Her freedom and beauty emerging from the cocoon of his suffering." That was Vincent, of course, not Blip.

"Maybe Greg is a shapeshifter alien, like Gorkus in *Revenge of the Drunes*," Sander (aka Beandog) suggested. The room buzzed. Thinking about Gorkus got his crew a whole lot more excited than discussing Kafka.

During this smackdown Justine looked like she was losing it. Then, when Beandog made his final insane comment, she started to laugh and I mean really laugh, like turning-red and tears-in-her-eyes laugh.

"Please!" she gasped. "Please don't tell me I have to convince you that Gregor isn't a cockroach. I can't believe you're serious. This is not a science fiction story."

Rose and Vince rode in from the west, providing hard, textual evidence to defend her, but the rest of the class wasn't buying it. Spanky, crazed with power, read a couple of sentences about Gregor crawling around on the ceiling. "Like, a regular person can't do that, but bugs, they have this sticky stuff on their feet so they can." He considered the case closed. It was wild. Justine fought like a champ with her posse at her side, but she was losing ground.

That's when I took a stand, and Hersch, I don't like to boast but you have to agree I was good, good like I've never been before. "Look," I said, "it doesn't matter whether he's really a bug or not. The thing is he feels like a bug and that's all that counts."

Justine gave me a smile that fired my insides. "Thank you," she said. "That's exactly right."

I stayed after class to talk to her—mostly to keep that beam turned on me. It was about halfway in my mind to tell her I was sorry about being such a loser and starting this ruckus, but she was so happy with me I couldn't. All I said was that I wanted to wake up some morning and find out I'd been changed from a bug into a human being. A real one.

"So you do know what a metaphor is!" She was way too excited. It was the ultimate English teacher triumph; her eyes were glowing.

"Oh, yeah," I told her.

Felt like a big man walking out of there until she called after me, "I hope you read *The Metamorphosis* someday—it's well worth your time."

Justine's parting shot had Hersch rocking the trees. You were battered and fried, mein Bug.

Hersch never faked it, claimed that would violate his integrity. Asked a question, he would tell the teacher straight out, I didn't do the reading. He and I debated the relative merits of our strategies without once considering the alternative: doing the work assigned.

Rose had that covered, Bug.

He shimmered the evening grass. Do you remember when Justine asked us, after we read the *Oedipus* plays, whether we would choose a beautiful life and a terrible death or a terrible life and a beautiful death? If those were our only options.

Everyone but Rose picked the beautiful life.

What would you say now?

His voice wind on the river.

I'd say Rose nailed it. Exiting in grief and terror strips the hide off the myth of justice.

We hovered there, over the recall of his death. And others that widowed my heart.

The absence of good fortune is much easier to discern than its presence, as I continue to learn.

Rose, at the end of high school, her gift to you? His voice wind in the pines.

Hersch, I'm tired, son. The present moment—which, I know contains time past—calls me to rest.

The way forward is the way back.

And persuasion is the art of unsheathing your opponent's will imperceptibly. The dead have an exquisite grasp on its hilt, summoning assent bloodlessly. Hersch had slit open the book to the page of Rose and me on the last day of school, beyond which lay Joaquin, the fire, Papito, Mamia, Lori, and Tiger, currently stretched across my thighs, purring. Their stories unreeled into the tall summer night.

For seniors, the last day of school is a seven-hour high…five, I began.

Oh, don't start there!

Rose!

Thrilled to find myself in your thoughts, Alex, among the dead and living.

Hersch conjured you.

And then left, as he is wont to do.

Granting us time alone, at school's end.

In that end lay a beginning.

My mind wandered off through the darkest grimpen of my realm. The agonizing truth was that the beginning of my metamorphosis converged with the end of Hersch. I owed my life to him as he owed his death to me. Yet whether this causal chain was essential or incidental I could not determine, fire and folly entwined as they were at the chaotic intersect of transformation. Nor could I see what I would glean from retracing my journey.

Because you start at a different point each time 'round, your understanding changes. Adds, stratum by stratum, to its depth, as your original memory is overlaid with all those since. You discern anew its place in the whole.

Which will, of course, change at the next juncture.

Our life goes by in changing, Alex.

Where would you like to begin?

At the swings, on the evening of our last day of high school.

Physics has shown that it is possible to be in two places at once, which psyche has always known. I am both present and absent from myself: here in the garden as the moon rises, and there in Vista Grande on the children's swings with Rose. Conscious of both, which, seen through the dual lens of the memory and the rememberer, inverts the image to bring what is distant to the fore, where the immediate resides.

2

"By Any Other Name"

Rose was on our favorite swing—the one that went the highest—when I arrived. A carpet bag of revelations waited at her feet.

I marveled anew at her verve, remembering us at eighteen remembering our childhood.

Rosie and I had had some exceptional over-the-moon contests in grade school, flying beyond Dragon craters to the peaks of Nautilus. Pumped our swings across the threshold of a universe private to us, unbounded but intimate, far from the Hunter Elementary schoolyard. We spoke beyond ourselves, words conceived as they arose, as if the casing of our skulls had flown apart on this galactic voyage, laying bare the inmost thrust of ancestral cognition.

Some nights even now I lulled myself to sleep in the hypnotic rhythm of the swings, Rosie's voice susurrating as she floated past.

A wrench like homesickness constricted my chest. The empowerment of our early years, flying through stars, slaying dragons, and ruling Camelot. A kingdom lost. That evening she summoned me to the swings, I had a wisp of hope that she was seeking to reclaim it.

The recollection dredged a smile at my teenish lunacy.

Of course she was not. Rose was seeking a realm untrammeled in a life unimagined. Having always lived by her mother's measure, Katherine's certainty that she had created Rose in her own image—

I was seeking the story of Rose that was my own, Alex. I was lonely for myself.

Unfathomable now, she went on, that on that last day of high school, I could not envision myself as anyone but the daughter of Katherine Susannah Stewart Hampton, the iron-willed aristocrat with an MD in psychiatry who surrendered her heritage for the love of Lou Best, my handsome father from tough-scrabble poverty who had swept her onto his horse during the fiesta parade.

A legendary tale in Vista Grande.

And whom she later blamed for luring her off-course, drove him cruelly out of the house he'd built and the life he'd made for us. A hand-crafted adobe, built with love and spectacular views. But no match for the stately Victorian manse in Connecticut and a summer place on Martha's Vineyard that my mother had left behind.

Not too far behind, Rose: you and she summered with her family on the island.

We were heading for the Vineyard right after graduation. You remember that's why I asked you to meet me at the swings: to say goodbye to my oldest friend, whom I had shunned the past several years. And in so doing, bid farewell to my childhood, which you defined.

The end of childhood. Words whose recall spiraled me deep into nostalgia. I am back in the garden amid lupine and honeysuckle, trumpet and silver vines, lavender, hyssop, and sage. Summer flowing riverine in my blood, the goldenblue of morning etched grand. Rose and I too fully absorbed to sense its passage, or our own, through reams of play, like the garden blossoming unawares, each whorl widening the sphere. Till the garden was submerged in adolescent reticence.

A sore beauty these memories roused even yet in my heart, the irredeemable pleasure of having lived them only once. In my memory it is always summer, the garden brimming. Rose, my Rose, how profoundly thinking of you carries me back and yet beyond where I have ever been.

Your soul, my friend, bordered mine at its inception, and you know it thus as none other can. Which is why I, that evening, entrusted you with my future, in sacred territory we'd shared, confident you would understand.

And you were on a mission.

More than one.

Rose bends down to pull a suede journal from the side pocket of her carpet bag.

"A sweet melancholy has gripped me these final days of senior year, Bug. Listen: 'Sometimes, when the afternoon sun pools in the classroom windows at an oblique angle and illumines our faces, I look around, overwhelmed with a profound affection for my schoolmates. What an amazing group of people, it strikes me. Joey, Lauren, Rene, Alex, Hersch, Vincent, the others. I've known them since I was four; we've been companions on the interminable road from childhood.

'And under the ruthless adolescent posturing, they are still my friends. No one else will remember me as they do. I wonder what will become of us, what our lives will be like. I wonder whether I'll ever be happy. I'm going to miss them. We'll never all be together again. Which of us is destined to die young? Which of us will live the longest? Which will be—then Beandog said something intensely dumb, the light changed, and that pleasant sensation of camaraderie vanished.'"

She looks up, eyes on mine.

"'But it left me with an idea for a valedictory address. In speaking about the particular journey we've shared, I decided to make this speech about them: really be their valedictorian. Gather their memories and through them tell the tale we've all written together, by being here in this place and time in history, on an odd little planet at the edge of a fiery spiral of stars.'

"What do you think?"

"Powerful. Eerie. I like the 'Odd little planet at the edge of a fiery spiral of stars.'"

"Thank you. But the class advisor insists I close with something more upbeat."

"Fool. Don't worry, though: you'll give a brilliant speech."

"The ending is crucial. It's all that most people will hear and remember. So now I'm inclining toward an excerpt from that poem Joaquin Stranger wrote for his chapbook, *The*

Fury and The Mire of Human Veins." She closes her eyes reverently and intones, "'Fill my morning bowl with lapis and emerald, float a few pearls against the amber and rose tailings spilled by the sun. Let me drink the early light of a summer's day and you will see how quickly my cells fly apart as I rapturous rise and fall under the seductive spell of the world.' That part of the poem should be upbeat enough, and it's so moving, isn't it?"

"Yes, it's great."

Rose had been infatuated with Joaquin.

Not him: his poetry.

"I'm seriously thinking about majoring in English," though I have not been till then. Pressing toward her conspiratorially. "Learn to spot a metaphor crouching in the bushes at midnight."

"Wonderful, Bug," though she clearly doesn't think so, frowning as she pulls away. "Be sure you don't bushwhack me while you're rousting it out."

"You don't need to sneak up on metaphors; they eat right out of your hand."

Not light-hearted this eve, my Rosie. When she speaks again, in the flat silence after my joke, her voice is rain and fire locked in passionate discord.

"It's been hard for me, growing up in a divided family and not being allowed to suffer. I am wealthy and intelligent—"

And beautiful.

"—with a well-laid path to follow. How could I possibly be unhappy, given all that? True, in one way, but the right to be miserable belongs to each of us, however unequal our circumstances. Class distinctions tore my life apart so I am at home nowhere. My mother's culture has no chamber in its heart for poverty. Nor has my father's any respect for wealth. The rich are assumed to be arrogant, ruthless monsters, self-serving and spoiled rotten. The poor, lazy parasites, lacking intellect and drive. And here I am, wrenched between the two—which is not the same as being in the middle, a class they say has all but disappeared. I'm more comfortable in the world of hicks but destined for the ivory halls."

"Some worthy knight might sweep in and rescue you." Hoping to remind her I'd once been her vassal Lancelot.

"There's no rescue for any of us at this late hour."

She flashes me a look implying I should know that.

"Every summer on the Vineyard, my joy in being there is tinged with a poignant knowledge that all too soon, when the polar ice cap has melted, it will be under water, along with most of the East Coast. We are living an end story, Bug, the final chapter of human history. Perhaps the last generation to grow up in this climate and geography, to experience these landscapes. I cherish my time among them, aware that I am both blessed and doomed."

"We still have some good years left before the end." Holding to my theme, as she does to hers.

"The view through that wide-angle lens makes whatever I do between now and then seem utterly meaningless, but at the same time infuses me with panic and determination to make this life my own rather than simply acquiescing to my mother's dream of who I am destined to be."

A sneer marring the exquisite landscape of Rose's face, "She hand-delivered my Harvard application to the head of admissions, gazing at him with the same look her father had in his turn: 'The building in which you are housed,' says the look, 'bears my family's name.' For centuries the Hamptons have been among those aristocratic clans who expect their children's applications to be merely an announcement of the next generation's arrival in the fall. It's a dreary rite that undermines any sense of accomplishment, which doesn't matter anyway since you have the clan name and money."

The light on the playground casts a golden spell that is about as far from Rosie's gloom as it can be. Dusky shadows stretch across the sand and run long into the mountains beyond us. A part of me wants to nudge Rose and suggest she take a look around at the present moment, which is grander than anyone could wish.

She sighs, scuffing the gravel.

"There's an old 70s movie *Mary, Queen of Scots*. The scene I love is when Vanessa Redgrave as Mary is riding toward England, thinking she'll be crowned when actually she's going to be beheaded. A strip of land separates Scotland from England, and as soon as Mary crosses into it, she spurs her horse to a gallop. For this short stretch, between kingdoms, she is completely free—free! That's how I've felt during the last weeks of senior year: in the border zone between two demanding lives, and for this brief span I can take chances and not worry about the consequences. Until I set foot on the hallowed grounds of Harvard, I am free. To be me. From being me."

The evening breeze stills. It recognizes, as do I, a moment of drama foreshadowing the denouement.

"Bug, do you remember when you were Lancelot, and I trusted you unconditionally?"

I smile, bowing my head, pleased that she does, too. "Yes, my liege, I do."

She King Arthur, I the Black Knight Lancelot in capes, boots, masks, rubber swords we got for trick-or-treating in first grade and wore till they looked like they actually dated from the Middle Ages.

"I'm going to trust you unconditionally once again."

We rein in our swings.

"I will not. Enter Harvard. I'm taking a gap year. Going to Scotland. But I haven't told Katherine."

A bold move, considering how steadfastly Rose has always played the game.

"She can't stop you."

"She'll try. I've already fallen behind in her view because I didn't finish high school early. I should be halfway through Harvard by now."

"My parents were hoping I might get in somewhere besides UNM."

Rose grimaces. "The checkmate on my board is the plethora of Katherine's relatives in Edinburgh and further north, in the Highlands. I'm going to learn more about my maternal lineage, embed myself with the Stewarts. Who are, as you can imagine, enthusiastic about my interest in their clan. How can she object to that?"

"She won't be in love with you taking a gap year, but she'll get over it."

"I'm going to do what I want for a change."

She is getting worked up, Rose is, and her toe kicks the carpet bag, which meows and plops on its side. Sauntering out, with an indignant yawn, the stripy cat surveys the playground. Rosie scoops it into her arms quickly and covers it with kisses I would appreciate much more than it does.

"I see you bagged a cat."

"This is the first pet that's really been mine, Alex, and the only being I love besides my father. I chose this kitten last fall and raised him entirely by myself. Isn't he beautiful? Like a miniature tiger. Which is why I named him William Blake."

"Of course."

"Oh, come on: 'Tyger, tyger, burning bright/ In the forests of the night.'"

My mind flips the pages of English textbooks, seeking Blake.

"Mystical British poet."

"Right."

William Blake shifts into a fifth-gear purr. His forelegs are on Rosie's shoulders, and he rubs his head on her cheek. It looks like a very affectionate hug.

"I was waiting till the end to introduce you to William Blake. You want to hold him? He's really sweet."

I've never been a feline aficionado, but Mr. Blake settles right down on my lap, licking my hand vigorously, which I try not to take as a comment on my hygiene. Rosie blows her cheeks out for a long exhale and grips the swing chains tight.

"It's more than a gap year. I'm not going to Harvard. Ever. I have to get away from Katherine, or I'll die. I am never coming home. And that's what you can tell no one."

Fierce pronouncements from my liege, but she inclines toward decrees. Not that I blame her for wanting to escape her mother, who has maintained a stranglehold on Rose. But what about me, her true and devoted knight?

"A courageous strike, Your Majesty, but when will I see you again?"

"When I have recreated myself in my own image and grown into someone I'm proud to be. A score of years at the least."

I didn't believe you, Rose. It was a bleak thought to be parting not only with my childhood but my closest companion from it. Like being thrown out of the house into the cold streets of anonymity. Of course it happens that most of us disconnect from friends of our youth when we head off into the world, but not intentionally, as Rose was doing from me. I shrank at the image of our meeting again in a score of years, exchanging awkward greetings at our twentieth high school reunion while we strained to recapture the ease of intimacy we shared this evening.

Her eyes are on mine while mine try to find someplace else to look. The cat seems a good option. I ogle his stripes, tickle his ears, and—

"Are you taking William Blake with you to Scotland?"

"No. I'm not. I can't." Tears in the vestibule.

"Well, he'll miss you, that's for sure. But the housekeeper will take great care of him."

"A churlish woman whom Katherine has taught to scorn me? She'll feed him to the coyotes."

"Lou will take him, good old Lou."

"He's allergic. He and his sisters are dog people."

"What are you going to do with him?" (I have to ask, though at this point I've deciphered whose number has come up.)

"All my friends are going to college."

"Including me."

"But you're going to be renting a house, aren't you? I overheard Joey talking about it with Hersch. The three musketeers and a cat."

I've been demoted from knight to musketeer.

"You've run through every other possible choice, right?"

"Look at how contented he is, lying there in your lap. William Blake is a super-cat, Alex. He's smart, incredibly loyal, affectionate but not needy; he's adaptable and good. He rides in cars. He does his business outside whenever possible. He's like a cross between a cat and a dog. Once he bonds with you, which I know he will, you won't have to worry about him running off. He's an amazing companion, and giving him away is the hardest thing I've ever had to do."

The iridescent blue of twilight chiaroscuroes the mountains. This is a time of day I relish, the hour of suspension between the inhale of morning and the exhale of night, when the world's breath lies at its core. We swing toe to heel, barely roughing the sand.

"You're going to love him, Bug. If he were a lesser cat, I wouldn't care so much about choosing the right guardian for him."

The Blakemeister's tail swats a mosquito off my arm. Not a bad trick. Yawns as if to say, That's nothing. You should see what else I can do.

"So let's connect the dots, Rosie Best: You come up with this scheme to vanish forever into the wilds of Scotland, and the only thing holding you back is Mr. Blake, and once you're down to me as the last sucker left to take him, you invite me to the swings to remind me that I'm your oldest-friend-darkest-secret-keeper-knight who's too close to say no. Crafty. But I've grown wiser since the days we were jousting with rubber swords. How much of this plan of yours is true?"

A pause, the three of us in dusk-lit tableau unswinging.

She Mona Lisa's me. "All of it," her enigmatic smile fueling my doubts.

WB shoves his head against my palm, implying Hey, Lance, how about a couple of strokes? I'm en route to oblige him when Rose intercepts my hand in mid-air.

"Forget William Blake if you don't want him even though he is a truly outstanding cat and it would make me so happy to know he's with you. I can put him up for adoption."

Indubitably a ruse, Sherlock, but this is the first time she's held my hand since we were seven. Immediately I cave.

"All right, all right, I'll take Mr. Blake. Hope our landlord accepts pets." More likely, I'll talk los parentitos into keeping him. They love Rosie. My father, strutting his minimal Shakespeare, likes to call her "By Any Other Name."

"Thank you, Alex. You really are my oldest friend, oh faithful and virtuous knight. If I come back before he dies, I will take William Blake off your hands, if you want me to, which you won't."

And here's the charge, I vow, for services rendered. When she wants her kitty back, she will have to take the whole package: Blake plus Bug, or nothing.

Rose in the arbor of the present, stirred. I knew you were in love with me, Alex, and used that to my advantage. But I had to find William Blake an excellent home.

A rush of warmth tingled my body. He was a gift of inestimable value, Rose. Tiger has saved my life at least once and in many ways.

My thoughts encircled that evening as I breathed in this one. So love-struck I had been.

The first person to whom we give ourselves unreservedly we call true love. True meaning assured in the belief that this love fulfills the dream of there being one right person destined for each of us. Implying thus that we will, as promised, live happily ever after. I knew absolutely that Rose and I were each other's halves, bound for a day when we fitted ourselves together. Naively unaware that as there are different means of being joined, we already were then.

"Whatever happens to me, Bug, doesn't matter now that I have entrusted William Blake to your care."

The misery in her voice seems out of place given that we're talking about a cat. It's time to try again to brighten the lilt of this conversation.

I smile, then drop my voice to a Godfather low. "Remember that when you go off on your great escape, I will be waiting for word of your whereabouts. And," I add, "from here on out, in secret missives address me as X. Not Bug, not Alex. Just X."

She blinks, grappling with the eccentricity of my request.

"It's the universal symbol, R. B., versatile, with a long and noble history. X marks the spot. It prefixes *excellent, exquisite, exotic, extreme, Excalibur*! Our very *existence* depends on this legendary letter. It's more than the end of my name; it's the beginning of my *exploration, excavation, examination* of the identity I intend to claim as my own." I arched an eyebrow at her. "In my end is my beginning."

That forces a laugh from Rosie. Then a terrible sigh. "Please give me your word that you'll remember me fondly no matter what I do, X."

Her hand drops onto William Blake's back, a cat's-breadth above my thigh.

The dire cadence of her voice rouses a new fear. What hasn't she told me? What is the real plan? And what if I don't see her ever again?

That drew a laugh from Rosie in the present. Oh, the absolutes of youth! Never and ever and always. The lesser hues of passion are distractions from the fervor of our intense reality.

Which seems absurd in retrospect but may be what we miss most in later years.

Remember me fondly no matter what, she said. "Fondly" is not how I'll remember Rose, I know, but ardently, devotedly, and yes, erotically in the shameless realm of my dreams, where she is mine.

William Blake jumps down from my lap and trots off to a bush. Rose shifts her hand to mine, clasps it a second time this evening, as her eyes brimming chide my selfish heart.

"X?"

"You have my word."

A promise sealed in a twined handclasp as darkness cloaks the schoolyard on our odd little planet at the edge of a fiery spiral of stars.

First love retains its idyllic fire regardless of the outcome. Thus chance meetings between erstwhile young lovers decades later can rekindle their desire, perhaps for who they were—and still are, longing to be recognized beneath the folds of age. Seventy-year-old widows and widowers may find themselves clambering back into the arms of their high school sweethearts, as though fated from the outset to end up together, not simply reclaiming the self-image they've secretly cherished.

But at eighteen in the schoolyard where we parted, the idea that we might not marry till we were ancient held no appeal. To have foreknown then that I would lose touch with Rose, and that years hence, when our paths crossed again, we would both be profoundly changed, would have devastated me. With William Blake, whom I privately renamed Tiger, under my arm and the memory of Rosie's hand still caressing mine, I waved goodbye assured of the future I'd planned for us. Sunday morning, Rose, valedictorian extraordinaire, closed her speech with Joaquin's poem. Listening through tears, the audience heard his words as hers and lauded her poetic gift. But Joaquin wouldn't have minded; by the time we graduated, high school was the receding terrain of a boy he once knew. The voice of his story rose in my mind.

3

"The Fury and The Mire"

You float the spoon between her lips, holding her eyes so she will swallow. Her yen for death is a powerful reflex that incensed, spews your attempts to thwart it. Why are you constantly stuffing her like a goose, she seethes. She is full, full, her stomach bursting with your damned soup. She thought you loved her, your old grandmother on her deathbed in this wretched place where her drunken son and his miserable wife would not even notice her passing till she out-stank them. Why won't you leave her alone, you, the only one who cares for her and knows how tired she is of this terrible suffering? If you someday grow old, Joaquin, which she hopes you never will, you'll see then what a mercy it is to be let go. When she has exhausted herself, you slide in another spoonful and she cries out, "Torturer!"

You do love her, and you are the only one: she is right on both counts. At most you are able to feed her a small bowl of soup daily, the rations of one in a prison camp, which is how she and you both regard this place that you are forced to call home. Where you are compelled to live by your mutual refusal to abandon each other. But there is no blame. She is so old, malnourished, her stomach swollen tight, her limbs skeletal, her frame shrunken to a girl's. She would fit inside the playhouse her once-husband built for you, into whose window she would poke her head, crouched in the dirt, to see if you were having fun. Sometimes she snuck cookies and chips out to you, treats you were not supposed to have between meals. But her visits were rare; even then she and your grandfather did not feel welcome in their son's domain.

They wondered what they'd done wrong to raise such an unhappy, liquor-addled man and what he'd done right to win such a forgiving wife and tender boy-child. It was her ranch he'd inherited, his wife Clarice's, almost like a dowry from her father, a widower consumed by his new love. Your grandmother had wanted you to come live with them in Pennsylvania, on their dairy farm, and your parents did let you spend a couple of summers there, but your mother needed her son, the one good thing that she could rescue from this disintegrating union on which she inexplicably maintained a tenacious hold. When Frank wasn't drinking, she'd flared at his reproachful parents, he was a terrific rancher, knew stock and crops and could coax the best prices out of the most stubborn buyers. Handy, he could fix anything, mechanical or motorized. And the music he pulled from the strings of that flea-market guitar, which seemed tuned to his vocal cords so that they sang together. Wooed and won her with his mellifluence. And the great Stranger wit that just the right amount of booze brought out before he waded in so deep he drowned loved ones in his troubles. Growing up with him that way, you were less inclined to find any saving graces in your father's self-sown hell.

You rode out the early years, raced through the middle ones, and ran from them in teen age. You entered realms where Frank would never find you and Clarice would not think to look. Dove into poetry, whose soulful barings and veiled labyrinths thronged your clefts and nourished there the life of significant soil. Magnetized by your charismatic outpour, which the girls revered, a group of studly wannabe's hung with you, the Outlaw Poets, you named them with casual irony, as if poets could be other. Gave readings and gave heartache, thrilled your teachers. Created an Outlaws chapbook titled "The Fury and The Mire of Human Veins," a line from WB, the Irish bard. Lived as far from home as the line of command allowed, sleeping overtime when they reeled you in. Harsh was the monotonous clamor from Frank and Clarice; nasty was your own. Broken only by an occasional unguarded intimacy you shared with your mother. These sudden illuminations stirred a latent familial vein in your heart that too soon would clot and immobilize you. Retreat was the only way forward, and so you both scurried back into your hideouts, salving the tender spots your surprise alliance had exposed.

You and your grandmother, in shared love, both wanted her to die, she ardently and you guiltily but justified by her suffering, which was not conventional pain but a loss of interest in life. She was no longer curious what the future held, for herself and for you; she didn't care to see how it all came out. Lost were her sense of place and belonging in the world. Awakening in the morning was a profound disappointment, for every night she prayed to die in her sleep. What sort of god would compel an old woman to go on and on doing nothing? You, though a mere boy, understood her feeling of uselessness, prayed with her. She was an existential crisis: Sisyphus, unwilling to push the rock back up, forced to refuse with vehemence continuously. No need to wait for the afterlife to dwell an eternity in hell, she complained to her grandson. Here I am already.

In unspoken covenant, you labored with her to find a gentle way for her to die. She had a stash of pain killers, strong ones from when she'd broken her leg decades before you were born, and she thought about taking the whole lot of them, which she hadn't needed then because her great reserves of energy made for a quick comeback. The pills had expired so long ago that you feared they wouldn't work right, could just leave her a mental cripple still breathing, or worse, and persuaded her not to try. She wasn't really set on the idea herself, didn't trust suicide, at which an aunt of hers had failed. Unless it was something natural, like starving to death. Again you dissented, for the sake of your heart and humanity.

To die well is an art as much as living well, the one we cultivate. Yet there prevails a sense of helplessness in the dying realm, which, along with an abiding terror, insists that the only good death is the one staved off. Thus all our efforts are geared toward prevention, none toward the grace of conduct and spirit that would elevate dying to art. Grief drives the sense of intrusion, injustice, punishment, that the end has come in the middle of things. We do not forgive death but invent stories to assign blame for mortality to our primogenitors' failings.

You read to her as she once had to you, whetting your hunger for a wider life. Romanced your questing mind with tales and epic poems of adventure, valor and honor, high-grounded fealty. *Ivanhoe, The Three Musketeers, Les Miserables, Huck Finn, The Once and Future King,* "The Death of Arthur," *The Iliad* and *Odyssey.* Greek mythology was a particular favorite of hers, and you came to know the gods as companions of brook and meadow. Summers with her you voyaged through this expansive terrain where danger heralded a call to action, escapades, glory. Wrested your character from stories, grew secretly under her tutelage to a boy of righteous moral sturdiness who dreamed of a chance to be tested by a noble cause, prove himself a fearless warrior for good. In time learned to endure the ignominy of a narrow life you barely tolerated. Buried your appetite for redemption in poetry, from whose nurture you drew the incessant ache of hope, aggravated and quelled by applying to college, an Eden whose apples were for eating. An Eden on which she, who had first awakened you to the immortal garden, had now closed the gate, her love of learning undermined by her loss of appetite. She fidgeted listlessly on her pillows when you read, would stop you with a gesture in midsentence to ask the time or hide away in seeming sleep. Her favorites annoyed her, conjuring better days, and new tales bored. "How does it end?" she would peeve, urging you to go directly to the closing pages and be done.

Your own poems were the only ones that summoned pleasure in her, but you had so few, never enough. You wrote for her, to rouse and entertain, by which you both profited. You sang the words to her, your own tunes, plucked from the guitar. This talent an inheritance passed down from grandfather to son to grandson, whole and unspoiled. Music came easy to all three, who, times you could number, had sung together and made a family of their silver notes. More often she had coaxed evening duets out of you and Grandpa on the broad, screened-in veranda of their Pennsylvania farmhouse, where you'd learned to play just as your father had. Not really learned: just come into your birthright, like having a prominent nose. Nights pullulating with the still heat of the day, crickets keeping time with you, and Grandma's arms flung rapturously, declaring the portal of heaven cast open to let the angels harken to your songs. It was the image of those nights that rose when you sought a quieting place to lay your thoughts and go to sleep.

Frank now only played drunk, in the barn, you strumming indifferently a few bales down, knowing it didn't matter how you played. But she, a discerning listener, she expected the best and you delivered. In rare spurts of forgetfulness, she would sing along with you, as she had back then, a few bars, till she heard the quaver in her flimsy pipes. Nonetheless encouraged, you always arrived guitar on shoulder, eager to coax a duet out of her. But these efforts, too, she finally wearied of, and you were left with soup and misery.

Despite your premonitions and her intentions, she survived the winter. People die in the dark of the year, she reproached you. Like your grandpa, out chopping wood before breakfast, keeled over dead, and I didn't even know it. Gone sudden, gone so much longer than I expected, all these years of loneliness. Why am I still here, Joaquin? Spring banging around the house enraged her. Its raw demands, thick with seed, howling and seducing the land to green. I cannot face another summer. This must stop, please, stop. She and the wind haranguing each other, each begging for a different kind of mercy.

One broody afternoon when you went in with her half-bowl of soup, she waved you to her, eyes lit. She could feel it coming, at last and way too late, a heaviness at the core, a remote pulsing in her blood that signaled the time was nigh. And in fierce pitch claimed she'd discovered the thing left undone that had kept her alive this godforsaken long. Did you know a decent lawyer? You must. It took an impatient minute for you to think of the father of one of the Outlaws. You'd met him a couple of times, a nice guy. It wasn't much of a lead but she grabbed it. Make an appointment for us, quick. My will. Nothing to pass on, I thought, till yesterday, when Frank slithered in, first time in months, smarmy venom dripping from his fangs. He must have sensed my dying and come to lay claim to his inheritance, which he'd have got if his greed hadn't recalled it to me. His ugly intent was plain, but I lured it out of him, he pulling up stakes for some fantasy life of a tramp singer in a spend-easy town, ten acres and a cabin owned clear, no strings but the six on his guitar tying him down.

That land up in Trove, Colorado. A forgotten dream. It's going to you, not Frank, much as he's counted on it. You're the one deserves the chance; it's real pretty land, Joaquin, and that cabin built by your grandpa on a hill outside of town to be a summer place in our golden years which never came. A fresh start for you one of these days. My only way out, you told her, an exaggeration that felt true. I can pay the lawyer with that turquoise bracelet. Clarice won't wear it anyway, ranch-woman, saddled with a bum who never takes her out anywhere fancy. Make a better marriage than your mother did, for god's sake. I'm sorry I inflicted that man on you all, except that he fathered a wonderful son. Don't know where Paul and I went wrong.

Calling the request urgent garnered you an appointment two days later, a Thursday afternoon. You'd been conjuring byzantine plans for sneaking out, none of which proved necessary, with Clarice off for supplies and Frank on horseback checking fence lines. The nice guy took one look at you, a gaunt pair of desperados with turquoise bracelet and deed in shaky hand, and wrote the will pro bono. He knew more than you'd have liked about your trials from the poems you'd delivered at Outlaw readings, too deep inside them to realize how much of you their words exposed. Besides, it was simple: a couple of pages with the witness signatures. He promised to file it, give you a copy for your grandmother. And you were back, tucking her into bed unnoticed. For once and contrary to the creeping onset of the scythe, she swallowed each spoonful with vigor, then fell easily asleep. Maybe worry-free she'll grow stronger, you thought, knowing better.

The final week was a happier one, though, in which sweet memories cradled her. After school, she had stories saved up to tell you, some new and others worn. The last evening you sat with her conscious, the two of you laughed about when they got an indoor bathroom at the farm, and great-grandpa, unfamiliar with toilets, laid his pipe on the rim of the water tank and walked away, after which it fell in and he thought his pipe had disappeared and none of the rest of them could figure out why the darn toilet had broken so shortly after it was installed. You sang to her, old folk songs and your own set-to-poem tunes. One night she closed her eyes and didn't open them again, leaving her body by degrees over the next three days, until it hit zero and she was gone. You were the one who found her, of course, and you found yourself unweeping but selfishly yearning for more time together. You opened the window to set her spirit free, in accord with an archaic belief she'd come to embrace. You stayed with her then, as so often in the late afternoon, and grieved the two years she'd been forced to spend here, dragged from the farm when she was informed that she could no longer take care of herself, knowing, as you did, that she wanted to stay and die where her husband and his family had for generations. The farm had passed to Grandpa's nephew and she to her son.

You tried to fix your thoughts on her, whose life was over, keep her memories whole and vibrant, but more than not you were the one they turned to. No one to tell about your day, complain about your parents with, read your poems and sing to. No one to comfort and be comforted by. Being free is no gift when being needed is no burden. Yes, you could go on to college now without worrying, but what did anything you could do matter just doing it for yourself? In the gnaw of those early weeks of spring after she died, you wrote letters to her, stashed them in the old lockbox that had lain empty under her bed.

Empty, that is, till a couple of days before she died, when you hid the copy of her will in it and stuck the key in the toe of an unmatched sock you still hoped to find the mate to. Not that these precautions were necessary; the nice guy lawyer had the original, along with the deed to the cabin and the turquoise bracelet, in his office. He'd be the one sharing the news with the family, as she had wanted it to be official and indisputable.

The mountains breed storms at every stage of life. Childlike whorls that kick up out of nowhere and rain havoc but play out fast. Young buck adolescent storms, a crack of lightning out of sweet morning blue, flooding arroyos with a gush that hauls boulders and cottonwood limbs into culvert swill. Strong, wild, erosive, a show of power no good to anyone but exhilarating nonetheless. The older storms: those are the treacherous ones. They mass slow over the peaks, thunderheads towering like capricious deities. You have plenty of time to watch them building, around here from 70–80 miles off, scenic awe at first but as they gather in the cowering sky, obscure the mountains with their swell, you know to brace and pray that the rooted bowels of the land hold firm. And that none of the lightning bolts they hurl strikes close.

Frank listened politely as the will was read, which didn't take five minutes, asked the nice guy how much he owed him and when he heard nothing, stood, shook his hand, and guided you out the door. Clarice had the bracelet on her arm, and you could see she was touched, more so than her mother-in-law might have guessed. To be thought of was a change for her.

At the car Frank paused to square eyes with you. "All that soup and ass-kissing paid off for you, son. Maybe. I wouldn't get too cocky about taking possession of that land." You could feel the air cooling hard. When the storm broke, you'd be up far gone into the hills at a meadow you called Heartsease. There you used to go regularly to get clear and quiet, compose poetry, read, spin wishes. Your mother would know where you were, but he wouldn't nor imagine she did. She'd be too smart to hang around anyway. Your pack was ready to slip on and you to slip out. It would take him an hour or more to get liquored up enough to kill you.

It was a good plan but not much trouble for a sober man with a history of escape to see through. Opening the back door, you nearly walked head-on into the bullet end of his rifle. There didn't seem to be any question about how serious he was and unlikely to respond to any deterrents. Nor about his skill as a marksman, even drunk. You followed the wave of the barrel toward the booze cabinet in the living room, took off your pack, and sat down. You were a decent shot yourself but would be dead before you had time to extract your pistol from the long-johns where you'd wedged it in your pack.

You were overdressed for indoors but feeling temporary. Frank's guitar stood against the bookshelf in the corner, and it egged you to remember the first song you two had played together. One of the classics. "Puff the Magic Dragon." "The Rainbow Connection." "This Land is Your Land:" Of course that's why your mind went to it. All those books were Clarice's. She'd wanted to study literature and do some writing, but the ranch got in her way. Just as it might yours. Not that it was a bad life. As long as it was a short one. The storm was crackling frenzied, hair on your arms jittery, air darkened. Swiveling toward the thunder, you tried to translate its bellow into a language you recognized. The gist was familiar; you'd heard all this spumed before, but what it meant for you, churned unknowable.

Where was Clarice? She'd headed directly for the barn. Gone for a ride. Outrun the storm, as you'd intended to. Not that she could subdue it, but together she and you formed a subtle windbreak that absorbed the impact. That she'd deserted you at its outset meant you would not survive the blast, meant she'd chosen not to witness your demise, sure it was coming. Or that she trusted you to get away on your own: mother and son fending for themselves. Regardless, you could have done with a burst-in of Clarice just then as the squall reached her entrance in its tale, the same story it told whenever fire raged in its veins.

Of how, growing up on the Pennsylvania farm, duty-bound to slopping hogs, plucking chickens, milking cows, plowing fields, cutting wood, checking fences, shoeing horses, birthing and burying and all the rank, bloody, gritty rest of it, he with his clarion voice and native gift for musical invention dreamed of heading out west to fame (and above all, fortune) as a singer-songwriter. LA, Hollywood. Got as far as Vista Grande, where he paused to earn some bucks, found a steady gig playing at the saloon on Abbott Road, becoming a local star when he danced with a gal whose prairie eyes he roamed searching for his reflection, fell full out for her tempered grace, but more than that: her emanations of freedom. Like she didn't care whether or not he did. Like she was all set, the luxury afforded a woman of independent means and spirit. And she sure as hell seemed to be, owning a ranch, five hundred acres outside Vista Grande nestled in the embrace of the Sangre de Cristos, which he took to signify she had money, more fool he, which is how he ended up in the life he'd set himself to leave, only not milking now but cutting, roping, branding, castrating, and loading the damn black angus to sell and saddled with a kid to boot, which he sometimes did, out of bed and into the corral to give him a goddamn hand. In debt and under gut-clenching pressure to keep the dwindling herd going through droughts and fires, make those interest payments, do more and get less. Meanwhile growing old and no songs written, hardly ever even playing, only friend a guzzle-and-puke bottle, the world against him, screwed, today, by his own fucking mother. One last chance at happiness to grab onto in spite of everything that spoke for not bothering to because she couldn't live forever, jeezus, ninety-three, bedridden but still here in their spare room, tightening that screw till it bolted him to the doom of a failed rancher nobody could endure. Trove. He'd held on and out for that ten acres, his father's glow baiting the hook from youth, but promises to take him along annulled by his own headstrong run to the West and then the early years romancing Clarice, learning to ranch, drinking, getting stuck so bad he couldn't think his way out before his father died and nothing more of Trove was said. Out loud. To himself, to gentle his heart, it became the bride of his salvation. Oh, he'd been there now, secretly, found the deed in public records, stayed in the cabin, assured it was all but his, and got acquainted with the town, a jackpot of a place to start over. Money? Yeah, he'd skimmed and scrounged through the years, enough to launch. Whatever the old lady claimed in her half-assed will, Trove was his.

Simple: You would sign the deed over to him, get it notarized, and he'd be gone.

A plan that easy, it seems to you, shouldn't have required getting drunk.

In the momentary cessation of wrack, the storm drawing breath for a new assault, you understood that it wasn't the idea had driven him to booze but its fulfillment, which rested on your agreement. The why and the how: those pesky villains that have scuttled a world of grand conceptions. Given, as he knew, that you would not freely sign over a toothpick to him, what inducement could he muster to coerce you? The rifle suggested his strategy, a clumsy one that would garner him, beyond a life sentence he felt he was already serving but this one in prison, nothing.

Or you have a fatal accident. Your pack gone and you out of here an hour after you got the land, eighteen, no one's going to doubt you ran off. They'll never find your body, and when you don't show up in Trove or thereabouts, that deed will pass to me as next of kin.

"Seven years before a missing person can be declared dead."

"I'll wait, up there, in the cabin. Who's going to evict me?"

"I guess they won't suspect anything."

"Yeah, that you're a good-for-nothing teenage runaway. Happens all the time."

"The original deed is still at the lawyer's. We'll have to get it in the morning for me to sign over to you." —Standing up, as though the conversation, for now, were over.

"Fucking shithead. You signed your death warrant with that dumbass move."

Blazing, the storm pitched itself at you, who, grossly out -weighed, -gunned, and -hated, slammed against the wall, muzzle hard into your chest, its bulleted shaft supporting Frank more than threatening you till he regained his footing.

"Outside!"

How fastidious, refusing to spill your blood in the house. And less trouble to clean up. But that was just one detail among so many he hadn't thought through.

For instance, what if you refused to go outside to get shot?

"Move!"

Cocked, aimed, safety off: your life riding on an intuition that he wouldn't kill you in the living room between the sofa and the entertainment center.

"Last warning."

How drunk was he? Your life riding on an equation: degree of inebriation over difficulty of cleanup times desperation.

"I can do it once, neat, outside, through the neck, or here, a bunch of shots, balls first."

You knew him as angry, defeated, reckless, but not cruel.

"Torch the house after, blame it on you."

Clarice's birthplace. As cars are projections of virility, so homes, this one for sure, can be vessels of fertility. Her consciousness of being was embedded in these walls. Splattering you across them and then incinerating the house to destroy the evidence: she would cease to be.

The battle had drifted into slow-motion as you negotiated with Frank, generating a sense of foolishness that he was unaware of. Time has no dimension in a whisky glass.

You were drained of energy to prolong the outcome. Fighting over a chimerical place called Trove where neither of you would ever dwell. You wanted only for him to go away, which meant you had to. Weariness slacked your bones as you yielded. Inertia shuffled your feet toward the door, foregoing a command from your brain. Windows on both sides of the carved oak entrance revealed slant rays, the departing sun. It was still spring, you noted, still your favorite season, still two weeks from your eighteenth birthday, and the fruit trees not yet in bloom. Might bear this summer, the one fruit year in seven that was all they expected around here. How your grandmother had hated over-wintering, despaired at the onset of lilacs and forsythia. It would be good to cease missing her.

Graduation in a month, college in four. Another chimerical place you'd never see. The leafing, the return of hummingbirds, monarchs passing through, piñons candling, light spooling into evening. Cricket songs and bird flitters, meadowlarks, grosbeaks, doves, jays, hawks. Run-along days of streaming, flying, that pulled you into a wilderness of desire to erupt and soar free of old ways and needs, to lean into the wind, to shed your habitual skin and bank naked into the currents of dream.

What you would do after opening the door and stepping through into spring was wheel suddenly and knock the rifle hard against the frame, knee Frank in the balls, grab the gun, sprint to the corral, mount Strider, bridle him if you had time, and be gone. Remember to close your eyes before you wheeled to keep from being sunblind. Wished you'd kept the pack on but you'd make it anyway, one night. The way to Heartsease was imprinted in sense memory though you weren't the rider Clarice was. Maybe she'd be there, stocked up, campfire lit. Summer and so much beauty near, the attempt was worth making.

But she wasn't there; she hadn't any thought of it. Was here, waiting at the door. Hadn't counted on you getting away to join her elsewhere. Hadn't left you in mortal danger. What mother would? Surprised you'd not learned enough about mothers from tending Ruth to know that. Even cowardly and peaceable ones will strike to defend their offspring. Although she could have done so sooner. Frank was set to shoot you in the living room if it came to that, and where would she have been then? Blazing through the door, of course, but she knew you'd be out and he wouldn't kill you till you were. She was your mother, spoken indignantly, as if that explained how.

You in mid-wheeling when she shoved you to the side, struck Frank a furied blow to the head with a log, yanked the rifle from him, hit him again twice, and as he buckled, whipped him with a horse crop about the neck and back, a beating that would leave scars. She had her pistol trained on him in case her assault failed, which it did not. Breathing steep, she ordered you to grab his other boot, and together you dragged him from the threshold before he'd bloodied it irrevocably. With rope she'd left beside the door you trussed him, then slid his heavy, stinking form onto a tarp and pulled him to the barn. He was moaning now as he regained consciousness, and you knew shortly he would writhe and roar, but the prospect did not unnerve Clarice, so you held firm. Into the barn you rolled him, padlocking the door from the outside, though trussed he could hardly have managed to escape. Your mother gave then, and you leaned slumped together staggering back to the house.

Tomorrow? You had fixed tea, chamomile with honey and cream, sitting now as victors after the siege at the kitchen table, shaken but euphoric, adrenaline coursing. You, mostly she, had defeated the monster who had ravaged both your lives for far too long. But what now? She, the mother, and you should have known she would, had a plan. Go to the nice guy and tell him your story, get a restraining order that won't let Frank set foot within a mile of either of you. Divorce him quick. If he didn't agree or asked for anything at all, take him to court for assault and battery, intent to kill. Prison or banishment were his only choices, and he could forget that damn land in Trove forever. That's the one thing you feared he would not do, even with an order compelling restraint. But the promised land was a war that lay many tomorrows hence. Closer battles loomed.

Your mother, who very likely had saved your life, now turned to you. It was too much. She couldn't handle things alone. To save the ranch, you had to team with her as Frank once had. Take the lead instead of follow orders. Even after she sold off fifty acres to a developer who'd been at her for a couple of years, a move she'd desperately resisted but the interest on those loans was killing her faster than losing a chunk of her homestead would. She grimly cut the herd to eighty head, knowing she might have to auction a few more after the coming winter. To you it seemed unwise to persist in the illusion that she could make a life ranching, though it was the only way she ever had or wanted to, but you'd been doubtful since the onset of adolescence when you saw that your parents' incompatibility ill-fitted them for any risky venture undertaken as a duo.

College? Your financial aid package was terrific though you'd still end up with loans. Next year, with the further losses you anticipated from the ranch, it might be even better, depending on who else, more desirable than you and needier, applied. No guarantees on money from year to year, though they would hold your spot. Never count on things, Clarice taught you, a lesson that experience had already done a brutal job of inculcating. This time she softened *never* by promising that it would only be a year and that she would see you through college thereafter no matter how many acres it took to do so. In truth, the ranch was yours, someday, your home, your inheritance, your destiny, she hoped, and why would you contradict her, your just-now nearly broken savior?

And thus you, not by nature a nurturer, became the caregiver for older women kin, soup-spooner for your grandmother, ranch partner for your mother, both strong women, both wounded, both disillusioned, both facing unsavory prospects.

The truly formidable challenge of this new arrangement with Clarice was not the work, to which you were accustomed and which in some ways would be easier to do without Frank despite his prodigious skill, but the effort of stanching the resentment that threatened to leak from your mouth and eyes. To sound, look, and behave as though you cared about the well-being of cattle you were raising to be slaughtered. Tightening fences to be sure they didn't bolt or die unprofitably in the jaws of a cougar. To fill water tanks and harvest grain for these same damn cows whose death was your livelihood. To be convincing in a role you played with no conviction. At times you were sure she saw through you but then at the next moment seemed oblivious, as though she believed you were just fine, maybe even happy. Did she fool herself or cling to the pretense to ward off guilt? You and she both play-acting for each other? The absurdity of that idea provoked your high-speed suicidal runs in the truck out to the farthest reaches of your cow-stubbled, cow-trampled, cow-shat property. You ate as little meat as possible to ensure your labor wasn't worth the effort.

At least, you told yourself, when the swell subsided, at least you had time to write this year, get your portfolio in good shape, make it a work of art to present for admission to poetry classes. Submit to literary magazines, establish an online presence, a following, credentials. Make yourself discoverable. Ranching had exhausted Clarice and Frank, but you were young and could go without much sleep. So you put aside the college folder, books you'd planned to read, remnants of high school, and in the clearing, lit by moon some nights, enshrined your journal. Spurred yourself through grimy days of dust and muck with the image of silver hours composing lines. When they didn't come at first, you appeased yourself with cautionary whispers of patience. "And indeed there will be time / there will be time / there will be time" murmured timorous Prufrock. You doodled, stuttered, scrawled the hollow pages of night after night. Only words from your limited sphere came to you: iron, leather, wood, fur, hoof, bawl, fork, tractor, corral, fence, boot, shit, blood, sear, afterbirth, rope, hay. Dirty words with frayed jeans. Words with no imagination, symbolism, or lyricism that you could detect. Nothing to think about. You wrote them all down and drew a diagonal line through them. Move on, but you couldn't. That was all the vocabulary you had left.

Barren of thought, you headed for bed and found the sleep of the damned dreamless. You grew taciturn, stopped speaking in sentences, stopped talking altogether beyond manure and flies. As your mother and Frank had: orders, questions, information, no frills. You regarded Clarice with the pained sympathy of a fledgling adult. Ranching didn't wear out the body but the mind. No refuge nor reflection: just the wearisome trudge into oblivion.

Most of the time it was impossible to be alone here where both of you were isolated and desperate. Joined if not connected. The end that was once in sight had lost its meaning. When the day comes to leave for college, will you go? If so, will you fail as so many ranch boys do, coming home with a shrug and sashaying back into the corral. Learn to compose cowboy poems, forcing the sagebrush range into metaphor. Building similes from homilies. Turning gruel into grit and churning rustic into romance. American Primitive. All so transparent and predictable. Best not to go to college at all. You would not become who you thought.

And for her? The end that lay perilously near would sunder spirit from flesh. She would become whom she never thought: landless sellout, living off the stock market rather than her stock. No more at home than a mustang in a circus ring. No more alive than a winter-sapped pine. She would go on for lack of choice like his grandmother but young enough to spoon her own soup when she remembered to be hungry. Hers would be the deepest loss, and you knew she knew and thus spoke obliquely to her of the future, foreshortening it to a week. As did she, blindered by the implacable dissolution that awaited both you and her.

The one person left to talk to was yourself, and the sole story you told yourself began with your grandmother's end and led to castrating bulls. You told it constantly, adding the rare day that mattered, as a way to make sense of it. At the departure point, when what comes next was the present moment, a small ribbon of silence, then it began again. You could hit pause for hours at a time, pick up exactly where you left off, whether you liked it or not. It was clear nothing else occupied that space where your brain once resided.

Until the disk stopped playing or the machinery broke down and the silence curled on and on.

When you are truly alone you lose the sense of your existence. You cannot hear the music because you are the music, cannot see the sky because you are the sere veil of blue between earth and infinity. To exist means to stand out from, and you do not because you are a part of, not apart from, the world. It is an inert state of being in which, unbounded, nothing is asked of you: you do not exist as a self. Neither free nor captive, neither coming nor going, neither chafing nor resigned, neither conceiving nor perceiving, neither growing nor diminishing, waking nor dreaming, desiring nor disdaining, but simply widening with the morning light. Alone because truly *you* are not.

Alone you pass for a shadow of the unmoored night. Alone you breathe as a mountain does, over centuries of imperturbability. Alone you forego nostalgia as ice in a glacial cavern yields to the tongues of sea. Alone your embrace is wind and your memory sand. Alone you have no loss to grieve, for what you have been is nothing you will ever be again.

June, and your eighteenth year was gone. Frank wrote to say that he was in a rehab center in Albuquerque, an easy drive, and had reached AA's Step 9 of the 12 in which he needed to apologize to the people he'd hurt, Clarice and you, his son, and ask their forgiveness. He could call or he could meet you in person at a place of your choosing. You said forget it, he wouldn't see you any more as long as he lived—except at the business end of a loaded gun. You exhorted Clarice to follow suit but knew she'd cave, as she did. The siren lure of their early days still sang through the prairie grass; she'd never ceased wanting him as he was then, nor she herself as the unbridled young woman. Once you saw his inevitable return in her eyes, you jammed your stuff in the pack, the same one you'd filled on that spring night a year ago, shouldered it and your guitar, took off for college. Clarice's protests that she would drive you there come fall swept aside, gently but surely, you hit the highway west, thumb out, a good-looking kid, throwback to the sixties, the kind of guy who can get a ride from anyone and easily make it out to the coast, where you hitched up scenic Route 1 going north to Seattle. Within a week you found work in a coffee shop, which bloomed here like chamisa back home, golden wild and ubiquitous.

July, you started playing guitar when the boarding house noise would drown out your chords, a tentative strum with no words. Occasionally caught a faint reflection of yourself in the mirror. Near month's end read Keats, Shelley, and dared their passion to breach your granite ramparts.

August, you wrote a fragment, spindle-rooted in a fertile clot of longing for a voice you'd not heard before, nourished by the persistent trickle through subterranean veins. Your spirit yawned, rose to greet you, shy but eager, like a rediscovered friend. You stood on the verge of *maybe*, beset by doubts but unable to repress the will to hope, fiercer than its counterpart, surrender. You planted yourself intently in affirmation's generative loam, still new enough to be easily torn up but sturdy enough to hold on.

September, you entered the university, not counting on anything but your resolve.

4

Rubbish Dreams

Moon cresting the hills diverts my eyes but not my thoughts, still focused on a night long ago. I strain to hold the present view, resting in my summer quarters amid the sibilance of crickets and aspen. But the stream of memory that Hersch let loose has a current stronger than the mountain wind this eve; its hold holds, and I am swept back to Vista Grande, to the fire and other losses to follow. A season unlike this one, of fearsome drought.

The wait for rain is a dun stillness in New Mexico. We rivet every cloud with an eye for swell in its girth. Spray the larvae of bark beetles devouring our piñon trees. Curse the gusts sucking the last bit of moisture from every pore. Rejoice at stray drops that come of a sudden, thinking now it's beginning, just as they vanish, parching the land with yearn. Maybe next week. Next month. Spring. Summer. Next year. Hope is a dream we dare not relinquish nor water.

Parched hills calling for rain can conjure its nemesis: fire.

For which we also wait, in dread of its ravening teeth. Each day is both a reprieve and a knell. We will not escape, but how grave will the punishment be?

I have lived always in a dry land. Its shorn plateaus and basins expose folly and jolt the observer. In time, the eye learns to differentiate brown from beige from buff from amber. To see datura and sage, cholla, chamisa, and scrub oak. To hear chickadees, bluebirds, the ubiquitous crows and jays, a shrill of coyotes. To see undulating depth in the hues of light and shadow.

This, my twenty-third summer, marks the cruelest drought I have experienced. Since May, wildfires have burned thousands of acres in New Mexico. Crews are exhausted, budgets tights, water scarce, fears enormous: all of us are on high alert. The air is heavy with smoke and dust. We wait, like rabbits cowering in their warrens, praying for the fires to bypass us.

But even that which is awaited arrives unexpectedly; even that which we expect catches us unprepared.

Or so it does me, in this case, asleep in the sweltering pulse of this mid-August night.

Tiger regularly finishes his killing spree about 4:00 in the a.m. and demands to come in so he can give himself a vigorous tongue bath in the comfort of my bed. He has to clean up any scraps of flesh, guts, and blood stuck in his long fur. None of this is a source of comfort for my head, where dreams of slashing eyeteeth and carrion terror eviscerate the last hours of sleep. Ravaged mice families, gutted bunnies, disemboweled squirrels, and headless gophers plead for mercy. Their haunting wails echo through clogged synapses, underscored by vague worries about bubonic plague, rabies, and hantavirus.

Still, it's better now than before I got a screen and he would bring the dying in with him to crush their skulls behind my sleeping knees.

So it's 4:00 and Tiger is yowling at the window and I stumble over there, cursing him as always, when I smell smoke drifting in on the wind. Smoke. Not a barbeque, not a cigarette, but fire smoke. You grow up in New Mexico with your nose tuned to that frequency. Grabbing my cell, every fiber alert, I obey my primordial instincts and call home.

Not a great message to leave los parentitos but really important. I shout it into their garbled landline answering machine, hoping to shock them into waking up. My heart's ripping along like the fire's inside me, while Tiger, gorged and oblivious, is licking the blood and sinews off his face. I hit the internet to check out the news.

The fire has already burned ten-thousand acres and yes, it is only three miles from town.

We are supposed to prepare for evacuation. For me that means my harmonica, computer, a backpack of clothes, my journals and books, and of course Tiger. It will all fit into Pacman, my rattletrap VW bug, which is parked down at the end of the street, where the battery apparently died. It's an awkward time to ask the neighbors, scurrying in and out of their houses with arms laden, for a jumpstart. This time I call Hersch. He hasn't gotten the news. He is scared, too. He'll come for me as soon as he's packed up.

Fire is total anarchy. When it catches hold of very dry, overgrown, windy high-desert hillsides, fire can burn at a phenomenal speed, leaping from tree to tree, jumping gullies, blazing through underbrush, spitting flames like dart throwers into the wilderness ahead. There's no telling which direction it might head, and you can get surrounded very quickly. The fire makes its own wind, which in turn revs the flames.

The crews who go out there to fight it push themselves to superhuman levels of exhaustion, digging fire breaks, beating back flames, burying embers, all the while trying not to get trapped and keeping an eye on the helicopters above them spraying retardant (when the winds subside enough to let copters fly). Their equipment weighs over fifty pounds, they're wearing masks so they can breathe, and it's hot, all the time ball-busting hot. Killer work.

Evacuating is a very weird thing to be doing early in the morning on too-little sleep. You anthropomorphize the fire and rail against it, like this disaster is some Wild West gunslinger villain who has it in specifically for you. And then you think about not seeing your house again, the one you grew up in, or maybe not being able to live in this town again till you're an old man. That thought makes you remember that the premier nuclear lab to the north could also go up in flames and release enough deadly radiation to wipe out several Western states, maybe more, maybe the world. And then you wonder why you're evacuating and to where.

And somehow, this thought connects to another, even as you're wondering what the hell is taking Hersch so long and the smoke smell is getting stronger, slipping in through the cracks around the windowsills and door, heightening your sense of urgency and creepiness—shouldn't your parents be worrying about you? Are *they* okay?

Now you're freaking yourself out. Where is Hersch? Call him again. No answer. News? No update. Parents? No answer.

The next time I call Hersch he's in panic mode. Slow going to pick me up. Streets are clogged. Masked and angry cops detouring traffic, trying to maintain order in the midst of mad confusion. Bumper cars. Honking. Lawlessness. Terror and rage. Hersch shrieking that he's going to die. "I'm coming, homie, on my way, but you're in the thick of it— Christ! Hang on!" he screams, then adds, "Hey, Bug, I love you, man." Major crisis time.

I sprint to the end of the street where my worthless Pacman squats like a toad. It sputters, rousing false hopes, chokes and quits. I kick the tires, pound the hood, curse it. The radio comes on, blasting static. Summoning all my mechanical know-how, I put the toad in gear and start pushing, turning the key with my right hand. Tires against the curb. "Die, you piece of dung!" I yell. "Dead," the static hisses back.

No good, this running. The air is being sucked out of me. Can't breathe right, dizzy. Have to clear out of here. Hersch'll never get through.

I stumble home, dodging neighbors carrying crying kids carrying mutilated teddy bears, and just as I crest the steps here comes Jack the drug dealer with another load of contraband in his arms. "Hey, man, what are you doing? Not a good night to be out for a run. Evacuate, man. Grab your goodies and go." He nods, pleased by the advice. And suddenly a new thought strikes him: maybe I'm not out jogging at five in the morning while Vista Grande burns. "Hey, man, you need a ride?" Accelerating from Jackass to Jumping Jack Flash.

I watch him cram the drug paraphernalia into his car, stashing baggies in suitcases and dumping what looks like half a pharmacy of pills into the trunk. Jesus, not his smartest move, but given the desperation of the scene, he might clean up on sales. I myself could use a little chemical boost about now. And a ride; I have to get out of here. Put off death as long as you can, that's my motto. Tiger, my pack, and I squeeze into the passenger seat; forget seatbelts: there's barely room for us between the hookahs.

Hitching a ride in a car loaded with enough contraband to put us away for life, with Jack, who's also loaded, is not my smartest move, either. For one thing, cop cars with flashing lights and bullhorns are cruising the neighborhood, ordering us to leave at once. For another, there's the car itself: a 1975 chartreuse Cadillac convertible with white leather seats. High visibility. Jack, six-foot-five, red dreads, and fluorescent shirt, shares that trait with the Caddy: you can spot him a mile away. His motto is "Hide in plain sight, no one comes looking for you." We differ in that view. He reads a lot and binges on movies, Jack does, and he spouts a maniacal stream of Hunter-Thompson-esque freestyle babble when he's stoned, also a lot. Now, for instance. That, too, makes him stand out.

"Apocalyptic, man. Surreal beyond the fringe zone. Driving straight into the fires of hell, or Mexico, man, seeking asylum for the insane. It's scifi and Fellini—you ever see *Satyricon*? A wicked brew, reality and illusion like no place I've ever been. We're in a new time zone, man, tune in. Harmonic dissonance. The devil melting like paraffin. Beanstalk Jack sucking the giant mama's tits while the drip drip drip of eternity on sidewalks breaks my heart. What did you say, man?"

I'd said something about not taking out the refugees hurtling down the sidewalks, but he'd rambled right past me, and fortunately them as well. Straight, Jack is a marathon driver, glued to the road, rolling like a pro in and out of lanes, outstanding. Stoned, he can still go on forever but he's a menace who tends to drift. Across lanes, shoulders, into fields, onto rail tracks and loading ramps. I knew this before I got in the Caddy. If there'd been an alternative besides death (which I'm seeing now as a risk either way), I'd have grabbed it. This thought becomes neon in my head as we pull up to a checkpoint where the cops are directing traffic.

"End of the line, Al, last night on the planet, it's all going to blow," Jack shouts to attract a little more attention to himself. "Let's drive to the mountaintop and watch the flames. You ever see *Dr. Strangelove*? Where Slim Pickens rides the nuke down like a bronco? Yippee! Yippee-ai-oh. Let's go down with the ship, man. Come on, honey, dance with me." The man in blue with a big pistol, also loaded, approaches, and I'm preparing to flee when an accident to our left distracts him. Jack guns it and roars through, waving his arms and singing, "You know something's happening but you don't know what it is, do you, Mr. Jones?" In his copious free time, he's also mastered Dylan's repertoire.

"On a night like this, man, hurtling through conflagration, old light hangs in the mind. We should know so much more by now. No one makes this voyage, not this late in time." He waves his arm, like he's clearing the smoke away. "Our eyes are trained on distractions, man, but they can still be surprised and never know what was missed or miss what's gone." His face contracts. "Fucking rubbish dreams."

Among the random words Jack strings together, some are excellent. It's like that old theory about how when you put an infinite number of monkeys in front of an infinite number of keyboards, one of them will write Shakespeare.

"Reality or truth, man, how do you tell the difference? The source of our confusion is we're all reading by one star, not enough illumination to decipher the stones and signs or pick up on the myriad visions lost to sleight of hand. We used to be magicians, man; now we're just clowns who fail to see the failure of not seeing."

We're headed toward Ponderosa Ave, which puts me in mind of a destination besides hell or Mexico: los parentitos, my natal home. Home safe. I try to call again: no ring at all this time. Why don't they ever turn on their cell? Or call me? If I can persuade Jack to turn onto Pondo, we'll go right past the driveway to their house on our (his) way out of town. I can walk from there.

"What what what? North, man? Turn north? I'm experiencing a moment of cognitive dissonance here, Al. Why would I go north to get to Mexico? North is like hick cowboy bars spurs spitting slaughterhouses rattlers rednecks geysers guns—"

"And Canada," I put in.

"Canada, man, we are so fucking far from Canada. Run out of gas way before then. North, shit. You've got a Tiger Tiger, burning bright, in the fires of this night. He's a beast, man, lying to the lambs, fanging the roar of old growth forests, churned into butter for our popcorn mania. You've got a Tiger by the tail and a glacier to hobble away on, ripe dude, nursing your wounded dreams of mastery. Tiger trumps tundra. Moose, grizzlies they'll rip the flesh from my carcass—car and cass, cool, how that unites us in the grim jaws of reaper teeth. Canada, man, that's a dream."

"Okay, well how about just as far as Farolito? Then you can cut across to 358 and go south. My parents live up this road; you'll be shed of me. Traffic's bound to be lighter going that way. Turn here!" Pushy, I know, but he doesn't have a route mapped out, and Ponderosa is clear. Whereas ahead down Ventura, we can see more flashing lights.

Ponderosa is in fact very clear in the direction we're going. We have a clean, straight shot, a nice change. Coming toward us the traffic is much heavier, which makes me wonder what's up and makes no impression at all on Jack. Neither does the smoke, which is getting thicker now, coating us like an acrid fog. He's singing the chorus to "Like a Rolling Stone":

> "How does it feel
> to be on your own
> with no direction home
> just like a rolling stone."

"Hey, Jack, man, how about pulling up the cover on this baby and putting on the a.c.?" I am choking on the words the smoke is so bad.

No answer for a long time, way longer than a normal pause. "This is so rich, so magical surrealism, man, like wonderland gone to weirdland. We could start seeing, like, you know, gargoyles and vampires rising from their graves. Don't say that, man. It's so easy to see shit like that when you're on…what am I on?" He gives me this bewildered look and I grab the steering wheel and point us back at the road. We are within a mile of my home when the cop lights start flashing. No sweat. I can make it cross-country from here. If he slows down—man, what a maniac. Braking not at all as we head directly at the police barricade.

Have you ever hit a moment of total lucidity in the midst of total chaos? Like the smack of a dust devil it whomps me just then, and what I know in this crystal moment is that everything is wrong. Jack and Caddy, both loaded, my pack and my cat, los parentitos, the fire, the flashing lights, the direction we're headed, the screams I'm now hearing: all wrong.

"North? Go north, you said? Al, you stupid shit, north is—holy crap!"

The reality of our screwdom finally strikes Jack, too, and he flips out. North is where the fire must have begun, someplace up there in the national forest, and we're driving straight into the heart of it. North is also HQ for every cop within driving range, including, no doubt, a couple from the narco squad.

Furious, Jack hits reverse, curtailing the life of his tranny, pounds the accelerator, and backs up, swerving dizzily till he crashes right into the concrete barrier at the roadside. Both of us so adrenalined we don't feel the whiplash. Paralyzed everywhere but our eyes, which watch the cop come up to the Caddy, glancing suspiciously at its contents. His hand slips down to his pistol, face hardening. Desperate, I throw open the door and flee, holding Tiger under one arm and dragging my pack with the other. Running for my life into the crowd that inexplicably has gathered behind a second barricade that I don't notice till I hurtle directly into it, where another cop grabs me.

Meanwhile, back at the Caddy, Jack seems to have come up with his own scheme for survival. "Stop that man! He's a drug dealer!" he yells. "He forced me to drive him. Watch out—he's armed!"

With a cat? It's theater of the absurd: Involuntarily I explode into laughter and tears, fall to my knees, pleading my innocence and screaming for mercy. Jack is stunned by my impromptu performance; even I can't believe I'm doing this.

"Sorry, I'm real sorry," the cop says. I don't look at him, just nod, and hold out my backpack hand for him to cuff. He grabs it and helps me to my feet. My mother is standing in front of me.

"Sorry, I'm real sorry." Like a complete idiot I repeat the cop's words. First the fire and now her son's a convict. I truly am sorry—and outrageously happy to see her. Still sobbing with relief, I take her in my arms. The cop steps away from us and fades into the crowd. What the hell are they all doing here? Why didn't she call me, her first and only born child? Can she imagine the hell I've been through to get here? Where's Papito? Time for them to loan me some money for a new car. It's not like I ask for that much.

As I'm babbling at her, I notice that Mamia is not hugging me back. She is not reacting to my plight. Her face is the color of this smoke-stained dawn. She says flatly, "Oh, good. You saved Tiger. I lost Caleb. And the photo albums. And your father."

And then I have to focus, see the house I grew up in smoldering. See the neighborhood in flames. Hear the family I grew up living next-door to screaming. See the cops ferrying people away from the scene. Hear my mother's words. But I can't make sense of them, not of anything. They are stupid words. Meaningless. Lost Caleb the terrier? Lost my father? And the photo albums? What? She is always losing things that she's put somewhere safe, always looking for them. "Has anyone seen a folder marked 'Car Insurance?' My silver hummingbird earrings? The cell phone? My sunglasses? Scissors?" I was raised with questions like these roaming the house. Her anxiety and frustration. A frantic walkabout and the shuffling of objects, clothes, opening and closing of drawers, closets, doors. What's wrong this time is that she isn't looking. Just standing here. I was usually the one who found her stuff by knowing where to look, staying calm, not caring that much. So it's logical for me to go in search of Papito and Caleb. I drop Tiger into her arms; she grabs hold of him too tight, like he's a stuffed toy, he yowls, and I yell at her too loud: "Hey, Mom! Be careful!" and take off toward the fiery remains of the house.

Then there are a lot of shouting people grabbing me, and I yelp, trying to squirm free. "Just give me a minute!" I snap. "I know where they are. Let go!" Kicking, I break free, and run, but not fast enough. Trapped again. I growl, a Tiger-like warning before he bites, but they have me pinned. "If he's not in his study, he's in the back bedroom. The dog's with him!" I am really yelling now, out of patience with these jerks. "He puts on his headphones, see, so he can't hear anything but his damn music. Joni Mitchell. Judy Collins. Let go of me! Let go!" I call for Caleb, full volume. "If he's scared, he'll head for the road. Doesn't get that he could be killed. Someone should check. Christ, who let him out anyway? Old and dumb. Mom? What the hell is going on here?"

She's beside me now, holding Tiger upside-down, the only cat in the world who doesn't mind. "Alex, they're gone!" She's screaming, too.

"Where? Why the hell aren't you with them?"

She just looks at me, mouth hanging open.

"Shut up!" I yell. She hates the words. I was always forbidden to say them. "I called! You didn't answer. I called. I left a message. To warn you. You needed to come get me." She's still staring. "What the hell—are you deaf? Shut up shut up shut up!" And finally I do, sedated by a stealthy needle or just utter pointlessness.

Whatever it is takes out my mouth, but my mind keeps working. I see Jack the drug dealer being hauled off—bizarre thing to be doing, my mind tells me. Who cares? Stupid, incongruous, all of it. Who's living this scene? He's pointing at me, cursing, screaming something about getting even, words that make about as much sense as my mother's. Even what? Are we doing? Everybody's watching him, which gives me the break I need. Wrenching free of the police, drugged crazy, I lurch into the smoldering ruins of the house. And there they are, shadows in the smoke, haloed by metal sparks, shuffling forward, Papito with Caleb in his arms. Me barreling at them, tripping over a ceiling beam and crashing to the floor in what was once my living room, now become a crematorium.

5

Chimerical Sanctuary

When I awoke, it was winter and snow had piled the hole where I lay, silenced by frost, hearing the ache of wind rushing through my corpuscles. On the sere plains where I'd come to rest nothing moved but the wind. All gone. I was alone at last, and no more could be expected of me. I didn't have to show up at work, write a book, be nice to people, jumpstart the car, impress Rose, feed myself or Tiger. I didn't need to make a life. It came as a great relief, entombed under the drifts, to just let go. When I thought about the alternative, having to move on, terror and pain flared again, scorching the blankets, which then slivered to ice. To go on or back: there was no place I wanted to be. My mother used to say, after a fruitless search for something, "Well, this time it's lost forever." Well, this time it is.

From within my burial mound underlooking the plains or sky or a gaping white I'd never inhabited, I saw vague outlines, and watching them coalesce into figures, realized they were coming toward me, figures black against immeasurable snow prairie, coming toward me arms laden, their burden indecipherable to my night-infested eyes, their stance inconsolable, their progress infinitesimal. Cold registered, shabbily dressed as they were, figures bent and winded by the wind, shorn by snow, a homeless remnant band of refugees trudging toward chimerical sanctuary. Their stuff, now I could begin to make it out, old and broken but they treated it like shards of inestimable value. They with no hope of haven, for the closer they got, the smaller these figures became, like some irrational reverse perspective. They would never reach me and I couldn't move, interred in the opacity of a night beyond the sun. Nor, if they arrived, give them more than a grave beside mine.

Still I could not shift my gaze from them, clinging to a perverse conviction they would make it and when they came, we would all metamorphose, they, the plains, and I, released as adamantine notes in a dazzling song.

By the time spring thaw mudded the lowlands of my gut, I was in a different state, Colorado, and my mind much farther away. It was yet winter there, in the land beyond my interior compass, though unusually mild as I was told, a climate incomparable to the one where I dwelled. My mother was with me, and Tiger, too, all three of us living with my father's aunt Gertrude (called Trudy by her American friends, Tante Trudel by her German relatives and my family). A woman, my sluggish memory whined, that I had never cared for in a house whose smells I couldn't stand: she stinking of heavy perfume, it of cabbage and liver. She was enthralled with my father and obscurely suspicious of me. She was a first-generation immigrant from Munich who'd married a US Army serviceman. Widowed and childless, living on her own in Summerville, she filled her days with gardening, sewing, and volunteer work at her church. Totally Americanized except for her accent.

Well numbed on every plane of possibility, I lay in Trudel's guest suite, a bed and bathroom complex with a door to the outside. When my eyes began to focus on these surroundings again and show me the very small domain to which I was confined, I discovered Tiger banished to the exterior windowsill of my room, where he meowed futilely at his errant human. Because I was trapped in tubes, I pressed the call button, willing it to summon help. Trudel answered, my least sympathetic caregiver.

"Tiger," I whispered, turning my head toward the window.

"He should have gone straight to the pound, but your soft-hearted mother insisted on keeping him. She feeds him. He sits there and yowls for hours. Such a spoiled brat. What did you want?"

"Tiger," I moaned.

"No, no cat in my house. They carry the plague, rabies, scarlet fever. Very dangerous, especially with all your burned flesh. And I am allergic to their filthy saliva."

What I later learned was no cat outside her house, either. Trudel was murderously disposed toward those that went after her precious birds. Instead of garden gnomes, her yard was mined with elaborate feeders, baths, houses for her feathered friends. Armed with a beebee gun, she could clip a cat's ear at twenty feet. Inside or out, Tiger was feline non grata.

I had to wait till my mother came in to check on me to get Tiger pardoned for existing. Even then, it took some intense pleading in a broken voice to get her to represent me in the court of Trudel, where, after making many concessions and unconditional promises, she gained Tiger admittance to my room only, as long as he defecated outside, wore a bell, and for God's sake stopped howling. Trudel warned that the cat should not be allowed anywhere near my body because of the dirt and disease endemic to him.

Tiger curled up at my side and slept as only a cat can, for about four hundred hours straight, awaking completely refreshed, very hungry, and with no memory of his previous exile. It was for him that I first wobbled to my feet, with help, and forced myself to walk, to eat, to get rid of the tubes that had kept me going during my trek through the glacial nether-realm. My mother felt it was well worth the occasional cat hair on my dressings to have me back. From my perspective, the real victory was that Trudel now refused to enter our room.

While Tiger and I took possession of the guest suite, my mother was stuck in the sewing room on a day bed amidst mountains of Trudel's half-done projects. Here a quilt, there a tea cozy, everywhere a throw-throw. I'd been crammed in that room once as a kid and felt like I was suffocating. But my mother was so effusively grateful to Trudel for taking us in that she never complained about the clutter. "I have nothing to unpack," as she pointed out. "It feels reassuring to cuddle up among your beautiful things. Maybe I'll even stitch a few squares of a quilt together." But she didn't because she was tending me and ever so privately and painfully, herself.

My mother brought me meals and all the news she thought fit for me to hear. Thus, "Rose and her mother are fine, though the house sustained quite a bit of damage. Rose is in England. I know she'll be glad to hear from you when you're better. Oh, yes. Joey was in Albuquerque, so he's just the same as ever. He'll come visit when you feel up to it." *Up* was something I could not conceive of feeling. Scarred as badly as the bandages indicated I must be, cutting myself loose from all those who knew me before the fire was my private intention. All but one. "Hersch?" she answered evasively. I'm sure he's okay. He hasn't been in touch yet. Typical." Actually not. Hersch was loyal to the bone, and he was the last person I'd talked to before taking off. He would have checked back. But of course my phone was lost, so how would he reach me?

As cobbled bits of my strength returned, Trudel insisted that my mother stop treating me like an invalid. I had to join them for meals and walk around the garden after sundown to build up my muscles. I'd never been close to Trudel, just polite enough to get by, but now that she wielded the savior scepter, I couldn't find anything nice to say. Nothing mean, either. I didn't say anything at all to her, just did the minimum to keep her off my mother's back, slept a lot and ate little. Read. But not good reading, a page-turning, mindless shuffling through books. It was like I'd finally become the Kafka Bug of my nickname, lying trapped on my back, waiting for someone to slide a piece of cardboard under me and throw me out. Which Trudel was clearly ready to do.

And like Kafka's bug, I couldn't take stock of myself because they wouldn't let me peek beneath the bandages to see what had become of my face and body. If you've ever watched a horror film, that's a dead giveaway that you're a monster. The thickly layered bandages were secured in ways and places that made them impossible to unravel. "Wait till your wounds heal," Mamia insisted, refusing another request for a peek beneath the gauze. "It won't do you any good to look now." Nor was I allowed to touch the bare skin during the daily changing of the wrap—danger of infection. I did catch glimpses of the red swath banding my breast and belly like a saber-strap where the beam must have seared me, but that just meant I'd be wearing shirts for the rest of my life. My bare chest had never been a selling point anyway. It was the handsome mug that I'd always counted on to persuade ladies to overlook the rest.

What my mother and the nurse didn't get is that their faces were 3-D mirrors reflecting not only the devastation they saw in mine but the despair they felt seeing it. Their eyes were far worse than a simple looking-glass would have been. And they declined to talk with me about what scars I would bear once my wounds healed. Believing that they were shielding me from discovering how truly grotesque I was now, they left it up to my imagination to picture.

Scars were not something I'd really thought about having until now. Oh, sure, the little ones from childhood recklessness, the bicycle slid too fast around a dirt road curve, a gash from the piece of tin I didn't notice in the weeds (followed by the inevitable tetanus shot). Those scars were more like badges of honor than hallmarks of disaster. Most of them had stories I didn't mind telling because they involved some act of bravery, however pointless, or a ridiculous adventure that had become funny: So you'll never believe this, but there I was…

Acne was the scar-scourge of adolescence that I escaped unscathed. Great hormones— oh, how we'd loved saying that word, real slow, drawing out the syllables and working them into lascivious sentences. Yes, I'd been granted good genes and a measure of good luck. I tanned well, too, thanks to Mamia's vaguely Latin bloodline.

Until, after hurling myself into the inferno, I lay here coiled in gauze. My face had clearly become gouged terrain that I would no doubt have to mask.

The only one who seemed completely unfazed by my altered state was Tiger. He probably hadn't paid much attention to what I looked like before. Neither had I, often enough, but lying swaddled in fear, I turned again and again to that past self, enhanced till it suited my ideal of Alexander the absolutely Great, a teen idol in his prime. Walking, talking, eating, dreaming, I thrust my invented, charismatic visage into the world. And the beauty of this rendering became so familiar to me that I did not recognize the gruesome reflection I saw when they finally handed me a mirror.

I knew the day of revelation had come when the doctor did. He had the bedside manner of a gravedigger: workmanly, stoic, hardened. "You may not like what you see, but most of the time you won't be seeing it," he told me as he began unwrapping the bandages. "When you run and fall headfirst into a fire, you can't expect to be a pretty boy afterward."

Mamia winced at his comfortless words, her creases of anxiety deepening. She sought refuge in Trudel's eyes and found none. Yes, for this momentous viewing Trudel had treed her cat allergy and was standing by, fully armored in schadenfreude. Her presence and the doc's contempt forced me to match their toughness: show no horror. Whatever the mirror held, I had to stay at a great remove from myself and look without seeing. Later, alone, I could break my heart with an open-casket viewing.

As he peeled the layers off, my thoughts roamed to an episode of *Twilight Zone* my sophomore English teacher had shown us when we read *Frankenstein*: "Beauty is in the Eye of the Beholder." A woman who has undergone countless failed surgeries to make her less ugly is anticipating the results of the last procedure. The doctors unwrap her gauze, and voila: a gorgeous 1960s woman emerges, but it turns out everyone else in her society is what we'd call repulsive, so she's still the odd one out, too "ugly" to live among them. I would just have to get used to the screams of small children, the averted eyes of adults, find a way of seeing beauty where no one else did.

Merciless, the doctor raised the mirror to me, holding it closer than was necessary. Trudel leaned forward so she wouldn't miss the expression in my eyes. Blank 'em, Bug, I commanded myself. No one sees nothing here. Remember, whoever's face's showing up in the looking glass, it ain't me, babe.

I cocked my head and held very still, studying a reflection that absolutely wasn't mine. A wide vertical gash ran from hairline to eyebrow on the right, the edges puckered in a futile effort to close over the wound. Random lacerations streaked the rest of brow and skull, leaving the hair a bit patchy. Two of them crossed in a jagged X. As in a marked man, exed off the list, out, exterminated. Across the bridge of the nose another chasmic slash that would never fill in. It looked like part of the nose was missing. Cheeks and chin were pockmarked with red welts of varying sizes that would someday just be pink ruts in the landscape of a hideously damaged face.

From a distance too remote to rouse feeling, I delivered the verdict to my breathless audience, "All set for Halloween," and handed back the mirror.

There followed a plethora of instructions in the doc's voice of an indifferent god, a cluster of tongue-clucks from Trudel and hand-clutching from my mother. I lay with my eyes closed, willing my breath to slow. Only after Trudel and the doc left did I grant my mother the reassurance of looking her in the eye. "I'll be all right." Flat voice. "It's no less than I deserve. Would you let Tiger in?"

"You could be a teacher, Alex," she cried.

What?

"I'd always thought you'd be a great teacher. You're a natural, sweetheart. You have the gift."

I nodded sagely as though we'd been discussing potential careers, then asked (unkindly, I grant you), "But don't they bear their scars on the inside?"

Tearing up, she rushed to the door. Tiger the magnificent stalked in and leaped onto the bed, where he began assiduously licking his anus. I could have grown fangs and scales and he wouldn't have noticed or cared. Plus he loved having me in bed, where I made a comfortable bolster for him. Tiger was just the balm old Alex needed to keep a claw-hold on normality.

They left a mirror, back side up, on the dresser. It was dusk before I rose to scrutinize the face that had once been mine.

That guy was no one I remembered. A deformed loser no one would. The guy they'd loved was dead, as so many of them were, anyway. And the dead, I assumed, had divested themselves of faces and bodies. No, he wasn't me and I could no longer be him.

This was how others would see me, and whatever I did or said would be associated with The Face. Like a guy I once talked to down on the plaza: very smart, probably some kind of astrophysicist, with a gruesome birthmark covering half his face. I heard what he was saying, and it was brilliant stuff about parallel universes, but all of his words were filtered through the birthmark I couldn't not see. I kept thinking about how it would feel to be him, walking around with it all the time, wondering whether it could be removed or whether the skin grafts would be worse than the thing itself. Did he pursue the brainiest career possible to compensate for how he looked? He was big enough to be a lumberjack.

It would be vital for me to keep my sense of humor—and impossible. I could only be funny because I was good-looking enough not to have to be: confident that it wasn't an "at least." An ugly comedian smacks of desperation.

Wide awake that night, taunted by the after-image of the face in the mirror, dying seemed much easier than living on. Can a person will himself to die? I remembered debating that question in Justine's class when she put it to us in connection with *One Hundred Years of Solitude*. But that was magical realism, and my magical powers were a delusion of childhood, except as I could be a conjurer in writing fiction, which I no longer would, my desire to do anything that required an effort, including to will myself to die, having petered out.

I thought I should cry, but no tears gathered. In making myself a blank for my viewers, I had purged myself of emotion. Or maybe I couldn't cry because that was too paltry an expression of sorrow for what I felt. Most likely, I was in shock, denial. It was inconceivable that I would spend the rest of my life looking savagely repulsive.

The moon beaming through the window illumined the overstuffed chair where I'd piled my clothes. The chiaroscuro image suggested a human shape reclining against the cushions, which struck my blurred eyes as a separate self, the one beneath the skin who still persisted in my memory. The I of me keeping vigil, a protective spirit that would not allow my ruined exterior to destroy the inner being crucial to preserving my soul. That would allow me to continue living within myself. Profoundly heartening, the strength it granted me, and I clung to this notion the moon had unveiled.

Dreams that night were of the kind that feel wakeful. I was sure I had not slept at all but was merely wandering amidst thoughts until I came conscious and knew I hadn't been. In and out I meandered, along passageways of my childhood, adolescence, young adulthood. Words streamed clearly, fragments of conversations, my lines often the perfect responses I hadn't given but that now rose easily to my lips. Everyone I cherished showed up, glad to see me. We joshed, hugged, told stories and played upbeat tunes. To discover that they were all still with me, these awesome people and moments, was exhilarating. Dawn found me giddy, still immersed in a world unscathed by the present truth.

Among the times I'd visited was one in which I as a young child was pulling an ornate box from my closet. I think the box had once held a gigantic Lebkuchen that Trudel sent us, but whatever, it was mine now. My mother called it the Later Box because we filled it with projects and stories and drawings I'd started but not finished. "You might want to come back to this one later," Mamia would say. "Put it in the box." When the box was full, we'd take an hour or so and go through it. I really liked those times, both of us sitting on the floor in my room, sorting through the box, talking about each thing. Some stuff got tossed, other stuff left out to work on, and always there was a small pile that went back in: the Still Later Things.

Time now, the dream sequence intimated, to make a box like that in my head. Whenever you come up against a problem or bad memory or scar you're not ready to think about, drop it in your mental Later Box. That storeroom will come in handy when you are scrabbling for ways to stay sane; it will shelter the man beneath the skin. Sure, on those edgy nights when you can't get back to sleep, your mind may reach involuntarily into the box and start hauling stuff out you're not ready to deal with. At two in the morning, you can't keep a lid on unnerving thoughts, a stubborn, repetitive, whiny mumble that's worse than a dripping faucet. But for the rest of your hours, postponing confrontation with anguish and uncertainty will be a saving grace.

The separate self, the inside man closeting pain in a box: My night's ramblings made brilliant sense until I checked the mirror again. There was no escaping that devastation. Past solace, past rescue, I gulped a couple of pain pills and went back to bed, riveted awake by my untenable situation. Scoured the corners of my recall for cheering scenes to inhabit. But the mirror was irrevocably etched on my inner eye, and the self I loved had slipped into an immense cavity. Descending, I realized that instead of conjuring a mental refuge, I, bereft of anything I could deal with now, had become the Later Box. I had stored myself for later, to be finished or discarded, which in this case amounted to the same thing.

At least I knew where I was. Which you must be sure of to know who you are. Nowhere, nothing, nobody. Negated, abnegated, abdicated, abrogated. Not two selves but zero. Dead despite my vital signs, which were meaningless. If only it weren't so hard to give up and un-be. If only we didn't fight so hard to make something of nothing.

Sequestered in the box of no present nor future, no here nor hereafter, stripped of that deeply human faith that things will get better, nothing was left of me for now. The Later Box implied a future, which I had none. What I needed, the tendril to which I might cling for my life, was that which I'd been and done once in the long gone by. An Earlier Box, like the one I'd fallen into through a dream last night—its origins thus hidden somewhere within me. Time past contained within the time future, the end in my beginning. Groped frenzily for a handhold, collapsing the Later into the Earlier Box, before the scars.

To be within a box that lay within: not a plausible deed physically or conceptually, but even less so to be the box within the box within. Hard to visualize. Had to be accepted unthought, where it was as likely as any other mode of being.

It was so roomy, so easy to breathe inside the Earlier Box that I yearned to stay there and there only. But of course that was impossible. People would expect some facet of me to be part of their onward world. Yet if in the consoling darkness within me who lay within the box he was, I could turn the mirror to reveal the terra cognita of happier outcomes, then the root of my identity might hold. I could go on living as disparate selves, one the guardian spirit self essential to me, the other an invention demanded by obdurate reality.

The outside Alex required to interact with others would grow opaque, tougher, drier, more cynical. A fatalistic cowboy rather than an affable pal. Stoic, taciturn, I would quote from "Ozymandias," explaining that buried ruins confirmed my view that our advancement was a cyclical illusion closely resembling the spiral of a vulture over carrion, wherein we are both the bird and the corpse, feeding on ourselves till there's nothing left. The energy we generate drives the energy of our destruction. Believing ourselves a separate entity from the planet earth, we take nurture from the life source by killing it. Thus we consume heedlessly that which will consume us until ultimately we swallow ourselves up.

Inside, where reflection is the mind's eye, I could continue to summon the free and playful Alex I had been before the fire. Alex the beloved who danced in the arms of good fortune. I would be at home with that Alex, dream as Alex, jest and behave as old Alex. But for the world I had to face, that had to face me unboxed, the world that held unfathomable despair, the un-me others stare at would take the hit, be the one who would never rise and shine again, regardless of whether he got out of bed. Who stopped caring. Whom nobody liked and who had no promise. Who would have been better off dead. He would be the one to suffer the ugliness I could not bear. "Who I am" and "whom others see me as" would be separate and unequal, each in his own realm.

Those nights when the Earlier Box rose in me were spectacular. I romped on the high school quad, jumping Hersch and butting Joey, stealthing across the roof of the admin building to erect a huge plaster penis, or zipping swords in a childhood duel with Rosie, partying with random dates. And I wrote masterpieces whose words shone like a divine gift and were erased upon awakening. The freedom to be happy, as I saw it, was the ultimate gift, and as they say, it's not ours to keep.

Mine was torn away by an overheard conversation between Mamia and Trudel. Spring had crested the mountains and was gliding into its summer hues when their words ruptured the hull of my secret pleasure. They were sitting on the patio in the garden and had forgotten that my window might be open. At least that's what I at my most charitable believe. Not like the days to come when they spoke directly within earshot to make sure I'd hear.

On this evening in May, they were speaking of how slowly the months since the fire seemed to have passed; in Mamia's view, it felt like years, which Trudel claimed was due to the need to distance herself from the tragedy. Actually made sense, I grudged her, I who had stashed the whole thing in the Later Box.

"His father's death. He hasn't said a word about it."

True.

"Doesn't ask about his friends. Vista Grande. What happened. I don't think he's even been on his computer."

Well, I had, but not looking up that stuff. Watched some classic movies, checked out masks.

"What's wrong with him?"

"He is living in his own zone." Another point for Trudel. "For him, the only real thing are the scars he has to wear. But the mirror he has put away in a drawer. Maybe he thinks if he doesn't look at them, they'll disappear."

"It's more like he's the one who's disappeared. Oh, Trudel, I feel as if I've lost both of them, Harvey and Alex. Should he be in therapy?"

"Therapy! American nonsense. He just has to pull himself together, face reality. You should talk to him, Michelle, tell him what you are feeling, how much he hurts you when he never speaks of his father's death. He must stop acting like a baby, thinking only of himself. He has the scars, from now on, ja, but so much worse happens to people in war. They lose legs and arms, eyes, their whole families, they are paralyzed, they starve, no one cares, they lose their country, are refugees, and still they go on, start over and build a new life from ruins. In war a young man who has his mother and aunt, a nice house, food and care would feel so blessed. A few scars—what are they? His father would not mind having them if he could live."

Papito. If he could live. She had no idea how badly I yearned for his resurrection.

That night offered me no plane of escape from their words, which looped in my head, sucking up all the air in the room. I breathed thinly, my body flexed and spirit waning. In an unmoored hour of the dark I became aware of a nebulous presence in the room with me.

"Mamia?" I whispered, sitting up. Not she, but in a corner of the room an amorphous haze elongating into a power I didn't recognize and yet knew to be my father. Devoid of his human shape but retaining the force of his being. What had to be called his ghost, this fire-hewn specter, a phenomenon in which I did not want to believe that was viscerally terrifying as he approached my bed. Snapped on the lights to eradicate him. No longer visible and still somehow there. Dangerous to me.

I feared what the ghost was after and why and that I deserved its vengeance. Sweating guilt, I dashed out of the room and hurriedly shut the door, thinking foolishly to confine him. As if.

As if it weren't just the opposite, I whom he had trapped.

As if I could lose him now that he'd found me through my hunger for his return. And no will has a greater lure than that of a dead father. When the old man's shade falls on you, white against a midnight sky, you have to pay heed, accountable or not for his death. Even though he would be a far more tenacious opponent if you had perished before him, resolutely dragging you back into his world, as he would and will, living or dead.

Because you wanted him to, wanted to be with him on any sphere of existence.

The ghost was extremely agile, emerging in low light from a corner to envelop the room in opalescent smolder. During the day he would enter lamps and curtains and wait for me to walk past, then come after me. The ghost was always in the house, but I never knew where till it was too late to evade him. A shape-shifter, the phantom could easily get to me, who realized with growing dread that my external identity provided only a veneer of safety, my internal identity a roil of vulnerabilities.

Harried night and day, my constant vigilance to elude Papito's spirit wraith led me to construct means and rules for fending off ghosts.

To begin, those you encounter are unhappy ones. People who died too young, too suddenly, violently, senselessly, brutally. The injustice of their demise haunts them, and they in turn haunt you who miss them most. You provide a smooth conduit into the land of the living, where they have unfinished business and seek to remain. If you have any sense of guilt about their death (and don't we all, in some way, feel implicated in the death of others, whether we are blameless or not?), they will fuel it.

Second, keep your hands tucked under the covers or in your pockets. If they get ahold of either hand, they can pull you over to their side, the underworld or afterlife or cosmos. Maybe having you join them proves that, in whatever arcane manner, justice has been served. Or maybe they're lonely. Papito's ghost kept slyly after my hands, trying to catch them in a naked moment on top of the covers. He went for them in my dreams, too, there very aggressively, and I was given to understand that if he grabbed one of them in that sphere, I would never awaken. Once the ghost even shifted tactics and tried being my friend, comforting me, to which I was ready to succumb till he reached for my hand.

Meantime, back in Summerville, while I was fleeing my father's specter, Trudel and Mamia had become allies. Trudel nursed my mother back to health, treating her like a fragile vase that needed fresh flowers daily to brighten her smile. "Live," she would tell Mamia. "You have many good years left. You're only fifty-two, not like me, already a crippled old woman with nothing to look forward to but the grave. Harvey would have wanted you to be happy, to find someone new. He was so generous and good, my nephew, and look how well he provided for you. The big pension, the insurance money, social security—you're a rich woman. Travel. See exotic places. Make a new life for yourself."

My listlessness was driving them nuts, or more specifically, driving Trudel to hound me to enlist. With a fort just down the road and recruiters hungry for fresh meat, even my disfigured carcass, it was a surefire remedy. In Trudel's view, young men my age were married and suitably employed with a decent car and promising adult futures. For us wayward, overgrown adolescents, the military offered a buzz-cut road to success. Mamia knew better, but she was going through her own agonies, and I was no help to her, hanging around slack-jawed and aloof, a withering reminder of her loss. With the burn scars and dour attitude, Trudel assured her that her son would be perfect for the army.

"They both ran into the burning house!" Mamia's voice hung between exasperation and despair. "Harve to rescue Caleb, for heaven's sake, a fifteen-year-old dog that was on his last legs anyway. A good dog, sure, but worth dying for? And Alex, just like his dad, headlong into the flames to rescue Harve *and* Caleb." My mother emitted a laugh like a caw. "It's like that song about the old woman when they say, 'I don't know why she swallowed the fly, and then a spider to catch the fly and then bird to catch the spider and then a cat and then a dog and a cow and finally a horse—she's dead, of course.' All of them are. Even Alex. He needs to make an effort, Trudel. I'm suffering, too. He's in suspended animation, and so am I, because of him. Was it heroic of them? Were they heroes? Should I have gone in after them?"

"No," I answered inaudibly from inside the box, scrambling to my feet. "I'll free you from my misery."

"Ja," Trudel answered quite audibly from her position of unwarranted authority. "They were heroes to run into the burning house. Heroes act without thinking. Anyone who stops to think for a minute will not do such foolish things. Women are not so often heroes because they use their heads."

She sighed. "My Merle, he always argued with me that heroes more than anyone have focus sharp like a razor; in one glance their minds see the past, present, and future, but their actions go beyond the limits of time. He would say I just didn't understand what a hero is because I had never been in combat. He had never been in combat, either, but I didn't say that. He was a good man, my Merle, and he believed above all in defending the USA from its enemies. I have the higher faith, the one in mein lieber Gott. Ja, ja, your Harvey was a hero, also a very good man. Alex, who can say: he might turn into something yet."

The unholy alliance between my mother and Trudel, the relentless pursuit by Papito's ghost, the futureless future I faced here impressed on me the need to get out of Dodge, to go somewhere that no one knew who I was. And soon, before I went totally nuts or was conscripted for service in some corrupt, bloody, oil-garnering invasion and had to take Tiger with me so Trudel wouldn't dump the best cat ever at the pound—or murder him.

One pinhole, enough to let in a gleam of hope, penetrated my acute sense of futility. Its source was Joaquin, who'd been a twelfth grader when I was in ninth, not your typical high school hero but a brooding gypsy poet. Rose had idolized him. She even used one of his poems in her valedictory address. He was a loner, kind of quiet, except when delivering his poetry; then he'd soar. Even Hersch and Joey couldn't find a way to mock Joaquin.

So there he was, after Vista Grande'd been torched, living in the mountains outside of Trove, Colorado, no more than four hours from where I was warehoused. Joaquin posted that he needed some skilled labor to finish building a passive-solar cabin on land he'd inherited from his grandparents. Subsistence farming while he built: off the grid and at peace with himself.

Still wiped out and enormously uninterested in life, I nonetheless sent him a message that I was coming, and without checking for a reply, loaded up my pack, grabbed Tiger, saluted Trudel, kissed Mamia, and headed off. Then I turned around and went back.

"The thing is, I need some money for a bus ticket. Sorry to have to ask but it's—"

"Alex, you had four hundred in the bank before the...and I've already added the five thousand your father left you. My own inheritance is—I'll buy you a car."

It was good to hit the road in Pacman 2, a restored classic that even had a USB port. Tiger curled up beside me, listening to a folk-rock 60s mix, I shed some of the lunatic guilt and fear that I'd been trapped in. Maybe Joaquin would be a friend who could see past the scars. Maybe working with him would ground me. Maybe escaping the Ville, I'd lose Papito's ghost. Maybe I'd find a way to unbox myself and live in the open.

6

"Aim Past the Wood"

There are days so lazy we can't even remember having lived them. The sun slows its course to an amble; late afternoon feels like midmorning. Hours lose dimension, swelling windily in the ponderosas but headed nowhere. The sediments of the day lie on our backs, hardening them to stone. We pause, in love with the interior quietude of granite and the ease of stopping, the irresistible allure of torpor. And wait for nightfall, a change that may revive our impetus.

It was on such a one that a shadowless figure made its way along the dirt road. Though his eyes were fixed on the fields and the mountains beyond them, he could sense that an aerial view would have revealed the immensity of the land he still had to travel through to reach human habitation. The same view would have shown how great was the distance he had already come from a broken-down VW. Yet from his limited perception he was walking in place. Beside him strode a cat.

The lone figure halted to try his phone again, which still didn't pick up a signal, take a slug of water, give the cat a drink from his hands, and adjust the sweaty bandanna wrapped around his head (and wish he had a cap), then trudged on. The day seemed to be growing longer as he and his companion moved through it.

What he couldn't see was the spool of dust following him down the road, soon to overtake him. The cat heard it first, raising his head to alert his partner. As the vehicle neared, the walker scrambled to the side of the road and hoisted his thumb in the universal hitchhiker's plea. The cat remained beside him, tail waving high. Then they saw the flashing red light. It meant nothing to the cat, but an instinctive fear punched the man. He hadn't done anything wrong, nothing he remembered, but the lights, the last time he'd seen them, signaled trauma. Devastation.

Frighteningly thin, exhausted (he always was these days), uncertain of the future and unable to lose the past, he couldn't withstand another blow. On top of which the desolation of this place, a thousand film scenarios, some primordial dread of authority gripped his bowels.

The black-and-white came to a stop. Rolling down his passenger window, the sheriff scrutinized him, shook his head. Noticed the cat. "Headed somewhere?" His voice sounded menacing.

It was hard to talk without breathing. "To find a friend," I muttered. For as you guessed, it was I on that infinite summer day, traipsing the road to what I hoped was a new life.

"That your cat?" I thought it was obvious but curbed the sarcasm and nodded.

"Car break down?" That, too, seemed obvious. I nodded.

"Passed it a-ways back. VW. Classic. When they're running. My buddy Floyd, he owns a repair shop."

I forced the air back into my gut, although my hands were still fisted. Classic bullshit. Get the kid's guard down with small talk before you nail him.

"Who you looking for?"

Should Alex rat out his pal? Yeah, it wasn't going to take bamboo under the fingernails.

"Joaquin. He's my friend. Building a house."

The sheriff's face remained impassive. He reached over and swung the passenger door open. "Get in," he ordered. "I was just going to see him."

Hanging on to Tiger like he was a stuffed animal and I was a little boy, we rode the washboard. *Get in. I was just going to see him.* Busted. Hey, Joaquin, it's me; I made it. And look what I brought you. What a sweet gift, huh? I'm a generous guy, always have been. That's why people run and hide when they see me coming—too much largesse.

"You old friends?"

It was too complicated to explain. That we'd known each other in a facial-recognition way when we passed in the halls during high school but hadn't seen each other in years. That he might not be thrilled by my showing up—I wouldn't be if it were my house. But I wouldn't be here if my house and most of my hometown hadn't been burned to the ground.

"Sort of," I said, and added for no good reason, "I'm here to help him with the house."

"Yeah?" The sheriff sounded skeptical as he sized me up. Very skinny, shrunken, white, with scars on my cheek, nose, lip, and chin (the bandanna covered the big one on my forehead). I didn't look like the kind of guy who could do much of anything. "You a builder?"

Prison whore, yes; carpenter, no, his voice implied.

"I know my way around nails," I boasted, trying to sound tough and seasoned, thinking, yeah, I've been hammered a lot.

"The cat?"

"Plumbing and plastering." If I was going to get whacked by this guy, might as well be for a joke. When he snapped my spine, would he crack a smile?

"I got a sink that's draining sluggish. Maybe he could take a look."

Leave 'em laughing when you go. I risked a glance at his face. No sign of amusement. He slowed down, signaled, and eased the cruiser down a steep side road. My bandanna was soaked through.

Ahead of us lay a broad meadow valley rimmed by ponderosas, spruce, firs, and aspen. Peaks rose beyond them, cutting a jagged line in the azure sky. If this was the last thing I saw, it was a majestic panorama to hold in my dying eyes.

The sheriff pointed to a half-finished two-story log cabin (let's call it a chateau) under construction on the high slopes across the valley, bordered by pines. "That's it." His hand slid over the butt of his pistol and onto his thigh. Now I saw a few other dwellings set far apart along the wide back of the hill, a few more down in the valley where a river oxbowed its way south.

I let out a deep breath. "Awesome." Dead or alive, I was here to stay. With that resolved, the terror uncoiled and I smiled.

"You fish?" I asked the sheriff, reaching for some guy talk.

"Not around here; it's all private. City folks. Summer homes. Mostly Texans. Where're you from?'

My hesitation made whatever I said next sound like a lie, but I didn't know what to say. "Vista Grande," I said at last. "Was. Born and raised. Just now, Summerville. Nowhere any more. Here." I struggled to focus on the beauty before me.

"Down about two miles is public. They bite pretty good on power bait. Smelly cheese. Worms after it rains."

I felt like we were past the torture stage. My death, when it came, would be quick and clean.

The cruiser was riding the high middle hump and the side heading up the slope, trying to clear the ruts, but it took some tricky maneuvers. Tiger rode the bumps and dips like a pro, shifting his weight to bank with the car, while I surreptitiously mashed the door handle.

"You hunt?" The sheriff asked me. Once again the answer seemed fairly self-evident, given my physique, but I tried to make my answer sound like a choice.

"Not much lately. I rely on Tiger here to keep us in meat. Of course his tastes run more to rabbits and mice than elk or bear."

This time the sheriff grinned. A reprieve! I stroked Tiger vigorously. Thanks, man. Right on cue, a meadowlark trilled and Tiger pricked up his ears.

The cruiser's red lights flashed across Joaquin's house as we pulled in. Despite all the friendly banter, I couldn't repress a twinge of uneasiness. Like a bad dude heading for a shootout, the sheriff strode forcefully toward the door, which opened to reveal Joaquin trundling out to greet him with a brotherly hug.

"Hey, Jess, how's it going? Come on in." He stopped, frowning lightly at me.

"I picked him up on the road," Jess explained. "Said he was a friend of yours. If he ain't, I can plug him, throw him in that open lime pit out back where we stow the bodies. But," he added, "the cat's a keeper."

"Alex," I said quickly. "And Tiger." Waited for the light of recognition. "I told you I was coming."

Joaquin nodded uncertainly. "Didn't know you were bringing a cat. Lots of coyotes around here." No open-armed embrace for Tiger and me.

"He's tough. He'll be all right." As if to prove my point, Tiger stalked off toward the woodpile in quest of rodents or a private spot to dump a load. Both, I figured.

"His car broke down a-ways back," the sheriff told Joaquin. "It's going to need a tow."

Joaquin shook his head. "I don't have time for that today. Can Floyd get it?"

"For the right price he'll do anything." They were talking past me like I wasn't there, which made me feel like a kid again, Papito and Mamia solving my problems in a resigned and exasperated tone.

"I've got money. I can take care of it," I cut in sharply.

"Your stuff's all bagged," Joaquin told Jess. "Want to come in?"

"Hey, yeah, thanks, man." Jess followed him through the door. I tagged along like he'd included me in the invitation.

Wrong. Joaquin wheeled around. "Listen, Alex. This is private business. It's legit but what happens here is strictly between Jess and me. Got it?"

The sheriff adjusted his handcuffs and sidled his hand along his holster. The fear that had paralyzed my vocal cords back on the road slugged me hard, making my head reel. Prison, the pit, the man who never came to dinner, car abandoned on the road, never seen again. Being a stranger here (albeit in paradise) a new worry possessed me: who'd take care of Tiger?

"I'll wait outside," I muttered, shuffling toward the woodpile as though I were already in leg chains.

"Oh, hey, man," Joaquin relented. "I didn't mean to weird you out. You might as well know if you're going to be here. I'm just saying, discretion is critical. Come on." It was as much of a welcome as I was going to get, and I accepted it.

The interior was dark and cool with only a few windows in place. The living room and kitchen had the intimate tranquility of lovingly handmade spaces. Wood reigned supreme: log walls, ceiling beams, wide pine floorboards, and through the two windows, a view of aspen and ponderosas. It was like a man-den in a forest. Finished, I could tell it would be nirvana, a place where I'd like to stay forever.

Joaquin was handing the sheriff a plastic bag of weed. This was not on my radar as a standard transaction with the law.

Jess put his arm around Joaquin. "That's really going to ease her, Joaquin. You sure I can't pay you?"

Joaquin laughed. "With what? All that coin you've got stashed after the doctor and hospital bills? Don't give it a thought."

The sheriff's eyes were trained on some point beyond the walls of the house. He was seeing things I couldn't, but following his gaze I took in the wildflowers carpeting the meadow that ran down to the river. Daisies, penstemon, some small red bellflowers amid long grasses undulating beneath the run of the wind. When you're new to it, you can't see beyond the beauty. But who needs to see more? I watched the field dapple as cloud shadows passed, grasses arching and swaying like a cat's back under a full body scratch. Where was Tiger?

"There," Jess said. "Looks like he's scored." Staggering towards us with a gopher locked in his jaws, Tiger had procured his first dinner in Trove.

"Got to get going," the sheriff said abruptly. "Head over to Miles' place, see how he's doing after the accident." He slapped me lightly on the back. "You're a lucky kid." I knew that, I really did. So many bad things could have happened on the ride over here.

"Not everyone survives a fire," he went on. Right. "Or has a cat like Tiger." True. "Or a friend like Joaquin. We're both lucky on that account." He tipped his hat to Joaquin.

Leaning out the window of the cruiser, he called, "Floyd'll get your car to his shop and fix 'er up. Let you know when she's ready. Pay him in cash." He waved off my thanks and saluted Tiger, struggling into the yard with his kill.

"Come around back," Joaquin said when we were alone, "so you'll understand."

The greenhouse was finished, tight, in primo condition for the couple of hundred marijuana plants thriving in its hot, moist microclimate. "I'm a licensed distributor," Joaquin explained. "Not getting rich, but it's a living." He fixed me with a very explicit eye. "Jesse's wife is fighting cancer. Trying experimental treatments not covered by insurance, along with the standard torture. Way over his head in debt. He'd do anything for her. Or us. He's a superhero."

Talk about not seeing things. I wondered whether the fire had blinded my heart's eye and I no longer had insight into the suffering of others. Maybe I couldn't read people any better than I could books now, just turning the pages without deriving any meaning from the words.

"I guess you didn't see my reply after you wrote me." Joaquin was leading me around to the yard, where Tiger was ripping into the belly of his victim, discarding the organs he didn't care to eat. No, I hadn't—and on purpose in case he asked me not to come. "I wrote back and asked you not to come." He was trying to gentle his voice. "Because I realized I could hire help locally and that would be better. I've been worried that the locals would object to my greenhouse, or maybe the opposite: raid it. It's not a secret, but I don't talk about it much. Still, you have to trust the people you're sharing this stretch of the planet with." He paused to give me a chance to say something, which I didn't. "There's this brawny kid, some great-nephew of Floyd's, with a back of iron"—I sensed an unflattering comparison with my wasted physique— "who needs the cash. I can call him when I need him."

We could try California, Tiger and I, become beach bums while my five grand lasted. Maybe Tiger could learn to fish. Or we could disappear into Mexico.

"I don't need steady help. Just someone at critical moments." Joaquin was dragging out this farewell thing ridiculously. "The main thing is I'm kind of a loner and I—"

"No worries, man. As soon as the car's fixed, we'll be gone. Is there any place in town Tiger and I can stay till then?"

"Here, stay here." Hearty, relieved. "It's not going to be more than a couple or three days. I'm a lousy cook, though, just warning you."

Three days. "I'm a good one. Worked at El Oro, hung out a lot in the kitchen. Omelets, enchiladas, barbeque, even a few veggies." Joaquin looked half-starved, which I also hadn't noticed before.

"I was ready to fight Tiger for a chunk of that gopher. Might have to go to town for supplies. Show you what I've got."

Joaquin's larder was very bare and very moldy. I made a mental list. Three days, maybe more. You never know which of the random skills you acquire is going to pay off.

After a quick trip to Trove in Joaquin's truck to procure supplies, I rustled up enough grub to satisfy three large men that night, and we ate most of it: pan-fried steaks, cowboy potatoes, soft rolls with butter, and even a couple of sliced tomatoes, all of which I bought, and Joaquin sprang for a twelve-pack of Mexican beer. He ate nonstop for nearly an hour, savoring every bite and packing away enough to add several pounds to his skeletal frame. I ate more than I had in months, and Tiger added a mouse to his rodent death toll as well as devouring scraps of steak fat. He and I hungered for more than food, but sharing a good meal was a start.

There'd been only one snag: when I went to light the wood cook-stove, I choked. Couldn't strike the match. I was bullying myself into doing it when Joaquin stepped in. "I'll get it. The stove's totally safe; you can count on that." If he hadn't seen me wince, I could have done it.

Sharing a good meal. Sitting around a table, cutting bites, chewing, washing them down with beer: That's the key bonding agent for creating good will. Food is a conversation lubricant, a kumbaya peacemaker, a bridge builder. Every culture knows this; hence, all holidays revolve around sharing a meal. Meet greet eat. From cavemen roasting mastodons to eighteen-course state dinners, all of us understand this basic principle for forging friendships. Joaquin and I, stuffing ourselves and chatting between forkfuls and slugs of brew, taking in the mellow notes drifting down the stairs from his sound system, began to clear a passage through the dense overgrowth that had complicated the beginning of our day.

"I didn't realize how badly I needed a decent meal," he said. "It's way more than decent, I mean, a feast. You sure can cook."

"Staff of life. I get a kick out of fooling around with new combos of ingredients. Herbs, spices, sauces. It's all cool."

"You go to college?"

"Yeah."

"Where?"

"UNM."

"Major?"

"English." I could see that caught him off-guard.

"What was your focus?"

"Southwest literature. I wrote my honors thesis on Abbey's *Monkey Wrench Gang*."

Joaquin smiled. "Great choice." My street cred was on the rise, and it seemed like it might be my move when Joaquin leaned forward, his eyes pinned to mine. "Do any writing?"

"Some. I won a prize for a short story junior year." Check. My turn. "You still writing?"

"Some. Not so much right now, but I will be when the construction's done. Just me and my greenhouse, six feet of snow, clear, quiet days." He smiled. "A woman next spring if I get lucky."

"Ah, a woman. Always an attractive addition to a homestead." (Of course that was out for me now, the ugliest freak in the world.) "And personally I'd recommend a cat. They're very inspirational to poets. You are still writing poetry, right?"

"Oh, yeah. I get impatient with narrative."

"You were amazing in high school."

"I was a kid in high school. Making it up."

"Blew my mind, the words that poured out of you. Beautiful. Totally uninhibited."

"Alienated. Totally egotistical. Fishing for love with a line of verse."

"You hooked a bunch of us."

"A lot of that stuff was crap. I reread it sometimes, to keep myself honest, and can't believe how self-indulgent I was. What are you working on now?" His move. I ducked.

"Nothing really, since the—"

"A novel?" he pursued.

Okay, I could talk about that since it didn't amount to anything.

"Kind of. Probably have to start over now."

"Who's the protagonist?"

"Well, he's this guy called Noland Chance. Eccentric archaeologist. On the fringe."

"Conflict?"

"His very separate view of common reality. You know, I haven't gotten very far into it. More of a concept with some random notes in quest of a voice."

"Annie Dillard says write as if you were staying up with a dying friend. Make it the most important thing you have to say."

"And aim past the wood for the chopping block. She also says that."

"You just need the first paragraph, according to García Márquez. Everything else flows from that."

"Joan Didion claims that by the time you've written the second sentence, all your options are gone."

"Keep it dramatic." Robert Frost.

"No pissless prose." William Gass. I choked back a laugh. Pissless Gass. What a combo. "None of it helps. You just write what's in your head the best you can and then edit it into submission."

"So the fire really nailed you, huh?"

The game was getting stale. Hadn't I already told Joaquin this story? I hated repeating myself. Suddenly I was beat.

"I dove into a burning house. Not too smart."

"Who were you trying to save?" A perspicacious fellow, that Joaquin. I chewed on a hunk of steak a good long while before answering.

"My dad. And our old dog. I was way too late."

"That's the story you ought to write."

"It's a very short one. You just heard it."

"That's just the tagline, not the story."

"Half the people in Vista Grande have already written their tragic fire memoirs."

Into my mind fell an image from the time I don't like to talk about: a journalist sitting in Trudel's living room prying details out of Mamia, trying to probe me. The two women were spilling their guts, but I didn't say a word. My story (their version) might already be on the market.

"No one can write your story but you."

"What about yours? What happened to the ranch, your folks. How you ended up here."

"Incredibly boring. What's going to happen, the life I'm planning to make, that might be worth telling. We'll see. What's your plan, going forward?"

I laid my fork down, feeling a sudden hunger that steak wouldn't quell. The wind blew through, leaving me light-headed. It was my move. I stared at the board, wondering how I could put off losing the longest.

Time widened, the chess of our conversation drifting through interstellar galaxies sustained only by faith in the idea of destination, in the hope of a purpose to be ultimately revealed, of secrets we could not fathom, a darkness so utter memories were indistinguishable from dreams, and laughter had no echo.

Checkmate. I had no plan going forward. Except to keep going away away away, as far from the fire as I could get. To defeat the brutal exhaustion of that horror.

Any moment I was going to fall asleep at the table. Pushing my chair back, I grabbed the dishes and headed for the sink. I'd already filled it with water and a stack of dirties when Joaquin put his hand on my shoulder. "Leave them. Morning's soon enough. As my gramps used to say, let the water do the work." He ducked into the living room and returned to the table with a guitar.

"Hey, Mr. Tambourine Man, play a song for me…"

I grinned. Back in the land of Papito, who gave me a harmonica when I was ten and got me playing along with Dylan. Forget bed. I grabbed another brew for both of us and pulled my harpoon out of my dirty red backpack. Joaquin gave me my cue: "In the jingle jangle morning I'll come following you," and I cut loose on a solo that shook an admiring "You rock!" from the man. Put another checkmark in the "he's a keeper" column next to my name.

Joaquin was polishing off a six-pack and neither of us was feeling any pain when the salamander walked through the kitchen. A salamander, about a foot long, maybe more counting its sleek, undulating tail. Two-tone, black and gold, with those prehistoric amphibious eyes. We froze. Following the scent of the river, maybe, it swept out the front door and headed down valley.

"A tiger salamander," Joaquin whispered. "A blessing upon this house." He looked at me with something like reverence. "Could be you, bringing it upon us."

I've been called a lot of things but never a blessing. My divine new status emboldened me. "Hey, I'd like to be the one. I'd like to stay."

Silence. Too blunt, too pushy, too soon. But then I was merely a blessing, not a saint.

"Did that just happen? Did a tiger salamander really walk through the kitchen?"

I nodded.

"Out of its range, I think. Endangered. Incredible. Definitely a sacred moment to write a poem or song about."

"Songwriting is one of my many talents, along with cooking and the harmonica. I do laundry, too."

"All I want is peace. We don't have much time left on the planet, and it's my aim to make each day I have beautiful, serene, fully lived. Make the time count."

A gust of night wind flapped the ties of my bandanna. I reached up and slid the filthy, sweat-stained cotton off. Joaquin's face registered shock as he took in the grotesque red welt scarring my forehead. Zorro couldn't have zapped me worse than the fire did. "Sorry, I forgot," I said, struggling to retie the bandannage again.

"Don't worry about it, man. I look just as bad on the inside." He paused, weighing the words he was about to speak. "This is the best place to heal that I can imagine."

Yes! A fountain of gratitude burbled up through my sinuses and spilled into the corners of my eyes. I was in. Home safe.

"Here's one I'm working on. Need another verse," Joaquin began to pluck the strings, minor chords, a sweet tune. "She turns her green eye on the hills / gives them the will to live again for a while, in their way. / She brings a rainbow afternoon to wander / where across the skies I fly overnight."

The longing in the words and purity of his voice carried me to the threshold of a realm I had not entered since college, when I went on a solo camping trip to get over a girl who'd dumped me (not my first but definitely my worst dumping). The Truchas Mountains. I fished and hiked my way back to sanity. During that spell, the world seemed infinitely melancholy, and I sank into elegiac dreams of a land where no one had ever set foot. Virgin territory, pure, pristine: wide open. I slipped inside stones and could hear the ponderous beat of the mountain. I crept onto aspen leaves where shivers of wind fondled my skin. A brilliant marriage of harmony and yearning. Nothing was out of place and nothing was lacking. One evening this stately old buck and I exchanged a soulful eyeballing and hokey as it sounds, he gave me the "It's all cool, man" high-sign message that restarted me.

"'I need the darkness, I need the river / to set me free for the moon / ah, summer dreams.' That's as far as I've gotten." He kept plucking the guitar, humming.

My turn to be generous. "Listen, I'll leave whenever you say the word. I don't want to screw up this sublime thing you've got going here. I'll pull my weight for as long as I stay. Keep me honest."

Joaquin nodded once. "Deal." He was still inside his song. "My wings seek the moon / summer dreams will awake and I'll fly…" He was free-styling, making it up as he went along. To have such images at the top of your mind, not buried under a lot of garbage: that's what I needed.

"'Where the hmm-hmm scent of dew on dust / lifts the willows into wings' something-something then go to: 'Summer rising on the something night, my life…' I'll come back to it tomorrow. My brain's too addled with booze to get the words right."

"Don't you have to write all that down?"

"No, I've got it. Still revising anyway. It's a song to this Luna moth that was on my wall. Spectacular. They only live one night, you know."

My sinuses began oozing afresh. "I was looking to get the hell out of Dodge when I came, but I hadn't really considered the possibility that I might end up in paradise. I feel like I've got a chance to get it together, and thanks for that man, Joaquin." God, was it ever time for bed.

"Wait'll I put you to work." He smiled, then grew serious. "I mean it. This is not a vacation home. And there are a lot of folks you need to be friendly with if you want to make it around here. That part drives me crazy," he added, "all the socializing."

I was beginning to see the role I'd be playing: cooking, cleaning, shopping, gossiping with the townsfolk. It reminded me of the housewives on the '70s reruns Tante Trudel watched faithfully to keep the existing world at bay. Mom: I could do that. For a while. "Dinner's ready, honey. Wash your hands, please." Okay, not that. But this thing was going to work.

"Hey, I'm good at that stuff, high-level neighborly chitchat. Menial, unskilled labor: that's the easy part."

It was late enough to be a Saturday night date, and we were both beat, but neither of us moved. The wind, chilly by now, rippled through the house, and in the east window above the sink a horned moon rose. The silence was so vast that even the crickets singing in the dark did not pierce but deepen it. Peace-peace-peace they chorused. Yes, this is why I came, oh ye gods of hills and forests. The bandanna is off: I'm out, undisguised, the full Alex. And so ready to crash.

I was gathering the will to stand up when a savage howl rent the serenity of the night and a killer stalked through the door: Tiger, dragging the salamander, its neck in his murderous jaws. It was half his size and could have put up a good fight.

"No!" yelled Joaquin, lunging at Tiger, who began to growl ferociously. Wrong tactic, as any veteran of the feline battlefield can tell you.

"Wait!" I yelled, lunging at Joaquin. "Wait. Let me do this."

Years of saving half-dead victims from the stranglehold of Tiger's jaws had taught me that if I panicked, so did he, clamping shut his deadly fangs. Forcible extraction was out. Flattery and deceit were my only allies in this rescue mission. I softened my voice to a purr.

"Wow, Tige, you really did it this time. Good kitty-kitty, let me see, you ruthless assassin, good boy, you are a monster, I can't believe you did that, good Tiger, let's see what you've got there, fellah."

Stroking him with one hand, I fastened the other around the hinges of his jaws and expertly squeezed them open between my Fingers of Life. The salamander (which was too large for his mouth anyway) dropped to the floor, and I grabbed it, keeping Tiger pinned with my stroking hand. The salamander twisted in my grasp, trying to wrest itself free: yes, still alive.

I laid the mander on the table where we could examine its wounds more closely. Punctures, but none that went clear through. He might make it. On the other hand, what did I know about salamanders?

More than Joaquin, as it turned out.

"I think," he ventured, "that reptiles need water."

"I think," I ventured, "that salamanders are amphibians." He frowned. "But whatever," I added hastily, "he still needs water."

Joaquin filled a hammered aluminum basin with about an inch of water, and we placed the mander in it. "Let's keep him overnight for observation," Joaquin said grimly. "You better observe the cat as well. Tomorrow you can try to release him downstream, beyond the cat's range. If he's still alive."

That was one of those unclear pronoun references that can make you uneasy.

"I'm really sorry about this, man. I should have figured Tiger would go for it. But, don't worry, everything is going to work out just fine." As much a prayer as a promise.

Joaquin propped his guitar against the doorway. "We'll see." As much a warning as a threat.

Tiger, who had seriously jeopardized my blessing status, glared at me, then narrowed his eyes at the basin. It was going to be tricky to pull this thing off. Best would be to stay awake on guard duty all night, but I would have been the "he" who might or not still be alive unless I got prone very soon. The sofa in the living room, whose cushions had been compressed into placemats for the springs, seemed to be my designated bed. I lay down gingerly, covered the basin with my bandanna, balanced it on my stomach, and wrapped my arms tightly around it. Not ideal, but hey, since my survival depended on the salamander's, a brief night of discomfort was not much of a price to pay.

I took a few deep breaths and tried to relax. But don't let go, I instructed my brain, and don't let me turn over. Hang on to this basin like we're in the middle of the ocean and it's our life raft.

Tiger jumped up on my legs and began walking toward the life raft. I kicked him off, both of us growling at each other. "Get out of here," I snarled at him, a futile command since cats owe no man obedience. It was up to me to keep him at bay. And, brain, I admonished, don't let the cat near us; treat him like he's a killer whale. Come on: think ocean, drowning, jaws of death: hang on to this damn basin no matter what. And wake me up if the salamander goes into cardiac arrest.

Lying on my back (conversing with my brain) with the basin on my belly, I gradually became painfully aware that my bladder was still loaded with beer. I knew I should get up and relieve it, but I couldn't face the effort. Luckily, on a camping trip in my childhood I'd learned Papito's trick for silencing the urgent cry of the urine: Imagine myself on a desert with only this water left, and hold on to it with all you've got, keep it in. He persuaded me of the completely erroneous idea that if I didn't pee, the sludge in my bladder would be reabsorbed into my body and keep me hydrated all night long.

Now, from the mature plateau I inhabit, I can see clearly that he simply didn't want to get out of his bag and help me get out of mine, unzip the tent, shine the flashlight on a potential site, then wait for me to overcome my fear of lions and tigers and bears, oh my, and lay down a thin stream of pee that could have waited. So, thanks to my old man, I'd cultivated a bladder the size of Delaware with the forbearance of Gandhi.

However, the issue with Papito's metaphor at this particular moment was that I'd been conditioning my brain to think ocean, and switching to desert might fry my mental circuits, leaving me vulnerable to the normal flailings of a sleeper, as well as give Tiger free range.

And there was also the problem of my ghostbuster gloves, zipped into the side pocket of my filthy red backpack slumped in the kitchen. White and ridiculous, I'd taken to donning them in case my hands slipped out from under the covers while I slept. They were an old pair of Trudel's she'd given me to protect my hands from the sun, and as with everything in those bleak days, I didn't protest. But tonight, either wearing them or not wearing them posed hazards. There was no way to explain them to Joaquin if he chanced to catch a glimpse. Then again, quite possibly without them I would be dead before morning.

Or would I? The room felt clear of my old man's ethereal presence. No white mist in the corners. No thickening in the air. No murmurs from another world. Not a whiff of his terrible shaving cream. Leaving as abruptly as I had with only a vague notion of where I was headed, had I, as hoped, given Papito's ghost the slip? I lay very still, checking and double-checking for signs of him.

Maybe I was free. Or maybe I'd be leaving at daybreak, hauling a new amphibious ghost with me. We'll see, Joaquin had said. No guarantees. Tiger began to make retching noises on the floor. He was well on his way to winning the El Grotesco contest in an unreality show. Are tiger salamanders poisonous? What a fragile hold I had on this brave new world, I thought, tightening my grasp on the basin. My bladder screamed for mercy.

A quick aerial snapshot of me by that photographer-of-the-absurd, the mind's eye, started a volcano of laughter, which was not conducive to repressing urine. "No," I said firmly, to my salamander-pressed bladder. "I have to stay. You wait till morning."

At that moment T. S. Eliot walked through the door. "The faith and the love and the hope are all in the waiting," he intoned. "Wait without thought, for you are not ready for thought." Great: some advice I didn't need coming unbidden from the master. It's an English major thing; all these famous writers have time-shares in your brain.

My back itched. Very carefully I scootched up and down the sofa, trying to scratch it. The water sloshed in the basin, spilling a mini-waterfall onto my belly. "Faith, hope, and love. What about charity, oh Thomas, stern Eliot?" He stooped and gently scratched Tiger's back where mine itched, then with a wan smile, faded from view.

Come on, I said to myself, just stand up, use the john, and start over. The sunburned scars on my face throbbed, and I knew I ought to slather some of that cream stowed in my backpack on them. Get the gloves. My bladder was on its knees.

"You're in a desert," I explained wearily, "keeping me alive."

7

A Wind of Light

Sunday, a month in, I rose early, affirming my new way of life. I felt good, soul-deep whole for the first time since before the fire. Since graduation from college. The slender oxbows of the Rio Sol shimmered in the valley below; a dawn breeze set the white and purple slopes of daisies and penstemon undulating. My bones ached with a flood of exaltation I could not contain. Here it all stood, the world which made room for us, and here I stood, for a rare moment feeling utterly at home in it. The place had chosen me, and I belonged where I was. Having been granted a morning of transcendent grace, it flashed on me that if I could float in this moment along the time/space axis through an infinity loop, I'd forego living on to see what happened next. Become the embodiment of Nietzsche's eternal return, except that I wouldn't be coming from or going to anywhere. I would be the essence of *is* and absolute of *here.*

Kundera described it as "the unbearable lightness of being," an emptiness that is the antithesis of loneliness, that is release and ecstasy. But unbearable because it cannot be sustained, can barely be remembered as more than a yearning. "Happiness," he says in a passage that broke my heart, "is the longing for repetition. That is why humans cannot attain it."

I wondered what kind of a day it was when Jesus rose from the grave. When he returned, stepping out of the cave-grave on a Sunday in spring, was it a magnificent morning? And after dying, surpassingly exquisite, he seeing things as if for the first time as he walked forth at the top of the hill, arid slopes coming into bloom, and beyond them the sea. Was the leavetaking harder after the resurrection than being crucified? That time, he would be back before long, if he was right. This time, because he was right, he would not. Surely he loved life as much as the rest of us. How could martyrdom have been more tempting than the curve of the gulf, the sparkling sea, and the smiles of earth? He'd done his job, suffering horribly to immortalize his father; he deserved a reprieve. In some theologies, Jesus returns at Pentecost to bless his apostles, which from this vantage point I see as longing for the earth. He made up some excuse to persuade his father to let him walk again along the luminous shore, watch the fish leap, the sea birds dive and soar. His heart was torn with desire to dwell eternally in this moment or live beyond it: to remain immortal or join the dance of transience. One time only for everything. Unbearably sad and ecstatic, what we get to have, what we don't. Each allotment incomparable, incomprehensible.

But Jesus was a good son and did not forsake his father, purportedly redeeming us thereby but mostly redeeming his father. Unlike me.

Tiger stretched front and back, shook himself, and yawned. A quick scan revealed to him the secret murmurings of field mice, rabbits, and prairie dogs emerging from holes. All manner of feast bustled on the valley slopes beneath the surface calm that held my eye.

The sun was just cresting the saddleback next to Indigo Peak. A meadowlark greeted me with its honeyed trill, a song of keen poignancy that never failed to hold me in its thrall. One of my clearest memories was a noonday stop in Kansas, in July, in Pacman 1 (no a.c.). I stepped out into the breathless wall of heat and heard a meadowlark. The song changed misery to euphoria, and all the resistance I'd put into fighting this blast furnace melted to gratitude for such a singular call to consciousness of beauty.

Hummingbirds were awake, too, whirring around Joaquin's many feeders, which, at my suggestion, I now kept filled. The ruby-throated were the more aggressive ones, diving at my red bandanna, then sheering off at perilous angles. Hummers had always been Tiger's nemesis. He'd endured humiliating defeats at their wings, banging into tree trunks and slipping on rocks. The failure to nail a single hummer was no doubt why he turned his murderous attention onto rodentia.

I have been feeling awake in ways I had never expected to nor known. Rising early on my own. This time of day used to be my nemesis, when for a spell I lay as if entombed. I called it the hour of the Grog, which I pictured as a beast primordial: squat and warty as a toad with the jaws of a slavering crocodile. Sitting on my head, the Grog would devour me if I moved. It had, I was certain, already injected me with paralyzing venom. I lay immobilized, smashed, crushed in a place whose dimensions did not include time. It was no-when, nowhere. Gradually the light of day would grow raucous and the rheumatic cough of my neighbors' truck would restore me to my bed. The alarm would go off, and I would discover Tiger stretched out on top of me, purring and kneading the blanket, fixing me with a hard and kibbled look. It was unnerving to come to in the sights of a killer cat, but it was also a relief that Tiger had vanquished the Grog.

All that was before the fire. After, I was roused daily by the alarm in my head, screaming catastrophe, demanding I get up and do it right this time. You know what not to do, cackled the alarm, so do something smarter than you usually would. And I did, over and over again. I tried out one plan and another, following each to its desired end. Then a flaw would come to mind, and I retraced my steps, choosing a different route at the point of miscalculation. Or started over. But never yet had I been completely satisfied with the outcome. Too many variables; too much for me to manage well. One day my primary goal was to do no harm and survive. The next, to perish (fully this time) having rescued my father and dog and whoever else I could. I didn't know which would make me happiest: to continue as the get-by-guy or to go out as a hero-slash-martyr.

Only in the last few days, here at Joaquin's, have I begun to wake up before the mental alarm, coming to myself in silence: the silence that is birdsong, dawn wind in ponderosas, a distant bell, the fall of the river. Only recently have I awoken in a clearing, my eyes wide as I open them, ready to go forth unresisting into the sunrise.

Years ago my father told me that Buddhist monks take special care with the moment their feet first touch the ground every morning. That point of reconnection with the earth must be attended to, insist the monks. In the past I had more urgent matters to attend to first, and then it was too late, and most mornings the thought never grazed my consciousness anyway. But the notion stuck with me and now it had become part of my arising. I paused before I placed my feet on the ground. Then, obeying some instinct deeper than ritual, I turned slowly as I stretched, greeting all four directions of the morning world. Having a new way of entering it gave me the sense that I had changed. And being able to change of my own will engendered a sense of control I lost in the fire—or perhaps never worried about having.

Nor did I imagine I had changed from Bug to man by magic, as satire, or out of rage. I had allowed, I had initiated, the change because it was essential and I was ready. "Ripeness is all," oh, yes. But to pluck the moment of ripeness cloistered among the tempting gilded ones requires an attentive heart. To make it fruitful, a valiant spirit. So much easier to yield to the forces of entropy.

Trove was in the third year of a severe drought. There was no ambient moisture left in the soil; the only source of water was rain, doled out parsimoniously by the clouds: a few drops for these hills, a cupful for those. The river was low, and for Trove, at 9000 feet up in the Rockies, temperatures were high. The drought formed the heartwood of every conversation, as I discovered on my forays into town, but the tone was desperation, not complaint. A big fire the year before had wiped out whole mountainsides of white pine, ponderosa, and aspen. Where the devastation began and ended was a trick of the wind—and of course, the efforts of extraordinary hotshot firefighters. Where the flames had prevailed, blackened slopes exposed the vulnerability of this tough alpine landscape. The longing for rain was tempered by a fear of erosion and rockslides. Joaquin's meadow had been mercifully spared, a gift of uncertain duration. We clung to predictions of a cold, wet winter: the return of El Niño, a miracle more welcome than the Second Coming.

Fire, rain, or whatever might lie ahead, after four weeks in Trove, I was in love. I wanted to stay. Here, with Joaquin. But the odds were against that. I'd taken to rising early to prepare myself to face the question he was bound to ask: "So, what are your plans?" I knew he expected me to move on, but every day my resolve to stay grew stronger.

Because I could see myself creating a life of purpose and meaning here with Joaquin. Because I could imagine a profound healing that would both liberate and season me. I would learn to be a true friend and in time grow to be a sustaining force in Joaquin's life. I would buy land close to him, find a woman who would love me, love the scars that saved me despite myself, a woman who would love Tiger, have children with me. Joaquin and his family would be our closest friends. Our small colony, dwelling in the mountains, would cast our joy and faith into the common pool of Trove's grace.

The hungry dream of a haunted man.

Over the course of this month, I'd discovered I had a natural affinity for gardening. In the greenhouse lay a magic that advanced through the black earth in quest of food and community. My hands could sense the tendrils (what a great word for them) binding themselves to one another, creating a web of great strength. I traveled their journey as though it were that of my own blood coursing. I checked the green and gloss of their foliage, nipped off suckers, encouraged the stems to extend their growth. Tending them required me to remain mindful and attuned, to treat with reverence their astonishing power.

No, I was not hanging out in the greenhouse getting stoned, as X-Mann the Bug would have. I worked in this bonanza of cannabis for hours daily without ingesting a whiff of it. These plants were Joaquin's livelihood and my passion. He was the tester, the taster, the harvester. He prepared them for distribution. As the caretaker of the greenhouse, my job was to keep the plants healthy and growing. Their well-being trumped getting high. I had, as it were, turned over a new leaf.

This week he also began trusting me to make deliveries, which were not simple drop-offs but involved conversations with his clients. Joaquin's weed was distributed primarily for medicinal use, and those who received it were eager for consultations. They described symptoms, reported progress or decline, asked about blends, and sometimes sought an informal check-up. Could you take a look at this rash? Neither Joaquin nor I had any training in this line; strains of marijuana were said to have properties that alleviated various pains and maladies, but everyone reacted differently, so there were no standard guidelines. Mostly these conversations arose from loneliness, poverty, fear, and despair. A lot of our regulars were old timers who had lived hard on a thin margin and were aging badly. The nearest doctor was a half hour or more away in Encanto, which made us much easier to consult. Joaquin charged just enough to keep himself and his greenhouse going, and he scaled his price to the buyer. Recreational users, on the other hand, paid a premium. It would have been a good model for the U.S. economy: humane, sane, sustainable.

Still, the point was that Joaquin had been doing all this without me for the last three years. My building skills were pathetic; I could hold and carry stuff, but couldn't saw straight. The mortar I mixed was too thick or too runny and didn't set up well. I was scared of heights and rarely drove a nail in straight. I wasn't bringing anything to the table except decent meals. And while he ate whatever I cooked with gusto, food was not a focal point in his life.

We did have great conversations, which I think we'd both been missing. And we made beautiful music together, also very satisfying. Both of us were fair card players, and both of us loved to read. The evenings were good. There seemed then to be a reasonable chance that he would want me to stay, at least through the winter.

On the other hand, I also brought with me a menagerie he in no way wanted: a killer cat and a wounded salamander. The latter was in recovery, well caged and well fed but not happy; the former was rampaging unrepentantly through the local small furry animal population. In the dark of early morning, lying sleepless on the torture rack that passed as a couch, listening to Mander trying to dig his way out of prison and stroking Tiger with my gloved hand, I'd taken stock of the benefits and losses I contributed to the situation. It would be better, of course, if I announced I was moving on than if he had to ask me to go. My thoughts roamed across possible options for my future: the California beach bum thing; a return to Summerville; a cross-country trip with no goal in mind, couch-surfing where I could, picking up restaurant work where needed, letting the winds take Tiger and me whichever way they were blowing. None of it really grabbed me. What I wanted to do was to stay here, maybe not with Joaquin, but in Trove. And that, I had decided, is what I'd do.

Staying in Trove meant finding gainful employment and a place to live, both in short supply in this small burg with the tourist season drawing to a close. Trove was a summertime town; winters were rugged, and staying alive was as tough for human residents as for animals. The liquor mart was larger than the grocery store. I could put in my application both places. And my credentials as a waiter were sterling, but Gregorio already had that position wrapped up at the only year-round café. Greg was one of the folks in town I'd gotten to know well. He and Floyd, both masters of their trade, took the pulse of the town daily. If there were any jobs to be had in town, they would know, and knowing I was serious about staying, they'd help me out.

It occurred to me that I could teach school. A magpie cawed derisively. Creaking to my feet, I watched sunlight crown the valley.

Tiger was far down the field now, visible only by the wave of his tail. Backlit stands of aspen glistened in the sprightly wind. A hawk dipped into a wide circle. All of us are hunting something, pursuing that state of fulfillment in which we are complete. I had reached it there a little bit ago, the bliss that could only be sustained by not living on.

Now that I had the beginnings of a plan, I could go in and fix us breakfast. Joaquin was up; I smelled coffee. Sunday was our big breakfast day: eggs, bacon, flapjacks, fresh oj. The greenhouse was calling; soon the roots would stretch out, seeking their daily fare of water and nutrients. Yes, everybody's hunting something.

In the kitchen Joaquin had converted one end of the table into a music composition studio. Strumming and humming, he had papers and pen strewn before him as he searched for lines. Writing songs conveyed a familiar intimacy; Harve and me, sometimes Hersch made three, sitting on the floor of my bedroom picking out simple tunes that were fun to sing. Me on the harmonica, trying to drown out Hersch's futile attempts to hit the top notes that screeched out of his range. Unlike us, Joaquin had a mellifluous voice that could have lofted him into the big time if he'd wanted that. I was glad the harmonica kept my mouth busy so he wouldn't hear how bad I sounded next to him.

Right now, every part of me was busy fixing Sunday breakfast, my favorite meal.

"Morning," Joaquin smiled. Another favorite thing of mine, that he regularly awoke in a friendly mood and greeted me.

"Good morning. Sleep well?" I always asked; he knew better than to, given the couch from hell that was my bed.

"Yeah. Hey, listen." Was this it? Was he about to pop the question? Laying the bacon in the pan, I clamped my fears with tongs of nonchalance. Whatever. "Remember that song about the Luna moth I was working on? That exquisite moth we found on the portal that your cat tried to eat?" Tiger non grata. "I've got this line toward the end but need one to follow it. Here it is: 'My wings seek the moon, summer dreams will awake and I'll fly. Summer rising on the wings of night, my life. Summer rising…da-da-dum-dee dum. Summer'—I don't what."

"A wind of light. Summer rising on a wind of light."

"Beautiful, man! How did you come up with that?"

"Hearing you sing."

"'Summer rising on the wings of night, my life. Summer rising on a wind of light. Summer on my wings tonight.' That's it. Got it. It's done." He scribbled the lines on a sheet, then sang the whole tune through, twice, the second time as though he'd grown wings himself. A swell of elegiac passion rose in me. That's why you live on after the moment sublime. Else you would miss this and further next-bend glories. Pancakes, eggs, bacon, fresh melons, and oj.

Friends have come easily to me since childhood. An only child who was never alone. I'm a get-along-go-along kind of guy who keeps it light on the surface no matter what's happening inside. During college I turned into a closet scholar, reading on the sly, taking extensive mental notes, especially in English classes. I kept quiet about graduating with honors. And so far, I'd told no one but Joaquin that my sights were set on writing a story big enough to be a novel, of which the first chapter was emerging on my computer.

In Joaquin at last I had a friend to talk with about writing. He hadn't known me before the fire, except maybe as a goofy ninth-grade face in the hall. He had no reason to hoot and say, "You, Bug? Get off it." Evenings, when we weren't composing and playing songs, we wrote, sitting at far ends of the portal, he in his notebook and all poetry, me on my laptop, narrative. Joaquin made it acceptable, *normal,* to check in with each other, ask for help, share what we were writing. We waited to speak if the other was in the midst of a thought. Most important, and hard for me at the start, we were honest with each other: not brutal, not superior (like my prof in the only creative writing class I took, thanks to him), just straightforward. That we were working in different genres no doubt helped, but Joaquin was the main reason we succeeded. He did not view writing as a talent you had or didn't but as an affinity that could be honed. If he'd been my teacher, I might be much more skilled and confident than I was. Our writing sessions left me charged. The energy I drew from them drove me, and Joaquin was its source.

"How did you learn to do this?" I asked him one evening.

"Unlike you, I was an only child who spent a good deal of time alone. I invented, not really an imagined friend, but another half, a you and I, with whom I read and wrote and conversed freely. Our camaraderie gave me the freedom to recite my poetry at student readings; I was so used to hearing the words spoken to an audience (the you of me) that it felt natural." He smiled. "I first had the pleasure of a real 'you' during fall semester of junior year when my roommate and I occasionally read our work to one another. Then he left for a semester abroad and never came back to school."

The you of me is exactly who I wanted to be for Joaquin. Exactly why I didn't want to leave. Forget the move into town, a job. I would not bring up my departure until he did, and when that happened, I would be on my knees, abjectly begging for a reprieve. Which would, of course, change everything between us and force me to go. My best course was to prevent the subject from coming up. Make myself increasingly indispensable.

The morning opened into a day brilliantly forecast by its dawning. I lucid-dreamed my way through it, yearning still for eternity. Please, nothing change, and don't let me forget this sensation, I prayed to the elements as I entered the greenhouse and commenced my daily patter of flatter to the hungry plants.

"Top o' the morning to you, my beauties. Well rested? Sweet dreams? Who's doing the most growing around here? Ah, my prodigious friend, you are the MVP of shooting right up and soon enough Joaquin will be dunking you in the basket. What's this? A tender newbie hiding under her mother's skirts? You must be what we call an unexpected addition to the family. You like the misting, don't you? Rainfall from paradise, eh? Or on it. Well, my beauties, indeed you are well, nothing eating you. No nasty little bugs creeping up your stems. Sound in mind and body, and ready to share your mellowness with others.

"Let's snip those suckers and tuck in those toes: good posture is elemental to good production, dearies. Don't let me catch you drooping, leaning, splaying, or sagging. Chins up, leaves out. Excellent. Ready to begin our morning thinning?"

I was at the far end of the greenhouse, focused on separating two plants that were so entwined neither stood a chance and still quietly celebrating my inspired "wind of light," when I heard the door open. "Hey," I called without looking up, "dropping by for a whiff of the green?"

"Uh-huh," he said, but he sounded strained like something had gone awry.

"Just one sec." I was making the final moves to free one and extract the other for transplanting. His footsteps crunched on the gravel. I could see I would have to tear more roots than was healthy to get the plants apart, and the question was which one to rob of the better chance of survival. They were of equal size and strength, and though immature, both in great shape at this point. I pulled gently, steadily, and the transplantee's spindly-white grasp on this chunk of earth yielded. Not too damaged to make a comeback, I soothed, tenderly laying it in the hole I'd prepared nearby, spreading the roots comfortably, and pressing the dirt firmly around it. You babes can still see each other, chat, pinkie-shake your roots maybe when you're bigger. So intent was I that I hadn't noticed Joaquin come up beside me till I felt his breath quivering my neck, goosebumping my arms. Another one of those stop-time moments that had chosen to grace this day.

"Don't move," he said, and the moment flipped to panic. I didn't recognize the voice.

Frank flashed through my mind: the evil alcoholic father who had tried to kill Joaquin once and promised to get it done the next time. Who believed the land was his and didn't give a damn about the restraining order that should have kept him from getting anywhere near Joaquin, who was probably already dead and now here Frank was to off me. The small garden spade I'd been using lay in the soil about twenty inches from my hand. A quick lunge and I could—what? Thrust it into his eyes? I wasn't much of a weapons handler except for the sword: years of fencing would have made me a dangerous man if I'd worn one buckled to my waist wherever I went.

"You guys got a nice set-up here. Lucrative. I'll leave you enough to start over. Just barely enough." The voice was too young to be a father.

I lunged for the spade, and as I did, hit the gravel facedown, hard, so quick I didn't catch myself. Before I'd recovered from the shock, my hands were bound behind my back, my feet tied up toward them at a wrenching angle. Pulled the bandanna around my forehead down to blindfold but not gag me since it didn't matter because he knew no one would hear me cry out, which proved that he'd overpowered Joaquin. No crime of passion this, but of greed. Stoner or stone-cold businessman, but either way, bent on robbing us.

"How did you know about us, this greenhouse?" My terrified motor-mouth kicked in.

Snort. "Everyone in town knows. All you got to do is ask."

That was true, but only for Trove people, not drifters or tourists. "Told them I was a veteran in need, on my way home but lost my 'script. They drew me a map."

Kind folks, those Trovers, and a good number of vets among them whom Joaquin served. Such an easy mark, generous, too. I heard sacks being opened. Frenzy seized me.

"Home, so where's that?"

"Denver. But it's not where I'm headed."

"Great town, Denver. My mom and aunt live in Summerville. Both widows. My uncle was career military."

"Anyone stupid enough to join the military deserves to die."

"So you're not a vet." I knew that, of course, but something in my wired psyche told me to keep him talking. Mission Distract and Annoy while I tried to figure out how to save the greenhouse.

"Of the pen, yeah, I'm a veteran con."

"What's the best heist you ever pulled?" I don't know where that came from.

"This one. The one you're pulling is always the best. Now shut up."

Rip. Shower of dirt. Screaming like he stuck me. This asshole uprooting my beauties. More screaming, volley of curses, stops ripping to murder me. Kick to the ribs, shriek, curses, something yanked off his head: bandanna, like mine. This one for a gag.

He bends to stuff the reeking cloth into my mouth. I spin my head at his right hand and bite down hard. Hard. Jaws clamped tight like a bulldog. Hang on, teeth bolted into flesh, his thumb, palm. Jerk it under me so he can't straighten up. My hold rigid. Come on, crunch through that hand, your bones cracking his. Who's yelling now, gutbucket?

His rush of pain and confusion opens me to roll onto his free arm. Drag bit-hand with me, its skin broken, blood pooling. Slicks my teeth. Grip fixed. Don't let go. Kicks, writhes, shouts, bangs his head on mine. Adrenaline pumping pain killer. Groin him with my bent knees, lucky shot stops him hard for breath. Blindfold loosening. Rub it off. My tough assailant's just scrawn and bone. If I get free of the rope, I can take him. He knows it. Desperation stokes a vicious shove: his pinned hand slammed against my head. Cracks my head back. Bite jarred, hand slips from my grasp. Blood spewed, gagging. No air in the windpipe. Screwed. Waiting for the shot, slo-mo.

In the old Westerns, heroes facing death go silent. You assume they've tapped an inner reserve of stoic calm, and really, at the end what is there to say or do? It's less an act of courage than an empty plain. Guilty or innocent, ready or not, they're through living. If you have time to know it's coming and right now, death is a force that settles the conflict, quiets the spirit. Which is why it shocks me to feel the reverberations of a terrible cry, not a bullet, shatter my heart.

And even more startled to realize that it ain't me howling but the intruder. And even far more stunned to discover what's aroused the howl: Tiger, my faithful, intrepid compañero, standing on the scumbo's back, claws lodged in his thin flesh, back arched, snarling. Unrepentant killer that he is, I've never seen Tige take on a human foe—or defend me from anything more vicious than a moth he wanted to eat. Then again, I haven't needed much defending, except from myself. The scrawn sucker hadn't seen T coming and can't figure what's attacking him. My move, time on my side.

Summoning preternatural agility induced by Tiger's aid, I extract my arms from the rope and slip it off my feet. Yank out the handgun in a back-pocket wedge of the doofus's skinny jeans. Jam the barrel right behind his ear (isn't that where they jam movie pistols for a ready kill?). He freezes. No trembling, I warn my hand, and look to Tige for back-up. He turns, stretches, real casually kneads his claws into the jerk's butt, down low enough to suggest where they could strike next.

"Get that fucking beast off me," numbskull moans.

"Don't move," I threaten. "He's a trained assassin."

What next? Scan through my crime films file and lay down a possibly risky course, but having Tiger embedded in dumbass's rear fuels me. I rise, put my foot on the moron's neck, pocket the gun, grab the rope, and deftly (no kidding) tie his legs together, then bypass T and run the last of it around his neck. Unorthodox, but it gives me a sense of control, like if he tries to move his legs, he'll strangle himself. The free arms bother me, but the right one's covered with blood and I shift my stance now to the left, standing on his fingers. A pro at neutralizing criminals I'm not, but in this position I can catch my breath. I've got to get him out of here.

For the first time in a month I wish Joaquin had cell service.

Tiger lies down and without moving his paws, relaxes, starts to purr.

"Listen," I growl, and I'm savoring this rare moment of star power. "I could shoot you or I could drag you by your neck. Or you could shuffle out, hands up, in front of me, to the house. If you've hurt my friend in any way, let me repeat, in any way, I will sic this killer cat on your balls and he will, I swear to you, pulverize them. He eats balls and spits out the semen. Yours won't be much of a meal, but they'll take the edge off. What'll it be?"

"Hands up, walk out."

"All right. Rise and shuffle, screw-up. Baby steps. Any faster and you'll hang yourself. Me and the assassin will be right behind."

Tiger and I are perp-walking the creep between the plantbeds when Jess, pistol cocked, eases stealthily through the door. He lowers his weapon, grinning. "Joaquin, you got to see this," he calls over his shoulder. A proud moment for the dauntless duo, only one of whom had not for a minute doubted the outcome.

"Only lost a couple of plants," I report. The taciturn hero, downplaying a major victory. I hand the criminal over to the authorities, adding, "He's got a record."

"Alex, you are awesome, man," Joaquin effuses. "How did you do it? He knocked me out cold."

Jess ties a handkerchief around the guy's hand to avoid getting blood on himself. "I know the cat's got his shots, but you been tested for rabies?" he asks me, grinning.

"Haven't brushed my teeth recently," I nod. "Maybe that bite'll get infected."

Jess unwinds the rope, handcuffs and leg-chains the perp, shoves him into the back of his patrol car, collects the gun from me, and climbs into the driver's seat. "I'll bet that cat's the one who did the heavy lifting," he winks. "He's a natural born lawman."

Right he was. Without Tiger, I'd be dead. My head reeled through the scene to the moment when I waited for the fatal shot. Casting off my mantle of heroism, I threw up that fine Sunday breakfast. I felt a bit more justified when Joaquin downed four aspirin, the most medicine I'd ever seen him take, and iced the bump on his head.

Joaquin urged me kindly to wash up and rest. He'd constructed a makeshift outdoor shower whose water flowed through a small solar-heated tank, which I drained and then kept on showering, oblivious to the icy well water pouring over me until Joaquin came back and shut it off. He handed me a towel, led me into the house, gathered midwinter clothes for me to put on despite the summer day, then made sure I lay down and took four aspirin myself. He was right to get me prone, but I was far too wired to sleep. My heart still raced with my thoughts, legs jerked involuntarily, and I twisted side to side, ostensibly trying to get comfortable but really trying to get up. Tiger was restless, too, prowling the room in quest of hapless bugs.

At length (and not much length) we both gave up and went outside, where the noon heat reared up and nearly knocked my feet out from under me. Went back in, stripped to shorts and a tee, headed for the greenhouse, Tiger at my side. To Joaquin, staining boards under the tree and still nursing a bad headache, I said, "I'm better off resting in the greenhouse." Outwardly, the tranquil green showed no signs of the morning's violence, but I could sense the disturbance in the roots. My plants needed soothing as much as I did. The ones that piece of garbage had uprooted were wilting; Joaquin had stuck them back in the soil but hastily, and not watered or tamped them down properly. I widened their holes and gave them a fresh start, coaxing them to dig into the soil and try again. Tiger was sniffing the area where we'd fought, and I joined him to examine it. The blood was gone, thanks to Joaquin. A white scrap under one of the beds caught my eye, and I crawled to retrieve it. A piece of paper with a hand-drawn map to our house. His own or someone else's rendering? On the back was a greasy fingerprint, Floyd's trademark. Or Floyd Junior. They'd be wrecked by knowing what their friendly assistance had instigated. We'd have to figure out how to tell them without conveying any blame.

But now it occurred to me that a sizeable number of inmates at whatever prison this schmuck ended up in would probably hear about this place. Best to warn a few people on the front lines not to give directions to anyone before checking in with Joaquin. Let Gregorio, the town crier, and Jess pass the word, which the story of the fight would help spread fast. Joaquin had to get a phone.

Time didn't intrude in the greenhouse, where the work absorbed and nurtured me till sundown. Joaquin insisted on cooking dinner that night, treating me like a hero-invalid. I knew we'd be eating red chile, his go-to meal. Joaquin told me while he was cooking that the dirtbag had come up behind him when he was sorting nails and cold-cocked him with the gun, expertly knocking him unconscious in a single blow. He'd tied him facedown to the door handle but didn't notice the snippers in one of Joaquin's jacket pockets, which he could reach with his hand to free himself. He worried that the scumball, who was clearly armed, had gone for the greenhouse and was after me, who he hoped had surrendered, and made the snap decision to run like wild to Jess's place and get help. Which he did, in record time. Meanwhile, back at the greenhouse…Joaquin felt bad now about the choice he'd made, but who knew how things might have turned out if he'd rushed in at the wrong moment. I didn't blame him. No blame on anyone.

"At first I was afraid the guy was Frank," I said as Joaquin added more garlic, unnecessarily, to the pot. "He was the only one I could imagine coming here with hostile intentions."

"He's too arrogant and bull-headed to sneak up on me," Joaquin countered. "Frank would drive the valley drunk, probably run his truck off the road and stagger the rest of the way. I'd see that cowboy hat coming. Jess would, too. I've shown his picture around in case he stops in Trove first to get another fifth. Everybody knows to look out for him. The only time he could catch me off-guard is at night, sober. I sleep with a gun and a flashlight for that reason; maybe I never told you that." He hadn't. "And I have a bell that's attached to the top of the bedroom door to tinkle if it's opened."

What about me, downstairs on the hammered sofa? I thought, and intuitive as ever, Joaquin answered.

"All you have to do is flip on the light and give him a look at your face. He's after me, not you. There's your guard cat, too, and it might be a good idea to shove Mander's cage close to the door so that if it were opened at night, whoever would trip over it when they came in."

"Great idea," I agreed. "I also think you might want to get a phone. Not just for protection, like it would have been nice to have today, but also for business."

"I'll ruminate on that one," which was Joaquin's way of saying "maybe sometime."

He dumped in more flour, then turned toward me and stopped stirring. It was sure to stick to the bottom, take a lot of the chile with it. I winced. Joaquin was oblivious. "You know, in general I don't believe in the concept of owning land—or much of anything. Stewardship, stepping lightly, sweeping my footprints to leave the earth trackless: those are my guiding precepts. But my grandfather, who loved this place fiercely, and my grandmother, who loved me fiercely and bequeathed it to me specifically so her son wouldn't lay waste to it, passed on to me an obligation. Or that's how I see it. A duty to treasure and caretake this little patch of the earth while I live and to let it go when I die. I've got a will in safekeeping that creates a conservation easement on the land, which requires maintaining free and open passage on it, letting the structures be until they crumble and the meadow returns to its wild state forever.

"When things were really bad during my childhood and insomnia had me in its clutches, I'd dream myself into an idyllic place of safety. I imagined it as a hillside with a beautiful log cabin halfway up. Below, wildflowers amid tall grasses descending to a stream. Rolling on into the forest at its flanks, ponderosas and aspen, whose soughing would gradually lull me to sleep. It looked a lot like this place, Alex. Which is why, despite my beliefs, I call it mine. For now. And will defend it, literally to the death, against Frank."

We ate for once without conversation, each reviewing the day's tumult. His red chile was tolerable, too hot and thick with bottom scrapings, but tasty. I drank more than usual to no effect. Tiger downed, sans gratitude or surprise, the extra can of cat food I gave him for saving my life. He commenced grooming himself on the floor next to me, emitting gross snarfling noises as he licked his nether regions till I escorted him out. Not long after, we soaked the dishes and followed him into the sunset.

Sitting on the porch in the golden rays of evening, I basked in listening to Joaquin play his new song with my line in it. My reserves of adrenaline had not yet been replenished, and I was so tired I felt a deep kinship with the wind of light. Ready to lift up and waft into the hills on a sylvan breeze. He invented variations on the melody after the song was finished, turning it into a curliqued baroque tune. Then stopped abruptly with a single strum, rested the guitar on his knees, and studied me.

"I'm going to talk to you about the subject you've been dodging, elaborately. For how long you are going to continue living here. A month ago I said three days, right? In the meantime, you've made yourself as useful as possible, cooking and doing housekeeping chores, but especially tending the greenhouse. You've got a rapport with those plants that surpasses any level of productivity I've been able to generate. I can sense them perking up when you walk in the door. It's magical.

"You're no help with the building, that's the truth, and Tiger is, well, he's cool but he's a ruthless predator, and I'm not fond of that. Prefer wild animals to domesticated ones, as you know, probably a way of repudiating my ranch-centric youth. Today, you two saved the greenhouse and that's big, Alex. If I had to start over, I don't know. But more than that, you put your life on the line for it, which humbles me. Not sure I could have mustered that degree of courage, devotion, whatever it took."

Joaquin rested the guitar beside the chair and stood up to lean against a post. Silhouetted by the burnished light of sunfall, loose hairs purling in the drift of wind, he looked exactly as I wished I did, never would. The poet king, ruling his beneficent spirit with a generous, untamed heart.

"And beyond all that," he went on, "you've become a solid friend. I've grown to count on seeing you the next day. You've given me a lot of refreshing ideas to contemplate as I hammer and nail. Our shared passion for literature and writing has spurred me to create new work instead of postponing that gratification till the house is done. Before you showed up, I'd forgotten how profoundly the interplay of body and mind strengthens both. I'm getting far more done on the house than I have for the past couple of years because my mind is reignited."

I rose spontaneously, eager to gush over the far greater inspiration Joaquin had provided, but he held up a hand to stop me.

"So here's what I'm thinking at this point. Next spring my girlfriend, I hope she will be my mate for life, is supposed to come out to join me. When she does, the two of us will need to start our world together on our own. Alone. But till then, till spring, I'd welcome your staying here with me. If you want to go on living in Trove after that, I'll help you find work. In fact, I'd like to hire you myself to keep taking care of the greenhouse." He paused. "Fair enough?"

I came here in quest of a home, but my limited vision assumed that was a place. I came to escape my hideous self, to be a new man making a fresh start with no history to those he encountered. Yet even if no one else knows you, you still know yourself.

They slap the label restless on my generation, but youth by its nature, in every generation, is restless. What they, we, are looking for is a home. One we may never find, dying unquenched midstride in pursuit of becoming ourselves, of discovering within enough familiar qualities to call some place home, the search a constant test of our willingness to be who we are: To say we've gotten it right, and here we'll make our stand, thereby granting the place leave to define our boundaries.

Only a lucky few are born into themselves, settled within, able to claim the world as home. They belong wherever they choose and know the place they belong because they are the home that they do not need to seek. Those who come to know them seek refuge in the shelter of their friendship. As I have in Joaquin. He is the home I sought, the friend exceeding my notion of what that could mean. To find a true friend is to come home, be at home, have a home. In the embrace of Joaquin's friendship, I tried to emulate the ease with which he spoke and acted. He was uninhibited, not for lack of self-consciousness but because he had made peace with who he knew himself to be; uncompromised because there was no bargain worth losing himself through.

I was aware of the potent yearning to mold myself in his image, realizing adulation was not what he wanted but likewise that I might not be able to resist. He was by no means the first person I had loved nor the first friend I'd had, but in my life as a so-called adult, the only one I trusted and believed in unconditionally. If I had been less the immature slacker I was in ninth grade, I might have won him as a friend then. Joaquin didn't play by hierarchical adolescent rules. But I also would have had to be writing—and willing to share what I wrote—to be outspoken about my views (to have views to begin with), to accept myself. None of the above applied. Years wasted in which we could have been friends. Joaquin would not want me to think that way, either, preferring as he did gratitude for what is over regret for what is not. His beauty lay in salvaging from a dump the joy of a stunning view.

Nine months, the span of human gestation. By then my bearings would be set, my forces gathered, my head cleared, my game planned: I would be ready to emerge into the world reborn and begin my life anew. My mouth wriggled giddily. "All right with you if I buy a new couch?"

8

"Blue Shadows 'long the Trail"

Fall in Trove is a palette of saturated extravagance. In a land where water is scarce, air and soil thin, the radiance of aspen gold nestled in deep pine green against skies lavish blue dazzles the heart's eye. A lifetime of southwestern hues hadn't prepared me for the powerfully moving gift of Trove's autumn.

Joaquin and I had established a productive routine that charted our days. Having shed the fear of expulsion allowed me to revel in the present, each morning a welcome confirmation of my place within it and an assurance of more luminous dawnings to follow. It was on one of particular glory that I flung myself open and ended up impaled on my heedlessness.

I'm in Trove, stocking up on supplies, which is code for coming to town to spend a few hours kvetching and gossiping with my new friends. Now that the tourists have gone, it's a sweet little town. Three streets long by five wide. Driving down the main street, called Main Street, I pass the Trove City Theater, the Trove Inn, and the fish hooks store, hardware center, knick-knack shops, and park in front of the Watchman's Café for a cup of java and the news of the hour.

Stepping out onto the sidewalk, I take a minute to check out Pacman 2. A sleek and gleaming '69 bug, in perfect running order. Ah, the irony: in a town three by five lives the world's premiere mechanic, bar none, and he cut his teeth on John Muir's *How to Keep Your Volkswagen Alive*. Floyd loves my little Pacman 2, lavishes care on all its parts. Wants to buy it from me whenever I'm ready to sell, which I have no plans to. Sometimes I pull into his shop just to chew the fat, as he says, and most of what we are masticating is Pacman talk. It's like taking a child for parental visitation rights. As we chat, Floyd polishes Pac's hard body with a chamois, wiping off dust. Looks under the hood just for the hell of it, and fastens an eagle eye on the interior to detect any signs of abuse. Given his scrutiny, I've become a model car owner. Floyd is teaching his firstborn, Floyd Junior, about Pacman's care and feeding; I have every reason to expect this little putt-putt will outlive me as it passes on down through generations of Floyds.

Baskets of pansies and petunias hang from the ornate street-lamp posts. That's the kind of thing people can do when they only have one main street to dress up. Paint the storefronts purple, red, blue, green with white trim, murals on the sides of buildings, decorative handmade signs with the store names, which are themselves old-school quaint: Trove Trading Post, Ye Olde Ice Cream Shop, Crescent Gallery, Trove Sweet Stuff Shoppe. One end of the street heads straight into the mountains, and the other end southward through immense bluffs, down to Norton, Encanto, and in four or five more hours, to what used to be Vista Grande, now a black, toxic scar in the Sangre de Cristo Mountains.

I hear they're trying to rebuild: Good luck, uranium leaching into the water and soil, radiating death for the next fifty thousand years. Or is it million?

"Hey, Gregorio, what's up, man?" My friend Greg, our local Argentinian, is the owner and all-purpose guy at Watchman's. Takes customers' orders; makes coffee, lattes, smoothies; serves meals; runs the register; busses, even does the dishes when Shirl isn't around. Lonny and Shirl help out several hours a week, when she's not making scented soaps and candles, which he sells in a shop at the corner. During her shifts at the Watchman, Shirl gets to pick the music piped into the café, too, folk-rock mellow. The rest of the time Gregorio throws on some Latin gypsy beats. It's a small, clean, and quite excellent operation, breaking even.

At an elevation of nine thousand feet, winter lasts fourteen months of the year, which doesn't leave much time for the tourist season. Summer and fall are magnificent for the brief spell when they flourish; spring is more like a calf trying to figure out which end to suck on. Freezes and thaws, confounds the buds and the birds and human residents.

How do I know all this, having lived a grand total of three summer and fall months in Trove? I talk to folks like Gregorio, who has the scoop on whatever's happening. I ask questions and listen.

Here's one other interesting bit of lore I've picked up: Everyone in Trove is a poet. Some are out, others in the closet, but every one of them is penning lyric lines in their heads or on the lined pages of the notebooks our True-Value hardware store sells. Not a lot of it is magazine quality, but it's down-home good and heart-cockle-warming. Poetry's a tradition that goes back to Trove's beginnings, as you'll see if you book a hundred-year-old fishing cabin at any of the ranches around here. There's bound to be a rhyme mounted on the wall, just above the leaping trout lamp. The opening verse of my favorite one:

> A feller isn't thinking mean, out fishin'
> His thoughts are mostly good and clean, out fishin'
> He doesn't knock his fellow men
> Or harbor any grudges then
> A feller's at his finest, out fishin'.

"Hey, Alejandro, que pasa?" Greg pours my coffee without waiting for me to order it. "You know who was in here yesterday? That old vet, the crazy one who lives all alone and was almost killed driving over Slurry Passage, yes?"

"Sure. I'm making a delivery to him today."

"So he's one of Joaquin's customers." Thoughtfully Gregorio flicks some lint from my new Indiana Jones hat, shaking his head. "I wonder how good is that, a man so unhappy, all alone. Like a hermit he lives in that cabin. He is never one to come in: never. And then, here he is. I was a tiny bit nervioso, but he ordered the burrito con extra chile, which is so good, and drank many cups of coffee before he asked me did I know someone who wants to buy a cabin for a hundred dollars. He's leaving, and can you imagine why?"

I couldn't.

"It's haunted, you see, the cabin. Driving him loco mad. He cannot sleep, he cannot eat—that's why he came here for the first time ever—he cannot do nothing without the ghosts creeping up on him, swirling fogginess around him, getting into his ears, screaming and crying. Every day it gets worse. He's a desperate man. They want to kill him. They are," he lowered his voice, "Vietnamese. From the war."

"He must have gotten into some really bad scheiss over there."

"No, it's not stomach sickness but fear."

"Fear's a kind of stomach sickness, man." I tried to shake the threatening gloom out of my head. "It won't help for him to move, now that they've found him."

"But he cannot stay!"

"Ghosts stick with people, not places. They're after him, and they'll keep on him wherever he goes. Unless the place itself is the source of their grief."

"You know so much about ghosts, eh?"

I drop back. Greg is the town's lips; he shares all. "It's just stuff you pick up. You know, ghost stories, Greg."

"But some tribes of indios, they close up the house where someone dies and trap the ghost. Then they never speak of the dead one again. They erase the ghost, like."

"Yeah. Maybe that works if the person died there. But the vet's being haunted by folks from across the world. If you believe him. He's seriously ptsd'ed."

"Como?"

"War sick. We call it post-traumatic stress disorder. Guilt, horror, shame, all the atrocity of battle that you can't handle comes roaring back and devours your soul."

"You want to eat something?"

Bad transition but good timing. I point at a sweet roll on the counter; they're made fresh daily. He brings me the one next to it.

"This one is better, made with the fresh peaches. Jimmy, he brings us two boxes of peaches from Duran on Sunday. Dulce como los besos de amor." He blows a kiss and waits for me take a bite. I make sure my face reflects ecstasy as I munch, which is not hard since the roll is superb.

"You see? Delicioso. To eat so good is like making love."

Gregorio is a Romantic poet, given to long odes about the women and men he has loved and lost or left. Sometimes a line or two of Neruda slips in when he's wooing a new one. The ecstasy and the agony. For him poetry is a medium for seduction, though he hardly needs it; most of the townsfolk, of every gender and age, are in love with Greg. His poems are just icing on the cupcake of his charms.

"Alejandro, when Joaquin's girlfriend comes in spring, where will you go?"

And where did that question come from, I wonder? Out loud, after a healthy pause during which I appear to be chewing on his query as well as the sweet roll, I say, "Why? You have a place in mind?"

"Do you plan to stay here, in Trove? What will you do with yourself?"

A question I have deliberately avoided asking myself, settled as I am just now. Spring might never come, or a more likely hope, the woman won't. No need to figure things out yet.

"I'll give it some thought. Just now I've got to shove off." I lay $5 on the table. Acting like he doesn't see it, Gregorio scrutinizes me.

"Your scars, hombre, is not a glad sight. Are you being safe with the care?" He examines the red slash across my cheek and nose, the X across my brow. "Ay, ay, ay. You must wear hats. And smear fat cream upon the skin."

"I'm going to the doc's this very morning, Greg. I'll pass along your advice."

"It's no good, mi amigo. You never listen to him."

"Doc's purple jumpsuit shattered my confidence."

Doctor Darrell of Encanto. My mind conjures a C-grade sci-fi movie in which everyone in the science lab is acting diabolically normal but the spooky music tells you to get the heck out of there before you end up a zombie or a blob or wearing a fly's head. Doc Darrell's office has that feel, minus the evil genius motif. He's a weird man, sure enough, but since most of his patients are as wacky as he is, they don't expect too much of one another.

The good thing is that he's willing to treat a variety of species suffering from all manner of ills: no case so enigmatic or bizarre he won't take a crack at it. Working solo, sans receptionist or nurse, Darrell is a total service, one-stop-shopping medico.

The clinic, a low-slung prefab set a-ways back behind the Shell station, is easy to miss. Pulling open the door, I find myself reeling back from the onslaught of a patient on his way out. Like many of Darrell's walk-ins, this mountaineer has clearly foresworn all the little niceties of civilization, such as bathing, changing his clothes, shaving, brushing his teeth, cutting his hair. Lunging onto the metal stoop, he calls over his shoulder, "Okay if I pay you in goat meat?" The doctor shrugs. Why not? It might even be fresh enough to eat.

Darrell leaves the door open for a bit of aromatherapy from the crisp alpine breeze. We smile at each other, he taking in old Scarface and I the bulging lavender jumpsuit and coke-bottle glasses that he wears in place of a white coat and stethoscope. Elevator music drifts through the clinic, Darrell's way of inducing calm in the insane. I follow him down the hall to an examining room.

How Doctor Darrell ended up in a doublewide in Encanto no one asks, but it can't have been his primary ambition in medical school. If, that is, he attended one. The certificate on the wall has a Photoshop quality to it, and John Doe University doesn't do much to inspire awe. But Darrell has a monopoly on medical care in the area, so there's no point in questioning his credentials.

"Alex, Alex," he puffs, his voice breathy from the exertion of the walk. "How are you?

"Shall we undress and get up on the table?" Which sounds like a proposition more reminiscent of b-grade porn than sci-fi.

The doc thrills at the chance of running his fingers over my scars, but since it's the only physical human contact I get, I try not to mind. "Yes, this one is healing nicely," he murmurs sliding his hand along my chest. "Are you using that cream I gave you?"

"Every day," I lie. He nods, pleased. There's not much he can do for me.

"I don't think you're getting enough protection from the sun," he worries, fondling the scars on my face. "Are you wearing your sunblock, Alex? A hat?"

"Sure am," I lie again, indicating the Indiana Jones hat that I only wear for special occasions, like a visit to him. "But, Doc, all day, every day, out there, hammering nails, I'm bound to catch some rays." He's right: the scars on my face (where the bandanna didn't reach) were an ugly red. Wear a hat, moron, I remind myself. Even though the part about hammering nails is also a lie, I am out in the sun a lot. Do not go bareheaded into that good light.

"How are you *feeling*?" Doc's tone matches the muzak.

"Good. Fantastic. Better than ever." Hyperbole, but truth is, I am closer to happy than I've been since the fire.

"Turn over so I can check your back, Alex. Say, how's our little reptilian friend?"

That's why I go through with this dubious examination once a month. Darrell fixed up Mander after that long, grueling night. Within a week the critter seemed pretty much back in shape, for a salamander, but I'd decided to keep him until he was fully healed and now that the temperatures were dropping—well. With a little help from my friends, I made him a cage (let's be honest: a luxury condo), filled it artfully with vegetation and rocks, a lounging pool. Caught fresh meals of bugs for him daily. It was a salamander paradise, especially compared to my modest quarters. Remembering my part in Mander's near-death experience quelled my envy, but Tiger had no such remorse. Having a gourmet meal captive on the front porch that he couldn't get to was exasperating. It wasn't that T-cat was undernourished, given his daily rodent and rabbit intake, but the idea that he should be denied *anything* he desired was an affront. Leaping onto the wire top of Mander's condo, he whirled dervishly, his eyes lasering through the glistening reptilian skin. A feline of infinite patience convinced of his inability to fail, he danced up there for hours daily while Mander soaked in his pool or dozed, wedged beneath the shrubbery.

I am one of the few who pays Doctor Darrell in cash ($20), which is another reason he's always glad to see me. Coin of the realm means a safely edible meal for him.

Speaking of dinner, I've got to pick up some groceries at the Belle Star. Frying chicken and rice, some kind of veggie. Watermelon for dessert. They have a three-minute melon season in Trove. Beer. Then home. But I've got these two deliveries to make first.

My first one takes me to Norton, retracing my path fifteen miles back toward Trove. An easy cruise in a vehicle so stellar. Mountains illuminated with gold-leaf. The weather gurus claim we're in for a cold snap tonight, maybe even a bit of snow, and there's a soupçon of brittle in the air. More, you'd say if you weren't from around here, pulling on your new down parka. The thing is, if you weren't from around here, you would have gone home a month ago. Trove is well-nigh buttoned up after Labor Day, except for the hunters. First hard freeze can come as quick as mid-September. It's the early descent of frost that gilds the aspens and refines the lens to bring the land into ultra-sharp focus, so it's welcome, if also a warning. I'm curious to see whether I have the grit to hang tight as the subzero temperatures gnaw my bony carcass.

And, as I told the doc, in many ways I really am in good shape. *Fantastic* may be overstating it, unless you compare it to being a quadriplegic in a bombed hospital near some war zone. *Fantastic* is the goal, and beginning to seem possible, given how well my relationship with Joaquin is progressing. He and I are like a cross between close friends and partners, even in business. He selects the strains of marijuana to grow, I tend them, he cuts and dries, I deliver and collect. A beautiful alliance. We're writing a barrage of songs together, he granting me a place in the kitchen composition studio since "wind of light." When winter comes and we have the expansive darkness to hone our musical and literary gifts, it's going to be legendary. Emerson and Thoreau. Simon and Garfunkel. Lennon and McCartney. Ginsberg and Kerouac.

Along the way, I've learned a few things about myself that would not likely have been revealed elsewhere. For instance, I'm terrific at splitting wood. Joaquin forgot to tell me that it was a difficult thing to do, so I just did it as though it weren't. Used my revered Annie Dillard line to "aim for the chopping block; aim past the wood," and was not at all surprised that it worked, given her prose. Besides, I like the huskiness of the phrase "splitting wood," set against my puny physique.

One of the greatest pleasures is that when I'm alone with Joaquin, I often forget about my scars, how ugly I am, all day. He sees beyond the wood.

Yes, I know, it sounds like I'm living a fairytale out here in the rugged hills above Trove. That's why Greg's questions about what I was going to do come spring were so aggravating. I'm doing what I want to do with my life, just now. It's good. I'm more who I want to be than I've ever been. I have no plans beyond keeping on. Oh, and maybe adding a room to the house for myself. It's something I plan to bring up around mid-March, casually, over a beer, when we've survived most of the winter, maybe just after a particularly stimulating critique of each other's writing. Meanwhile, my main objective is to do all I can to see that nothing changes.

Although I am wildly thankful to be free of his ghost, I wish Papito could be here now. He would get what's so right about this life; he would love it. I can hear him strumming along with our songs for all he's worth, head thrown back, ear-hugging grin. Or down at the Watchman with Gregorio, trading tales on stuff neither of them knows anything about. He was made for Trove. "You did it," he'd have told me. "You found yourself the perfect life." Then he'd toke up—oh, yeah, he was a wannabe hippie, and there are plenty of real ones around here for him to hang with, still inhaling, forever young: immortalized by Dylan.

If he hadn't died, he'd have bought a cabin here with Mamia, a summer place. Joaquin and I would've cruised over now and again for a free meal and some parental adoration. I miss their cooing. From what he's told me of his childhood, Joaquin needs it even more than I do. He and his mom have good moments and lousy months. It's closed-off part of him that looks like independence from the outside but is really just a means of walling off hurt. Mamia would have dismantled that façade with openhearted kindness, while Papito would have eased Joaquin into our circle with his guileless benevolence.

Near the outskirts of Norton, an eighteen-wheeler roars around me, stinking up the air. Pacman 2's filtration system isn't up to repelling the big trucks. I hold my breath till he's out of range, then roll down the window. A shaft of icy air plunges in. Should have worn thermals and a parka, at least my vest. Turning into the strip mall's parking lot, where I'm making my delivery, I spot Ida and Ruth, already there, also dressed like it's summer. They're tough, those two.

Ida and Ruth live so far off the grid that even Google hasn't mapped it. No one is allowed anywhere near their place, which is why we meet at the Walgreen's end of the mall's parking lot. Ida, the one with the prescription, should be on weed 24/7. An amputee whose left leg is gone from mid-thigh on down, she prefers her ill-fitting prosthetic leg to her crutches to her wheelchair but doesn't like to use any of them.

I pull up next to their ancient little hatchback, which looks like it's been dug out of some scrapyard, and wonder how long they've been waiting. With nothing clocking time for them but the sun, they just take a rough guess at when to come in and are sometimes here for a couple of hours before I show up at the appointed hour (you have to appoint some hour, I've explained).

"Hey, there, medicine man," Ida calls, gingerly sliding out past the duct-taped car windows and loose-hinged doors. I offer her a hand, which she ignores. The prosthetic leg, already dressed in a sock and shoe, lies amidst a heap of jackets and bags on the back seat. "How they hangin'?" She props herself against a convenient dent on the hood, throws her head back with theatrical flair, and pulls a cigarette from the pocket of her sweater, coughing as she inhales.

I hadn't known Ida smoked. Ruth sees a quick shadow cross my face, grins. "It's not like she hasn't tried to quit. Went three weeks one time." In her faded work-shirt and flat-topped hat, she is the tailbone of the sixties.

"Went crazy is what you mean," Ida cuts in. She stares unabashedly at my scars, her eyes giving me a low score on the suffering scale. "And that damn nicotine patch."

"Forgot she was wearing it. Just about tore her apart."

Ruth has the money ready for me, takes the bags, a quick exchange. "You and Joaquin are real lifesavers, you guys. This stuff's the only way she can get to sleep."

"Whatever works, I'm glad of it. Everything okay out there on the range?"

"Plugged a bear cleaning out the apple trees. That's our winter's meat."

"My birthday's next week," Ida throws in. "Going to be 51. 51." She shakes her head like she can't believe it. I can't, either. She'd look a lot older except for the thick mane of chestnut hair without a fleck of gray. Still, it's amazing she's made it this far.

"Yup," Ruth affirms. "We best get going." She's already halfway back in the junker when Ida decides she has to pee. The nearest public restroom is way at the end of the strip mall, quite a hike for a one-legged woman.

Ruth gets out again, and I expect she's going to get the leg or a crutch, but instead she walks over to Ida and turns her back. Ida tosses her cigarette, salutes so-long at me, grabs Ruth's shoulders, and they start off across the parking lot, Ruth walking in front and Ida hopping behind. They act like this is a totally normal way of getting around, like they do it all the time, and maybe they do, but for me, watching, it's an eye-popper. So much more work than screwing on the leg.

Or they could have just driven over there.

But, doing it the hard way, they make it; then Ruth comes back alone, puts the hood up, and starts messing with the car. I should take off, might as well already have for all the attention she pays me. Key in the ignition, worried about Ida getting stuck in the bathroom and watching Ruth check the oil or something, I can't leave yet. Then Ida appears around the corner of that faraway building where the restroom is. I look to see whether Ruth has noticed, and when she gives no sign of going to get Ida, I lean out the window and say something innocuous like, "Well, there she is, ready for the long walk."

Just then Ida takes off solo across the parking lot. Her arms are outstretched, like wings, and she's flapping them up and down as she hops toward us. Perfectly balanced, even with the stump. Tiny ankle, wearing a sparkling slipper on her foot, and as insane as it is, she's really very graceful. She makes it look easy. But a single misstep—it kills me to watch but my eyes are glued. Over that whole parking lot, hopping like a bird, she just keeps coming.

Ruth sees me dumbstruck and says, "She's good, right?"

"Incredible."

"See ya next time, kid." And I head out, astonishment trailing me up the road to Trove.

All the miles to my next delivery, I can't get the image of Ida hopping across that asphalt out of my mind. Gloriously, obnoxiously risky. What a show-off; what a champ. Why didn't I run over there and offer her my back? Had I become wiser or more of a coward since rushing in to save Papito? Or more aware of the precarious balance of every scene, alert to how readily I could throw things off, might have toppled her. I didn't trust myself to intervene, knowing how much harm I could do. If Ida had fallen and broken her good leg or a hip, I'd have felt somewhat to blame. Action and inaction hold equal responsibility for consequence.

But Ruth had clearly been sure Ida needed no help. Hadn't even looked up. Treated it as utterly routine, which it may have been at the yurt. Nor had Ida asked for help. In fact she seemed euphoric about the crossing. Seeing again Ida's wide-winged performance, it struck me that she must have been a dancer once. Only a dancer could venture such a flight and carry herself with a grace that made me feel weightless. Or hold such indifference for her post-dance body.

The epigraph of Atwood's *Alias Grace*, which I was reading last night, pops into my mind. It's a haiku by Basho: "Come see real flowers of this painful world."

My next delivery, the crazy vet who Greg says wants to sell his cabin, is less a flower than a wounded crab the tide of humanity left behind. Winding along the road with the Rio Sol on my left and the steep bluffs on the right ("Watch for falling rocks," warns the sign: just speculating here, but it seems likely that by the time you've spotted them, you're getting crushed.) A few miles southwest of Trove lies a rickety wooden bridge that looks better suited to foot traffic, but Pacman 2 will go anywhere. On the other side, I accelerate up through the pine and aspen stands, following what's no more than a memory of a road, until I get above timberline to a rocky outcropping just below the summit. That's the vet's so-called parking lot, identified by his rusted jeep decked in camouflage paint. From there I have to hike to the cabin, which rests fortress-like at the top. Where it's always ten-twenty degrees colder than anywhere else, I note, berating myself again for dressing carelessly this morning. A challenging delivery of a hundred-dollar baggie.

I spot the barrel of the rifle from a good ways off because I'm expecting it. Unlike the first time two months ago when I'd boldly walked up toward the cabin, thinking about what a haul this must be in winter, and he'd leapt from behind a tree, rifle cocked and pointed at my head. "Hold it right there," he'd growled, which was my second choice after evacuating my bowels and ducking for cover. "Who are you?"

He'd advanced on me, still ready to fire. I'd raised my hands in the age-old gesture of surrender, the bag of weed dangling from one of them. When he was close enough that the whites of my terrified eyes filled his sights and I could smell his rotting gums, he'd uncocked the rifle and rested it on the ground.

I was considering the advantages of breathing when the old guy had flared into a military posture. "Attention!" he'd yelled, saluting me. Now, even though I've never been a military man, I have seen enough old war movies to know the basic commands. Belly in, chest out, ramrod up the backbone, and salute (with bag of grass swinging free over right eye).

"You here on a mission, soldier?" he'd barked.

"Yes, suh!" I'd spat out like a cross between Forrest Gump and Private Ryan.

Scrutinizing my scars, he'd frowned. "Mekong Delta?"

"Where?"

I'd jerked my head to the left, hoping that might signify somewhere, but it didn't suffice.

"Tet Offensive?"

"Yeah, Tet, suh," I'd affirmed. Whatever that was.

"At ease, soldier. As you were." I relaxed just in time to get feeling back in my hand.

"So what's your story?" he'd demanded, slinging the rifle over his shoulder and nodding for me to follow him to the cabin.

Seriously? I had not been up to inventing some war story, and the bad movies had taught me that some vets just don't like to talk. "I got no story," I'd muttered, breathing hard from the climb. "Shit happens."

"I been there, buddy. Tell me about it. Just rough it out. How'd it go down?"

"The scars are the story, but nothing—"

"Scars mean you're healed, pal. I'm still bleeding."

"You should see my sucking chest wound."

He'd grinned and slapped me on the back. "We both got burned, soldier."

His cabin was surprisingly light and well laid out, very clean. It looked ready for inspection but gave off a good vibe, anyway, and I'd looked at the vet with new appreciation.

"Call me Chewie," he'd said; I'd heard the nickname, but only a chosen few were allowed to call him anything at all. Our eyes caught. "On account of my hairiness," he'd added, shaking the tangled brown mane on his head. Between that and the beard, Chewie's face was mostly obscured.

It shouldn't be so hard to deliver his bag of medicine after that introduction, but I have to go through the cocked-rifle welcome every time. Now, like then, I say, "Chewie, man, it's me, the maimed delivery boy. From Joaquin's greenhouse to your lungs, express service."

A grunt, followed by the reassuring click of the rifle being uncocked. "You're eighteen minutes late."

"Hey, sorry. I got held up at the doc's."

"Stay away from that snake-oil salesman, soldier. He's dangerous. They ought to string him up for quackery."

"Well, see, Chewie, the Hippocratic Oath doctors take—"

"They take an oath to be hypocrites? Figures."

"Hippocrates. Ancient Greek doctor's name, the first. It binds them to the promise to do no harm. Doc Darrell holds to that, don't you think? He may not do much good, but he's pretty harmless, right?"

Chewie comes up close again, checking my scars, which like the doc and Ida, he seems unreasonably attracted to. "Here's your medicine," I say brightly to get us past this moment. "You owe the man a hundred."

"It's good stuff, worth the money." His first positive comment. "This shit is the only reason I'm sorry to leave."

"You're leaving?" Feigning ignorance is the best way to get the straight story.

"Right now, by which I mean walking out the door right now. Duffel's packed."

"What about your cabin?"

"Weather-tight. Just close this sucker up and drive away. Course I am trying to sell it. You interested?"

I'm not, but Chewie is still leaning on the rifle, barrel up, using it as a kind of crutch. "What are you asking?"

He lifts off my hat, lets his eyes rove across my scars, very slowly, taking in the red welts with a warped amazement as if he himself had inflicted them. I'm glad I never made up some phony story for him to study them by.

"For you, soldier, wounded in defense of our great nation, a one-time offer, good this moment only, of just a hundred bucks."

He waves the bill he'd pulled out to pay Joaquin back and forth in front of me like a flag. A hundred bucks. It's my kind of desperate, a bar set low enough so I can step over it without lifting my feet. A hundred bucks equals three bags of groceries loosely packed.

"Deal." I hold out my hand but instead of shaking it, he pulls the hundred out of reach.

"Let's get the papers signed and notarized. Won't take long."

He darts in to get his stuff, his gestures furtive, his back hunched. Retreats as quickly as possible, striding ahead of me down to where our vehicles are parked.

"It ain't the cabin, it's me that's haunted," he wheezes. Exactly what I'd said to Greg. "They just tracked me here, so I got to head out, sweep my footprints clean. Bad leftover war karma juju."

Is there any other kind for us vets?

It's a stupid thing to do because I really don't want the cabin. But for a hundred bucks it's a stupid thing not to do. Or maybe that's how it seems to me just now when I've been thinking about my folks having a summer place in Trove. Sentimental transference.

Of course transferring the deed and getting it registered takes longer than predicted, even skipping the finer points, which at that price we could. When you add Gregorio's Latin intensity to Doc Darrell's congenital creepiness, multiply that by Ida and Ruth's surreal stoicism, factor in Chewie's squirreliness, and throw in about four hours of paperwork, you've got an equation for exhaustion. I was beat.

But it occurs to me that by recounting this day, which turns out to be a critical one, I may have given the impression that Trove is composed of the flotsam and jetsam belched forth by some post-apocalyptic tsunami. And that's wrong. There are plenty of healthy, powerfully organic and good folk in town, those who run successful businesses and hike for joy, those who are performance and visual artists with a true eye for beauty and a beautiful eye for truth, virtuous families raising happy children, people simply hanging out digging Trove. It's just that the line of work I'm in, and my unnaturally warped soul, brings me into mano a mano relationship with the traumatized denizens on the outer circles of society and the inner circles of hell. The kinship is irresistible.

But that's also not an accurate picture of my Trove. The vital, significant sphere around which I revolve is Joaquin. True friends are a rare find; soulmates a dream. From my current vantage point, my great fortune has been to have two of the former—Rose and Hersch—one of the latter and the only one I expect to have in this lifetime, Joaquin. While I gave much of myself, certainly the fond chambers of my heart, to the first two, I could give myself wholly to the last. Maybe the crucible of the fire made it possible for me to do so; more likely it is Joaquin who did. Hersch, of whom I can no longer speak and not yet think, though I'm still convinced he's beaching it in Zihuatanejo, knew me like a brother, and I loved him like one despite our being very different people. Rose I simply loved.

Rose reminds me that I actually have more than one soulmate: Tiger. May he have enough lives to last through one of mine.

By the time I've waved vaya con dios to Chewie and picked up the groceries, the sky has turned to dusk, and a cold wind has risen. Late dinner tonight, but Joaquin doesn't mind. I'm on my way home, thank god for home, headed out of town with the radio playing Willy Nelson when it hits me that I, Alexander Mann, at a mere twenty-five years of age, am a homeowner, by accident or design, king of a craggy realm in the high country. I have a room of my own. Not the summer cabin my parents would have chosen, but ten acres of mountainside that go with the cabin, thoroughly uninhabitable but mine. Tiger and I could raise goats or swallows or bighorn sheep there.

The drive home is the heart-crushing-beauty part of my day. It takes me through open pasturelands and hills, riven with rivers, softened by pines. Broad-backed, open slopes of grass laced with a final burst of gold and purple wildflowers. I've seen eagles surfing the wind currents, the occasional buck or bear. The stone-faced mountains looming above timberline range away into the sky. Those who look closely might see swaths of pines in the foothills have gone from green to brown and gray. Bark beetle. Drought. Fire. The dead and dying may soon rival the living in number. In a few years this landscape will look more like Wyoming than Colorado. In a few years or maybe overnight. I'm a big fan of setting the bar low, too far down for even the most thigh-studded limbo dancer to get under.

As I'm maneuvering through this welter of thoughts, I see a woman trudging along the side of the road looking lost and thoroughly worn out. The fatigue in her back, bowed under a heavy pack, and her unsteady legs by far trump mine. She is too lightly dressed for this frigid evening, her windbreaker and hair battered recklessly by the tempest that is determined to conjure snow from a halcyon day.

Braking to offer her a ride, the last piece of the imaginary equation that is my wishful future quivers through me. My home plus a wife equals my life transformed. In one day. Too much happiness to bear.

"Can I give you a lift?" I call out, gallantly unlatching the passenger door as I struggle to keep the jubilant trill out of my voice.

"Maybe, I guess." She hesitates. Am I leering or is it the trill? "I'm not exactly sure where I'm going."

Excellent, yes. I'll set you on the path to paradise, my soon-to-be-betrothed. "Well, I bet I can get you there," is what I actually say, trying to sound cheerful rather than psychotically indifferent to her destination.

"I'm sure you know everyone here and where they live, including my friend," she smiles. "It's such a small place. But I don't want to put you out."

"More than ten miles there'll be a delivery fee, of course."

Score. She's looking very grateful and relieved now. I get out and help her shove her pack into the nominal back seat of Pacman 2.

"It's so kind of you to give me a ride." The vast weariness in her voice reminds me of my own entrance into these here parts not so long ago. She is shivering crazily, and I turn the heat to high. Her gloveless hands seek the vent, warming themselves as if it were a fireplace. Even disheveled, she is magnificent. Ebony hair, skin white as snow, nose red as Rudolf's. Her eyes, I noted when she smiled at me, were mesmerizing blue.

I touch my pulled-low hat courteously and affect a drawl, hiding my desire behind an ebullient wit. "The creed of Trove is kindness, ma'am. We do not leave anyone stranded on the road, especially not a lovely damsel-in-distress like yourself, at nightfall."

"This place is incredibly beautiful. I just can't believe it's real. Look at the moon! Colder than I expected," she sighs, "but still glorious. You're so lucky to be from here."

Bingo: the first time I've been mistaken for a native. "Line!" I yell at my inner director, who, as usual, has nothing for me.

But Buck Homer does. KRZY's host for Classic True Grit Western Music Hour starts up his theme music, a ballad crooned by The Sons of the Pioneers:

> Shades of night are falling
> As the wind begins to sigh
> And the world is silhouetted
> Against the sky.
> Blue shadows 'long the trail.

At this moment, it's the most romantic tune I've ever heard.

"Perfect," she smiles, right on cue.

Yep, sure as shootin' is, for the blink of a happy eye, until I pop the question.

"Now, who's that friend you're going to see?"

"Oh, man, I'm sorry. Here you are idling and I relax like you know where I'm going.

His name is Joaquin, Joaquin Stranger. He's building a house somewhere around here. Do you know him?"

What's this, what's this? My bride delivered to my door? I start to say, Know him? Hell, I live with him. He's my best friend, but before I can draw breath, she goes on.

"I'm so tired I can't even think straight. Feel like I've been traveling for days. Which I have, leaving Seattle at 11:00 last night, getting to Denver in the middle of the night and taking a bus to the depot to catch another bus to Summerville, then changing again in Dell to get to Arroyo, where I thought I'd be stuck and have to call Joaquin and spoil the surprise. But while I was having a burger somewhere, I happened to overhear a couple talking about Trove and I dared to ask them—it's not the kind of thing I've ever done—if they were headed there today and they were, in a big SUV, so they didn't mind giving me a ride. Shared the back seat with their hound dog, who was big and slobbery but nice. The man is a hunter; he and his wife have a cabin on a private ranch south of Trove. They were willing to drive me all the way through town, but I could tell they were hoping just to call it good at the ranch. And who could blame them, two elderly folks driving up from some place in Texas, Amarillo, I think; even though they took a couple of days to get here, it's quite a haul. I thought we were closer to town than we were, must have walked three, four miles, and I was losing it when you came by. Is it far to Joaquin's? I don't want to put you out."

I open my mouth to again assert primacy in terms of my relationship with her friend, but suddenly my inner director taps my brain. Don't say anything yet. Find out more about her first. Surprise the surprise. And drive slowly.

And during the small pause while I'm taking direction, she starts talking again, stream of consciousness exhaustion babble.

"God, I can't wait to see him. It's been much too long. I wish I'd never taken that job, just gone with him right away. Thought I needed the experience to get ahead but what I needed was to get my head on straight and hold tight to the man I love. More than anything in the world. The only one ever. He taught me how to love. Him. Oh, God, I ache all over just thinking about seeing him."

The hot pricklies scamper up my back and arms whispering, his bride, fool, not yours. This is the fabled woman who was supposed to arrive and supplant me next spring. But faithful to my director's admonition to listen before spilling my guts, I just nod, casually, "He's not expecting you, right?"

"No, not yet, anyway, not till April. I just couldn't wait, I really couldn't. So here I am. I hope he won't be mad at me; he doesn't like being caught off-guard, but I can tell from his letters that he's been missing me as fiercely as I have him."

Razor-edge shock draws blood to my face. He hasn't said a word to me about missing her. Let alone "fiercely." What have I been missing?

"There's a problem with me coming now, though, because he has this guy with him, Alan, Aaron, Alex, something A, who showed up out of the blue. They've been building the house together, though I guess the A-guy is doing more housework than work on the house—that's what Joaquin says."

Of course I'm offended, but I play along. "Well, everyone needs a wife."

"That's true, but not one that screams in the night like this guy does. I guess he has terrible dreams; wakes Joaquin up with his groaning. Wears Sunday-church-lady white gloves to bed. He needs a shrink, for sure, which J is not."

Señor Incomunicado, why did you never speak to me of these night terrors? This is far more information than I want, or want her to have, but her loosened tongue seems to have spun out of control.

"Plus he has a killer cat, which is kind of rough because Joaquin is big on birds. In fact he says there's a death zone around his house now that keeps all the wildlife out. The idea of a no-rodent zone actually appeals to me—and I actually love cats—but it's hard on him."

What's next, slander the salamander? But no, a scrap of kindness drops from her lips.

"Though A-something, I just can't think of his name, is a wizard in the greenhouse, Joaquin says. He has some kind of Zen power over the plants, which are thriving like never before. Of course I'm pretty good with growing things myself. But anyway, they've come up with a shared workload in the business, and it's awkward for me to break in and take over. Really awkward. But I don't see him living with us when we're just starting our lives together. Especially if there's shrieking in the night. I'm a nurse, and I'd feel obligated to take care of him. All I want to do is be with Joaquin."

Whether my director's advice was sound or not, nothing I can say will rescue the situation now. She and I are rivals in our love for Joaquin, though its quality and nature are of a very different kind. I will fight her and lose, as friends always do to lovers. It occurs to me I could drive her off the road, bind and gag her and throw her in the river. No one saw me pick her up. No one but Joaquin would recognize her, and he doesn't keep up with the local news. She'd just never answer his letters again and never show up. Too bad. How sad.

"The A-guy is a totally lost soul who's latched onto him, which seems to happen a lot to Joaquin. But how to get rid of him at this juncture, you know, in a nice way, very tricky."

I yawn to cover the murderous thoughts I'm having. Vital links between my wounded heart and shattered mind seem to have been severed. She rubs her eyes, throws her head back against the seat.

"I don't know why things always have to get so messy, you know? I'm here. Joaquin and I are going to spend the rest of our lives together. It's time for this A-guy to get on with his life and he should just realize it."

He does now. Maybe Gregorio, the prescient town crier, was trying to give me a heads-up.

I turn off at our home road (hers now, formerly mine), the two ruts across the valley where once I thought Sheriff Jess was going to dump my body. She stiffens. "Where are we going?"

"To Joaquin's place."

"Wow—this is a road?" First-timer nerves: twilight, eerily odd driver, hairy road to nowhere. So tempting.

"You don't have to take me all the way to his door. I mean, if this is the road to his place, I can walk the rest of it. With my trusty North Face flashlight. Seriously, I don't want to put you out." I can tell she's ready to jump.

"No problem. It's just another mile or so." My voice, like my future, is flat and grim; it sounds nothing like that of the dapper, courtly gentleman who picked her up.

"I mean, your family must be expecting you. It's late. Do you have kids?"

"No wife. No kids." I turn full-face to her and yank my hat off, letting my scars catch the last light of the day. She gasps, trying not to. Didn't Joaquin mention the scars? I gun Pacman 2 over a rock; hard crunch and a sideways lurch.

And then, despite my worst efforts, we're pulling up the driveway.

She recognizes the place (from photos, most likely) and emits a pathetic little squeak of joy. "Wow—right up to the door service. You're awesome; thank you so much. I really am grateful. I never would have found it on my own, especially in the dark. Thank you ever so much, um, I'm sorry, I don't think I even know your name." She's already halfway out of the car.

"Alex. Or Alan maybe. The A-guy."

Joaquin steps out onto the porch; he would have heard Pacman 2 coming from a ways off and might could be wondering why I'm so late. Surprise, baby.

She stops dead. Joaquin, seeing her, does, too. The three of us make a striking tableau that Tiger stalks through the middle of. I draw a ghoulish smile from the rage that's been mounting.

"Brung you sumping to go wid dinner, Joe Queen. This here woman was hitchin' to get to ya and jes happen to stick her thumb in my erectshun—oops, I mean direcshun."

He looks at me, thoroughly baffled, which is just the effect I'm going for. Meanwhile, she melts into a puddle of shame and regret. "Oh, God, I am so sorry. I can't believe I was so stupid. I should never open my stupid mouth when I don't know who—oh, my God, I am so sorry."

It's one of those interesting moments I'll have a hard time forgetting. So is the next one.

Joaquin flies off the porch and into her arms. His face—I have to say it—billowing with joy wider than I've ever seen in him. "Lori!"

"Joaquin."

Horror flick to pure cheese. They hold each other desperately, like their ship's about to sink. Watching them, I know mine has. That's what you get for coming into someone's life unsought.

And they don't let go. He doesn't turn to me and say, Oh, Alex, this is Lori and what a terrible way for you to meet and please join this hug-fest, my best friend who is always welcome here, nothing has changed.

Snow begins to fall, a fresh layer of lost hope. I am alone in a world where I don't belong, as I never did. At least I can leave unnoticed in this blizzard of desolation with its silence for cover. I jerk her pack out of the backseat, unload the groceries, and dump the bags beside the car. Slumping past them to my sofa-sized quarters, I shove the few belongings I'd arrived with into my pack. I pause at Mander's cage and shake my head: have to travel light in this weather. Outside, I see two blurred figures whose mouths appear to be moving, whose hands reach for me. I evade them, focusing on Tiger: right, yes, Tiger's still mine. With a flicker of interest I watch my cat lift his leg and pee on the woman's backpack. Good boy, I commend vaguely, and the thought emerges as a word I hadn't meant to utter: "Goodbye." Speaking brings the others briefly into my hearing.

"Alex, you don't have to leave," the man is saying. "Let's have dinner and talk about this."

I want to tell him there's nothing to say, but it's an impulse I can't act upon because all my momentum is driving me away from them. I have what I'd come with, if not what I'd come for, and I'm freezing in this winter grief. Go, go, go, and then I remembered the rest of it, what the bird of passage said: "Human kind cannot bear very much reality."

The snow has smoothed the road and Pacman 2 skims over it like a sleigh. I hardly recognize the landscape in this new guise and have to idle for a while when I reach an intersection. It crosses my mind that the car has lights, which might help me find my way if I weren't blind. Best maybe to get out of the car, lie down somewhere and sleep. Let the snow bury me as it was meant to. I wish Mamia were here to tuck me in.

Tiger, stalwart companion of the road, sensing we're doomed, climbs into my lap and begins giving my rigid left arm a good lick-over, warming it. Left? What's left? I'm left. Left bereft. Go left, young man, go left. Yes, sir, Mr. T, left it is. Till we fall off the edge of the world.

Something in the act itself—of making a decision, of turning the wheel, of finding a logical response between my foot depressing the accelerator pedal and the car lurching forward—reconnects my brain to the present and I spark back to life. Switch on the headlights and take stock of where I'm going and what my prospects are. As long as this business of existence continues to demand a reasonable plan, I am obligated to come up with one. We are headed away from Trove, toward Slurry Pass and Rivertown. Why?

Sure, me and Tige could spend the night in Pacman 2, but we could also turn around and spend the night with Gregorio, who has a guest room and loves company. But he might already have some, and in any case staying with him would involve telling him the story, which would then be broadcast throughout the town. The wound is too fresh to bear probing. Who else? In slow motion, like a battery almost out of juice, my mind flashes through the faces of people I know and finally, on its last whir, replays my day. The sixth face it illuminates is Chewie's, and seeing it I slap the wheel, startling Tiger with this sudden exclamation point. The cabin. Against a halo of crepuscular rays, Our Hundred-Dollar Cabin of Saving Grace. Providence ringing the bell. Good juju. Karma. The cavalry. Ye olde skyhook. Chewie, to whom and by whom we have been delivered.

Of course I don't want to live there, but it's a place to spend the night and get my act together for the trip to that California beach where Tiger and I were headed all along. This has been merely a rest stop on the road to our true destination.

And of course I realize that getting to the cabin, which is treacherous in daylight, might prove fatal at night, but so what if I don't make it? I won't be missed long or by many, Floyd and Greg, maybe, but I'm really just a blip in their lives. The rewarding thing, in a Schadenfreude sense, is that Joaquin and what's-her-name will be wracked by guilt. It will surely end their relationship. Joaquin will throw her out as damaged goods, then start writing obsessively, drinking heavily, punishing himself brutally. His poems will be exquisite in that tormented, confessional way, and all of them will be dedicated to Alex.

With the heedless gusto of a man whom death cannot daunt, I gun Pacman 2 up the faint track to the vet's—no, my—cabin. Tiger, less suicidal by nature and species, growls. "You can get out and walk if you don't like my driving," I mean to growl back but my right rear tire is spinning in air. I jerk the wheel to the left—go left, young man—and feel the edge of the tire scrabble for a tread-hold. Not a LeMans driver, I gun the car again, which puts me into a sideways slide down the hill. I have no idea how far up we are on the mountain: Would we just roll a couple of times and end up maimed or spiral airborne to a clean, fiery death? Adrenaline squirts involuntarily through me; I let up on the accelerator, drop into first gear, gently brake while easing the wheel toward the right, and Pacman 2 grabs the road. So much for going out with a bang. For Tiger's sake I have to make a reasonable effort not to get us killed.

Chewie's—my—parking place looms ahead. Pulling in, I discover I'm shaking. What an incorrigible wimp I am, never able to live up to the coveted image of myself as a man of courage and sangfroid. As if—no, because—he can read my thoughts, Tiger huffily leads the way up the last steep haul to the cabin, eschewing the flashlight that the wimp keeps zapping all over the rocks.

At the porch I stop abruptly and begin patting myself in the age-old gesture of man searching for house keys. I let my thoughts rove back over the title transfer and related bureaucratic horse-piss. Nope, nowhere in there had Chewie handed me a key. A final humiliation but at least a private one. I plop my backpack on the porch and try the door anyway. It gives. A quick scan reveals that there is no lock. Well, yes, of course, when you've got nothing to steal and a high-powered rifle to defend it, who needs a lock on the door?

I am about to barrel in when a thought chills me. What if someone is already here? I really don't know what kind of renegade banditos might be hiding out at Chewie's. If I can stand to one side and shove the door open while flashing my light around the interior, maybe I—

As I am plotting my strategy, Tiger shoulders the door wide open and marches in, tail waving high. Step aside, Wimperella; I'll handle this. Swathed with shame I pad after him, illumining his feline fortitude. He checks the corners for mouse holes, examines the woodstove for gopher nests, and unearthing nothing to massacre for dinner, flattens his ears and walks back out. I shadow him, feeling ridiculous, but without Tiger I don't think I could stay. The place seems eerily thick with Chewie's ptsd, as if he had loaded it to the brim with craziness before fleeing.

The porch will have to do for tonight. I spread out my bedroll and sit down on the weathered bench to unlace my boots. Resting my head against a log of the cabin wall, I breathe deeply for the first time in several hours. I, demented Scarface, have lost and found a home, driven in and out of a snowstorm, ascended and nearly descended a mountain. Now it's quiet, the moon sliver overhead. Now there's nothing further I have to do. Now I'm excruciatingly sad. And while it was horrible tonight, experience has shown me that it will be worse tomorrow. I've had a second chance at happiness; nobody gets thirds.

Snow has quieted the land, whetting the cold. I slouch into an old-man stupor on the bench. It was dumb to have fled here. Dumb to think I was a woodsy self-sufficient macho man. Like right now, when I should go in and start a fire, my first since…which is why I won't. Should grab my stuff and Tiger and drive to Norton, rent a hotel room for the night, get some dinner: ought to have done that in the first place. Or I could just keep sitting here and freeze to death, definitely my easiest option—and most probable given the lure of inertia. Over these despairing thoughts the soundtrack of Lori begins to play when from the other end of the bench issues a faithful warning growl. Without any interest in what has aroused the feline ire this time, I squint into the dark. Coming up the hill, silhouetted against the deeper darkness of the rocks, is the figure of a man. Only Chewie knows why I might be here. Odd that there'd been no sound of the jeep.

Pulling myself forward, I raise my arms as if they were holding a rifle. "Hold it right there! I've got you covered," I snarl.

The figure keeps on coming till I can see him grin. There's no mistaking the goofball who wears it. "Hey, Bug, got room for one more?" Hersch asks, stepping up to the porch.

9

"Death's Other Kingdom"

"Hersch!"

This is the moment when things turn around for our tempest-tossed hero, Alexander, the Not-So-Great.

That's what should have happened, what I expected, because Hersch showing up was the veritable cavalry from the old Westerns. The deus ex machina of every story I loved. "Just when things were looking blackest..." cue the violins from *Peter and the Wolf*. All breathe a sigh of relief. Hersch is back: the dynamic duo, as Papito used to call us—or the Three Musketeers when Joey was along. I wanted to be rescued so badly Hersch couldn't even begin to fathom it.

How he found me: that's what I'd ask if I could get my vocal cords unjammed. Genius, that's how: that's Hersch. Two years after the fire he tracks me to this dilapidated one-room cabin on a mountaintop outside of Trove. Epic, man. Still trying to speak, I crank my arms up, crooking them to hug him. Hersch, Hersch, you dude.

His face is not quite what I remember, I see now. One side of it appears to have shriveled, and he's, wait: he's bald. When did he shed that girly white sandwich-shop-manager skin for red? Ruddy, let's call it, like the hue of a port-swilling English baron. It's okay. I know I look just as bad to him. Dude: Most of his ear on the funky side of his face is missing. Hands are stumped: I'll have to get him some cool gloves. It's freezing, man. Snow thickens the air. Where's all his stuff? How did he get here?

On the porch, Hersch curling back his blackened lips in what I want to believe is a smile, me speechless, he extends his stump toward Tiger, solid buddy of yore. T hisses, back arched and hackles rising, ears flattened. Baring his teeth, he makes a wild dash past us and with an unholy yowl flees into the glowering forests of the night.

What the hell? I laugh at the sheer absurdity of his flight. Tiger and Hersch were bros. They had the same mellow kind of rocking-chair outlook on life and the same killer attitude toward procuring food. If Tiger had been able to stand on his hind legs, he would have worked alongside Hersch building subs and eating up the profits. And Tiger had never been too fussy about appearances or hygiene, which is one of the reasons we all got along so well.

Maybe it wasn't Hersch. Maybe it was something from the way beyond that freaked Tiger out. Cats see things that we don't see. God, it's cold. Time to go in, light a fire, eat something, hear the story. "Tiger!" I yell, full voice. "Get back here. We're going in." Silence. Hersch cocks his head and shuffles past me, heading straight to a far corner of the cabin, where he sinks to the ground, arms dangling from his knees, head down. Why hadn't I noticed he was totally worn out? I grab a couple of logs the old codger left on the porch and close the door. Tiger'll come back when he gets cold enough.

This is not the triumphant reunion it promised to be, heralding a cornucopia of adventures that would dwarf our adolescent exploits and mend my broken heart. No, it's grim, blighted by Hersch's mute suffering, which eclipses my pain. Given the aura of doom he's dragged in with him, starting a fire seems essential: I just do it. The wood catches; light and the hope of warmth take the edge of death off the room.

"Hersch, man, you okay?" I ask in the face of irrefutable evidence that he is not. "I've got some stuff to eat out in the car. Hey, it's Pacman 2, bro, I'm still a Pacmaniac, but this one is sweet. You'll see when we truck around in it tomorrow. Everything works. It's all about maintenance, dude." I sound like my mother trying to put a cheery spin on a plate of okra.

This whole day is spinning out of control. It began so well and has fallen so totally apart. A good reminder of the reason not to buy the trust thing Joaquin tried talking me into. Fool me twice, shame on me.

Hersch raises his head, watching me fret around the cabin. "Hang in, you're going to make it," I chirp. His look bespeaks grief beyond the losses he has manifestly endured, beyond the possiblity of recovery, beyond the skein of resilience. It is a look I snapshotted to store in my personal museum of horrors.

The firelight illumines a single chair pushed against a rickety table, a single bed with a thin, stained mattress, and the woodstove. Nailed to the tarpaper wall is a picture of a cherub torn from the packaging of Charmin bathroom tissue. There's no place like home.

"You're beat, man," I say too heartily once again. "Stretch out on the bed here while I bring in some stuff from the car. Yeah, um, see if I can rustle up some grub for dinner. You want to get warm by the fire? Okay, well, yeah, I'll be right back. I'm just so damn glad to see you. How'd you ever track me down here? You're a bloodhound, man. Yeah, so we got a lot to talk about. Be right back."

The door sticks, and my foot is raised to kick it when Hersch speaks. "I've been looking for you for a long time, Bug. All over. I looked. I could not stop till I found you. I found you." His voice is the rumble-whisper of a zombie. The hair on my neck rises, and I suppress the urge to yowl and flee as Tiger had. I do not turn around.

"Yeah, yeah, you sure did, man, sure did. Wow, you're quite a looker, I mean tracker. Here we are, together again, homes, two years past El Fuego Grande, and we're going to stick tight from here on out. I should have tried to get in touch; sorry, man, I should have. I don't know what was going on in my head. I was pretty screwed up, you know, kind of tried to disappear. It was wrong. I should have been looking, too. I get that. Sorry, man. Hey, I'll be right back. We can talk. Get comfortable. Stretch out on the bed."

I escape out the door. Blurry images follow: remembering that Pacman 2 is parked down the hill and I'll need a flashlight but what for, since I'd left all the food for Joaquin and whatshername; all I've got is what's on the porch: my coat and sleeping bag, a blanket, flashlight, my backpack—not enough survival gear; yelling for Tiger; hurling the beam of my flashlight through the trees; the snow getting serious; wind rising; the opacity of absolute desperation.

Stumbling back into the cabin where Hersch, exactly as I left him, continues to pin me with his uncompromising eyes. Me blubbering about no food, no cat, no plan, nauseated by exhaustion; him with no words, no give. Draping the blanket over him and noticing for the first time that he's wearing only a white t-shirt, the kind he always used to wear, every day, which is reassuring and terrifying. Too many things are off about this scene, but none of it really registers: I see without feeling or caring. Except for Tiger, my Tiger, Tiger in the night.

"Forgot about me, didn't you?" Again, the monster growl. I answer from a thin shelf on the outskirts of sanity, a perch so remote I don't have to listen to what I'm saying.

"I knew you weren't dead, man. Never believed that phony baloney RIP tribute on Joey's FB page. Mexico, right? Zihuatanejo. On the beach. I knew you were hiding out there and I should have come right on down to join you, but I was pretty fucked up, homes, with the scars and I didn't really—"

"Think, about me. Forgot as soon as you copped a ride. The guy you called to come save you. Like I wouldn't. Or at least Tiger."

"You're invincible, bro. Walk through fire like that dude we read about in Justine's class."

"He was a phantom, remember? Not flesh and blood."

"Hey whoa, man, way too literary for puny-brain tonight. Let's hash it all out in the morning, what do you say?"

He doesn't. Where is Tiger? In the forests of the dead. I should get us all the hell out of here. A phantom: Hersch, the firewalker, burning bright. Tiger ran not because Hersch was there but because not-Hersch was. How had that possibility eluded me? Fear is the enemy, of which Hersch, my friend, is an outward manifestation. I am afraid of something I don't want to know. Then without even checking the spittles of fire, I scramble terrified for the cot and into the sleeping bag, plunging down broken, rickety steppingstones into a hallucinatory nightmare.

They are sitting on a campfire, Harve and Hersch, guitars in fine strum, six-pack between them, talking music and breaking into fragments of song. Neither of them has ever been any good at remembering lyrics. That's my job, along with busting a few chords on the harmonica. "Hey, Mr. Tambourine Man" is my winning number. I try to step into the fire to join them but can't get any momentum in my legs. It's cold and dark where I stand, freezing. I call to them to let me in, but they don't hear me. Or choose not to. I yell, stomp, kick dirt at the fire. Throw my harmonica at Hersch's head, where it lands above his blackened ear nub and bounces off, tumbling back against my boot. I don't exist, which seems grossly unfair given how real they are, haunting me. Papito, that is. This is the first I've seen of Hersch. Or thought much about him, which hurts worse than anything I've done because it isn't in the service of love. I shiver, my extremities gone numb. In the tone of Hersch, a ventriloquist who doesn't move his lips, I hear him say, "You're a cold dude, Bug, just now figuring that out."

Weariness suffocating me in that glacial realm of horror without rest, I understand what Hersch had meant by, "Got room for one more?" If only they would let me into the righteous compass of unkindled flesh.

"It wasn't completely my fault, you know. I was trapped in gauze and shit for months. You might have sent a message." But Hersch doesn't do things that way. He just shows up. Like here. Then whoever he's with has to figure out what to do next. Or should have called him off. I've done neither. But what the hell did I do to bring him here, tonight? Went freaking nuts with loneliness, and Hersch would have sensed that. He is a most intuitive dude. "I've missed you, man, you hear that? Got nothing but love for my bro. The be-here-now guru." Though at this moment I wish he weren't. Wraith in a room of human dimension, where I, locked in a state of hyper-anxiety, struggle to flee some uninhabitable truth. Never warm again, don't deserve to be. Warmth belongs to the honorable, not the heedless.

I swing up on my elbow toward the corner where he crashed and recoil. Hersch is rising, free of gravity's hold, his head lodged among the ceiling beams, his crucified arms stretched way out, much longer than ordinary appendages, resting on air. His face widening beyond the cabin's reach.

Too dizzy to look, I wait for teeth and fingers to close on my throat. Weeks from now, they'll assume I froze to death. Joaquin and whatshername who wasn't supposed to come till spring will feel guilty for a while, but they'll tell each other it wasn't completely their fault. The game of blame: is it really about having shirked your duty or is it about clearing yourself of it? If you feel terrible about what you haven't done, you're forgiven, by the living at least, your conscience salved, and you are freed from further obligation.

It's no use asking anymore who's responsible but who cares. Mine is not the work of undoing past follies but of going on despite them. Till now. Seeing what I can do with what's left. Or was. Picking through the squalor of options, the refuse discarded by blind incendiaries, cobbling together scrappy tropes from broken limbs. Yet my brain, operating independently of my will, is a conflagration of anguish and self-justification, scourging hope of unconsciousness with trauma.

I dive into the flames to save him, a sacrifice that defies life and logic. He is my best friend, and in that dire moment I discover that I love him more than I'd reckoned. He is my other, my double, my not-me and I his. Our paths, though different, are never separate because we walk them wholly aware of one another. Measuring each other's stride, sometimes critically, sometimes compassionately, but not indifferently. Beyond the biological, we are each other's keepers. And I have to go on, even when instinct cries against it. It is the only brave thing I've ever done.

"Harve, beloved Papito, was my man—"

"Harve? I was speaking of you, Bug, you who called when the fire hit. Hersch. Hersch Hersch, save me! And I had to go on when I could go no further, when the roads were blocked, when the place was in flames, had to go on when it could do no good, served no purpose except the urge to save you, who were already saved, saved yourself, which I didn't know, had to go on because I could not bear to leave you behind, to let you down, go, go go with the inexorable impetus, eyes clotted with smoke, into the fire, breaking through the barriers of common sense, oblivious to commands by police, undeterred by the likelihood of failure, on, go on, go, go, go into the bitter inferno. It was the only brave thing I've ever done."

"My keeper."

"My brother."

"My father."

"My friend."

"Harve."

"Hersch. It was me you called when the flames rose, you whom I drove through the firestorm to rescue, you whom I risked everything for. Hersch, Hersch, come get me! Help. Screaming for me, your friend. It was I who chose to go on when I was meant to go no further—turn back, the cops bull-horned get the hell out of here—I who tore through the barricades of common sense, the commands of authority, undeterred by the horror before me. I who went on and on, refusing to leave you behind when you called for me, your friend, your lifelong homeboy, I who found your house, the roof already flaming. I who ran in to look for you and found you gone, I, who having come against all reason to save you who had not waited nor called to say go back, not on, I'm safe. I who found myself trapped as I thought you were, with no way out. Back or on were walls of smoke, concealing flames. The paths we walked separately but together were severed, and I, Hersch, had been left on the one marked 'no exit.'

"Coming to your rescue was the only brave thing I ever did, and no one knew. You never knew, my keeper, my brother. You went on, went on without me, without wondering, without seeking, without regret. It's been a long night's journey into this one. When you can no longer deny me."

Restlessness shakes me, the desire to snap apart, bone by bone, and feed myself to the wasteland hungers bred of injustice. I am wrong, more: I am the wrong, insatiably capable of wronging, and the poison writhing in me would kill any who might hope in vain to suck grace from my marrow.

Vain, meaning both arrogant and futile, as were my attempt and I, both vains. And horribly, fatally mindless—less and less and less. Even the blessing of a good death escaped me. No martyr, I, just a fool.

"Who you are is so much less important than it once was. You're not the friend I remember, not the one I set out to find, not the one I hoped you'd be, but the one who left me behind hurtling into the flames to save him, the deserter who plundered any hope of redemption."

Hersch standing over me, rage in his firelit eyes, his blackened lips curled back in a snarl. Am I waking in the dream, dreaming that I am awake? Have I not slept at all? Hersch with that face is not imaginable. The stench of ash and old sweat. I am awake and terrified, like Victor Frankenstein when, on the night of its creation, his eyes open to the monster towering over him. But unlike the monster, Hersch isn't trying to smile; he isn't standing guard but keeping vigil. He wants me to die.

"It's time. Last rites include your confession."

His fury presses down on me like stone. Hersch, Cool Dude, Master of Imperturbability, the Jokester who chose to read *Harold and the Purple Crayon* at our high school senior dinner instead of a tear-jerker speech of gratitude to his family and friends. Hersch, the sandwich-shop manager and condo-owner, the rock: my best friend before I thought Joaquin was.

Hersch wants me to confess and die. I hear a bell ringing. No idea where it is.

"To bring evil into the world, to inject the malice of abandonment into a friendship built on loyalty, decimates both the perpetrator and the victim. Annihilating trust is a form of murder so cruel it defies the usual punishment. Faith broken, the loss of breath is irrevocable. What does breath matter when all it inhales is despair and decay?"

Tiger, Tiger, burning bright, in the forest of tonight.

"I came for you, I came when everything argued against it. The fire was like fog, impenetrable. I smashed through police barricades, ignoring common sense, all the warnings, the instinct to save myself. I came for you because I could imagine you and Tiger stranded in front of that funky little house, in the area where the fire was entrenched, trying to start that no-good, piece-of-crap car. Envisioned you two clowns there, the radio stuck on some screechy tune while the neighborhood went up in flames. So I came for you, even though it killed me; I wouldn't have been able to live with myself if I hadn't. You called and I came and you were gone, and there was no way out."

The proximity of death fills the cabin. I scan the room for Harvey's ethereal white formlessness. Hersch pulls my eyes back to his. Even that slight shift of focus hurts; a preternatural cold has risen through the floorboards and slithered into any exposed flesh. Wind hisses at the flimsy window, tonguing my scarred cheekbone. The bell is still clanging. And Hersch, the executioner, in his t-shirt, seethes above me, waiting for an answer that is not an excuse. I have awakened to a nightmare worse than the one from which I awakened.

"I didn't know we were the kind of friends who would die for each other."

"Neither did I."

"Or die together rather than leave each other behind. Because that's what would have happened."

"The whole mission was pathetic and pointless. I should have turned back when I told you to grab a ride with a neighbor, as you did, and headed as far away from town as I could get. I had a clear shot south. We'd both have made it."

"Zihuatanejo."

Ringing and ringing. I force my brittle arm out of the bag and press the flashlight switch. The flare of pain coinciding with the flare of light just before I enter a desolate space of sordid terror. The end. Whatever happened next I've barred so tight I'll never find it again. Did I scream? Turn off the flashlight? Throw it at him? Bolt? Lose consciousness? Probably. Probably several of the above. What I see is the door to the cabin flying open, snow cannoning in, and the roof lifting off. Untethered, I ascend on the updraft to a stratum sere as light, beyond recall, flying off the compass into an interstellar solitude. So wide within that my atoms split open and become vessels for tidal drift.

Alone, I ride the undulations of air beyond the contours of earth. Farther, where nothing breathes and no reflection pierces, where neither direction nor destination matter (though it is hard to lose the sense of going somewhere). Where I could fall without descending, merciful for me to whom heights had been a dread, soaring beyond fear and folly, beyond guilt and blame, beyond myself in recognizable form. Space, they call it, but measuring infinity, it is just as much non. Euphoric, unhurried, I sail over canyons of aurora borealis and glide down the belly of a solar wind. Then I am beyond all familiar galactic phenomena. Death's other kingdom.

Matter into energy, bobbing unsuspended through the stars.

If we could remember only the best of ourselves with integrity, return buoyant to this vindicating moment or that act of generosity, see ourselves flourishing and beloved, hear ourselves praised, believe ourselves good. The rest, while not forgotten, lying dormant unless summoned and even then vague and evanescent, slipping like minnows over the dappled streambed. If then, Hersch and I in solid camaraderie would lounge on the quad, on his couch or mine, forever doing nothing but dwell in the bliss of our sublime youth.

Or if we could pretzel memory so that every wrong turned right. Recalling our transgressions is far worse than committing them, the loss of faith in ourselves growing with each recall. We end as a tenuous elder, scared of a misstep, having made so many, a fragile hull of warnings and worries.

These dark meanderings of the heart thin as I furl past nebula. The nebula give way to fire, the fire to ice, the ice to silence, the silence to expanse, the expanse to dissolution which then purifies into un-ness, the original quiescence at the core, where the blindness of nothing to see yields a vision conjured by the inner eye yet undeniable: a crystalline aperture into which to float. From its jagged edges protrude thoughts, though none demand thinking. They can be grasped free of effort, known without being taken, and kept: they are mine.

Nothing here requires action. It is the unbeing undoing, unfeeling, unmeaning, undreaming, unsundering of self and soul, of perception and reception, of dissembling and disclosing. To fall so wholly into the interior, expecting absolute blankness, finding instead a luminous chamber unshadowed: that is the grace of submission. No fears, no doubts lurking in the dreams of the unbound traveler, who having entered because no other way lay open, now must continue in faith, leaving an imprint on the cairns. You were here, better than not to have been, perhaps, but regardless, pressed on. Although there is no movement in the land where memory has been banished, a borrowed grief.

Memory here no threat, simply an elongation of the aerie.

Memory is a trick of the imagination, and the mage who plays it on us is time. We believe the trick because the sleight of mind is so subtle. Distracted by a moment—the flash of a smile, the hollow behind our youthful ego of grievances, caught in a mirror we thought we saw through—we continuously reinvent memories in the making of them, schist upon schist, the original experience a fossil from which we take what skeletal meaning we wish. That is the deception of the sorcerer time, whom we mistook for a sage.

Memory and imagination are profoundly linked by desire and divided by time.

Are the sorrows we've dreamed more real than those we've lived, and aren't dreams as integral to our reality as conscious memories? Imagination is revered, sought, as a measure of brilliance and artistry, revealing higher truths. Imaginings are scoffed at, treated with contempt as an indulgence, but never taken seriously. You're just imagining things, meaning a false perception, an illusion, an untruth.

Memory and imagination: imagined memories, remembered imaginings. The borders are blurred, which is, to the rational mind, a sure sign of incoherence, madness: the growing opacity of my self-perception.

If memory is a measure of time (time thus a factor of memory) and time and space are a continuum, then I am on a trajectory a long way from home. The light is ancient and the darkness apocalyptic.

If time, however, is an illusion and space thus a fabrication, I am where I have always been: banging around in my head in a flounder daze. Here, which is also there, which is elsewhere, anywhere, wherever-where. I am everywhere I have ever been and nowhere I know. Nowhere and now here. Unable to distinguish possession from yearning, love from loss, hope from despair. I am on a course laid by inertia and entropy, unspooling along coordinates that bend toward oblivion. And rapidly approaching on the periphery of consciousness is an enemy vessel whose rockets are set to fire.

Fire is the key, isn't it? The no-man's-land where I wait for passage, pray for redemption or amnesia. Where I toil ceaselessly to extinguish my shame. If there were a divine finger stirring the cosmos that rose dripping with stars to offer me a cuppa infinite kindness, a universal pardon, a sweet draught of forgetfulness and unbroken sleep, I would travel all the light and dark lands of celestial eternity to accept it, say yes, thank you, I am here. But the inability to conceive infinity is what renders us mortal and our singular lives unimaginable.

"Time to go."

My footprint on the earth will be very shallow if I die now. Not much accomplished, not much left behind. Easy to forget.

"Nothing's holding you."

Who wouldn't agree? There is more for me in that nether world than in the one of substance. Mamia will miss me, but so much pain and distance has already grown between us that her sadness will be a ripple, not a tsunami. She will seek me on the shores of memory and find only flotsam and jetsam, with an occasional bright shell twisted into the seaweed. It will be an endurable loss that in the end will free her of all responsibility for and to the past. She can begin again on her own terms, owing no one and torn by no competing desires. Yes, even she will agree.

"Hurry up."

But I will not. Rushing has been the source of my fatal errors; I am not hurling myself out of existence.

"Too late for regrets."

The birds may miss me, their calls heard by one fewer, and the hills I so admired. Surely they will notice the loss of adoration. In the subterranean web of the greenhouse my absence will be sensed, a passing sorrow that will nonetheless be sung. There are winds that know my name, and the river that calls me by it. Dreams that will grieve at no longer being dreamed.

And Tiger. But he is no doubt gone ahead of me, as usual.

"Sweet Jesus."

All right, Hersch, let's go. I'm ready.

"There's no one here."

Then I am elsewhere.

"I'm going in."

Or nowhere.

"Watch your step."

A desperate banging at the gates of incomprehension stirs me from my reverie. I hear in it the tolling bell that, it's true, could be for me but is more likely a call from the known world. Given that I have no idea where I've been and the wind is picking up, it seems unwise to act. Easier to let come what may and become what will, surrender to the drift. With snow piling into my heedless mind, all I have to lose is consciousness.

"Come here!"

"Who on earth? What happened?"

"I don't know."

The known world, we like to call it: explored, named, mapped, and conquered. Known in the sense of owned. Preposterous as the idea is, the implications are promising: that there is an unknown world, or a barely known one, a half-known one, an unknowable one. Perhaps even an inconceivable one where memories dwell solely in the unlived experience and the insensate realm. Fantasies there are the coin of the realm, illusion the threshold guardian of truth.

"It's Joaquin's sidekick."

"Frostbit, real bad."

"But not dead. He's got a pulse."

"Good thing you wanted to come up to check on Chewie, after the storm."

"I wonder where he is."

"And how the hell did this guy wind up here?"

"More to the point, how are we going to get him out?"

Once you've been set adrift on a blind glacier, what can you do to keep yourself interested in where you're going? I wonder, but only remotely, whether another is speaking or only I with myself.

"Use the mattress as a sled. Roped between us, we can fly down the mountain."

I struggle to float again above the earthly plagues of guilt and ice. It took me some time to learn to fly after the fire. One night I was walking through a luminous spring morning and I simply rose, not very high, but definitely in the air, high enough to soar, and I headed for your place, Hersch. I was looking for you. In the last room, in your basement, you were sitting in a corner, grinning, with hot babes snuggling against you on either side. You nodded at me, said, hey, the bug is winging it, and I circled and zoomed off, feeling lightheaded and full of myself.

"Here, grab him under the arms."

A whisper of skin, slight as a phantom, grazes my hand as I spread myself wide at the brink. My hand, so carefully guarded all these nights, winces at the touch. I hear a shriek as we begin to fight, then several more, then quiet, a moan, a violent shock, a searing, scorching blast that's torn my head off.

The fire!

Screams, orders, hands. I flail, brittle, trying not to splinter.

Check the fire, the fire, the fire, the fire the fire.

"Easy, easy, man."

Hersch, my captor, my scorekeeper, who has deserted me to perish in the flames. As I did him.

I imagine I see his shadow ahead slipping among the flames that will not consume him nor admit me. At my approach the smolder hardens. Low and weary, my passage through its bones.

"Slide the rope under the mattress as far as you can."

Ashen, this place, dim and gray, skimming the frigid rock hollows and spires. Twilit justice drained of mercy. Granite bladed sheer with the torment of the dying. I am where I deserve to be, amid indurate and pitiless boulders that shun the suppliant.

"Okay, I've got it."

What are the odds of a stone opening to enfold me at nightfall? I knew you'd come home. Yes, it's just the way you left it. Go and rest now; then wash up for dinner. The tomatoes are fresh from the garden. As if there were some place for me, light and thick as a country loft beyond ruin.

"On the count of three."

"Hang in there, bud."

Where we could face one another unmasked. Naked, honest. Would we see thus clearly that masks disguise how alike we are or discern our unbreachable onliness?

"Wait. Stop."

My right side is crawling, like a thousand bugs skittering across my skin. Tickling and shivering me, snaking up my ribs.

"Oh, my god!"

From deep within my cavity emerges Tiger, the indomitable one. My savior, my friend.

"I was wondering how he survived. Seemed like a miracle, but it was the cat. Just enough extra body heat to keep him from going under."

Tiger, a miracle: synonymous. He climbs aboard my chest and spurs me over the callous realm of the unforgiven. Soul billowing, I purl into the void.

10

"Surely Some Revelation is at Hand"

"Things fall apart: center cannot hold…something anarchy is loosed upon the world—" Not a single blessed poem learned by heart, whole, straight through, not even the Yeats she drew bleak solace from. But loosing anarchy, yes, her specialty, moron, idiot, fool. And that blood-dammed tide: she, the record-holding award winner for mere, that's the missing word: mere stupidity. Her tongue run loose as a hunt-crazed rough beast. "A-something. A-something." How about A-assdumb, girl? Slouching toward an hourglass waste of sand when she could have walked in beauty like the night—Joaquin's first courting words. Lord Byron, a Romantic poet, and Joaquin, too. Not Yeats, whose gaze blank and pitiless was her inward own.

Out loud she said, "Happy New Year, Alex. It will be because you are going to start talking to me, open your eyes and say, 'Good morning, Lori. I'm feeling better, thank you, ready to eat and walk by myself. I appreciate the help, but I'll be okay on my own now.'"

Dusky wind threw a mouthful of snow at the window, full of Yeats' passionate intensity. Guilt had spurred her through the first three months, but with the year turning, impatience topped it. Not enough had changed to count as progress. Inert, mute, Alex had made no effort to come back to himself. To care that she had devoted every day to keeping him alive. To rise. Nothing stopping him, physically, Doc claimed. If he'd set that powerful will of his to living instead of dying, already be well on his way to a full recovery.

But all his joints and sinews were stiffening as he lay there like a polished corpse in a coffin. She could hold a funeral for him and drop him in the ground and he wouldn't move a muscle. Easier yet, just don't come tomorrow. Quit. How many years can he lie there playing dead? Flashed on herself at sixty, shuffling over to empty the catheter bag.

That evening, three months ago, A-something had picked her up, jaunty gallant rescues roadside waif, where you headed, ma'am, and I'll get you there, hat pulled low so she wouldn't see the burn scars from the fire he'd run into to save his father, which his father ran into to save the old family dog, who she guessed was too senile to get out of the burning house on his own, or maybe didn't want to, he was that old, and like father like son plunging headstrong into the flames, from which neither father nor dog emerged but Alex did, seared. They shot old dogs on the farm.

He'd just stilled the death knell pounding his ruined heart, making a comeback with Tiger at Joaquin's in the hills above Trove when she jumped into his VW bug and commenced babbling about her true love who had to get rid of A-something so she and Joaquin could dwell in joy alone together. Instead of smiling flirtynice and asking about him, the way she'd been trained as a girl to do but had unlearned, that training for once sensible. She as heedless as father and son, plunging her gabble-maw into the doom of an invalid no more willing to save himself than the old family dog had been.

And in such a sweet room, lent to him by Gregorio out of the kindness of his incredibly kind heart. The cushioned rocking chair, ground zero for her vigil. The bed, brass framed and quilt laid, nightstand, lamp, and the white table for medical supplies. A wheelchair borrowed from the doc. Not that Alex needed it. He wasn't a damn cripple.

"Joaquin has this guy living with him, Alan, Aaron, A-something, who showed up unexpectedly who's got to leave so we can start our lives together."

His neck tense. The air leaden. She so loaded with stories she couldn't see past them.

"This guy has nightmares; wakes Joaquin up, his groans and yells. PTSD. Needs serious mental health care and—"

Clamped firmly between thumb and forefinger, that instrument of devastation would not have loosed the anarchy she was too keyed up to see coming.

"Plus A-whoever has a killer cat, which is a problem because Joaquin loves wildlife. He says there's kind of a death zone around his house that no creature dares enter. Me, I'm fonder of cats than mice, but it's stressing Joaquin out."

He could have mentioned Alex's scars, which she'd seen even with the light and his hat low. One bisecting his nose, pockmarks on his cheeks and chin. Not that Joaquin's tact absolved her.

"The guy is a sad case who's latched onto him, which seems to happen a lot to Joaquin. But how to get rid of him, very awkward."

After which, the discovery and Alex fled. Nothing but his summer sleeping bag to outlast his first mountain snowstorm in a decrepit cabin, and Tiger, whose body stretched alongside, kept him from death.

Fire and ice. If Alex pulled through, he would be a man of steel, tempered in the crucible of disaster.

Of course she couldn't quit. Even at the turning of the year, blood thick with freedom craving. Her hand slipped down to stroke Tiger, who rubbed her wrist and yawned. "You good kitty, you. The hero of the story. So brave." Picked up Alex's flaccid hand and slid it along Tiger, who wriggled under the familiar touch, began to knead the quilt. "Come on, A-something," she coaxed. "Give your lifesaver cat some love." The hand dropped away when she stepped back to survey the window. Snow mounding high. From the South, she felt meanness in the voiding white, a callous hunger that would suck your marrow. Wait too long and Joaquin's truck would balk at the run up the hill. She'd have to haul herself that last thigh-deep stretch, the carrion storm fanging her.

Catheter bag empty, IV bag full. Greg would be in soon to get Alex all set for the night. There would be a party in the restaurant, even in this weather, and Greg at the center of it. Man, could he dance. Oversized parka, mittens, fur-lined boots from a yard sale, thermal underwear, armed her for the journey. Which she shouldn't have had to make at all, given it was New Year's Eve with a monster storm chomping at the land. Tomorrow? What if it was still coming down? What the hell would she have to go through to return to this prison? Joaquin had suggested shipping Alex to his mother, who was living in

Summerville, but when the flattened widow with pale voice came, it was clear that caring for him would end her life before his.

Joaquin told her that like suspected terrorist detainees, she was being held without bail indefinitely, but in her case, on charges she had leveled against herself. She was both captor and captive. Her confession made and heard, she would have been free to go if she could have forgiven herself. Or if her victim had. The crime had by year's end been far diminished by her compensatory service. She owed Alex nothing more, but she wouldn't let herself abandon him. When would her sentence be served? It was his call. Joaquin, though: how long would her life with him wait?

"What do you do there all day?" Joaquin had asked a month in. She was not the ardent reader he'd always been, not the poet or musician. Couldn't draw or sing or dance. She was a small dark girl from a country home that wasn't even hers. Foster child, unclaimed, never suckled at the breast of her real mother. The folks that raised her weren't cruel outright, but they yelled a lot and made her feel the orphan. A charity case whose life they'd saved. Expected her to work her way through the days all of them counted till they were shed of her. She would have left sooner if she'd thought she could make it on her own. If she'd had a plan.

Well, she did, but it was pretty basic: leave home. Lyle, her older brother, fourteen, native to the family, was the primary cause. The torment she endured at his hands made palpable the ugliness of the place. She was eleven when he first caught her alone in the bathroom, just done wiping. He wedged the door tight with a matchbook and unzipped his jeans. Forced her to look, to touch his erect manliness. Then reached into her panties and poked his finger inside her. Jagged nail, grimy digit he wiggled around in her till he squirted a stream of white mucus onto her tee. If she told, he'd see she was sent back to the orphanage, forever. He could do it, too. His mother, whose mashed-potato face spumed rage at any upset, was easily swayed by her firstborn and especially against the girl. This place was bad sometimes, like right now, but the orphanage was worse. Here she had her own room at least, and she could lock it from the inside, get quiet and safe. And the younger boys minded her like a mother, given that the one who bore them was more an overseer. The littlest boy was a poorly diapered, crawling thing when she first arrived at seven, but big for a straight-edged girl to haul around, as she did, everywhere, with the other one trailing her, wetting his pants at four.

The foster dad had retreated to the fields and the bottle. Slept until winter in the loft of the barn. Had lost the use of words, grunted for the most part. Hard to tell him apart from the pigs he fed and ate. A sloppy butcher, the meat tasted of slaughter even after it was cooked. Her gorge still rose around pork. He was down to the bare minimum of human, the father. Stank and drank, as his wife snarled, not wanting anything more from him than a decent harvest. Lyle was meant to help him but too mulish to do him much good. None of them would be staying on the farm when the old man passed.

She took to wearing tees and jeans to school every day, hair pulled hard into a ponytail, though she was sixteen and should have been in dresses and make-up, loopy curls. Her foster mother scowled at her look, warned that she'd never catch a boy that way.

Good, she thought, just what I want to not do. Lyle still trapped her in unexpected places, finger-diddling her in the expected place.

College wasn't even a whisper in the piney woods where she hid from him, did her homework and sometimes peed, till the counselor at school proposed it. An ex-marine who liked to call her into his office and close the door, he breathed on her neck and ear while guiding her through the forms, the essays, the test prep. Made sure she came off pitiful and deprived, with enough oozy misfortune to make her a likely diversity candidate.

Treacherous as these sessions were, they paid off with acceptances from three schools. Her method of picking was the one farthest from home: the Northwest. Through the chancy hoop of fate Joaquin leaped at the same school she did. There, the odds of meeting would have seemed improved, but he was all English, learning the craft and honing the art of verse, reading, finally, as much as he liked unfettered from the daily call of ranch life: on the other side of the barbed wire, ascending the wide slopes of his mind. She, who had longed to be cared for, was drawn to the caring professions, to sniff out need in others and cure it, making herself thus needed, and she dared hope, loved. Healing, easing pain, giving life, making its passage sweeter, bringing it to a happy end, that was where she gravitated, and the nursing program took her in its eager embrace. She was unaware of the scarcity of those in medicine who were not seeking prestige and second homes in exotic locales. To be a nurse seemed to her the pinnacle of bliss.

These spheres, the poet and the nurse, had but one venn center: the infirmary. Where Joaquin, after particularly strenuous midterms for which he forsook sleep and meals, checked in, flu-riddled. It was first semester of senior year, and she, a promising student nurse, was interning under the close eye of the staff. She checked his fever, took his vital signs, signs that proved vital to their future trysts. She did not see his languid movements, sweaty skin, drooping eyes, nor hear his coughs and moans, but rather felt the depth of his presence, a keen and clear eye for the elegiac glory of the earth.

She invented a kinship of spirit between them well before he was able to focus on the comely young woman ministering to him. By then, the warmth and conviction of her fantasies enveloped him too utterly to resist. They went to dinner, to films, to his room, the quad, the library, went as a pair where and whenever they could, reveling in each other as lovers bound.

But it was senior year, and her studies continued while his did not. She was after an RN and a Master's in Public Health, widen her options. He began applying to an MFA program at the university, thinking it both fruitful for his practice as a poet and a natural way to extend their time together. It was a fiercely coveted program, and like many, preferred students who'd been out in the world a bit before resuming their studies. He was not admitted. He applied for a teaching job in the local schools, but without credentials or certification, he was not hired. He considered working for the university, a route many alums took, but by then there were no openings. And by then his father, who'd come and gone during his son's absence, was in rehab again, and his mother needed him. Grim, heavy-footed, he made his way home. She wrote and called daily. They kept the faith for as long as he could manage it before sinking into the swill of his former reclusive self. Poetry fled Joaquin's wounded soul, left him blank.

Did Lori give up on her man? That's a possibility you'd only raise if you didn't know her. There would be no other for her, as there had been none till he walked infirmly into her sphere. She was ready to camp outside his window, if need be, till she crumbled into dust and a good wind blew her into his pores, from where she would burrow deep inside him till he himself was dust and they commingled eternally. She was packing when they offered her a job at a prestigious hospital in the city. So flattered she couldn't say no. Didn't yet see that with her qualifications and innate gift for nursing, she would never be unemployed. Even her care of Alex was paid by the expensive health insurance policy his mother kept up for him. Work was everywhere, a fact of her life she'd learned early on. How to make her life work, though, eluded her.

One thing she kept deciding, she thought for sure. She was not going to spend another three months tending this mute corpse of a ruin. Who could get up and do for himself whenever he wanted. Who was so used to having things his way he was paralyzed when he didn't. She wasn't good for him any longer; she'd lost the empathy that was crucial for aligning will to way. Time to make a new plan. For Gregorio's sake, too.

She gave herself points for having done her best early on. The horror of her words still rebounded, slamming against the walls of her mind like bats gone deaf. Drove her wild with shame. A-something, something, thing, ing, ng A-some…. She'd broken him, though to be fair, he was cracked all to hell and had not mended cleanly. Didn't matter. She'd smashed him into a suicidal frenzy, as good as killed him. First weeks of service were expiation and recompense, prayers for mercy circling her clenched gut like a rosary of despair. Nights with Joaquin she waited till he slept to weep.

When it looked pretty certain that Alex would live, such as he was, after his vitals had been stabilized, her penance turned to restoration. Now she was in her element, the healer once again. She summoned cheer as her hands massaged and bathed him. She apologized to his limbs but wove a tapestry of bright scenes for the future. Of course he would stay with them. Forever, if he liked, or until he met the woman of his dreams, as he surely would, being as sweet as she remembered from when he picked her up that night and she behaved so deplorably, which she would never stop regretting. Ever. She herself would build him a room in Joaquin's house. They would be happy. Alex was a whiz in the greenhouse, she reminded him, which also spoke to his virtue and keen sensibilities. Hours long, days long, weeks long, she praised the inert, mangled flesh heap, accepting his silence as reproof and passionately set on bringing him back to the world.

Besides laying on hands, she read to him and told him stories, wrote his mother, invited her to come visit, and kept her informed of Alex's condition as she had not before been. They got on at once, a mother-daughter pair whose longing to be that was their bond. Such a wonderful mother, such a loving daughter: they opened up to each other, there in the room within Alex's hearing, had he bothered. All about the fire, all about the evening's drive to Joaquin's that ended in disaster, all about their fervent lost wishes for a different outcome. Their worries about the one ahead. Not a word of blame for Alex.

Why he couldn't go to Summerville: all the mother's fault. Why he would come home to Joaquin's: all her fault. Even if Joaquin didn't want her anymore, wherever she went, Alex would go with her. And she would always stay in touch. The mother would support him regardless of cost. Albatross: the undercurrent of their vows, while both reassured each other it was by choice. Did he imagine himself hanging from their necks even as they swore to care for him lifelong?

The mother left with Lori a sealed envelope for her son, the living dead man. To be given him upon his resurrection, should he roll the stone away from his entombed heart and walk among them again. If not, to be destroyed by Lori, a promise she would keep.

Reading the paper to him, she skipped the ugly stories, which meant no hard news. New Restaurant Opens in Arroyo, Will Parks and Grace Underwood Engaged on Indigo Peak, Homecoming for Mirabelle Aldorf's Hound Buster (a five-hundred-mile journey from where she'd gotten lost on a camping trip in Wyoming), Dell Police Chief John Lorenzo Retires, Twins Born in Truck Bed, Leda James Weds Seth Warren (congratulations—wish I knew you), and as the holidays neared, inspiring stories from the Christmas Angels fund. Hers was the Disney version of current events, where people whistled while they worked and wishes on stars came true. No one was injured or died in her news, not even friends like Jesse's wife who finally succumbed November 23, just before Thanksgiving. No stress, no sadness, no reason not to get back up on that horse. Cheered her up even if it didn't get a rise out of him. Alex must have deduced her strategy, if he was listening: the invalid, frail, to be protected from the world's pain.

Best of all, she told him one morning, Floyd had his VW bug all fixed and ready to roll. He'd simonized it, looked brand new. Floyd was driving it around the block every few days to keep everything in perfect working order. Whenever Alex felt up to it, he could slide in behind the wheel and cruise Trove. She faltered a bit on that last idea because it spun her to the fateful night when Alex was last at the wheel. Still, reclaiming his car, that would restore freedom and identity, his youth. But he didn't bite.

Joaquin came by a couple of times, tried talking to him. Made sure Alex knew he was welcome and always had been. If he'd just waited a minute that night Joaquin would have told him so. Which wasn't wholly true, and therefore hard to say, because once Lori was in, Alex would have been out, sure enough. No matter: Alex remained a passive lump in the bedsheets. The IV bottle dripped more life into him than Joaquin's words, which is why, after twice trying, he decided to spare himself the awkwardness and not show up again. When he came for Lori, if she was not outside waiting, he honked, a soft one to call her to him. Didn't see how she stood it every day of the week, and every as in seven, with only a rare exception when she could talk Donna, a retired nurse who wanted to stay that way, into taking a shift. Supportive in the beginning, Joaquin's patience had worn through faster than hers. He chafed at the daily loss and tried to figure how to wean Alex from her. Them. Thank whatever gods there be for Greg. The nightwatch. She made it easy duty for him, of course, but without him? Well, it might take that, pulling the supports out from under Alex. Or hospitalizing him in Summerville. Joaquin reproached himself for these ungracious thoughts, grew desperate for some providential hand to save him. Them.

He gave her books, thinking may as well put this lost time into the enduring beauty of literature. More common ground for the two of us, less reason to talk of Alex. A volume of Romantic poetry. García Márquez's novel, *One Hundred Years of Solitude* (fitting choice, given her circumstances). She began to share the words with Alex, who Joaquin said had also been an English major, and discovered the pleasures of reading aloud. Further in, she commenced discussing her questions and thoughts with the mummified form. When evening came, then, had fodder to launch Joaquin on a full tour of the ideas, which brought her into his realm, and what man doesn't love to teach his woman things he knows all about?

Evenings, after dinner, were their golden hours, stretching from table to bed. They would talk of his days (double the work, no time to write). Got Alex out of the way on the drive home or on her arrival there. After the first weeks, the reports were brief. His: greenhouse tending, interior work on the house, deliveries. Hers: no change, no response to whatever she'd tried. As Joaquin's resentment grew, she stopped reporting at all, said she'd tell him if there was anything new. Wanted to get on with their lives together, their half-lives, Joaquin called them. Of course the money she earned helped, but he was of a mind to have more of her, less of the lucre. "Just till he wakens" was her promise going in; then "Just till his mother comes to take him to Summerville," followed by "Just till the new year comes in." Till tonight. Another solution had to be found. But even that fell to her, by default.

The golden hours shone with music and book talk. Joaquin played songs for her, mostly ones he'd written but a few classics learned from repeated hearing. He was a ballads man, set the Romantic legends of Tennyson and Byron to melodies that glorified them. Also loved Blake, Yeats, Eliot. After she asked him the meaning of "The Second Coming" (raised evangelical, she was not sure what to make of WB's troubled account of the return), and once he'd explicated the poem for her, Joaquin turned it into a melancholy song. Tried to get her to sing harmony but she had no ear for notes. Knew only country tunes with three or four chords, folk, bluegrass, simple ditties that were the medium of faith and family gatherings. No one sang in her old home. The puffed, sallow mother didn't approve of any music but hymns; her children learned no nursery rhymes or game-playing songs. Imagination, a synonym for fun, bred indulgence, courted wickedness. That evil girl, overhearing forbidden lyrics on the schoolground, whispered them at night to lull herself.

When Joaquin sang the poems, she found herself memorizing phrases without realizing she had. Then she would speak-sing them to Tiger, who purred for sweet and sour notes alike as long as she scratched his ears. Once or twice a day they would leave their prison and take a walk, Tiger matching her stride for stride as he had Alex. She thought how lonely he must be without his man; she had Joaquin, but he had only her. Yet he was gravely genteel and kind, seemed thankful for her allegiance to this unhappy scene. All those haggard winter days Tiger was her only source of companionship, and she who had never had a pet grew more firmly attached than she would have believed to the cat. No matter what became of Alex, she would keep Tiger with her. He was a stalwart and true friend and would be treated accordingly. Hard to say how many years he had left. He would sleep with her and Joaquin, just as he had with Alex.

By the time their golden hours of evening wound down toward bed, they had both mellowed and talk had softened to affectionate murmurs. Sometimes one of them fell asleep in mid-thought, leaving the other to wonder what hadn't been said. Or would start sleep-talking words impossible to decipher. If a funny phrase emerged from the garble, the listener swore to remember it to share the next morning but never did. Nights came when the one left awake mourned the lost chance to make love. Still they managed it often enough to hold them close. He was pleased that she'd never been with another man (Lyle's grimy finger didn't count, though it had managed to despoil her), so he could teach her that, too. She an eager pupil in his arms, elated by his tenderness, his patience, the crescendo of arousal moving inward like a revelation. Back in college when they first made love, he asked her about every touch: "Does that feel good? Do you like this? Am I hurting you? Going too fast?" and gave heed to her answers, teaching her likewise to ask him his pleasure. To be mindful of lovemaking as a gift. Nights in Trove, in their bed, the discovery lay in variation, finding new ways to heighten the ecstasy. Neither had envisioned ever being so desired, so fulfilled.

Her growing conviction that Alex's withdrawal had an element of the deliberate in it, as in why bother, fed an unuttered irritation that at rare moments snapped like a gust-torn pennant. Flared at the wanton lump, then turned the storm on herself, hurling on her own head all the accusations and demeaning names she'd been whipped with growing up. Joaquin only had to see it once to shrug off any latent jealousy of Alex. No, his competitor was of a smaller, furrier persuasion. "Tyger…tyger, burning bright / in the forests of the night." He could have just let it go, but cooked up this notion that Tiger was the draw to Alex. Joaquin was clearly spending too much time alone, gone a bit muddle-headed when he arrived at the idea that getting her a cat of her own would shift her affection rather than widen it, which is naturally what happened.

A Christmas gift, in a basket, black ears peeping over the top. Quiet and regal from first saunter across the pine floor. The queen took possession of her lap and her heart in one move. Checkmate. How cats who know their stuff play. Montenegra, a name that came with her (said Joaquin, though his blush made that unlikely), given for her ranginess and hue. She was a year old, free of self-doubt and esteem issues. Had been Jesse's wife's cat, it emerged, and Jess couldn't keep her any longer after Stellita's death. They'd been a bonded pair, trio counting him, and Montenegra was used to be being worshipped while doing her share of the housework: devouring mice and other rodentia along with creepy-crawly pests like centipedes, which she mutilated ferociously.

It was a majestic gift, and a solution to a problem that created another Joaquin had not meant to solve. Thanks to him, Tiger would have a friend, too. A new bonded trio. She took Montenegra with her to Alex's, introduced her to the room where they would spend their days. And as she hoped, Montenegra sunnied the climate of the place. The cats took to one another like mates, with Montenegra the adored partner Tiger had not imagined he needed. She dominated but in the way that love rules those who, lonesome beyond hope, find it. The two ate from the same dish, curled into a tangle of fur and tongue, and both of them walked with her in the valley. Joaquin feared he'd lost all in his efforts to reclaim one. But she held her promise to him sacred. With Montenegra there, Tiger would just be the easier to bring home with her, which she planned to do this eve that marked the threshold of a new year.

She hadn't counted on the storm coming in such a rush, snow climbing fence lines and ponderosa limbs, turning the road to a plume of memory, the houses flanking it dim-lit hillocks. Up to Joaquin's, a miscalculation would strand her in a ditch, at the wrong spot might overturn the truck. He with no cell service or internet, no vehicle, and if the blizzard kept up, no electricity. They wouldn't be clearing the road on a holiday. She might not get home till the day after next.

How could he know she hadn't tried? Joaquin by himself, heading out to search for her, stumbling on a buried rock, falling, knocked out, over his head in drifts, found way too late to save. Unlike Alex, and yet not: he still lost. She strained to think of any way to get word to her beloved. A long walk but she could gear up for it. Wrap the cats in blankets. Tiger had survived worse. Maybe take the truck partway, see how far she could get. Floyd would loan her a headlamp.

It was an hour before her shift ended but near dark as she made ready to leave. Launched an advance trip out to sweep off and start the truck, scrape the icing windshield, turn on the heater, loop blankets into a nest for the cats. Thankful she bought those knee-high fur boots at the yard sale. Joaquin gave her his old down parka, extra-long on her, and a pair of minus-40 mittens with wool liners, winter stockings, goggles, thermal underwear. Dressed, you couldn't see any skin. She felt invincible but had been warned to know better. She was white by the time she came in, the snow mocking her efforts to clear it. Stupid to drive in this weather. Any fool could see. Joaquin would, a man of good sense. He'd trust her not to put their happiness at risk. Unless she didn't grasp the danger and tried. That worry would force him out to be sure she wasn't stuck somewhere, confident he would rescue her, but maybe wipe him out in the attempt.

Which was the case she made for going. Had to try. Couldn't leave the cats behind because, because how could she? Stupid and selfish, unless you remember her as a girl mother and see these two critters as fur children. The cats as powerful incentive to make it home. Think of the courage they added to her waning store. Wouldn't have gone without them. That alone should have flagged the journey. She was gathering them into her arms to wedge beneath her coat when a voice not her own purled into the room.

"Don't take Tiger."

Froze her bare.

"He's mine."

Who's paralyzed now? Head locked, unable to swivel, her thoughts shrapnel. Alex revived? Some revelation surely at hand. Alex revived. Or had been all along but not moved to let her in on it.

"I have been here. Trapped in my head. Shards floating echoes no core."

Had he spoken?

Laying the porcelain cats on the bed, hand on the wall to steady herself. Alex revived. Goose-flesh skittered up her arms.

"So many times I tried to thank you. You're the only one. And Tiger. Both leaving me alone."

"No." Scooting Tiger up against him. "He's stuck close to you all these months."

His eyes found hers, whose look had pulled deep into her head for refuge. For him, the wound was fresh, but where he'd been in the dateless rills of sundering had obliterated anguish. Seeing her was newly beautiful.

"Lori. Thank you."

She felt the tears rising, thought to quell them, thought to let them come, for him.

"We waited, watched so hard for you to awaken, Tiger and I. Did all I could. Never gave up. Then tonight—it's, the thing is, you spoke at just the right time."

Sitting up, hand on his cat.

Of course she wouldn't take Tiger away, even without his plea. He must have been suffering abandonment beyond her imagining. Ragged teeth gnawing his vessel as he roiled in the undertow off some foreign shore. Her faith in self ebbing. Ye of little. A nurse with a three-month expiration date. To hell with you, slacker. As long as he never knew how close she came.

Broodiness extinguished the town.

So here she was, Ms. Lori, RN, caught on a stormy night between patient and lover, longing to save both and fearing the loss of either. The cats as well.

"Alex—"

"You better get going. No cell or internet at his place. And you've got the truck." She was incredulous. Had he learned to read minds? He shook his head. "Look, you've got your gear on. You were wrapping up Tiger. And his girlfriend."

"Montenegra."

"I miss Joaquin." He stretched his mouth in an effort to smile, then crumpled. "Terrible idea, though, wrestling the truck across the valley in this storm." Didn't have to mention how small she was. "Can't believe it's still snowing."

For Alex, whom time had flung aside while spinning those conscious of its passage through daily cycles, the drive up to his aerie had happened only the night before. It was the very blizzard, hauling assassin winds through the mountains, that had nearly exterminated him. Would have been fine if it had. A scarred superfluity shuffling along because it was easier than not, but just barely. She'd taken in that self-loathing at the start, as kindred spirits do, but rejected pity as she made the acquaintance of his heritage. To come of age crowned by a loving court of family and friends, to have a mother so deeply his, should have armored him for tougher battles than disfiguring scars and cruel words.

"It's going to be quite a feat to just to go out and shut the damn thing off."

He was right: contending with the storm was a pointless act of defiance. Joaquin would expect better of her. Judgment. Restraint. The kind he exercised. Would not risk his own life to save hers. The idea fisted steel bands from throat to bowel. Was that the test of devotion she'd been unaware of seeking? For him to die trying to save her? Reckless courage, come hell what may bravado, hazard it all at any cost. He'd prove himself truer by holding fast, trusting her to, also. Not as showy as sacrifice, his a more durable affirmation of love.

Unconvinced but yielding, she tromped outside, catless, to the rumbling, well-heated truck. An amorphous hulk whose door should open long enough to extract the keys. Wind lashed her goggles, which fogged and froze at once. Grope, step, grope, step, brooming the headlights, which glared off the iced plastic shielding her eyes. The windshield streaming. Swept toward the truck door and over it, grasped the handle, cleared it for unlatching, reeled at the jerk. Scrabbled in with a caul of snow that commenced to melt in the roar of hot air. Off with her puddling hood and goggles, mittens. Ran the wipers, sat for one indecisive moment. It would be so easy to shift into reverse, turn and head down the street on a route she knew by heart and gut. Pressing the clutch, a surge of confidence burst the steel bands and she could breathe. Could "arise and go now, and go to Innisfree." Yeats, riding shotgun.

Grudgingly the tires plowed aside the drifts as she hunched over the steering wheel. Gauge the edges and watch out for buried cars, squatting like Norse trolls. The landscape had taken on a mythic ghoul of lurking deities and demons. Exhilarated but calm, she held a steady course approaching the ninety-degree turn onto the bridge. First gear all the way, 4WD, forget the brakes; in these conditions you just had to go slow enough not to need them. Eased across, tires grinding the mounds. She'd driven her first truck at thirteen, on all kinds of roads and off. Knew mud and marshy hollows. Joaquin taught her snow. Puny, but no pussy. She had a throbbing clench in her stomach that signaled certainty she'd make it. Toast the new year with Joaquin, their first of a lifetime, in their hillside home in Trove.

The climb out of town, a sharp ascent punctuated by a hairpin curve. The road was invisible, railings vanished, reflectors hooded with snow that fell faster than her blades could clear the windshield. She was driving blind, following sense memory up the hill. If she got stuck here, would have to leave the truck wherever it failed and walk back into town, still too far from home. Tracks lost less than a minute after she made them. Leastwise didn't have to worry about traffic: a hangman's joke. Careful there, into the turn. Gas it just enough to go forward without slip and slide. Think in inches, not miles. One ray of her eye scanning for any sign of Joaquin trundling through the storm in search of her.

Because despite it all, she wanted him to be. A medieval trial of love, the knight, the quest, the conquest. She ached for proof that he loved her more than life. As she did him. They were already a starbright wish fulfilled, so good it smacked of fantasy, which was why she doubted its permanence. Withheld complete trust, dread a knot wound like a noose in the secret chamber of her heart. She'd come to Trove looking for him, not he her, and while he'd welcomed her euphorically, suffused with happiness, spoke of time farther out than the range of their conceivable span, she wondered what would have happened had the pursuit been up to him. And here she was again, going to him, a grand, absurd gesture that he might read more as desperation than devotion. Stupid, scary stupid. But she exalted in grand gestures, especially those of love. Hers had been a life of small ones, diapers and chores, bedpans, IVs, bandages, and vaccinations, essential, yes, not glorious. It helped that Joaquin was a poet and his lyrical soul bent toward the ideal.

Slowing at the hairpin rise. She pressed on the pedal, a movement barely evident except to the rear tires, which started to skid. Steered into the slip, her foot rigid on the accelerator. Knew she was near the edge just as she bumped against the railing. A soft blow, a scrape, then a spittle of forward momentum. Blinked sweat out of her left eye, which swam. Safer to drive blind than let go of the wheel. The hairpin was the worst of it. Rope her way up one more cliffy patch and she'd be on the straightaway till Joaquin's hill, which it was plain she'd walk.

Think of his face when she stepped onto the porch, knocking off her boots and coat before crossing to the door. Her grin, his gape-jawed amazement, disbelief, much too belated fear, and then elation. He'd be so proud of her, scold her foolish daring but embrace her awestruck, gratified, beholden. Because he wouldn't have come looking for her, she realized being out in it. Less a knight than a king.

But he'd have to acquiesce to the transcendent power of their bond. To her love. And grant her a boon in honor of her heroic trek. She would ask for the one commitment he had been hesitant to make: a child. Her leaning was for two, his none. Didn't see any reason for offspring, humankind nearing the end of its time on earth. And given his hostile relationship with his own father, didn't think he'd be any good in the role. Maybe start drinking heavily and shout at everyone, like dear old dad. Why she wanted a family after all she'd suffered as a child baffled him. To do better than was done to me, to raise my own in the love I yearned for. Make up for things, balance the score. Do it right. It's easier to love a baby than not to, you'll see. And he would, now he knew how far she'd go to get through to him.

A hurtle of wind broke against the truck, caught her unprepared. Threw both of them off-course. The wheel wrenched in her hand, and the truck slid sideways. Turning into the skid brought them face down the hill, skating. Don't brake. She pulled the wheel over again, sheering sideways, just as another cannonball blasted the truck back around the direction she meant to go. Gas. Upupupup, you sweet beast. The tires spinning ice hit the rail, harder this time, god let it hold, heard the crunch, the crack, the collapse. Grounded. Stopped. Get a grip, she commanded both herself and the truck. Come on. And before either of them could think of quitting, eased her foot on the gas.

Babies, love, poems, firelight, songs, kisses, laughter, miracles, babies, hugs… Mantra-like, she spurred herself through images of grace, summoning the last trickle of grit from her dry veins. You could reach so deep and then you just unhinged. Died frozen. Like Alex, almost. The rear tires found a snow-hold and the front began wallowing the truck uphill again, very slowly. Needed more gas but laid on with imperceptible care. Feet channeling the guts of the truck. And the glacial passage resumed.

Twins would be the best. Suddenly two and no one to blame or praise. Two girls, or a boy and girl, but not two boys, please. She'd already been through that. Joaquin would not relive himself as the father of girls. But after the crunch against that thank-god railing, he wouldn't owe her anything: rather she him, for damage to his truck, whose body had been remarkably clean. Unless she saved his life. Or lost hers.

Cresting the hill, its steepest arch, the truck threatening to stall. Her foot like a bow on the pedal strings drew high notes from its bowels, which were straining tight. Hers loose. In the churning swell of leashed panic, she dripped and huffed unawares. Craned, squinting, as if that might help. Up and over, please god, onto the sinuous road to the base of Joaquin's hill. Walk home. On a loop, this vision played.

The tires started to catch, and she was on the rim of a hallelujah shout when through the white curtains burst terror in its spectral guise as death. Gliding toward her at a predatory pace, so bent on forward that it slammed, then flipped clattering onto the hood. Stopped her flat at the edge of the crest for an instant before the backward force kicked in and they were slip-rolling down the hill. She braked instinctively on impact, forgetting her precarious hold on the planet, and launched the truck into writhe. The tenacity holding her snapped. Let it go. Jump clear.

Laser-beamed eyes riveted, through the windshield whose wipers he grabbed, then slid into the glass. Hand on side-view mirror, clattering blood-red spit spewed broken goggles dangle the eyes the eyes locked on her and if only he would stop screaming. Everything stop. Joaquin, whipped across the hood, draggle-eyed, blood-wrenched, flailing. Her brain crept slower than the truck had, laboring toward a straightaway thought. Slouching toward Jerusalem. She would stay with him, in dying as in living. But kill him she would not. Lori, RN, would never kill him whom she loved most in all the world.

They were in free-slide mode approaching the hairpin, the odometer on the rise as they fell. Unbuckled the seatbelt, yanked up the blanket (dear cats, safe with Alex), hat, goggles, mittens, got her bearings. Steer toward the railing at the hairpin. Left one. Bouldered meadow runs for a stretch before plunging. She could jump as they plowed into the barricade, pull him down on top of her. Get him free whatever it took, hang onto him whatever happened. She'd carry him to Gregorio's if it came to that. Half his size but wild with horror. If he would stop screaming. Broke eye contact just long enough to check the rearview.

Back windshield had no blades, nothing to see. Had to gauge the hairpin, steer toward the left rail and not overshoot it or they'd drop into the gully, up-end the truck, Joaquin flying over it. How far had they slid while she was zapped out of her senses? Pure guesswork. Trust, which she'd absolutely proven was an unreliable measure in one so rash. Steer blind, blind faith, Jack and Jill, humpty-dumpty, the fool on the hill, down will come baby, hickory dickory dock. Turn the truck off. Idiot.

A jolt and screech of metal on metal, smashed glass, tires grinding. They had connected with the rail. Hooked her eyes on his, praying he could read them as she set herself to jump. Elegant, taking a bow, the truck arced to point nose down the hill. Drag a chunk of rail with it, impatient to deliver itself and cargo to the gully, the bridge, the frozen river, and end its mad labors. Or glide brilliantly all the way to town. She jumped.

Struck snow. Missed the uprooted steel fangs and rolled to clear the truck's swing. Snow caking her face and where was Joaquin? Truck now gliding on face-down the hill without her. With him? Still on it? A flash of movement. Scrambling. Had to catch it, scud on her stomach. Shrieking, screaming. Him under it? Caught something not a foot, and held on. Under the truck. Pulled hard. The truck gathering headlong momentum. Down, down, she lodging on a rock held onto the not-foot as the rear tires rolled past, veered right, gullyward, and she would not let go of the screaming as she crashed into him, the body attached to a ski. Who was Joaquin, or used to be.

Night so pitch thick and snow heaved that he was indecipherable. There seemed to be enough of him to make a whole, if it was all one. Tugged the leg parts toward her, rest of him came with them. Screaming. She opened her mouth to beg him to stop, found it already open, the shriven cry branding her tongue. Held her breath to quell it, reeling in the after-shock of soundlessness. Then a thud, a crack as the truck rolled over the embankment, catapulted into the valley. It would have been a clean drop, nothing but frozen river below. All her doing.

As was the mangled bundle of jacket and ski boots. She sought his face at the other end, found a mask, spread it apart, put her lips to his, blowing tremulous breath into it. Saliva, a wisp of cough, groan so faint she had to will herself to hear it. Calling his name over and over between breaths. He sprawled unresponsive in her grasp, taking a break from the persistent urge to live.

His leg was broken, she could see from the angle of incidence at which it protruded. What else? Maybe little that wasn't. But much longer in this disarray and they'd both freeze up. Had to get him into town. Dispel the panic, use her nurse brain. Make the best of it. If she failed, die with him. Which just then was vital consolation.

The cats' blanket had come with her, hooked on a bootlace, and keeping one arm firmly around Joaquin, she jerked it free, laid it out beside her, and began to open his limbs, form a recognizable arrangement she could wrap. Poorly. But it made her feel safer to prop him blanketed in her arms. Broken leg an awkward splay like a backwards L that she tried to secure under her knee. The idea was to be a human sled down the hill, then rush to the first house to get help. The Lamperts. She was sure of that part but not the sled plan, fraught with opportunities for further injury and overturns.

Didn't notice till she readied herself that the snow had stopped. Gaunt skein of moonlight, enough for the eye wide-pupiled to navigate by. It was all the hope her blood needed to surge. Free hand paddling, she launched them down the hill. Past the half-mounded tracks of the truck's felling. Had to brake with her leading foot as they neared the bottom. Joaquin moaned, leg scraping rock. She winced for him, then remembered to talk.

"My sweetheart. You'll make it. Hold on, my love. You're strong. I love you so much. Let me count the ways, you beautiful man, poet of my soul, dream of my heart, my dearest. Come, hold on, the center must hold, you must, we'll soon be safe and warm again. You are too good for this world to lose. And I love you so. Stay with me."

Like a midwife, journeying with him: coax, inspire, reassure, croon, embolden, sustain her beloved, whom she had broken but would mend. Lilting notes of praise.

Used everything she knew about driving, aerodynamics as they scooted into the turn over the bridge faster than she'd intended. Plenty of room to slip through, long drop to the iced riverbed. Also places to grab hold, done right, which, her record notwithstanding, she would do if they slid near the edge. Instead, though, focused on holding the center, banking and braking, one protective arm tight around Joaquin, one leg braced on his angled one. Skimmed cleanly across and into a snow pile. First piece of luck of the eve. Presaging more to come.

Saw the lights and heard the thrumming, hard to say which first. Too disoriented to make sense of either as they approached, overwhelming her after the absolute quiet she had conjured to enforce single-mindedness. Golliwog ho, we've overflown the bridge right into your lair. To shield Joaquin from its ripping jaws, she threw up her arm, leaned away from the oncoming besieger, cowered her eyes shut, ostrich fashion, praying not to be seen. Was, of course, since Floyd's mission was to find her, after getting word from Gregorio who had it from Alex, miraculously again among the speaking. The snowmobile stopped within feet of the muddle of bodies its headlights had exposed from some distance off. Not much else out there tonight.

Throttled down, swung out. Old, he was yet an agile man, born to withstand hardship. Don't scream, she ordered herself, still cringing blind. Till he called her name, said his own. Floyd, sent to find them, Floyd the invincible, Floyd the faithful, Floyd the shining knight in storm armor. He who peeled blanketed Joaquin from her grasp, supporting the broken leg, carried him to the mobile, while she staggered behind, ready to keel but resolved not to as she mounted the steed. Held her arms out for Joaquin, whom Floyd managed to drape over her, leg propped on the seat, secured there by her hand. Plowed through the snow like home pasture, years of turning it under his wheels. To Gregorio's, where Floyd's wife and family and the New Year's Eve revelers were gathered to receive them. Help, on all sides, lifting, carrying, arms over and under, cooing worry, amazement, wonder. Laid in Gregorio's bed, his little home behind the restaurant, a hostel hospital for friends and emergencies. Saint G, patron of the frozen wounded. Offering a snug-bedded path to salvation.

The desire to weep uncontrollably (how else, rescued after such a night) shook her, which they took for cold. Luke warm bath, by Floyd's wife, to bring her temperature to normal. She knew the drill, Nurse Lori did, held in the tears and flooded others instead with gratitude. Recalled how stupid she'd been, and Joaquin in grave peril because of it. That cleaned her out of tears. Stepped from the bath to his side, where they were rubbing his unclad body to restore circulation, daubing, bandaging wounds, keeping their distance from his leg, which she went straight to, thinking only of medical aid and not of whom the limb belonged to nor how it came to break. More luck: all her equipment, meager but wide spectrum, was here, had been for Alex's care. Caught a glimpse of the cats as she fetched it, stretched in a crosswise spoon on his bed. Luck abounded.

Only temporarily set, the leg, not the way it should have been but the best she could do. Floyd would bring Doc Darrell here on his snowmobile, holiday or not, tomorrow. They'd get 'er done right. Meanwhile, morphine, a slow warming, close observation. Hell,

Floyd had seen a lot worse and they came through fine. Probing hands had found no other breaks. Doc would be mighty pleased to see Alex back from his tomb of silence. For now, every one of us'll clear out, you have a mug of chamomile tea and sleep, the sure cure, right?

Drank it double-handed, still wobbly, but her restrained professional conduct in place. In place of hysteria, the scream ricocheting undiminished inside. Forced herself to ask the decent questions, offer profusion of thanks. Where would Gregorio sleep with both his own and guest beds taken? Upstairs, of course, in one of the two rooms of the restaurant's boutique B&B. Concerns waved aside, just take care of yourself and your man. Alex, his arms around Greg and Floyd, hobbled to the bathroom, then settled for the night. He'd been fed and fluffed, cats, too, nothing left for her but to edge in beside Joaquin in Greg's spacious bed, whose sheets were always clean, one of his many miracles, and keep watch over her suffering beloved till morning. Happy New Year. With Alex next door, a triptych of suffering, flanked by placid felines.

She lay stiff and trembling beside Joaquin, counting his breaths, fingering his pulse, gauging his temperature by feel. Hours, she deemed, had passed when Gregorio's miniature of Big Ben chimed a fifteen-minute interval. Morning lay on a shore too far to see, or perhaps there was none, only this one, and the long rowing across to no end. The blood-sear of guilt, the ravages of imagined horrors yet to strike, drove her after the next chiming from the bed. To pace, fret, beg the gods for mercy. So much good fortune despite her reckless efforts to thwart it, might be all that was due them. Joaquin the sacrifice on her impulsive altar. She hurt everywhere and it was not enough. Desperate for comfort, she sought Tiger, Montenegra, whose lives she had inadvertently spared.

Found them curled up with Alex, who was awake. After three months, done sleeping. Brimful of talk. She took up her familiar vigil in the rocking chair, Montenegra on her lap, and basked in the pleasure of listening to him. But rose at the first twinge of weariness to check Joaquin's vitals: the same as they had been. Crept back to Alex, for whom she was no longer liable and who was glad of her company, as he professed he had always been. Even remembered a few of the poems she'd read him. Something she had done well.

Punting toward midnight, Joaquin stable, morphine dulling his pain, but she, unable to relax beside him, laid her head exhausted against the chair, granting herself the absolution of sleep. Would have received the blessing had not her head lolled, jogging her awake. Again, then again. Alex, watching, called to her, voice muted to benign grandmotherly timbre. Room and plenty in his bed, where she was welcome, purely as a friend, as anyone would be. Nothing meant by it, nothing desired but her rest. She was already saying no when her body contradicted, moved her of its own accord to where the covers were flung open, Alex extending a smiling hand. Spooned but not seductively against his gaunt frame, she exhaled, and with that outrush from the cavern of her shame flowed at last the tears. Threatened to capsize her, their vehemence quaking the bed. And Alex, newborn as harbor, stroked her gently, murmured words of solace whose tenor was their substance.

He intended no more than that, to become the friend he'd known but had not been. Provide succor. That's how it often begins, isn't it? A small kindness accretes into a vast yearning. A few hours stretch into a long dream.

I I

"Mother To Son"

My beloved son,

Writing a letter to the dead, although perhaps you aren't yet, is not hard because I can tell you everything now without fear of judgment or condemnation or ridicule. I can say first of all that I am sorry I let go of our closeness when you became a teenager, that I assumed you'd no longer want or need me as you once had, that I shifted from a confidant to a watchdog, keeping track of your movements rather than of you. Narrowed my focus to grades and curfews, turned our conversations to chatter. I locked down just when I should have opened up the lines between us. I was following the script of American motherhood and stuck to it as you grew into a young adult. Never again did we talk and play and laugh as we had in your early years. Never more did we speak easily of our love for one another.

No, the curse is older, fiercer than an American myth: it's the story that has cast a long shadow over mother and son relationships through the ages, the story of Oedipus. The marriage of mother and son, unwitting and happy till the knowledge of their kinship undid them. Translated by later cultures to an unconscious yearning for incestuous union. I abjured intimacy with you and cast you off to save you from a hideous pseudo-prophetic warning created by men to keep us apart.

I never feared you nor myself, only the disapproval of others, the societal taunt of "mama's boy" that has so effectively severed natural ties. In dread of that, I broke the vow I made myself never to sacrifice our relationship to any competing claim. Broke it aware that I was doing so but dismissed the transgression on the grounds that I had been naïve to think we could remain as we were. And persuaded myself that you would not have wanted us to, would have rebuffed me as a clingy mother who needed to get a life. So I got one without being told, congratulated myself for doing so, and shoved our bond to the periphery. To my relief, others stopped asking me what I would do when you left for college, started your own life, as though it had not always been yours to inhabit. You accepted the distance as you do most buffeting: with unflinching equanimity.

I don't know much about you past thirteen. Photos of you clowning around, a good-looking guy with his friends romping through adolescence. Easy go lucky, what me worry, water under the bridge kind of guy whom everyone loved, so again I patted my back for having done the right thing and done it so well. I didn't know you were a writer, as Joaquin now tells me, that you were working on a novel. I was an English major, too, but craved the scholarship of the discipline rather than the penning. I didn't know that you have an uncannily green thumb, or that you were lonely. Lori and the doctor claim that there is no reason you can't be up and about again, back to yourself, more or less, but that you lack the will. I didn't know the boy I prided myself on raising had died, and the man grown in his stead ebbs on the dark side of the moon. I didn't know how much you loved your family till you ran into the house to save your father and the old dog.

That was an exceedingly courageous thing to do, my dear son, and I didn't know you were so brave. Well, foolhardy, too, perhaps, but no more so than your father. He was the only man I would ever have shared my life with, not simply because he loved me but also because he respected and admired me as a talented woman with a discerning intellect. We dreamed of having a houseful of kids, but you so fulfilled us we needed no more.

I did know how desperately you hated being here in Trudel's house with her lording it over you and reviling Tiger. I knew how depressed and sick you were, scarred inside and out, but after our years of deep silence beneath the chitchat, I did not know what to say. And I myself was as near death as I've come, not physically but spiritually with Harvey's loss and your terrible wounding. And the house gone, strata of memories that polished the bricks, rubbed the woodwork, burnished the walls, filled bookshelves and photo albums, file drawers and boxes marked "Alex Preschool," "Alex – Hunter Elementary," "Alex – Special Paintings" and on and on, saved for your children to adore and giggle over. More boxes under the bed with your very finest baby clothes and best books and toys, also for Alex: The Next Generation. And from our ancestors, too, those treasured keepsakes (what a rhapsodic work, that which is kept for the sake of those whom one does not know yet). Of course clothes and jewelry, letters, mementos of journeys and more, more things whose presence in the house was not even remembered but whose discovery would have been welcome. So much of my life disappeared in the flames, and so consumed was I with figuring out what was left of me that I did not fully reckon what was left to me. You. You, my beloved son, who should have been my first and foremost concern, you, the sole allegiance my heart owed.

Joaquin, Lori, Gregorio, Floyd, the whole crew down there in Trove whom you've known only a few months, have proved to be truer friends to you than your mother has. Your life-saving cat Tiger has proved more loyal than I. Tragically, your best friend from days of yore, Hersch, perished with so many others in the fire. I knew that during your time of recovery here but kept it from you to avoid adding to your pain. There are miraculous and excruciating tales to tell from that catastrophe, but they will wait or never need be told if you, too, are lost.

I have spoken of some of them, much of this, when I've been there, where you lie. I've talked to you for hours, kissed and stroked the ruined flesh of your face, grown a kinship with Lori, the finest nurse anyone could wish, scratched Tiger's ears and held him, wept belatedly for all you have endured without me, begged your forgiveness. I have sworn that if you gather the strength once more to live, I will be a true, faithful, and devoted mother to the end.

Trudel, too, has died, with terrible swiftness, descending from the flu into pneumonia, from whose grip she was not released till it had squeezed from her the final breath. Granted, at 91 she was of an age when the heavy tread of time was likely to fall on her. I was with her through those torturous hours in the hospital, and as I sat by helplessly, my guilt was redoubled with thoughts about those whose hands I had not held as they departed. Your father, my own parents obliterated in the plane crash. And I vowed to sit with you through to the end, but as it has not drawn nigh, and may not come for years, mourning prematurely felt ghoulish, predatory. Lori will call should you worsen—likewise if you return to the world.

Surprisingly, Trudel had squirreled away a good deal of money, which she left to me, along with the house, worth plenty should I decide to sell it. Right now, I am inclined to stay. All of her things I did not want have been sold or given away, the house renovated to my taste, and while I no longer feel at home anywhere, this is as good a den as any to hibernate in till I can imagine a path forward. I do not equate my suffering with yours, but our states of unbeing bear an anguished resemblance.

Trudel also left me a long letter (twenty-some pages) written for Harvey, to be read when she died, which she expected to do well before him, so as to preserve a record of their family ancestry. He knew some of it, of course, but as it turns out, of his father few facts and many hushed omissions. I have made a copy for you to read someday. As you will see, hers was a far more thorny and courageous life than you might have imagined after knowing Trudel only as an old woman settled into a fixed, narrow world. At age eleven she was instrumental in her family's escape from Nazi Germany, and decades later she was the only one to whom your grandfather confessed his complicity in the death of his pregnant girlfriend. The years in between were hardly uneventful. I think you will be greatly surprised to learn about your heritage. Her closing sentences, concerning you, are all I will include:

"In the known family, we have only Alex to carry the Mann seed, and you must watch with sharp eyes like an eagle to see he does not go astray. It may be, you should think about it, that the army is right for him, where order and discipline will keep him from derangement."

I laughed, Alex, reading that last urgent paragraph, as I hope you will, both read and laugh. In any case, you can see her wish that you join the military is an old theme with Trudel and had nothing to do with your condition as you recovered at her house. She did love you, though.

But it was not to induce laughter that I included that last cautionary excerpt. Never fear, my beloved son, that I will press you to keep the Mann line going. I expect nothing of you that you yourself do not wish. When I gave you life, it was yours, not to be reclaimed. The closeness I long to reestablish with you is not a subterfuge for redirecting your course, simply understanding it better and sharing it in a supportive way. Having children at this perilous time in humankind's future seems to me an act of stubborn optimism, with which you may or not emerge. Regardless of whether those of your age will grow to be old before the time of human habitation on the earth is over, our end is on the horizon, and we must adjust our expectations accordingly. *Carpe diem* seems more an acquiescence to the truth than a rejection of responsibility.

Perhaps that's just me, a woman whose faith was incinerated and who hopes only for no greater losses in the coming years. Yours, above all.

Should you reawaken, please come up to be with me a while, however long you can tolerate leaving Trove or staying here. If your spirit calls for new adventure, we can travel wherever you like. Visit Rose in Britain. Revisit Germany, though that may be too painful without Harvey. Or somewhere entirely unexpected. I am by no means urging you to live with me, only inviting you to if you wish. To find you at my door would be pure bliss. Or just call or email me hello and I will rejoice at your return.

In that Langston Hughes poem, "Mother to Son," she tells her boy to keep on climbing, not to give up because it's hard, as she knows, since her "life ain't been no crystal stair." I cannot compare my world to hers, but I grasp the sentiment, which is please keep going, Alex, as I have, against my will. To surrender to depression would be so easy, but would, I believe, dishonor Harvey by my lack of strength and independence, by allowing him to be forgotten sooner than he will be. Hard as it is to see and hear him in my mind daily, the silence of my departure from this realm would negate him. I will not pity myself more than I do him.

And that's one last thing I will tell you, who may be dead, that I would otherwise hesitate to do for fear you'd doubt my sanity. Harvey's ghost has come to live with me. Yes, shortly after Trudel's death, I became aware of another presence in the house, and hard though I worked to deny it, inwardly I knew it to be Harvey. Then one night I awoke to three distinct, loud knocks on the door, and when I peeked outside between the curtains, saw no one, but opened up anyway and called out to whoever might be there. I have nothing left to fear, you understand. No response. Several nights later I saw him, in the corner of the bedroom, unfurling from a whitish spiral. He spoke to me, we conversed, thought to thought. I could not bear for him to leave me, I told him, and he smiled, patted my hand reassuringly. He is not here always, but intermittently I discover his presence in a plant, a chair, a painting, a lamp, even in the garden. It is like a light wind buoying me from within, this sudden uprush that sweeps my interior. I have been far more deeply at peace since his coming. God, how hard I've tried to subdue my rage at the fire that hewed a merciless swath through our lives. God, how I have missed him.

And you, how I miss you. As I see now I have for years. An ache throbbing at the core that I took for the anxiety of aging but was the loss of true kinship with you.

Recalling what my father used to say, "Life goes on, but love remains," evokes ever wider spheres of meaning for me. I live in the remaining love. Come, my dear son, back, up, here. I wait for you, hand extended, to walk the onward lands and engender fresh sediments of memory and possibility.

All my love~

Mamia

I 2

Banished

Lori Lori Lori. A two-note mantra he sang to himself. Lori Lori Lori brought him back from the dead with a fast pulse and heart a-quiver. A lad of 25, his strength of will and limb were well matched. They kept mirrors away from him as he learned to comb his thin blond pelt and brush his teeth (you don't want to know how they looked after three months of no dental care). He who'd never had much of a beard, descended as he was from a hairless tribe, chose to forgo shaving. Lori had made that same decision some time before, finding the pale fuzz not worth bothering to trim. There was hardly enough to cast a five o'clock shadow.

Lori Lori Lori. Stroking Tiger and Montenegro with sensuous ardor. Exploring his body to make sure the key parts were still fully functional. Getting ridiculously clean. Eating, excreting, walking, and sleeping: within a week all his appetites were back, driven by the one. As soon as possible he packed his bag and declared himself ready to go home— Joaquin's, that is. With Lori. Racing to beat Joaquin back: a fortnight till Joaquin could begin to think about managing that, but knowing Joaquin, no more than two weeks before he crutched through the door. Two weeks to turn her heart.

His own had not wavered since the night he picked her up by the side of the road. He'd fallen for her before he knew who she was. She'd laid claim to him at first sight, admittedly unbeknownst to her. So this was not, Alex convinced his saner, doubting half, a fall-in-love-with-your-nurse thing or the first person you see when you awaken fairytale thing, or a baby duckling imprinting thing, or a proving his manly appeal in spite of his disfiguration thing. Nope, clean and clear love. Mentally check-marked himself; now he had to work on getting Lori to see she felt the same. Two weeks.

His mother did give her letter into Lori's keeping, knowing that the wise, compassionate nurse would put it in Alex's hands when the time was right, should that time come, as it had. Lori had called Michelle, of course, as soon as Alex awakened, and Michelle, overwhelmed with gratitude for Lori, for the miracle, for the grace of God (whom she believed in less than she did Lori) talked by phone with Alex, who was cheerful but put her off coming down until he felt a bit stronger (read: had won Lori). As soon as Alex declared himself fit to move back across the valley, Lori gave him the letter. The wiser among you (everyone but Alex) will pick up the subtext in that gesture: go to your mother, attend to her, let her nurse you back to full strength, as she yearns to do.

Our bright young lad did not open the letter, fearing it would distract him from his immediate goal, Lori Lori Lori. Yes, sir, he left it sealed, guessing its contents would in some way be a summons home. He did not open it until that summons was more a rescue than a request, until it was his only course, really, as it had been from the time of his awakening. But the boy never was a quick learner. He could not stop hurling himself into the flames of lost causes. Had not been blasted out of his illusions even by the toll of the self-rung icy death knell. He persisted in the faith that he could bend life to his desires and make of its twists a personal road to fulfillment. Lori. For her sake he wagered his scarred and mutilated flesh against the perfection of Joaquin.

With Alex at the house and Joaquin at Gregorio's, Lori reversed her daily schedule: days she worked at home, evenings and nights spent with Joaquin. Unless he needed extra attention, day and night. Alex became a highly useful member of the team as he tended the greenhouse, got the wood in, cooked the meals, shoveled snow, took care of the cats. Used the opportunity to refamiliarize himself with being upright, smoothing his walk, strengthening his muscles. He was running the place and Lori was mighty grateful, as was Joaquin. Didn't know what they'd have done without him. A real lifesaver. Moving into position is how Alex saw it. Check and soon mate.

He was surprised at how dense Lori proved to be. She was smart and had great skill in healing, which meant she read people sensitively. Excepting now, with Alex's passion for her. Missed all the cues and looks, the touch on her arm, the voice. Granted, Lori was exhausted. He'd been sleeping for three months while she hardly had and then been through a major trauma and without a moment to recover, right back into nursing along with making the deliveries. Lori's days a hectic back and forth and hither and yon schedule that would wear anyone out. He could see that, which is why he gave her neck rubs whenever she sat down for a minute and offered foot and back rubs, which she gently declined. Down to a week, desperation thick-knotting his gut, he had to try a new tactic to mate the queen.

The ploy he had in mind was a rotten one, taking advantage of Lori's goodness as he had depended on it unknowingly for three months (lost time, seriously regretted). He would conjure a midwinter night's mare, running choked and panic-shattered up to her room, fling himself onto the bed shuddering. He would invent some grotesque eruption of the unconscious that would dredge up her guilt for launching him at the cabin where he nigh froze to death. She'd have no choice but to draw him in, and he'd pretend to not even notice, just lie there gasping and shaking while she calmed him. As they were lying there, more or less in each other's arms, he would begin by thanking her, effusively, pathetically, for saving his life and tell her she meant more to him than any person on earth, and go on to say, throatily, that he had fallen in love with her at first sight, and he'd never been in love before, and he would be ever so slowly insinuating his body up against hers so that she would feel his prodigious erection (which he would certainly have) and get a sense of how well-endowed he was (lucky guy, Alex, hauling around an enviable penis that belonged to a much larger man, an organ big enough for a cathedral), at which point she would start to soften and he would use techniques honed in college to melt her. He loved the melt: with Lori, pure ecstasy. The only challenge would be holding his engorged state long enough to get her to the height of abandon. One night of lovemaking, and he intended to go all night, maybe longer, maybe they'd never get out of bed again, just die there in a state of euphoria, and she'd be his. Pretty flimsy, our boy's plan, especially transparent to someone as savvy as Lori. Who was in love with Joaquin. But it was the best he could come up with, given the torment of the constantly swollen organ mashed against his jeans.

A providential snow saved him the embarrassment of going through with his scheme, and bizarrely brought it, without artifice, to far less contrived fruition. She had to forgo the trip across the valley to Joaquin, relieved that she'd installed a phone so he would know why she wasn't coming. It shook her, though, the mounds of white, wind spits, early dark when the electricity went out. Alex made a fire, heated soup, offered cheery assurances. They turned in early, bade each other a fond goodnight, she upstairs, he still on the cushy couch he'd brought in last summer, musing on his plan, asleep before he could decide whether this should be the night of its launch. He had been feeling cold more than shrieky and disgruntled because the cats had chosen to go up to bed with her.

Lori was the one who woke screaming, from an authentic nightmare reliving the night of the accident, screaming as she had then, seeing Joaquin again collide with the truck. In the midst of this excruciating vision Alex was at her bedside, then at her side in bed, soothing her as he had on the night after they made it back to Gregorio's, saved from death but not the horror of it. Alex's arm protectively enfolding her, his voice a lulling solace in her ear, his warmth a comfort into which she straightaway fled. A more righteous scenario our devious concocter of schemes could not have sorcerized.

And it came to pass that small offerings of affection advanced into the realm of arousal, the groundwork having been laid by terrors of the deep, whose intensity at the jittery edge of weariness thrust unforced from careworn to carnal. Nigh imperceptibly, he slid into her, and she yielded as moist earth to root, he thickening, deepening, she fastening around him, on and on into the molten core of their beings, where lava poured from peak explosions that transformed their interior lands. Lori weeping, clinging to him, afraid of being swept into a seismic maw of passion from which she would never emerge. Alex triumphant, the crusader with chalice in hand, certain of his victory. The odds had been so daunting, every sane bet against him. And yet they lay, as one as two can be, his vows already secretly made. He mounted her again.

Good for Alex to have that night of surpassing glory. He needed it to regain trust in his powers and not become a torn skein. More than that, though: he needed to give himself utterly to someone other than himself. He needed to risk love, fully grasp its worth, measure his own by it. Of course it would have been great for him, as it would for all of us, to have and to hold that first true love till death them did part (though they'd both had their fill of death), but knowing it could have happened, living the possibility just one night, provided critical sustenance for the heart.

Had the turbulent yaw of desire not smitten him, he might have foreseen the outcome of their tryst: Lori weeping in the morning flogging herself with recriminations at her faithlessness to her one true love—how could she, with him laid up because of her stupidity and recklessness? Exhaustion was her only out and plenty credible after the trauma of New Year's Eve from which she'd never caught her breath but trucked on with a compulsive energy that would have brought your average spike-driving, weight-lifting hombre to his knees. Turning then her merciless whip on Alex: how could he, too, have been so faithless to Joaquin, who took him in at the nadir and gave him friendship, hope, purpose? Yes but…but nothing. He scrabbling to rescue a shard of the night's wonder, she smashing it, grinding its beauty into dirt. Accusations, rage, loathing: the onrush a blur of horror that was hard to remember, harder to forget.

Alex was so banished.

Flung out of the charmed circle, it did not take much for him to discern that he had never really been in it. To Joaquin he'd been a circumstantial friend: like, you're here and that's good for now until my real life starts. He'd made himself useful, which is different from indispensable and desired. Joaquin had tried to dismiss him the first day he came. Lori had let him know before she realized who he was what an impediment he represented to their happiness. He'd forced himself on both of them, desperate for a new life but even more so for a home. And beyond these obvious needs lay the craving for forgetfulness. None of which had been granted him, and all of which he had now to relinquish.

He loved Lori, who wanted only Joaquin. He idolized Joaquin, who loved only Lori. No one loved, wanted, or idolized Alex. He tried to tell that to his idiot child brain a million times but it didn't penetrate. He'd been banging his head (and other parts) with undeterred vigor in quest of a way in when Lori showed him the way out.

She ordered him to pack his scant belongings, made a motel reservation for him in Arroyo, told him to read the letter from his mother that evening and to do the right thing by her, the one person who loved him whole-heartedly. Lori didn't bother to swear Alex to secrecy. His doom crackled the air between them. Unyielding to the end, she stood by grimly as he hugged Floyd and settled himself in the car. He smiled; not she. Au revoir too good for him, likewise farewell, hasta la vista, aufwiedersehen, implying the hope of seeing him again. All she said: "You can't have our life, Alex."

But wait: it wasn't as easy as that for her. Every silver lining has its cloud, as her foster mother always said at a glint of happiness. The cats. No way Alex would leave Tiger behind and who would expect him to, but Lori did sacrifice her cool by asking, gave him his only shot at contempt. A good cat is hard to find, he said, knowing she wouldn't get the reference. Tiger was far more desirable than Alex in this scene and would have said so himself if he hadn't been utterly lovestruck, an enthrallment Montenegra fervently requited. Tiger always landed on his feet, Alex thought, a bitter pride between his teeth. But for once, he had a prior claim. He counter-offered, his only snideness, to take Montenegra with him and keep the cats together: Solomon says, who's the real mother? Not Lori. Her gorgeous feline would find another; the likes of Tiger were commonplace.

But she was lying and they both knew it. The likes of Tiger were not to be found again, nor Montenegra. Nor Lori, nor me, Alex protested. She outraged that he'd ruined everything; he aggrieved that she didn't love him—after a night like they'd had, a defense that reignited her fury and shame. Neither of them up to the brutal cleaving of the felines. It was a wrong that made nothing right. Treats in hand, the executioners steeled themselves for the wretched task. Their victims lay unawares, curled purring into each other, sun-glutted innocents on the corrupted bed. They had never been apart since their first nosing a month ago (seven in cat years).

Coax-voiced, stealth-paced. Their hypersense kicking in to signal a threat, the cats woke suddenly and laid back their ears, oblivious to the treats. They did not favor a splitting of the blanket. Clawed and yowled, a first, as Alex tried to pick up Tiger and Lori Montenegra. Twisted and slithered and grappled to escape human arms and tear off together to some thicket impenetrable. Maybe for good. Both were adept hunters; no babies to feed ever: they'd survive. Alex had to bag Tiger in a pillowcase to get him out of the house and into Pacman 2. Lori had to trap Montenegra to keep her in the house and out of the car. It was a hurt that surpassed their own.

The roads had been plowed but were not clear of ice, and skidding through the tortuous Palisades, unsteady yet on the pedals, made sliding into the Rio Sol a plausible, and thank god final, detour for Alex and Tiger. Still he fought to get to Encanto, salute the doc as he chugged by, get on the straighter, wider road to Calhoun. But strangely they'd had more snow in that area and the road was even worse. He got stuck behind a trio of cars moving with fearful caution and couldn't risk passing them.

In his head, playing on a damn loop, was that damn Lori Lori Lori mantra. The tone of longing had a few additives out of his control, a volatile mix of anguish and anger, exasperation and ecstasy, desire and despair. He hated her with a love too sharp to breathe. She hadn't once said what a powerful night it was, an orgy of sex transcendent, an experience that would never be surmounted, with Joaquin or anyone. Knowing what could be, had been, she would have to fend off the shadow of dissatisfaction from here on. Unless she came back to him, unable to live with less.

The hour's drive to Arroyo spanned four, the sun lowering as he pulled into the motel, where he had planned not to stay because Lori had arranged it. Shun. Rhymes with done, goes with I am, done, with, for. Checked in, bagged Tiger the Terrible (speaking of shun: he'd ridden in the back hidden from Alex's view by a pair of boots, instead of shotgun, the seat he owned), and slopped his backpack on the sad, kempt bed.

And we're off to K-mart, to buy a cat harness, indignity heaped on injury, so you can pee, ungrateful beast. Then to some take-out that I'll be just ever so delighted to share with you, Mr. T, if y'all can just summon up a whet of appetite after losing your lady love. He couldn't, either, the two of them staring at the gone-cold burger and fries, wanting to throw up their contracting hearts. Unfortunately, they would not perish of a dinnerless night, might in fact have added to their lifespan by not eating the larded rot before them.

Put on the TV, grabbed the remote, and watched whoever was on, spouting whatever garbage-of-the-day was stinking up the can of popular culture. Switched channels. Laughter, sports roars, prayers, news talk: an indistinguishable mass of noise that emptied the room. Darkness enveloped him. Tiger had crawled under the bed. Alex slumped, thinking he should, at the very least, make an effort to cry. As Lori had done, effortlessly. Release the pressure, reset the emotion gauge. That, however, would require feeling something. Our hero, whose sexual prowess the night before had the adored Lori gasping and moaning, writhing, wide open erotic and then floating his name on the afterglow currents of quenched and incessant desire, had turned into a numb hump, impenetrable. He could replay every moment of last night, as though he'd been an observer as well as an engorged perpetrator of euphoria. He could call up her face this morning, their parting. Heartsore, he could call up New Year's Eve, when she'd come to him freely, in need. Three weeks and he was dead again. How many lives did he and Tiger have left between them—six or five? "Hey, T, we're running through them." No answer. His mother's letter sat benevolently above the weatherman's face.

The thing is this, he told the ripped envelope, they would have thrown me out anyway. Wouldn't have let me just hang around vegetating, or stay on companionably. They'd have sent me home to my mother either way. I was on a limited visa to their golden country. At least, at most, I had the one night in paradise. I was master of my happiness, and Lori's, a title they would never have conferred on me. It was the right thing to do. Yeah. Got to give the boy credit for trying. Circumstantial friends, not lasting, not true, not Hersch. He took his mother's letter to read at last. "My beloved son."

They got a late start because why not. Tiger was on a hunger strike, drank just enough water to survive, and Alex choked down a stale sweet roll and coffee: continental breakfast in the lobby of the motel. Not interested in being good to themselves or each other. The cat left a nasty dump in the room for Alex to clean up while he was in the bathtub shower making a futile effort at presentability. The backpack shouldered, Tiger hidden under his jacket, Alex trudged to the car and headed north toward Los Olmos Pass on a road that defied attempts to clear it. Arroyo was a walk-in freezer and snarly gray. He revved Pacman's heater up to full blast.

Gramps: the bad seed. Killing his pregnant girlfriend. Odds were that Alex wouldn't have that kind of girl trouble now. More likely to get picked up as an escaped convict. The fam: theirs was a tale worth reading one of these days, and that thought alone kindled a faint light in him. Something he wanted to do, other than wrap Lori in his embrace, or die young. Wished he could imagine himself living his days as a high-spirited cavort, all principles suspended, writing, drinking, doping, humping, a Grampsian cum Hemingway art and life romp to the finish line. Much easier than to bear another fifty years. Give Joaquin a novel to write about him, or at least a song Lori couldn't sing.

The first time Alex spun his mother a story that she believed he was five years old. They were out on a walk in the arroyo by their house with their old dog, Jonas. As always, they were holding hands, a gesture he still liked but no longer engaged in. Without any clear intent or destination, Alex began telling her about a walk he'd taken here by himself a few days before. In the yore of then, when the area had not yet become a neighborhood, Alex was the sole child and the child of everyone, welcome wherever he roamed and thus free to do so safely, Jonas at his side. On the occasion of this adventure, he'd been alone as he climbed the hill across from their house, up and on over the top to the other side, where an old cabin lay weathering in the sun. Went inside—at this point his mother slowed, stiffened, suppressing the why-you-don't-do-that speech that would follow—and found a ragged man curled up on a bed with a gray blanket over him. It was cold inside. The man wakened, sat up, and began talking to Alex in a growly voice that was not mean. Alex sat at the rickety table as the man asked him questions, invited him to stay. He'd been expecting Alex, he said, and he did seem familiar. When he closed his eyes and fell asleep again, Alex left.

Mamia freaked the fuck out but very calmly so her son wouldn't. She explained in her dark voice why what Alex had done was very dangerous and asked whether he could take her and Papa to the cabin. Alex smiled and said (as he remembered, with enormous though subdued pride) that it was just a story he'd made up. Took her a while to believe it, but convinced at last, after a thorough interrogation, she was enthralled with his imagination, sure she had a budding writer by the hand. Of course it might have been a dream he was recounting, but even that was quite a feat for a kindergartner. Her enthusiasm had embossed the experience on his memory—not just the story but the walk, the scene, his kid-sized, ramble-voiced telling of the tale. Thinking back on it dredged a smile from him. Also made him consider, in an academic way, whether he might have been seeing a prophetic vision of himself in old age; he liked that interpretation of the scene but not its content. Again, what are the odds of my growing old? he comforted himself. She was right: it had been long since they'd really talked. He had new stories to give Mamia and means to make her believe them. He could splice fact and fiction with an editor's trained eye for intercuts and credible sequences.

Harvey's ghost: that would keep him from hanging around the Ville too long. The trick would be to leave Harve there when he moved on. It stung to hear how much she loved the ghost, how good he was to her, patting her hand, smiling, when it was an avenging fury to him. Justice served in the afterlife, which was apparently an eternal postscript. But surely you lost interest in the world of the living as the years of deadness grew long and everyone you knew was on your side of the river. The question was, did mercy come with death? Would Alex's demise quell Papito's anger and give him a peacelove absolution blessing?

Pacman 2 was built for sturdier '60s antecedents, those who eschewed a.c. and cushioned seats. Heating was minimal, and the speakers tinny. Alex hadn't cared four months ago when he identified with the dawn of Aquarius, but now the deep-freeze was fracturing crucial outposts: his feet ached, his butt felt numb and splatted, his bladder writhed, his shoulders balled into iron knots, head pounded. The roads were better after Willow Springs, but with a top speed of thirty-five, he had hours to go before he slept. Might stop in Dell for the night, call her, say I'm coming in tomorrow. That's how he urged himself onward, knowing he would do nothing of the kind. His arrival was going to be a surprise, and she'd love it. No prep: just go with the flow. Alex is back. Woohoo. Tippecanoe and Tiger too.

Well, she was rich now, or well off, as the discreet say. Taken care of. Another few years (how old was she exactly?) and she'd collect Harve's social security, which had to be pretty good, along with the pension due him. She wouldn't have to worry about anything except Alex, and it was his intention to lift that burden from her soon. He would be strong and good and consoling and able to get on with things, and that's what he would do. This intermission at home would last only until he'd figured out what to do next, which was likewise its sole purpose.

He pulled over at a rest area south of Dell and peed, leashed Tiger for a brief jaunt to the bushes to take his turn. The leash was the ultimate indignity, for both of them, that blared Tige was a captive. He'd always come back readily to Alex; now they both knew he never would again. The war between empathy and irritation added one more friction to Alex's grave discomfort.

Homestretch to Summerville. They'd come up about once a year to visit Trudel till he graduated from high school. Eaten lunch in the car. Pulled over at that rest stop. Papito had told him the same stories about his great-aunt Trudel's fly-ins from all over the world for his birthdays. About her skepticism when he married a woman from Vista Grande and left Texas for the badlands of New Mexico. She hadn't been to Vista Grande ever, which heightened her wild speculation—and Alex's relief. He felt that she left an air of herself behind at every place, and he wanted his home to be free from breathing it in. After his recovery in her house, he carried an imprint of her weighted tread of disapproval, along with the whiff of incontinence. Eau de age. She may have saved the family from the Nazis, but as the clan came down to him, to what end all this suffering? A chronicle of losses whose memory had descended to an inchoate fool. It would be very hard for him to miss her: guilty, Your Honor, but defiantly so.

A vicious wind had settled under Alex's collar like a biting memory. He did not want to explore it at this unsteady juncture, so tugged at the leash. Tiger pulled back. No hurrying a cat, an angry one pretending to root about in the bushes for the right spot to lay down a trail of waste.

Memory born with consciousness but shaped by experience, not only of the event but of the moment of remembering. A recollection seen in the pale dawn of love is altogether different when viewed from the battered ramparts of defeat. And not just where or when, but who at that moment the rememberer perceives themself to be. And not just the memory of one lifetime but of inherited memories as well, the stories we are told and by whom and how we relate to the storyteller, at the time of first hearing and with each successive hour as we claim them. Memory, like time, may spring into conception through the development of a self, but it evolves and endures through experiences. Understanding those experiences makes meaning of memory, new in every tick and turn, altered by previous rememberings of the memory, schists laid down, stratified and embedded with the fossils of all that has, or may have, or we wish had, been.

How many times had he and the folks pulled in at this rest stop? You pee and pee and pee again, going to or from the same places, urinals measuring the circular, pointless waste of your journey. Eau de despair. Into this stained porcelain receptacle he emptied himself of any illusion of progress. A fitting place to be buried. Soon.

When the hind side of Center Mountain came into view, he pulled his act together. His mother needed a son with still some hope to share. Prepared a cheery script to greet her, pathetically brief with no follow-up. He could claim he was worn out, needed to rest, and escape to bed. Or hungry and worn out, eat first. Praising Mamia's food always a winner. With that reassuring thought, a lesson from his one college drama class popped into view. The prof, a sadist who hated non-majors, instructed Alex to enter the room and take charge of it without speaking a word. As the student least likely to succeed on all counts, Alex came in puffed up with his body fiercely set on look-at-me, you lowly peons. I own you. Nothing. Deflated, he sat down to watch the prof do it right: Enter the room with all his attention focused on the students, his eyes sweeping the crowd. Focus on others to gain control of them, he explained, which he could have done without humiliating Alex first. But the lesson did stick. He used it as a waiter when exasperation had him teetering on the edge. Now here it was again, a rabbit pulled out of recall to charm Mamia. Into overlooking him. He'd ask all about her, get her talking, give her the chance to unburden herself of the loneliness from which she'd suffered without him. Relieved, confident, he headed down toward ex-Trudel's abode. It hadn't even snowed in the Ville.

Then, like a brick through the window, cool turned to consternation. Tiger. He hated this house from where he'd been shunned, his life threatened, an obnoxious bell hung from his neck. One look and he'd know that not only had Alex traitorously ripped him from the bosom of his lady love, but he'd done so for the inexplicably cruel pleasure of bringing him to hell. Wouldn't take Tiger but thirty seconds to scale the fence and be gone. The only thing that had kept him here the first time was loyalty to Alex.

U-turned Pacman 2 and got on Escondido, heading south toward town. Car lights heralded the early dark of a winter night. Walgreens used to be on Mountain Avenue. He didn't know the Ville well. Eyes straining to spot any kind of store that would have a cat box and litter. Tiger just hadn't been the same since the cabin, he could hear himself say, forgetting that Mamia had seen T when she came to Trove, and of course Lori had emailed her pictures of Tiger with Montenegra. No matter: Alex was the lead player in this drama. Don't forget cat food.

Still there, right where he'd left it years back: good old Walgreens, no apostrophe needed. A light corn snow swizzled the air, but at this inauspicious hour parking was no problem. Inside, the fluorescent lights suffused the aisles with a pallid glare that mashed their products into blur. Alex found himself squinting geezerlike as he lugged past the sanitizing products and down the electrical aisle toward a sign for pet supplies. All the basics in place, good old Walgreens. He could have used a basket but not enough to traipse to the front and back here again. Tucking the litter box under one arm, litter bag clamped inside it, and squashing wet 'n dry cat food between his other arm and his chest, he plowed toward the cash registers. Barely avoided knocking over an end display of Valentine's candy as his litter-bearing arm banged against a customer hurrying toward analgesics. Alex gripped the box tightly, refusing to lose his load, and muttered an apology. Should have been a blip forgotten in the next ten seconds, but the guy grabbed his shoulder and spun him eye to eye. "Al!" way too loud is what Alex would have liked to claim, but the chills rising from his buttocks to his hairline denied him that out.

Jack. It was Jack the drug dealer, last seen being hauled away in handcuffs from the fire ravaging the Mann house and lives. Jack, who would no doubt have cleared the Mexican border if he hadn't given his worthless neighbor Al a ride north. Jack, in a wool suit and quality tie, muted gray shirt, hair trimmed, no tats showing, gold watch, handsome shoes, teeth whitened into a big grin. Clean, elegant, slick. Nary a trace of the ex-con nor the crazy-assed sky-high dealer nor of the vengeance-reeking maniac Alex had feared he'd run into one day. The litter box with bag clattered to the floor, where the bag split, regurgitating its scented clay bits onto the linoleum.

"Al, man, it's good to see you, man. Looks like you came through that fire alive, mostly. What are you doing up here, bud?"

Still in a wonderland daze and uncertain how much to give away, Alex shrugged, "Visiting. An aunt." He tried to juggle the cat food cans awkwardly into his other hand before surrendering them to the cat box on the floor.

"Hey, that for your wild cat, what was his name? Butch? Man, that was a helluva ride, am I right? I thought we'd both be dead by now, me in prison, you in that blaze. Here we are, in Walgreens, a couple years later, buying cat food and aspirin. Lord God, life is beautiful." He leaned in, exhaling mint-cool breath. "You want to know what happened? We could grab a brew down the street. I got half an hour before meeting my lady for dinner. She is something, Al, I mean, beautiful outside and in. Curls and curves, man, like you could just keep rolling around in, and a pious nature to go with them. Goodness and good looks in one sweet, rare package. Got it made, am I right?"

Of course Alex wanted to know what happened. He also wanted to get out of here and finish this terrible journey. Faking exhaustion was no longer necessary. His nerves throbbed, sending dark trills of pain to every cell in his body. But if not now, then later, and he had no desire to meet with Jack again. Nodded, letting the dry food bag slip down his leg. "Sure. Tell me about it. But I don't have a lot of time; my aunt's expecting me."

As if he had summoned it, Jack reached around the corner and grabbed a cart, loaded all but the open bag of litter into it.

"It's the hand of God, I swear, Al, which He laid upon me and led me out of the darkness. I hope you've accepted Jesus Christ as your Savior, Al." A narrow look that Alex countered. "So, here's the story. Here it is. Yeah, they convicted me when they saw all that shit I had in the car that night I saved you instead of heading to Mexico. Judge sent me to the state pen, max, and had in mind to throw away the key. But three awesome things changed my fate in three months, Al. One, I found an old buddy there, a con with connections on the outside who got me the deal of a lifetime, I mean the dream deal, the kind you only need one of to be set. Two, I found God, and I promised Him I would put a good percentage of my drug money into His church, which I did: got my name on this plaque when you go in, so He forgave me. Three, the state of New Mexico was so cash-strapped after that season of fire that they were giving non-violents with a good record early release. I was a prince of a con, Al, especially after my baptism."

The snow had picked up and Alex's patience was waning. Jack's voice, blaring in the silence of the empty store, unnerved him. He shifted his weight and the cart rolled, nearly spilling him next to the cat litter. Jack paused, took stock of his wasted body.

"Hey, man, you need to sit down. You're wobbling."

"I've got to get going, Jack. It's an awesome story."

"Oh, that's just the start of it. Here, man."

Again, Jack the magician yanked a couple of plastic lawn chairs from the shelves, opened them next to the cart, waved Alex into one, and plunked himself into the other. The impromptu bizarre theatre of the scene jumbled Alex into submission.

"It was a miracle, for sure, Al. I got out, got rich, got religion. Moved up here to where Christians rule and found myself a community of true believers. What more do you need, am I right? Well, one thing more, at least I did, and that was like a legit career. I'd been turned, you might say, and God infused me with the will to be an upstanding member of society. But doing what? Well, the answer came to me one night in the voice of the Lord. Just one word, big enough to light the room and wake me up: Property. That's all He said: property. Man, I prayed for understanding, prayed and prayed and prayed until it was made clear to me: Real Estate. That was my calling. I've always been a salesman, right?"

Tiger would be getting very cold under the seat in Pacman 2. He was a survivor, no doubt about that, but Alex couldn't handle laying more guilt on the stones that were smothering him. He spread his lips in a smile-like configuration and rose partway, hands clamped to the chair old-man-like.

"Congratulations," he squawked.

Jack popped a mint into his mouth, offered Alex one from the tin. "I'm clean," he said. "Went cold turkey. For Jesus. And Ramona."

Slumping back, Alex sucked the despair out of the mint. Why was he in such a hurry to go to the next stop on his road to nowhere?

"So I got my realator license, started selling houses, and for me, Al, it commenced to be easy as selling dope. Everyone wanted what I had to offer; it was just a matter of connecting them with the right product. So, yeah, I'm golden. And now, man, with the open drug laws in Colorado, in addition to being a realator, I've got me a legit shop where I sell some truly fine weed if you're in the market. Hard to fathom, but I can boost that shit legally for so much more than I used to on my own. It's a beautiful world, am I right, Al?"

Creator, destroyer. Grace, catastrophe. An inferno of those proportions could ignite and incinerate without any moral basis. He was glad that he hadn't ruined Jack's life. He was glad the story was over now and he could wallow again in his own miserable one.

"You're my hero, Al, man. You got the ball rolling for me when you asked for a ride that night. If there's anything I can do for you, anything at all, Al, just name it, it's yours, anything but my woman."

On his feet, stiff and musty, Alex croaked a laugh. "Nope, not your woman. Good running into you, Jack. We're both going to be late now."

Jack leapt from his chair, overturning it and texting as he folded it up and leaned it against the shelf. "Come visit me, man," extracting another mint from the tin. "My shop's out on Airport. Sweet Deal. Check the website. I can set you on the path to Christian righteousness, Al, born again in grace and love, which it looks like you could use a little of, am I right? God bless." He paused. "Have you thought about some tats on those scars? I've got a friend who's a genius with needles. Turn your face into a work of art."

Paused again, on his way out, to yell, "Hey, Al!" and hurried back with a bouquet of pink roses. "Take these to your auntie. Make her so happy she won't care that you're late. Same goes for Ramona." Much smoother than Alex the new Jack was, with an eye for pleasing others that it would be well worth our young stumblebum cultivating.

Tiger had defecated in Pacman, infusing it with a nauseating stench that Alex welcomed. At least T wasn't martyring himself; he cared enough to punish his onetime friend. Curled up on the back seat on top of Alex's sleeping bag, he hissed when Alex tried to cover him with a jacket. Vengeance, not recompense his mode, but the dump was a step toward opening negotiations. Weak logic, yet the only card Alex held and persuasive enough to get him puttering through the snow toward Mamia's reclaimed home. More pressing at the moment, to bed.

Roses and shit fought for control of the VW's limited, frigid air supply, slowing Alex's brain. A genius with needles. Make his face an artwork. More like turn him into a freak, not that he wasn't one already. What was he going to say first when Mamia came to the door? Should he take the roses with him? Tiger? Then unload the car right away before she could ask about anything? Clean up the car tonight or let it really harden (and ripen) till tomorrow? How little would he have to do to be polite before sleep? Dinner? Had he eaten since Arroyo? He wasn't hungry, but Tiger might be. What if she had a new dog that hated cats? What if she had company staying in the guest room? A body-wide groan wracked him. It was overwhelming to contemplate all the separate steps and possibilities required for his arrival. Whatever script he'd worked out before seeing Jack was lost—just as he was, having driven past the Meadow Street intersection and headed now, it appeared, to Utah. A motel sign neoned through the snow: he could stop here for the night, try again tomorrow. To drive the what? five miles to her house. It was 6:30. He turned the car around for a second time tonight, disgusted by his boundless ineptitude.

Predictably, his homecoming was far simpler than imagined. He didn't know, and she didn't tell him, that Lori had called ahead with the news. Lori's explanation: Alex was improving physically but remained emotionally unstable. She had urged him to visit his mother, who knew him better than anyone and could help him through this very bad post-trauma depression. She also mentioned the tragic parting of the cats and hoped Michelle would make Tiger feel as much at home there as possible. Thanks to Lori, Lori, Lori, a pot of chili was simmering on the stove, the guest bed was freshly made, closet emptied and aired, carpet vacuumed, towels hung in the bathroom, everything in place, which, Alex, still a child in his mother's house, took for granted.

Hug, big hug, come in, Tiger wrapped in welcoming arms. Unloading the car was a single trip for the backpack and cat stuff. Leave the shit. Collapsing in the kitchen with a full bowl of her signature chili while T ate ravenously, two cans of wet, nothing more asked of either of them as they bedded down, the cat opting to sleep with Michelle. Out cold, both travelers, motionless, dreamless as the night winds streamed by, hurling the snow into Kansas. Plenty to come to terms with, but fortune and misfortune alike bow to nature's dictates, namely, rest and the assurance that tomorrow is, after all, another day.

At noon the sound of a male voice wakened him. "Shelley," the voice pleaded, "don't take on too much. He's a grown man. You've got a life of your own."

Coming out of a molasses slumber, his sinews were remarkably lax. Unwilling to tighten despite the urgent signals his brain sent them. Danger. Get up now. Shake off your hopes for a soft landing in Mamia's world. Prepare to defend your territory. Prepare to vanquish the intruder. Prepare to discover you've already lost. Prepare to move on.

13

Flotsam and Jetsam

The suspension of time is a gift mesmerizing. A wave that swells unrushed to its break, gathering from its chasmic interior an enormous power that will undertow all in its domain. Watching it build arouses delicious thrall, the end being known, as long as you are high on the shore, but if you've waded too far in through bravado or carelessness, sparks panic. The daredevil or a child of the sea may deem themself immune, the oft-plummeted swimmer stroke landward rapidly. Whatever course the players of this quiescence take, they will be aware of the alluring freedom of time's inheld breath: the interstice between moments freezing as it awaits wave-break.

I lay idling in such an abeyance, knowing that I would soon have to act and that my actions would have a colossal impact. Whoever this man was, he could not, so soon, slither into Harvey's place beside Mamia. Why did the ghost tolerate him? Why was there no mention of this intruder in her letter? Why was he, already, trying to get rid of me when Mamia had begged me to come? Bullshit. First pair of pants to cross the threshold.

But just now, I did not need to do anything. Lie in bed, let the wave mount. I sensed a cavernous release in sinew and bone, my body melting into slack. Mamia was at the helm. She would feed Tiger, take care of him. With Trudel gone and Mamia pampering him, he probably wouldn't run away. Screw him if he did. Bigger worries massed on the horizon. In the kitchen. Where this man was telling her he had to go set-up and rehearse, promised he'd be back tonight after the show, and he guessed she wouldn't be able to come what with Alex here, too bad. She agreed. Next weekend she'd be there for sure, yes, Alex, too. I'd love to come, the wave-rider sneered to himself. What's your bit? Clown? High-wire? Shame if you broke your neck.

When the male voice no longer gnawed the air, I heard Mamia chatting up Tiger, washing dishes, then very softly approaching my room. Feigning sleep, I let her sit on the bed, her hand light on the quilt, before I groaned, wriggled, as though her presence had brought me to consciousness. Smiled at her through slitted eyes, rasped, "What time is it, Ma?" She sat down, stroked my forehead, tenderly as she would silk.

At eight I contracted a vicious case of the flu that threatened to turn into pneumonia. Stayed home for two weeks, feverish, coughing, ears throbbing. In my recall, I hurt everywhere, severely. Unconcerned about her own health, Mamia stayed with me most of every day and many hours of the night. She sat on the bed, soothing me with her voice, giving me cool water to sip, stroking my forehead. Her love alone diminished the pain. After the fire, wrapped in bandages, I had conjured her hand on insomniacal nights, flowing toward my hairline. With every pass, I softened.

"I've been so lonely down there. Without you, Papito, Hersch, my home world. My friends in Trove, they're great and I was lucky to find them. But they don't really care. I'd never really belong; that's the kind of town it is."

"You're not going back?"

"I don't have a place to stay, stuff to do. Lori and Joaquin are together now, you know; it's a one-bedroom. I've been sleeping on the sofa, living out of my backpack. Which was okay before. Greg, he's a superhero, but he needs that guest room. It's not just a place like somewhere to sleep and eat; it's a place in the bigger sense, you know what I mean."

"You're going to stay here with me, sweetheart?"

"If that's okay."

"Of course. You don't even have to ask. It's as much your house as mine." She lifted my left hand and kissed it. "How long?"

"I don't know. As long as you can stand me, probably. I don't have any other plans."

I scooted up and back, pulling my hand in. "Unless there's no room for me here, either, with your new boyfriend."

"He's a friend only, Alex. I knew him when I was young. He's headed to LA in a couple of weeks."

"Before Papito?"

"Last year of high school. He was a musician, singer. I had a crush on him. All of us did. It was one of those silly teenage girl things, and nothing came of it."

"Why didn't you mention him in your letter?"

"There was nothing to tell. Maybe I wrote it before we ran into each other. I can't remember. What matters is that it's been fun having him around, kind of revived me, got me out of the house. I've been lonely, too, my son."

I had that reprimand coming. And as they say in court, once I'd opened the door, she felt free to walk through.

"Not one email, call, postcard, anything after you left for Trove. You acted as though I died in the fire."

"I owed you too much to be kind."

"You know how I kept up with you? I found Gregorio online and he was so generous about writing to tell me how you were doing. Always upbeat, that man, sharing stories in whose mesh he caught the underlying current of what was going on. And then, after the cabin, Lori. She was so good, embracing me as if I were her mother, calling and texting, welcoming me when I came to visit. I was, am, boundlessly grateful to her. My dream is for you to find a woman like her."

"Ditto."

"Not even two minutes to send me an email."

"It wasn't a question of time."

"Trudel?"

"How can I love you who are so much a part of me when I loathe myself?" I drew back from the confession as if stung by its honesty. The language sounded like Joaquin, awkward on my tongue. Rushing to cover, "What's his name?"

"Frank." Braced herself for the pounding roar: "Frank Stranger."

My outrage crashed foaming down her.

"Frank Stranger. Joaquin's father? The guy who nearly killed him?"

She fought the riptide.

"He's different now. Sober. Straight. Divorced. Ashamed of who he was but taking full responsibility. Hasn't seen Joaquin in ten years, remember."

"A dangerous, ugly man. Violent temper. Abusive. Mean. Unpredictable. A homicidal maniac failure who could fang you like a rattler but with no warning. Joaquin said."

I swayed to my feet, tottering over to the chair under which my socks and shoes were stashed. Mamia rose to help me, was rebuffed with disdain. "I'm getting him out of here today. Where's he staying? Did he sleep in this bed?"

"No, no. His airstream is parked out back of the house."

"Convenient for him. I'll bet he has a key to the back door. Easy in, easy out. Rich widow, lonely, traumatized, vulnerable to the memory of a teenage crush. Jeezus, Ma, you're so naïve. Why the hell do you think he's hanging around here after he abused his son and his wife? They had a restraining order against him, you know. He's the reason Joaquin has a gun. Oh, shit, I probably shouldn't have told you that. Don't warn him. I just can't believe you're harboring a psychopath." I flared at her. "He goes or I do, but I'm not leaving you here with him. I may be a screwed-up mess, but I'll get the police, whatever it takes, to move him out. Change the locks. How could you do this to my father?"

Filthy with spume, she retreated. I glared her away with an alternating current of contempt and despair that each soured the other. She opened and closed her mouth repeatedly to answer me, but like a beached fish, drowned in the effort. There was too much to say; there was nothing to say.

"You must be starving. Let me make you some eggs and bacon." Slipped quickly out to the kitchen to cleanse herself of the assault. Tiger glanced at me, then followed her, tail up in my face.

Calmer but no less angry after a meal, which I gulped without savoring, I stirred the cream and honey into my coffee to hide the shaking. "Okay, tell me: how did it happen?"

She struggled to match the frigidity of my tone. "Very simply. When I was a girl, Frank came through Vista Grande on his way to the West Coast and got a gig playing on Abbott Road, at a place that we all frequented. He was terrific, playing the songs he'd written—"

"I got that part, from Joaquin, what I need to know of it, and the crap that happened after Clarice had the misfortune to win the jerk's heart. I'll fill you in if you care to find out why he's out of here tonight. Tell me about how he managed to track you down and snake you into letting him squat in your yard. Ours."

"Frank had a gig in Denver. He needed to supplement it, so he found a place to play in Summerville. I heard his performance advertised on the radio, recognized his name, went to hear him. The early show. Introduced myself afterward. He asked me to coffee. We had fun rehashing the old days. He told me he was divorced. I invited him to the house for lunch. We ended up talking for ten hours straight. About everything. It just flowed. Felt good to talk someone at last, besides Trudel. So, yes, I know about his past. I also know he's sober, filled with remorse, a man who's faced his demons and wrestled them to the ground. Not that he's pure and perfect but that he understands how and why things go wrong and has a clear sense of whom he wants to be. He's a far stricter self-monitor than anyone I've met, but he says he has to be. I don't know whether he can keep it up, but he counts each day as bettering his odds. I have days when I feel like drinking myself into oblivion, but I can't bear the idea of a hangover. Pills, then, I think. The longing drives deep, Alex, to numb the pain, even end it. I'm in no position to criticize someone who's trying his best to fight it."

She carried my dishes to the sink and rinsed them. Unobserved, I raised the jittery mug and chugged the cold coffee. Frayed nerves and hot liquids were a bad mix, but more than that, I did not feel secure in showing weakness. She could not be allowed to see the remnants of her invalid son who lay, a month ago, inert and helpless. I had to be ready now to transform myself into an agile Zen-master who could pulverize her foolish vision of Frank without damaging her. Or risking her love. I had too little of that to lose any more.

"Thanks for the delicious breakfast." My mouth clenched in a smile, my hand skittering over her shoulder as I put the mug in the dishwasher. Ignored her pleading look. No forgiveness, no acquiescence, no resolution. Not from her wounded son whose only shot at winning was, against all odds, to stay in the game.

Bereft and desperate, I shambled off to watch daytime TV (anathema, bane, trash) while I came up with a strategy to best Frank.

The soap opera featured a woman, Lola, torn between her husband and her lover, the former of whom had a gun and threatened to kill her or himself—he was still undecided about which was a more fitting punishment. The lover, on the other hand, claimed he wanted nothing but the chance to make her happy, an unproven assertion. Lola had just discovered she was pregnant, something neither of the men knew yet, and of course she didn't know which one of them was the father. Near the close of twenty-two minutes of melodrama, hints were strewn that the lover might be bisexual and equally in love with husband and wife. A ménage: the easy solution, but of course it wouldn't be. I recalled Papito telling me of a cousin Matilde (on the Dresden side) who had lived with two handsome, attentive men. She was the envy of all those who didn't know the men were gay in an era when homosexuality was a crime and were using her as a beard.

Choosing my foremost goal: that would determine my move. Avenging Joaquin or saving Mamia? Both noble and gripping causes, but the latter had the more immediate claim. Both would be accomplished by Frank's death, but I'd have to pay for that, not only by doing time but by losing Mamia's faith in me. Dearth of lethal weaponry was an impediment, too. Had my old baseball bat made a sentimental journey to Summerville? Or my sword from fencing; dull though it was, it could inflict some harm. But after three months in bed and only three weeks on my feet, my Lancelot agility in hand-to-hand combat might be as blunt as the sword, especially against a man Joaquin described as a rage-fueled eighteen-wheeler.

On the saving Mamia front, I was hampered by the many inexcusable wrongs I'd done her. Really, a call? an email? An acknowledgment that this extraordinary woman who'd been a mainstay in my life for most of it was still loved and cherished by her only child? If any kid of mine treated me that way, I'd grab him by his frost-tattered earlobe and throw him headlong back into the snow. See if you can do the job right this time, I'd yell. Do us all a favor and die. Of course I wouldn't, but could I still love myself if I were my son?

Yes, our boy was stumped. A pitiful sight, drooped in the comfy chair in front of a talk show on a storm-weighted day, flailing at ludicrous schemes for altering a situation into which he had blundered. And as long as we're being completely honest, helped to create. If he'd been at his mother's side, taking care of her instead of himself, Frank would have had no access. Shove that airstream of yours where the sun don't shine, mister, and bowleg yourself on down the road to oblivion. No room for you at this here inn. We're full up with men.

My swaggering thoughts were cuffed by a breeze silting over my neck. Door open? Frank coming in? I was so ready to go at him. I muted the TV, cocked my good ear at the kitchen, but nothing. Mamia somewhere else. Again the breeze shuddered at my back. I scooched down in the chair, hunching my shoulders against the caul of air. Was preparing to tighten my robe when the draft crept down, fingering my chest. I froze, suddenly aware of the source of cold. Not emanating from living blood, this ghost wind. An icy touch that numbed the skin it overran. Harvey, crawling toward my hands, which unprotected lazed on the chair arms. Winked them into the pockets of the robe, which clearly offered no safety since the ghost had already seeped into my esophagus, rendering me mute. I'd not worn gloves since that night in the cabin, had forgotten about them in fact. Papito could have killed me any time.

Survival dictated flight, but fear pinned my carapace to the suede. Where was Mamia, who loved her ethereal departed? Focusing on her halted the specter's progress toward my hands and nethers. My breath gathered, surged to stricken vocal cords: "Ma!" Pathetic. "Ma!" A squeak whose wince would not summon a hiccup. She must be in the back, probably making up my bed or collecting laundry—or calling Frank. "Mia!" Yelled bigger than the house. She appeared hastily, phone in hand: "I've got to go. Call you back later? All right."

Eager to clasp the phantom breeze, arms widening. "My love, look who's here with us. The family reunited." Harvey withdrew his eerie ectoplasmic grip from my body and vaporized, freeing his son to tear scream-laden to the coat closet, where I scrabbled my deformed hands into the mittens stuffed in my winter jacket.

She stood aghast, phone dangling, where I'd left her. Who'd she been talking to? If it was Frank, their talk would have to wait till I eviscerated him.

"Who?" nodded at the phone.

"Lori."

Paradise lost. Yesterday.

"Why did you—"

Time and overdue to free myself of the malevolent haunting I'd endured. "Papito's specter. Not a fan."

"You should be honored, Alex. The guardian spirit of your dear father, my beloved husband staying close to shield and comfort us. Why are you wearing gloves?"

It would be long, long before she could hear the story whose fatal grip cowed her son into taciturnity. Maybe I'd leave the whole of it for her in a letter after I'd gone somewhere, as I would have to do.

"Need to rest."

She stepped resentfully aside as I slopped back to the bedroom.

The great escape, eh, lad? When the going gets rough, put on some gloves and go to bed. Inertia as your problem-solving modus operandi. I was tired, truly so, but not a fatigue that sleep could cure. Tired of the rubble, shorn hopes and battered cairns. Tired of trying to make sense of a wasteland where I sat fishing with a baitless hook. Tired of being the kicked bucket and scorned revenant.

Yesterday. The scene played out between the restive nodes of my interior stage. Lori'd had to break the news of my departure in a way that would garner Joaquin's sympathy and lay no fault on herself. "You know it's been hard for me, these months, tending to him. And then with you there and him here, my patience gave out. I can do as good a job as Alex in the greenhouse. Floyd Jr. will handle deliveries. We can cover everything without him till your leg heals. And you'll need to sleep downstairs for a while anyway. Me, too, with you. Don't worry. It's just such a relief to have him gone—and he ought to spend some time with his mother. She needs him. I don't know whether he'll ever be back. Not with us, I imagine."

Joaquin would have been understanding, of course, though sorry that Alex had left when he was needed most. Wouldn't say that, but Alex knew well enough the chagrin his friend would feel. Two weeks more, a month, till Joaquin could take over running the business again. He'd have inferred from her waning patience that Alex didn't leave of his own volition and wondered why she chafed so at having him around for a few weeks more. He could have slept upstairs, for one thing. Those were logistical problems easily solved, not like the crop, which had languished in the absence of Alex with his gift of green. Lori could keep the plants going, as he himself had managed to, but thriving? Unlikely. Still, she had every right to bow out of caretaking Alex, a role that had exasperated her despite her penance. "Can you get me home tomorrow?" I imagined as Joaquin's sole request. But she'd have heard in it his resignation to a tough battle of uncertain outcome. Been sorry, too, although she knew he couldn't have stayed after the last night. Alex was for her synonymous with an intractable guilt.

I myself could spew a gut-load of synonyms, none of them bearable facing either past or future. The bleak trail I'd hewn had closed up as I passed, and the terrain ahead was a pillar of salt. No friends, no destination. No triumphal return awaited me anywhere.

A soft cry and furry feet landed on my chest. Tiger, hidden under the bed, knowing as ever how to time an entrance. He feared ghosts, too, I remembered, so we stood united against the headwind of Papito. Despite how differently we'd been torn from the women we loved, we were allies in despair: each other's stalwart comrade for the run of our days. Or so I, clinging to a fur belly at the top of the waterfall, hoped.

I felt the gush coming before it flooded my sinuses. Years since I'd sunken into its debris. Tumble-plummeting through sobs that Tiger muffled, not begrudging, as he never did, human grief. Definitely the larger of these two souls, charity being native to him. Though still wounded by the separation from Montenegra that I had wrought, Tiger was perhaps fixed in the habit of acquiescing to his erratic companion or perhaps ultimately, a cat: born with a highly flexible backbone that could twist in midair to right him when he landed. Wet with my eye splatter, Tiger began to groom his fur and licked in the process the mitten that stroked him, a pleasurable touch he recompensed with purring, which put us both to sleep.

Darkness overtook us in that unspun time. Mamia awakened me with a gentle invitation to dine. Snow milled in the trees, sociably piling into empty cones and crisping the air. I asked for another bowl of chili though she had an array of delectable edibles to offer. She worried about my emaciated body, but I reminded her I'd done nothing but sleep and rest today, no reason to be hungry. She ate with me, after feeding Tiger, who needed no cause to eat. Talked quietly of inconsequential things, details of the house renovation, a movie, the new mayor. I listened as though attentive, hearing the lonesome notes below the chatter.

"How's Ari? Did she make it?" A question that arose from nothing, but flushed a smile from her withdrawn visage. Ari, Ariadne, had been her closest friend in Vista Grande, a woman she met casually at yoga class, then grew close to over the years. Ari was triumphantly single, unrestrained in her opinions and consciously self-indulgent when she chose to be. She freed Michelle to share an intimacy she'd never dared.

"Ari came through fine, her place, too. But she'd had it with fire country. Moved to Vancouver Island. Loves it there. She wants me to come visit." A rare light in her smile. "Thank you for thinking of her, Alex." Such a little thing to ask. I had to yield the right of way, give her a chance to get on with her life. Sans Frank.

"What did you mean, you owe me too much to be kind?"

Even as she spoke, she knew the answer. That love is a gift to be bestowed, not a commodity to be lent and repaid. I knew that, too. But when you feel indebted beyond any hope of providing restitution, it's hard to be generous. You're in the hole no matter what you do, a mean and bitter place for a young man to dwell. Especially one who has committed more wrong than his mother can imagine, than he himself can abide.

"I don't know; I was worn out, just talking. You have done so much more for me than I have for you, and I feel bad about that, which makes me, I guess I meant, unkinder than I ought to be. I'll never do enough to make things right."

"Alex—"

"Not the point, I realize. It isn't a rational equation. Great chile. Thanks, Mamia. I think I'll get cleaned up, take a shower."

"I washed your clothes."

"Thanks for that, too. And for feeding Tiger. Taking us bedraggled refugees in."

"It's not a debt, sweetheart. I'm just so glad to have you here. What I hope, when you're stronger, is what I said in my letter: that we can get back to the way we were in earlier years, close and natural companions who can and do talk unconstrainedly about everything."

"Yes."

It was 10:00 before Frank knocked on the back door.

"Hey, Shelley?" I opened the door, hating that Frank used her nickname.

"Okay if I come in?" The snow flung itself at his back, skittering into the kitchen. I grudged him barely enough room to squeeze past. Not be mistaken for a welcome.

"My mother Michelle has gone to bed. I want this time alone with you." I led him into the kitchen, transforming my ragged gait into a wide-legged strut.

"Sure." Too easy. She'd warned him. "Mind if I make some tea? Want a cup?"

"As long as it's straight tea."

"I don't drink any more. Thought you knew that."

"It's a good story. I've heard others."

Of the many ways to elicit a confession from the enemy, provoking him is the route I chose. Madden him, get his fists swinging, his temper blazing till he pulls that flask out and chugalugs. If he ripped me up in the process, all the better. One more scar would be well worth the pleasure of throwing this gold-digging scumbag out.

"It's been ten years, kid, since I tried to kill Joaquin. Pains me that that's the single most enduring memory he has of me, and the way these things go, it's gotten magnified over time. You got an earful of the killer dad version of me, I can bet on that. No excuse for what I did or who I was, but it's not the same person you're talking to now. I'd give anything for a chance to show Joaquin how sorry I am."

The kettle whistled and Frank, with grating familiarity, extracted two chamomile tea bags from Mamia's store in the cupboard. Set mugs on the table for himself and me, with spoons for each and the honey bowl between them. Stretched yawning, then sat up and looked his inquisitor resolutely in the eye. Assuming he still had a voice whose resonance approached Joaquin's, he'd be an attraction. Dressed in fringed leather and jeans, tooled black boots, he was the poster cowboy for a rugged C&W singer. Sandy-haired, with gray at the temples, blue eyes, clean shaven, six-two: he'd groomed the image and made himself at home in it. I could picture him at the mirror, sweeping the forelock back lightly so it would fall just right across his brow when he leaned over his guitar. A little bit of shirt untucked beneath the leather fringe to suggest he was unaware of how he looked. Maybe needed a little help dressing, ladies, their hungry fingers dying to tuck him in. Such phony baloney. Seriously, Mamia?

"Yeah? Why haven't you given anything, at all, to do it?"

"Restraining order first, the—well, no. I didn't have the nerve, or maybe the right words to get him to trust me. No blame on him, of course; I'd be just the same if I'd had a father like me. I can't see how to make up for all the suffering I caused him."

Tiger strolled in looking like the sheriff swaggering down Main Street. He sniffed his empty bowl, then leaned against my hitching-post leg. Frank laughed.

"So that's Tiger. Shel—Michelle has told me some humdingers about this fur-boy. Sounds like a bonafide hero, loyal and true, what I'd call a real dog of a cat."

If we hadn't been enemies, I would have grinned. Instead, "He'll snag you by the eyeballs if he feels threatened."

"No doubt, kid, but I'm no longer a threat to anybody, as I keep telling you. Here's the deal: when we get done talking tonight, if you want me gone from your mama's, I'll hitch up my trailer and be out of here in the morning. Spare you the trouble of working yourself up to tell me to split. Good as done, that simple. So that aside, what's on your mind?"

Forewarned, absolutely, or he'd never have been able to checkmate me in a single move. Since nothing Frank could say would change my stance, we could talk about whatever or not, just go to bed so he could get an early start on clearing out. Too abrupt to call it a night yet: what would I tell Mamia? That's it: what do I need to know about Frank to justify kicking him out? Beyond his past, which should have been plenty but clearly had not.

Rising slowly, I sauntered over to the fridge and pulled the bag of cat food off the top of it, refilled Tiger's bowl and gave him fresh water. Then leaning on the counter, exuding a sense of control, "Tell me about the good man you've magically become."

New game, my realm well guarded.

"Starting from where Joaquin left off the night when I bottomed out and tried to kill him. I reckon you know I took off and checked myself into rehab. Out of options. Dead man walking. I don't remember much from that time, the detox and the counseling. Didn't think I was salvageable as a human being. Mostly just didn't have any fight left in me, kind of sucked along like scuzz in a river. Got clean but not motivated to make another run at a life. Those folks down there in Albuquerque went to considerable lengths to set me back on my feet, secured me a part-time job as a custodian at a preschool, where the work was easy and I might come to terms with myself while sweeping the floor. They let me go on staying at the rehab center, keep up the counseling and group sessions. I did whatever they told me to, just like the preschool kids lining up to go out to play, washing their hands before snack and brushing their teeth after, circle time, games, stories, finger-painting. It was all one span of time to me, lighter or darker, but unchanging in my head."

I poured myself a glass of water and took a seat opposite Frank, leaning away from him. Tiger, steadfast witness, jumped in his comrade's lap, tail holding the beat. Going to be a long one, we both realized. Maybe that's his strategy, I mused, wear me down, filibuster straight through the night and get an extra day out of it. Not a chance. Besides, I slept most of the day and I've got twenty-some years on him. I flashed Frank a savage "go on" leer.

"So one night this guy checks in to the center"—classic lead-in to the conversion—
"and he's way more messed up than I ever was and looks like he's come from the gutter,
reeking and homeless filthy, but dragging under his arm a guitar. The folks there knew him;
he'd been in and out of the center over the years. Nobody's story is private down there,
so when I asked, they told me right off he'd been a well-known singer and mentioned a
few of his hits, several of which I recognized, as well as his recording name, Staley Ray. In
time we got acquainted, exchanged tales of woe, though at first there wasn't much to them
besides that old devil booze. He'd been on his way up when it destroyed him, couldn't get
work anywhere now, just playing on the street for spare change to get wasted. After he
nigh busted his guitar trying to get in the door at rehab, I took hold of it and on a whim
commenced to play. Surprised us both mightily to discover I could still pick out a tune and
hadn't lost my voice after all that crap I poured down the gullet. Ray taught me his songs,
and I recalled some of my favorites from the old days. Made us both so happy to hear me
sing and play. What all those good folks' work to motivate me hadn't accomplished this
old drunk's guitar did. I was back, kid, ready to try again.

"Of course, after years of AA indoctrination, I knew I had to make amends before
moving on. Step 9. I'd lied and skipped it, gone on to complete the rest with Clarice and
Joaquin weighing down my heart. Step 9 is the biggie for most alcoholics, who would
sooner die than apologize sober. Especially when you know damn well there's no reason
for you to be forgiven. The things you've done—well, that's why you're here, and that's
why you started drinking long before here. It's a viciously stupid cycle: you get drunk and
do god-awful stuff that you hate yourself for and then you have to drink some more to
forget it and you commit another round of ugly deeds that send you back to the bottle.
When you unwind that pattern and trace your steps back to where you started drinking,
it's your own failures that were the cause, not the folks who got punished for them by your
alcoholic lunacy. But living with the mess you've made can be easier than cleaning it up.
Until it isn't, and then you've got to: no other option, just like when I arrived there, but
this time, heading out. To make things right.

"I wrote to Clarice to ask if I could see her and Joaquin, and that's when he left. But
Clarice and I, we'd had some good years together early on, and I guess she still harbored
enough love to hear me out. Things at the ranch were shaky; she'd had to sell off a piece
of it and some of the herd, needed help. So while I was dead-set on making a career of my
singing this time around, I stayed with her a while to give her a hand. Slept in the barn,
not to assert any rights, you know, husband, owner, none of that, despite her offering to
put me up in the guest room, and I only took meals with her when she invited me. Till
winter, when I had to move inside. You can tell Joaquin I never went near his room; it's
however he left it, unsullied by his dad, when you see him. And tell him I'd sure like to
apologize for all the wrong I did him."

"Write and tell him yourself."

Frank studied me. No softening in the kid's demeanor, I hoped is what he saw, me
still whetting the hostile edge.

"You're right, I should. I will. He's in Trove, right? Living on the land my mama left him."

Abruptly I swung forward, all teeth. This was the part I'd been waiting for, when Frank tried to lay claim to Joaquin's land.

"Need his address."

"Nice try." I sneered. "Just send it to general delivery to Trove. Everybody there knows Joaquin."

"I bet. He's the kind of guy everyone wants to know."

"And they'll stand up for him if you get anywhere near his place. The sheriff lives one hill over. He's fully aware of the restraining order against you, just like most of the permanent residents. It's a small town; word gets around fast. You won't be made welcome anywhere in Trove, better believe it."

Frank cocked his head, attentive to the venomous tone of this warning. My rage was clearly a reflection of Joaquin's. In the intervening decade, the image of Frank as a murderous villain had been preserved in every detail, magnified into a legend. Odds of completing Step 9 with Joaquin were long; maybe on his father's deathbed he'd grant him a pardon. The gulf between them had rawed a sore in Frank's throat, one that elicited an old man's catarrh and caused him frowning pain every time he swallowed another reminder of how virulently Joaquin hated him.

"You won't believe me, Alex"—using my name for the first time— "but I'm saying it regardless. I've got no interest in that Trove place any more. It was a blessing unintended, my mother leaving it to Joaquin. Set me free, which is what I've always craved being. Clarice and me, we're divorced. I got the truck and the airstream, my stuff, the guitar, and that's it. I'm heading to the West Coast, as I meant to do thirty years ago, try my luck singing. This time with more weathering, ready to stay the course true in heavy seas."

Tiger curled into a ball, kneading my robe, the steady throttle of his purr welcome solace as the night drew late. The stronghold of wrath I had erected to decimate Frank was keeling, but I maintained my position. I'd heard Joaquin say that his dad could sweet-talk the devil out of taking his soul, words learned from his grandmother, who knew her son's duplicitous power.

"Here's how it looks from where I sit, Frank"—using his name for the first time— "arriving to find you in my mother's house, which she has opened to you without reservation. You're divorced and scraping by, a middle-aged man with nothing going for him. She's a lonely, wealthy widow who has remnants of a girlish crush on you, the old recapturing–your-youth thing that's easy to fall for. You oblige that vision, happy to be the the-one-who-didn't-get-away this time. Oh, sure, you'll go on out the Coast to fake a career for a while, then come back here humble and let her nurse your broken ego, make her think she's saved you, and about the time she's used to having you around, you'll pretend you don't want to take advantage of her any longer and are moving on. Then she'll be devastated and invite you to stay, a fateful error that you'll jump on with some crappy line about never wanting to leave because you've fallen in love with her, but not feeling right about pushing her into a relationship like this. Then blah blah blah you'll get her in the sack and get a ring on her finger, and big fat checkmark, you are golden. Play your gigs here, in Denver, wherever, but no worries about supporting your delusions of making it. My mother is stuck with you when you start drinking again and life gets ugly. She's a loyal woman, like Clarice, and will hang on even wounded and bleeding. I'm not going to let that happen, which is why you're out of here in, oh, about four hours."

I had never been much good at games: chess, checkers, cards. Got impatient or folded too soon or had too many tells. Harvey had tried to teach me about bluffing, watching other players' cards and moves, developing a long-range strategy. But his son was not a player. Made irrational gambles; tried and failed repeatedly to shoot the moon. Didn't matter. I took defeat in stride and didn't prize my wins. Just now, though, I wished I'd gone a few more rounds and let the pot grow before making the call. With more at stake, Frank might have buckled. Instead, he got a close-up look at the hand I was playing: I'd bared my bluff in one virulent tirade.

Frank stretched, cracked his knuckles, rubbed his face. It was a long sit for a man in his fifties who'd played two shows. Getting this kid to understand required a muster of his waning reserves. I watched him fake a yawn as he concocted a scheme to insinuate himself into the lad's head and find a way to talk to him from inside.

"Growing up, you always had good friends, it sounds like. Rosie, then Hersch. Cavorting through high school with them, down in South America, and more, I expect. Lots of good times, happy memories." Anecdotes that Shelley had told him replayed on fast-forward as he sifted them for the right approach, then, seeing me harden, moved on. "And after the fire Joaquin. That's a great thing, having friends. I was raised on a farm, only child, like you, but a good distance from others my age and anyway, there was a constant supply of work. Not complaining about that, my folks were great, but I did come to manhood lonely. Lots of stuff I couldn't talk to anybody but myself about, jokes and sex cravings and dreams of being famous. Kept so much secret that it was a bad shock when I up and left for LA to become a singer. Should have forewarned them but I didn't know how to say what was going on inside me.

"Having no friends, I didn't learn how to be one, which I speculate might have been at the root of my problems with Clarice and Joaquin. I'd drink in place of talk. At the rehab center, you had to discuss your issues forever, and since I was going along with things, I learned how to say what I thought and to get a better grasp of it by doing so. Years of stuff came up. Then old Staley Ray and I, we got to be friends, in a desperate frontier kind of way, and stuff came out I'd never share with the group. I think it could be claimed a true friendship sprang up between us."

From the darkened living room behind Frank, a white amorphous mass rose. I widened my view to watch it while still seeming to look at Frank. For once I discovered that my terror had been displaced by an urgent desire to see the ghost massacre Frank. His hands were looped behind his head, propping it up, and thus easily accessible to Harvey. Grab him! And the thought ignited a wisp of a grin that I quickly extinguished, but not before Frank misread it.

"I know. Friendship with a guy hanging onto life by a toe is not much of an accomplishment. He would have talked to anybody, never remembered my name. But let it be a start. Your mother, she's an amazing woman, as you know, the finest human being by a mile that I've ever spent time with, your mother told me right off she'd like it if we could be friends. Nothing other, no romancing nor lovers' hold on one another, no long-term expectations besides the natural, warm bond shared by friends. I could not imagine what it would be like having a woman for a friend, since I'd only ever been a bedmate or a husband and done both shabbily. She got the conversation rolling, telling me about her life from the time she first heard me play till now. We covered a wide range of territory, laughing and I'll admit it, shedding some tears. Shel—your mother—is the first real woman friend I've ever had, and that means so much more to me than having another honey or wife that I would do nothing for anything to violate it."

The ghost wending toward those diamond-edged words. His last, and I granted him credit for ending well. My mother's stance was thoroughly believable, her generosity in taking him in, her faith in his character. That closing sentence, though, stretched my credulity thin. How long could a predator like this guy keep his hungry bulk off her? The ghost jutted over Frank, a diaphanous spume on the verge of enveloping him. Despite strict orders to my eyes, I looked up. Grab his hands!

That striking, deceptive smile of Frank's broadened as he turned in his chair. "Harve," he said. "Been a while. Have a seat between me and your boy. Maybe you can boost my ratings with him." Tiger, alerted to a crisis by the tension in my legs, opened his eyes and seeing the ghost so near, yowled and fled, a back-foot claw leaving a bloody gash in his insensate host's thigh.

The ghost oozed over Frank and stood at the window, where he was sharply highlighted against the black beyond. "Harvey, you know how it's been between Shelley and me. And I would never dream myself fit to take your place in her life even if she wanted that, which she doesn't, and me, neither, if it meant losing her as a friend. Can you help me out here? You saw how lonely she was, even with you around, how hungry for conversation, to tell someone her own age what she was going through. And willing to hear me out. Not to give advice, that was such a relief for me who's had folks recommending I do this and that nonstop. She's let me figure it out for myself. I hate to leave, but if Alex here can step up and be a friend to her, why then I feel a little better about going. What do you think?"

Frank cocked his head at me. "He's a comfort to your mother, but not much company."

"It'll be me who goes. I can't live here with my father's ghost. Not after—" and again those illuminating tears of unbearable guilt quivered my eyes.

I pushed back my chair, and head lowered, prepared to charge away to my bedroom. "It's fine, really. I get it. Stay as long as you like. I believe you. Don't worry about me."

"Whoa, kid. Slow down." He yanked a tissue from his pocket and handed it to me. "Here." In mid-rise, I paused, hearing Frank say, "You've got some unfinished business that needs settling. Not with me, I'm guessing, though it's mighty good to know I'm not being evicted at dawn."

I slumped back as Frank crossed to the sink, ran cold water over a paper towel and soaped it, pulled a dry one off the roll, and turned on the kettle. Gentle and sure-handed, he wiped the cut on my thigh clean and laid the dry towel on top to absorb the blood. Carried our mugs to the counter, submersed new teabags in each, poured boiling water over them, and returned to the table. Loaded up his spoon with honey and commenced stirring. I watched him, numb, thankful for the chance to do nothing. Aware, also, that my tears (why did I have to keep crying?) had fueled an all-nighter. The ghost withdrew, melting courteously into the white wall at a far corner of the room.

"I have a keen sense of what we looked like, a couple of stubbled old drunks squatting in a corner, rambling on and on, Staley Ray and me. If you walked by, it might sound like we were mumbling jumbo, just keeping each other propped up. But if you'd gotten down right next to us, which no one did, you'd have heard some true wisdom spouting, along with confessions and questions and sore regrets we couldn't get past. After a month or two, I felt safe talking to Ray because he didn't remember long and had none other to tell my secrets to in any case. I expect he felt the same, though I recall a good deal of what was said, because it mattered."

Frank offered me the honey and spoon. Ordinarily I'd have refused them, but on this interminable night I hungered for a rush of sweet. The perception that within my cells the air had widened and could carry them off like puffs in the wind kept me rooted to the chair, my hoary tailbone grinding into the wood.

"It mattered to me getting a hold on why I'd turned into a booze-hound and getting clear of the muddle I'd made. It comes down to forgiveness, son. Genuine and honest and durable. When you've done something—let's say it right, when you've done countless things—that are unforgivable, or at least you deem them so, you can reach the point that the burden becomes too heavy to carry and you turn mean and angry or you drink a lot and get violent. In my case, I did both, and worse, to Clarice and Joaquin. To my mama and daddy. To anybody I'd screwed. Sounds ass-backwards and it is, but you punish them for your misery, which you caused yourself. Weirder still, unless you're drunk or born stupid, you know you're perpetrating this craziness against them while you're doing it, and the more you keep on, the less you're able to stop because the unforgivable shit just keeps piling up."

Frank grimaced as if the words were triggering physical pain.

"You know you're bound to lose this war, Custer, but if you can come up with a decent excuse not to suicide, you'll raise the white flag on yourself. Meet on the battlefield, unarmed (and it's damn hard to face yourself sober) and open the negotiations. Draw up the terms of your truce, and make sure both of you sign before you head off seeking ways to forgive yourself. That done (or begun), you can proceed to let go of the anger you harbor toward those you have wronged. And that done, you can ask and pray to be forgiven by them as well. There's the ultimate freedom, when you are pardoned for causing the unhappiness of those you love."

Frank exhaled deeply, his triumphal catechism recited fluently, then was quick to add, "You know I'm not there yet, not by a long shot. Joaquin, foremost. Too late to make it up to my folks. Others. Can't move on clean, the way I'd like to, but I've learned how to forgive myself for as much as I can. And to unburden myself now and again, by speaking freely of my wrongdoings to kind-hearted listeners like your mother. And you, now, if I may."

Tenacious though my mind was, I could sense it shutting down as Frank went on. I heard the litany of the older man's betrayals in a trancelike state, not asleep but lodged in an ancestral vein that held prayer. Sitting at my mother's kitchen table, with my father's ghost spooling in the corner, and Frank confessing to me all the grievous harms he had wrought, I felt churched. Bless me, Father, for I have sinned. Bless me, Father, for I have sinned. On and on it went, time having lapsed into a dream.

Here, at my side, the erstwhile detested father turned father confessor, Frank Stranger, whose judgment would be as merciful as the one he sought. Frank, to whom I had never spoken before this night. Frank, who sang cowboy, dressed in buckskin. Frank, who'd almost killed Joaquin. Frank, an alcoholic chasing stardom at fifty-something.

And here I was, the scarred wreckage of mindlessness. I, who had called Hersch to his death. I, who'd crashed my father to his death. And the old dog. I, who'd seduced my best friend's woman. I, who had abandoned my mother. I, who craved pardon for my unforgivable crimes.

Yes, here we were, the two, flotsam and jetsam, washed up in deceased Tante Trudel's kitchen on a snow-spun winter dawn.

And here is the untold story whose fiery, icy grip had ravaged my guts, making me taciturn and erratic with those who loved me. Occasionally cruel, too, bowed under the load of all I couldn't admit: a weight I'd not borne pre-fire, when for years transparency had been a hallmark of this genial boy.

It began with Tiger, my savior ever and again, alerting me to the twists of smoke funneling through my open window. Or it began with Pacman, the VW that never ran. Or it began when I couldn't reach my parents, by text, voicemail, message as the smoke thickened and the neighborhood was ordered to evacuate. Or when I called Hersch to come and rescue me because of all of the above.

But the crime itself began thereafter, when I took off with Jack, the dope dealer, and didn't let Hersch know I had. My best friend then, a rescue ranger, self-designated, his Halloween costume even as a junior in college, who I knew damn well would come at any cost but hadn't calculated what the price might be. Unforgivable: I forgot completely about Hersch as soon as I had a ride. Hersch, who died trying to save me. In the cabin, where the ghost of Hersch finally caught up to me, I was good with dying. It was the least I could do, and of course the most. Like Frank in rehab: I was done with fighting, but in my case, my conscience, my guilt. Hersch was exacting eye-for-eye justice of the kind we swore as boys would be ours whenever some kid wronged us. Being miraculously rescued, which Hersch would have applauded, had left me wondering whether his death sentence had been commuted or whether Hersch was biding in Zihuatanejo for the right moment to appear. Doubt made living a consciously precarious enterprise, and as such, diminished my enthusiasm for doing it.

The ride with stoned Jack was insanity—I knew stepping into the convertible it would be—but most of my adrenalin was fueled by rage at my parents: why weren't they frantically trying to reach their only child? Not even returning his text? It did not occur to me they could be in trouble, my natal home on fire. I was going to inherit that house, which I loved, marry in it and raise my own kid there. My folks would build a guesthouse on the property for themselves, be the grandparents from heaven. For a seemingly footloose lad in his mid-twenties, I had a pretty solid hometown plan to sustain the future. All I needed was income, a career, but I'd get one of those in the seasons ahead when I'd ripened.

Nonononono. No. What was everyone looking at? It wasn't. It couldn't. Not permitted to happen. Not to me, not to my family, not to my home, my plans. Oh no. No, no. The umbrous red glowering within commanded a mesmerizing power. I couldn't turn away, couldn't bear to comprehend it. Mamia, face riveted to the open doorway. Where was Papito? The dog? He went after the hundred-year-old dog? Rescue ranger blood prevailed. I dove in. A heedless, pointless, needless, thoughtless, but irresistible call. The one Hersch answered, and Papito, and me. The difference is they had clear missions; I had nothing but a compulsion pounding in my veins.

Plunged heartbroken into the inferno, where all around, my harbor, my future, my childhood snapped and flamed. My living room, the games, home video land, music center, where we laughed and played and made ourselves a family. The bookshelf fallen, its volumes embers. Sparks, wires popping. Smoke harsh and toxic where summer winds rode yesterday. You grow up in Vista Grande, you bear a primordial dread of fire but believe yourself immune to it. Like earthquakes for Californians. Incredulity obscured my vision more profoundly than the smoke. Standing in the midst of a fire-struck room, I still could not believe I was. Until the silhouette of my father emerged from the hallway beyond the living room, carrying the dog.

He was motioning me back, yelling "Get out!" as I catapulted forward screaming "Papito!" Could not stop the headlong rush toward him. I had to help, to rescue the rescuer, to be the kind of son who would guide his father through the flames to safety. But he didn't need me; he was doing fine. He was on his way out of the house with the dog. Mission accomplished. Until I, blinded by the elation of discovering him, stumbled against the pillar where they used to measure my height to show how much I'd grown, and it gave, bringing down with it a viga that fell directly on my father and the dog, crushing both of them, while I fell over the beam.

I couldn't stop my tortured rush through the shouted words, writhing in Frank's embrace, banging my head on his chest, jabbing his ribs, scream-moaning a deluge, absolutely present in myself and the bottomless cataclysm of that moment. He unlike Papito holding fast, murmuring an undertone of croon. He did not give way; I did not bring him down. In his arms huddled, confessions heaving unfettered from me, shuddering gradually to phrases, coagulating into incoherence, a vowel, a spew, a hiss, as the fire burned out. And he cradled me, patient, quieting, as day came on and on.

Waited, Frank did, till he was sure I had nothing left to say just then. In the sparest language told me what he had heard: panic, love, shame. Guilt, the vengeful judge intruding in the darkest chamber of our hearts, rears up afterward to silence pleas for leniency. An uncompromising bastard, that judge is, and his verdict slays us inwardly. As long as we give him full reign over us, we will continue to serve, dead, a lifetime sentence without parole.

They were big on religious indoctrination at the rehab, but Frank came away with a doctrine of his own, founded on love, yes, and trust in the power of good and forgiveness. "Forgive me" were holy words that would grant you peace. And love, yes, and good will. Make a heaven of life, not after. "Forgive me," truly meant, would disarm the spiteful judge and free you to begin anew, in the natural course of a life gilded with suffering and beauty. "Forgive me" marked the border between hope and despair.

Who's being asked to forgive you? A rhetorical question he answered by circling around to his earlier dictums about forming a truce with yourself, agreeing to your own terms for a pardon that you can abide by. You have to be the one doing the forgiving of yourself, though another can set you on the road, as he was trying to do. But it was a temporary stay. Only you could commute your own sentence.

Nodding, resting, deep breaths. His voice rumbled into the core of my being. What I heard, without yet fully taking in his doctrine, was empathy. Having committed acts of unintended murder was different from being a killer. I'd told myself that often, but guilt had mocked my justification, as Frank had not. The rock of his unconditional mercy absolved me. He forgave and forgave and forgave. Which, that morning, and despite knowing I had to do the same, on my own, for myself, restored hope.

My mother, who could not have helped overhearing, had the grace not to enter this scene for some time after its turbulence had subsided. Time! It, too, left me alone in Frank's arms, withholding its incessant press until Mamia came in and took me from Frank, into her embrace. She pardoned my absence from her life, and Harvey's death, and every other act of willful stupidity or arrogance. Forgiven by my mother, absolved by Frank. Both more generous and loving than I had ever been. I had arrived here yesterday weakened by evasive maneuvers intended to keep the horror at bay. Thanks to them, a surge of possibilities bolstered me. UnTroved, what did I want to do now? Could have been the last squirt of adrenalin following an all-nighter, but whatever: it felt great to feel good.

The sun broke my mother's hanging window crystals into twirling spectrums that flitted across the hazy essence of my father's ghost. Could the dead forgive? Suffused in shards of color, he looked benign.

"Just ask," Frank my telepathic sage advised, unaware of the risk. "You don't have to say it out loud."

Seemed a shame to die on a morning of such promise, but then again, what better time? I recalled a day in spring, azure and gold, sprawled on the patio amid lilacs, Tiger curled under a chair, a time so utterly blissful that I thought, I could die now, content. Far better to depart at the pinnacle than slink out at the nadir.

Took off my gloves, laid them on the table. Crossed the room with even step, my eyes pinned to Papito's ghost. Walking toward him whom I had run at through the fire and away from ever since. Extended my naked hand, hidden from him in dream and waking combat, thrust it straight into the translucence. Gripped chill, but did not budge. Asked him, unafraid of the inevitable. Freedom is a shape-shifter: for some forgiveness, some solitude, some escape, some death. For me, haunted by guilt, any form would do. The icy film shrouded me. No protest. I had abdicated the right to choose.

Sharp and strong, my father called to me from within my head, and I opened my eyes. Time to get on with the day. The pall had cleared. I stood shaken, whole, taut. The ghost was impatient with my loitering. My father, el beloved Papito, gave me a conditional reprieve: Let it be, son. Wake up and move on. A call to consciousness, overdue. And I understood, on a frequency beyond reason, that his ghost's route into my cowering psyche was one I myself laid in my quest to grieve.

Tiger stalked hungrily into the kitchen, surveying us for the most likely candidate to feed him. His nonchalance signaled what I already sensed: Papito's ghost had departed for the realm of the dead, at least insofar as his guardianship of me. I would go unaccompanied through the world from here, which seemed on that rugged morning harrowing. A second death. It ached me, beyond any assurance that mortality plays no role in the span of love and friendship. Yet at whatever remove he dwelled now, he would remain comingled with my thoughts. I would miss him outright, and in time I might learn to call upon him as he had these months called upon me.

Tiger eyed his errant caretakers. Frank broke free of the tableau and poured him a bowl of kibbles and fresh water, then hauled out the largest iron skillet and laid down a row of bacon slices. He was humming a tune I didn't recognize, likely one of his own. Who would we be to each other now, he and I?

14

"How Do I Love Thee?"

"'Hail to thee, blithe Spirit!'" Illumined by a crag of winter lightning. Fair maid, gowned in velvet cream, sumptuous Victorian dress lent by the Trove theater to augment her dramatic entry. Thrall of oblique sky-fire, out of season, titillating each nerve and hair, the latter coiled in sweeps about trim breasts. In jeweled hands a silver platter, borrowed from Gregorio, princely ally, heaped with splendor: roast goose, carrots and peas, potatoes, honey and orange sauce. Adorning the table, champagne, candles, and at the far end, cast leg reclining on a stool, beloved Joaquin, whose spirit hailed must feast blithe now on her love.

Responding with like formality: "Lori, dearest one, to dwell a moment in the glory of this sight is more than recompense for an eternity of death. You give credence to beauty as truth, truth beauty, and all I need on earth to know is you."

Truth, no, alas, soul cringing within a gown that could not conceal toothy guilt of cuckolding the best of men, no excuse excuse that sordid plunge into depravity.

"A holiday banquet of your own conjuring, my love? I say we celebrate New Year's always on the 25th of January."

"It's the vision of such a revel that drove me to the wheel to chance the blizzard—vision, or call it obsession, foolish and nearly fatal." She laying the platter before him, with knife to cut the goose as she held it steady. He sealed in an envelope of lush aromas purling from the silver repast and the cream, his adored one fragrant with lavender. Melting him.

Fine for now, but later she wanted him hard.

The lash of thunder gave eerie intimace to the feast. It was late afternoon, the time of sunset, but tonight sleet pelted an early dark. Romantic though not the Wordsworthian "beauteous night, Calm and free" she'd planned to cite. They ate and drank, he with gusto heartily, she neat smidgens, as befit a woman in loaned velvet. He toasted her, she bowed her head modestly. Her air of innocence felt sham yet so tenderly put on it was intoxicating. Together with the champagne and the anomalous storm.

Let Dionysus' grapes enkindle him. Let Zeus's bolts draw his sword.

Beneath her feet, the ebony cat, Montenegra, awaiting scraps she knew would come. No hurry. After-dinner buffets had little appeal now that she dined alone. She bore her loss impassively, giving no outward sign of the emotional havoc their separation had wrought. As a cat, it was incumbent to get over it, which she did not doubt Tiger had done. They might wish their lives otherwise, but the nobility that had impelled them to each other ruled their desires. Meet each day free of expectations: What comes is what must be.

The gem crowning their repast was apple pie but not merely: The recitation, standing, candle-shadowed, of the boldest love sonnet of the Victorian era, from whence the style of her cream velvet harkened, written, apropos tonight, by a woman to her man. Not verse of divine Shelley or eloquent Keats origin, but the gift of Elizabeth Barrett Browning, now gilding the tongue of Lori.

"How do I love thee? Let me count the ways."

Smiling, open-armed, into the mist of his eyes.

> "I love thee to the depth and breadth and height
> My soul can reach, when feeling out of sight
> For the ends of Being and ideal Grace.
> I love thee to the level of every day's
> Most quiet need, by sun and candlelight.
> I love thee freely, as men strive for Right;
> I love thee purely, as they turn from Praise.
> I love thee with a passion put to use
> In my old griefs, and with my childhood's faith."

Plummeting into the final four lines, oblivious to where she headlong landed.

> "I love thee with a love I seemed to lose
> With my lost saints—I love thee with the breath,
> Smiles, tears, of all my life!—and if God choose,
> I shall but love thee better after death."

And he, whelmed brimming, was, this once, the one without words.

Every syllable, every phrase and line, in place: "The whole consort dancing together." The only one she'd learned straight through. Though she had more up her velvet sleeves to gift him if she could figure out how and where to work them in. She'd pieced together sequences to speak for her these last nights marooned in their upstairs bed while Joaquin slept on the couch. He, pilled for pain, drifting off early, left her hours free to converse with poets, secure their words in her mind. She roamed the shelves and desk drawers in the bedroom seeking lines to rouse his passion. Halted by the photo of nine-year-old Joaquin at the Bosque del Apache in New Mexico, a refuge for sandhill cranes. Flocks rose thick behind him, and she, a cavernous stare full on them, could hear, in her shorn childhood recollection, their marshy cries.

Cranes. Often in those younger days she had wished to be one of them, live by their devotion and loyalty, their faith in the migratory route. They evoked the yearning of this loveless girl: to dwell among friends, to belong to one, to have a path leading both ways home. Brecht's "Duet of the Cranes," which Joaquin had read to her senior year (in the original German first), then set to a melody of his own with alternating lines for her to speak, had caught in her throat and stuck there, a pang she cherished and cultivated for its elegiac soar:

He: See there two cranes veer by one with another
She: The clouds they pierce have been their lot together

Joaquin changed Auden's translation to suit himself, and she preferred her man's lines:

He: See yon cranes paired lifelong together
She: What clouds those two as one have weathered

Then, continuing with Auden:

He: Since from their nest and by their lot escorted
She: From one life to a new life they departed.
He: At equal speed with equal miles beneath them
Both: And at each other's side alone we see them…
She: On through sun and moon's only too similar shining,
        In one another lost, they find their power
He: And fly from?
She: Everyone.
He: And bound for where?
She: For nowhere.
Both: So all true lovers are
        True lovers are, true lovers are
He: Do you know what time they have spent together?
She: A short time.
He: And when they will veer asunder?
She: Soon.
Both: So love to lovers keeps eternal noon.

When Joaquin introduced her to YeatsAudenThomasBrechtDickinsonStevensEliot FrostPlathBishopMerwinRichPinskyCollinsHeaneyOliverGlück, she recognized in them an inchoate familiarity of sentiment and circumstance. Disillusioned, bitter, hurled into the cruel abyss of the twentieth century from a chimerical idyll reigned by justice and virtue, their outcry gave voice to hers, though she could not have told you what they or she meant to say. Which is why she worked so hard to memorize their poems, to get it, berated herself for holding only shards that revealed piecemeal truths.

These lines in Glück:

> It has come to seem
> there is no perfect ending.
> Indeed there are infinite endings.
> Or, perhaps, once one begins, there are only endings.

And Eliot:

> At the source of the longest river
> The voice of the hidden waterfall
> And the children in the apple tree
> Not known because not looked for
> But heard, half-heard, in the stillness
> Between two waves of the sea.

And Collins:

> You are always the bread and the knife,
> not to mention the crystal goblet and—somehow—the wine.

They unlocked her bewildered chest, a cavity wherein she wandered dark and nostalgic.

Joaquin, sweet dreamer undeterred by his grim youth, preferred the Romantics, and once you got used to the archaic language, their metered verses with steady rhymes were easier to learn.

Keats:

> Bright star, would I were steadfast as thou art—
> Pillowed upon my fair love's ripening breast,
> To feel forever its soft fall and swell
> Awake forever in a sweet unrest

Or Shelley:

> I have never heard
> Praise of love or wine
> That panted forth a flood of rapture so divine.

Hard not to love as Joaquin himself, with their lofty odes and spirited lyrics, grand epics and soaring elegies. Still inclined she was to recalling chosen fragments, not the whole of their poems, oft of daunting length. He, her darling, spoke and sung them as though they'd sprung from his own breast, glorious. These nineteenth-century kindred verses the surest aphrodisiac.

Hours not devoted to verse she burned through another volume, which he had brought from college and showed her when they began to play with erotic variants for lovemaking: *The Kamasutra*.

Little Lori, RN, made brazen by anxiety, devoured the images, glutting portions of her memory not reserved for rhyme with sinuosity of limb. Fitted herself into the illustrated postures, a pillow simulating Joaquin. Rehearsed alternately sonnets and sex, double essence of arousal for this tryst. Her mission irrevocably set, she did not repudiate her lust, her devious scheme, nor entertain the possibility of failure. Had to trust her wiles, his tender spirit, their love to prevail over his broken body.

Eagerness disguised as adoration, she spread wide her arms in air's embrace.

He, glorying in his fortune, reached his hand toward hers, the easier for her to go to him as though unplanned. The easier for her to rest his head on her velvet, letting their hands stray clasped toward her nether region. To press into him, ripple suggestively but seeming unawares, let the moment's swell his manhood engorge, rise toward the inevitable. He groaned.

"Let me do it, my love. All. You on the sofa, me on you, my happiness to please thee, thy happiness mine. Come, come away."

She to be one crutch, much dearer than the metal one jammed in his pit. Leaning bowerlike upon each other, shuffle-glided toward urgent consummation. Yet not shy of ritual. At sofa-bedside he stood, she disrobed him, caressing each revealed sphere of nakedness as it was bared. Sweater and shirt, his chest, back, neck languidly kissed, sucked, licked; his trousers ankled, she on her knees the good leg fondled as her hand deftly slid the underworn pants off around his swollen member, then gently mouthed, just enough to turn desire to fire.

Laid him on the sofa, stronger than she knew, murmuring, "Teach me half the gladness / That thy brain must know." Looked past the contours of his surface landscape she'd mutilated to the unblemished stratum beneath where true Joaquin abided. Removed socks, slippers, eased off pants, stroked the whole of his body unclothed save for the leg-long cast. He breathing like a soul upon the pleasure rack as she withdrew hand and lips to demolish the alluring fortress of cream velvet.

Wind bansheed the cabin, rattling panes. In the far keep of heaven, bolts seared ionized clouds, which grumble-bellied sought to reclaim their shape. Hurtling the pines, dogged sleet built to a crescendo. A bit early, she chastised her confederate gods, unless uproars are your opening notes. Shook back her curls and willed herself seductive. Button by ribbon by hook uncovering her own treasures, from breast to bush, stepping lithe into the heaven's angled light an easy hand's length from him. Thunder sounded her oncoming as she brushed his flesh with hers and arced her leg high over to mount him.

Or nearly did. An aerial view would have revealed the complexity of achieving intercourse with a broken-legged man in a way her imagined act had failed to do. Nurse

Lori's determination to make love to Joaquin overrode her polished understanding of the human frame. Muscle, sinew, bone, their placement in the anatomy have ne'er been realigned at will. His cast, thigh high, would support not even her slight weight, and its heft immobilized the leg, as indeed it was meant to. She tried to make herself the hypotenuse to his right angle of torso and pelvis, but couldn't situate herself above his erection without endangering the leg. Squatting backward, she facing his feet and he her buttocks, an erotic pose the *Sutra* had commended, deprived them of lip and eye arousal but offered him the carnal spice of seeing her unseen. His hands rose to part her buttocks and expose a fuller view.

Maneuvering quickly, to keep him inflamed, but cautiously to keep him unharmed, aware always of her exigent goal, this its sole probable shot at fulfillment, Lori's own desire vanished. Though she made a great show of hungering for him, body and moan, whilst she guided him in and closed over him. She drew into her, along with him, the power of earthy gods, whose boundless lust fueled her own. Undulated sutra-like to simulate intensifying heat as she slid him deeper in, breath quickening to bring him to a climax before her quiver-arms, unused to upholding her astride, collapsed, or he, still convalescing, did.

A cry, she echoing falsely, and it was done. Deep, deep, as near her womb as she could thrust him, no matter the pain. A blast of thundersleet avalanched the window beyond them, its timing, she mused, right as the celestial conductor brought his baton down. Below the storm's dying voice, Joaquin's, calling her, wanting now, after he feasted on the sight of her nether lips, to press the tonguing ones against his. And she, locking her inner passage tight, loathe to release him, touched his hand, but he was not content. "Come, my love, come lie beside me."

Dismounting then, nimbly and swift, clutching him as he withdrew, she rippled into the narrow edge of the sofa left her. Murmured "Smile on our loves," a line she'd steadfastly prayed to the star of evening. His ardent kissing of her mouth and neck wrested from her at last a true climax, at its height she pulling his sperm upward, closer and closer to the hoped-for union with an egg.

From the abandoned table, a soft munching neither lover heard. Montenegra, pawing the goose carcass for rich morsels, lapping water from their glasses as she wove between candles spilling their golden wax onto the (fortunately not borrowed) cloth. A repast bountiful enough for two.

15

Let Unfold What Will

"**A**in't got a woman in any port
waitin' heart breakin' for me to court."

The flashy redhead slid her breasts across my meager chest, then pranced into a turn, circling under my arm. I swallowed a laugh, which came right back up and erupted, gagging on the distaste I harbored toward strutting to a C&W tune with an overripe floozy.

She dazzled, mistaking my croak for pleasure, and swung toward me, wrapping my arms around her and rubbing her broad, girdled rear against my parts. I shuddered, giving her yet another unintended signal, and she sidled into me nimbly, grabbed my waist with her hand and scooted my arm over her shoulder. Engulfed in a noxious cocktail of suffocating perfume and belched beer, I gave the band a glare: time to wind down their hard-luck, hardly bearable tune. They revved into another stanza.

I'd done some serious dodging to avoid the dance floor in this cavernous Western joint. Met no woman's eye, kept moving from the bar to the bathroom to the shadows to the door, sticking close to the herd like a young wildebeest running from lions. The number of aging solo women here tumbled me back to middle school dances, boys in a protective huddle, girls sidelined by our terror but stalking the lone stray. This was far worse because the women, too hungry to be coy or courteous, were in full pursuit of single bucks. The target of numerous advances, I kept backing up, desperate to melt through the wall, when I found myself flanked by the redhead, who paraded me triumphantly onto the dance floor.

"Them lonely days on the road,
and the hurting nights full a woe—woe, oh yeah,
but no woeman in sight
no love to set things right."

If you judge yourself by how others see you, I'd judge myself a halfwit loser with a rotten disposition. There were far better dance partners at the Cowboy Round-Up this evening, even some charming, non-predatory women like Mamia. I could have asked one of them to dance and had a pleasant, uncomplicated conversation with her, then said goodnight and no more. Maybe it was because of Trove that this place felt so tawdry and stale. Remembering the clean green of my cannabis plants in their loam, the waft of rain coming down the mountains, sun-heated ponderosas, notes of the meadowlark and the thrush, I yearned for Joaquin's porch. But these images led me inexorably to Lori, the reason that world was lost to me, and above all, she, whom I could not conceive of spending much more of my life without.

Frank and my mother sashayed by. They weren't dancing close but with the ease of a couple who knew each other's moves. Unlike scarlet o'hair-a and me. "Fun, yeah?" Mamia winked. I nodded, but where I wanted to be was in bed with Tiger stretched out on my belly. The floozy zipped me toward her for a lascivious belly bump, and I went limp, trying to pass out.

"You okay, hon?" she asked, whirling me around.

"I'm feeling kind of sick. Think I better sit down."

"Aw, you'll be fine, doll. All the guys get a little light in the head when I dance with them." And the band played on.

> "Just need a corner of your heart
> be a good enough place for me to start
> a fool—oh, yeah, a fool for love
> like me to start."

A week after my arrival Mamia had coaxed me to come with them, hear Frank play a set, have a drink, maybe dance. It was not even on the list of things I didn't want to do: off the Alex grid of coordinates ranging from always to never. Frank joined in, the man to whom I had confessed my mortal sins and been absolved by and who had then gone on to treat me like a regular person, a fine new friend, who had brought my mother the first bit of light and kindly love after my father's death. Confronted with their eagerness to show me a good time, I relented and braced myself for a one-off at a C&W joint.

Like his son, Frank was a charismatic musician, his voice honeyed umber, the rich chiaroscuro of tones arcing into the listeners' marrow. He played the guitar like one who'd been born strumming and crafted the pacing of his songs to arouse keen emotional impact. His own melodies wove an intricate spell, but the lyrics, predictable and a tad corny, fell far short of Joaquin's eloquent visions. Still, I could see why Mamia the girl once had a crush on Frank and why the woman cherished his friendship. I wasted an inordinate amount of thought formulating a way to tell Joaquin that his father had become an excellent man whom I admired. Or maybe just tell him that he had nothing to fear from Frank in terms of the land and his drinking. For now. To alcoholics, *now* was the critical measure of success. It would be so much easier to explain about Frank in person—Frank, who would only be around for another week, I reminded myself.

Come on, Bug, try to have a little fun. What happened to your sense of whimsy, you, the ironic master of the universe, who can turn trauma into a joke? Who can argue both sides against his middle? Who would have made a tall tale of this fiasco, exaggerating the horror to get laughs? Where did that guy go? Jousting in senior hall, Bug and Hersch, with ninth graders on their shoulders, devising elaborate excuses (that took twice as long to invent as the homework would have taken to do), adding turgid organs to pictures in sober history texts, sneaking three-course meals into the library, slithering out the window when the Spanish teacher was at the board, dating two girls in one night without either one finding out—and on and on. The guy whose infamous motto was, "It's not due till sixth period." God, I missed him. Where did I leave that cool scofflaw whom almost everyone loved?

Even in college, when I discovered how much I'd missed by not reading Kafka, Ellison, Faulkner, Solzhenitsyn, Vonnegut, García Márquez, T. S. Eliot, and Shakespeare, powering through them on the sly; when writing metamorphosed from chore to euphoria; when learning became my ardent quest in everything from partying to critical analysis; when I learned the art of threading carefree time through my days without compromising my studies. And the freeform trek internationally with los guys, cavorting through bold adventures in our cloaks of youthful invincibility. Home again after college with no plan, waiting tables at the café, light duty that gave me time to cruise: reflect, read, write, and fool around. Not much came of my efforts to write a novel, and my situation felt very temporary even as it drew on, spanning two years of extended adolescence. Bitter restlessness fringed my romps during that time, but never interfered with my sense of play. And destiny, the faith that I was headed somewhere incredible, bound for the laurel wreath. Or I would be as soon as I was launched into action by a peal of significant celestial thunder. The fire that decimated my hometown was not the call I awaited. Murder and mutilation were great material for a great writer but more than I could tackle. Yet.

They did launch me, though, in a convoluted way, by driving me to Trove, where the many loves of my life lay. Despite what I told Mamia about my being finished with the place, that's where I longed to be. Romance, friendship, writing, music, tending the green-growing world: all manner of beauty and virtue were wedded there. While here I, expelled from Eden and humorless, sought to press a new future from the dregs.

I could think of nothing I really wanted to do anymore, except loosen the grip of the crimson-headed floozy now that the last mournful chords of the song were dying a hideous death.

She sighed, way too close to my face. "You danced right off with my heart, loverboy. Now how am I supposed to go on living without it?"

"You got your pick of hearts in this place," I boomed, way too loud. "Me, I've got to mosey on home to the wife and kids. Those twins are an ornery pair."

Her spongy hand made a grab for mine, but with more agility than she'd expected after my performance on the dance floor, I slipped her grip and backed away. "Can't go home smelling too strong of your sweet perfume, now can I?"

"Hey, Polly." Mamia was at my shoulder, Frank behind her. She smiled at the flooz.

"Shelley!" She moved possessively toward me. "Take a look at the young stud I roped."

"Meet my son Alex." Mamia to the rescue. "And I don't believe he's available. We're headed home," she added to me. "Ready to go?" I nodded furiously as Frank handed me my coat.

Polly made a quick recovery. "Y'all's son? No wonder he's such a looker," she smirked. "Who's the lucky lady that got a ring on him?" She glanced pointedly at my ringless finger.

"Let's get out of here," I muttered, taking Mamia by the arm.

Slumped in the back, eyes closed, while they talked, I thought about what it would be like when I was in driver's seat after Frank left next week. Who and how would I be with Mamia? What was I going to do if I stayed around? Not many other options on the horizon. The glamor had worn off beach-bumming in southern California, so far from Trove. Lori. I didn't want to commit to anything too permanent, in the Ville or elsewhere, in case somehow I was granted a pardon to return to my true home. Had she told Joaquin what happened? No more than I would, neither of us willing to risk losing a man we loved—deeply, in different ways.

Frank's departure, on a bleak February morning, wind-seeded snow threatening, left Mamia and me adrift. I grabbed Tiger and retreated to my bedroom, fighting to quell the uncertainty that shrouded the day. How alone my mother had been before he came: abandoned by her lousy son who was too saturated with guilt to mourn with her; left to care for and later bury her husband's aunt. My mother who went on with no assurance that her future held relief from sorrow. Yet she did not reproach me nor insinuate I had anything to apologize for. Instead, she wrote, opened her soul wide to enfold me, dead or alive. And as the second winter of loneliness veiled her, an unlikely reunion with Frank breached the dark fabric and restored to her a crepuscular happiness. Even that spindly light I resented, punishing the one who had embraced me. Now the source of good cheer was gone and I the cause of misery dwelled with her, ye persistent albatross reminding her not to enjoy life.

Frank had invited her to visit him in LA. She'd perked a smile, then hesitated, glancing at me. Rather than encouraging her to go, I raised a deformed brow and shrugged. "You, too, Alex," Frank, being far too nice, proposed. "LA's a great town. You'll like it. Lots to do. Surfing, clubbing, music, whatever floats your boat. A laid-back place but hopping. Hey, Tiger can clean up at the beach, digging clams and crabs and all." There it was, a shot at one of my dreams, plattered and served with the man's characteristic gusto.

"Sounds good," I mumbled noncommittally.

"We'll stay in touch, won't we, Shelley? I'll send dates and hope you make it. And at some point I'm bound to be back through here. It's been so good to spend time with you, both of you." He hugged her the way a good friend does, close and tight with no lecherous undercurrents. Same way he hugged me, same sentiment, delivered with a sincere welcome to call or write whenever I wanted and a friendly admonition to stop tormenting myself and have some fun. He left and the Sulkmeister fled to his room. So he wouldn't have to comfort his mother. Pathetic. Swinging up and out of bed, I got dressed, grabbed Tige, and resoluted into the kitchen, where Mamia was finishing the breakfast dishes.

I gave myself a month to learn how to be a good son. Emerged no paragon, but passable, C+, maybe B- range: a dutiful fellow whose heart wasn't strong enough to validate his efforts. She was an easy grader and ranked my efforts much higher than they deserved to be. When I made her tea and we sat and talked for an hour, she was elated. When I made dinner (which, if you remember, I did nearly every night at Joaquin's), she flooded me with compliments. Likewise shopping, cleaning, helping out with little stuff like changing the bulbs in ceiling lights. With nothing else to do, I was gratified to find uses for my time. Couldn't get interested in writing and only sporadically in reading. Between chores and errands and surprise treats for Mamia, I knew myself to be in suspended animation, waiting for my life to change.

In the beginning she trod cautiously on inquiries about my plans but realized as the month doddered by that she needn't because I didn't have any. Only then, and in a casual way, did she begin to make a case for her old dream of my becoming a teacher. "You were so happy and successful in high school. I think you'd be an inspiration teaching English to kids that age." Didn't laugh, didn't choke, didn't scream. The good son. She emailed me information on a local alternative teacher certification program that relied as much on interning in a classroom as on taking courses. But she refrained from pushing her agenda with follow-up questions or suggestions. Took a different tack, apologizing for trying to rush me out into the world. I should spend as long as I needed recovering, and if I felt up to it, maybe the two of us could take a trip together. Start in LA but go on to Hawaii, then into the South Pacific. Fiji, Bali, who knew, we might even fly over to New Zealand and Australia. We had time and money: why not spend it on a grand adventure that would give us both exciting new experiences and perspectives to revel in. She had me at Hawaii, but the subtextual core of my brain, which was a close replica of hers, knew that she was offering this bait as a means of getting me to figure out what to do instead. She, too, was waiting for my life to change. Neither of us acknowledged this shared understanding but talked avidly about our route and destinations. In the meanwhile, as the snow gave way to young greens, I was recovering my health and strength, unconsciously getting in shape for a journey of my own devising.

The postman came early to Mamia's house, often before I'd shuffled into the kitchen for coffee. It shouldn't have mattered when the mail arrived since none of it was for me, but I couldn't stop hoping. This morning, unseasonably warm like April in March, for the first time I walked past the pile without looking. Had decided on a course of action that night, in and out of sleep: a purpose and direction that I grasped as worthwhile.

"Good morning, sweetheart. Did you see the letters for you?" Mamia smiled, her ready hug my welcome to the day.

Two of them: one from Joaquin, one from Lori, separate envelopes, both mailed from Trove. Tear them open and race through them? Or keep them for later, savoring the anticipation? Though they might both be ugly condemnations, extinguishing any chance of homecoming. I slid them into the pocket of my robe and took the cup Mamia offered me. Studied the headlines of the local paper as if they held critical information: "Homicide Suspect Arrested"; "Charges Filed Against City Clerk"; "Teachers' Union Calls for Strike"; "More Winter Weather on the Way."

The longer I waited, the less important the contents of the letters became. I had resigned myself to whatever. Only the fact that they were not sent as one interested me by midafternoon when, resting in my bed with Tiger sprawled on my stomach, my fingers worked the edges of Joaquin's envelope. His would be first, I had decided; he had less cause for venomous recriminations.

It was warm, in fact, though brief, scrawled in seeming haste. Simply an update on his condition, a hope that I was well, an assurance that he missed me alongside a wish that I had not left so abruptly (okay, a slight reproof there) but of course coupled with his understanding of my mother's need for me. One paragraph, lines widely spaced to fill the front side of a page, and signed "Ever your friend, Joaquin." He didn't invite me back outright, but he didn't close the door on that possibility, either. No bridges burned. As I folded it back up, a PS on the other side soared me: "I'm working on a new song and need a line:

> 'Gentle friends who pass within my mind
> Have you seen the golden winds below timberline?
> Time after time
> dee-dee deeee dee dah…'"

An open hand extended to grasp mine.

Emboldened by his words, I tore apart Lori's envelope. Even shorter, likely written at the post office without Joaquin's knowledge when she was mailing his, it was an unadorned apology for evicting me from Joaquin's—twice—and a somewhat grudging recognition that Trove was as much my home as hers. The last two of the four sentences she wrote were the key to her missive: "Joaquin and I are expecting a baby. We're so in love."

A baby. *When* she didn't say. Hard not to wonder whether our illicit night might have been procreative. If it had happened then, she'd be about ten weeks along. October. Joaquin had written nothing about Lori being pregnant. He had to know. Maybe she'd conceived earlier, like in December. But the fetus surviving that New Year's Eve crash, not good odds. And Joaquin could hardly have been in lovemaking mode with his leg in a thigh-high cast. I was possessed by an unequivocal certainty, rereading the words, that it was mine, and that's why she'd told me. But how to get a message to her privately: Am I the father of this child? No way other than in person. And why would she tell me? Well, if the kid looked like me.

I awoke from a dream that night holding the image of an immense flower with a single, circular, indigo petal. As I watched, it opened, revealing another, crimson. That one gave to azure, which flared wide to expose orange, to turquoise, to gold, to ivory, to crystal, which I could nearly see through, for I stood at the center, naked. The grandeur ringing me blazed my eyes. Slowly, with great care, I caressed a petal. At my touch it withered. Another. And another. "Stop," I cried. "Listen to me! You're mine!" Several shriveled. I stood rigid, ashamed, then subdued: Let unfold what will. Do nothing but behold with humility. Be still.

Divine guidance or wishful thinking? Who knows the source of visions from the dark side of the mind, emanating from an unfulfilled yearning to dwell at the heart of beauty enraptured? I grappled with the ethereal as petals fell away and I was left, exposed:

so much to say and none to hear me. Yet whatever I wanted to tell them fled with the mirage.

The problem with the Zen-like commands the image delivered is that none of them meshed with my plans. Though their counsel may have been worth heeding given the chaos that doing things my way had wrought, I had no patience for complying. It was time to get on with my life, an impetus I acted on the next morning.

One of the local community colleges offered courses in a program called TESOL, teaching English as a second language, which would enable me to apply for jobs in foreign countries. Yes, it meant teaching simple language and grammar, not literature, but it would put me far enough away to dim the temptation of returning to Trove. An easy out and an appealing one. I could sign on as a substitute teacher at high schools here, while taking TESOL classes, to get my bearings in the classroom (and to see whether I could stand it). Subs were in high demand, as the classifieds indicated, qualifications as minimal as the pay. Mamia could travel with me to wherever I was hired so she'd have a piece of that trip she seemed keen on. I wouldn't mind teaching on a South Pacific island. Maybe they'd have an American school and I could get a real job there. Lots of research to do and plenty of time to do it. A man without a schedule in no hurry.

Before heading into the kitchen for coffee and a meaty conversation about my prospects, I typed a short reply to Joaquin. "Great to hear from you. I hope you're healing well. So sorry I left you in a lurch with the greenhouse care, but you're right: my mother needs me. And it's time for me to get on with my life, much as I'd like to keep feeding off your dreams, which nourished me through a rough time. We're going to be traveling, pretty soon, my mother and I, and hard to reach except by email. I'll send a postcard or two along the way. Greetings to Lori." There I paused, not on Lori so much as on what I'd planned to say next: "and from Tiger to Montenegra." What about Tiger on our world trip? I'd never leave him behind, but what kind of a life would it be for him, crated on the plane, then confined to a hotel room if we could even find a cat-friendly one? Quarantined at Customs? Lori would think of that, too, and offer to take Tiger back. I deleted our travel plans. We'd figure it out. The less said the better to them. Signed it "Your grateful friend who also misses you" and added my own PS, an inspiration of the moment: "Time after time / calling me to pine."

Regrouping, for the sake of T, I announced to an elated Mamia that I was going to look into her alternative licensure program (and sub as I took classes, my own idea). At the same time, I'd check out American schools in other countries where cats were welcome, Europe more likely than elsewhere. What if I went to Germany and honored my heritage by becoming fluent, marrying a German girl, having bilingual kids with dual citizenship and a home in each land? The possibility of adventures zipped up my spine, fortifying it. A man on the move.

Which is how I ended up in a twelfth-grade classroom at a modest charter high school in the burbs. First to hit me was the scent of teen glands gone wild, a familiar odor from days of old, much less noxious then. Cinder block walls abutted low-hung acoustical tiles; the windows looked just right for an old Western shoot-out, an observation I unthought instantly so as not to put it out to stray psychopaths loitering in the schoolyard. The room's regular teacher, Mr. McKee, was a slob, his refuse strewn across the desk and bookshelves. Dregs congealing in a toxic mug, empty soda cans, half-eaten sweet-roll, dead plant, a crust of filth on every surface. The center drawer stuck, the side one squealed, and neither held a pen or marker. On the floor, under desks, and near the overflowing garbage bin lay wads of used Kleenex and paper. With kids' backpacks hunched in the aisles or on their desks, the place had the transient feel of a bus station waiting room whose occupants were on stand-by. My eyes roved this mess as I handed out quizzes and scrambled to quell my panic at spending the day imprisoned in it.

The students were recognizably bored, lamentably passive, utterly immersed in adolescence. I picked out Hersch, Joey, Beandog, Spanky, and Blip, but no alas no Rose or Vincent, and withheld judgment on which one was me till deeper into the class. They were meant to be discussing a short story, "Upstream," none had read—well, one boy, George, had (definitely not the me), a kid I soon learned had gotten into the Air Force Academy, an achievement that motivated him to excel. After the quiz (for a banal, transparent story that I read as they failed) and a fruitless attempt at discussion that was simply an exchange between Boy George and me, I shifted gears.

"So, what do you guys do for fun around here?" A good question for teens anywhere outside of glam cities, although the answer is a predictable "Nothing." However, asking it showed them I was ready to blow off the academic portion of today's learning. They lifted their heads, focused.

"You new in town?" Beandog countered.

"I am. Living in my deceased great-aunt's house with my mother since the family home and my rental burned down."

"Is that how you got hurt?" Blip plunged in. Of course that's what they'd really want to hear about, and knowing my audience, I accelerated into an heroic tale without any hesitation.

"So, yeah. I lived through the fire in Vista Grande three years ago. The one that took out most of the town." Dramatic pause. "Killed my dad when my folks' house burned to the ground. Our old dog, too" (a heartstring-puller for teens who loved their pets more than their parents). "I tried to save them, but—" I shrugged, indicating my scars. Riveted.

"Lost my best friend in the fire. He looked kind of like you." I nodded at a kid in the back, who popped out red. "It was a wicked blaze. Middle of the night. Ate through the town like a demon monster. Any of you ever been in a fire?" I narrowed my gaze at a pair of disbelievers near the window. Heads shook. No one spoke. "It's like getting thrown into hell. You're cruising along, everything's cool, go to bed one night, and wake up to smoke, alarms, people screaming, trying to get out with some of your most valuable stuff. My worthless junker car wouldn't start, never did when I needed it, got a ride through the flames with an ex-con. My neighborhood was on fire as we pulled out. Smoke so thick we couldn't see headlights of other cars till we were on top of them. It was a death trip. By the time we got to my folks' house, where I grew up, it was almost gone. I ran in to save—already told you that part."

I paused again, leaned on the white board, legs apart, head back. Now that I had them, I could take my time, let the story swell with tributaries as it meandered through the fertile vale of their desire for thrills.

"I hear they've started to rebuild Vista Grande again, but I'll never go back. For me it'd be like walking into an open grave." I started pacing, erratically.

"I was out for a long time, months, healing the burns. Didn't come to till spring. Then I took off. Thought I might go to the coast, bum around Venice, Long Beach, somewhere with lots of water like an ocean." A few titters, as I'd hoped. "Stopped along the way in the mountains to help a friend finish his place and stayed on to work in his cannabis greenhouse. Best weed you've ever tasted." I grinned. "Great painkiller." But of course they all knew that; several of them, I saw now, were not so much rapt as profoundly stoned.

"I'm writing a novel about the fire," I went on, spinning my facile lies. "Got a connection with an East Coast editor who'll help me get it published. It's going to be big, totally awesome movie material. And of course a fat lot better to watch on screen than to live through—for those of us who were lucky enough to make it." A solemn pause and a choked cough, underscoring how hard it was for me to talk about this.

"One super thing: my woman was in Scotland, still is, working on her PhD dissertation, so she's fine. We'll get married when she comes back next year. Childhood sweetheart. We went from preschool through high school together. So, like, she knows me from way before the scars, when I was a swaggering dude. Hard to picture, but I was a player back then, pretty cute, the kind of cool bro you would have gone for"—tapping a front-row blonde on the head. She cringed, then giggled. I winked. Laughter skittered. I stepped back. "And my woman, she's beautiful, star quality, and incredibly smart. Harvard grad."

"Is that where you went to college?"

Snort. "Nah. I had way too much fun in high school. Didn't get serious till second year of college. Here's the deal, kids, and I'm not fooling with you: Seize the day. You heard that? Saul Bellow said it first. Seize the damn day. It means enjoy being young while you are. Make it good. Don't waste your youth getting hung up on school and other stuff or griping and wishing you were an adult or a child again. You've got a choice between souring out and making the worst of things or having a blast, which is the road I took and the one I'd recommend. Your call, but don't blow too much time deciding because it's over real quick. Take it from El Hombre del Fuego."

Five minutes left and I was hardly warmed up. Exploits from my storied high school and college days flooded my mind. Post-college travels with Hersch. I'd keep that dude alive—more: make a giant of him. Could have reeled out some recent tales, like that of the murderer I overpowered in the greenhouse. But I held off, won their allegiance with a parting kindness.

"So if I tell you what this story nobody but George read is about, will you keep quiet about my doing it? George?"

"Of course." His response unanimously affirmed.

"Here's the gist: Boy discovers he's adopted, runs away, upstream, saves a kid from drowning, figures out he's the kid and his adoptive parents saved him like he did this kid. Theme: self-discovery, with a dash of salvation thrown in. What's due tomorrow?"

"We're going to keep discussing this story and write on it in class, as always."

"Wow. Okay. Good luck, y'all." I saluted them.

They were pokey getting out the door, pulling their stuff together in slow motion.

"This was the best class I've had in a long time. Thank you."

"Yeah, you gave me a lot to think about, Mr. Mann."

"Seize the day. Make a good tat for my arm."

"You're The Man. El Hombre del Fuego."

"Thought with the scars you were a vet. We've got a lot of them in this town. Your story's way cooler."

"Hope you come back. It'd be so great to have you for a teacher."

"I think you're still pretty cute."

"Thank you, Mr. Mann."

Brilliant! I'd hit my stride in the first class of my first day of teaching. I'd be a rock star before the week was out. Except McKee came back and the next class I subbed for at a different school was very well prepared and discursive. They hardly needed me once I'd taken roll. Still, I knew now that not only could I do it, but I was a natural-born high school teacher. The classroom, stinky, drab, restive, would be the stage on which I'd play the lead.

The courses in my alternative licensure program were a cakewalk after my serious academic pursuits at UNM. Their value arose from providing common ground to relate to experiences in the field. In a district hamstrung by the scarcity of instructors, several students were already teaching on waivers and brought in problems of the day for us to dissect. It was the best kind of education for a novice; my untested confidence grew, feeding my impatience to begin. May lobbed that opportunity into my court.

McKee was undergoing emergency surgery and would be out the last three weeks of the year. His senior sections had clamored for me to return as their sub—small wonder given my golden day with them. I was hired as a long-term sub rather than a replacement teacher, which is to say, cheaply: fine. I was in. Bye-bye, McKee, I thought-sang, your realm is mine now and forever.

That weekend Mamia and I went in armed with cleaning materials and a vacuum, spent three hours making the room tolerable. Threw two large garbage bags full of disgust into a can at the rear of the building. It wasn't a showroom when we finished, but I'd laid claim to the space in the process. My final act, a clear declaration of revolution, was to move the desks out of rows and into a circle—albeit a big one, but far more amenable to honest, animated conversation. I had newbie status on my side if I got in trouble.

Imagine, if you will, the classic homecoming of a legendary warrior whose courage, might, tenacity, and skill have vanquished the enemy: not an altogether exact analogy but that's what I felt entering the classroom (a theatrically late entrance) the following Monday. Not only cheers and applause, but a standing o, caps in the air, yeah, even hugs from the least fettered of the crew. Here's what you can't fully imagine, even if you will: what that greeting did to and for me. I've had some exceptional orgasms in my time, but this surpassed them all in terms of sheer ecstasy. I grinned and grinned, bowed, called in vain (to my delight) for them to quiet down. They were talking over one another, all about how they insisted on my coming back and how cool was the circle and like, what had I already done to this trashy room, and I was the greatest teacher they'd ever had and now they had something to look forward to besides the end of school. More than the end, even. Forget warrior: I was a god.

Three weeks in May of senior year is no time to get into heavy work mode, but that's what McKee had planned. They were to read *Crime and Punishment*, a tome that George himself was balking at. A dreary way to punctuate their high school careers, and I immediately freed them of that burden, promising once again to summarize the novel and let them sparknote it in further detail for the standard final exam, which I'd be required to give—but then, I'd be the one grading it, too, I assured them. No hard-ass, I, not in May with these adoring fans, who quickly spread the word so that subsequent sections were jubilant upon arrival.

Apart from indulging in plenty of story time, outdoor lazy classes, a field trip (aka, creative writing exercise) to the nearby breakfast burrito café, I did have a novel in mind to share with them but knew I'd have to buy it myself and swear them to secrecy about reading it. At least initially, until I ferreted out the limits of the approved curriculum, which looked stunningly dull from what I could uncover. I decided to get the book first, make it a surprise they knew was coming, let the anticipation grow, and then bingo, bring it in, each copy in a brown paper bag to emphasize its illicit and racy contents. What would they find, pulling it out? Hunter S. Thompson's wacky, maniacal *Fear and Loathing in Las Vegas*. Drugs, sex, rock and roll. Even for pot-smokers who consumed impressive amounts of cannabis, the range and quantity of drugs in this depraved saga would knock them sideways. A few of them would have seen the movie, but reading and discussing the book was irresistible fun. Thompson and I would sneak tidbits of sophisticated cultural and political knowledge into their unsuspecting minds along the way.

Friday: copies procured second-day air and bagged, I stood beaming pierce-eye rays at the class until a profound, explosive silence froze the room. Among the many things that amazed me, about myself, about teaching, is that facing these kids, I was not conscious of my scars. They were part of who I was, a man whose distinctive persona the kids loved. Their acceptance became mine. They became mine. My moods, my whims, my passions were theirs. I could lead them because I could read them (my private aphorism).

This morning I was in total Hunter mode and regalia: bright Hawaiian shirt, ridiculous safari jacket, hat, and shorts, hiking boots, dark glasses, cigarette holder. Ray-bombing them, I thought someone would recognize the gear and call me out, but no: a circle of stares, enthralled, watched to see what I'd do next.

I strode the perimeter, muttering, then leaped onto the desk, waving my arms, shouting, "We can't stop here. This is bat country," and ducked. Held the crouch for the count of five, then straightened, swinging my finger around the circle at each of them. "Anybody? It's a line from? Hello? Buehler? Buehler?" Yep, times were not what they were.

Indeed, they examined the bagged books I handed them like the relics from a lost culture that they'd become. A few had indeed seen the movie and recognized the title, but even they didn't know it was made from a book. So not bat country but terra incognita. In fluent Hunter S. Thompson (which I'd spent nights learning in high school), I read the opening chapters to them, sidetracking to explain the premise. Got them to when the doctor of journalism and his attorney threatened to tear out and eat the lungs of a scag baron, at which point they were hooked. For added incentive, I finished with, "No quizzes on this one. Read it for the sheer magnitude of Thompson's savage journey to the heart of the American dream. And remember, keep it in the bag and don't tell anyone I gave it to you—unless you want a new sub in here next week."

"When's it due?" George, pen poised.

"You tell me," I fired back.

"Monday!" Beandog yelled enthusiastically.

"Or whenever we're done reading it," proposed Hersch Junior, true to his forebear.

"I say we all try for Monday," Beandog insisted. "It's not like we're doing anything else."

Nods and murmurs of assent. I would have given them a week.

I stayed on schedule with *Crime and Punishment*, summarizing the chapters they should have been reading daily. Made sure they kept lists of characters, themes, symbols, and related literary elements that would come in useful for the final. A crisp ten-minute jog at the start of class that they hung in for, aware of all they weren't having to suffer on account of my largesse. Then we'd get into the real stuff: arguments over the choice and quality of drugs, cars, Las Vegas acts. I'd pull over on the shoulder of certain passages to dive into meatier discussions, such as on page 18, "How can their journey be described as an 'affirmation of all that is right and true and decent in the national character'?" Or echoing Thompson's question, "But what *is* sane?" And "Do you believe that 'somebody—or at least some force—is tending that Light at the end of tunnel,' as he says on page 179?"

The kids especially liked skipping around in the novel, talking about whatever caught their attention, letting that topic lead to another. It was, as they noted and I already knew, like having a real conversation instead of a contrived discussion with pre-designated questions. I was always in the mix but not obtrusively, let the ball pass naturally into my hands. Until one of them casually mentioned that he'd gotten a little lost on page 73 when Raoul Duke is reading the newspaper before escaping the hotel, and his comment launched my first rant.

"What Thompson is comparing here are the atrocities of the Vietnam War—outrageous torture and racist murders of our so-called enemies, denigrated as 'slopes,' brutal crimes that were never punished, comparing all these horrors with the five-year prison sentence given to the greatest boxer of all time, Muhammad Ali, for refusing to kill 'slopes.' The injustice of that punishment validates Thompson's destruction and deceit:

why bother playing fair in a country so lacking in humanity? Given those headlines, his cynicism is justifiable.

"On top of that Ali was a black man, their favorite color to imprison, and his being a celebrity made it all the better and being a great, big, intensely strong man better yet. They could get good press mileage out of jailing him, like, nobody goes free if you don't go into the service when you're called, and get some good work out of him to boot. Prisoners are the current slave labor force, working for a quarter an hour at whatever job the wardens choose to give them. It's an industry, just like they say, mostly run by private corporations. Got to fill the beds to make money and got to get work done for token pay to fatten their profit margin. It's the new Jim Crow—a new form of legalized slavery.

"When I was a senior in a Vista Grande high school, not that long ago, we used to take a field trip to the state penitentiary in the spring. The year I went they let us walk into a solitary confinement cell, and it was like being trapped in an animal cage. Designed for breakdown. I would have gone nuts in there in a day. Then I thought about night, everything pitch black, and how lonely I'd get. It broke my spirit just imagining the terror and dehumanization of that kind of un-life. The inmates had one hour outside, in an exercise cage, on weekdays. They took us to the death house, where the last prisoner was executed, IV still set up, clock stopped at twelve, and after we saw solitary, I could see why the guy volunteered to die, meaning he stopped the appeals process. You're dead either way, slow or fast, and there's no way out of the pain. Oh, they try to indoctrinate the prisoners with religion: great audience, very receptive, but what a fraudulent way to recruit believers, hauling the hopeless into your ranks."

I paused, just long enough for a breath. "The question not yet conceived when Thompson wrote this is whether five years in prison is worse than five years at war. What's the relative PTSD rate for one versus the other? Who has a better shot at a life, coming out of that scene? It's a bust, either way. You guys, have you had to register with the selective service already?"

Of course they had. "Just a piece of brotherly advice: have a back-up plan."

The air had grown heavier, as though it bore rain. I knew I'd been talking too much, too long, in a vein too dark to leave open. But the kids' confusion had touched a nerve for me, though I hadn't realized it, because Hersch's uncle almost died to save himself from being drafted and then killed in Vietnam. He used to get frothy telling us stories about those days.

"My best friend, the one I lost in the fire, his uncle was drafted to fight in Vietnam. The draft back then was a numbers game: you were assigned a number at random (so they claimed), and when it came up, you had to report to the nearest draft office to see if you were fit, and if you were, off you went to basic training and from there into the jungle to fight a war with no good reason why. It wasn't like a Hitler ruled Nam; all our government had was this domino theory of Communism taking over the world. And what they really were after was a way of boosting the military-industrial complex that churns out overpriced weapons of destruction.

"When Uncle Will's number came up, he wished he could take off for Canada, where lots of young men found refuge, but he had family obligations that held him back. He also had a very sure premonition that he would die in Vietnam if he went, and he couldn't fathom a more meaningless death. Not one to put his neck meekly through the noose, he headed into the draft office with a desperate plan, which worked out differently than he'd intended though in some ways was even punchier. He took a razor with him, and he meant to slit his wrists with the recruiter sitting there, watching him. But the recruiter left the room, left him for a good while by himself, and he got restless and slit them then, bled all over the asshole's desk, who, when he came back, called 911 and gave my bud's uncle a 4F, which means unfit to serve. But to have to attempt suicide to free yourself. Why is this a culture that breeds and rewards so much violence in young men and then jails them for practicing it? So a second piece of advice and then I'm done: Keep your eyes open and a friend at your side.

"Hey, class is over. Wow, I really got on a rant, you all. Kind of a downer. Sorry."

George came up to me as they filed out, mostly quiet. "I learned more in the last twenty minutes than I have in all my years of school," he told me, sincerely. "Thank you." He walked to the door, turned back. "I know you think I'm insane to join the air force, but it's a free education and a terrific one. And I've always wanted to learn to fly. It's really a good deal for my family."

That was the part I left out, the way the military kept itself going on poor-kid volunteers: the rampant economic disparity in this country. Didn't work back in the 60s or even the 90s when those on the bottom rungs had alternatives. But all of this sad, heartless century it kept the maw of war glutted with hapless bodies.

"I don't think anything, George. You'll be great whatever you do. They're damn lucky to have you." I high-fived his grateful hand.

"Keep ranting, Mann," Beandog called from the doorway. "We love ya!"

They did. And I them. It was the fulfillment of a dream I hadn't even dreamed. I swore to use this unexpected gift with care, to sustain it, let it multiply and go forth, as the Hebrew god commanded Adam. Was I the created or the creator? Who had been made in whose image? I mused, and striding headily to the teachers' lounge, decided: both.

The last week was a wild ride, beginning Monday with an unprecedented snowstorm. Late May, lilacs in full bloom, baby fruit on the trees. A foot of the white stuff that melted in the spring sun by noon but nonetheless spawned a snow day. It was a miracle, for which my students credited me, and I accepted their accolades with exaggerated pomp. Global warming was of course the true cause, and we should have mourned this further proof of the chaos to come, but being remarkably short-sighted humans, we celebrated our Snow Day in May rather than grieving the end times that loomed.

Friday was laden with year-end festivities: a bacchanalia before exams, climaxing with the debut of the all-mighty yearbook. In contrast with Monday, the weather was ideal for romp-and-gambol. Sitting on the athletic field signing books for my kids, I granted myself the freedom to be one of them, wrote playful and flippant and ridiculous things, all lines from *Fear and Loathing* I knew by heart. A bit impersonal but clever approach,

I thought, and quick. "Never cross the Great Magnet." "Do it right; remember Horatio Alger." "It seems entirely reasonable to think that now and then the energy of a whole generation comes together in a long fine flash." "Hang on to that fantastic universal sense that whatever we're doing is right." "We had all the momentum." "We were riding the crest of a high and beautiful wave." "Indeed. But what is sane?" "Good god! You just backed over that two-foot concrete abutment and you didn't even slow down!" Later I was sorry when I read theirs: heartfelt and devoted outpourings of admiration, effusive promises never to forget me, and honest hopes that they could be like me someday. Very personal, warm farewells that still moved me when I read them years later.

On my way to the lounge to collect my stuff that blissful afternoon the principal, Morris Wright, asked me to stop by his office. Could have been anything but I was not concerned. Hadn't I come in during the last inning of senior year and scored a major victory? Whether or not he knew it, the kids and I did, and we were the ones being educated, the reason this whole system existed. If someone had ratted out my deviation from the prescribed curriculum, so what? But far from chastising me, Morris invited me to return in the fall, teaching English full-time to the seniors on a waiver while I completed my licensure requirements. He'd been besieged by requests to hire me. McKee would not be returning. Yes, yes, yes. Ecstatic, I agreed before we'd even discussed salary. I'd done it, become a teacher by being myself, bold and unabashed. Broken the rules but taught truths. Mamia had been right, and now she, too, would be liberated by my success to do as she pleased, once she discovered what that was. I floored Pacman 2 driving home, zoomed up over the 25-mile speed limit by exuberant force of foot.

The final exam I gave was breathtakingly easy, in part due to McKee's limited imagination (or indifference) and my alternative approach to learning. He asked, "On a scale of 1–10, how well does Raskolnikov's punishment fit his crime?" And "Explore a major theme that connects this novel to our previous readings this semester." That's one you could use annually no matter what you were teaching. My question was, "What is the American Dream in Thompson's novel (written in 1971)? Use specifics from the book to develop and defend your position. Then explain what the American Dream is now in your view."

Since McKee kept terrible records, which Morris verified, I graded the kids on the last three weeks and the final only: all A's. Felt like Raoul Duke himself, screwing the system. Wouldn't get away with that again, but just once was so sweet.

At prom the following Saturday, a cluster of my kids had gathered around me. I thanked them for their gracious words in my yearbook, and they thanked me for their A's—the first some of them had ever made in English. What a tight-cheeked culture we are, doling out scarcity with self-righteous sadism. The Founding Fathers would never have heard of grades, and here we treated them like received wisdom from the divine. Yes, I did say some of that.

"Mann, I love that we never know what's going to come out of your mouth."

"I came to school these last weeks just to see what you were going to do or say. It's amazing to have a teacher who's not, like, totally predictable."

"But totally smart. And willing to put it all out there. You're a wise Mann."

Basking in their adulation, I couldn't help sharing the news about next year with them. Hands slapped and clapped, congratulations flowed. They bemoaned their leaving just as the greatest teacher ever arrived: why does the best stuff always happen after we graduate? (I recalled saying the same thing my senior year but shrugged benignly instead of telling them that.)

"I wish you could get a job at my college."

"Thanks, but I've got a job to do here. Whole new bunch of eyes to open."

"Have you met the juniors? They don't deserve you, Mann, no way. A snarky bunch of deadbeats."

"It would be such a rush to have you again."

"Oh man, yeah, like a miracle. I'd even major in English."

"I thought you were planning to anyway, Dune."

"He just said that to make you love him."

"This way, kids, you get to come back and visit me. Give those deadbeat seniors I'll be teaching your sage advice about college. Show them the road ahead. Maybe teach a class with me."

"Want to dance, Mann?" Beandog (aka Melanie) of course. She grabbed me and there where I'd never wanted to be again I was, but this time with a hot teen shaking her booty at me to a killer beat. I grinned at the upheld phones of my groupies and strutted into the undulating horde.

At graduation, Sonora, the luscious blonde I'd embarrassed the first day, hugged me. "You rock my world, Teacherman. You're the heart at the heart of it." She'd been quieter than most of the others during this year-end love fest, which I thought was due to my inept start with her, but not. The scent of the roses she was carrying trailed me as I hand-shook my way through the festive scene.

One last look around the classroom, all alone. Even after the cleanup it was shabby and plain. With Mamia's help, I could get some more color into it this summer, bring in some plants and funky posters for the walls. Spiff it up a bit. But the key to its beauty was the kids, their thinking and laughter, triumphs and struggles: all the moments that transpired within the barren cinderblocks. It was weird to feel bereft. Never had I greeted the summer with ambivalence; never had I been impatient for school to begin again. Strange, how my aimless quest to escape from the longing to return to Eden had led me to the discovery of paradise: a place where I belonged. Rejuvenated, transported to a timeless realm where my companions were always eighteen, I could revel in the illusion of eternal youth. Sure, that might be harder when I was fifty, but I had decades to go before decrepitude.

Spiraling around the circle of desks to the middle, it struck me that this was clearly the place to be, at the heart not the head of the class. I had gone there instinctively and been enormously successful, but next fall I would do it consciously: Lead from the center.

16

"So Quick Bright Things
Come to Confusion"

"**X!** I am on the lam. In Scandinavia, the exact location to remain undisclosed even to you, my one true friend."

Friend, not love. But nonetheless tantalizing. Her baroque script on the envelope had been immediately recognizable, but Mamia had pointed out that there was no return address. Since it appeared unlikely that Rose's missive held a confession of her eternal desire for me, I decided to read it aloud to Mamia, who was watching me as she dried the lunch dishes. She had, after all, known Rose as long as I had and stayed in touch with her during my comatose months.

I skipped the salutation since with Rosie alone had I shared my secret name, X.

"I am on the lam.

"In Scandinavia, the exact location to remain undisclosed even to you, my one true friend."

"You two have been so close since childhood. Perhaps someday you'll end up together," Mamia commented, reiterating my nigh-forsaken hope.

"I've long feared I would have to go underground, but I thought it would be to evade my domineering mother Katherine, not a suitor. He was the perfect man for me to wed, and I had to run for my life. My life: that possessive pronoun is key, for it would have been forfeit had I succumbed to the wishes of Mr. Very Right, shored up by dear Lady Fiona. She, till now my closest ally in the clan, was already preparing the engagement announcement. Now she will surely never speak to me again."

"Intrigue and ignominy! Rosie always was my favorite storyteller." Mamia had left off drying and taken a seat across from me at the kitchen table.

"What prompted me to hazard this vertiginous fall from grace was the disparity between duty and passion: too much of the former and not enough of the latter, on my part. He, on the other hand, was love-struck. That knowledge and the cowardice of my flight do weigh sorely on my conscience. But nonetheless, I am glad to have escaped what would have been a dreadful union, though from my previous missive, when our wedding seemed a likely prospect, you'd have no reason to think so."

But I will think so because you didn't marry this dream guy. Friendship is a type of love, and liking each other seems a promising route toward loving. Just two letters off, ironically. Maybe I could try that joke on Rosie the next time I proposed to her.

"Alex, the suspense is killing me."

"It's been several months since I wrote, so I can't quite recall how much I told you about Bruce McLellan, the über-handsome, brilliant professor of medieval literature I came to know when I entered Cambridge for graduate studies last fall. Introduced to me by Aunt Fiona, Bruce began escorting me everywhere and proved to be a gracious gentleman. Though he is nearly twice my age, we seemed ideally suited to each other. He was smitten with me, and I, flattered and dazed, thought myself wildly in love with him. At Christmas he began seriously courting me.

"In the months after, as our companionship grew more routine (though never drab), I began to wonder whether my likely betrothal to Bruce would be the beginning or the end of my life. Metaphorically, Alex. Within the insular, privileged halls of Cambridge, as the wife of a revered professor (as perhaps one myself when our children were old enough to board), I could foresee young Rose cruising on a sea of glass, a life so utterly unperturbed by the Sturm und Drang of the world outside that I might persuade myself it didn't exist. Over time I would lose empathy with the unfortunate souls trapped in war and famine, come to see poverty and disease as divine retribution or simply Social Darwinism. I would live and die as though no one beyond my gilded keep mattered at all. It seemed a devilish bargain that would bereave my soul.

"American that I am, I missed in Bruce the rebellious fire that would have pursued a gypsy girl, and abandoning his post, gone nomading with her across Europe. Longed for a dramatic sign of nonconformity to expectations: daring to disturb the universe. I yearned to be swept into a future whose course was not mapped and which I as co-captain would help navigate as we plunged into terra incognita. Oh, certainly, one could say that's true of any future and in a narrow way it is, but the marriage that lay before me lacked spice and danger. More, I gradually realized: it lacked, on my end, heart, the ardent throb we call love. Bruce was a terribly nice man, highly intellectual and academically ambitious, good-looking, and unexciting. The personification of fortified beef stock.

"Getting out of the foregone conclusion that I would marry him was even trickier than escaping home seven years earlier. The eyes of the clan were upon me, not just Katherine's, though she had been duly informed, and while she may not have shared in her family's elation since it meant I would be staying in Great Britain, she conceded that Professor McLellan was a brilliant choice for me.

"Glen Aerie, which you may remember is Aunt Fiona's estate in the Highlands, appeared to be the chosen site for Bruce's proposal of marriage at the end of Lent term. We were both going there for a fortnight's Easter holiday. Though Fiona had not spoken of it to me, I gathered the wedding would also be held at Glen Aerie, a triumph for my doting great-aunt who had adopted me as her heir. Abandoning Fiona was my one regret, but I could think of no way out other than to disappear, cowardly though it was.

"I was done with the academic term a week before Bruce and so planned to train to Glen Aerie in advance of his coming. Of course I would never get there—my escape called for heading directly to the airport in Edinburgh to catch a flight to Oslo, where I would vanish. Know that I am traveling under a false name with a forged passport obtained from a friend of one of my myriad cousins who thought it a gas to keep several identities handy. I have chosen an androgynous first name and a common last name so that I can look as I please and meld into anonymity. My hair is cut short, dyed, and I wear whatever comes to hand: sometimes a big sailor's cap, jeans, a loose top, boots; others, a hippie dress, scarf, and bangles. I keep my head down, travel light, use cash only, and speak little. My aim is, as it was when first conceived, to be no one.

"The night I was to leave, Bruce came by my room. Always solicitous and kind (yes: he was much too good for me), he brought fruit and a new book for my journey, by train a full day's ride. We sat at the window, with a lilac-scented wind pouring in, and spoke of beauty, serenity, the widening light of the season. My hand was in his, and in the waning of our conversation, I noticed his grasp on it had closened. Just as I did, Bruce dropped to one knee and proposed. He prefaced with an apology for not waiting till we were in the paradise of Glen Aerie but defended himself by saying he couldn't let me leave without expressing his intentions and knowing my response. Caught off-guard, what could I say but yes, Alex? And with that 'yes' my escape plan suddenly looked absurd and immature. Was I running from a life with Bruce or still running from Katherine? Was I eighteen or twenty-five? What did I really want? How did I hope to make a life for myself better than the one at my feet? I was a self-indulgent idiot. Forget Oslo. I would train to Glen Aerie in the morning and share the grand news with Fiona, who would certainly understand (applaud!) his jumping the proverbial gun. We would begin planning the wedding and welcome Bruce a week hence with a great, private feast. Then Fiona, our bridal patron, could send the invitations, a traditional role among the clan fulfilled in lieu of maternal parents under some circumstances, such as mine.

"He kissed me, with the deepest tenderness, and I, virginal maiden that I truly was, responded with demure lips as he pressed me to him. I could feel his desire rising but trusted he would save lovemaking for the wedding bed. My hand still in his, we walked together to his car, where, under an ancient yew, we bade good-night. He offered to escort me to the train station the next morning, and why wouldn't I have agreed? After a prolonged leave-taking on this perfumed eve, I returned to my room to pack.

"Whatever they call it—a dark night of the soul or wrestling with the angel—such were the hours that followed for me. I had no one to talk to as I struggled to decide which route to take, packing as though headed for Oslo but nothing I couldn't as easily have used at Glen Aerie. My thought from the start had been to leave as if I'd be coming back, as though I'd simply gone on holiday, to avert suspicion, though I realized that doing so guaranteed they'd look full-out for me. It was in keeping with my cowardice to depart thus, but also practical since I couldn't travel with a roomful of stuff in tow. By four in the morning, burning adrenaline, I decided not to decide till I reached Edinburgh whether I would there disembark for the airport. It was impossible to be a traitorous runaway with Bruce's eyes on mine—if indeed that's what I chose to be.

"Too enthralled to even notice my fatigue, Bruce saw me onto the train with fervent professions of love and the sorrow that my absence, be it ever so brief, wrought in him. He found a window seat for me on the platform side so that we would not lose sight of each other till the train pulled out. A devoted soul, he, who trusted he'd found his life's mate and was bound for the realm of happily ever after. En route to Edinburgh, I chastised myself severely for not sharing his conviction or at least giving it a chance to grow in me. There was nothing not to love about this debonair, erudite, and courtly man. The irrevocability of my choice tore at me: Leaving Bruce now, I would never get him back, or if I did, our relationship would henceforth be clouded by doubt and subterfuge. In Edinburgh I would decide my fate, by what means I could not then divine.

"My dear Mann, it has, so far, been a journey made perilous more by my fear than by actual consequence. I look as I'd planned to, an innocuous young vagabond drifting through the summer, one of a horde I noticed for the first time. Seems to be quite the thing among the youth, traipsing aimlessly through Scandinavia. If Interpol or private detectives are seeking me, I have not caught wind of it. Nonetheless, whenever I see someone looking at me, my skin crawls with presentiment. It is a nerve-tinder experience, being on the lam. Once, a man who appeared to be following me boarded a commuter train one car down from mine. I jumped off just before the doors closed and stepped onto a train going the opposite way.

"Traveling in friendless anonymity, thus being of no account to anyone, is, however, profoundly disconcerting. That, in turn, has caused me to question whether I made a mistake fleeing from a world wherein I had a leading role. The freedom gained not worth the affection lost. 'So quick bright things come to confusion,' the Bard reminds me. And yet, I reply, in all this time I have never missed Bruce.

"And why should I care whether I'm apprehended? I am a woman in her mid-twenties, have not committed a crime, cannot be incarcerated nor dragged home against my will. I care because of the dishonor of facing the clan and my jilted fiancé with no story to tell that has the least plausibility. Running as I am from country to country, alone under an assumed name and holding a forged passport—disappearing, mind you, after withdrawing a considerable sum from my bank account in advance—how can I claim to have been abducted? Or to have contracted amnesia? Or lost my mind overnight? To have done anything but deceived them all and fled? No, legal retribution is not what I dread, but shame. Utter and unconditional humiliation. Followed by banishment to the homeland and Katherine. The horror of disgrace keeps me lamming. I will not be captured, however long it takes for them to give up.

"Do not even think of joining the chase, Alex. If in the past two months I have evaded Bruce and Katherine, you will never find me. I have cut all internet ties and use only burner phones, which I discard frequently. And I've no idea where I will go next—Russia, Denmark, Germany, or further south to Portugal or Spain or Italy. I book no advance passage but simply go where whim takes me whenever the time seems right.

"I am writing you, and you alone, merely to relate my tale and assure you that at present nothing untoward has happened to your friend Rose. However, if you've received no further word from me a year hence, you may assume that that is no longer the case and inform Katherine of what you now know. My remains will likely be irretrievable. I trust you will write a heartrending eulogy.

"My dear confidante lifelong, may all be well on your journey toward a brighter future than mine appears to be.

"Your Rose

"PS Please share this news with your dear mother. If only her compassionate arms enfolded me, I would feel utterly safe. Remember how we cajoled her to participate in our Camelot dramas, stepping into the role of Guinevere or Merlin or whoever we needed her to become? She took our child's play seriously and of course raised the bar on our enactments. I adore your mother, X, and privately think of her as my true one."

I smiled at Mamia. "A well-deserved endorsement to close on."

"Rose is wonderful. I'd love to call her my daughter."

Keep the faith, Bug. Maybe she'll marry you for your mother.

Mamia sighed. "I hope everything will work out all right for that dear girl."

Through the window I saw William Blake spring elegantly from a low bough to sink his teeth into a pocket gopher. Score!

"Don't worry," I assured her. "Rosie always lands on her feet."

17

"The Father is the Son of the Man"

A thick-ring year it had been, vertiginous growth but rived with catastrophe. A year that left your marrow dull, your heart gaunt, pores flattened. You'd thought you had another decade of youth, a good three of middle age before you contemplated old. Instead, doomed prematurely to retrospect, a lingering existence. You would have preferred a slighter year.

Snip snap. A plant too leggy, your leg too bony. The washcloth heat asphyxiating as you take the stem and leaves in hand: trim, disentangle, tuck, harvest. The soil's moisture level heavy. Once so easy to stride to the other end of the greenhouse and shut off the faucet, a dread now, your careful steps limped. You, limping along.

The summer before, you were prospering, a man of twenty-nine with his own land, building a house, business, friends, a welcome place in the community. Writing songs, cultivating a crop of value, a life of your own desiring fueled by good work and pluck. You could envision fulfillment, your soul branched wide with a lofty sense of purpose. You woke at first light, hungry for the day.

Yellowing here, wilting there. Too much water, too little. Hard to find the right balance unless you mind-meld with the plants, like Alex. Part of the weave, that guy, hyper-linked to this place. And to you, after you let him in.

It was your idea to start the cannabis enterprise, the greenhouse hand-built, finally getting some use out of your ranch boyhood. Knowing likewise what not to do: borrow against the hope of big profits; squander what little you did make; brazen your way through sales deals that often went sour; blame the world for setbacks you engendered because of being an ignorant, drunken fool.

No, you'd been careful and quiet, sure-footedly trading on the quality of your product instead of boisterous charm. You'd done your research, bought topnotch seeds, started small, asked a reasonable price, been generous with those in need. Like Jess. He got the word around that you were a man to be trusted, a decent, humble young man who wanted to serve, not exploit, the community. In three years you'd hit your stride, establishing yourself as the local supplier, stocking a couple of shops in town and filling a growing number of individual orders.

More of them for pain than pleasure among residents of Trove, mostly recreational for tourists, who bought marked-up and fancied cannabis items from the stores. Your identity was kept secret from vacationing strangers, whose impulsive cravings might well lead to a raid. Like the assault by the con, from which Alex (and Tiger) had saved the greenhouse. Head down, you went from newbie to known entity mighty fast for a town whose interior and exterior were rigidly walled off one from the other.

Damn white flies. Thought you'd wiped them out but here they come again. Squish what you can, then mix up more of your magic potion; that's another trip in and out. You, just limping along. Evenings silent, you and Lori polite, reproachful, you still sleeping downstairs, by choice. She so large and sluggish that each day is a chore. Hefting guilt like you do the leg, which you've forgiven her for. But not the other.

These days, you've become Trove's lame hope for the future. It's you and those few like you of the next generation that will take over one day and carry forward the little town's personal history. You're family, sharing privileges and responsibilities commensurate with your youth and skills. The limp attests to your heritage: nearly everyone's got at least a digit missing, if not a limb, has bad knees or shoulders, scars, along with unseen damage like a weak heart or diabetes, cancer, impaired lungs. Your wholeness had made you feel (secretly) a cut above them, not so much proud as exempt. That illusion shattered with your femur.

What's happening over here, huh? Some damn bug eating the leaves. Grasshoppers caterpillars, what? Here we go: aphids. Where did all those ladybugs and mantises disappear to? Never had problems with bugs when Alex was in charge. Jesus, so much damage so fast. Pay attention or you're going to lose a big hunk of this crop. Just when you were hitting your stride, sure you'd make a slim profit this fall.

Hitting your fucking stride. Sure-footed no more. Screw those walking idioms. Invented by people with two well-matched legs. Nothing you'd thought about before the accident but they're everywhere.

You had dared to let your mind leap ahead, conjuring days, years, when you would rise early to tend your crop, then come in for breakfast with Lori, go to your study to write till noon, send a trusted assistant out to make deliveries and collect payment (a job you hated) while you put in a couple hours sorting the dried plants into bags and whatever else needed doing. Time by mid-afternoon to read and snooze. Dinner, then kick back, play and write songs, get a full repertoire going so you could cut an album to market in town. Once in a while you'd have to play a gig to stimulate sales.

What would happen when something hit, your poetry or your music? You'd deal, of course: take a nom de plume, stay totally away from the public eye, which you thought of as not unlike the eye of Sauron: you didn't want it on you because it would corrupt and ultimately destroy you, turn you into its slavering minion. Disguised by a name, you could move unbesieged among your adoring fans and brilliant readers. At some point you'd write your memoir, to be published posthumously. Then all who had known you would remark on their good fortune, and those who had been unkind would lament their ill treatment of you. Childish dreams, vindictive but so satisfying that you had not been able to view them clear-headed till now when they had no chance of being realized.

Two weeks ago you turned thirty, marking the start of your thirty-first lap around the seasons. Birthdays were not really occasions you honored, nor did entering a new decade seem especially portentous. It was a passage on which to reflect: to, if possible, view the "past and future with an equal mind" and find oneself along the imagined trajectory.

You'd been eager for this rite of passage, turning thirty, becoming indisputably an adult to be taken seriously. But your reflections that day were acrid and venomous. You were an old-timer with a bad leg and a narrow, worn life ahead. Your poetry, should you ever write again, would be small. Your memoir profoundly ordinary, relating how little happened and how much did not: a history of petty grievances lodged against the injustices you'd suffered. The one epiphany that entered this thicket of dark musings was an understanding, finally, of your father's bitterness at his thwarted life. Maybe you would turn to drink, too, but more likely weed, to blur resentment and remembrance. His urgent yen to run was yours as well. Get out, vanish before the birth, leave the whole screwed-up mess in Lori's hands. She deserved it. Not the whole mess: your limp would go with you.

The doc gave you a series of exercises to do to strengthen muscles not used to doing more than their share. You were spotty about keeping them up; Lori helped at first, while you two were still in love and she slept on the sofa with you, rubbing your leg till you drifted off to sleep. God, she was good, those hands so wise and sensitive, drawing the soreness out till with a renewed hope for vanquishing the pain, recovering to normal, you let go. Nights dreamless, days harrowing as you struggled to hold on to yourself in this excruciating state. Give it six months, the doc had said, but by then her pregnancy had exposed her deceitful seduction, and you realized you would never recover yourself again. Even more painful than the leg was the townsfolks' fixation on the love they believed you still shared. Neither of you would disillusion them.

Your romantic, tragic story had become legend embellished with each retelling: how each of them, hearts longing to be together on their first New Year's Eve, took off through the worst blizzard ever in Trove and found each other head-on at the top of that hairpin curve; might have killed them both if Floyd hadn't rescued them in the dead of night. That's how he got the limp, yeah, it's permanent, doc done his best and Lori even spent a considerable chunk of her savings to take her man to a specialist in Denver, but that break, it was too complicated, whatever they call it, a compounded fracture, see, to grow the bones back straight. Love of Lori Limp, a triple-L, is how it's known around here, among ourselves, and we say it about other young men who are gone on some gal. Drive up that road and you'll come upon a little marker we created, two hearts in a field of snow, Lori and Joaquin written on them, and below is a little four-line poem Floyd's wife Dahlia wrote to commemorate the romantickest story ever happened here.

Embarrassing, being the tragic hero. You see less love and more stupidity in that night, with debilitating consequences. At least for you. Leg was set as well as local resources allowed, but the femur broken ragged, tibia snapped dead center and above the foot, the leg healed crooked. Yeah, it's pinned, but the damn thing hurts a lot; you have to be careful turning too fast, climbing and descending stairs, let alone ladders. Haven't been hiking since it happened and surely couldn't go far or fast. Had to get a truck with automatic, not nearly as good as standard around here. Doc says your balance will improve as you get used to the shorter leg; he offered you a lift to wear in your shoe, but that threw your knee and hip out of alignment, shooting pains down the leg. Nothing to be done. Not a goddamn thing to be done. I'm the guy with a limp. Lame will be my primary identifying characteristic.

Spindle-thin at this corner. I wonder if it's the light or soil. Moisture's good. Throw in some more compost, drape that gauze over them, see if either helps. Alex would have felt out the situation, made the right adjustment instinctively. That guy had such a knack; new to the greenhouse scene but a natural at it. What do you think's wrong with these plants, Alex? Wish he'd come back. Hear yourself saying that? You who were ready to turn him away at a glance.

A scarred, emaciated wreck, he sought refuge in the life you were constructing, begged an unfathomable second chance. Grateful, willing to shift into whomever you needed him to be, he excavated a role to fill, quickly became vital. You contrarily slow to give way to him, protective, suspicious, yes, even nasty. Your vision had not included this desperate soul who launched himself at you, who cried out at night, who couldn't light a fire, who brought along a killer cat, whose only plan for reincarnation lay in being admitted to your world.

What he could do was tend. Suddenly you were eating well and regularly. The house was cleaner, tidier. Errands no longer nagging at your days. Deliveries made. And most important, the greenhouse prospering. "A wind of light." That's how he vanquished your guard and sailed in. Even so, you didn't grasp that Alex was the companion you needed, the wife in all but bed. You saw him as a stopgap till Lori arrived. How fervently you awaited her coming with the spring. Dreamed your joined lives into a wondrous union, enfolding that of Eros and Psyche but surpassing it in soul. You wrote her immense letters billowing with your vision of incomparably glorious days to come. She replied briefly, awkwardly, nurse not writer, rendering as passionate an accord as she could: yes, yes, yes the gist. You didn't comprehend that you already were living as you wished to be, sans romance. Seduced by the myth of eternal bliss to forfeit love of a friend for that of a mate. If only she'd held herself back another six months.

Arriving instead on an unexpected autumn evening, wounding Alex, who had offered to drive her to his doom, with words he was never meant to hear and she should have known better than to speak. In her beginning lay our happily never after end. Alex nearly dying, a rush to oblivion that you also now understand, often tempted to freeze as he did in his cabin, more deliberate than he to make sure you were beyond reawakening. She, remorse-laden, stuck with caring for Alex, rightfully and yet for the next three months, he, comatose, dominated your lives. The damn cat Montenegra knotting the tie to him rather than, as you intended, loosening it. She hubristically trying to drive your truck through a riptide storm, when it would have been so sensible not to. A few minutes and you would have been at her door, ruddy, intact, to celebrate the new year.

Best forgone, a celebration of this year, as its passage has been a maelstrom. Dawning with the unconscionable act that destroyed your belief in the woman whose integrity was the cornerstone of your devotion. Raised as you were with lies and acrimony, son of a marriage built on gamesmanship and defensive strategies, your deceit radar was perpetually on full alert with everyone but Lori. Yes, even Alex continued to get cursory scans until she felled him. Early on in your relationship, her unrestrained adoration opened a hidden wellspring of trust in you to which only she had access. She knew how critical it was to preserve this pool when she mercilessly sucked it dry. Clad in a gown of cream velvet seducing you, or raping as you sometimes feel, to breed. You, suspecting nothing but an urgent passion, yielded gladly, thankful that even with bound leg you had the sexual dynamism to arouse and fulfill your woman. Her sheer wickedness cannot be pardoned nor your naïve faith be restored.

You can find an element of mean-spirited justice in the outcome that does nothing to alleviate your rage. You sacrificed Alex's future on Lori's altar; she sacrificed yours on this baby's. These babies. Two, yes, curled into each other but with separate placentae. Her craving to be a mother greater than the foundation of your union. While you were just beginning to heal from her previous blunder. A duplicitous woman bent on getting what she's after at any cost. You did not consent to conception, to becoming a father. You did not want children, as she knew. You will not marry her; you will not take part in rearing the children; you will not care if things fall apart; you will not love them; you will not relent ever.

Shit. Tore up that good bunch with weeding. Oppressive heat is making you careless. It's always been a sauna in here, but global warming has upped the temps. Someday you'll be able to grow year-round without a greenhouse. Not. In this lifetime. Maybe her kids when they can't figure out anything else to do. Grow cannabis amid the Sonoran cactus. If the valley hasn't burned up or down by then. It's not going to get easier.

Your house will have to be enlarged for her kids. At first they can sleep with her upstairs; Floyd already offered to rustle up a couple of cribs. But those outgrown, they'll need another room. Bathroom, too, since you don't want to share with them. Footing, frame, windows, plumbing, electricity, roofing. More time and money you don't have. An awkward addition: Your house isn't designed for expansion. A lot of work for an old man, lame.

Morning, noon, evening, morning, noon, evening. You find yourself in the same place doing the same things. Days, weeks have ceased to matter. The sun locates you but provides no sense of direction.

Most mornings you wake at dawn, slump into the kitchen to get coffee and hobble on out to the porch to let the caffeine seep into you. Head back in for cereal, a banana or apple, then to the john to do your business if you're lucky. Old man, that's something you never had to think about before; something in your guts twisted up. Before you cripple your way out to the greenhouse, Lori usually comes down to greet you. You don't let her sleep with you anymore partly because of the leg, mostly because you don't want to lie next to that lumpy bitch. You prefer the sofa Alex bought and passed on to you by default, along with his grief. You prefer Alex, as a friend.

Some mornings, after a bad night, you don't speak to her beyond a grunt. Won't let her touch you. Just shuffle on out to the greenhouse. Back at noon for a lunch she's readied and may eat with you, depending on how unhappy or uncomfortable she's feeling. She may be gone, at a doctor's appointment or running some errand. You don't ask, don't care;

besides, you've got deliveries to make, which Alex used to do after tending the greenhouse. She offered, give her that, but you wouldn't let her near your stuff. Didn't want to get dependent on her since soon enough she'd be totally out of commission with those twins on her tits. Your lives would be separate then; best start getting used to it now. You still eat dinner together, for convenience, but generally in silence, her efforts to add music to the dreary table a failure.

Other mornings you do share a perfunctory kiss. She quivers, ridiculously hopeful over and again that you've softened and a wisp of affection has escaped from the stronghold of abstinence. She tries to open a conversation, always a mistake she regrets. Whenever you look at her, you remember how long she waited to tell you she was pregnant. Whenever you look at her, you wonder how one you loved so profoundly has become so ordinary. She'd be a pleasant acquaintance you might buy supplies from, talk with about the weather, not sure of her name.

Morning again, noon then, evening. Same pattern, like living one long day a thousand times with minor variations. You remember that description in *The Stranger*, from which you, disaffected Joaquin Stranger, used to distance yourself. Meursault stagnating in prison for a year feels he has lived a single day. You recoiled then at the thought of such a purposeless, undifferentiated life, now yours. What was once exciting has become a rut. Once a plan now an encumbrance. Is that how Frank got stuck? Did your mother trap him with a son? Could that be why he wanted to kill you? His life a song on a trajectory of freedom to roam and discover the breadth of his talent. Ended abruptly, noosed to a ranch, doing exactly what he had intended not to do. At least you had chosen your life, though it's no longer one you want.

You might have opted not to be born if you'd known how things would turn out. Shambling sweat-runneled into the house for a bottle of water and the dreary lunch your nemesis laid out for you to eat with her or alone: the latter increasingly your preference, while she sits reading in the other room. Or pretends to. Today, though, she's doing something real, unexpected. Beside the table where your sandwich rests, a suitcase, a backpack, her saddle-bag purse. Lined up, ready to go. You can hear her tread upstairs, moving across the bedroom, in the rhythm of a conscientious guest departing. Make the bed. Wipe down the dresser, nightstand, bathroom surfaces. Straighten up pillows, leave the place looking as if she'd never been there. She was going. Where?

Sit down. Guzzle water. Eat your sandwich. Cool and indifferent. It's her choice, better for both of you at this point. In fact perfect, her timing. Get your house back, your hope, music, poetry, your life, what you've been after, isn't it? Smarter than you thought, Lori, knowing when to go, if not when to come. But how's she going to get out of here? Small glitch: you'll have to drive her somewhere, and not too far. Bus in Arroyo most likely. An hour in the truck, hunting for ways to part on a friendly note. Write a check and stick it in her bag. It's the least—

"Skip the charity." She's on the stairs, watching you. In her eyes you see dearth where your reflection once shone. Like windows boarded up. She's already left. Driving her to Arroyo will be redundant if necessary. Relieved your goodbyes have been said, you void the check and toss the book into the bowl where it's kept. Tear off another bite of sandwich, gulp of water. Like she's not there anymore. And you no longer need to resist the fierce urge to hurt her.

Car pulling up the driveway, which is what you call your side of the valley. Jess. So few vehicles come up the road you know the sound of their engines. Checking on you, good man. He senses your unhappiness, not rocket science for a friend, and doesn't get it. Love-of-your-life expecting twins on your first try; he and Stellita, deceased at fifty-seven, childless. Not likely to marry again, Jess, he at an age when he'd expected to have grandchildren. Loyal even though your reaction to Lori's pregnancy was incomprehensible. He was missing the key piece in the story, of course, but even that wouldn't make sense to a man yearning for offspring. Seduction by his beloved cause for break-up? Crazy Joaquin. You understand his position, sure, from the outside looking in. He'd have to learn so much more about your interior to, perhaps, get it.

"Jess." You rise to welcome him though he's motioning to you to sit, sit. Sweeps off the police hat, nods at Lori, not surprised. So she arranged for a ride. Thoughtful, embarrassing, unnecessary. It's the least—

"Coffee, Jess?" she says, coming the rest of the way down, her massive bulge at the prow.

"I'm good." He turns to you. "How's it going?" You shrug. He's here to take your erstwhile woman away, and you're about to make that awkward for him. Them.

On cue, "Lori asked me to drive her to Arroyo."

Right. You nod. The bus. Whereto? Elementary, Sherlock. Back to the Northwest, the hospital, her old job; she'll be in the care of a horde of doctors and nurses who love her. Get a place with one of her baby-tender friends. Much better scene.

"Hey, I can drive her. Got a delivery in Calhoun, that monthly guy, you remember. Halfway to Arroyo."

"I would sooner Jess took me." Brusque, eyes on the sheriff. "If you don't want coffee, we can go."

She stoops to lift Montenegra to the counter, where, you notice belatedly, a brand new carrier sits.

"You're not taking the cat on a bus?"

"Not taking the bus." She guides Montenegra in, strokes her, latches the door.

Gotcha. You want to know what the hell without begging for it. Jess has her bags and is heading out the door. "Give you two a minute to say goodbye," he mutters.

"Let me drive you." This time you mean it.

She shakes her head and slides the cat carrier onto her hip. Won't stay. Tries to maneuver it under her arm. Nope. You're heartless, sitting there like a bum. She glances at you, finally. "Thank you for everything," she says primly like a houseguest who stayed overnight. "Good luck with your business."

"Lori." You sound mildly desperate because you are. For information. "What happens when you get to Arroyo?"

Over her shoulder, halfway out the door. "Shelley's meeting me."

Rise and hobble, boy: this is news. "You're going to stay with Shelley? Alex: does he know?"

She's hurrying away from you. "Because it can't be good for him, having you there."

She sets the cat carrier gently on the back seat and seatbelts it in place. Montenegra mews once and is quiet. Jess stands by Lori's door to help her into the car, a gesture that implies you're a jerk for not. A wild panic constricts your chest. So fast. Gone. You came in for lunch as usual. That's all you did, and the rest was done without you.

"Hey, Lori," You're at her window watching her strap in, not easy around that bulge. "I'm sorry. We should talk sometime, at least. Stay in touch. Let me know how the birth goes."

Her eyes are fixed on the road across the valley. You'll never see her again. The woman to whom your love and life belonged six months ago.

Going to stay with your closest friend, her victim. Who didn't hold grudges, who had tolerated your abuse with humility. Who kept reinventing himself with every loss. Alex would absolve Lori of her wrongdoing, and each of them would incline toward the other's need. They'd marry and raise the children in Summerville, Shelley as grandmother, maybe invite Clarice into the family circle as well. A tight circle, dwelling in the grace of unilateral virtue. Even you would not be shut out though never allowed fully in, a father who callously abandoned his children and their mother. You will remain Stranger, an onlooker devoid of the requisite generosity and selflessness to love. "The child is the father of the man." Right.

Your grandmother? Outcast ally. You called your solidarity with her love, but she made scant demands of you beyond those of caretaker. You don't have a knack for tending, like greenhouse Alex, nurse Lori. Interlocking puzzle pieces on a skewed backdrop. Things could have turned out so differently. Loneliness will make you a good poet.

Freedom, grim but soothing. You'll grow accustomed to being on your own, become more adept at managing your limp, try the lift again. Things will get back to a mutation of normal. She'll be a phantom memory in a couple of years, an old tale they'll weary of retelling. When your work's published, songs played across the nation, your image will metamorphose into the brilliant, misconstrued writer/composer, and they'll appreciate you for yourself, not merely as one half of a fairytale couple. Much better this way.

Disappeared behind a curve in the valley, Jess's car bearing Montenegra, Lori, your babies. Knowing her, she'd left nothing behind. Sleep upstairs again, in your bed; lead a cat-shit-free life. A nap, then deliveries. You'll have time. Light till 8:30. Try the bed.

You lurch toward the house, yearning to find it cool, afraid that somehow the heat of your blood will have infiltrated the air. A line of a new song surfaces:

> "The face in the water could have been mine
> If my memory had grown forever innocent of time,"

it runs, which sounds pretty mellow for a guy who's just disavowed all connection with others. Why would Mr. Self-Sufficiency be thinking about innocence? Change it to "cynical" or something. It won't be a song you can perform around here, maybe nowhere, written just for yourself. That's how you'll be living now anyway.

Before you begin to, a final backward, salt-rendering glance as Jess's vehicle crests the opposite side of the valley, heading onto the main road through Trove. Folks will notice them going by, and when Lori doesn't return with him, what will they say? She left him; he treated her badly because he didn't want kids, don't know why, blamed her though it takes two to tango, you know. Going to live with Alex and his mom; it's all pretty confusing, but at bottom Joaquin's fault. Twins! And him rejecting them: go figure. You'll be a pariah, the fool on the hill. Even Gregorio will revile you because he adores Nurse Lori. Everyone does, that's the problem. When she was in town caring for Alex, they got used to coming to her for medical advice and treatment, or just to talk. She has a deep reservoir of empathy.

A crash of black, sprawling body-drop into a waterless well. Blasts of agony spurting, blood on fire, bones jarred, screeching nerves. Shouts, screams, hollow in mind's cavern, help none. The earth quakes. Rumble, crumble, boom. Sprues loose. Bolting molten up from furious veins, underground. Leave me be, leave me free. Leave me me.

"Honey? Are you hurt?"

She's come back, she's sorry, she loves you. "Honey?" No, no. Listen closely. "Come here, baby." Not Lori. Mom's voice. Sob wallow, blood scrape, lip burn. Mom, Mom, Mom, pick me up, hold me, hug me. I missed you. I love you, Mommy! Hurt hurt. Hold me. Grab her leg. Wet in your mouth, a tooth hanging. Mama, please. She hauls you into her arms. Safe. Then swift, stinging pain, anger, fear. A stiffening. Down.

Mountaintop's gonna blow. From the chasm growls, belches, fumes choke the lungs, rasping for breath, exhale turbulence, originating within, a violent eruption, the spew of guts foul vomit bile, these dry heaves that strike like illness but are the advent of sobs. Rising volcanically from the inferno that is your denied misery, your inheld clutch for rescue. Sputter, hack, gagging nausea. Hold me, hug me, pick me up. Hideous retching from a magma chamber whose plug rusted shut is forced by the onrush to yield. Prostrate, unattended, face buried in spittle and dirt after tripping on a rock in your path, you begin to weep for the first time since you were four. Mama, please. Save me.

Your parents had gone away for a night to celebrate their fifth anniversary, left you with a sitter. When you heard their car pull in, you burst with joy to greet them, running tripped, fell hard on the flagstone path. Surged into tears, scrambling up arms extended to your mother, who took you in hers. As you clung sobbing to her, your father gave you a sharp spank, yelled at you to stop bawling and grow up. You did as you were told. Learned to live apart from yourself, to stop expecting comfort or solace, to channel need into art, *I* becoming *you*, so much easier to get by at that remove.

To have the wily endurance that you cultivated merely land you here, face down on rock again, sobbing like the child forsaken. Your four-year-old tears roiling within would surely have erupted into brutality when you own child cried. You could have explained your fears to Lori but confessing would not have stopped the explosion. Might not have. Telling yourself has released some pressure. But the lava keeps flowing and may not stop for years, centuries.

You've got to pull yourself together now, get up and wash off, change clothes. Deliveries to make. Got to, yet cannot, stuck here in the grit of this seismic torrent. Purged of yourself by yourself, stranded far beyond recall. You who in vain sought refuge offering it to others, guardedly. You so quick to withdraw love, so slow to give it. Cry, Joaquin, cry and cry. Sate your blighted spirit with tears.

I will.

18

"The Place of Solitude Where Three Dreams Cross"

Bill, Toni, Annie, Franz, Jane, Albert, Kurt, Arundhati, Ernest, Mary, TS, Ralph, Ed, Nadine, Leo, Junot, WB, Jean-Paul, Alan, Carlos, Margaret, John, Hermann, Jhumpa, the Bard…snip, snip into pile of assorted cutouts. Red, yellow, green, black, purple, orange, gray, blue, white, pink…ka-thunk, ka-thunk into stapled latticework multihued across the vast bulletin board. Alex and Mamia, the collage artists with scissors and stapler. Teamwork. Our first artistic collaboration since my kidhood. Forgotten skills unleashed from overlong confinement.

This is how it used to be. A rainy day: check; us alone together in the house: check; shapes and glue, paper, scissors, markers spread across the table: check; a tape of jolly tunes on the boombox: not anymore, but still in our heads, Mamia humming "The Rainbow Connection" by Kermit the Frog, me whistling along. Joy billowing from our endeavors. Still now, vortex of laughter whirling in my gut, a kind of homesick ecstasy. So rare as an adult, to be thoroughly content with what I was doing, to be sure of it. Collage was ever my medium of choice.

Mamia had brought in plants to humanize the tall, gray file cabinets lining my classroom. Notice how easily I took possession of it. *My* classroom, chipped cinderblock walls, stained carpet, tattered acoustic ceiling tiles, pen-engraved tablet desks, and all. Amazing, the pace at which such a room can be demolished by its spirited inhabitants, each of whom wants to leave a literal mark on it. I remember carving an "A+" on the underside of my desk, to stand for my winning Alex self and for the grade I strove to claim without effort. Hersch tattooed his desk with a leering satyr whose large erect member kept any of the girls from sitting there. Maybe I could work that story into a pointless reminder to my students about not writing on their desks. The students were *mine*, too.

Rain flew splat at the windows. The storm was quickening, a welcome respite from the summer's drought. I paused to watch Mamia staple a colorful basket-weave of construction paper along the upper edge of the bulletin board. She was a craft genius who could see the creative potential in any scrap. I was the idea man in this partnership and she the one who knew how to realize my vision. As with this project, when I wanted to transform the bulletin board from a random pin-up place into a work of riveting literary and artistic merit, Mamia suggested the cutouts of famous authors' heads. When she saw the board itself, littered with marker sketches, she added the paper backdrop. And another idea, which I wish had been mine but give her full credit for: to leave spaces among the authors for inserting images of the students. Put their heads up there with the literary greats to encourage them to think of themselves as writers—and, of course, to give them a reason to love the board. Brilliant concept, and fun. What a team Mamia and I were.

When I was five, she gave me a stack of *National Geographic* magazines to cut up. Papito was slow to get on board with their destruction, thinking they might someday be valuable like old baseball cards, but when he checked the price of back issues, he shrugged off the lost fortune that never was. I had an art box to store all the cutouts for a rainy day or whenever I felt a collage coming on. Mamia added wrapping, crepe, and tissue paper, very odds and total ends from the ragbag. I could cut and paste with unwavering enthusiasm all day, my attention span mysteriously waxing over a hundred times longer than at school. Mamia hung in there with me during these creative binges, playing at making her own collages but never gluing anything down in case I wanted to use it. She sketched a lot, and when I asked, taught me the rudiments of figure and landscape drawing. Her great talents, art and patience, though it was literature she truly loved.

While we collaged, we talked. Stories, dreams, family history, religion, philosophy, life and death questions: all were fertile ground for cultivating. I could ask her anything, tell her everything. We built a fortress of intimacy large enough only for ourselves. Once settled inside it, no interruption could breach it. She'd answer the phone, put in a load of laundry, then come back, and we'd go on as if her absence had never happened. It was so easy till I became conscious of others' view in from the ramparts. Embarrassed, I took off with the marauding hordes of adolescent boys, left Mamia holding down the fort of our collage days.

As she was still doing, the bulletin board now a tapestry of color. The radiant focal point of the room.

"Fantastic!" I applauded her.

She bowed appreciatively. It was an immaculate weave, tight and bold. The joins, staples, were nigh invisible. For a flash I pondered whether we should just leave it at that but of course not. Bring in the clowns with markers and it would soon be graffiti. Stay with the plan. Even so, some of the authors would soon have unusual facial hair, horns, fangs, who knew what all. Yet less room for the crude on a bunch of faces. I scooted the pile of cutouts toward Mamia, who began idly arranging them. The fun part, which she was only amusing herself with till the master artist put his hand to it. Never expected to be this happy again.

I wished Tiger were here with us, stretched out on the frayed rug purring, or stalking the corners of the room for edible insects and leftovers. The incorrigible hunter who had never regretted a kill. I admired his absence of conscience and certainty of purpose. He was a critter on a mission that surpassed the mere survival imperative. He took pride in sating his predatory instincts for their own sake, hunted to hunt, slew to slay. And he was a rabid advocate of torture, god love him. Though he had slacked off a bit since the arrival of Montenegra.

It had been a week, Lori and La Negra showing up with the late summer rains, storming fierce every afternoon. Lori, here, with Mamia and me, pregnant with twins, having split irreparably from Joaquin, who wanted no children. It would have been a dream come true if at least one of those babies wasn't mine, not her preference and the reason she'd lost her greatest love. Nothing I'd learned from her directly, mind you. She was speaking to me like a houseguest I barely knew, courteous and reserved. Mamia—Shelley—she treated like the mother/friend she always yearned for, a woman she trusted and adored unconditionally. All I learned about what had happened and why Lori was now staying here came filtered through Mamia, earth mother goddess.

We'd had some warning, I'll bet more than Joaquin had. Letters to Shelley, deep phone calls, I'm sure lots of talk about me because even though Mamia didn't know about our tryst and the baby that likely grew from it and my hasty eviction, she was around during the coma months, which is when she and Lori got very close. The story of the pregnancy, as passed along to me, opened with Lori's seduction of Joaquin, a terrible plan launched by her fear of losing him and the absurd conviction that he would want a child after his near-death encounter. She hadn't been in her right mind, nor had he, still wasn't, but his fury had become unendurable. He hated her and her unintentionally two babies. I had once again emerged from my ruinous course unscathed. Confession time shadowed me, its reproachful footfalls echoing through the dank halls of imprisoned conscience. Where would I go after Mamia threw me out?

Shake it off. Hold on to your collage-a-rama sweet spot. Snip-snip. George, Zaide, Oscar, Vlad, Elizabeth, Aldous, Jorge, Scott, Anne, Nathaniel, Leo, Alice, Hunter, Fyodor, Emily, Charlotte, Sherman. Remember how good it is to have your own room separate from the house, which is now the women's territory. Hated that room where you'd lain after the fire, listening to Trudel talk smack about you with Mamia. Where you'd holed up after Lori exiled you. Remember how much you like that space over the garage, the privacy, its simple furnishings and layout, your stuff uncomplicated by layers of others'. Had Lori to thank for that. And having her here: it was good to be around her even as a distant housemate. Montenegra and Tiger, reunited like they'd never been apart. Like they knew they always would be. I could hardly wait for the babies.

"Are we going to let Joaquin know when she goes into labor?" My question cut the silence.

"She's sure he won't come." Mamia paused to look at me. "He's your friend. I think it's up to you to decide."

"It's up to her."

"He's hurt her so badly she won't do it. But speaking as a woman, I believe she'd want him to her side."

"Speaking as a man, I can't believe he wouldn't want to be."

Mamia smiled. "Then do it. She'll never know you did if he doesn't come. And if he does, maybe they'll find their way back to each other and become a family."

Mamia, the indefatigable optimist.

"You'll get your chance, sweetheart. And when you become a father, I promise to be the most attentive, doting grandmother any child ever had."

If she only knew. What a pig I am.

"Hey, well, you'll get a shot at it come October. The d.g., designated grandma, to the twins, only grandma Lori's kids will have."

"There's Clarice, don't forget."

"She's the one who's forgotten. Hasn't been in touch with Joaquin in over a year."

"I intend to phone her, with Lori's consent. See if she'd like to come up from Vista Grande for a long weekend, get acquainted with the sweet woman carrying her grandchildren. They might grow to be very close."

The indefatigable optimist.

"Frank?"

"I don't know. We still email intermittently. I'd like to tell to him, after the birth, but that's really the family's call, Clarice, Lori, and Joaquin, if he comes. If he doesn't, I'd be more inclined to invite Frank to meet his grandchildren, which of course he'd love to. I think. It's a complicated family."

"You can be sure that if Frank comes, Joaquin won't. He's not a forgive-and-forget kind of guy. I mentioned in an email meeting Frank, said that he was a changed man; Joaquin replied, 'Watch your back.'"

Mamia shook her head. "He may find, as he grows older, that grudges become too heavy to carry. I can't bear to hold one for long anymore."

"Frank did try to kill him, would have if he hadn't been so drunk. That's bigger than a grudge."

"Oh, yes. But I still believe the twins can bring about some kind of reconciliation."

"An uneasy truce, at best."

Lightning flashed us, baring the sky and its torrential outpouring. Aroused me, as fear that thrills can. The heavens crashed in headlong thunder, a satisfying rumble. I'd have to confront Lori, talk honestly with her before spilling my guts to Mamia. Or I could also do nothing.

"Lori told me once that if Joaquin had been a girl, he would have been named Miranda," Mamia continued. "She'll use that name if one of the twins is. And she insists on giving her Michelle as a middle name. If either is a girl."

"I hope they both are. 'Stranger' as the surname?"

"Yes. It's a lot better than her own."

"Which is?"

"Mud. One 'd.'"

"No one ever said it. I see why."

"She wouldn't use it even if it were lovely. Her foster family was awful to her."

I stood up. Done. On the table we marked off an area the size of the bulletin board, laid the heap of cutouts right at the border. Mamia moved aside and sat down where I'd been to give me the prime arranging spot. Serious collage design work about to begin, oh yeah.

"I hope you and Lori get to know each other and become friends, Alex. She took such extraordinary care of you." Mamia was gathering my cutout scraps into a pile to throw away.

"To a large extent you owe her your life. I know you're angry with her for leaving Joaquin—well, for putting him in a spot where she had to leave him—but she's a very dear young woman. Please give her a chance."

The shadow looms. Another perfect opening to tell Mamia the truth. And then what? She's terribly disappointed in me, but she insists I tell Joaquin and recast Lori's actions in light of mine, the end result being that both of them hate me and Joaquin is even less willing than before to take responsibility for the kids.

"If I'm the d.g., you're the d.f., my beloved son. Or at least a sort of father/uncle."

"Like Oedipus?"

"Like many men who take over when the male caregiver is out of the picture. But Joaquin may show. They could make you the godfather."

"Scarface. That works." I moved WB next to Annie, then switched him for Oscar, the wild man. Mamia slid Jhumpa and Kurt toward me. Good call, their heads a striking contrast.

"I just had a thought, Alex. Why don't we put a shot of your head in the midst? For the kids to discover as they scan the images. It might make them ask if you're up there, why shouldn't they be on the board, too? That way it's their idea; they're invested in it rather than having you do it for them. They could even supply the photos, which you were planning to take."

Perfect. I high-fived her. "Who's the born teacher here?" She laughed. "This is the most fun I've had in quite some time, Mamia." The rain pounded affirmation.

We paused for snacks she'd brought along. PBJ's and apple slices with peach-mango smoothies, healthy and sweet. Chatted about the authors, the exterior view in relation to the interior that emerged in their work, so often the two disparate. Mamia added some stories about their lives to my repertoire. She asked about my writing, which at present was not happening and not imaginable. An amiable conversation, easy and safe. So much to say unsaid, but the currents of good will continued to buoy us.

The literary heads aligned themselves with remarkable compliance considering how ornery many of those wearing them were. Except for Hunter, the fringe-rider, who ended up dead center, leering cadaverously at Mary like some figure out of nightmare, which didn't seem fair to her. As I was contemplating a different placement, Mamia took and printed some pics of me, one of them goofy enough to face down Hunter's smirk. I moved us both to the left and gave Mary her beloved Percy to ogle, bowing to the romantic Romantics, a gesture Mamia heartily approved. "There are so many captivating tales to tell the students about those two."

By midafternoon our masterpiece dazzled in the fresh sunlight that, in typical southwestern fashion, had effortlessly shoved aside the storm and claimed the day. Drips a-shimmer, drains a-gurgle, streets ablaze and drying fast. The air was still cool but weighted with a rare humidity. We took several shots of the collage's pristine beauty, then set about washing and disinfecting every surface in the room. Mamia had awakened the urge to start clean, and we knew no one would get there as thoroughly as the two of us. The rows of desks became a circle, one for me among them. Tables lined the east wall, and off to the side squatted a large, ancient, wooden teacher's desk Mamia had unearthed at a used furniture store. Scrubbed, stained, waxed, and polished to sheeny perfection. My headquarters: I felt instructive sitting in it. Less than a week before school started, ready to go.

Late afternoon, weary but triumphant, we returned home to find Lori stirring a pot of chili stew she'd made. I remembered that it was the one dish Joaquin knew how to make and had taught her. The meals she'd learned to cook from her foster mother were not worth sharing, sprung as they had from parts of wild and domestic animals that folks wouldn't eat if they could afford better. She'd been twig-skinny for more than one reason growing up.

The stew wafted a delicious scent through the house, a fitting but unexpected welcome for the hungry art stars and janitorial staff. Mamia was effusive in her praise, and I joined in, a harmless setting in which to speak warmly to Lori, who brightened in the stream of our compliments. Going back for seconds, I passed her in the kitchen, said quietly, "It's nice to have you here. Please let me know if there's anything I can do to make your life easier." In reply she gave me a stricken look: a woman starved for kindness. If Joaquin had only said those words to her once.

"I didn't mean to take your room."

"Glad you did. Living above the garage makes me feel like a man."

A wan flicker. "The cats have things worked out."

Of their own volition, Tiger and Montenegra split their time between my room and Lori's, gifting us each our fair share of their company, like kids of a divorced couple. The garden, however, remained their favorite spot when it was sunny and unsuspecting prey happened by. Not that our majestic pair of felines hadn't laid claim to the entire neighborhood: they had, other cats watching them furtively from porches and bushes. But while all the lands as far as they could stalk were theirs, the heart of their territory remained the garden. There they washed each other, swatted insects, slept entwined, play-boxed like kittens occasionally. The only ones with a perfectly harmonious, idyllic relationship, I noted with a twinge of bitterness. And absolute faith in being reunited despite the unfathomable stupidity of their humans. Or perhaps, in some highly advanced way we couldn't grasp, they had remained connected when they were apart, physical absence a manageable impediment to their happiness.

"I'm glad they're back together."

"It's so good of Shelley, and you, to take us in."

Ah, a crack in the glacier that I intended to widen into a fissure, ultimately melting enough of the substrata to plunge into a real conversation with her. Start from an oblique angle, talking about my new career to both her and Mamia: show them the curricula I was mapping out, solicit their advice, allow the exchange of ideas and stories to become a natural part of our days. As she got used to talking with me, I could begin to get a little more personal, first about her health and the advance of the pregnancy, offer to drive her to the doc's when Mamia was busy, cook dinner with her, slipping in a few savory techniques as I did, invite her for an evening walk afterward. Mamia would back me up fully, pleased to encourage our friendship. As September drew to mid, see if I had a sufficient clearing to apologize for the part I played in the babies' conception, offer to go public with my guilt and accept the blame and contempt sure to follow.

Would she allow that? Would she ever consider a DNA test to see who the babies' father might be? One of each is what I think we both suspected, but what would be the consequence of knowing the father's identity? If it were Joaquin, I'd never have to confess. If they were mine, I would and then take full responsibility, try to woo Lori into a platonic marriage for the sake of the children. I could whittle away at the platonic part, and in a decade or so, she might relent, even if she never came to love me. Getting ahead of yourself, Bug, as ever. Just get the dishes done and head up to your room—after, don't forget, kissing Mamia goodnight and thanking her again for all her help. She's amazing. Like a magnet for those in need: we all stick to her.

The first day of school bore down with an inexorable rush. Oh, no, oh, yes: here it is. Opening ceremonies, welcome back and introduction of new teachers, step forward, smile and bow, then on with the day. Seventeen seniors in my first section, thirteen in the next, then fifteen, eighteen, and twelve more in my AP English class. Two other teachers, to my relief a woman who was only moderately popular and a middle-aged paunchy man, taught the three other sections of seniors and the seven junior sections. I had met both and intended to blow them out of the water, politely.

The reputation that preceded me from last spring needed some undoing and updating. I was the teacher who gave everyone A's and didn't assign papers and told the greatest stories. All true, yet not how things were going to go this year. I decided to set the record straight right off by telling them to address me as Mr. Mann, took roll assiduously, warned them I might be assigning seats (ever an effective way of ending sidebar chatter), then launched directly into an overview of the curriculum, handing out textbooks and assignment due dates, the first an essay by Stephen Hawking on determinism, due tomorrow. Only after this barrage of information did I ease into a story about how I sat through the wrong English class my first day of ninth grade. I ended class with a prereading mystery game to fuel their interest. It was a successful strategy, I decided, as I steered Pacman 2 toward home. The Mann is no pushover but still fun. He has a wicked sense of humor, and he's young enough to *get* us. Alexander the Conqueror. A+: my Day One takeaway.

An expansive replay livened the dinner hour. Too full of myself to have much of an appetite for Mamia's green chili enchiladas, I dominated the table, giving big answers to little questions. For dessert I served tomorrow's reading quiz; both members of my captive audience had generously agreed to help me out by doing the reading assigned to my students, and now both took the quiz, perfect scores for each. Mamia followed up with excellent suggestions for clarifying a couple of the queries. Lori, who had said almost nothing till then, asked why I chose this piece as the opening reading, a great kid challenge that I was glad she'd reminded me to prepare for, and it took me a couple of minutes to smooth out my explanation of the connection to Tralfamadore, where Vonnegut's *Slaughterhouse Five* hero Billy Pilgrim spent his happiest hours. Over the dishes, which we did together, Mamia asked where I wanted tomorrow's discussion to go and how I'd get it there. It was nearly bedtime when we finished, but I felt kite-high, adrenalined to charge into class on zero sleep. The cats striping my bed shifted my mind to off, and I was out before I was drowsy.

A week in, I felt more confident than ever that teacher blood coursed through my veins. A congenital gift, imprinted somewhere on my DNA strands. The kids who felt most comfortable (read alpha boys) ventured to call me TeacherMann, and in turn I gave them nicknames, eschewing the ones they already had in favor of my superior tags grown by observation. "In my class you're Boney. Put on a few lb's and I'll change it to Beast." I was, in education parlance, creating community.

And at home, continuing industriously to slither my way into Lori's good graces. She was enormous now, still six weeks out from her due date in late October, but the doc was convinced the twins would be born in less than three, which was within the normal range. She was slightly dilated and dauntingly active for a woman carrying such a load. When I could tear myself away from TeacherMann, I learned quite a bit about pregnancy and birth. Procedures, positions, processes. I could talk stages of labor, Lamaze breathing techniques, a thinning cervix, breach baby rotation, water breaking, the episiotomy, crowning, and placenta, knew the pros and cons of the epidural, a Caesarian section, of Pitocin drips, and circumcision.

Lori was firmly opposed to any intervention in the birthing process. She had assisted in the delivery of many babies during her nursing days, and back on the farm, of piglets, pups, and kittens. Her preference would have been to give birth at home, but with twins, the risks were too high. She'd seen women lying helpless, numb like slabs from the waist down, while the doctor brought their babies the easiest way for them, the mother simply a receptacle rather than the vehicle of birth. That would not be her experience. With Joaquin out of the picture, this was her one chance at motherhood, and she would bear her children with minimal assistance. No anesthesia, no drip, no forceps, no cutting her belly open: none of that for Nurse Lori. Mamia and the doctor tried to soften her position with any-means-to-an-end arguments, but Lori was uncompromising. She wanted to be fully present throughout, to give birth rather than be delivered of her babies. She rubbed her stomach constantly. We all three were aware that the time and Lori were ripe.

Thursday evening of Week the Second, as we were finishing our roast chicken and pesto, Lori caught her breath. A sudden pain had rippled across her features, light sweat erupting on her upper lip and brow. Mamia had her coach's bag packed, was ready to walk out the door, but Lori held up her hand to wait, wait a minute. The sharp jab passed, and she could breathe again. Her water hadn't broken, no need to go yet. But it was a sign that put us on high alert. She let me walk her to her room, then wanted to go out and walk along the sidewalk lane behind our garden, which led to a pocket park with a bench under a silver maple tree. We walked gingerly in silence, her arm in mine, both expecting another stab and a small deluge from between her legs. At the bench I helped her get settled and let her rest before seating myself beside her.

"Full moon tomorrow night," I noted, well aware, as was she, that more babies are born when the moon is full.

She inclined her head toward me, facing the evening wind, eyes closed, and inhaled deeply. As though we'd entered the viewfinder of a movie lens, the surroundings blurred and the camera zoomed in on a close shot of the duo on the bench. Right on cue she opened her eyes, directly into mine.

"Go ahead. You can talk about it."

Not taken in by the friendship dance, little Lori. She'd known from the start that I was circling ever tighter around that night, our night. Looking for the time and means to address what had happened then and since.

"I'm sorry, Lori. I'm really sorry." Felt so often, never spoken.

"It takes two."

"You were in shock. Unfair advantage for me."

"I wish you'd told Joaquin that."

"Thought you were on birth control."

"I use a—I would have been if I'd imagined—us."

"How could you have? Or that you'd been whirling in the maelstrom of my consciousness for weeks, months, your voice, hands, breath. I knew you, woke up in love with you. And I remain so."

"Sleeping beauty."

"Ugly. And I remain so."

"Woke up to save Tiger's life, and Montenegra's, from my stupidity."

The intimate flow between us encouraged me to wade in.

"Lori, I want at least one of these babies to be mine. So bad."

"We'll never be sure." She pulled away. "I don't intend to find out."

"What if they—"

"No!" Abrupt, vehement, punctuated by a struggle to rise without my help.

Always pushing your luck, dumbo, flying without big ears or a feather. I stood up, tried to catch her elbow, she twisted to get away, staggered, and like a boulder, toppled. On her stomach, on the babies, on the concrete. Before I could grasp the magnitude of her fall, and how would I ever get her back on her feet, the water started to pool.

"Ma—Mamia—help!" Screaming into the night while I yanked my phone from its carrying case. Lori's body constricted in agony, her face torn. Babies, oh, her babies. I swallowed down the bile, crouched beside her, whispering her skin with my hand.

Mamia, the ambulance, the EMT's, us following them at high speed, the IV, surgery center, me shut out behind the doors, Shelley going in, walking beside her at Lori's insistence. The antiseptic bathroom where I threw up, gagging on snot, on rage, on fear, moaning desperate prayers to a god I'd never heeded—please don't let them die, please, please, save them, my children, my children, my children, don't let them die, my father, my Hersch, my children. Staggering against the toilet, door, sink, clutching the stained steel, shaking in a frantic effort to empty myself of craziness, untremble my voice before hauling out the phone to call Joaquin. To say she's in labor, she had a bad fall, come, be with her, I don't know what's going on, you need to be here, Joaquin, Joaquin, hurry. Then breaking down again when he says he's on his way. A cramped, pleading ball on the tile floor.

Drifted into a vision that opened a door into the breezy rocking of a golden rocking chair. Moved slowly up the ornate spindles from behind. Heard before I saw the tots, their gurgles and squeals, a man's voice cooing to them, tufts of his hair cresting the chair's oaken back. Peeked noiselessly over his shoulder at my own frame, in my arms on my knees the twins rocking, cherubic pink and blue, to and fro, and while the motion lasted, all three of us sublimely happy, together alone, to remain in the eternal present. I eased into the rhythmic sway, comforted by the promise of the scene. "All will be well and all manner of thing will be well...."

Pitched forward by the clangor of a phone in my grip. The phrase, I charge you with disturbing the peace, rushed through the gape in my memory, directed at the floor. Time had fractured, and I had no hope of piecing the slivers into a coherent, sequential whole. Cases in point: When had I called Joaquin? I remembered sitting beneath the maple with Lori, but why were we there? At what time of day? And now? What caused her fall? We were at the hospital, but how did we get here? Were the babies born? I'd just seen them, little Miranda and the boy, but that couldn't have happened yet. It seemed unlikely. Who could fill the ragged edges where the splinters of time no longer connected? The phone.

"Alex, where are you?"

"The place of solitude where three dreams cross."

"Where?"

I reconsidered the question. "On the floor."

"Which floor? I've been up and down every floor."

Floors were not vertical surfaces to scale unless there had been a great change in the tilt of the earth. I wondered how to ask.

"Which room?"

There you go, an easy one to lob over the net. "The bathroom."

Silence. Had I made a mistake, disclosing my location? Or did they call this space something different now? "The room with the stainless steel sinks and urinals and toilets behind doors and soap in little oblong dispensers and paper towels to pull down from a black rectangular dispenser and—"

"Just keep talking, sweetheart. I'll find you."

"Mamia?"

"I'm coming."

"The babies?"

"I'll be right there."

One conviction I knew I'd had before opening the door was that if the babies died, I would, too. A man can only take on so much guilt before his conscience bursts.

She brought an orderly in green hospital clothes with her, a soft-limbed fellow who helped me up without bruising my raw core. The orderly and my mother guided me to a room with a bed, so thoughtful of them, I wished I could have told them, but now that I was back in their world, I had lost my voice. I pondered whether we should return for it, no doubt rotting in some corner of the bathroom, unless I'd flushed it down the john. An image of my voice with a balloon yelling, "Help me! Save me!" as it was sucked into the drainpipe made me laugh. A prick. Then the blessing of void.

19

The Granite Abyss

It was morning, and Mamia was still with me, haggard, drooping, in a stuffy chair.

"Alex?"

She smiled, tight, wary.

"How are you feeling?"

I hurt. Alive.

"Would you like some water, sweetheart?"

"Okay."

They'd gone back for my voice, which had been lost. I recognized it as mine. "Tell me."

She scooted the dumpy chair closer to the bed, took my hand.

"What happened? Did Joaquin come?"

"Yes. He's with Lori. She's fine."

I had failed to consider the possibility that she might not be.

"The doctors urged her to have a Caesarian as soon as we arrived, but she was already in labor and wanted so much to try for a vaginal birth. It was slow, so slow, not really but that's how it seemed when we were counting every minute. Very dangerous, the waiting, and so traumatic for her little body, lurching through contractions. No epidural, no relief. She wanted to experience the births naturally. I was crazy with fear, but Lori was committed to it, against the doctor's advice."

Mamia gulped the water she had offered me. I knew we were headed into perilous terrain.

"Then, thank all the gods that be, the first baby's head dropped and she could push. Joaquin came in just in time to see it crown. We watched the body emerge and slip out, neat as could be. A beautiful, perfect baby, five pounds, three ounces, a girl, Miranda Michelle, aspirated, crying, she and Joaquin and I, my tears and his euphoric. He held her as they cut her cord. His baby girl. My own designated granddaughter. Lord, what a miracle."

I breathed, as I hadn't during Mamia's tale, expecting tragedy.

"Number two child, the other twin. Less willing to follow its sister into the world, did not come and did not come and after an hour the doctor forcefully recommended a C-section. He urged us to convince her it was the safest way, the surest. I started to, but Lori reprimanded me; I was to be her advocate, and she wanted to give birth as women were meant to, without intervention. Joaquin was desperate but held his tongue. The doctor and nurses were monitoring the baby, still getting a heartbeat, so they let her labor on. Oh, my god, Alex, I was as worried for Lori as the baby; it was awful to watch her suffer so fiercely—and unrelentingly. Finally, finally, it entered the birth canal, and as it did so, as it was dropping, as she was readying to push at last, the heartbeat grew faint, grew fainter, everyone panicked, terrified, I nearly passed out but forced myself to stay conscious, breathing with Lori, the doctor worked that baby out as fast as he could, it crowned, a little boy, perfect, also."

She paused. I readied myself for a hallelujah shout.

"But dead. Neither the doctor nor his staff could revive him. God, how they all tried. He would not breathe. His heart would not beat. He turned blue. Stillborn. Died in the birth canal. Miranda's brother. Despite my fears, somehow I believed till the end Lori would triumph, but she didn't. Should have had the C-section. But who knows what might have gone awry there? It's no one's fault, Alex, not yours nor Lori's nor mine, Joaquin's, the doctor's, not anybody's. He could have crowned a few minutes earlier and been fine. You just don't know."

This was not how it was supposed to turn out. I'd rocked the twins on my knees, rocked them in a golden oak chair, cradled in my arms, laughing. How could one of them have died since then?

"Her fall must have weakened him. Done some internal damage. If she hadn't fallen, he would have made it."

"Alex, my dear son, you're such a dualistic thinker. Life is not a simple bifurcation of alternatives. There are innumerable possibilities that lead to consequences. If Lori hadn't fallen, she might have gone into labor at 3:00 a.m. and I might have been so groggy driving her to the hospital that we got into an accident. Or a million other things. Harvey might have tripped and never emerged from the house. You can't keep laying the blame for the worst outcomes at your own feet. We all play many roles in one another's lives, and each has its own effect and each modifies the infinite paths that converge and diverge as we walk them. You are not responsible for her baby's death. Please believe that."

Mamia quivered to her feet, turned to face the rising sun. "He was perfect. Beautiful child. Still warm, at the threshold of this world. I've never, I've never seen a dead baby." Choked on a sob, let out a keening breath. She was exhausted, her shoulders drawn inward to constrict the grief. Not everything's about you, TeacherMann. Get out of your head and give your mother the comfort she deserves. Hold her. I did, soothed and let her weep. I'd never seen a newborn at all, could not conjure the image of one dead. But this one, which I knew as one knows certain unknown things, was my son whom I had rocked beside his sister in the golden oak chair, I had to see. Now: the desire swelling to urgency, before it was too late.

"Where is he? What's going to happen to him?"

Mamia's sharp look warned me off. "He's in the hospital morgue, I'd guess. Why?"

"In the morgue! I have to see him." Too cold down there for a newborn.

"That's ghoulish, Alex. Why torture yourself?"

"I have to go to him. Right away."

"What about Miranda? And Lori and Joaquin?"

I pulled on my pants and shoes, ran my fingers shaking through my hair.

"I'm sure you'll need Lori's permission." But I was out the door, forcing myself to walk, act calm.

Of course she was right, a hurdle I was unlikely to surmount. Lori would know why, which didn't mean she would agree, but what would Joaquin think? And I could not, now or ever, tell him, a man converted to fatherhood, his earlier resistance and cruelty forgiven in the whelm of love. The three of them in her room, a tableau of redeemed harmony, parents bending toward their child, who slept in the sweet assurance of her welcome. Who would have the gall to enter that charmed circle and demand to see the son who wasn't there, the dead other? Though the sear of his loss lay just behind the ecstasy in his mother's eyes, flaring shame and anguish. He could have been saved.

There might still be time. I needed to talk to her alone, persuade her let me see the dead other. "Hey, Joaquin, if you need to take a break, I'll be happy to take your place for a while. You've been up all night. Go on, get some rest. They've got beds."

Wearing a smile too big for his face: "Thanks, man. I'm fine. Can't leave my women. I'll crawl in next to Lori when I get sleepy." His widening smile defying the laws of physics, "My mom's on her way here to meet Miranda. And Lori."

Lori jumping in, "Shelley was planning to invite Clarice up here so we could get acquainted, but it, she didn't get a chance to." She cocked her head at me. "I think of Shelley as the mother I would have loved to have, so she's like Miranda's maternal grandmother. Our little girl has a wonderful family." The clock was ticking.

"That makes you in effect her uncle." Joaquin must have swallowed the Cheshire cat. "Would you like to hold her?" He vacated the chair for me, laid the swaddled Miranda in my arms.

For the first time I took a close look at her, and yes, in the realm of babies, she was spectacular. Not that I had any to compare her with, but true beauty is singular in nature. Her hair was light like mine, her eyes, when they opened briefly, blue like mine, her nose and mouth, ears, chin—all modeled on mine. She burbled, yawned, and the way her lips and face moved was a double for baby videos of me, which I'd watched with the parentitos ad nauseam. Not only was the boy my son, but Miranda was clearly my daughter. The thought that I was rocking one of the children I'd fathered shivered me. I tightened my grip on her blanket.

Joaquin, hovering observer, "Are you okay?"

My god, I could never give her up, hand her back to her wrongful father, who had not wanted her be born. If he'd had his way, she wouldn't have been. Neither of them; he was probably relieved to be down to one. Whereas I was profoundly dedicated to them both from the moment they began life in the womb. This baby, and her brother cooling too fast in the morgue, belonged to me. I'd have to tell him, get the DNA test, prove my parenthood, assert my rights. She was mine. They both were. I would not surrender my children.

"Alex, man, you look bad. Here, you're the one who needs rest." He reached out for Miranda, and I rose, prepared to defend my claim. Alerted suddenly by my face or her new mother instincts, Lori swung out of bed with astonishing agility and took Miranda from me.

"Get some sleep. It's been a long night." Firm, icy. Her mouth set hard.

"Where's the other baby, the boy no one's talking about?" I stepped toward her.

Joaquin, rigid, poised to spring. Lori furious. "Get out."

"In the morgue? You're just going to leave him there to rot?" And I heard my fangs gashing her but couldn't stop. "He could have been saved. He could be here now, lying beside his sister: he should be and you just let him slip away and now his name will never be spoken again so he'll disappear from memory. His name—you didn't even know his name: his name was Yeats Eliot Stranger. I rocked him, Yeats and Miranda, in a golden oak chair, laughing, and this was not how things were supposed to turn out. He was mine and he didn't die: you killed him, you threw him away, you gave up on him, he would have come around if you'd laid him on your stomach held him given him a fucking few more minutes but you had the one you wanted and he was the extra, the discard, the other, my son I should have been there, let me go to him maybe it's not too late to save but so cold down there where you let them put him in the morgue in the ground cover him up. Aren't you tired yet of covering him up, making believe he's not mine, my flesh rotting in the morgue because you're a coward and a stubborn bitch who had to have things your way even when, no because, you were sure to lose him? Did you hate me that much, did you? Kill me then, not him, not one of my babies. They're both mine, they're mine, he was mine, mine, hell of a way to make me pay for my sins, sacrifice my son, and now you think I'll let you take my daughter, you—"

Lunged for her, lunged fast, but Joaquin stepped between us, shielding her.

"You're glad he's dead, down to one, wanted them both dead you never wanted them at all murderer don't deserve her give me—"

And the room was suddenly full of people, Mamia coming in with a cropped gray-haired woman and a different hospital man grabbing me roughly and suddenly my knees buckled, and everything was sudden now, me shrieking into the dark, dying, of which I was glad, to join my son if I could just tell them to lay me next to him in the morgue, we could go away together and no one will ever know he was mine, glad to be rid of us.

"Alex, Alex, my dear son, why must you torment yourself so?"

Wrong. I'm the father, not the son. Too late now to save him, tagged and bagged in a drawer of the morgue. If Tiger had been here…but that was a glacier from another age. Where was I now? Where were any of us, carrying on the daily pretense that we knew where we were, living on what we believed was secure ground, wading unaware deeper into the corpse-stratified quicksand grave of living on.

In the room that was my own, over the garage, in my bed, with no memory of the passage from there to here. The cats straddling a patch of sun, whose eastward origin pointed toward it being morning, another one. I had to come back to consensus reality, take up the walking stick of my given role, and shuffle on. Apologize, be nice, predictable, write off the chimera of happiness that had propelled me across the desert. I had no children, no lover, no prospects. I was a scarred, mean 26, and in a decade would be a bitter middle-aged. My life would be ebb, the vacancy of expectation, the sterility of imagination, the absence of desire. When Mamia died, I would remain alone in this house that I hated, ill-kept and ill-kempt, rocking barren-armed to dust. I rose and dressed to begin the countdown.

Mamia, of course, with breakfast on the table, glad to see me though I needed a thorough scrubbing. She spoke quietly, perhaps to avoid reawakening my frenzy. Made sure I knew she loved me, my bedrock mother. Talked about, literally, the weather. And when I'd eaten my fill, less than she hoped, added without reproach, "I called the school yesterday and told them you wouldn't be in: family emergency. Monday, too, so you have a long weekend to recover."

I had forgotten yesterday was Friday. No notes for the sub; they probably just screwed around, gleeful not to have homework. My schedule was off, and I'd have to do some reclamation work to get us back on track. What would I tell them about why I'd missed class? Nothing, very little. It was nobody's business. Or I could make up something outrageous, tell each section a different crazy story and let them compare notes. That would be the fun teacher way to go. Better get rolling. I had a lot to do.

"Thanks, I mean really thank you, for calling in for me, Mamia. And, just to say it for openers, I am so sorry about last night. The night before last, I mean. And yesterday. The whole thing. We can talk more later. And I'll send Joaquin and Lori a letter of apology, too." I hugged her; she did not withdraw from my foul-smelling embrace. Not my mother.

"You can tell them yourself in person," she smiled. I recoiled. Hadn't thought where they might be. In the hospital, I guess.

"They're staying here with us just till tomorrow. Lori thinks she's strong enough to travel to Trove already. The doc can look after her. I understand, but I had so much hoped to have more time with Miranda. Clarice is going down with them, which it's her place to do, of course."

Mamia was squeezing the apples in our fruit bowl to hold onto her composure. "Lori promised to come up and visit me with Miranda whenever she can. I know she will. I just wish she would rest a couple of weeks and let me take care of her before leaving. But she's eager to go home. And Joaquin has to get back to tend—"

"I've got a lot of work to do for my classes, especially after missing Friday." Shuttled my dishes to the sink, poured a fresh cup of coffee. "I'll catch them on their way out."

"What about din—"

"Thanks for the great breakfast." Halfway over my shoulder, gone.

Reading over my notes was profoundly impressive. I created all this? What a genius, only 26. My curriculum had rhythm, had flow, had weave, had thematic unity and layered intent. A brilliant creation. Someday it would be a book: required reading in every education department. I would become one of the gods of this field, in urgent demand on speaking tours and at very high-level conferences. I could tell them about my little room above the garage, the classic artist's garret where I planned and wrote my first masterpiece: Year One Curriculum. With this lofty vision driving me, I set about tinkering with it, trimming the fat and adding perfection to slower moments.

I rested from my labors only when the dogs of hunger growled in my belly. On the verge of heading into the amazing self-replenishing kitchen, I remembered that they were here and might be hanging around. Texted Mamia not to count on me for dinner, then zipped off in Pacman 2 to get a pizza and a six-pack. Saw Mamia watching me out the window; too bad, but I'd outgrown curfew.

Sent one more text while I was waiting for my pizza, to Joaquin and Lori. It felt like a safe distance from which to say, "I'm really sorry, J n L. Was out of my mind, a place I go too often. Congrats on Miranda. Wish u 3 a happy life. Your weird friend and uncle ~Alex"

The plan for tonight was to wolf the pizza (choice bits for the cats, of course, if they stayed with me), medicate myself with beer, sleep long and prosper in the unconscious. Morpheus was the greatest of my gods. With luck, the Strangers would be gone by the time I awoke, and I could begin pretending this weekend never happened.

The iridescent blue of the near-dusk sky lit my way to the stairs. Pizza to my chest, six-pack dangling from the right-hand middle fingers. Looked up as I mounted the bottom step to find Joaquin seated on the top one, obviously waiting for me. My heart turned around and left while my legs kept trudging toward him. Exactly what I'd hoped to avoid, the one-on-one. I should never have sent that text.

Joaquin rose and stepped aside to let me enter my room, then followed.

"Want some pizza? A beer?"

"No, thanks, but you should go for it while it's hot. And cold."

Good: that would keep my mouth full of something besides venom. I popped a top, slugged half a beer, shoved a wide slice into my maw. The big problem being that I wasn't hungry any longer, my stomach contracted into a wad.

"You deserve to know what happened," Joaquin began. So did he, but I'd been stripped of vindictiveness. "And to know that you were right about a lot of things that had best been left unsaid. Medically speaking, yeah, Lori did let her son die by not allowing the doctor to perform a C-section. But the whole time she was working full-out to bring him into the world, give him a life begun right. She's stubborn that way; her abusive childhood perhaps explains it. And her origins unknown. When he arrived—and we both would have loved to name him Yeats, call him that in our heads since you spoke his name; Lori whispered, 'Things fall apart' over and again after you left when we were alone—she did what you said she should have: held him on her stomach, rubbing him to bring him back. After the docs had a go at reviving him, she took him to her again: tried mouth-to-mouth resuscitation, massaged his heart, would not let them cut the cord, would not let him go. She was sobbing, screaming. Shelley took Miranda out of the room to keep her from hearing her mother's pain. I tried to comfort her, but my efforts were suspect because— right again, Alex—I'd forfeited my rights to be her helpmate, I who'd wanted both babies aborted early on. Who shunned his beloved when she continued to carry them. If you hadn't called, I wouldn't have even been there. Thank you for calling, my friend."

Bile rising again from the cancerous secret in my gut. Should have bought a 12-pack.

"When we finally pried the utterly and truly dead baby from her, Lori begged to have him in the room with her, which was against hospital rules. Once again, your question about why he wasn't there with us struck home. I spent, the hospital chaplain spent, hours reassuring her and gently redirecting her attention to the living child, to Miranda. There she came to rest, from there the joy sprang, to there she fled and with a refugee's desperation for a new home, pinned her focus."

Joaquin shifted, then stood and faced the window, a sky-drawn silhouette in the dark room. It was better for both of us not to flip the switch. "I've never had a baby in my arms, this one mine, which I never expected to have. A girl, yes, a delicate girl child. Humiliating as it to admit, I much prefer a daughter to a son, a break from the patterns that made me revile fatherhood." His voice dropped low, redolent with tears. "I am happier with one than two, with Miranda than Yeats. But if he had lived, I would have opened my arms to him. Tried to emulate my grandparents, who were so good to me. I could have done it, once he was in my arms. I'm not a monster."

Would that I could say as much, popping the third top.

"The point is that you should know you were right on, Alex, and your words broke our hearts, something only one who genuinely knows us could have done. I wish you hadn't spoken because it hurt so much to hear aloud the terrible questions and accusations we had leveled silently at ourselves."

Time to apologize with so much more than a text. The reckless damage I'd done was irreparable, as whatever I did to those I loved proved to be. The babies were Joaquin's; my balls were no doubt frozen in the cabin, or fried earlier. The rocking chair an image conjured to assuage my guilt. Rise, ugly man undeserving of mercy, sorry for everything, sorry, sorry sorry. But he—

"Alex, nevertheless, we want you to know—yes, Lori, too—that you are Miranda's uncle, our closest friend, and if you want to come back to Trove, you're welcome in our home, our family."

—stripped me of my intended apology by offering forgiveness where condemnation was due. Homecoming in place of exile. Friendship for enmity, and I had said Joaquin was not a man of that ilk.

No words to return to him, only my beaten self, which rose without volition and lurched over to embrace him, as I had never done before. Both of us in tears, hanging onto each other as I could not have imagined two straight men doing, especially being one of them. From the eyeless safety of his shoulder I confessed the harbored dream.

"I'd been thinking I'd be the babies' father, raise them as my own, after being the worst son a good man ever suffered become the best father the twins could wish. Watch them grow, hear them call me daddy, fill their lives with love and happiness. But it wouldn't have worked anyway because Lori would never have allowed me to be a father to them."

"Oh, in time I'm sure she would have."

"No, she'd never have forgiven me."

"For what?"

This was the moment to tell him. The truth. Nothing but. Or forever hold my peace.

"For not being you."

A simple truth, whole enough. My night with Lori was not itself to blame, though it had been the catalyst for our labyrinthine passage to this moment; it was my irrational assumption that at its end she would love me as she did Joaquin. Her love was what I'd sought through entering her body. So pathetic a delusion. Even if Miranda was biologically mine, she would be his in all ways that mattered.

He stepped away from me. Still awash in tears, just visible in the ebb light of day. Stood and let empath silence speak, time dry grief and heal memory. Bridge the riving.

"Even so, you called."

I did, and if I hadn't.

"And saved me."

The crickets loud and monotonous drove weariness into my skull bones. Joaquin bade farewell with a second embrace and slipped out the door. At the top stair, he turned. "Please see us off in the morning."

One more scene and I could get back to my life. My classroom. My teaching. Coming up: *One Flew Over The Cuckoo's Nest*, whose inmates were certifiably sane. Constructing a reality in which the outcomes commingled poignant injustice with a sharp hope that elevated the readers' humanity. Rather than cursing the gods, they sat among them, gazing benevolently on the noble, unmerited suffering humankind inflicted on itself.

As the next morning, when I joined Mamia in wishing the Strangers a safe journey and sweet homecoming. Met Clarice properly, she assuring me of no need to apologize, Lori warm and kind, knowing our transgression sealed impermeably. They wreathed us in extravagant gratitude and enfolded us with bountiful hugs. Three-day-old Miranda passed from Mamia's hand to mine, babe of placid grace, and they departed with Lori's promises of frequent returns and Joaquin's effusive invitations to visit them in Trove. I draped my arm over Mamia, trembled by the leave-taking, waving, smiling, recalling how in days of yore los parentitos had stood just so to see me off.

"You all right?" I asked as they disappeared around the corner. Mamia buried her face in my shoulder.

"I'm going to miss them." Her voice like cracked stone.

"We'll go down soon. Don't worry." Patting her arm solicitously. "Can I do anything for you?"

That vaulted a smile from the granite abyss.

Alex, taking care of his mom, thinking of others before himself, a grownup Mann at last. Nevermore to be scarred and spurned by impulsive stupidity. Bodes well for his career and possibly even at some point his legitimate fatherhood, wouldn't you say? But as Mamia has occasionally, in jest when he was nearly late to school, reminded him, he was slow being born and had been slow ever since. Slower than molasses in January, Papito adaged.

Assumption junction, Hersch threw in whenever Bug got ahead of himself.

20

"Where Thou Art, There is the World"

"Alex, my faithful and virtuous knight," Rose's letter began. I was sitting in the garden, watching Tiger hunt lizards. "It has been a year since I last wrote."

A year? I had received her letter only a few months ago. I jolted to my room and pulled it from the nightstand drawer. No date on the letter, but the postmark on the envelope read June of the previous year. Clearly it had been as lost as she was. I returned to the garden and continued with her current missive.

"Justine Lake and I were wed on the Isle of Skye. Yes, beloved Justine, our erstwhile senior English teacher, is now my wife and I hers, in a sublime state of marital grace. Life, my dear first and always friend, which I can now claim as mine, self-conceived and of love made, has begun. Consider me back in the world, and as promised, you are among the first to know.

"I can feel you rereading that paragraph, X. Take a short break to get yourself a beer, settle William Blake on your lap, and start over."

Right.

"Before I tell you the story, which is a grand epic that you will relish, let me say that if I had wanted to marry a man, it would have been you. I was never in love with one, but I loved you more than any. A part of me wishes you could have been at the wedding as my Best Mann, which you are. You would have loved it, Alex, being there. After a week of rain in Edinburgh, we took the train to Inverness, stayed overnight at a sweet wee inn that I'll tell you about later, and the next morning drove west past rain-swollen Loch Ness into sun-clad Skye, its green hills lightly heathered, gulls and eagles cavorting in the billowy air. It was a day the gods had set aside for themselves to frolic on pinnacles, gazing oceanward, as did we, clasping the Isle whole and pure in our euphoric embrace.

"I had a dream once, wherein I envisioned myself dressed in lavender and leather. Well, on this occasion I was, in a flowing dress that echoed the hue of the majestic slopes. Gray suede boots and silver earrings, my hair adorned with garlands of wildflowers. You'll get a photo soon. Justine, oh, my exquisite mate, was in green and gold, outshining the leaves of birch and briar. She carried roses, I marguertine, oracle of the mountains, and these we exchanged with our rings and vows. It was only the two of us, and an officiant (our friend, a pastor himself gay), abreast a mountain overlooking the Atlantic. We danced, in trio, and sang romantic madrigals that prospered in our hearing as wine flooded our veins. Then picnicked on salmon and asparagus, my favorite meal of summer. Fresh pastries for the sensual finish, and a good loll, hand-in-hand, in the sun on our garden quilt. Late afternoon, which on solstice is more like noon in the day's arc of northern Scotland, we drove down to the harbor at the far western edge of Skye and took a boat ride into the bay, where orcas swam in number and puffins squatted on rocks, diving at will for fish. Among these rare and stunning brethren of the deep we traveled jubilantly, blessed by their acceptance of our vessel. At day's end, near midnight, we celebrated once more at the tiny inn of Inverness where we had stayed the night before. They have a suite of rooms upstairs, whence we by candlelight ascended well into the early hours of tomorrow, but neither of us yet wearied of this day. The rain had stopped, and for a brief stretch of darkness the land stilled. We lay together, occasionally dozing but never asleep, unwilling to let go of our absolute and impermeable bliss. I need words exceeding any description I know of joy-wonder-gratitude-ecstasy. Juliet, a rose by any other name, says to her Romeo,

> "'And yet I wish but for the thing I have
> My love is infinite. The more I give to thee
> the more I have.'

"Yes, something approaching that effusive cry.

"You can't be shocked, my friend, hearing me attest to my adoration of Justine, you won't be; I'm sure of that. You were a close observer behind those hoodied senior-year eyes and must have discerned even then that I worshipped her. What neither of us understood was that mine was not merely a student crush on an outstanding teacher but a true passion, on every level of being, that did not manifest itself until I ran into Justine in Berlin, which is where my story begins. This leg of the tale, in any case. It's been a long journey for us from Vista Grande to the Isle of Skye.

"When last I wrote, I was in Oslo, under the assumed identity of Sydney Jones. Drifting through Scandinavia, I waited out the summer, then headed south in fall to Germany. What I did not tell you is that I knew through email exchanges with Justine (yes, I'd kept up with her) that she was coming to Berlin to study at the university, working toward a doctorate in modern German drama, focusing on Bertolt Brecht. (Read his plays sometime, Bug; they're amazing.) I'd had my fill of anonymous Sydney and was eager to be myself for a spell, converse with a good friend.

"It was in this state that I arrived at Justine's door in Berlin. Autumn tinged the broad avenue of chestnut trees on a late afternoon of rare warmth when I knocked, hiding a grin at the anticipation of her shock on seeing prim little Rose so disguised. What I did not anticipate is how delighted she would be to see me in any guise. She'd been pining for New Mexico, loneliness soughing through her as it had me, both of us feeling, cast by our own hand, into alien winds. Justine's was a purposeful challenge, an honor, in truth, to be accepted into a doctoral program at the University, and though difficult and intense years lay ahead, she would come through them with a tremendous education, a far greater fluency in German, and quite possibly, a coveted position at a university here or back home. She had been in Berlin a mere two months; soon enough her congeniality would win her a covey of friends. I, by contrast, was rootless, Justine my only contact. But what a splendid one: She invited me to stay with her till I found a place of my own and made certain I felt welcome—more than: awaited. That evening on her narrow balcony I knew at last I'd made the right decision to flee from Bruce.

"How we fell in love I will not relate in a letter beyond saying that we did, profoundly, and so tumble-turn swiftly that I now understand why 'fall' is the chosen verb for love. Justine discovered me, uncovering who I never knew I was but yearned to have been: Rose free of duty, of assumptions, others' expectations, fears—all manner of constraints that bound me. I was at last at peace with myself, though I'd never thought I'd been at war, but how I could have known I was until I was not? A fountain of vibrant joy poured from my spirit, replenishing itself endlessly on its own rapture. By all accounts that winter in Berlin was dreadful, gruesomely cold and dark, but for me the city sparkled, and its chill never penetrated my happiness.

"While Justine was at classes, I attended a language school to learn German, which I am now speaking well enough to pass as a native with foreigners. It's a marvelous language, Alex, and you should learn it to uphold your heritage."

The daydream of a sojourn in my paternal homeland, a German wife and children, flared and withered in an unvoiced laugh. Rosie had lived that fantasy, as so many of mine in which she'd figured and that had never come to pass.

"At Christmas Justine and I moved together to a larger place and each gave the other the gift of a kitten, Russian blues from the same litter, mine named Sydney (in memory of my former identity *and* the Elizabethan poet), hers Bertolt, or BeBe. They are the dearest pair, clever, inventive, and so affectionate. But be certain they are no match for William Blake, who is a god among cats. I wonder, does he show any signs of age? I long to see both of you again, to hold one of you in each arm and thank you for your enduring loyalty to me. Others were not so kind.

"The following spring, once again lilac season and just as glorious in Berlin, Justine persuaded me to return to Britain and apologize to the family I'd abandoned. It was doubtful they were still searching for me, and I worried they might have thought me dead, but she assured me we would reappear in time to prevent their declaring me so. Notice that I said 'we,' for I would not have had the courage to go without her. And I was right to be apprehensive: the clan I'd deserted, mainly Bruce and Fiona but myriad others as well, were outraged and unforgiving.

"We traveled first to Glen Aerie, stopping overnight at that wee inn by Inverness (the same one we stayed in our wedding night—this is when we discovered it), where, after a hefty shot of whiskey, I called Fiona. Her greeting was terse, uncharitable. She suggested we visit the following afternoon from 4:00 to 5:00, making clear we were not invited for dinner or overnight. She asked no questions concerning my whereabouts nor expressed any pleasure at my return. She also failed to mention that Bruce was there, on break, as he would have been the year before, planning our wedding, but this time recuperating from a suicide attempt for which, we learned, I was to blame.

"Fiona met us at the door and guided us stiffly into the garden. It was a fine afternoon, right for tea on the lawn, which her housemaid served us. We spoke of nothing personal—current news stories, the queen's impending visit to Edinburgh, the weather.

She had made herself a distant relative on whom I was paying an obligatory call on my way elsewhere. Just as the hour was up, Bruce appeared at the garden door. Fiona rose hastily to shield his view of us: impossible, of course. He joined us with a dignified, formal greeting, seeming very much in control except that he was in a nightshirt with hair askew, as though he'd just awakened from a nap. Shocked by his unkempt appearance, I braced myself for a terrible scene ahead.

"When my aunt's endeavors to prompt our departure failed because Bruce would have none of it, she tried to take up the mindless conversation we'd been having, which also failed. His eyes harrowing me, he asked all the questions I'd expected from Fiona: where I'd been, what I'd been doing, what my plans were. His tone was professorial, a show of interest in a former student whose answers he would not remember. I found it hard at first to breathe, but as the interrogation went on and my voice grew more robust, the familiarity of such a conversation lured me into believing all was well. He'd recovered and moved on. I smiled, sat back, and the instant Bruce noted that shift, he pounced.

"'Had you decided to leave me when you boarded the train?' Fierce now, claws and teeth bared.

"'No.' That pacified him briefly.

"'When, then? You must have had a plan.' Not waiting for a response, he assaulted me. 'Why, Rose? Did you think of me, how I would feel? No word—you're just gone. Saw only what you wanted. Selfish bitch. I loved you, I trusted you, two become one, happy, a life, blessed by children, all my dreams, I had no thought of losing you. Why? If you had told me. Declined my proposal. No decency, no grace. You are a monster, and I am desperate to spurn you. If I could rip out my heart.'

"A sudden wind ravaged the garden, overturning cups, hurling napkins and sweets across the lawn. Bruce was on his feet, shirt and hair flying. Justine later called him a mad Lear, which was too harsh, but the transformation was shocking. With energy drawn from the wind, he advanced on me screaming, 'I did try to, but it would not come. What matter? I am already dead.'

"His screams rose to hoarse, wracking sobs as he stood over me, hands clenched. Justine, o brave my beloved, grabbed him from behind and shoved him down. There he lay huddled, all moan and wail, shaking. My aunt rushed to his side, baleful glare fixed on me. I gathered myself to run off, arm in arm with Justine, when the cruelty of my deeds struck me full on, and I dropped to my knees in the whistling grass to apologize to Bruce and to Fiona.

"'Too late,' she spat. 'Get out. You are not welcome at Glen Aerie nor ever will be.'

"'Too late,' he shrieked. 'You have mortally wounded me and will not be forgiven.'

"I collapsed, horrorstruck by my guilt. Too abashed to plead for mercy, nor was it offered. This exceptional suitor, my fiancé for a night, had been diminished to a shuddering hysteric. My desertion, as I heard more about from others afterward, had been unimaginable within the compass of his globe: rendered him unable to see himself in the mirror. The only way to be sure that he still lived was to kill himself, an attempt that failed but only physically. His spirit was indeed dead, murdered. He lived a recluse at Glen Aerie.

"When I fled, he'd taken a leave the intervening year to search for me, though Fiona made it amply clear that I had forsaken him. Because I'd had no chance to disguise myself before reaching the airport in Edinburgh, I was easily traced as far as Oslo, where the trail vanished. Bruce railed against her, went to war with the evidence in the absolute conviction that flight was not in my nature. Had I gone freely, I would have left him a note. Had I not wished to marry him, I would have refused him.—And why hadn't I done both or at least one of those things? What would it have cost me to be kind?—He was fixed in his belief and pursued my ghost all over Scandinavia. It was a miracle we didn't bump into each other at some remote train station—had we, my life would have taken the established course I had foreseen: I would have lied, returned with him, proceeded to become his wife. The near-miss of that reality dizzied my head, bile rising to my throat. At the next instant shame blanched me, seeing what misery I had wrought in Bruce and also in Fiona, who had become as a mother to him and was herself brutally disappointed by my faithlessness. I left terrible carnage in my wake, dear Alex, and will pay for it in the grand reckoning."

Good to know I'll have a friend in hell.

"Of the clan whole, only one family was genuinely glad to see me again, that because of a new member—and he a complete surprise. Lou. Mr. Lou Best, my beloved father. Living now with a widowed cousin of Katherine's, Heather Maxwell, and her two daughters, Barbara and Emily, in Edinburgh. She had taken him in as a boarder, but the relationship had unfolded into romance. What was Lou doing here, his first trip to Europe? Of course. And like Bruce, he'd hunted quite assiduously for me, but unlike Bruce, he relinquished his claim on the runaway when my intention to get lost was undeniable, and unlike everyone else, he was certain I'd be back. Thus vindicated, and rejuvenated by love, he celebrated my appearance with biblical generosity: homecoming of the prodigal daughter. Justine met with warm acceptance by all, and the evening after my return, we sat down to a providential meal.

"As he carved into a sumptuous dinner of roast lamb, my father seemed curiously at ease with my liaison with Justine. Having two sisters and a daughter, now two more prospective ones, Lou was accustomed to being a man among women, his ways softened by them. But a lesbian was outside the Best family traditions, and I expected a cooler reception from him till Barbara spoke up. She was twenty, attending the university, living at home and elsewhere.

"'It's a grand relief to have allies in the family,' she began, directing her words at Justine and me.

"'Her girlfriend Innie is trans,' Heather added, without the slightest discomfort or animosity.

"Justine cocked her head at Heather in clear admiration. 'So you don't mind a bit.'

"'She's a lovely young woman, Innie is. I would only object if she were unkind to my Barbara.'

"Like yours, Alex, an amazing mother. My eyes swam with gratitude—and longing. Justine's parents, too, had supported her when she came out to them at nineteen in a less tolerant era. Only I was cursed with a wretched one—blinking, for a nightmarish instant I thought I saw Katherine at the dusky window. Dropped my fork, startled, and reared back. Lou, the benevolent patriarch at the table, followed my gaze.

"'It's a mulberry with odd branchings. I've sometimes caught her silhouette in it.' He grasped my hand. 'You can guess she's not really happy with me.'

"'I've given Lou full permission to trim the offensive limbs or contour them in my image,' Heather added. This woman is imperturbable, Bug, gracious and witty. I want to be her daughter. Or Shelley's. It's possible that a woman like me needs several mothers.

"The evening grew boisterous as we switched from champagne to whiskey, retiring to the drawing room, where we sprawled across the sofas, chairs, and cushioned floor. Stories flowed, laughter, memories hard and tender, weaving us into a new-knit family. I thought of Glen Aerie, my abiding love for it and Fiona, wishing them well, yet so relieved I was here instead. Bruce, too, yes, and others I had wounded. In an eddy of contentment, I sent blessings to everyone streaming. May all manner of thing be well.

"I surfaced from my reverie when Justine, stretched out beside me on the floor, drifted her hand across my cheek. She wore a face-cracking smile, her head resting on one arm, as she began.

"'You all know I taught this beautiful woman when she was a senior in high school. I was a first-year teacher, unsure of myself but elated to be embarking on a new career. The first day my hands shook so badly that I waited till near the end of class to pick up the stack of syllabi I'd intended to pass out to the students at the beginning. In retrospect, I have no idea what I said or did during that period, but I do remember the one girl who opened a discussion I'd not thought possible to have so soon. She was brilliant, raising questions about the nature of reality and its role in the text assigned for summer reading. I was deeply impressed and ever so grateful to you for diving straight in, Rose.'

"'We didn't get very far as I recall. Sander asked, 'What is reality?', potentially a rich question, but Hersch countered with, 'What isn't?' Everyone laughed, and that was the end of that inquiry. Still, I knew from that first day that yours would be a real class.' I kissed the hand caressing me.

"'What you didn't know, my dearest, is that during that opening class, I fell in love with you. Yeah, right then, in an utterly impossible situation. My dreams, day and night, brimmed with you. Your name echoed through the inmost chamber of my heart like a long-drawn yearning. Oh, the will I had to summon when you came to my office to review drafts, when you began to confide in me. Never allowed myself to touch you or even sit too close for fear an ardent breath would give me away. It was torture; it was bliss. I couldn't stand to be near you nor bear not to be.'

"Alex, imagine how she suffered, and I never guessed."

Nope, neither did I. My teen-boy take on Justine was that she had to be in love with me, despite my pathetic performance in her class. Maybe because of it, you know, her saving me from failure. And since I was in love with Rose, who was in love with all things elusively English and anything but me, it looked like one of those doomed romantic chase triangles. As a teacher now myself, in daily contact with nubile adolescent girls who worshipped me, I could empathize with how much restraint Justine would have had to exercise, and way more than if she'd been in love with me. Back then Rosie might have been flattered, but she wouldn't have been ready.

Several pages left to go. Could be a two-beer letter, but Mamia was in the kitchen, starting up dinner, and I didn't want to sit down at the table drunk. I grabbed Tiger on his way to accost the legs of Shelley the Soft Touch Scrap Dispenser and forced him to hang in with his compañero.

"Justine extended her drained whiskey glass to me. 'Just a tipple more, would you mind, sweetheart?'

"Of course I obliged, getting refills for myself, Heather, and Barbara as well. My father still preferred ale, but tonight he was too full of joy to imbibe anything more. On my second trip back with glasses, Justine swung up as though to stand, took our drinks and set them aside on the floor, put her hands to my hips to arrange me directly before her, standing. I had not yet registered her intent, but all the others had, rising now to form a loose circle around us. She smiled, laying my left hand in her right, raising it to her lips, kneeling with one leg up in courtier fashion. I understood at once and flushed crimson as my namesake, answering the question she'd yet not asked.

"'Yes, yes, yes. Fervently and ever yes, my sweet love, I will marry you, marry and marry and marry you, renew my vows with every breath, strive to make you as happy as you have me. I want nothing that is not you and everything that is. Yes, and ever yes.'

"Did I say all that with the family's eyes upon us? Yes. Justine was glad of them, chose them to bear witness, and I saw the power of their encircling our love. A blessing that did not need to be sought but was granted by the affirming communal spirit of the clan. Justine rose to kiss me, and as she did, Emily's voice rose in a song of love set to Shakespeare's line from *Henry IV*, 'For Where Thou Art, There is The World.' She is a meadowlark, her trilling notes pure and euphonious. Mesmerized we stood, tears welling, as she held the last elegiac tone. This is my family, new and old, Alex; these are my people now. In the after-moments when we embraced each and all, I knew our union presaged other happy ones soon to come: my father and Heather would surely wed, as in time would Barbara and Innie. Little Emily, still too young to follow suit, would be surrounded by happy pairs whose love would lead to hers.

"You can see what an evening it was, my friend, surpassingly glorious. The only shadow marring it was that treacherous figure of the mulberry resembling Katherine's. Without question Lou would trim it, I said to myself, preferably tomorrow morning, to ease the creepiness.

"When at last we tripped upstairs to bed, very little of the night remained and no surprise, for we had claimed the greater share of it as our own, to keep eternal tender in our souls. How I slept at all I do not know, my mind reeling through the fulsome celebration. Justine was breathing slow and evenly beside me, and I followed each inhale deep within her, bearing her scent inside me, snugged myself into the heart-core, like a secret child who would not come forth until gushed back regretful into the world with each exhale. Thus I lay, my head resting on her shoulder, thanking all the deities humankind has ever created to thank. It's a comforting safeguard to direct our gratitude to a higher force, both specific and universal. And as Meister Eckhart reminds us, 'If the only prayer you said in your entire life is thank you, that would suffice.'

"A rustle from the doorway caught my ear, and I smiled, thinking it a member of my family come to gaze lovingly at the fortunate couple. At first I pretended I was asleep, then opened my eyes as though just awakened and sat braced on my elbows to welcome the night visitor. But the face and form would not resolve itself into any that I recognized, and a peculiar dread iced my toes. I sensed more than heard my name being called, a ghastly rush of 'o' and 'z.' Tried to persuade myself I but dreamed this horror.

"The invader glided into the room, a dense smolder, clearing as it reached my bedside, to unmask her visage, the fiendish Katherine. That mulberry was no mimic, nor had I imagined her there. She had watched us from that dusky vantage point, and waited seething for the hour of my death. Which now reared above me, silver blade aimed at my heart, and I, still like a child in her thrall, too overcome to scream or move. Inexorably slow, the downward plunge of blade toward my breast, as though she were standing at the remove of the firmament above me. Yet the only hurt I suffered was the vindictive thrust of intended murder by a woman whom I had not loved nor trusted for years. She bore me but could not bear me.

"I swatted away her knife, stirring the air, touching naught but it. Hissed at her amorphic rage. My scorn blew wide through her and willed her back into the darkness from which she'd emerged. At the door, wisping toward oblivion, she raised her bitter hand to speak.

"'My hopes for you were fearfully high, Rose, and thus have had a very long way to fall. You are my paradise lost, my dreams disgraced, my faith shattered. You have made me the demon you believe me to be.'

"So saying, she swept into the hall. I did not awaken when she left because I had not slept. This was no dream, and yet, clearly she was not here in flesh or I would have been slain. Neither flesh nor fleshless, but in some realm between the ethereal and the real, and I cannot explain it. I do not believe in ghosts, nor was she one. Whatever trans-substantial form she inhabited, it was a torrential relief to have her gone.

"Such a woman is my mother, Alex. Now think of yours, so tender and so true. She has infused you with her goodness as Katherine robbed me of much of mine. My peace of mind lay in shards, and unable to calm myself, I had to wake Justine to garner her comfort after this wretched encounter. She surmised, rightfully, I think, that however dreadful it may have been, this visitation freed me from any obligation to my mother beyond the most superficial greeting card. Thus, I will not be returning to Vista Grande until after her death, though I will visit you."

Rose closed with a passionate exhortation: "Go forth urgently in wonder, O knight, as if each hour were a river whose swift currents you are navigating, hues and jewels catapulting past. Plunge into the tide of every moment, scoop what you can of its bounty. Chase the last sweetness from its ephemeral passage and sunder the ancient cry of despair with exultation. There is more and more and more to live, yet never an excess to squander ungrasped. Dwell ever on the farthest edge of your capacity, and don weariness as laurel testament that you have run the breadth of your days.

I am ever your loving and devoted friend,

Rose of the Roundtable"

She hadn't called herself that since second grade.

A searing restlessness kept me up most of the night. Like a hybrid of jealousy, yearning, tenderness, and resentment it churned. By morning the rhapsodic joy that filled me when I finished the letter had reversed course: I felt hollowed out, a concavity that slumped purposeless on Trudel's knick-knack shelf. Those I admired and loved had, like arrows, found their true path and struck home on the gladsome swell. Each was ensconced with a lover surpassing dreams and aspirations. Except Hersch. Don't forget me, Bug. As if.

In this slough I decided to stay abed as long as I could. Coffee would have been nice; many's the morning I'd wished for a preset timed machine to brew it in my room, preferably within reach of my outstretched hand. I resigned myself to sipping the days-old glass of water on the bedside table, as Tiger had also done at some point, leaving telltale hairs along the rim. A grudginess set in that made me decide not to share Rose's news with Mamia just yet. Crammed the letter in the bottom drawer of my nightstand on top of her earlier one and a host of miscellany. I had a caffeine-deprivation headache and a grumpy hunger. With Tiger draped over my arm, I shuffled off to scrambled eggs and bacon with a mammoth cup of coffee.

2 1

"Ripeness is All"

"What is it your grandparents most want from you?" Brief silence. "When you visit them, what do they hope for from you?" Wait for it, but I didn't. "What can you give them that makes them happiest?"

"A hug. Even when they smell funny."

"Okay, a hug. Why would that be the thing that makes them happiest?"

"Because they don't get many hugs. Like I said, they smell funny."

"Right. But even when they smell good, why don't they get many hugs?" Molar extractions can be more painful for the dentist than the drowsing patient.

"They're old. No one loves old people."

"Aha! So the greatest gift you can give an old person is love. Agreed?" A ripple of nods. Jerri stretched as she reentered the earth's atmosphere. "Hello, Jello. Guess what we're all doing here."

"Yeah. Loving old people."

"Do you?"

"Fake it pretty good when I need money."

"Well, well. Despite yourself you've given me a great segue into the first scene of *King Lear*. It's a play, JellyBelly, and you are supposed to have your copy in front of you, and yeah, that was today. Five points off."

She sucked in her blubber gut and whined, "It's at my mom's house, and I didn't have a way to get over there this weekend."

"Lear at eighty years old had been king for a long time. Like Queen Elizabeth had when she died in 1603. She had no children to inherit the throne, so they had to bring in a Scottish king, who became James I. He was openly gay, though married, and a fervent witch-hunter who burned a ton of women at the stake. Some scholars accuse him of being a misogynist."

Turning on Flynn, who was checking his phone, "Imagine us having a foreign president like that."

"Cool," he sneered, trying to stuff the phone in his jeans pocket.

I nabbed the phone. "Come get it at the end of the day. If you can find me."

"This is, like, so unfair. My dad's headed for Iraq. He's supposed to text me when he gets in."

"And right now you're, like, in English class, in school. What does *misogynist* mean?"

"A constipated baboon. Kangaroo cheese. Shit, I don't know."

"Okay, out. Six-hundred-word essay due tomorrow on James I. And not one word of it better be plagiarized, Fartface. And read Scene 1 of the play."

"What play?" he muttered, slopping through the door. Five-beat count, back in. "Can I have my phone now?"

"Get to work."

"You didn't tell us what *misogynist* means, Mr. Mann." PitSkin accused.

"Can you make an educated stab at it?"

"Like something about a regulation?" No one offered him a lifeline.

"Use context clues, you knucklebutts. What I said about James I clearly implied that it means someone who hates and mistreats women. Who's prejudiced against them."

"Why does it matter to know about this? I'm really asking." Katrina, one of the few salvageables.

"Lear was written in 1606, under James I's reign. Knowing the social backdrop of the play gives you a wider understanding of one of its central themes, the power dynamic between Lear, his daughters, and their husbands. And raises questions about allegiance to a source of authority for any nation, which in turn leads us to ask what qualities constitute genuine authority. For Lear's three daughters vying to inherit England from him, that authority is their father, a bond that muddles their relationship to him as king, and his to them as his successors."

Class was half over, Scene 1 of Lear is long and complex, and entropy was setting in.

"Okay, let's start reading and talk more as we go along. Bitcoin, play Lear. Scammer, Kent. Hairball, go for Gloucester. PitSkin, Edmund. Nerdnuts, Edgar. Jello, you've got Goneril."

"Gonorrhea…"

"Okay, thank you for stepping up, Poopyhead; you're a ringer for The Fool."

Boney laughed. He hated Poop, who ridiculed him.

"Boney-boy, you've got Oswald, Jello's servant." A good match physically, but no one wanted to serve that seam-buster. "And you, Nelson, you're her long-suffering husband, Albany."

He nodded. One of the good guys.

"Hazel, you're Regan. Sasquatch, you're Cornwall, the lucky—and evil—dog who's her husband. Katrina, you're Cordelia. For this scene anyway. You'll get a bigger part when one of the knucklebutts flakes out. Barbs, read the servants' and knight's lines."

"I can't read Shakespeare," Hairball complained. "It's all gibberish. We should read it in real English."

"Go SparkNotes, you fool."

"I'm not the Fool."

"Okay, everybody. Here's the deal: Do your best and don't worry about missing some of the words. We'll double back and I'll make sure you get the gist of what we've read before we move on."

"Let's double-back first."

"Read, Gloucester."

"Where's Edmund?"

"PitSkin, you're up."

"Ah, man."

"I thought the king had more affected the Duke of Albany than Cornwall…" and we were off, blindly, lamely feeling our way to Dover.

My brain was fraught with lines of literature these days, burrowing through texts with such excessive care that the words of the classics had become embedded. Escaping thus also the terrors of the classroom, where I was hourly defeated.

First, third, fourth, and seventh: I'd lost them, how and why I didn't know, but that brilliant rapport I'd begun with had faded to a murky brown. True, the curriculum I'd devised was, in teacher-speak, challenging, over the heads of all but the top tier and the AP section, 6th. I wanted my students to reach, to strain, to surmount their limits and discover the full range of their intelligence. They wanted A's and no homework. They wanted to get into college and leave home. They wanted to party, get high. Same things the Bug wanted as a high school senior and told them stories about, featuring his goofy pal Hersch. When Mr. Glass-Housed Mann, who was supposed to be on their side, had mutated into a sarcastic tyrant, his adoring minions galvanized into surly and audacious rebels. If all their grades were low, that would reflect as badly on him as on them, and there'd be parents to answer to, what with college looming.

Of course, to their chagrin and his relief, they weren't all low. That sparse upper stratum in the regular sections not only enjoyed meeting his demands but pressing beyond them, and likewise enjoyed seeing their classmates' sloth penalized. It was about time that papers were due when they were due, quizzes required close reading, discussions exposed the unprepared. For on the flip side, those who excelled were rewarded by the Mann's favor and I myself spared the unpleasant task of writing college recommendations for the unworthy masses, reserving my talents for the best regulars. The major difficulty here was being outnumbered: in the regular sections the best, already outsiders, were prone to silence in the face of their popular classmates' onslaughts. I was an undefended champion of the brightest, and as such condemned as an arrogant ass. Their view afflicted my own and made me so.

The AP class was my salvation: Twelve razzle-dazzlers, all girls, minds honed to a blade, no duel left unfought, no idea unexplored, no question unpursued. These were the students for me, and I reveled in our forays through sumptuous intellectual terrain. Always rested and ready, each wanting the lead, courteous but competitive. These were the students that gave me the courage to experiment with strategies, texts, and ideas; they went with me through Rilke's *Duino Elegies* and Eliot's *Four Quartets*, Dostoyevsky's "Grand Inquisitor" and Camus' *The Stranger*. Still to come were Ellison's *Invisible Man*, Goethe's *Faust*, Kafka's *Metamorphosis* (going back to my former nemesis, whom I had learned to admire), and Forster's *Passage to India*. None of which were in the prepackaged AP curriculum, but the test itself allowed students to write on a given set of works or any others "of comparable literary merit." All of mine were, and the students' embrace of my choices affirmed my faith in myself as a teacher. We were having a grand time together, they even more daring and open than I. Whatever complaints the bottom-feeders in my other sections might have would be offset by the 5's these girls would score on their tests.

Most gifted of the twelve was Vivienne, who met with me regularly before or after school, sometimes off-campus, to probe intensively along pathways we'd opened up in class, to work on her college essays and drafts of critical and creative papers for me. She was an insatiable student of the best sort, one who pushed and trusted me. That her beauty was as brilliant as her mind made her irresistible as a tutee: I hungered for our times together. Fortunately, my salacious thoughts had not osmosed into a "wolfish visage" since she continued to approach me with earnest confidence and seemed thoroughly at ease during our meetings. Perhaps it was unimaginable that Scarface could have the passions and hormones of other men.

One afternoon as the October light huddled in a storm-swathed sky, I was concerned about Viv getting home and suggested we break off our discussion early. Her smile mutated to a grimace.

"This storm? This is nothing, Mr. Mann. You should see what's waiting for me at home." She rocked forward uneasily, a flash of pain striking her features. "Can I tell you something in private?"

That's not a question but a call for conspiratorial silence, which a teacher should never agree to, and of course I did.

Her father, she confessed, had abused her sexually. He was a violent man, but he was also the D.A. in this town, powerful and esteemed. Her mother basked in the reflected glory and implicit threat of his position. Did she know what was happening to her daughter? Viv thought so, but they had not spoken of it.

Dumbfounded, I tried to swallow this revolting gush of knowledge, but it stuck in my craw, making breathing hard and speaking impossible.

"You don't need to say anything, Mr. Mann. I'll be gone to college next year, and I'm never coming back. It's just that I appreciate everything you're doing for me, much more than any other teacher has. I feel like I'm really learning how to write and think from you, and I love your class. It's—we have a special relationship, so I wanted to tell you. Probably shouldn't have."

Her regret snapped me back. I who had kept a wrenching secret far too long had to support Viv, my favorite and finest student. Suppress my lust and become her advocate. And (no sacrifice) work with her as late and often as she liked. As I told her, my promise fervent and my commitment firm: Whatever she needed, whenever she did, I would be there for her.

Clearly, I knew that as a teacher, I had a legal obligation to report the abuse. I could be prosecuted for failing to disclose it to the authorities. But then, the chief authority to whom this crime would be reported was the man who'd be in charge of prosecuting the case: Vivienne's father. No good would come of telling anyone, though her father— parents!—should not go unpunished.

The other AP girls, too, clandestinely shared their troubles with me in writing and in person, though none were suffering as Viv was. I thought how easy, and in truth, seductive, it would be to become a priest, privy within the darkness to confessions from the darkness within. At first I was uncertain about how to respond to the girls' revelations, but rather quickly I got used to them, looked forward to the intimacy they offered, even found myself topping off grades on papers that bared delectable or dreadful secrets. Whether or not I was provoking these divulgences, I was open to them, and regardless of my hideous face, the girls seemed eager to win my affection through exposing themselves.

Vivienne did not elaborate on the abuse she bore, in fact did not refer to it again. When I asked her how things were going at home, she simply shrugged. "Terrible. I hurt a lot." And moved on. Thinking about her after our meetings, my conscience tormented itself: I should do something to protect her; I should not be aroused by the image of Viv in my arms. Even though I was not much older than she, I had to be the good father, the one she deserved and craved.

Her mind: that was the only thing I should rightfully be attracted to. This lissome young woman of burnished red-gold hair was an intellectual marvel. It was to her scholarly gifts that my allegiance belonged—and wasn't the challenge her incisive questions posed what exhilarated me as a teacher? For instance, I recalled, our conversation earlier that day about whether Meursault's lack of introspection in Camus' *The Stranger* made him a child or a sociopath. She had little sympathy for Meursault and favored the latter interpretation, which drove me to dig into specific passages that raised compelling arguments in his defense. At times like these I was completely absorbed in the excavation of literature, thinking beyond myself in the quest to make meaning, and Viv reveled in the ideas we unearthed. She was drawn to the best in me, drew it out of me, and such potent exchanges were the most durable and significant aspect of our special relationship. Yes, it was in the academic stratosphere with students like Viv that I thrived.

To hell with the slackers. Maybe I was just not cut out to teach second-rate public-school students. Maybe I was meant to be at Exeter or St. Paul's. Maybe college. Or maybe I should divide the regular students up for the rest of the year, let the babies read YA titles with their ear-buds in and give them kiddie quizzes: "Why did Constance break up with Trevor after she saw him kissing Georgia?" and five-paragraph essays on the pros and cons of social media. Meanwhile, the serious students and I would read and discuss the good stuff. I wouldn't even need to give them quizzes, and I could assign complex, writerly essays that would be a pleasure for me to read. Track 'em within the classroom, that was the answer. As Lear's godson Edgar says, "Ripeness is all."

Worthwhile long-term strategies to explore. My immediate problem, however, was that Rose and Justine were coming this first weekend in November, staying with us for a week, and both were intent on observing three days of my classes. More to the point: observing me teach. I had to pull off a series of amazing lessons, and here we were botching *King Lear*, Justine's favorite Shakespeare play. And mine.

My gut had been to go with *Lear* for the AP only, *Midsummer Night's Dream* for the slacker classes, a quick and fairly easy romp through the Bard laden with magic and romance and comic twists. Dissect a few speeches, watch the movie, write an in-class essay, check it off the list. But perversely I chose to make things impossible by jumping all of the classes into *Lear*. I loved the play a lot and harbored the ludicrous conviction its tragedy could win over the most obstinate learners. My regulars had mangled the opening, first and seventh even worse than third and fourth. At the rate we went today, it could take weeks to get to Dover, let alone the Act V dénouement. And with the resistance I'd met, it wouldn't matter when or whether we got there: the kids would have dropped out the first time we hit a stile. What was I going to show Rose and Justine? Oh: and Mamia, who had been acutely aware of my burgeoning frustration and had, since October leafed in, stopped asking me how my day had gone. She'd begged me to tell her, please, whenever I liked, assuring me of her desire to know. With the visitors here, she mentioned the possibility of tagging along to a class or two if that didn't prove overwhelming. My Greek chorus, staunch supporters until the fates turned against me and I was thrown out of the citadel on a dark and stormy night.

How to make three days of this travesty go well was my fret that evening, sprawled on the bed next to the cats. Yes, the cats stayed with me when the Strangers departed. Lori had read disturbing accounts of cats' intolerance for babies; sometimes their behavior, she told us anxiously, bordered on the malicious. Since, as you may recall, Joaquin was not a fan of these wildlife assassins, he backed up her hesitation about taking Montenegra back to Trove and away from her beloved Tiger. So for now, a long now in my calculation, the cats were mine. Rose, fervent aficionada of the feline, thought I came out way ahead. I could work up a strong defense of her position at moments like this, when, desperate for a sounding board with a neutral ear, the cats proved to be indulgent confidants. Their genuine indifference was a comfort; nothing I said shocked or disappointed or excited them. Only an occasional tail flick indicated their impatience with my whining, easily fixed with a back scratch. They took the liberty of licking their assholes while I described my possible strategies to them.

A trio of left-behinders, we spent nights and weekends hanging out in my room or the garden, I admiring their kills, noting a certain resemblance between, say, a lizard tail and PitSkin, or the organs of a mouse and Fartface's oozy gym bag. The cats' impassive equilibrium calmed me, and they appreciated having free access to my room through the screenless window I left open for them. Till winter. I could foresee myself trundling into a hermitic middle age amidst cats, shielded from despair by their complacency.

"The first thing you have to understand is that most kids are stupider than they were a decade ago. Hell, than the seniors were last spring. Also lazier. And meaner, some of them. Not all, mind you, a few are terrific, a few. But the rest, they don't want to learn all the amazing things I could teach them. So that limits my options on this *Lear* thing."

I caught Tiger's nonchalant eye between licks. "I mean, maybe I should skip the enactment, show the movie for the next three days, give an in-class essay Friday, return it with erudite comments and advice on Monday when Rose and Justine are there to watch me, then move on to some provocative short story we read as a group. Or I could save the in-class essay till Monday and tell R and J to wait till Tuesday, not return the essays but go right on. I could read aloud "The Ones Who Walk Away from Omelas," which will keep their attention and not leave much time for discussion. For the Wednesday finale, I could, let's see, I could take everyone outside on the field and choose somebody to be the Omelas suffering kid, let them decide whether to walk away or stay. Choose the unlucky kid by drawing lots. Make the rest justify their decision to go or stay. That would be our discussion. And look for contemporary parallels. Wow, that's good."

Fingers skating Tiger's fur met with a tail slap upside of my head. Don't. I'm working here.

"Or I could borrow some costumes from the drama closet and beef up the Lear performance. Secretly tell Kent and the Fool and Edgar and Cordelia (maybe Albany, too) that every character but theirs is stark raving mad; they are the sane ones. Have those few kids wear ties, kind of a clandestine symbol for sanity. Meanwhile, I'll tell the others that this is a power war between young and old; whichever side wins—in effect, makes a more persuasive case that they would be better leaders, no matter what the outcome of the play is—gets to take over the class for a day, run things. A dangerous ploy. I'll think on that a bit more."

> Doodle-dee-do
> Do-do-dooo.
> Doodle-dee–do
> Do-do-dooo.

The theme song from this Clint Eastwood spaghetti Western back in the sixties that Papito loved and we watched a hundred times when I was a kid: *The Good, The Bad, and The Ugly*. Anyway, that's how I mentally divided up my class sections: AP the good, of course, in fact the great; third and fourth the bad; first and seventh the ugly. Given that distinction, I would invite R and J (and Mamia) into fourth and AP only. Eat lunch with them in between.

I rolled over on my side, spooning Montenegra, who scooted a little closer to Tiger, not offensively but indicating a clear preference. Seven o'clock. Had to take action. Make a decision about *Lear*, follow through. All my options stank. Inertia sat mountainous on my ribs. Go to sleep now, get up early, as in four o'clock, figure it out then. I set my phone alarm and lay snow-angel-limbed across the bed. Maybe the answer would come to me in a nightmare.

The school, hazy in predawn darkness, projected the soft aura of a beneficent matron, casting a spell of luxurious quietude I burrowed into like a kid snuggling under the covers. Whenever I could propel myself here early, it was enthralling. This morning I'd gotten to school before anyone but Principal Wright, who lived there, bedding down in a swank private suite deceptively marked "Custodial Closet." He greeted me as he would have a stray dog wandering onto the property, and while not brooming me off, his grimace sabered a thin, red line across the transgressed bounds of the school day. Aha, Sherlock, skidding 'round the corner: so he has a woman in his pied-a-terre and I a juicy tidbit for the teachers' workroom at break.

Slipped into the costume closet, my form an imperceptible blur at the periphery of dawn. The stench even at this chilly hour was reeling. Mouth-breathed into the pong, arming starched and silken garb, flutters of bright scarf and tie, zany wigs, a jester's cap, swords and swash. Using the bundle of loot to ward off further onslaught from the Wright, staggered the halls to my classroom, leaning against the doorway while chinning the wretched garments to dig out my key. The door gave before I'd inserted the shaft in the lock, hurling me inside as the lights blared to fluorescent attention.

"Do you have Augie's permission to abscond with his costumes?" Wright!

Blindsided by my shield. And a mounting din of complaints from parents, which he, the honorable Principal Wright, had attempted, I had been informed, to divert but would soon require a more formal hearing. An annoying buzz my indignation had been swatting away. Greatest English teacher their kids had ever had the good fortune to learn from. Writer to boot, a nascent bestseller smoldering on his desk.

"Ask forgiveness, not permission?" I countered emerging askew from the adolescent sweat-embalmed heap.

"From Augie?"

Right. But keep the lines taut, Bug. "The play's a month off. I'm, my classes are, enacting *King Lear*, and I thought costumes would add a dimension of verity to the reading." I was impressed with my coherent breakfastless defense.

"Be sure you check in with him before first period this morning." Abrupt, underwhelmed, irritated by my break-in. As if these flimsy, reeking duds were sacred apparel. Perhaps they'd be of interest to an archaeologist in a thousand years when they were exhumed from the dump where they belonged, but now they were tolerable only to kids wrapped up in playing a part in their gaudy public and private dramas. Nonetheless, with elaborate care I draped them across chairs and desks. Studied the effect from the viewpoint of the door swung open: brilliant, enticing. Might inoculate them against the recollection they'd be reading Shakespeare for the next several days. Might rouse admiration from R and J—so creative, that Alex, such a natural teacher. He knows how to keep them in. And I had plenty of time to scoop up coffee, OJ, and a Ville-style breakfast burrito from Lorca's.

Pumped, I was strutting back to my classroom an hour hence, key shaft erect and ready for insertion, when from the cluster outside the door it became evident that word of my coup, my theft, my genius had already spread. Kids gaping at the array through the window, then at me.

"All the world's a stage, my minions. In with you, and choose a garment befitting your role. Kent, Fool, Edgar, Albany, and Cordelia, the ties are reserved for you." Going all the way with my bed-laid plans.

"I don't remember who I'm supposed to be." Ah, Jello, lucky I wrote it all down.

"You want us to *wear* this crap?"

"It stinks. God."

"That's 'cause Augie doesn't have them cleaned after a show. If you wear one for the next show, you have to get it cleaned, if it matters to you. Some of the boys' stuff is so gross." Florence, a wannabe drama queen, passed along that unsavory tidbit.

"None of this junk would fit me." An arch response from Barbie-doll. Anorexically thin and barely literate, sporting multicolor nails and copper-stranded poodle hair, convinced she was laying waste to her modeling career whiling away her teenhood in high school.

"New do for the hair, Barbs: sweet. Highlights the chartreuse in your mini—or is that just a long tank?"

"Put this shit on, you'll smell like rat-piss all day." Fartface, who would anyway.

"The whole room's gone skanky." Ah, Poopyhead, like you would know skank.

"I'm waiting outside till this garbage is removed." Bitcoin, my designated Lear, stalked off, the court obediently trailing him to the grassy knoll under the cottonwood where, on my charitable days, we held class.

Checkmated by an ugly bunch of juvenile jackasses. I stood routed at the door, my reactions disabled. Katrina, Nelson, and Hazel waited with me, offering to help take the costumes back to the greenroom closet. I hated to give up so bloodlessly, but they had a point, undeniably about the rank odor emanating from the room, and now that I knew these costumes bore the grime of last year's perspiring thespians, I didn't want to spend the day with them, either.

But the scoundrels who'd walked away were not off the hook. Once reassembled in the classroom with autumnal breezes sweetening the air, albeit mingled with car exhausts from the road beyond, I proceeded snappily to a drear Plan D.

"Next three days in class, you're reading *King Lear* silently to yourselves. Friday, the test from hell, which will go on your second-quarter grade. And none of the answers can be found online, trust me on that. Monday, in-class essay on the play. If you're absent for either one, the make-up will be harder: you can trust me on that, also. Oh, and all phones and laptops off and in your backpacks. No electronic devices in sight this week. Now get on it."

"What if I have a question about something?" whimpered Crusty, hoping to throw me off, but I'd thought about that while lugging costumes back to their lair.

"I'll hold study sessions at seven in the morning tomorrow and Thursday. Show up here and ask me whatever you want. About the play."

"Seven?"

"Good ears, Boney."

"But, Mr. Mann, you know I have to read all my books on Audible."

Of course Hairball did, or claimed to. "You sit over there, yeah, the far corner there, face to the wall, and listen on your headphones. I'll be checking from time to time to—see how far you've gotten."

I turned my back to them and headed for the white board to list where they should be in the play by the end of each class session in order to finish before Friday. What they didn't get done in class was homework. I had to write slowly so my rage didn't squiggle the lines. Word would pass to the other sections, who would come in armed with gripes. Screw them. Except fourth period; I'd be nicer to them, sympathize about the jerks in first period who spoiled everything. Needed their good will for next week's observations. And of course my prized APers would enact the play, as planned, brilliantly. With discussion, they'd be in Act III when R and J showed up.

Making my vengeance test was twice the work that teaching the play in class would have been. I hunted down obscure details and checked them against online sources, then added a few questions about historical context: the information I'd delivered Monday before the whole enterprise collapsed. Fartface would have been able to answer these at least if he'd written the paper I assigned him, but the insolent idler had shrugged it off: "What's another F to a guy you call Fartface?"

The few who showed up at seven both mornings were the ones who didn't need to, of course: Katrina, Hazel, and Nelson from first, Tony and Lyndel from fourth, Rickie from fifth, Bella and Reese from seventh. Excavating the multifaceted depths of *King Lear* with them, I decided on Thursday morning, when they had all finished reading the play, to show them my respect and gratitude by letting them write their own quiz, together. "Address what you consider the most important and enduring ideas in the play. You can add interpretive questions as well. Work on it in the library during class today." They all eight belonged in AP English, but it conflicted with Honors Chinese and other advanced classes.

Friday about half of the kids in The Ugly periods were done early with my spite test, which is to say they gave up before class was over. Of those who kept trying, some were doing it just to write stupid answers, a few vaguely amusing but most nasty and insulting. The Bad got further with the test and a number of them made a serious effort, though none aced it, as I'd made certain was impossible to do. The Good, of course, were in the heart of performing Act II, with pauses to explicate key speeches, such as Lear's "O, reason not the need!" in Scene 4. I stayed late that afternoon to grade the tests, a laborious undertaking because of the number of students and questions involved. Wanted to be done before R and J arrived tomorrow. The kids wouldn't get the tests back till after my revered scrutinizers were gone, and at that I'd probably have to curve the grades, but I wanted to rid my mind of beasts so foul. For the next few days I needed to be the gracious and ebullient Mr. Mann, turn my Hyde into Jekyll.

When Rosie and I used to play together in childhood, it was usually at my house, where Mamia watched over us with loving eyes, but occasionally at hers, where the maid kept us in distrustful view, particularly me, a rubber-sword-brandishing boy of five. Rosie's palatial estate held one bathroom that petrified me, the guest bathroom, which I was supposed to use. I would approach the closed door with trepidation and stand there, reluctant to turn the knob. An ominous tension radiated from within. I feared that opening the door would reveal a pirate with a knife in his chest, or a griffin poised to spring, or a river of blood spilling from the toilet, or a witch, her clawed fingers shooting out to grab my neck. The space felt deadly, and I have no idea why. When I did go in, once or twice, goosebumps rising on my arms and back, I couldn't force myself to shut the door all the way. Being in there exacerbated my irrational dread, and on the third expedition to that door, I stopped cold, unable to enter, even at the risk of wetting my pants. Skipping around the corner, Rosie found me doubled over, crying. I whispered my dilemma to her, at which she grabbed my hand and tugged me to her bedroom, its private pink bathroom just beyond, in time to save my pants from disgrace. "You can always use mine, Lancelot," she offered "when you need to."

I was buttoning my jeans when the maid appeared, furious. "What have you been up to in here, young man?" She gave my undone jeans a hard glare. "Exposing yourself to Miss Rose?" Advanced on me, yanking me out of the room by the elbow. "I'll be sure to report this infraction to your mother, to both of them," she hissed. Then pinching my shoulder, warned, "Don't let me catch you in Miss Rose's bedroom again." I didn't know what "exposing yourself" or "infraction" meant, but I understood that I should feel ashamed of whatever I'd done. Tears welled again, and the maid squeezed my shoulder harder. "If you cry, naughty boy, it proves you're guilty." Of what, peeing? But I clamped my face shut, said nothing. Rose tried in vain to defend me (from what she didn't know, either). We filed out of her bedroom hangdogging our heads, played CD's instead of games for the rest of the afternoon. I vowed secretly not to come over to her house anymore; she vowed secretly to get rid of the maid who'd humiliated her best friend. We each succeeded, thus double-solved the problem, but both of our actions were taken on my behalf, not hers. And that, I saw now, readying my garret for their arrival, was how it had long and often been. She was the caretaker, I the cared for. I would have said that changed when she bequeathed me Tiger, but no, he'd simply assumed her role tending me. He and Joaquin and Lori and Mamia and Frank. Even Papito and Hersch were on the guardian team, and for a short spell Justine, helping me graduate from high school. I was the perpetual baby they took part in raising. Why did they bother? What had I ever done for them?

And why was I unable to grow up?

Had been unable to. My mission this week, besides teaching masterfully, was to demonstrate self-reliance, to show them I was the beacon guiding my ship, the wayfinder and wayfarer, sailor and port. Odd metaphor that toddled into my head, but it vesseled a lyric truth: the double self, the inner I and you constantly in dialogue, had achieved the essential symbiosis for making an adult of me. Thanks for everything, y'all—no, I mean it, thank you for your concerted efforts to make me one of you. You triumphed. Now, what can I do you for? I'd out-mature my confederacy of women. Out-hand-stretch my handlers.

And the sun rose and the sun set on my week in the fettered outskirts of hell, and behold, it was Saturday, gold and brisk.

Rosie, arms a profusion of fresh fruit and vegetable, charged breathlessly into the kitchen as I was fixing a redolent stew for lunch. "Farmer's Market is marvelous!" she huffed, strewing the counter with her gleanings. "Oh, and that smells fantastic, Alex! Can you use any of these veggies in it?" She paused to open her arms in a smile. "Oh, Alex, my dear, dear Bug! How happy we are to be here. To see you again after so long, after so much! Letters, miles, Justine and I married, you a teacher, here we are, isn't life wondrous?"

Hugging Rose, I grinned at Justine, realized anew why the gang and I had had a mad-assed crush on her as seniors. The years had only hewn Justine's beauty deeper. For the first time in a good while I was embarrassed by my scars. But she greeted me with a sincerity I could scarcely muster nowadays. Facing the extraordinary woman who'd been my best teacher, holding the extraordinary woman whom I'd loved for twenty years, I was overcome by a euphoric loosening in my groin, like the feeling after climax, an afterglow their presence stirred that I yearned to prolong.

But Rose had swung around to embrace Mamia, just entering the kitchen. "Oh, Shelley, my dream mother! How insanely lucky we all are to have you!" Her joy festooned our little home with gala spirit, turning an ordinary morning into a holiday. I uncorked the champagne Mamia handed me, and we drank to one another, to happiness, to friendship, to reuniting, to the future, to life: L'Chaim! There'd be no work done today besides feasting, the meals only one aspect of our bounty, inebriation a state of mind not purely alcohol-induced. Story after story rolled over the hours into dark, tales well known and those never told, about ourselves, others, memories, dreams, fulfilled and foregone. The hole at the center of our blazing circle was death, a welter of deaths, to be keened another time. More due: Katherine, it appeared and as we had already heard, was suffering from early-onset Alzheimer's and would need full-out nursing care, probably confinement in the shadowy halls of her natal family, as Rose was here to ascertain.

Asked how my teaching was going, I offered the gallant response I'd prepared: "That's what I'm hoping you'll tell me after you observe." I put them off till Tuesday with suave apologies that roused no suspicion; besides, Rose had concocted a dizzying tour of Summerville and vicinity, a harried, all-inclusive seeing of sights for which Mamia and I declined to join them, falsely asserting that we'd been everywhere. Off the hook and with two days to over-prepare ways of revving up my kids, I settled into the stuporous bask of evening. It was a gift just to look at these two. Seemed unfair to have deprived two good men (I being one of them) of their conjugal love, but at the same time it was impossible to begrudge their happiness.

Sleep came easily, for once. Tiger at the back of my knees, Montenegra beside him, a gentle caress of purr and fur sheltering me from worry. But late in night's migration the path led across a scathing desert, I bowed under the weight of a pack, with no sense of destination. Apprehension lay thick on my tongue. I had very little chance of getting out whole. The pack began to writhe and bulge, its seams ripping, and in my hair the clutch of a hand as a small figure heaved itself onto my shoulders. As though expected at its perch, the creature ruffled my head. "You don't have to walk," lisped in familiar tones, "when you can fly." The body of an infant swept upward in a wind of light, hovered just above my reach, beckoning. "Come on." I flapped my arms, the baby laughed. "Not like that. Deep breath, hold, release it, let go." Yes, of course, I remembered how, and floated up beside him. His hand in mine, we rode the currents of windsong over the plains.

"How did you find me?"

"You've been carrying me."

"Where are we going?"

"Away."

"How long is our journey?"

"As long as you hold on to me."

"It seems more that you hold on to me."

"Each, for the other, an anchor."

"Yeats?"

"Yes, Father?"

Elated, we streamed upward, light as wisps, rarefying.

"Why did you not come to me as a ghost, like the others?"

"I died unborn. There is no trace of me upon the earth to inhabit."

"How is it, then, that you know my language?"

"It is rather that you know mine. 'The communication of the dead is tongued with fire,' and you learned it from your father."

"Do you share my memories?"

"I live in you."

The sky ahead darkened. Great black whorls of cloud approached, riven with lightning.

"Yeats?"

"Yes, Father?"

"The storm. We must go back."

"I see nothing of your world."

"What will you remember of our flight? Of me?"

"Only what you do."

"That I love you?"

"That I love you."

"That I will not let you go."

"That you let me go."

"No—"

A crack and bang of imminent danger tore the word from me. Swirled under by enormous waves of air scourging my shoal. Through the torrents I clung to the phantom hand. His grasp thin, voice faltering.

"Yeats?'

"Yes, Father?"

"Will I see you again?"

"I am never and ever with you."

"My son, oh, my son, my son…"

Breaking through the window, its first rays skimming my eyes, wet, and I still calling him. Tiger yawned, padded up to lay himself next to my face, where I inhaled his fur with every breath. Alex the Weird off on another nocturnal odyssey; time to reel him in. Nobody did it better than my compadre. Even when, as on this morning, I fought the lifeline he cast for me.

This new spectral vision was not cause to don my white gloves again and keep my hands tucked: just the opposite. I longed for him to return to me, fruitlessly willed myself to discover him, to see his wraith in the corner, at bedside, on the ceiling, to come upon him in my closet or the shower or the garden, to see him rise from Mamia's tall Italian vase or fly to my arms when I opened the fridge or the windows of my car, to find him squatting on the bookshelf in my classroom or hovering at my elbow as I graded papers in the office. I wanted him to make mischief in my life, to turn my head wherever I went, to take me wherever he went, even if it were off the earth. I slept with my hands bare, palms up, above the blanket, waiting for his touch, imagining the feel of it as it had been in my dream. But I was on my own, reeling unguided through the storm of living on.

22

"Thou Art the Thing Itself"

And now it was Sunday, Mamia and I alone again after a shining breakfast plaited with exuberant flavors. Rose's contagious felicity spiraled through the house, banishing night visions and bourgeoning dread. Until they set off on their adventures and I had no choice but to fight back nausea, lay a course, and secure the ship. Arm the rifles at every porthole. Swab clean the deck of old blood. Fly my colors boldly into the seas of scoff and sloth. If my mission proved victorious, they would clamber aboard and dance the jolly hornpipe in celebration with me.

Among the faculty at the school I had one friend, Terry, the physics teacher, with whom I could talk openly. She was a veteran with a rich storehouse of tales from the frontlines whose many years had bladed her wit and refined her perspective. I admired her steady hand, loving nature, imperturbable tolerance of all manner of adolescent shenanigans. In Terry's windowless matchbox office we often lunched together or rehashed the day at its end. It was she with whom I shared my triumphs, bewailed my defeats, she whose advice I sought and took. After the grisly Days of Flail and Failure, as I came to call them, she tried to console me with an analogy of teachers to parents. We are *in loco parentis*, emphasis on *loco* for taking on this massive extra unpaid job. When children feel unsafe in the classroom or at home, they are generally very docile and obedient around outsiders, Terry explained, because they can't risk the consequences of acting up. When they feel at ease, safe, then they can be little hellions to test the limits of their elders' patience. Even if they exceed those bounds and provoke your anger, they trust that nothing awful will come of it because you love them—that your punishment will be in keeping with their transgressions and your forgiveness is assured. So I should laud myself for creating an environment where students know they are safe and cherished. It was bullshit in my case, but I needed to hear this kind interpretation, this exonerating fairytale. The truth was that they hated me and had made vengeful use of the observers to humiliate me. While I was overpraising fourth period to win their allegiance during the observations, building up my relationship to our venerable guests, they were plotting their resistance. Terry invited me out for a beer, first time, a welcome delay from facing myself head-on. The decision that lay before me, as I saw it, was major reclamation along the lines Justine had counseled, or resignation.

The Days of Flail and Failure began on a resplendent autumn morning, Tuesday. Unseasonably warm. Ruffle of wind shimmering the aspen leaves, whose gold illumined the cerulean sky. An auspicious salutation from the earth. I walked determinedly tall into the classroom, strapped first and third to their seats with horrendous threats, and delivered a gripping read of "Omelas," laying particular emphasis on drooz, the magical substance that keeps the townspeople mellow. Chastened by my draconian measures last week, and yesterday's in-class essay, and the need, after all, to get decent grades first semester of senior year, the kids were unusually cooperative, nicely droozed out, as I thought to myself. They even raised a couple of intelligent questions during the five minutes before class ended. When I promised them a field trip tomorrow (saving, till then, the joke about it being literally a trip to the field), they left nearly buoyant. An extra gift: third was released two minutes early so I could welcome my guests, who saw the happy campers departing, several hand-slapping me on the way out. Looking good, Bug. Fourth is gonna soar.

Sour. One letter off and a terrible inversion of my expectations. Of course I wasn't able to terrify them with grave consequences at the start of class, which might have been the key to my success in the earlier periods. Instead, I praised and cooed, introducing them as the finest and fairest in the land, to which they responded with uncharacteristic apathy, despite which I graced them with a charitable smile before launching into "Omelas."

The opening paragraph of my reading stunned them. I hit the bass notes of wizardry, the fluted lilt of seduction. By this time I had the story partly memorized and could look up to underscore a dramatic phrase. Initially, their eyes met mine; my gaze held theirs. But a couple of pages in, the drumming commenced, lightly at first, then insistently. Astor, the wannabe rock star drummer who improvised his beats on the desktop: no punishment had won his silence when he was hungry. I had even allowed him to bring a snack to class (a concession the others resented but understood). He'd showed up with it the next day but not the day after, because, he explained, he'd gotten hungry in second period and eaten it then. I prescribed two snacks, which he tried once successfully before forgetting. My fallback was to have him sit with our ancient, oversized encyclopedia weighing down his arms. In front of the visitors, I couldn't bring myself to expose this bizarre tactic, sought instead to gag him with my eyes and finally with a gentle reprimand whose ominous undertones were lost on him. Score one for Astor in the disruption category.

Others were more subtle, making their points in the annoyance and disrespect arenas. I caught Siobhan texting, Coltor snoozing, Bella painting her nails, Marley eating, and Victor made a ten-minute foray to the bathroom. In every case I had to choose to stop the reading and focus on the infraction, deliver severe threats as in the other classes, or ignore them as if these were irrelevant teenage behaviors, to be expected and disregarded. That seemed easiest, under the circumstances. However, as soon as they realized they could get away with pretty much anything because of the observers, my merely bad fourth-period class redoubled their efforts at distraction, adding sidebar whisperings and giggles to their array of wrongdoings. I raised my voice, walked among them, a futile approach that only disempowered me further. Carpe diem, my pretties, but, oh, are you going to get it when we're alone again. There was no time for questions at the end, no friendly laughter as they departed, no hand-slaps. A vengeful gleam of triumph in the eyes that grazed mine. The more I'd buttered them up, the more freedom they'd known they had, and they had abused it mightily.

If fourth was, generously put, a crushing disappointment, lunch thereafter redefined awkwardness. My favorite diner was closed for repairs, so we had to eat at a sleazy, crowded fast food place that myriad students frequented. To save me from humiliation during this ordeal, we talked about things other than the class. They asked about my work on the diversity committee, what I thought of the school's principal, the holiday schedule. Topics as bland and uninteresting as the food. Driving back to school, a too visible cloak of doom hung over me, and I had to fight my self-loathing to step back into the ring. Opening the classroom door, my visitors trailing, I persuaded my heart that the APers would restore its faith in me. Slipped into my teacher guise and beamed at them, the suave confidence Mann. Introduced my guests, whom they welcomed with genuine courtesy and pleasure. We were deep into Act III, as I'd planned, about to begin Scene 4, which held Lear's eye-opened speech about the "Poor naked wretches" he has "ta'en too little care of," followed by the imagined trial of his daughters. Juicy: the stuff of AP guts and glory. They rose to their places on our classroom stage without needing to be asked.

Kent, played heartrendingly by Beatrice, had spoken her first line to Lear when the door swung wide and a ridiculously handsome young stud trod in.

"Cyril Raj," he announced. "I'm new."

Curly dark hair and chiseled features, intensely blue eyes set in unblemished olive skin: "velvet over stone, granite over bone." Athletic frame. Wide-mouthed smile, hard to read. A sight that silenced. Number 13 in AP, the only boy. He would change everything, create a whole new dynamic, alter the energy, destroy the intimacy of a group of brilliant girls with a scarred teacher who prompted no erotic fantasies. These thoughts whipped through me all in the brief span during which we sized one another up. Then he strode over and handed me his schedule with admission to this class.

"Cyril, nice to have you join us." My voice constricted, like that of a man who's kicked away the chair.

"You can call me Raj. Everybody does. So what were you all in the middle of? Sorry to interrupt." His voice sonorous.

As noted, a sight that silenced. My gregarious wunderkinder had lost the power of speech. What they were in the middle of was the staring at Raj. Lustfully.

"*King Lear.*"

"One of my favorites. Saw an awesome production last summer at The Globe."

Rose jumped in. "We saw that one, too. It was spectacular!"

"We're at the start of Act III, Scene 4. Grab a book off the back shelf and have a seat," I told the kid, fighting to regain my authority. "Beatrice, go ahead."

She did, but flat, small, abandoning the spirited zeal she'd read with before.

The next line went to Irene, my Lear, a drama star who read Shakespeare as fluently as if it were her first language. She, the class anchor and inspiration during this enactment, suddenly balked.

"I've been reading a lot. Why don't we let Raj play Lear? He's seen it performed, and it would be fun to hear someone new take over."

"Yeah," echoed Beatrice, enthused afresh.

"I'd be happy to, though I'm sure I won't be as good as you've been." A chivalrous fellow, this King of Handsome. He stood up, gliding toward Irene's place on our classroom stage.

Two options lay before me, the wise and the foolish. Wise would have been to go with the flow, trust the girls, climb aboard the Raj bandwagon. Foolish, which I chose, was to resist and impose my own will.

"Let's give Raj a chance to get his bearings before plunging in. Show him how it's been going."

Their faces closed like a curtain between us. "I thought you said we'd change Lears at this point anyway. Janie was supposed to take over because Cordelia doesn't come back in for quite a while."

"But I love Cordelia," Janie protested. "And I don't feel very well today. I think I might be getting sick, so I'd rather just watch."

"I could direct," Raj offered unhelpfully.

My job. I wasn't about to have him show me up in that role.

"Let's take a vote!" From Vivienne, until that moment my sidekick who staunchly defended every move I made. No need to vote, of course: Go straight to the concession speech.

"Looks like we've got a new Lear." I nodded toward Raj.

He grinned. Checkmate. My girls dissolved in mental swoons.

Predictably arresting, a gifted thespian, fearless in his portrayal of the mad old king. I found myself unable to stop him to analyze key moments and speeches, as I'd previously done. Studly had claimed the room and all in it. What had once been my kingdom became his realm, which I would have to armor myself to regain. My bevy of AP noblewomen were his. Even Mamia, Rose, and Justine's faces were alight with the pleasure of watching this delectable, unselfconscious hunk perform. Pathetic though it was, I looked forward to his death at the end of Act V.

"Thanks," he said, departing the class, and this time I detected an arch in his tone. "I hope we're going to go back into some of the more important speeches in those scenes. Seems worth doing."

"It does, doesn't it?" I shot back, straining to arc my hauteur above his.

He paused at the headshot collage of authors and students. "Nice." Flicking his ultra-blue eyes over them. "Where's Charlie Baudelaire?" And with a shrug wandered out the door, the girls I'd thought were waiting to chat with me trailing him like maenads.

"How fortunate that this young man showed up, Alex!" Rose gushed as I attempted to escort my visitors away against the influx of seventh period, which I definitely didn't want them observing. Sensing my urgency, Justine hurried out, but Mamia lingered.

"I'll see you at home," I scooted her into the hall with a quick pat on the shoulder.

"We forgot Baudelaire." Sincerely abashed.

"So many more writers and poets than we have room for." But I knew she would find a portrait of him to add to the board, and I'd have to decline, not really for lack of space but because there was no chance in hell I'd let Studly McHandsome win another round.

If there had been a way to avoid going home, I would have found it that afternoon. Wished I could fly again with Yeats far beyond the storm of my defeats. Instead dawdling in the cramped English office, laying out my battle plan for tomorrow, scanning online critiques of *Lear* for new insights, questions, angles to bring to the discussion, and bracing myself with a crust of feigned assurance for the review of the observed day that awaited me when I crossed the threshold of Mamia's abode, which these ruminations put off till near sundown. Luckily, the three women were deep into a bottle of merlot when I breezed into the kitchen.

"Something smells delicious." A reliably flattering opener I'd learned in high school when my plummeting grades required a diversionary tactic.

"Roast lamb with potatoes, peas, and carrots," Mamia enthused. "These dear women are culinary artists!"

"Standard British fare," Justine smiled. "Not much artistry involved but good nonetheless. Can I pour you a glass of wine?"

"I'll stick with beer, thanks," grabbing one from the fridge.

"You must be exhausted, sweetheart. I can't imagine how you teach five classes a day." Mamia's nightly expression of concern, which I nightly shrugged off, usually followed by a hug and a retreat to my quarters.

"You do have your hands full," nodded Justine. She shook her head. "Being there today made me remember why I decided to pursue my doctorate. Simply didn't have the stamina, or courage, or whatever it takes, that my parents did, and you do. The volcanic energy of adolescence overwhelmed me. I was just your age when you were a senior in my class, Alex, so I should have been up to it but…" She drained her glass, refilled it. "Here's to you!"

We toasted, Justine and Mamia cheering, Rose clinking my beer half-heartedly. She had a lot to say but was waiting, crafty Rose, for the right moment to pounce. I warned myself not to be alone with her but knew she would corner me in some impenetrable byway and give me, well, face it, my due comeuppance.

At dinner Justine turned the conversation from the dismal teaching they'd observed to the content of the classes. *Lear* offered perennial terrain for the literary explorer, and I tried out my ideas on them, for instance, that in a world of disguises (Edgar as Tom, Kent as Caius), Lear learns to see through to the real man: "Thou art the thing itself, unaccommodated man is no more but such a poor, bare, forked animal as thou art." Stripping down, he uncovers, literally and metaphorically, the truth about how and who man is. I would come back to this theme when we read Lear's speech about "Through tattered clothes small vices do appear" and against the backdrop of those discussions, let them respond to Lear's assertion in Act 5 that he is "every inch a king." This would be just one through-line to pursue, but it seemed a fitting one given the theme of social justice that anchored my AP course.

"As well as the regulars," Justine pointed out. "LeGuin's 'Omelas' story is right in line with the social justice theme. I love your reading choices," added warmly. What a mensch my former (and still) teacher was. It occurred to me that I could invite her to guest-teach tomorrow, but she must have seen the thought spring Athena-like from my mind because she put her hand on my arm, saying, "It's such a treat to simply observe, not be in charge, Alex. Thank you for granting me this privilege."

One more day. I wasn't clear on their plans after tomorrow, but what did it matter as long as they didn't involve sitting in on my classes. They'd be back in Scotland soon enough; we could stay in touch periodically, Mamia and I might visit them in several years when we could laugh about what a lousy teacher I'd been, and everything could go back to normal between us. Keep it together tomorrow, Bug, leap and bound but trash those naïve expectations of success.

By the time fourth period rolled in, the students all knew that the mysterious field trip meant walking out to the field where they played soccer and ran laps. Its green charm was dimmed by schists of lost games, broken bones, coaches' yells. We gathered under the lone spreading tree that pre-dated the field, and I laid out the activity, which the students likewise already knew, and not only: they had prepared a strategy to undermine it. No one would walk away, and their reasons for staying painted a detestable picture of the contemporary teenage outlook. I had, however, promised not to doubt their motives when they shared them but to accept them as valid and truthful. Hard to do, knowing they were lying to show the guests their worst side and blame its hideous aspect on what'd been taught by me. Vicious little bastards they, now fallen in my estimation from "bad" to "ugly." But given their current vile state of mind, I could argue merely a few literary points with them, not the critical moral ones.

Halfway through this sham class Peterson Hathaway stumbled into our cursed circle under the tree. His eyes were bloodshot, hair and clothes rumpled, he stank of unwashed teeth and skin, old sweat and something curdled. I couldn't quite make out what drug would have leached from his cells with that foul odor. The venom I'd suppressed shot hissing from my fangs.

"Slippery Pete, man with no timepiece, wanders in. How's the weed or whatevs you're smoking cooking snorting shooting ingesting these days? Long night, Petey-pie. Shame school had to get in the way of your party. But no worries, you can do college ripped."

I spat all this out while he shuffled over to me with his admit slip from the front office. I glanced at it; anyone could get one of those with a parental note (usually faked, rarely checked). This one said "family emergency," which was almost as common as "feeling sick." The voracious homework-eating puppy had gone out with the twentieth century, though pets still died at a freaky rate on test days.

"My mother's appendix burst. I was in the hospital with her and my dad all night. She had emergency surgery; it was touch and go. She's still in the ICU. I just left. Probably shouldn't have come—I'm pretty wiped out. But I didn't want to go home."

Sassy, savvy Mr. Mann shot down. His formerly passive-aggressive students now united in open rebellion. Most of them didn't care much for Petey, but my offensive attack had made him a hero to be defended, his cause theirs, and they rose up against me in churlish contempt. Forget "Omelas." Here's the suffering kid none will walk away from but all will walk away with. They smothered him in condolences and offers of help. Discussion turned to appendixes and mothers, stories of other family illnesses and ways they'd coped with them, an array of warnings and remedies. Everyone, it seemed, had dealt with an emergency. Everyone understood what he was going through. Slippery Pete basked in the sympathy. The class, such as it raggedly was, ended. I was the one they shunned without a backward glance, despite my attempts at rectifying my ugly accusations.

If lunch was awkward yesterday, today it was just plain dismal. Rose still held her tongue, but her eyes were dark fire. When she trapped me alone, as I knew even more surely now she would, she'd fry me. I was already wallowing in guilt, though I couldn't yet say out loud what a rotten failure of a teacher I'd been, couldn't yet dissect the scene we'd just lived and analyze how and where I'd gone wrong and what I should or could have done, why they hated me and whether it was my self-loathing that provoked their hatred. Lots of territory to excavate, and at that point I was too shaken to start digging. Unlike Pete, I wanted to go home, quit my job and go home. Then get out of town and disappear.

Instead, I hid my shame and barreled into AP. An excellent discussion of *Lear* might resurrect my withered confidence. I had to best Studly McHandsome in plumbing the depths of Act III, Scene 4, and win back my devotees: that was paramount. My opening question about whether "unaccommodated man is no more than such a poor, bare animal" would get the class going, and I had a dynamite rejoinder to their likely agreement that yes, he is no more than this. Revved myself up again to press onward.

He walked in splendor through the door, surrounded by his entourage, all of whom vied animatedly for his favor. Irene plastered me with a baleful look, which made it clear that, of course, *everyone* knew about the incident with Slippery Pete. I had been repeatedly amazed by how quickly tales tattled across the school, while homework assignments intended to be shared with missing students grew cement feet. No cover for me, though I would proceed as if untouched by that petty disgrace.

Dove in, my voice tolling Lear's indictment of man. Vivienne's lips parted and she drew a breath, ready to assent, as I figured she (they all) would, thereby launching my follow-up about the nature of self-consciousness and why an animal would require it. But she exhaled without speaking, cocking her head at McStudly, deferring with that glance to him. He smiled, waited courteously to see what others might say, but they sat mute, counting on Handsome to deliver an unassailable verdict. I felt the bile of an ill-digested burrito in my throat.

"Vivienne, what are you thinking?"

She shrugged. "I don't know."

Liar. So much for pinning her to her unspoken response. I moved on to Beatrice, who always had an opinion and never hesitated to defend it.

"Beatrice?"

"Lear's a mad old man in a rainstorm. How can we assess anything he says?"

Playing a game she knew not to. I was scrambling to find an inoffensive way to point that out and challenge her to think about the question itself when Stud spoke up.

"Well, of course the question is not really about Lear's sanity but about his discovery of the true nature of man and society when he himself is stripped of its trappings. And whether he's saner at this juncture than he was as a ruler in the opening scene is one of the big issues of the play. 'Reason in madness,' Edgar calls it later, which I'm inclined to agree with."

Gotcha. Stepped on my lines, SMcH did, but as it was in a noble cause, I forgave him.

"Well said," bestowing my approval on his lean frame. "Now, Jocelyn, what are your thoughts about the original question?" as I wrote it on the board.

She was a shy one, still not convinced she belonged in AP, doubting the validity of any position she held. I generally had to push her, though until yesterday it had seemed that less was at stake. Sitting next to McH, she lowered her head, shaking it. No chance she'd venture an opinion.

He, cloaked as the gallant Señor Empathy, sped to her rescue. "It's pretty clear that man must be more than an animal to be able to ask such a question. The fact that we are conscious of ourselves as entities separate from one another and from nature, that we can think about ourselves, is indicative of our status as more than an animal, though that Lear could believe we aren't raises the dramatic issue of whether he is conscious of himself at this point"…blah blah blah…

Madness clouded my reason. I couldn't think, couldn't speak, couldn't move, couldn't listen to the usurper of my domain spout my words any longer. Stood watching his expressive face move, watching every girl in the class watching him. Gazing with unabashed adoration upon him, I mean. Fury paralyzed me. He had stolen not only my girls but also my ideas and my position. Who was I now anyway, an interloper who occupied the empty space at the front of the classroom? How was I here? What difference did my presence make? Did they even see *me* anymore or just a superfluity in the room that had ceased to matter? He had devoured my authority and purpose, my will, which to regain I had to get him out of my sight out of my class out of my life. Murder crept into my imaginings, a glorious resolution to this injustice that I, a conscience-made coward, would not act but devoutly wish on.

Tuned back in when my nemesis restored me to the present with a bull's-eye, his to mine. Something about him wanting to retrace ground we'd covered before his eminence had graced our lives, a speech near the start of Act III.

"It ties in to whether Lear has any sense of who he is once he's been thrown out of the kingdom. The speech when he commands the gods of the storm to discover their enemies—a great way of telling them to expose the true demons. But here, it's hard to be sure if Lear is including himself among the wicked. Is he talking to or of himself when he says, 'Tremble, thou wretch,' (thou being the familiar form of you),

'That hast within thee undivulged crimes

Unwhipped of justice. Hide thee, thou bloody hand,
Thou perjured, and thou simular of virtue
That art incestuous.'"

He paused for maximum effect. "If he is, then he is confessing that he falsified his own virtue and that in fact he was incestuous. Committed incest." Waited for the air to flee the room. "That might help explain why the two older daughters have no compassion for him. At least it casts them in a different light."

I had passed over that reference because I thought that it was misread—that too much was read into it. Jane Smiley with her *Thousand Acres* tome had pretty well scraped the bottom of that pan. Since no one else suggested any misbegotten liaisons between him and his offspring, and since he would presumably have been pushing seventy when they were pubescent, I considered that whole line of inquiry a titillating distraction and had rolled on past it. Now I saw in the girls' faces the assumption that I'd missed this vital theme.

What I should have done is explain to them what I just did to you. What I did instead was laugh. A wind of disapproval rushed back into the room, humming from twelve throats. The storm had broken. My once-faithful Vivienne rose on its torrent to expel me from the kingdom.

"It makes sense of everything that's happened so far. The violence, the cold relations between them, the vengeance."

"The evidence in the text—"

"Is ample," she insisted. "We could go back now and find all the clues easily." A pause, her eyes hard. "I can't believe we missed that line."

How sharper than a serpent's tooth it is to have a thankless student. Vivienne of the red-gold tresses and green orbs, on whom I'd lavished hours of care. Those college essays I'd revised with her, making them soar high enough to fulfill her Ivy League dreams. The early-morning conferences to hone her understanding of difficult passages in our texts. The SAT practice tests. But what a sublime couple they made, she as fair as he was dark and both glistening with youthful ardor.

"Look, the thing is that regardless of whether he's speaking of himself or to multitudes of sinners, the issue is power. That's one of the central themes of the play. Incest is about one person overpowering another through sexual force; it's just one form of subjugation. We've seen here the power of rule, of truth and lies, of family bonds, of loyalty and betrayal, hate and love, of rights and wrongs, youth and age, and not just in Lear's situation but Gloucester's, too. It's power that's at stake, and that's what you need to consider rather than whether Lear committed incest."

I willed my mouth to shape itself into a smile, disfigured though it might be by ire.

"You're downplaying the importance of incest." Vivienne, giving no quarter. "It colors their personal relationship, and as you said earlier, Lear doesn't seem to be able to keep the private and public realms separate, who he is as a father and who he is as a king. Maybe's he's been raping the whole country, maybe Kent and Cordelia have like Stockholm syndrome and love their abuser."

So far out on a weak limb that she was sure to fall. My smile grew genuinely condescending. Poor baby. Let Prince Charming rescue her if he wanted to, but he opted instead to watch the bough break.

The others had come around now, recognizing, which they inevitably had to, my superior authority. Crepuscular rays, I imagined, fanned out behind me, as the storm blew off across the plains. Still the Mann.

"Well, okay, that might be going too far," she continued, hanging on to the twig, "but still, if Lear raped his daughters, at least the older two, who could have protected their little sister because that happens, like sacrificial victims to keep him off the baby girl, it's so much easier to understand why they would throw him out into the storm to die. And I mean, he did the same to Cordelia, in effect, and then forced them to take care of him. He's a monster, really. The incest thing just makes everything make sense."

Raj stretched, extending himself fore and aft in a leisurely fashion. My stomach tensed. But he said nothing, merely turned to Vivienne, letting his eyes caress her face, his manifest support urging her on.

"You know, I can see how it would for you, Viv, being an incest survivor yourself."

Flashcrashboom. The room went dark except for Vivienne's face, which was a neon scarlet, lashing me.

"Mr. Mann," rasped, quivering, "I told you that in confidence. How dare you!" And she ran for the door, gusting tears. Three girls rose to follow, and McStudly mobilized to go after them, then torsoed around to face me.

"'As flies to wanton boys...'". Sneered, turning to the class: "Best be wary of what you tell the Mann. I suspected as much, only one day under his rule, but never thought he'd go so low as to exert his power to mutilate us."

"He loves to ferret out our secrets." Irene emboldened, threw the accusation at the witnesses, my friends and mother. "The sexier the better."

"I know. When I told him about Marina sleeping with Duke, while his girlfriend was, like, taking a bath in the next room, he frenzied. Made me tell him all the gory details." Thanks for sharing Beatrice, who everyone pretty much knew was the scrub-a-dub in the tub.

And Jocelyn chimed in, why not? "That's how he gets his kicks, through our lives. It's kind of an emotional rape." Audible gasps. Yep, over the top and out of line, that, and she realized it, quickly softened, no doubt conscious of hanging on the cusp of an A- with six weeks of good behavior left to go. "But that's also how he gets such great writing out of us. We open a vein for him and the stuff that comes out is our true inner selves. I mean, he's the best writing teacher I've ever had."

Whether she meant that last part or not, she was right.

The bell rang, merciful shriek, postponing the denouement till tomorrow, granting us all time to recover, gather ourselves, and find a safe path toward forgiveness to travel together. I would arrange a meet with SMcH, get him on board or overboard. It would all be so much easier once we were free of the committee's scrutiny.

Drove home in shock, straight to my room, not ready to talk, not able to eat, not willing to remember. Just sprawled on the bed, eyes shut, one cat on my chest and the other curled against my underarm. Heard the text come in but didn't pull out my phone to check it. Neither slept nor moved, a state of torpor from which I could not rouse myself while night crept into the room and blurred all but memory. At some point I must have liberated myself from even that scourge and gone to sleep. I did not want to reawaken, or if, then only to an utterly changed world. Nothing would dare to be the same.

The text was from Rose, and when I came to with a start at the insistence of my 5:00 a.m. alarm, its message got my blood churning: "J and I will be with Katherine the next two days. Evaluating the situation. We are taking you to Trove for the weekend." Not a chance I'd be going with them. The thought was even less appealing than heading back into the classroom.

And of course the only thing in the world that had changed was my hunger, gone from nil to ravenous.

Go in straight, I directed myself, be nice, smooth things over like it was no big deal, yesterday's news. Turn Slippery Pete into Peter the Great, a promotion that would more than satisfy him. The kids would be over him anyway; he'd been a designated weirdo since ninth grade, so I'd been told, and would, after his unexpected canonization, return to that lowly status. Checkmark. I assigned the fourth period their second in-class essay of the week, this one an analysis of the primary theme of "Omelas," its relevance to our society, and in relation to that analogous state, the motives for their actions in refusing to walk away. It was intentionally an oversized task for forty-five minutes, and as I collected the essays, I informed them these were drafts I would review before they rewrote them for a final grade. This strategy, devised on the spot, was far more punitive for their misbehavior and preventative of any future rebellion than a lecture would have been, in part because it required them to think and in larger part because the other sections, which had been astonishingly well behaved, did not have to write the essay. The ultimate rub was that they couldn't whine about it because they knew the reason for this extra work and didn't want to hear me lay it on them.

Trifecta.

AP, I feared, would be tougher, and I had an in-class prepared for them, too, on whether Lear is a man "more sinned against than sinning," as he claims. But I didn't need to use it, yet, because they met me in a subdued frame of mind, clearly anxious to avoid any more fireworks. Vivienne would not look at me, but she also chose to sit elsewhere in the room, left McHandsome to fend for himself, which was easy for him as he once again read Lear. We moved on. I realized that the fault lines of indignation and distrust still brewed beneath the surface, likely to cause another eruption at some point. I owed it to Viv to straighten things out with her, apologize, reassure her of my fidelity, try to justify my betrayal on the grounds that she had stubbornly shifted from literary analysis to psychoanalysis, which she knew was not valid. Or something like that—the right words would come to me.

At the end of the day I texted Rose back. "Can't make the weekend trip. Thanks though. Have fun." It took her less than thirty seconds to reply: "It's not optional, Bug. Pack an overnight. Be ready at 7:00 on Saturday." Jesus. Who did she think she was? My fingers were poised to send an acid rejoinder about poor working stiffs with papers to grade and prep to do, but I didn't want to go there. Easier, in the end, just to be sick this weekend. A lesson I'd learned from my kids.

But Friday night when they got back from Vista Grande, Rose intercepted me. As I was about to text my apologies for a sudden onset of the dreaded crud, she, telepathing my intent, called.

"Alex, I understand your reluctance to go with us, but please spare me some transparent excuse. This trip is not meant to be a rare and exquisite form of torture for you; rather, I would like your assistance as one who knows Trove, which I do not."

Okay, there's a bend in the river I was not anticipating.

"The truth is, it had been my plan to keep this news a surprise. To tell you along the way. However, I don't want to drag you down there in a foul humor, too irate to be decent company."

Rose, the soul of tact.

"Are you already in bed?"

"Half asleep." I snore-yawned.

"Well, wake up, please. Here's the story I meant to tell you en route. You'll see why it concerns you."

She drew a long breath, gathering her tale. I lay back on the bed, my hand stroking Tiger. Rose was a storyteller, not one to cut to the chase.

"Centuries ago, when Katherine was a dewy-eyed bride looking to spread herself across the Southwest, she pried loose some Hampton family trust funds to buy property in far too many idyllic locales. A ranch along the Pecos River that she leased to a wealthy wannabe cowboy for a while, then sold at an enormous profit; an old adobe near O'Keeffe's home in Abiquiu, used for mental health seminars and retreats; a ski lodge in Aspen, and oh, a variety of other prime spots including a spacious cabin on a picturesque hillside near Trove." She paused, waiting for a reaction I inheld. A spacious cabin in Trove, the kind of home I had once so ached to own. "Managers looked after all these properties, keeping them tiptop for her rare visits with Lou. My father was especially fond of the Trove cabin, whose proximity to wilderness nourished his soul and whose exquisite views, he told me, were a dream vision of pristine beauty."

Oh, yes, I know.

"When my parents divorced, Lou could easily have claimed half of Katherine's holdings, New Mexico being a community property state, but the dear man was too proud and modest both to take his due. He asked simply for the Trove cabin, which she quickly deeded to him before he came to his senses and scrabbled for more of their estate, she having been a fool not to protect it with a pre-nup. He walked away—from the house he'd built on the land he'd bought—with nothing else, made a clean start and a successful comeback, business-wise. As a man, he limped along, his spirit broken, for some twenty years until he met Heather in Edinburgh. May the next twenty restore his joy in love.

"And now I come to the part that especially concerns you, Alex. Since Lou plans to stay in Scotland with his new family, at most vacation in the Southwest, he gave me the Trove cabin as a wedding gift, did so in truth gladly (since he's had to pay for its upkeep). I need to go there to register the deed in my name and inspect the place, which has been empty for too many years. I want you to rent it from me next summer for a very nominal fee. You were so happy in Trove, even with all complications that arose. You should have another chance at living there, if just for a season, in a place of your own. Maybe your dear mother will want to go with you. In any case, that's why you need to come with us tomorrow, to see the place and decide whether you'd like it for the summer."

When I did not speak, she added, strategically. "If you're not interested, I may sell it."

Pause.

"Alex?"

I lay silent, my hand at rest on Tiger's back, not because I knew better than to interrupt her outpouring but because I had nothing to say. A jumble of emotions wrenched my stomach. After sealing off the yearn and memory, here was Trove again, ripping through the fabric.

"Are you asleep? Alex?"

She wouldn't yield, I knew that, but neither would I. Tag along with them, look over the cabin, and then after seeming to give it careful thought, say no to her summer place.

"I'm coming up to your room."

Thrust enough air across my unwilling vocal cords to tell her, "Okay, yes, see you in the morning."

23

Answer Your Heart's Call

We headed out beneath a flinty sky of roughened clouds that matched my sullen mood. Justine drove the rental, Rose riding shotgun, chattering, Bugman in back, eyes closed, unresponsive. The broody landscape of a gray morning did not invite watching. I thought about the last time I'd made this trip, summertime a year ago, Pacman 2, Tiger beside me, hoping to restart my life working with Joaquin. Who didn't need or want me. Rose laughed, stretched across to give her beloved spouse a kiss. She didn't want or need me, either. Lori had her man and her child, never had wanted or needed me. Mamia was the only one who did and likely ever would. Until she died. Unless Frank came back for her, which he'd probably do when he got tired of the road. So no one, ultimately. And who could blame them. I'd spent some time staring at my face in the mirror, ole scars and stripes I called it privately, tried changing expression, talking to myself, imagining how I would look coming in for a kiss. It was bad. I myself wouldn't have wanted to be at the receiving end. Erratic mood swings didn't add to my charms. Quick to anger, given to jealousy, resentment, negativity. A nasty wit. There was very little to love.

Rose picked this moment of self-denigration to nail me.

"So what happened? When did you turn into a...a—"

"Prick?" I offered.

"Worse. A mean-spirited sadist. You used to have a sense of humor; now it's just spite."

"Easy, my love," Justine cautioned. "Having observers in the room changes the dynamics. We should have left when the kids started acting up. I knew that. We owe you a big apology, Alex."

"Those were the most obnoxious classes I've had this year." What a relief to say it.

"But why did they feel compelled to behave so horribly with us there? If they were fond of you, respected you, trusted you, surely they would have done their best to show you off to us. Not humiliate and defy, like abuse victims in front of witnesses."

"Rose!"

"It's okay. She's been waiting for days to beat me up. Go on, slugger, take your best shot." I jutted my chin at her.

"Last spring you'd found your calling; everyone loved you. Hired by acclaim. This year, you stink. Sorry to be so blunt, but I am devastated. What the hell happened?"

"Look, I had awesome kids in the spring. The best. Unbelievable. They warned me about this year's bunch. And maybe they spoiled me for the regular goofballs. I did have great rapport with the AP class till Studly McEgo showed up."

"He is tremendous, and you know it, a gifted actor and scholar. He just exposed your insecurity. You're way too possessive of those girls."

"He's a phony with a shallow intellect, but it looks like he fooled you, too."

"You know what the hell happened? You turned into Mr. Biggs. That's right, the English teacher who tried to make us his disciples. We hated him, but fear of his caustic tongue inhibited us from speaking our minds, *our* minds, which he wasn't interested in anyway unless they were mirrors of his. Required us to worship him and do everything his way. Think his way, write his way, interpret literature his way. Those who did were admitted to his charmed circle and could do no wrong. Talk about an ego!"

"Usually the cute girls who wore their skirts short and hair long. And the really smart girls. We called them the Little Biggs. I don't know what you're complaining about. You were one of them."

"Only because I was such a grade-hog. Had to have all As. It also kept Katherine from showing her fangs. But I didn't like or trust or respect him. He thought he was the best English teacher in the school, the one who really taught students how to write and think. We knew it wasn't true, but we didn't know how terrible a lie it was till we had Justine."

"That's right." I snatched at this point of agreement, hoping I wouldn't have to yield to all the others, which were likewise undeniable. Rose had named my faults accurately and cast them in a light we both recognized.

She whirled to face Justine. "What was it you were telling me about having 'power with' rather than 'power over' to form a community that's greater than the sum of its parts?"

Of course they'd been talking about me, probably with Mamia as well.

"A writer named Kreisberg put forth the concept that power is an energy to be used as we will. When used for good, sharing power increases rather than diminishes it, like the power of love.

> 'The more I give to you
> The more I have
> for both are infinite,'"

Rose put in, quoting Juliet from her balcony scene; then she added in case I'd missed the point, "The more power the students have, the more the teacher does. You just have to trust them and yourself enough to share. Like Justine did."

She stopped herself before making an unflattering comparison to my spotlight-hogging strut, but it was in her voice.

"Alex, Rose, I know you're close friends, and I don't like to interfere in your conversation, but I must speak up here. My darling, instead of punishing Alex as you have, perhaps you could suggest ways to alter and remedy the situation. Or if you can't just now, perhaps you'll allow me to?"

Rose nodded. She was breathing hard, her pale skin flushed with outrage.

We were nearing the exit to Willow Springs. Halfway to Trove.

"From my view, Alex, teaching is about discovering how to further students' ability to learn. Since this process requires their full cooperation and participation, it's not about making the students do your will but assisting them to develop their own through your guidance. This may sound hyperbolic, but in the richest sense you are serving to unveil their happiness, which I believe is commensurate with learning. Chief among their desires is to be loved. Your role as their teacher is not to make them love you but to love them, which ironically, will bring them to love you."

Justine's calm, persuasive words breached my defenses. I hadn't realized I was shaking.

"Our first afternoon you explained that you'd given up enacting *Lear* with the regular students because they weren't able to get or appreciate the play." (Babbling Bug, shooting his mouth off in the false belief that he had everything under control for their observation.) "What I wondered then, but reminded myself to wait and see who these kids were, was whether they'd had a voice in choosing how to study this magnificent play.

"Resistance tends to melt in the face of responsibility, Alex. So you didn't know how to teach *Lear* to your regular sections though you thought it worth doing? Ask them, find out how they learn best, use what you can of their suggestions, which automatically gives them a stake in the venture. If you evaluate them significantly on the development and implementation of this study, they will work hard to make it engaging, worthwhile, and fair. So they all suggest different things, learn differently: natural enough. Well, then, you work collaboratively with them to develop a plan that synthesizes aspects of their strategies and offers them a variety of opportunities to succeed. Give them agency, leadership, in this enterprise, let yourself learn from and with them. You will discover the joy of seeing them awaken to their capabilities and make education the joining of individual will to common understandings.

"Put simply, it's good to remember that you are their advocate, not their adversary. Their guide, not their commander, he who beckons rather than blinds. Learn with them, from them, and they will do likewise with and from you. And—give yourself time to experiment and space to fail, failure being one of the greatest teachers. You will find your footing." Justine glanced over her shoulder at my tormented face. "Sorry to go on so long. I know you know all this."

"I do," my earnest response, quiet. "I know what I should be doing. You taught me."

She waved aside the compliment, focused on getting us through Willow Springs to Arroyo.

"If you know, Bug, then what's made you so mean?"

Justine parried Rose's accusation, "We understand things long before we are able to act on that understanding. It's like learning a new language."

Rose, undeterred: "Shelley thinks it was the loss of that baby boy you'd planned to name Yeats."

"She told us that in confidence!" Justine reprimanded.

"It made things worse, but they were already rocky," I acknowledged. "Last straw kind of deal. Stripped away any illusion of happiness."

"A talented, bright, disillusioned young man does not a good teacher make."

"So? You have an elixir to transform me, a magical restorative vial I can down? Some way to persuade me against all reason and evidence that life is beautiful and I can become a good teacher?"

Rose smiled, wide and kindly. "Maybe," she said, "a summer to write and think in a place you love will help restore your faith."

The alpine horizon beyond Calhoun promised a halcyon day. Gone were the clouds that had bullied the sun into another region. Despite my fears about returning to Trove, site of the Icarus odyssey where I'd peaked and plummeted, my heart opened to ache as we neared. So glorious, so beneficent, so irredeemable my sojourn there. I craved and dreaded our reunion, pangs I'd only known for romantic love in the past. Back to Trove, coming home to my beloved. It was the place, not Joaquin nor Lori nor the rest, I yearned for.

Main Street. Floyd's (no one there). The Belle Star. Dry creek bed under the bridge, a bare remnant of aspen gold hidden in the folds of dark green. Candles, olive oils, toffee, fossils, art galleries, outdoor gear, post office, theater, hotel, fishing gear, hardware store. The crowning joy: Lunch at Gregorio's, superb as ever, prepared as if (!) by advance notice especially for us. His genuine delight in feeding and talking with us, me above all since he was just meeting R and J, made the re-entry sweet. When we finished dessert, were sipping another cup of coffee to mellow our bulging stomachs and prolong the ease of doing nothing, Floyd, Jess, and other townspeople I was close to wandered in, as if (!) they knew we'd be here and came by deliberately to chat. Even though I'd left without a word of farewell, they were glad to see me. Welcome home, welcome home rang in their voices, a greeting I'd never heard except from los parentitos.

Rose and Justine left me with my friends at the café while they went to the county courthouse to register the deed in their names, an unorthodox transaction on Saturday, arranged by Rose with her charm and deep pockets. Like a time traveler, I slipped back nine months into my former cadence, chatting as though I'd just come in for supplies. Floyd was concerned that I'd let Pacman 2 fall into disrepair (meaning I hadn't been scrubbing its innards and polishing its outtards regularly; he was right). Jess wanted to know whether Tiger was still a big game hunter and was treating Montengra in the queenly way she deserved. Belle scolded me for leaving her with an overload of stock since she'd increased her orders after I started cooking for Joaquin. And as if (!) summoned, he pushed through the door.

We'd seen each other in September, but maybe I hadn't really been looking at him. Joaquin was haggard, gaunt, bag-eyed, a man with too much work and too little time to eat and sleep. Wince-limping. Deserters' pangs struck my guilt-laden conscience. I had screwed this man whom a year ago I'd idolized. Rose's accusation, "a mean-spirited sadist," burned verily. I stood to greet him, and on impulse changed my handshake into an embrace. Which he returned, gratefully (or wearily) sinking into my arms. If it weren't for his family, I realized, I'd ride shotgun back to his place, fix us a big dinner, and roll right onto the couch tonight.

It felt so natural to be here, with friends, and profoundly stirring to discover that I was still at home among them.

The return of my traveling companions broke up our love fest. It was midafternoon, and Rose was eager to drive out to the cabin.

"You're going to love the place, Alex," Gregorio assured me, Floyd and Jess nodding in assent. "And we will love having you here in Trove again." So everybody knew everything, of course, but their treating it as a foregone conclusion would make it harder for me not to.

Floyd clapped me on the back. "Better get going before the light does." His hand gripped my shoulder. "Hey, and try to take care of that sterling vehicle of yours till next summer." I saluted him.

"See you for dinner!" Gregorio called after us.

Docile and eager as a rescue critter, I followed Justine and Rose to the car, opened the back door, but Justine stopped me from getting in. "Rose is driving this last stretch. You're shotgun." She smiled. "We want you to have a clear first view of your potential summer home."

And I did. Up the fateful hairpin and on out of Trove west on 833 toward Slurry Passage, we cruised past the sandstone bluffs, the very Broken Arches motel, and the Three Sisters restaurant. Off to our left a road I'd traveled only once, when Joaquin wanted to fish the reservoir at the headwaters of the Rio Sol. The next road to the right was Joaquin's, and two miles later the road we took, winding through a valley and up a hillside from which rose a two-story log cabin with a wide veranda overlooking the Rio Sol and a spectacular stretch of the Rockies towering over the broad glacial valley. Much like Joaquin's but, truly, even grander. Rose laid a hand on my arm and squeezed. Trembling, I scanned the forested hills behind the cabin.

"Wilderness," she said. "Protected, though some of the land is used for grazing." I knew that but was too stunned to remember that I did. Steady and calm, Rose navigated the well-banked road up to the cabin, parked under a roofed carport, got out and motioned me to follow suit. Unfortunately, I'd lost the use of my legs. Ignoring my paralysis, she unlocked the front door and walked in, knowing I'd have to stand and follow.

Chest constricted stopped my breath. Heart bounced erratic in its airless cage. Dizzily grabbed a post and hauled myself up. What a shame it would be to have a heart attack just when the chance of a reprieve lay before me. A jittering blackness rippled through my head and disappeared. I stepped inside.

Immaculate, stunning, and why wouldn't it be, belonging as it had to Katherine and Lou? The comfortable living room with a fireplace at the far end, dining room, and kitchen spanned the breadth of the house. That was exactly the layout I liked: sitting, talking, cooking, and eating in a shared common space. A small entry-room for winter gear and cleaning supplies. Large south-facing windows swept the landscape, guiding the viewer down the hill to the river and beyond toward the scooped valley within its alpine shelter. To the right and left, woods, below them the road to town. FWD in winter, but that was anywhere in Trove. Rest of the time, Pacman 2, my steadfast ride.

Beyond the wide first tier of rooms, two baths and bedrooms, a laundry nook, and stairs to the second floor, which was one large, carpeted space that could be cut up, or could and would be, for me, a bedroom and study, a place to gaze and write and rest. Again the views, even better up here. It was more house than I'd imagined living in, solo, more than I'd dreamed of when I conjured a future house and family one hill over from Joaquin. Here I was a good two miles beyond his turn-off, enough distance so that I would not have to be part of the Strangers' world.

The cats! Oh, man, they'd be in heaven! Back in the country, five acres of it theirs, roaming freely or sprawling with me in the sun on my study floor carpet. To be as happy as my cats: that was an estimable goal unlikely to be fulfilled.

The cats would never want to leave. Nor would I. And therein, Shakespeare, lies the rub. If I accepted Rose's offer, the felines and their attendant were here to stay. At least for their lifetimes, maybe mine. Was I ready to commit to Trove? What would I do here? I recalled Gregorio asking me what my plans were and I shrugging off the idea that I had to make any, yet. Later, sure, trusting my friends would help find me work of some kind. I was thinking in months then, not years.

We walked the land as the shadows grew, discovered up behind the cabin an aspen grove and rested there, watching the light ebb. While I am fond of all species of tree, the aspen is my favorite. Their few remaining autumnal leaves susurrating gold, lithe-limbed white against the dark hills. If I were able to reincarnate by choice, it would be as an aspen. And here, in this grove. Though for now, next summer, I would sit in their midst, read and nap and breathe.

"Well?" Rose asked in the tone of one who knows the answer.

"How much?" Not that it mattered. I still had most of the money my father bequeathed me, and Mamia assured me of plenty more from Trudel.

"Hundred a month. That's what Lou's been paying to have someone named Dooley check on it, keep the place free of rodents and insects."

I nodded, as though contemplating. It was a ridiculous sum. She could get ten times that a week in season. Though it seemed perverse of me not to leap up and say yes, the long-range view made me hesitate.

"Let me think about it." Spoken sincerely, received indignantly.

"For how long?"

Trick question at that moment, which Justine diplomatically answered for me.

"Why don't you ponder the idea tonight, Alex? We can come back out for another look in the morning."

"Yes, thank you." I extracted Rose's thorn and gave both of them a grateful smile.

Evening brought the curtains down on our expedition, and we drove back to the café in silence, watching the colors dim. While Greg was enthusiastic about serving us dinner, and our taste buds salivated at the offer, the digestive organs rebelled. They still had a load to get through. We thought about a stroll around town, but with the descent of the sun came the sudden chill of mountain climes, marked by a harsh, storm-scented wind, and the Trove Hotel was right across the street.

Early though it was, we went directly upstairs to our rooms. I sat in front of the TV with the sound low, whipping my indecisive mind with recriminations. "For how long" haunted my thoughts. I'd promised myself to be a good son, take care of Mamia for a change: for how long? I'd declared myself a teacher: for how long? I'd called Trove my heart's home: for how long? Returning, it seemed no less so than when I'd left. A summer in my own place might be the essential catalyst to affirming my attachment. And if not, I could leave. The cats had proved themselves adaptable: they didn't rule my life any more than I theirs. I drifted off still in turmoil, woke up hours later to the voice of some TV historian reading the names of the Civil War dead in a somber monotone guaranteed to keep them in their graves.

A sumptuous feast that broke our scant fast greeted us at Gregorio's the next morning—itself a feast of beauty. I'd thought of November as an indistinct month, adhering to no season and of no particular weather. This year, in this Rocky Mountain hamlet, it was, on the contrary, a time of all seasons whose weather held the full bounty of the year's possibilities. Last night I would not have predicted this mild, vibrant day, one that called for an extensive meander through the hills and meadows of, I was more confident now, my next summer's home.

After warm farewell *abrazos* with Gregorio, who reiterated his excitement at seeing me again soon, we headed back to Rose's cabin for a second look. The morning light swept grandeur through my upstairs study windows. From the veranda, meadow grasses, pines, and aspen wove an enchantment over the land. I remembered surveying a like scene from Joaquin's porch, a hungry exaltation coursing through me.

Get this, my heart warned my mind, here we are going to make our stand. Yes, I replied inwardly, yes. Although my tongue still lay leaden in its cavity.

"Well?" Rose prompted me, exasperated but certain.

Justine shifted the focus. "What is the source of your doubt, Alex?"

I thought about inventing some complex, esoteric concern but gave it up. "Not about coming but leaving here. I can't imagine how the cats and I ever will. And leaving my mother, whom I had sworn to myself to take care of. Our life together. And what I'd do in Trove, in the long run." My voice had risen to the break point.

Rose melted. "Oh, Bug, I'm sorry. I thought you were just being obstinate to thwart me. The summer is merely an opening gambit; in truth you can stay here as long as you like. I'm rather hoping you will. You can talk with Shelley about your moving here, but I'll tell you that when we spoke with her, she was enthusiastic. Who knows but that she might join you in Trove? Have faith. If you answer your heart's call, as I did, you won't go wrong."

"Isn't there a school in Trove?" Justine chimed in. "There must be, here or nearby. You could apply to teach. Hone your craft among people who already know and trust you."

Right, of course they were, on all counts. My yes rebounded from the hills, its joyful cry echoing a thousand times yes.

Then we were driving back to Summerville and when we got there, it would be Sunday evening once again, and they were leaving tomorrow morning for Boston via Vista

Grande, with Katherine in tow. I never wanted to go back to school. Quit, move to Trove immediately. Justine outmaneuvered me, rousing my conscience and helping me create a plan o' the week as she drove. I took down whatever she said on my laptop, but kept a slide show of my Trove home running on screen alongside the lesson plans.

Out of the corner of my ear I also took in some further advice she offered, realizing how pertinent it was to me.

"As you return to the classroom," Justine began, "beware of the temptation to mold the class in your own image."

"Like Ms. Kimbo, remember?" Rose threw in.

"We called her Ms. Bimbo." A vision of the flouncy science teacher who promenaded around the lab zipped past my brain. Everything we did in class was about her.

"Let me suggest that it is instead the role of teachers to measure their own success in terms of the independence their students achieve. At best, by year's end the teacher is nearly invisible, though crucial, in their learning process. Granted, it's hard to give up center stage, but doing so is the key to awakening the yen to explore and interpret ideas, which are in turn the keys to the growth of a critical mind. The beauty of it is that once free and awake, the mind cannot be closed again. It will exercise the right to think for itself in every sphere."

"I am still amazed by how perfectly Justine read us while we thought she was simply teaching us how to read books." Rose laid an affectionate arm on her wife's. "Like she knew you were better than you knew you were, even back then. Tell him."

I grinned, shaking my head. "I don't think I gave you much hope for my redemption."

Justine responded seriously. "Alex, while you indulged in the cool adolescent antipathy for schooling that many of your ilk did, I could see that you were making considerable effort not to engage that fine intellect of yours. You exhibited far greater depth and curiosity than you were able to hide. I always knew the day would come when your gifts would win out against your disclaim of them."

How could she have seen any promise in the Bug, who got his nickname from mangling Kafka, who turned in crappy, one-draft essays, who invented deplorable excuses for late work, who never had worthwhile questions or ideas to bring to the table? If a goofball like me could become an English teacher, and possibly someday a good one, who among my current students might harbor undeveloped talent I could nurture? "Don't get stuck at assumption junction," Hersch warned me. Time to stop deciding who my students were and discover who they could be. My new resolve illumined a glint of hope.

"Make this year a great success, Alex," Justine concluded, "and you'll be able to return to Trove as a destination, not a retreat."

Back in the Ville, Mamia was delighted that I would be renting the cabin for the summer—and likely beyond. Her eyes kindled. "Not only will it give me a chance to be with you in that magnificent town, but I'll have a place to stay when I visit Miranda." A bashful moment later, added, "I may go to Los Angeles first to see Frank. He's been urging me to come." Unspoken but implied: I'd been holding her up, inhibiting her journey. As usual, failing to see a point of view other than my own. Life as school, teacher as learner with so much to learn.

Rose gathered me in a genuinely loving hug, did not pull away at the prescribed moment. At length she sighed. "X, take better care of yourself, please."

I grinned into her neck. "You calling me X?"

"It's your power name. And you need to summon all your powers for the next stage. X is tempered steel, the man of fire and ice. A *man*." She pulled back and grabbed me by the eyes. "We'll come visit you in Trove one of these years, you and the cats, and I expect to find you ensconced in the good life, *la vida agradable*, as Señora Chavez used to say. I foresee you sharing your hearth with a woman who loves you, maybe a child. Tiger will be a hundred and still vigorous, with elegant Montenegra at his side. You may even out-happily-ever-after me, X, though not likely."

The rush of tears caught me unguarded.

"I'm still in love with you, Rose."

"I love you, too, my oldest, dearest friend."

Then it was Monday, and I braced for first period. Anthology of short stories from around the world, beginning with Tolstoy's "How Much Land Does A Man Need?" Ironic, given my weekend, but easy to teach now that Rose's homestead provided all I needed. I went in early, as always, to stay ahead of 'em. Got my coffee, dodging the Wrightmeister, who was in a closed-door meeting with someone loud and unhappy. Scuttled back to my hole and pulled my neck in. Time to check my thoughts against what some of the critical gurus had to say about the story, which we'd be reading in class and discussing after. It was a straightforward tale of human greed, but how did it compare to others and what contemporary parallels resonated?

I was deep into an analysis of these issues when a harsh rap on the door of the office startled me. Glanced up to see Wright, full frontal frown, with a tall, rubicund woman who looked enough like one of my kids that I deduced she was a parent. With equal skill, I reasoned that she was very angry at me. For what? The possibilities were overwhelming.

She blasted into the office, turning my comfort zone into an inferno. Behind her, the Wrightster offered gingerly, "This is Mrs. Kablinski, Vivienne's mother. She would like to talk with you. And so would I before the day is over. Find a time." Gone: a cowardly retreat. I motioned to a chair; she did not sit down.

I knew well what this was about and that I had it coming. When she'd exhausted her litany of threats and flogged me bloody with shame, we got down to the assault Viv "claimed" she had endured. Her mother thought Viv was being overly dramatic, impugned TV and some YA book for planting these ideas in her head. A cry for attention, of which she got plenty. Don't believe everything you read, young man, and never shoot off your mouth without thinking about who could get hurt. Vivienne's father is the well-respected District Attorney of Summerville, revered by the city. She, his devoted wife, would not stand for any rumor of misdeeds to plague him.

Moreover, she'd heard that I was always digging for dirt on the girls, prodding them to reveal intimate stuff no teacher should know. That I got my kicks from prying into the details of their sex lives and family relations, that I liked to strip them bare of secrets. She'd told the principal about the kind of voyeurism I indulged in, and if I didn't cease and desist immediately, I'd be summarily dismissed with a negative recommendation and a lawsuit on my head.

Sincere apologies, given humbly, vows to mend my errant ways, further apologies, praise of her daughter, to whom I'd already apologized for outing her in class, gratitude to Mrs. Kablinski for coming in to discuss the situation with me and giving me an opportunity to improve. No excuses, no defense. Didn't argue with her about Viv's assault claim, which I fully believed. She was mollified just enough to leave the office, though her parting hiss warned me I'd be under close surveillance for the rest of the year.

Numb-fumbled through classes, my zombie copilot teaching for me. The kids had an inkling I'd left the room and were alternately obedient and ornery, trying to get a response that was not forthcoming, after which they tuned out. None of them cared how much *land* a man needs when there were far more urgent needs, like lunch and a passing grade on the sixth-period physics test. Hook-ups and break-ups, new gear, a win against Melrose High.

I came to only briefly during AP when Vivienne apologized to me for her insane mother's visit. She wished she'd never said a thing to her mom, and actually she wouldn't have if Raj hadn't encouraged her to explain why she was feeling so stressed. Thanks, Studly. But hey, I deserved all the punishment he could dole out. Let him run class today, be Lear and the director. My acquiescence shook him up, but he regained his composure and stepped into the role with fierce authority. They were at Act V, Scene 3, and suave Raj led them onward, stopping at key moments for discussion, such as after reading Lear's famous declaration to Cordelia that they will "take upon's the mystery of things, / As if we were God's spies," delivered by Raj with searing pride. He was amazing, this young idol, as Rose had said, his excellence one of the "mystery of things" that I would have to take upon myself, not merely bear but nurture in league with the forces of light and good. My mouth thanked him at the end, the tones issuing from it warm. He grappled my limp hand from under the desk, shook it, and in turn thanked me for entrusting this class to him. You're an advocate, not an adversary, Justine had reminded me. Maybe I taught best when I was too dazed to speak.

The meeting with Wright was quick, a simple bifurcation of options: Shape up or get out. I should feel his eyes on me at every moment. I was tempted to salute but instead thanked him for giving me one last chance and promised to make the most of it. No more shenanigans, no sir. Marched straight-backed and tight-legged out of his office like he'd given me a wedgie, which, face it, he had.

Excused myself from dinner with Mamia that night, too much to do, and ordered in Thai, which the cats like. Cracked a beer I didn't drink. Stared at the tube, volume too low to decipher, let the shadows engulf me. Slept fully dressed, covered with a blanket and cats. Pitched headlong into a dream.

It's before McStudly showed up, and I have the AP girls all to myself. We're sitting around a picnic table. I'm giving them a creative writing assignment: But today, I instruct them, "I want you to speak your pieces, not write them. Speaking short-circuits the mental editor, allows you to be absolutely honest. Go deep: go to your most private place and let it all out." Secretly in the throb of this dream, I know I want to see them bleed. Up my sleeve I'm holding a mat knife, blade open, and as each girl's turn comes, I reach under the table and cut her. None cries out, though they are in acute pain, and all are bleeding. They speak and speak and speak, each word dire. The blood pools and seeps in rivulets toward my shoes. I try to rub it into the darkening sand, which thickens to sludge. The last girl I come to is Rose. I hadn't noticed her before. She refuses to be cut, swats the blade from my hand, and hurls it across the yard. "What kind of a brute are you?" she yells. Her outcry echoes around the table. All the girls rise, pouring blood, and curse me, the sadistic abuser who's been tearing them apart, cutting them up to make them hurt worse than he does, engorge his power, absorb his terror, and pacify his ego. "Keep your wounds to yourself, your scars are not ours," they shout. Their frenzy grows to a scream, and they advance on me, the dripping blade held high in Rose's hand. The scream becomes mine, awakening me wild in my throat.

I jolted from bed, slammed the lights on. Churned into the bathroom, wrenched water from the shower, let it run cold over me, then scalding, pummel the nausea. Scoured my flesh with a loofah. Red raw, unappeased. The blade still ghosted in my hand. What kind of sadistic brute am I? Emphasis on *sad*.

Not just with the AP stars but my regulars. I had gone in smug, assured of their respect as my due after last spring's triumph, hadn't done a thing to earn it. When they didn't bow down before me, I punished them for their failure to recognize my greatness. Leveled the blame at them for my not winning their slavish devotion. Called them names, obnoxious inventions bequeathed to embarrass and subjugate. Ignored the plaintive voice (whose was it?) early on, asking could they read about a good person that faced hardships but emerged victorious: someone who taught them how to live rather than how not to, like most of the books we were reading. There weren't any on my list wherein good prospered, but I could change that, try Proulx's *The Shipping News* or Abbey's *The Monkey Wrench Gang*, Morrison's *Song of Solomon*, Hesse's *Siddhartha*, and add some nonfiction, biographies of great people. I could still do it, would. And call my students by their rightful names, stop bashing their appearance. Why had I been so oblivious to their wishes, so stubbornly, righteously attentive to my own?

No more, nevermore, not ever again. This vow alone, wrested from the headwaters of my shame, granted me the strength to go forward into the ashen schists of dawn. I would bind and mend. Guide rather than goad them, and let them guide me so that together we would mold this brief communal span into a transformative education. I would learn through them to become the teacher I could be, cultivated in their image of the ideal. They would learn from me how to forge a beginning from an end.

24

A Threefold Spoon

You push your tongue into the slit, engulfing the labia of the plum with your mouth. Green: not the hue of ripeness, but a clever species, this, disguising its sweetness to repel thieves, such as you are, and she. You devour another and a third. Your chin runs wild with juice.

A tiny hand grabs your ear: hey, where's my share? Tenderness exceeding what was the frontier of your capacity squeezes the last pulp from the third plum and sends a finger-load over your shoulder, where it is sucked between new teeth and toughened gums. Her language of bounce and wiggle is plain: More, more. And she is learning the rewards of expressing her desires plainly: you give her more. The gratification as potent for you as for her.

You think of the woman at the other end of life you used to feed. Spoon by unfulfilling spoon, your grandmother. Oatmeal, soup, tasteless nurture for sunken expectations. Staving off death by not much. Why were there no green plums for her?

"Bucket coming down.

She clutches a branch and bends as far over as she safely can, regarding her beloved partner and child from a perch in the foliage. Miranda and Joaquin. Joaquin and Miranda. These two, a gift surpassing any image of happiness she'd conjured in childhood fantasies. Glows, watching him finger-feed Miranda, her Joaquin an ardent papa who's come to trust himself to love their offspring, no longer fearful that role would unleash an abusive gene inherited from his father. How glad he is to have a girl child, Joaquin tells her, which bolstered his confidence that he wouldn't repeat old patterns, not do unto her as had been done unto him. Not, she assured him, that he'd ever needed to doubt. Abuse a form of self-punishment, in her experience, for which Joaquin has no longer cause. She, too, a victim once of cruelty, whose torment seeded a devout resolve to give Miranda the childhood denied her. So far, a luscious one.

"Careful, Lori. You're way too high." Your damn leg keeps you earthbound, what should be your job hers.

"Spent a lot of time hiding in trees, my love. I'm part robin." She laughs, makes a wing of her free arm.

"Skylark," you think. "Teach me half thy gladness, blithe spirit, thou scorner of the ground."

You tip the bucket of plums gently into the sack, already more than half full. Leaning over not so far as to slide Miranda onto your head. She's burbling, her grasp shifting from shirt collar to hair. Your body revels in her uninhibited touch. A perfect child, yours and Lori's, who is creating you in her own image. You will be for her the meaning of parents, both real and ideal, hers, to make and remake as she comes to know you, grows into herself. She who entered the world as a stranger and a Stranger. In whom your happiness now resides. And in Lori, as hers in you and Miranda lies, a family. The word originates from Latin, you looked it up, for "servant," specifically "household servant," and yes, you are in service to one another and to the love that binds and nurtures you in the household you share. None here the master.

Climbing has ever been her refuge. Learned young how to camouflage herself amidst the leaves, quiet as a shadow. Once fell asleep in oaken crook, hauled back to consciousness by the mewling of little boys who needed her to hang from. A hybrid of monkey, bird, and leopard, she skittered up and down old wood, arbored in the upper story of branches, for views, freedom, safety. The plum tree, though at thirty feet unusually large for its kind, rooted perhaps in an aquifer, is no challenge for Lori. Footholds to the top, where branch-loads of plump fruit await. Retrieving her bucket, she nimbles back up, higher than wary Joaquin can abide.

"We have plenty," you call to her. "More than we can get home with."

She turns her face to yours, blows you a kiss. "Just one more bucketful. These are so gorgeous. Miranda's going to suck your fingers off!"

"As long as her mother gets down safely with them." You're grumbling now, vainly. The morning is a confluence of loveliness. Make that your focal point. You imagine it as an expertly sculpted jewel, from the lapis lazuli sky to the silver quivers of aspen leaves, deep shades of turquoise blue-green spruce and field grasses, highlighted with penstemon, daisies, lupine, and sage. You live in a work of art, unassuming, unrestrained, unsurpassed. Wide-angle lens reveals a mere sliver of it. Beauty that cannot be overgazed. Teach Miranda to look and look.

Splendor of place is the one thing you have a surplus of. Otherwise, you're at the edge. Month to month, hovering at zero, the last five dollars stretched so thin the paper microfissures. Rough winter and spring in the greenhouse, bugs and a leak that froze a swath of plants. Half the crop you'd counted on. Lori knows, she works with you to get by, putting up fruit like these plums, making granola, bread, and large batches of chili that are extended. You're both used to a shoestring life. As are your friends in Trove, everyone aware of your struggles, those with a bit more than you offering invites to dinner, bringing by some extra of this or that, like too much casserole for them to eat, tamales, turkey hash. Or Jess letting you pick fruit from his orchard, of which you'll give him a large share of the chokecherries, plums, next month's apples. When Lori gets back to professional nursing, it'll be easier, and you both know it, but for the next ten or twelve moons, her nursing's reserved for Miranda.

"Whoops!"

An overripe one plummets toward you, glances off your shoulder, and explodes on the ground.

"Boom!" from Miranda, a word she favors.

"Sorry, love. It was just out of reach."

"Boom, mama!"

"No, no, Mama no boom."

Miranda tugs your hair and leans abruptly over toward the bucket. You grab another plum, bite into it, scoop the flesh onto your finger, and stick it into her eager mouth. Conversant in the language of entreaty, this little one. You give her more. You want to give her everything she wants, and in that impulse the two of you are united. Thankfully at this age her wishes are few and easily fulfilled. Not so in years to come.

No inheritance, like Rose has and Alex will get. Nothing to pass on but your house and land, the gift of a home. Love. Though Michelle has been deeply generous to her adopted grandchild. All the gear and furnishings of babyhood have come from her, and a lavish stream of toys, stuffed animals, books. She will see to it that Miranda's larder of delights is always stocked full. Trove friends, too, giving you boxes of outgrown clothes whose filaments bear the history of the town's offspring.

Your leg is hurting, baby-weight pushing on it, and you slide the backpack off gently. Extract Miranda and set her on the ground, then lie next to her. She crawls toward a daisy, buries her face in it, sniffs and rears back smiling as if she's inhaled an ambrosial scent. Lori must have taught her that, to smell flowers. Mouths a dandelion, sniffing. A picture flashes in your memory, one you saw when you were—what, twelve?—and your parents had gone out to dinner, left you alone. You crept into their bedroom, where you were not allowed, and started snooping. In your mother's jewelry drawer you discovered a photo of yourself, at—what, three?—holding up a bouquet of dandelions you'd gathered, and sitting behind you your mother, both of you grinning. Some visitor must have taken it because your family didn't own a camera. You stared and stared at it as the room grew dark. There were so few pictures of you as a child. You have no memories of yourself being happy, nor your mother, but here you are, triumphant, your lips and hers widened in full smiles. Why was it hidden away? And yet among her valuables, a keepsake she treasured. You wanted it but didn't dare. Perhaps growing up with no pictures of yourself in a house of few mirrors freed you from self-consciousness in adolescence. Still, a small album would have been comforting. Alex said he'd had a shelf of them before the fire, so many you could rifle through them like a flipbook.

Miranda has circled back toward you, comes up alongside your head, and lips your nose, sucking it. Gums and baby teeth. No one has ever treated your nose like candy, and you chortle, which she imitates, saliva running down your cheeks. Her goo is a salve that returns you to the moment's play. She sits back and pulls a wee handful of grass, dumps it on your chest. Pats it down, gets another and another, mounding you in grass. You stroke her hair, pat her back, and she crawls on top of the grass, facing you. Her mouth bobs all over your chin and cheeks, giving you her version of kisses. This is far more joy than you'd imagined knowing in your life. It blossoms expansively through you, an ache so vast it takes your breath, yet you would sooner die than relinquish this euphoria. Your own child, arisen from your seed in Lori's fruit, a daughter who loves you utterly. It is the most natural of outcomes, to have a child, and boundlessly miraculous.

Miranda, you her Prospero. Illusion now must be real, all the palaces and so on, for her to explore. Cannot be simply a magic trick, this world. Too cruel. You long to show her everything. True, our little lives are rounded by a sleep, but within the circle between them a life full of promise. Of plums and poems and poems of plums, which you will teach her to write. Though you are not doing much of that yourself these days, writing, now that you are so content with living.

Another plum whooshes down, bringing a leafy twig with it.

"Don't worry, I'm being careful," she says to forestall admonition.

He chafes at being grounded by the leg, risks injury more heedlessly than she ever has. The wound to his independence slow to mend, as her guilt. She burdened by far more regrets, privately held terrain she wanders at unexpected hours, rocking Miranda in the lee twixt midnight and dawn, or harvesting peppers and kale, or strewing wildflowers over Yeats' grave, where she often goes, alone and with Miranda, but not Joaquin. This death hers to suffer.

Though once she found Alex there, eyes closed, murmuring. He, too, unhealed. They spoke of the lost child, what he might have been like, or rather who, for both understood that Yeats was Alex's son. What lingered uneasily and unspoken was whether Lori had someway known that when he was in her womb and been reluctant thus to birth him. An implicit accusation from Alex, a staunch denial from Lori that her persistent doubt undermines. Had she? And if Yeats could only have been Joaquin's, would she have spared no measure to save him? But if that, neither baby would have been conceived. Perhaps none ever. And what would have become of him and them had he lived? So many strata of complexity that they dared not excavate. The grief inheld, they talked instead of his likely irascible nature, their child making mischief and gamboling in the hills of the afterworld. He did not tell her of his ethereal flight with the ghost nor she of her dream visitations with Yeats. They did not ask nor receive from each other forgiveness. But no longer enemies, these sojourners in heartache. Their trespass a stone they would be buried with.

What she does not admit, at any cost, is that sometimes Miranda looks at her with Alex eyes.

Stop now. The bucket almost too heavy with fruit to carry down. Yet so hard to leave any behind. The jams and jellies, puddings, bowlfuls of help-yourself ripening plums on the kitchen table. Living at the hover of scarcity makes free pickings a cherish. Little else of plenitude in their cupboards but love. That, the constant thought she holds opening the doors on emptiness. Which breeds reluctance to cease when plums are still at hand. Or nearly, cat-stretched along the limbs.

"Storm's coming. We better start for home, Lori."

Between the leaves to her right, where a far mountain range undulates, she can see the dark billows puffing. Still miles off but their pace hard to calculate. Half hour? Two? Might veer north and just whiffle them. But so fine to get a warning across panoramic skies. In her childhood holler, weather crept up and banged onto them sudden, like Lyle jolting surprise in some nook when her mind had strayed.

Storm aside, she understands Joaquin wants her to come down to him. The risk of fall a steel hoop constricting his breath. He doesn't know, has never been told, of her long-ago fall, how it came nigh to killing her at thirteen. A humiliation she's sought to burn away. Dressed in tan jeans, outgrown the year before but not replaced, walking to the schoolyard for noon break, a pair of creeps trailing her, their snickers menacing but unexplained till they were out of earshot of adults.

"Blood." Like hounds on the track. She feeling the wet in her groin and knowing then that it had blotched her pants. Her first period. At least she'd been aware to expect it someday, just not this one. The hounds gaining on her, their slobber breath clipping ponytail and neck, she in desperation bounding toward the mulberry tree, shimmied up lithe as a trapped possum or raccoon. The blood coming harder with her exertion. She wouldn't be going back in today, hang out here till the bell rang and all the kids left the yard. Outwaiting being the same tack that other prey critters take.

These hounds advantaged over canines by their opposing thumbs, with which they scooped up pebbles to stone her. Ping. Not big ones but their velocity wounding. She more vulnerable to hurt with the blood pool between her legs and stomach cramps. Higher was the only way to escape, and so up she went, the mulberry a very old tree, maybe sixty feet to the top. They pinged her less often as she climbed out of reach till discovering that, backed up on a hillock, they had a better crack at her. Circle of jeers now goading them on. "Bloody Mary" the chant, emphasis on *blood*. Sickened, climbing higher, still hit and once bad on her hand, which she jerked away, lost her hold, tried to catch another branch on the way down but her momentum was too hurtled and she landed, sideways flung, in the grass at her tormentors' feet. Unconscious. The onlookers milled off far enough not to be implicated when the Principal Fulton showed up but still close enough to get a solid view of the action.

The hounds, envisioning solitary prison cells and public shame, kneed themselves around unmoving her. "Sorry, Lori," one hound bayed. "Don't die. Don't tell Mr. Fulton," the other begged, a contradictory plea. Their voices tumbled over and over these hapless rosaries of penitence, "Sorry, Lori." "Don't die, don't tell Mr. Fulton," till she regained consciousness and opened her eyes.

Their prayers answered, the hounds glided to their feet, eager to clear the scene yet newly realizing that her restoration made silence crucial to avoid a severe Fulton beating. Gently helped her to sit, she internally gauging bones, which remarkably seemed whole, and the dizziness subsiding. Arms and face scratched, blood to mingle with the other and turn it from embarrassment to injury. She ignored the hounds' solicitous inquiries, their pathetic handkerchiefs wiping at her arms, but did not rise before she could do so on her own. And walk from the school with just the occasional wobble, grossly aware of her soaked red buttocks, the focus of her departure.

The significant point being that she could survive a fall from great heights intact. This plum tree represents no real challenge to her agility. It is Joaquin's uneasiness that tugs her back to the ground. Miranda would shortly want to nurse, too, start fussing. Unless she was plum-full and dozed off.

"All right, love. I'm on my way back down. These are the best yet."

"Good," you say, both to the plums and her coming. Storm is near, riling up the wind, and you have this laden sack to haul. Miranda in your arms, you kneel and lower her into the backpack, then slide it onto your shoulders, and stand up. She is as charged as the ionized air, her little hands on your neck, in your hair, legs churning a kick-and-bounce: let'sgolet'sgolet'sgo. Miranda and the swelling breeze both geared for action. When she's older she'll want a pony, and you'll find one for her, a sweet-tempered little bay.

Stretched full out, no inch of reach left in her between fingers and foothold. Cup the trunk with her hand, bucket in the other coming around to meet it. Bend at the knees till she can grab that low branch there and hunker, then the foot heads down to its next lodging. She's calculated everything but the wind, which gusts up sudden and yanks at the bucket, pulling her off-balance and tipping it just enough to spill a plum, whose fall is broken by leafy intertwigging right by where she plans to hunker, which she does, hanging onto the trunk while leaning far as can to snag the plum. Ha! Drops the foot, solidly planted, and she descending after, within view of the ground now, though still some fifteen-twenty feet to go.

The wind slaps a branch across her face. "You dirty little slut, slinking home with virgin blood smeared all over. If you're pregnant, I'll shame you in front of the whole town." Like she hadn't already been. "Filthy whore!" The old man who never spoke to her gone to rage. Don't cry, she ordered herself. Don't you cry. The mother knew what it was, told her to get the borax and scrub them jeans like hell. Can't afford new ones. Whyn't you stopper yourself with a rag? Or stay home and bleed out down by the creek? Stupid girl. She scrubbed so hard the jeans bleached around the crotch, but better white than red. The old woman gave her one of the boys' worn diapers, permanently shit-stained, to wrap between her legs till the next time they had money to buy some female hygiene, a word that meant nothing to Lori. No questions about her day and nothing would ever have been said if Lyle hadn't heard the story from friends and waited for an inopportune moment to share it with his mother. "Stay out of them trees, you hear? You're too old to be climbing. It ain't ladylike." She refrained from saying that if Lyle weren't always at her with his nasty finger, she wouldn't have to hide in trees. He was worse than ever, aroused by the blood, which he was determined to poke up into and swill around in, taste. She shamed twice over.

A growl of thunder, ushered by wind, heralding rain.

"Mamamamama!"

"It's okay, sweetheart," she calls, and her foot rutches down to catch the next branch, a sturdy limb but just out of range of the one she's hanging onto. Monkey-bars her way to the trunk, wind chittering the leaves, prepares to slide down the couple of inches she needs to reach the big branch. Quick handhold shift and she's got it, bucket still upright, leaning safe on the wide arm of the tree.

Miranda's fussing on the verge of tears. Joaquin rocks soothing to quiet her. A spit of rain.

Come on, she goads herself. Faster. And descends another leg-length. The cilia on her arms shiver a warning and nigh simultaneously a crackle and clash of tumultuous air masses. Her baby screams. Her hand falters. She grabs at a small branch, which snaps off and leaves her dangling for a breath before she falls, on her back, toward the ground. Even so, clutching the prized bucket.

You can see her, your dread turned to disaster, your body working free of thought to shield her from the ground. And keep Miranda safe as you absorb the crush of Lori's body. Whirl to position yourself under and facing her, and as you do, Miranda's soft-boned forehead swings straight into a low branch. Shrieks bursting into hard tears. Alive, but for how long? And you can't take your eyes off Lori, who will be on you in a second. Crouching, back arched, to keep Miranda away from the impact, you open your arms to cushion your beloved's fall.

So slow for Lori. No life she's lived flashing before her eyes; instead, the one she hasn't yet. Might not on this sphere. Joaquin's brow creased, hair silvered, Miranda a fair young woman, drawn to each other by loneliness, the place they'd always held open for her. She heard once, from a math professor, that the first real number is three, one and two being just points, three the requisite connection between them. How dearly these plums had cost her! Would she haul this bucket repentant through eternity, her singular damnation for greed, for hubris? Broken-winged, knowing the grief she'd caused her family whom she loved above all else? Dying this day over and over?

A knotted limb punches her abruptly hard in the back, flings her onto her side, jarring loose the bucket, and tossing both her and it into a cascade of downspinning leaves. She curls, fetus-like, head tucked, muscles softened, shoulder braced for the crash.

Which is the right way to fall if you must.

To her the ground seems to give so that she rebounds. Enough to break her fall rather than her neck: a thudded not a splintered hit. Breathless for a moment, afraid to look, the first sensation when it comes that of arms rounded under her. The first sound Joaquin's "Lori!" and Miranda's cries. The first reaction from her a flip to her back as she tries to sit up to tend to them. The first sight, their pain, which annuls hers.

"It's okay. I'm okay."

Testing carefully her movements to be sure she is, and miraculously hale and saved. She reaches for Miranda. Then becomes aware of Joaquin's arms holding her. He is the rebound that padded her landing. Her man, her knight, the one she'd yearned to be rescued by on New Year's Eve when she nearly killed him. And now again, might have an inch or two to the right.

"And you? Are you okay?"

You are, extracting your arms, which though bruised and sore, will recover. And she likewise, your supple skylark. Miranda, too, must be, to complete this glorious save. In Lori's trembling arms, your child, and on her brow the scarlet lump throbbing. A dire wound, still likely to be fatal. So in saving one, you killed the other. You extend your hand to comfort Lori, afraid to touch Miranda.

"It looks worse than it is, believe me. Lots of blood vessels there, but she'll be fine." Nuzzling her mother's breast, where her tears are suckled away.

You wipe the drizzle from your head. Bloated gray, the cloud overhead threatening to spill its guts. Go ahead, you challenge it, do your worst. No one here gives a shit about getting wet. We're together, we're whole, we're fine. We're thankful beyond any garbage you might dump on us. Although, you concede, it would be a twisted shame for the family to have come through this nigh disaster and then be struck by lightning.

You shift positions to enfold Lori, your legs outside hers, her back resting against your chest and groin, your lips on her neck, your arms cradling her. Her arms cradling your daughter. A threefold spoon amid grasses and leaves and plums. This is an image to keep in your memory's jewelry drawer.

His mouth on her neck, the baby's on her breast. Together they stir a quickening in her blood. She turns her lips to Joaquin's, their kiss a long-drawn nectar.

"Let's get married," he says. "Right away." It's not something either of them had thought or talked of doing, an extraneous tie that could not bind them closer. "Just us," he goes on. "At the courthouse. No hoopla," he urges, then reconsiders. "Maybe we'll have a big party sometime later, invite everyone." What he doesn't add but they both know is, when we can afford it. "Will you marry me?"

"I did, love," she says, "back in college. The first time we kissed."

"Will you marry me again?"

"Shelley is coming down next week. She can be one of our witnesses. I'd like her to be."

"Alex can be the other. I'd like him to be." She says nothing. "That is, if you'll marry me."

"Officially, you mean."

"Yes, officially. Till death do us part."

"We nearly missed the chance to say that, officially."

"Twice." His lips brush her neck, arousing a flutter at her erotic core.

She settles deeper into him. "A lifetime is not long enough for all the love I have to give you."

"And I don't have a ring," you add, your mother having refused to give hers up even after divorcing Frank, your grandmother's having disappeared down Frank's whisky-drenched gullet.

"Nor I." There was none for her to inherit, nor would she have wanted one that had sat on any of their miserable fingers.

"Maybe someday I'll get you one, after you marry me."

"You're the only man I've ever loved, ever will."

"You're the only woman." You breathe in her hair. "Grandma said only marry a woman you love. Implying, unlike her son Frank, who loved no one. A mean and unhappy man. Some things can't be forgiven, my love, especially the way he treated his mother. Also mine. And me."

Her mind wanders back to a year ago when Joaquin wouldn't speak to her, when she had to leave him with the babies growing in her. Well, she thinks, maybe.

You can feel that remembrance emanating from her head. You were cruel to her, Frank-like, and would have lost her if Alex hadn't called. That's three times you almost missed being able to speak the marriage vow to stay together till death you did part. Which now that she is your life, that you have been in flesh and soul made one, is, ironically, impossible. Living without her would be your death. That realization sparks another: her happiness is your profoundest desire. To fulfill her fulfills you.

"Do you want to have another child?"

Her breath catches. Him asking, which she never expected he would. Not that she hasn't thought about it, not that she didn't always want two, not that she doesn't believe in the importance of growing up with a sibling, but that she is so grateful he asks. He who she knows does not want another child, who resisted Miranda till she was born. And this, too: she had her chance. It would be a betrayal to Yeats to have another. At least that's how she feels now. And how she feels now, at this moment, is so utterly blissful she cannot imagine wanting anything more, which frees her to give him the answer he seeks, knowing, as she does, that she is answering for more than this moment. He won't ask again.

"No," she says, "no," and hearing the word understands that she means it.

"Lori." You gently lay her head back on your shoulder and swivel yours around so you are looking at each other. "I can't get on my knees without letting go of you, which I am not about to do, but I'm asking as though I were. See me on my knees, armor clanking, my hand extended to yours? My lady, my love, will you marry me?"

"Yes," she says, seeing the time has come to say yes, "I will, I do, I have, again and again and all the days of eternity. As often as you want, wherever you like, courthouse or field or dark side of the moon. I am wedded to you fiber and cell, my dearest one, you indivisibly knit into my soul. I love you beyond all measure." Her thrust into his arms nearly dislodges all three.

The bulbous vessel of rain, impatient with your exchange of vows, splits and begins to dribble, then to stream. You've had enough of things falling this afternoon, but she laughs up at the cloud. "I get it. Had to let it drop, you did. Well, come on down." Catches some rain in her mouth, exhilarated by the growing intensity.

You watch her unlatch Miranda's gums from her breast, wrap her tight and slide her into the pack, which you slip on despite the fussing. Lori's on her feet, steady, rubbing her tailbone, which clearly hurts, as she looks around for the sack. "We can come back for it," you tell her. "Let's run for home." Lightning swipes the clouds, thundering them.

But her nimble hands are collecting the plums that spilled from the bucket, assessing straightaway which ones are worth taking after the fall and adding them to the sack, which is of course far too heavy to lug running through the rain.

"No," she shouts above the burgeoning torrent. "Let's just go hide beneath that overhang." Pointing up the hill to a narrow ledge of stone, under which you'll barely fit. She grabs one end of the sack, expecting you to pick up the other.

"But, Lori—" you start to protest. She laughs again. "We'll be fine. It's a one-bucket storm."

25

"Turned Around Rightways"

"Talk among the aspens was lively at evenfall. Spindles of natter whirring up trunks and down limbs. From the elders issued tales of winters savage enough to fissure rocks. Cautionary tales for saplings: hoard your sugar, shed your gold. Store your energy for the long hibernation to come. See shadows lengthening into night, earlier than yesterday? Hear a floodtide of wings susurrating south? Smell our kindled ancestors twined with the wind? Feel the rich tapestry of fungi webbing your roots? The light is cloaked, sturdy rod in hand, forth on its hemispheric odyssey to the nether end of world. Turn inward, children, and make ready. Only the most prudent of you will taste another spring.

"At your right there, strolling through day's remnant beams, tread muffled by cast-off foliage, our idolizer. He who would be tree. The joke, passed wood-wide from aspen and birch to spruce and pine on the fungal threads, set off tipples of laughter, which his ears translated to a pullulating yearn. He knew their laughter, just as he knew their songs and chatter, their keening. Sensed that their language was as variegated as his own. They shared good news and bad, water and sun. Certainly, there were ancient enmities, but the epic friendships towered over them, roots dense-woven and crowns interleafed. Imagine, as he liked to, friends whom you stood with for centuries. How entirely you would know one another, how integral the life of each to each. How agonizing the loss of any, in the course of things or hewn unfeeling.

"He felt welcome in these woods, which he was so simple-minded as to call his. Where he was no more than a mayfly in the immense span of their arc. Sensed a likening, a kinship, believed good will for him dwelt here. The arboreal community trusted him, made light of his reverence but knew it was genuine and of the many relations they'd had with humankind, by far their preferred mode."

Strike that last paragraph: mawkish tripe. Do you want the trees to love you because you are in love with them, Señor Anthropomorphizer? It's a common pitfall, this attribution of feelings that reflect our own to other species. We invest with human qualities that which we hope will recognize and appreciate our humanity. Is it a form of self-aggrandizement or a genuine desire to recover an affinity lost in the course of our ethnocentric avarice?

Just love the woods, Mann, and let it go. Love them whole: the ants sucking honeydew from the asses of aphids and the fungi sponging hollows that woodpeckers dug. Burrowing parasites and blood-necked click beetles. The eco whole where you daily ramble. Hallelujah your good fortune. Don't make mystical gumbo out of it by imagining they requite your devotion. To be a good steward to this span of earth is your role, and you have plenty of talent for it. To wit, Joaquin's flourishing greenhouse. To double wit, the abounding health of these five acres designated, for now, as yours. You have an unparalleled ability to screw things up in the human world, but you're like Superthrive in the natural one.

Puzzling that we set ourselves apart from our environs by calling it "the natural world." By implication ours is, then, unnatural. We, God's divine creation, set above and apart from nature because we possess a consciousness of self and of our mortality. Rilke says we are "the watchers: always, everywhere, / looking toward the all and never from it!" and asks, "Who has turned us around this way, so that, no matter what we do, we look as though we're leaving?" Exiled by ingesting the very knowledge that sets us above and apart. We who live here now estranged, seeking a sense of belonging to the world, a way of becoming at home in it.

The cats face me with eyes of the world, turned around rightways. Tiger and Montenegra know the territory and accept without question that they have come home. Days when I can find them I keep them in, for the birds' sake, but nights they roam freely. At nearly eleven years by human count, Tiger could have settled into a gentile middle-age, snoozing most of the time, indulging in an occasional leisurely explore. But like Floyd and other elders of Trove, he refuses to yield, sets forth each dusk to reaffirm his hunting skills on an unrestrained killing spree. After all, he has a gorgeous, young dame to prove himself to, and while Montenegra could take him in a catfight, she instead gives him the lead. As I witnessed one night from the veranda. Tiger had used his sparse remaining teeth to bring down a rabbit, which he dragged up the hill for my viewing pleasure—and no doubt to rub his machismo in my face. On a grassy knoll they ripped apart his victim with courtly grace, he giving her first go at the choicest morsels, she making certain to save some for him. Very loving in a savage way. Their nightly safaris have led them as far as the Strangers' homestead, where Lori welcomes them affectionately, Joaquin less so. She overfeeds and coddles them, but they always return here: a small victory for me.

Joaquin stopped by soon after I moved in. Reiterated his offer of employment in the greenhouse, which I declined. Expressed interest in the writing I told him would be my focus but was unwilling to discuss. When I didn't ask about Miranda, he recognized that I had no desire to reclaim the closeness of our friendship and kept his visit brief. Leaving said, "If you ever feel like noodling on some tunes, come on over. You're always welcome." Points for trying, which Lori hadn't. Or more truthfully, I hadn't let her. When to my chagrin we met in town, she greeted me, I nodded, eyes down, and moved away. If I spotted her at Yeats' grave, where my obstinate feet led my unwilling head, I would fade back into the trees and wait till she was gone. Though once when I arrived before she did, we'd spoken uneasily about the lost child, our unacknowledged son. From my end, they remain awkward neighbors, our boundaries crossed only by the cats.

And by Mamia, who visits every other month, alternating with Clarice. The surrogate grandmother and the biological one invited back into the charmed circle after a distance of years. Mamia stays with me, of course, Clarice with them. Early on, the grannies coaxed me, respectively, to have the Strangers over for dinner or go to their house for same. If she chose to invite them here, I told Mamia, I would be elsewhere, and it was easy enough to simply demure from accompanying her to their place. I know I sound pretty hostile still, but generally I haven't been, and my refusal to befriend Joaquin's clan anew was made in the effort to avoid reigniting dormant grief. Juvenile but true, that out-of-sight, out-of-mind adage, and I needed to fill my headlands with buoying companions.

Such as my ghosts. Again, I know how that sounds, given how I struggled to banish Harvey and Hersch, but here, with the woods for them to play in, the river and wind and solitude, my cramped heart swung open to welcome these spirits of erstwhile torment. They made themselves comfortable among the trees, and presumptuous though it may be to speak for them, they have found a home amid the spindrift of this realm. My sense of their spectral presence is infrequent and transitory, a slight thickening of the air beside me and on my shoulders, where baby Yeats likes to ride and fiddle with my ears. None speaks to me any longer—or their voices have grown so faint I cannot hear them. They are ever more absent from the world of the living, ever more at peace with being dead. Their visits fall like a blessing into my meandering thoughts.

This place teaches me continually my place, elicits the humility and gratitude of being alive within its teeming bounds. It teaches also that physical bounds and psychic ones are as densely interwoven as tree roots. The breath indrawn to the far hollows of the body cleanses the mind. The pastoral tranquility of the landscape engenders an internal counterpart. Storms surge me to a high pitch, blood-pulse like tidal waves thrashing my flesh. This earth has become my measure, and I dwell in enchanted accord with it.

Living so has granted me a fathomless reservoir of peace whose depths, I hope, will never be plumbed, for each morning it deepens.

You're sitting back now, glad to be able to leave me in bliss. To close the book on my harrowed life with a smile. Looks like our Mann came out on top. God's in his heaven and all's right with the world. True, he's thought he was here before once or twice, as you may recall glancing back over his escapades, temporarily, which evokes the risk that his current joy, too, might not endure. But he's no longer a novice to reality's flux, has acquired a durable sense of balance, knows about edges, the precarious currents of spirit, fragility of bone, the long reach of mindless actions, the claims of memory upon the heart. His revels are informed by past transgressions. It seems safe to trust him with happiness.

But consider this possibility: I might be luring you into a state of bask to spur you, my readers, who have grown up or at least older with me, through another convoluted struggle in this tale. Or not you but me. For I am weary of confessing my plethora of wrongdoings, as I am of looking at my flesh on which they are writ large. There's only one mirror in my house, in the bathroom of what has become Mamia's room for her frequent visits. You'd be surprised at how well you can get along without seeing yourself daily, repeatedly, at every turn. When I do, then and again, I am startled by how different I look from the man I expect to view. A stranger to my face, which no longer represents me. I seek my reflection in the faces of others, how they look at me, whether seeing me gladdens them. I seek in the run of my life now to gladden others and thus myself. So it seems wise to assume that I began this chapter among the aspen in order to remind and comfort both myself and you of how much beauty comes from the grace of attempting to turn ourselves round rightways, to look from the world as well as at it.

I returned to Trove with the set intent of being a writer in what I dubbed The Hermitage. Yes, I would maintain the friendships formed in my previous incarnation as Joaquin's housekeeper, greenhouse hand, and weed deliveryman, as well as a chatty gadabout in town, but my trips into Trove would be few and swift. Of course I'd stop at Gregorio's for a meal, at Floyd's for periodic Pacman check-ups. Groceries, gas, and home again. There'd be talk for a while, but they'd get used to my new ways as they got used to everything. I would write and read and write some more. Hike, tend my five acres, sweep and scrub the house. Keep my lands in order. Shrink my footprint to a wisp whose passage yielded to the lightest wind. To a wind of light.

Though I did not have a story readily at hand to author, one thing I was firmly decided on was that I would not write about myself. I'd spent all my conscious years thinking about myself, first one way and then another, and I was sick of dissecting and analyzing Mr. Alexander Mann. The hell with writing what you know. My novel would be about something I wanted to discover. And no more fractured chunks of time during which my thoughts scattered and I had to start over. I would create my novel in one tremendous outpour, as Gabriel Garcia-Marquez had his *Hundred Years of Solitude*: isolated, undistracted, oblivious to date or time, food or family, burning with inspiration—the only way to write a true and original masterpiece. GGM was coming home from a trip, driving his family, when, cresting a hill, the first sentence of *Solitude* sprang fully formed from his mind. From there he took off, the voice and the story writing itself. Similarly, it seemed to me, I was coming home from an extended trip, driving myself uphill and down to draw forth that sentence from the wellspring of my unconscious. Meanwhile I fiddled around like an idle shopper trying on garments he doesn't plan to buy.

The longer I waited, the greater my anxiety, as though I were working against a deadline, nonexistent. I could sit here for the rest of my life pretending to write, nothing to stop me, thanks to Mamia's support, enough to keep me going in a frugal way. The quest for a leading sentence haunted me, or rather began to hunt me, tracking me into the most mundane regions of my life. I couldn't brush my teeth or fry an egg without grand phrases crescendoing through my mind, only to be plopped into the discard bin when I reviewed them later.

Over my panicky thoughts crept the shadow of a character from another tale, Camus' *The Plague*. As the plague intensifies, the petty official Grand, whom Camus describes as having "all the attributes of insignificance," continues working on the opening sentence of a book whose content he has not yet conceived. His enkindling hope is for the publisher, upon reading it, to say to his staff, "'Gentlemen, hats off." Thus he continues to toy with the sentence, revising it from "One fine morning in the month of May an elegant young horsewoman might have been seen riding a handsome sorrel mare along the flower-strewn avenues of the Bois de Boulogne" to "One fine morning in May a slim young horsewoman might have been seen riding a glossy sorrel mare along the flower-strewn avenues of the Bois de Boulogne." "At last," Grand claims, "one can see them! Smell them! Hats off, gentlemen." What the tale is about is of far less concern to him than to write it beautifully. The absurdity of the old man gnawed at my relentless, futile efforts.

Paragraphs blossomed and wilted, each in itself a promising bud yet lacking momentum. Characters brewed from seeming randomness metamorphosed into Hersch and Harvey, Rose, Mamia. Excitement caught hold when the idea of fictionalizing Papito's remarkable ancestry emerged; I had the long letter from Mamia to get me started, and she could provide more anecdotes for me to embellish. It would be wicked fun to mimic Trudel's faulty English and self-aggrandizing style, as in this sentence from her letter:

"Back in Munich, Peter, my father, struggled to start anew, and total failed, leaving wife and daughters when, in 1939, he died, destitute. I, Trudel, his favorite always and most resourceful daughter, my mind to go from Germany made up, where life now was too dangerous."

The story was a guaranteed winner, rife with a daring escape from the Nazis, tragic deaths, serendipitous reunions, a new beginning forged in the New World, and the escapades of my legendary rodeo-cowboy grandfather, who impregnated one of his many women, took her to Mexico for an abortion that killed her (likely what he had in mind), and died young under the hooves of a bull without ever confessing his crime (except to Trudel). Yes, indeed: a tale destined for the big screen, with the big stars and big bucks. That was a plan I suckled for two months, fleshing out its chapters and assessing the gaps. But when I began to write, the voices sounded phony, especially when I threw in German syntax or translated idioms. I didn't know any of these people but Trudel and felt like a thief snatching their stories to make my own. Ridiculous paranoia since stories are drawn from the common well and these in particular from my heritage. But that actually made it worse because I was exploiting people to whom I owed my life.

I thought about writing a children's book starring my cats, gave it a clumsy try. Scooted over to nonfiction, going for "Trove: Walden of the West," myself cast as Henry David, but I'd never really liked Thoreau, who came across as didactic and arrogant, or perhaps unpersuaded and thus fiercely adamant. I wondered what a Walden would be like written in the present moment of uncertainty, climate change eroding our future. Species dying off, trees on a northward migration, fires and storms intensifying, water growing scarce. We would likely not outlast the century. The catastrophic upheaval of our environs echoed in the global ruin of our civilizations. And yet I was strolling through my days as though everything were normal, as though life were still beautiful, which here it was. I could write dispatches from this outpost of paradise not yet lost. My life alone in the hills of Trove. That thought brought me to the obvious realization that such a book, like Thoreau's, would end up being about me. The grating truth was that I had only myself to write about. It was the one story I knew.

Began my tale under the file name "Rosie and Bug," my angle being to trace our friendship from preschool to the present. Add romance, make the years-long separation after the fire heartbreaking. I'd end on a reunion, she with her wife Justine, me with my son Yeats, she an historian in Scotland, I a teacher, the memories of our youthful love welling unspoken. Very cinematic. In fact I would begin with a scene from our first trick-or-treating when out of the darkness loomed the towering hound of hell, his slavering maw open to reveal fangs that would impale us. We screamed; Papito rushed forward, nearly colliding with the Great Dane's owner, who had him firmly by the leash. Cool on screen. And finally I was launched, not on a Nobel winner but a good story pleasurable to tell.

I wrote daily now, or more accurately nightly. My schedule adapted itself to the cats', the three of us sleeping through the morning, awakening at noon to eat and clean ourselves, basking in the wide arms of afternoon till the sun drifted below the hogback across the valley on its way to other lands. As twilight curtained the land, we ate once more and set off on our divergent adventures, they abroad, I at my desk, where I wrote till first light. Perfect for the nocturnal felines, it did not prove a sustainable routine for me, but during the winter of my return year to Trove, it freed me from the urgency of time. I did not measure my output by the hours, let what would arrive at its chosen pace and go as far as the darkness reached. Nothing disturbed or distracted me in this untime. Free to wander mentally as I did physically the land, I did not heed where I was going nor worry that it might be nowhere or that I would lose my way because all ways offered the exultation of discovery. Rarely did I retrace my steps to see where I'd been but simply took up each evening my last thought from the dawn. Once I recall wondering as I paused over the keys how I would know when I was done. When you've run out of story, came the answer, and we both laughed.

But before I had, the world banged in.

There was very little overall for me to keep track of in this pattern, so I have no excuse for losing awareness of any element in it. Winter receding, a minute more of light every day, the woods boggy and meadow slushed with runoff. The slow greening as we rotated toward the sun. It was my first spring in Trove, and I was intent on seeing each bud, wild iris, stalk of grass. Even so, I had stores of attention left to notice Tiger's absence sooner than I did. Was it a day or more till I went looking for him? And how much longer would it have been had La Negra not attacked me?

At my desk in the waning hours of night, tapping an account of Rosie nestled in my arms after an ardent tryst that burned my fingers to record, I was startled by Montenegra springing unexpectedly onto the desk. She was not one to initiate contact though she accepted it graciously. I stopped, said hello, and as I reached out to stroke her, she sank her teeth into my hand. Not playfully, not fondly, but with a vicious wrath, biting through the skin to bone and blood. I yelled and on instinct raised my other hand to strike her when flashbolt, her message irradiated me. Tiger. Where was he? When had I last seen him? She released my hand, understanding in some arcane feline way that I'd been alerted. Then she led me to him, not out into the chill of nascent spring, but close by, under the bed in Mamia's room. Where he lay rasping, gravely wounded. I extracted him, my hand's fresh blood overlaying his blackened mats. A hole pierced his side. Deep. Gaping. Surrounded by smaller puncture wounds. He did not lift his head or make a sound. Time crashed in, taloned with fear and guilt. No vet within fifty miles. No vet at 5:00 a.m. Tiger was dying.

Montenegra slipped under my arm and began licking him. Why had she emerged from this attack unscathed? Why hadn't she stood by her man? As he would have, my brave Tiger, thrown himself into the fray and fought for her to the death. Coward. Why hadn't she alerted me to his plight sooner? I'd never formed a close bond with her; she was

Tiger's mate more than my cat. She was Lori's, inherited by me on behalf of Tige, who'd seen me through so much, to whom I owed my life. Lori's cat. Nurse Lori who loved Tiger. I yanked the throw off Mamia's bed and forced my urgent hands to be steady as I wrapped him in it and carried him to the car, laid him on his shotgun seat. Montenegra hopped in beside him, and I shoved her to the floor, loosing my anger at myself on her.

Lori, Nurse Lori, please save this dauntless scruff whose wounds I would gladly have taken on myself to spare him. I meant that. Scarred as I am, a damaged organ or two wouldn't matter. Tiger was my compass, always pointing true when I strayed. His equanimity kept my headlong impulses in check, sometimes, and when it failed, he went down the abyss with me. I hit the cattle guard too fast, winced as we thumped over it. "Sorry, T." A slight shudder—or an involuntary spasm—but a wisp of life for which I gave thanks as we puttered along the main road. Trove lay at the edge of spring, the planet tipping its northern face toward the sun, and by the time we pulled up to Joaquin's familiar veranda, the sky had lightened to stone. Their door was unlocked, as it had always been, but the interior had changed its aspect from rudimentary to comfortable. In a less desperate moment, I would have admired its transformation to a home.

I called for Lori, knowing it would waken them early, though not by much. Said nothing more when she scurried down, alarmed by my tone, and laid Tiger on the dining table, spread his blanket to expose the wound, gasped. Montenegra pressing herself against Lori's robe was not the annoyance to her I would have found it to be; instead a call to action. I was ordered to boil water, get clean towels from the cupboard, antiseptic from the medicine cabinet. Like a birth, this ritual preparation for leave-taking of my beloved soulmate. Joaquin appeared, and also wordless, stroked Tiger's head: a first in my recall.

If I could remember the surgical procedure with any clarity, I would tell you about it, but my heart was sick and my mind opaque with despair. At every moment I expected Lori to turn sorrowfully from him, tell me there was nothing more to be done. She was not a vet, not even a full-fledged doc, but a nurse who had no experience with the innards of a cat. I anticipated his death as one more that I would have to haul across the guilt-laden barrens of my life. Why should I be reprieved after committing manslaughter twice, and again on an unborn fetus? Now a fourth, my cat, who'd loved me inexplicably, given me undeserved loyalty, hung in and on despite and through it all. Me not even noticing he wasn't there until it was too late.

A kaleidoscope of blur is all I retain: glitter of fearful instruments, syringes and tubes, requests from Lori to Joaquin, who stood by her to assist as I could not bear to, sucking noises, sponges and antiseptic fluids, bloodied water and the towels I had managed to gather in a vacant numb, slowest dawning ever. Lori's hair longer than it had been, a cataract of dark waves streaming down her ivory robe, aromatic to breathe, and an instant's surge when the thought "she's going to save him as she saved me" grazed my icy spirit and glanced off, leaving it colder than before.

The memory that sticks from that terrible morning is Joaquin's arm on my shoulder, Lori's eyes catching his as a beam of sun caught hers, where wary hope glimmered. "I don't know, Alex, but he's breathing better. I've stopped the internal bleeding and stitched him well enough to make it to Dr. Roman's. We'll take you. It looks like a couple of ribs are broken, and the diaphragm torn, and I wouldn't want to say for sure that Tiger will pull through, but he could. He's amazing, you know." Instead of agreeing and giving her my profuse thanks, I broke down. Crumpled and sobbed, trembling violently. Had to be scraped off the floor and consoled when I should have been acclaiming and elated. Baby Alex, still unable to get past himself.

Dr. Roman was the one who extolled Lori's skills. By stopping the bleeding, she had very likely saved Tiger's life, so far. However, the damage was extensive, as x-rays revealed: organs punctured, diaphragm shredded, a bit of lung shorn off. The doctor speculated that Tiger had been grabbed by a coyote and shaken hard. How he had escaped was baffling; that he had, amazing. I glanced at my gored hand: maybe La Negra did intervene on her mate's behalf. And somehow, they'd gotten back to the house, or she had gotten him there. When? Logistics I hadn't considered fogged my mind.

The prognosis was not good, and the cost of surgery, after-care, would be exorbitant, the doc counseled us: me. And at that, no guarantee Tiger would pull through. In fact, the odds were against his doing so. A country vet unused to taking extreme measures to save an old cat, Dr. Roman clearly favored euthanasia. It wasn't as though cats were hard to come by or Tiger a rare breed. I forgave the doc's assumptions because he didn't know T, and issued hard-eyed orders to spare no expense, do everything in his power, go beyond the extra mile, bring in specialists or whatever it took to save my one-of-a-kind cat. Yes, he was startled by my emphatic response, but of course acquiesced. I'd be staying at the motel down the street, I told him, coming by frequently to check on Tiger. He was to call me the instant anything in T's condition changed. Crazy rich kid. But I didn't care what he thought.

The Strangers of course had to go back. Over her protesting whirls, they took Montenegra with them, knowing I didn't need the added responsibility of caring for her. Joaquin or Lori would give us a ride home when Tiger had recovered well enough to travel. None of us allowed any other option to intrude on our thoughts. Until alone in my impersonal motel room, the anguished breath I drew crushed me and I subsided into tears once more. The image of Tiger took on a Blakean hue, blood-choked and burning with pain, staggering out of the forest in the night, when the stars threw down their spears, water'd heaven with their tears. To which my own accrued the sum, twisted the sinews of my heart. Let the immortal hand that shaped your fearless symmetry imbue the courage needed now, my Tyger, I pleaded, garbling Blake while I hobbled sock-footed across the carpet. Like it's not worn enough without you rubbing the threads barer and shouldn't you do something? Call Mamia but not in this snot-crudded voice, always throwing yourself into her arms when you're in trouble and Lori will do it anyway and then she'll rush down here to comfort you. Is that what you—you know what I want. So get dressed and walk up to the vet's to see what's happening; it's been almost an hour and Tiger might be better by now. The thing that's so unfair is him staying with you by your side through your ordeals and you not: tell the doc you need to be with him, by his side, whatever they do you need to be there with him whatever they do by his side you need to be there with him inside at his side speak nicely now.

In surgery still? How much longer? Just started? What have—but can I go in? Like scrub or whatever they do and stay by his side? Well, after wait-right-here, I need him to be with me.

From a ledge further on down the week, I could see how wild I'd been, croaking half-thoughts at the receptionist in a waiting room that held two dogs and a cat whose owners held them. The nurse gave me an anti-anxiety pill from her own store, gave me an intern to guide me to a restaurant and order a meal for me. In a crisis, Tiger was much more self-reliant and composed than I, but the pill had restored enough control that I knew not to tell the intern I depended on my cat for sanity— stability—perspective—wisdom—clarity—fortitude…

They let me see him post-op. Dr. Roman was noncommittal about the efficacy of his work, but he was impressed with my cat's stamina up to this point. I begged to spend the night by his cage and was permitted to stay till eleven when an intern came in to take over my vigil, promising to call at the slightest sign of change. In fitful exhaustion, I bobbed along the shoals of light slumber, unsure of my surroundings awake and asleep. My beacon on this perilous journey was a mirage that rose nebulous, forming itself into a recognizable generality that became then impeccably singular: Tiger, curled into a ball. Through the night he hovered steadily, right before my eyes, all my undulating attention fastened on him. I had the irrational sense that if I let him out of my sight, he would perish, that holding onto his image secured his life. Later I discerned that it was instead a ruse to keep me alive.

As we both were, in the morning: he able to lift his head a bit to greet me; I allowed to stroke him, talk to him. His vital signs remained strong; there was reason to hope, not yet to celebrate. But for a few quick excursions to take care of base needs such as food and waste, I hung tight with Tiger all day. The medical staff were skeptical but accommodating; one told me, smiling, they'd never seen a pair of patients so close. They couldn't begin to imagine. From cage-side, I called Mamia, persuaded her not to come, called Lori and gave her an update. Found a reservoir of optimism to soothe both of them that had a like effect on me. Tiger was going to pull through. I explained to him why he had to.

Late that night, as I flailed on the motel bed, the intern called: spiked fever, indicating infection. Tiger was sinking fast. Yes, the Dr. Roman was on his way in, and yes, the intern had made sure antibiotics were still dripping through the IV. I scrambled to wakefulness as we talked, ran full-out to the vet's office haphazardly clad. Into the back, where T lay breathing hard. Implored him to fight, stroked his head, reminded him of the fire, of our night on snow mountain, of his invincibility. Of Montenegra. Of all the rodents out there waiting for him. Of naps in the sun-washed study, the veranda where he ate his kills, the river, the years still ahead. Of his exceptionally brave spirit and the need to summon it now to defend himself.

The doctor, who had been preparing to ask me to leave, heard my rambling prayer and let me come sterilized into the operating room with him. Tiger was sedated but mildly as Roman probed and found the source of the infection: an abscess that had formed on his torn lung, which I heard about but did not see, my eyes fixed on Tiger's face. Removing the offending ulceration, he hoped, would restore T on the path to recovery, but he warned that repeated doses of anesthesia and the trauma of opening him up again was a lot for a cat his age to overcome. If Tiger relapsed, that would probably be it.

In the steel of another dawn, we trudged back to post-op. I sat, cupping T's unresponsive head with my hand. A wind had risen overnight, banging tree limbs against the clinic's metal siding. I felt the pounding inside my head, and my fraught nerves recoiled at every hit. I wanted to strike back, beat the walls to protest, not the wind, but the tolling of a small, furred, most dearly cherished companion's encroaching death. My hand curled tight, throat moaned, tears clogged the spillway, all of their own volition, for I had dwindled into a bleak obscurity. I meant to be praying but at such a remove from any god, the wind carried my voice away. I meant to stay strong and clear, lend my will to live to Tiger to fortify his reserves. Instead sniveling, full of dread.

My hand twitched, another involuntary response. I stared uncomprehending at the fingers, saw they were not the twitch source, rather Tiger, whom I was now squeezing. Tiger had twitched, which was good, but because I was cutting off his air supply, which was not. I reeled in my brain. Focus on Tiger and forget your grief, the wind's clangor, all the other meaningless distractions, I chastised myself. Turn your thoughts catlike full on him and his return. Please, please. And remember not to be so quick to assume the best. For uncounted hours I kept a hand nestled loosely against his head, my own resting semiconscious on the frame of his cage.

It's a large cage, and from behind the bars the world ogles us distorted. Mirrors fracture the planes of space into transected strata of darkness, which our eyes pierce easily. Beyond the spikes, kaleidoscopic whirligigs and in the farthest reaches, blue: iridescent indigo whose clarity seems painted but resolves into sculpted depths. Waves of sand purling into ocean, and we breathing as though of water born. A mild sea but warmed by no sun, we enter there by no invitation, needing none, for it is the realm from which we'd sprung before the beginning. Perhaps. Or that for which we were destined beyond the end, and what did it matter which, since they were as indistinguishable as nothing is from nowhere.

Seductive, the blue soothe. Stirs a yen to be engulfed. Shadows beckon from the tranquil deep. Homecoming. Yield to the lush cessation of memory.

Unless there is another route. Compress ourself against the sterile metal flooring of the cage, calculating how to escape passage from the mesmerizing blue without being impaled on an opaque tilt of air. Slink by stealth, one crafty paw at a time, we inch forward, imperceptible except to the tides luring us into their sway. Not to be resisted, the siren call of primordial seas, and we are ready to give way—when a hand, blind and quaking, grapples for our nape. We suspended between these forces lie, imagining ourself elongated, fractured into strata of darkness, neither dead nor living. Cry out, mewling to be released by one or the other. The hand does not surrender, its grasp more desperate to impel us than the currents of indigo. And thus delivered unto it, we resurface, still crying.

I was roused by my voice, echoing a familiar meow: Tiger, whose journey from the underworld had been a double consciousness we shared. He lifted his head slightly, gave me an impatient look I should have been able to read. Water? Pain meds? He mewed again. Just call the doctor, bub. Which I did, gladly, the main message T conveyed being, let's get this show on the road.

Likewise, gladly done. Riding shotgun in Joaquin's truck on a sublime April morning, Lori waiting for us at the house with Montenegra, both in charge of after-care, as Tiger shortly informed me. Lori had made a tender bed for my *compañero adorado*. Montenegra greeted him with a restorative body licking, to which he submitted blissfully. My attentions were received with less gusto; Tige was not one for Mann-pampering. He grudged my daily checks for any sign of infection, preferring Lori's ministrations. We were buds, T and I, he the self-designated trailblazer of our team, and it was bad form for me to assume the lead. Keeping him cooped up, medicating him, insisting on excessive bed rest: all outside the scope of my role.

The more he shucked off my care, the fonder I grew of my extraordinary cat. We were preternaturally close, some rogue brand of guardians to each other. I'd known I loved him but hadn't realized before how central he was to my identity and equilibrium. I refused to imagine my life without him.

26

"Omens of Future Happiness"

Tiger's near-death revived my awareness of the fragility at life's core. The little world I'd treated as indelible had cracked, and I was assailed by edges, the proximity of danger. In the past I had always been the one at risk of annihilation, but my fear now was riveted on the loss of all I loved. The fortress of solitude built to protect my realm disintegrated, and I, assigned to a watch of which none relieved me, was on guard night and day against further catastrophe, bewildered by fatigue. Not that it served as a defense, this wariness: quite the contrary, for dwelling alone in a state of anxiety exacerbated my sense of helplessness. I needed readier access to comfort and reassurance than Mamia, at a far outpost, could provide. I needed to return to those I had cast off.

Repulsing friends, above all Joaquin, had left my spirit homeless. It had wandered my inward alleys, deprived of the sense of belonging I so admired in the trees, nourished by their interweave of roots. Thinking to liken myself to them, I had instead distinguished myself by withdrawing from kinship with my species. Certain I possessed my own fulfillment, I had cleared the land of those whose embrace would have firmly rooted me. Because I wrote by night and slept by day, my rhythms disjunct from those of the light, I was becoming peculiar. Out of sync, I grew inattentive, a failing that drove Tiger to the verge. My self-imposed isolation would end in lunacy, making of Mann a blithering recluse.

By good fortune, Tiger's ordeal had unbolted a gate between the Strangers and me that their kindness coaxed me to tentatively step through. Lori—and her cat—had saved Tige at the first critical juncture. The family had treated me as if we were good friends, staying the course with me, Lori still coming out every afternoon to check T's healing. The intense gratitude I felt was hard to convey in person, so I wrote her and Joaquin an effusive letter of thanks that echoed Dr. Roman's words of praise, as well as an apology for being such a lousy neighbor, asked their forgiveness, and promised to mend my ways as she'd mended Tiger's wounds. I closed with an invitation to come to dinner, which they hastened to accept.

Reentering a friendship is far more difficult than leaving it. The desire to retrieve what you formerly shared is doomed, for starting over you are burdened with the weight of prior knowledge and its encumbering expectations. At the advent of a new friendship, free of past entanglements, you explore the space between you in quest of common ground, whose periphery grows like a living thing beyond your joined terrain. Its character bred of a singular time will exist undiminished within that frame, its later articulations built on memory, dear but irredeemable. Over Joaquin and me hung the cast of our glorious three months together after I arrived in Trove. Within our current frame, we had yet to discover whether we could be close again.

Food is always an easy place to begin, and the feast I had prepared was designed to draw the compliments it roused. The ingredients recalled the first dinner that had won me three days' stay at Joaquin's, though neither of us spoke of it. Tiger and Montenegra were also a lively source of praise, they deigning to be fawned upon as long as our ministrations included tidbits. But once the guests' appreciation of the meal and the subject of cats had been exhausted, our conversation stiffened, given all that we couldn't talk about. Yes, I was working on a fictionalized memoir of my childhood, freewriting at this point, and sure, Joaquin, I'd welcome another set of eyes when there's something to see, thanks for offering. And of course, if they ever had an emergency—or needed a break, like a vacation—they could count on my help with the greenhouse. Miranda is a real charmer, cute and pretty as can be, what a smile, looks so much like both her parents, walking like a champ at nineteen months, seems quite advanced, touched by genius, even, signs of musical talent in those squeals. Happy you all are doing so well. Winding down into awkward as I served pie and ice cream. Disappointed that our exchanges held none of the dynamic spontaneity Joaquin and I once shared. Can't reclaim a spurned friendship in an evening, Mann. Hoped he hadn't stowed his guitar in the truck for an after-dinner songfest, where the clumsy air between us would be more obvious. Conversing with Lori, my only goal was to express humility and gratitude, which she intuited and helped me succeed in, but it was a sparse foundation for an evening, and we both realized it. As we were finishing dessert, she threw off caution and hit me with a knockout question.

"Alex, what are you planning to do when you finish your book?"

"I'm nowhere near done." True, if brusque, but spoken to end that line of inquiry.

"Well, I was just thinking. About the time when you'd begun teaching, when I lived with you and Shelley, before…you were so enthusiastic and smart. Maybe you should look into the possibility of, well, at least substituting at the school in Trove. From what I hear, they really need subs. And that might lead to more, like it did in Summerville."

Flushed, her words a mumble, uneasy about bringing up anything from that time. As I was, but the lid off the box, I had to face her exposed.

"It started well enough, that teaching year, got really bad, ended reasonably well. Still, I'm not convinced I've got the right stuff to head back into a classroom."

Joaquin stepped in, fixing me with his Yoda stare. "Once upon a time, not so long, long ago, in a galaxy not at all far away, you asked me to take a chance on you, and I've never regretted it." He would, though, if he knew how I'd abused his trust, his woman. Nonetheless, he was the closer.

"Yeah, okay, sure, I'll check it out when I finish my novel." And that was going to take far more time than I'd anticipated.

"Just let them know you're available," Lori urged. "You don't have to say yes whenever they call."

On that terrifying note, I fled back into my writing, revived as an impassioned channel for escape, digging a route deep and away from the friendships I'd thought to restore and their misguided vision of me. I was a writer, not a nascent substitute teacher. Poured myself into every sentence as though each offered freedom from any other obligation. Made my excursions into town more infrequent and slipperier, disappearing at the approach of anyone who looked intent on having a real conversation with me. Did not stop at Floyd's. Safely home, I buried myself in writing and reading, walking my cherished acres fervently.

Meanwhile, Tiger the Invincible, bathed daily by Montenegra's tongue, recovered his strength and emerged unchastened and unchanged from his near-death experience. He hunted and growled by the window till I finally surrendered to his demands and let him out again. My pleas to him to be a bit more standoffish around coyotes and other big game went unheeded, as did my stern warnings to Montenegra to keep him out of trouble or call for back up if he got into it. They humored me but did not obey. As summer ripened, T dragged rabbits, squirrels, gophers, and indeterminate carcasses up to the veranda to share with his beloved while I sat trying to meditate on the pastoral beauty of the hills. What he did outside my range of vision I quailed to imagine. At the same time, it was comforting to know that the score between us had been evened, and I settled into a tranquil acceptance of the understanding that Tiger's life, whichever number it might be, was his own, both our lives saved by each other and Lori. I did not own him or it, and he was as free as I to do what he liked. My responsibility was that of a caretaker of his bodily estate, plus the unreserved affection that sustained me more than it did him. Montenegra and I remained genteel friends, her bite a row of fading skewers on my hand.

Lori, on her periodic stops to check out Tiger, had the discretion not to mention the idea of teaching again. The absence of that subject hung between us, but the cats filled the space, both of them treating Lori as the savior she was for them. In the end, her staunch expectation that before the coming school year I would act led me to submit my application. I limited my availability to teaching English classes, only Tuesday through Thursday, knowing that those were the least likely days they'd need me. Principal Santistevan was nonetheless effusive in her gratitude. Experienced teachers willing to sub were a scarce breed. The pay was a joke; babysitters made more than subs.

I'd done a commendable job of forgetting about this toe-shallow obligation by October, when on a Monday evening I received a call. It was for teaching grades eight, eleven, and twelve. Their English teacher had left no notes, so I decided to wing it with creative writing prompts, of which I'd retained a large file to draw on, so I'd be playing on my home court, no excuses for doing a lousy job except my desire not to do it at all. Nothing about the prospect of teaching sounded inspiring, but I was in the mood to be disgruntled.

I rose and showered glumly at dawn, vowing to say no the next time the principal called. It was my good fortune not to need a job to support my modest lifestyle, and regardless of what others thought, I relished my freedom. It was a gift I'd been unwrapping these many months and had not yet exhausted. Loneliness did not weigh down my spirits; I was not hiding out, waiting for my life to begin. Nor was I waiting to answer a call to service. "One time only" was the mantra that got me out the door and into the classroom.

Trove is the sole town in River County, hence the seat of its government and site of its elementary and secondary schools, one each. Some seventy students comprised the whole of the student body in the middle and high school: a pyramid with the fewest members at the top. As a result, my classes were breathtakingly small: one section of five seniors, one of eight juniors, and two of twelve and thirteen eighth graders. That alone created an experience far different than I had resentfully sandbagged myself against.

Beyond the ease of teaching so few, several of the students were children of good friends of mine. Floyd's sons, Hal and Skip, in twelfth and eleventh, respectively. Belle's daughter Clancy, also a junior. I knew two of the eighth graders Jaime and Ed, from around town, and as more of the kids introduced themselves, I recognized connections to their parents. Thus, coming in I was a member of their community, treated kindly as a neighbor. Scrapped the writing assignment in favor of conversation about their lives in and out of school. At their request, shared some of my stories. The hours passed fluidly, unreckoned by clock time. This is how school should be, I thought as I prepared to leave: mellow, comradely gatherings of good will and intent. An informal environment such as this lends itself to learning.

I was sliding into Pacman 2 when the principal caught up with me. Mrs. Santistevan wore an apologetic, urgent look, one that told me before she asked that I would be back for another day. Refreshed as I felt by my time with the kids, it no longer seemed an onerous undertaking. Even when she, sincerely abashed, inquired whether I could sub for the rest of the week, through Friday, I didn't flinch. A brief span away from my writing might do me good, possibly become fodder for a scene. But with three days of teaching ahead, I'd have to do some planning. The regular guy, who was recovering from a car accident, emailed me his curriculum with profuse thanks for taking over and his assurance that I could use his lessons or do whatever. The latter was my choice.

Among the juniors a lad named Rio stood out as exceptional, and toward his sharp mind I steered my mini-curriculum. Instead of proceeding with *To Kill A Mockingbird*, I chose the story "Axolotl" by Cortázar, knowing it might short-circuit some of his classmates but would enthrall Rio. Afterward, I'd have them write on transforming themselves into the creature of their interior being, who they were turned inside out. Also a tough challenge, and yet engaging. I was eager to try out some new ideas on them, always a good sign. The eight graders would be reading a Bradbury sci-fi story, and with the seniors (no Rio's among the five of them but good kids) I would focus on narrative essays, analyzing some and writing one they could use for college admission, which might further their hesitant passage along that route.

At lunch I settled onto a patch of branch-dappled shade under a cottonwood in the dirt schoolyard. It was a good observation post for watching the students, some of whom were playing a loose game of soccer, others roaming as they ate. A few were paired up, neoned by the glow of first love. The currents of this scene bespoke peace, at least to the new eye. No doubt beneath them lay sediments of feuds and isolation.

"May I join you?"

At the periphery of my vision stood Rio, lunch bag in hand.

I flourished my arm to indicate a seat beside mine at the banquet table. "Please do." Grand, to be sought out by the student I admired most. Having him sit with me, I noticed, drew respectful glances from many of the kids and would likely confer favor upon me as well. In class he had been the one to whom others listened, whose judgment they trusted, and whose approval they coveted. The untitled leader of the pack.

Rio's charisma was the more astonishing because he was (and I speak as Scarface) singularly ugly. Tall, gangly-limbed, his shoulders hunched atop a skeletal frame, he bore crooked features and spindly shanks of hair that draggled over his ears and neck. With an ill-fitting wardrobe that matched his looks, Rio could have done a creditable job of playing the villain in the town's annual melodrama—or Caliban. But for his voice, a resonant bass whose tones were molten silver. And the ideas that issued from it spellbinding.

"Have you read Edward Abbey's work?" he asked, tearing off a bite of his large tortilla wrap.

"A good deal of it." I grinned at him. "You planning to blow up some roads or dams?"

"Not at all. I was thinking about his essay 'Aravaipa Canyon' from *Down the River*. At the end he talks about how we'll 'never get to the end of it, never plumb the bottom of it, never know the whole of even so small and trivial and useless and precious a place as Aravaipa.' Then he says, 'Therein lies our redemption.' I'm not sure what he means by that."

In his inside-out essay Rio had written that his interior self was a hillside near Trove, its surface and subterranean biota. Just as the earthen depths of the hillside could not be probed to their farthest reaches, his interior realm would never be fully known, by him or others. It was, as I'd expected, a sophisticated piece of thinking for a junior, and as I had not imagined, a lyrical essay worthy of a naturalist. For that was his goal, he told us, to study environmental science, specifically, the ecology of place, this one, about which he already knew quite a bit but shrugged off his understanding as cursory.

I pulled up Abbey's essay on my phone to reacquaint myself with its ending. There, in the paragraph before the last one that Rio had memorized, Abbey claims that the world is "infinitely rich in details and relationships, in wonder, beauty, mystery, comprehensible only in part. The very existence of existence is itself suggestive of the unknown—not a problem but a mystery."

Rio pushed on. "I wonder what Abbey thinks we need to be redeemed from," he mused. "And how not knowing the world whole would redeem us from whatever it is."

I had studied this essay in college, and the ideas we'd explored then still made sense to me, though they were no more complete than Abbey's understanding of the canyon. "If we knew it all through to the core," I began tentatively, "what would be left for us to discover? What would we do with our lives when there was no more mystery?"

He startled. "Nothing. It would be a kind of death." And ripped deeply into the tortilla, chewing on both the idea and the wrap. "So, yes, we are kept alive by comprehending the world only in part, redeemed by our limitations. It seems strange, but as I think about it, obvious."

Rio gave me a jagged smile, which I returned, adding, "We learn as we go deeper in, our own complexity growing with and from our growing understanding."

"When I walk that hillside, I often wonder what was there four hundred years ago, or a thousand, or a million. How different it looked, what lived here, what it was like for them."

I'd had similar thoughts about my hillside, perhaps a Trove-induced intimacy with the land that made us familiars in a realm transcending time.

Lunch period ended before our conversation did, each of us thanking the other as we returned to class. That night I decided to give Borges' story "The Garden of Forking Paths" a shot, realizing that the juniors would need plenty of help with the language and the plot line. The idea of ever-branching possibilities would appeal to Rio, whose enthusiasm I counted on to rope in the class. As it did, but he played a lesser role than yesterday because his classmates jumped on the idea by themselves. It was reminiscent of a "choose your adventure" tale but without an ending. Friday we followed up by drawing and labeling a vast maze of forking paths on the white-board that spanned one wall, some of which intersected while others led to unforeseen epiphanies. It was a kind of Dadaist "exquisite corpse" that got them (and me) excited about writing fantastical stories.

Word of my inventive teaching gusted through the community, and I enjoyed a heretofore unimagined prestige wherever I went in town. All the teachers at the school were devoted, but for some of the veterans, habitual years had worn passion to routine. They were fair and honest and predictable, trudging from Labor Day to Thanksgiving to winter break to spring vacation to summer. Measuring their lives in grades, the rewards of their profession diminishing with repetition.

No scene or chapter sprang full-grown from my head after that four-day stint in the classroom, but I drew from a well of recollections. At eventide, meandering among the aspens, I would enter a conversation with Hersch and Joey, Beandog, Spanky, and Blip, hear our banter replicated with flashback clarity. Hurried home to write it down just as spoken, never quite able to, though phrases remained intact. Well, why don't you record it? I chided myself. But when I did, the awkwardness of saying our words aloud spoiled the natural ebb and swell of the repartee. I tried iterating the conversation in my head over and over like an actor memorizing lines, something I was not particularly adept at doing. Nonetheless, these gleanings quickened the pace of my writing and provided a sense of assurance that I was headed somewhere. Listening to them was so much more rewarding than making them talk. What I would eventually do with these snatches of chatter I couldn't fathom but trusted that at an unforeseen point they would take their place in my memoir novel.

When the patter of my homies dwindled, a yen to return to the classroom seized me. Even though none of the students in Trove resembled friends from high school, they had sent me back to those days, and for that I was extremely grateful. I hadn't been attempting to mine them for inspiration, which next time I should do, I urged myself, quite certain there would be a next time, as indeed there was. The regular English teacher, as the kids called him (which I teased them made me the irregular one) emailed a week into November, explaining that he'd been suffering from bad headaches since the auto accident and his doctor had advised him to go to Denver for a thorough work-up. Could I take over for a week-and-a-half before Thanksgiving? The past month the students had spoken about me often, and they were eager to see me again. Yes, yes, and I them; no need for lesson plans. Laughed at my grouchiness about subbing the first time I went in, and at my mutability, which suggested that I'd better not trust my impulses. Yeah, Hersch, I got it: assumption junction.

Staying my lofty course with the juniors, I chose Carlos Fuentes' novella *Aura* to read with them. Bought the books myself, an investment that cost me two days' subbing. For the eighth graders, Greek myths that they could access online. More college application work with the seniors; deadlines were nearing, and I could help them complete the forms and their essays. Delve into some contemporary short stories for relief.

Rio's exhilaration was the focal point of my days. He bounded through the novella the first night, could hardly restrain himself from going beyond the assigned pages in our discussions. I pushed him instead to explain what he understood of this abstruse tale in which a young scholar who answers, as if summoned, an ad to edit an unfinished French manuscript, finds himself in a dark, timeless abode where an ancient woman has called back her youthful self, who was married to a man the scholar precisely resembles. Written in the second person, it seems an indictment of or invitation to the reader, whose selves of every age coexist. I am summarizing this directly but of course did not foreshorten the students' discoveries of truths they believed inhabited the tale.

Taken by the sense of destiny in *Aura*, when and why things seem fated to happen, Rio pursued the idea that our cultural myth about true love revolves around the belief that there is one person put on this earth who is intended or meant for each of us. And that we will know that person when we find them. But is it actually a coincidence that brings us together? And might there be others who would be just as right if only our paths crossed? He got a lot of indignant pushback from the believers on that line of inquiry, which he deflected with courteous but unyielding arguments.

I let him soldier on for a while, then turned the students' attention to a different matter. "What do you think the old lady means by these words on p. 83: 'They tell us solitude is the only way to achieve saintliness. They forget that in solitude the temptation is even greater.'"

Silence. I could see Rio waiting for his classmates to offer some thoughts, a patient fellow but poised to spring on the question when no one else did.

"The temptation to sin. To commit evil." He spoke with great confidence, standing on the threshold of the tale, its door held open for his classmates to pass through.

"She's like a witch?"

"Yes. You know how they say that someone who is in love is bewitched?"

Eyes popped. "But Felipe is in love with Aura, not the old lady," Clancy protested.

Astrid jumped in. "This book is really creepy, Mr. Mann. It's kind of a ghost story."

I smiled. "It is indeed. But it's a ghost story with many twists. For instance," I moved on, directing them to page 139, "consider what the narrator might mean here: 'You don't look at your watch again, that useless object tediously measuring time in accordance with human vanity, those little hands marking out the long hours that were invented to disguise the real passage of time, which races with a mortal and insolent swiftness no clock could ever measure.'"

As I drew another breath, Rio took up the reading. "'A life, a century, fifty years: you can't imagine those lying measurements any longer, you can't hold that bodiless dust within your hands.'" He shook his head, astounded.

The students' faces were blank but open, ready to dig up the buried treasures this tale holds, yet uncertain how to recognize them. I knew some of the words were too sophisticated, the sentences long and complex, major barriers to approaching the concepts they described. Rio, who had grasped the story whole, found in every paragraph confirmation of his understanding, but together he and I had to bring the rest of the class into the charmed circle.

"How old are you?" My eyes roamed across the eight of them, inviting anyone to give me an answer I already knew.

"Seventeen," Quade said, and the others nodded.

"So what happened to your twelve-year-old self? Or your five-year-old self? Vanished?"

"Yep," Skip agreed. Floyd Jr.'s younger son was a nice kid but a fairly slothful and ungainly student of literature.

"Of course not," Judith responded archly. "Everything that's ever happened to us is still in us. Somewhere. It doesn't disappear; we just can't get at it."

"That's a grim thought."

I laughed. "Yeah, know what you mean, Skip. Not ever being able to ditch yourself." The bell rang, inconveniently as always. "So just think about that idea in relation to *Aura*, everybody. Maybe it will start to make more sense."

"Mr. Mann, you made me think so hard already that my head hurts," groaned Clancy, squeezing her noggin between her hands.

"Thanks for giving us something interesting to think about," from Rio, earnest, sincere. "And for not wasting our time." At the door he waved. "See you at lunch."

Yes, it had become habit for us to eat lunch together, though with winter here, no longer under the tree. Our daily talks were the greatest boon of substitute teaching.

"I want to say it again, Mr. Mann—"

"Alex," I interrupted. "We're not in class."

Rio grinned. "Alex: Thank you for not wasting our time. It drives me crazy, learning so little over so many years when there's so much to learn. My whole youth has been devoured by boredom with petty tasks. Sometimes I'm tempted to pack up and go, but I don't know where because here's where I want to be, just not in school."

"College will be very different."

"Depends on where I get in."

"I'm going to go out on a limb, Rio, and say, wherever you apply. With a mind like yours, you can't miss. And you'll have the rural edge."

"Sure, for what it's worth anymore."

"Your first choice?"

He hesitated. "I haven't said it out loud before. Stanford."

"Let's start prepping for that, then." I heard the words rolling past my lips before I'd registered their meaning. What was I proposing, to tutor Rio for the next year? Or did I just want to seal my place in his heart, as his expression told me I had hereby done?

"You're a fair wind that blows only good, Alex." Bending the quote to his own purposes.

Well, I thought, I'll do it for a while until he realizes he can prepare himself better than I can.

As if he were retorting to my thoughts, "It's not the doing of it so much as the support and the sounding board."

Look at me, taking over Mamia's role, I chuckled inwardly. But as far as I know, personality plagiarism is legal.

"The distortion of time in *Aura* is wild," he continued, shifting gears. "External versus internal perception. The, the lack of conformity, or uniformity, in each measure creates a sense of unreality. Fuentes counters with all the precise details he gives us. Crazy stuff."

"What do you think causes that distortion?" TeacherMann inquired.

"I don't know. Maybe they've lost their way in the dark. Maybe the old lady has enforced a timelessness by her three-day cycle of death and resurrection."

"Yes, certainly. And when you consider her reasons for imposing this cycle, since she clearly would rather die?"

Rio chewed ferociously as he thought about that. "Not sure. But I'll cogitate on it. Are you going to tell the class that Aura and the old lady are the same person?"

"I'd rather not. Hope instead they'll tell me."

His eyes kindled, and I basked in their admiration. It was a Justine answer and had come so naturally from me.

"How did you get into teaching, Alex?"

Paused, gathering a quick, honest answer without a story. "Accidentally. Searching for something to do with my life."

"I don't think I'd be any good. Not patient enough."

Rueful wince. "I didn't used to be. But everyone deserves a chance to learn, even if it's in spite of themselves. And compared to the rest of your life, you actually don't spend very much time in school."

As the days wended toward Thanksgiving, my juniors continued to excavate *Aura* with astonishing tenacity, led, of course, by Rio. Why use the second-person "you" to narrate the story? Who was the narrator? Was Felipe really the old lady's long-lost husband? Had he been reliving every three days for eternity, as Aura had, but simply forgetting it, again and again? If he was forgetting that cycle each time, was he actually reliving it? On and on they went, ranging far afield. The students were crackling with possibilities, even the ones who normally sat out discussions. Seniors, too, were thriving, amazed at themselves for completing college applications, which had seemed a mountain too jaggy to climb. And the eighth graders were immersed in Greek myths, reading, enacting, drawing them, and writing their own. It was a happy crew that prepared to head home for a turkey feast.

Tuesday afternoon a storm blew in. Large, feathery snowdrops that clung and mounded fast. The weather guessers were bouncing off their charts with predictions of the storm's monstrosity. The onset was exciting, as the landscape of imagination ever is before we have to deal with real consequences. Twirled through the school day, said our holiday farewells. The kids expressed regret that I would not be coming back the following Monday, and while I replied in kind, inwardly I welcomed the idea of secluded writing time. My one disappointment was that the storm would prevent Mamia from joining me for Thanksgiving weekend. I had bought all the fixings for our dinner, which she and I were planning to make together. Well, I'd keep the turkey frozen for Christmas and eat the perishables. We'd talk by phone, in any case, as we did often.

I was erasing the board when Rio came in with his little sister May in tow. She was a seventh grader whom I'd seen on the playground but never spoken with. Half-hidden behind her scarecrow brother, her face spangled in anticipation.

"May and I are here on a mission." Rio's voice held an uncharacteristic shy note. "My dad and his current partner Chloe asked us to—"

"Invite you to our house for Thanksgiving dinner!" May burst in. "Rio says you're the best teacher ever!"

"You probably have other plans, but we thought we'd ask anyway." Giving me an easy out, which I was inclined to take but curiosity challenged my escapist tendencies. What was the father who had produced Rio like? This partner?

"Our dad is the best father ever, so that makes two bests! Please come!" May, who had emerged from the shelter of Rio's back, spoke in exclamation marks.

When I didn't respond, she continued. "We don't like Chloe very much, so we could talk to you instead!"

Rio stopped her with a cautionary frown. "May, it's not about whether we like her, but whether Dad does." Obviously embarrassed, he filled in the critical gap. "Our mother died of a brain tumor four years ago. He's been lonely. Chloe is good for him. They've only been together a couple of months. We don't really know her. Ought to give her a chance."

"I've been lonely, too," May, in a defiant whisper, added. "When you go to college, I'm coming with you!"

Rio angled his arm around her and smiled.

"I am!" she insisted, then to me, "Rio is going to be a famous writer about plants and animals! And I'm going to be an artist and illustrate all his books!"

"She's very good," Rio said, and meant it. "Listen, we don't want to keep you, Alex, with the storm coming on. Please don't feel obligated to join us. Just if you want to."

Thanks to May's chatter, I had had time to collect my thoughts. "I'm honored to be invited, truly. My other plans have been cancelled by the storm, so no conflict there. And if that same storm doesn't make it impossible for me to get to your place, I will come."

Rio knew I drove Pacman 2, which, though a sturdy little tank, was no match for several feet of snow. "I'll pick you up. My dad's truck is a high-rider with a snowplow."

Any seventeen-year-old but Rio had made that offer, I would have refused.

The Galicia home was burnished copper and cedar. In the firelight, its luster deepened the warmth of the family and their habitation. Rio's father Orlando was a master carpenter and stonemason who had fashioned nearly everything inside the house by hand. Orlando's grandfather, who had built the house of mammoth logs, had been a blacksmith, his artistry reflected in the umber of metal implements, pots, and the ornate door and window fastenings he had wrought. His son, I learned later, had run off with a woman from California, leaving Orlando's mother to raise him and his siblings, who then had followed their remarried mother to Wyoming. All but Orlando. He had inherited the house by default and refined its interior with his woodwork. The imperturbable faith of generations beat heartlike in this abode. Small wonder that Rio was taken with the study of local ecology, particularly the broad alpine hillside on which he grew up.

Over a sumptuous feast, I discovered that Orlando, self-educated far beyond the reach of local schools, had bred a passion for learning into his children. At an age much younger than most boys, Rio began reading the classics of literature while studying the local flora and fauna, the Rio Sol for which he was named, and the heavens reflected in its waters. May had imitated him but found her gift in sketching and painting from nature. She loved equally close-up details and sweeping panoramas, had a sharp eye for key elements at any scale. While they had been born in this house, for them it was simply a feature in the landscape that was their home. Altogether, these environs would prove a durable inheritance, one that would both anchor and launch them.

"Welcome, Alex," Chloe wrapped me in a smile after we'd been introduced. Her tone was warm but flecked with the uncertainty of one who has not yet established her right to be here. I returned her smile, grateful that she was able to look me directly in the scarred face on first meeting.

"Dinner smells delicious. Can I do anything to help?" My go-to, no-miss opener.

One outsider to another seeking a way in, she inclined her head toward the kitchen. "Sure. This way." Stooped to pick up a tawny cat, which she draped around her neck like a boa. Clearly its habitual ride. "Meet Catsby the Great." Feline folks, she and I: the fur that binds.

As I sliced green beans, we exchanged histories. Chloe had run a college bookstore at a state school in northern California for more than twenty years before returning to her home in the Rockies. She was from a town just a mountain pass away, but fell in love with Trove during a summer she'd spent interning at the gallery of friends of her family. Her ambition was to open a bookshop in Trove, a really excellent one that would become known for its eclectic collection and its leisurely ambience.

A tall woman, lithe and more youthful than her silver ponytail suggested, Chloe would be a kindred soul for Mamia. I could hear them talking books together on meanders through the countryside. The storm that had kept us apart had cast me into the sphere of a woman who could become her closest friend in Trove, help me lure her down here for good. Thinking about the two of them infused me with the light happiness due to these festivities, which in turn initiated a vivacious ease among us all. As the dinner progressed, we talked and laughed like old friends celebrating yet another Thanksgiving in one another's fond company.

Amid the clatter of silverware on heaping plates, Orlando passed an unexpected question to me. "What do you do when you're not enlightening my son, Alex?"

Since I hadn't had to answer that one before, I didn't have a smooth one-liner prepared in response. "I'm writing a novel," I told him.

But as I said the words, I immediately doubted their validity. So pretentious-sounding, so far from the discontinuous vignettes I'd written. "Rosie and Bug" was an improbable, schmaltzy tale, flawed from the outset because it had no core. Time to take a break, I chastised myself, reread what you've written, and either abandon or reconceive the whole project.

"I didn't know you were a writer." Rio's surprise was tinged with hurt. "What's your novel about?"

"That's what I'm trying to decipher." A weak comeback but honest. "It's not very far along. I'm simply exploring ideas to see whether they will coalesce into a good story."

May to the rescue. "If your novel has plants and animals in it, I can illustrate it for you!"

"These kids of mine are determined to create a book on the local ecology." Orlando nudged the spotlight off me. "Rio's writings, May's drawings. Though with the climate chaos we're in the midst of, it will be more like a history than a guide."

"I plan to incorporate the ecological changes as we go. Adaptation will be a central aspect of the book's focus," Rio corrected his father.

"It's good you have the courage and faith to trust in our ability to adapt. My own coping mechanism is just to be thankful for the grandeur of this place, knowing that by the next century, it will be no more. As Hesse says, 'So be it, heart. Bid farewell without end.'"

Chloe, who had relaxed in the flow of the afternoon's ebullient chatter, now threw off her newcomer status and emerged as an erudite and fiery advocate for resistance to despair.

"What troubles me more than the dire time we face is the complacency many people face it with." Waited for a reaction as we waited for her to go on, which she did, her eyes fastened apprehensively on Orlando's. "Even if there's nothing we can do to alter the course of the future (which I'm not convinced there isn't), we still have a responsibility to live fully each day. To take care of our little piece of the planet, to not waste the time we have. To not give up."

Orlando nodded vigorously, put his hand on hers, encouraging her to continue, which again she did. "Have you read Camus' *The Plague*?" At this rare table, everyone but May had. "Remember how, when the plague spreads in the condemned city, the people first turn to hedonism, then withdraw into passive desperation? The calamity kills them before they die because they are unable to live with its ruthless advance. Only a few intrepid citizens persevere and finally rout the plague. One of them says, 'We're all in this together,' and those words come back to me when I see people surrendering their lives to the oncoming planetary disaster." She stopped abruptly, though we were attentive and it was clear she had more to say.

Lowering his fork, Rio hewed the path forward. "Here we are, tucked into a little piece of the planet that feels remote from the chaos. And absolutely, the beauty of our refuge compels gratitude as well as action to protect it. But it can also create a false sense of safety because it seems inviolable. I wonder whether that's true for others who dwell on their own little fertile plot of earth. While those forced to live in a wasteland are overcome by hopelessness and despair."

"Yes, some have lost too much to care," she agreed, "and some not enough. And others are in blind denial. But nonetheless, we owe our lives the attempt to make them worthwhile. Even if these efforts will not prove historically significant because we are nearing the end of our story, we should strive to make them daily meaningful. Live them awake. I think I actually mean live them with love."

Orlando spoke a benediction. "You've brought added meaning to our Thanksgiving—along with preparing a magnificent feast, Chloe."

"Amen," from the guest who'd contributed little yet but his attention and appetite.

Chloe bobbed her head in appreciation of the compliments, then went on as if in dispute with herself. Listening, it seemed to me to be an old argument, unsettled.

"The problem with tending our own gardens is the inclination to fence or gate them. To make them ours by excluding others. To conflate responsibility with ownership, doing right with having rights. Somehow the earth ends up being property, thus commodity, investment in the crudest sense. And then it is traded on the same basis as other goods, its value designated by whomever it belongs to. What a travesty—I'm sorry," she murmured, "I get carried away talking about these things. Didn't mean to dominate the conversation, and lead it down such a discouraging path." Once more she sought Orlando's eyes for reassurance that she hadn't embarrassed him and took comfort in his smile.

My turn to risk a personal view whose truth I believed but had not fully articulated. "Trees have provided for humans since the beginning, nourishment, shelter, warmth." Waved my arms around, indicating the former trees we were sitting among in this gracious house. "We've claimed and cut and marketed them. But in the multitude of woods still standing there is an intricate subterranean web of roots through which they communicate and support one another. All forests are common ground that I'd like to think extends beyond any attempt to confine or seclude their reach. Maybe if we dedicate ourselves to the nurture of local roots, our efforts will travel through this wider net by means we are not consciously attuned to."

"You're right. I was thinking only of the human grasp, not beyond it."

"The earth won't end just because humans disappear," May stuck in. "Lots of plants and animals and insects will mutate and survive, maybe do better without people messing things up." She looked to us for affirmation, which we gave her.

"As areas that have recovered from human devastation have shown," her father added. "The napalmed jungles are back, and wildlife is thriving around nuclear plant meltdowns. We may be making the earth uninhabitable only for ourselves, which would be a terrible but ultimate justice. Still, it's comforting to think of the world going blithely about its business without us."

May beamed around the table. "I'll bet prairie dogs will be here forever."

In the laughter that followed, I saw May and Chloe exchange a look of admiration. Chloe uncloaked, heartened by this thaw. "You might try drawing a book of creatures and plants as you imagine them in their evolved state."

So saying, she rose to bring an apple pie and whipped cream from the kitchen. Rio went with her, followed immediately by his little sister.

"Teaching is a grand way to live consciously." Orlando, fluent host left alone with his guest, gave me an opening.

"Teaching Rio is deeply gratifying and worthwhile but requires no effort, so I'm not sure I'm actually doing anything of note."

"You are giving my son a kindred spirit, a like mind, which is setting him on fire. He's been pretty isolated on his journey, with no one to address his questions or share his discoveries. Except me. What he's wanted is a young person whose experience of the world is similar. That's you. And I am very thankful to you, for you." Orlando's face, carved as masterfully as the interior of his home, expressed the truth of his praise.

Late in the afternoon, when the storm had temporarily cleared, this acclaimed lad of highest attributes trucked me home. Sunset clouds blazed the sky and snow-laid hills, bound us in wordless awe. I framed the scene in memory, an iridescent coda of hues to end this day.

On the verge of bidding goodnight, Rio's face widened into a grin. "I figured it out," he said. "What causes the distortion of time in *Aura*. The moving force in the story's action. It's love, isn't it? Love, which is inherently unbounded by time."

"Yes."

"A very possessive kind of love, one that has come to possess her. When she laments that the world takes so long to die, it's because her love cannot die until the world does."

He clutched the wheel, exuberant at having unraveled the mystery.

"Yes, Rio. Brilliantly seen and said." Grinning back at him, my hand raised in a high-five, which his met.

That night, as the storm mounted a second assault and I snugged myself deep in my cat-bedecked bed, remnants of the afternoon's conversation floated through my tryptophaned brain. Love, teaching, tending gardens, making a doomed life meaningful, the subterranean web of roots. I recalled the day in my senior year of high school when I realized, with profound bitterness, that the world would go on without me, that I would perish and things would keep happening that I'd never experience. Unfair! my self-centered spirit cried. The world should die with me.

It was not as if I hadn't thought about my death before that day, but we were reading Rilke's *Duino Elegies*, a risk for Justine to take and a leap for us to make. In the first elegy of Rilke's ten, I was assigned to read part of a verse that inscribed itself on my memory and remained, each word raised like braille whose rub left a permanent impression. Lying in bed ten years later, the passage spoke to me:

> "True, it's strange not to live on the earth any more
> not to continue customs you were just getting used to,
> not to interpret roses and other such promising things
> as omens of future happiness, not to be who you were,
> cared for by infinitely anxious hands, and to put
> even your name aside, like some broken toy.
> Strange, not to wish wishes anymore."

I was desolated. So strikingly did Rilke expose the loss of things we treasure unawares, so powerful his conjuring of the feeling of being ripped from life, from ourselves, that it was as if I'd been poisoned. A grinding fear shredded my stomach, turning soon to gall. I remember looking narrowly at my classmates, wondering which of them would be at my funeral, resenting the possibility that I wouldn't be the last to die. It took the Vista Grande fire to irrevocably incinerate that childish impulse.

Now, given the chaos we had unleashed on the environment, there was a chance I would outlive the world, be there to know its end, which would then be mine. Far more devastating, I realized, than it going on without me, to see everything I cherished die. Rio and May should get to live long, full lives beyond mine. Others, just being born, deserved the world. It tore my heart to think of them lurching young into the void.

"We must love one another or die," Auden had written, then repudiated the line's obvious fallacy. Revised it to, "We must love one another and die." But no one remembers the fix because in changing it, he diminished the breadth of its meaning. It is not a physical death that the lack of love condemns us to but the death of our humanity, thus of our world, a concept in itself born of faith that we are who we think we are. Lovelessness is the end of us as we conceive ourselves in relation to one another. There can never be just one person left on earth because it would have no notion of itself, would perish of inconceivability.

Perhaps, I mused, the garden I tended could be my students. For teaching, too, is an act of love, and it was one that on this night I felt a surge of affinity for. To learn to be a good teacher, one who could be trusted, one whose devotion to making of his own and his students' a life worthy of its creation would nurture a hunger for good. The classroom would become a source of, not a distraction from, my writing. Rio had opened myriad paths of thought; today alone would lay the groundwork for my next week's pennings. While I might never again among my students find a Rio, who sprang Athena-like into my life and whom I loved fiercely, not in a romantic way but spirit calling to spirit, he had set the bar for my aspirations, and it would be my responsibility to hew from rough timbers ample minds.

I was drafting a cover letter to Principal Santistevan when sleep arrested my hazy epistle and trundled me off to its nether realm.

27

"There Is No Why"

Of a crisp July afternoon, the trees scattering droplets left over from a brief shower, I on the veranda glorying in the fresh scents, contemplating my class notes for a disussion with next year's seniors on memory as the irrefutably unreliable narrator, a truck I did not know pulled up in front of me, and a young woman swung out of it. Her hair provoked my first recognition: red gold. I saw but scrambled to overcome disbelief.

"Mr. Mann, hello!" Vivienne called, waving.

I propelled myself down the steps toward an unfathomed reunion with my student.

"I missed you. So I thought I'd come by on my way to—wherever I'm going next. How are you doing?"

I cast my arm in a wide circle around the house and land.

"Sublime." Viv had the look I remembered wearing when I first saw my home. Awe and hunger. Her love of the place won at a glance.

"Come on in," I urged her. "Tell me what's going on."

Viv and I had exchanged a few emails during the run of her freshman year of college. She'd liked her courses and turned in a strong performance, I gathered, but was not thoroughly persuaded it was the right school. That happens, I'd assured her, and students often transferred successfully. She hadn't replied to that email. Nonetheless, it felt great, her wanting to visit me. We'd parted on excellent terms, but still, who was I to her, really?

"It's good to see you, Viv." She had joined me on the veranda, lemonade in hand. "What brings you here? And how did you find me?"

"The guy at the café drew me a map to your house."

"Ah, Gregorio."

"I'm on a road trip. No specific destination. Maybe California."

"By yourself?"

"Welcome to the 21st century, Mr. Mann."

"Alex, please." The idea of Viv traveling alone to nowhere in particular smacked of desperation, a state I recognized as one who'd shared it arriving in Trove. Sensed a troubling backstory but cautioned myself to be patient and give her a chance to reveal it.

"Your dad's truck?"

"He doesn't drive it much anymore."

That rang another warning bell. I thought about my heated confrontation with her mother and had to ask, "Do your folks know you're here?"

"Not exactly."

Which we all understand means no.

"Do they know you're gone?"

"They will. When they read my note."

She'd taken the truck and split.

Harboring a runaway: good one, Bug. Self-preservation urged me to find her a room in town.

"Don't worry, Mister—Alex. I've got a sleeping bag, and if I can just crash in the truckbed tonight, I'll be on my way early in the morning."

Desperation to despair: another familiar pattern.

"Viv, I have two extra bedrooms in this manse. You're welcome to stay in one while you plan your route. It's no problem, none at all. Make yourself at home."

She was openly relieved, her taut features loosening. "Thank you, Mr. Mann."

"Alex. From here on."

"Alex."

Embarrassed but jubilant admission: "I brought dinner."

I laughed. Had I been that transparent to Joaquin?

Even more reminiscent than her showing up uninvited on my doorstep was the alacrity with which she fit herself into my life. The first morning we sauntered the land, talked ecology and conservation, subjects Viv was surprisingly well versed in. She was nineteen, I twenty-nine, but we spoke as equals. I thought how glad I was not to have to grade her anymore. After lunch we lazed on the veranda, chasing an observation sporadically. Another shower refreshed the earth and our energies, and we hiked up into the mountains, walked the sun down. Viv seemed stiff, her pace sluggish next to mine, which I chalked up to the altitude.

By the second day she'd found unfinished projects to dive into around the house: windows that needed scraping, touch-up painting, warped threshold repair—none of it urgent, all of it satisfying to see tackled. But most important, she proved herself a cat devotee, winning the affection of Tiger and La Negra with treats and strokes.

Viv was squatting over a protruding floorboard nail when I, scooting past, noticed an odd swelling on the strip of her back revealed by her upslid shirt. Paused to study it, which, as quick as she became aware, concealed. Too late, though, to disguise the welt. I held my stance, insisting without words on an explanation.

"I hurt myself. It was a stupid accident."

"May I see your back?"

She straightened up and faced me, hammer aloft, nearly like a weapon. I made no move to protect nor assert myself, and she surrendered, turning around, laying the hammer on the counter, and raising her shirt. It took knife-edged restraint for me not to gasp at the welts, bruises, and cuts.

"Your dad?"

"He thought we'd go on as before. I refused. He beat me. I left." Backstory, unembellished.

"Some of these wounds look infected, Viv. I've got to take you to the doctor. This is serious."

"I don't want anyone to know."

"Doc Darrell's an ask-no-questions guy. He took care of me."

She slumped into my arms, giving way to tears. I feared my commonsense might yield to outrage if we didn't leave at once, so lightly but steadfastly I hustled her out the door.

The Doc, too, was staggered but held his tongue. He took a great deal of care ascertaining that no bones had been broken, also took photos to document the injuries, wished for the confirmation of x-rays, which Viv declined, cleaned and bandaged her wounds, providing me all the while with a demonstration for how to continue her care at home. No Lori to lean on this time: I was to be the medicine man.

On the drive home I asked whether she'd had any contact with her parents. Even though she'd left a note telling them she was on a road trip and thanks for the loan of the truck, they were bound to try to reach her.

"I turned off my phone when I left the house. Haven't checked it since." She sidled a grim look at me. "Don't worry: they're not in hot pursuit. They know why I left."

Viv said nothing more about her father, only (after my probing) that her mother always disappeared when the abuse was going on and pretended ignorance of it. Let her daughter suffer in her stead, I thought, my anger swelling into a noose. When Mamia and I spoke secretly, she thought we should go to the police, have the man and his wife arrested. While I was strongly inclined to do so, Viv's reluctance to have any contact with her parents stayed me. She threw herself into obliterating the incident, as abuse victims will.

I wished I could share her sanguinity about their reluctance to come after her or turn her (and me) in, but by the fifth day, worry beat out my will to do nothing. Mamia fed my concern with hard facts from a lawyer friend. Accessory to the theft of the truck and harboring the criminal who stole it, countless years in jail baited by lifers with shivs: much as I didn't want to cause Viv more pain, I couldn't face the nightmares.

That evening as we rocked on the veranda I put it to her. We couldn't wait for the cops to show up with an arrest warrant, which, as she knew, her father had the lawful right to demand. Instead we had to take the fight to her folks. If she wanted, I would go with her to their house, confront them with the photos and our testimony of their abuse, threaten legal action if he ever touched her again, leave the truck with them so they'd have no claim on her. Mamia would drive us back down if Viv wanted to spend the rest of the summer with me.

With toneless stoicism she acquiesced, reconciled to the prudence of my suggestion and fortified by having me with her. We talked little on the drive up, each inwardly preparing for our role in the encounter, both keyed up and apprehensive. Guiding me to her house, voice constricted, Viv kneaded the photos, gathering resolve through fresh memories of anguish they reignited.

It was Saturday afternoon, her mother on her knees in the yard gardening, her father on a chaise lounge reading the paper. As they identified the truck, they stood and drew together, their faces clotted. None of us welcomed this reunion. I took the offensive, swinging through the gate, Viv on my heels.

"Mr. and Mrs. Kablinski, good that you're both at home. Vivienne and I are returning the truck she borrowed to escape you after the severe beating you gave her" (eyes on dad) "and from which you (eyes on mom) "did not try to save her." I stepped aside to give Viv a chance to speak, but her father overran her.

"That is a false accusation for which you can be hauled into court. She stole the truck, which warrants jail time."

Viv thrust the photos into my hands, her body palsied, mouth spuming. I strode them to her parents, remained directly in front of them.

Her mother, unable to face the evidence or the potential humiliation, stepped away, defeated. Her eyes met Viv's, imploring forgiveness. Not so daddy dearest, who snarled at the photos, at me, at his victim.

"Bullshit," he spat. "You did this to her, you ugly pervert. Can't lay it on me. I'm the DA. You have some kind of hold over Vivienne. One look at your fucked-up face and who do you think the jury will believe? Or the reporters? With your reputation as a hornball teacher, forget it."

"What about me, my words? You think they might believe me?"

Slowed him down, that did, for a minute scared him, but he plowed on, his wolfish visage bluffing and huffing in an effort to blow her over. "You won't testify against me. Me, your father? I'll put it back on your creepy boyfriend, making you do it to get him off the hook."

Viv swelled, her father menaced with his fist. The air between them felt bloody.

"Honey, don't—" Mrs. K squeaked, her voice trembling. Which honey? I wondered.

"You slut!" he shouted. Talking to which woman? Viv balled her hands.

I worried father and daughter might tear into each other—or explode. Slid myself between them and shoved the conversation to a plane intended to defuse the melee and put his guilt before a higher court.

"Mr. Kablinski, when you're given a child, you're given a chance at unparalleled love and happiness. It's a gift you ripped apart, destroyed. No way to undo the atrocious harm, the pain and grief you've caused your daughter. Vivienne is an extraordinary woman, a beautiful person who would have adored her father and mother. It's a terrible loss for you as well as for her."

Tears from Mrs. K did not move her husband, but my words had turned his rage intensely quiet. "Since you returned the stolen truck," he fumed, "we will not press charges on that count. But you do anything with those photos, I swear I'll annihilate the both of you. Now get the hell out of here."

We did, still riding the ferocious energy of this confrontation.

"Viv!" her mother cried. No response as we devoured the sidewalk and pivoted around the corner, heading for a coffee shop in the next block. When we'd gathered enough calm to restore normality, I'd text Mamia to pick us up.

I thought we'd burst into a replay and denunciation when we plunked into our booth but realized there was nothing to say. We were still absorbing the shock of the clash. We drank our coffee, regulated our breathing, and waited for my mother.

Later, as I reflected on the scene, I thought about how abrupt it had been. Her father must have planned out in advance what he'd say if she came back. Maybe he had various scenarios prepared. His abuse would have festered as a potential threat, but he knew Viv would be too ashamed to take action on her own. And if she did, his friends in the legal community would support whatever story he told them about the source of her wounds. Rejecting her soundly appeared to him to be a means of self-protection, but it could be interpreted as fear of reprisal.

I lay awake reliving the confrontation and where it left Vivienne. We'd cut those bloody ties, and I was glad of it, but that brazen act had cast her future into an oblique abyss. She had nowhere to go and no way to get there except to Trove with me. Whereas I had the year ahead mapped out, which she knew from our innocent first hike when I thought she'd be traveling on in a week or so. Indeed, as I told her with a mix of pride and trepidation, I had been offered a fulltime job teaching English at the one school in Trove. No, not in place of Alfredo Cisneros, for whom I'd been subbing, but alongside him. In May the other English teacher, Leona Far, had announced that she was pregnant and taking a year's leave. Thus I had her spot and was assigned to teach seniors, juniors, and freshman.

Viv had been effusive in her delight that I'd be teaching; despite my rotten performance during the fall of her senior year, she was adamant in proclaiming me the best and most valuable teacher she'd ever had. "You gave me a voice and pushed me to hone it. Then you compelled me to make the acts of writing and speaking important, meaningful. I saw a lot of students in college who had no idea what they wanted to say or how to figure it out, let alone say it, on paper or in class. That's part of what turned me off. No one was asking more of them, so they weren't likely to get any better except by accident. I'm so glad you're back in the classroom." She'd still hesitated to use my name, but her words were stored in my prized cache of compliments.

Recalling them engendered a sense of urgency. Had to get to work on the curricula, on themes and assignments. I threw off the blanket and turned over my sweaty pillow. The air wafting in from the windows was far too hot for a summer night in the Ville. Even in July this thin alpine atmosphere cooled quickly after dark, granting relief from our intense sun. It was a cycle I'd known all my life but one that appeared to be eroding thanks to climate change, the sinister shadow that I reminded myself of whenever I banged into a seemingly insoluble problem. Take the long view, X; keep it in perspective. Your dilemma of the day will be of little account when we run out of clean water to drink on an earth pulsing with unbearable heat. Won't make any difference what you do or don't. Yet this reassurance was no help in the moment. Things just kept on mattering.

The obvious course, really the only one for Viv now, nigh penniless and with no plans, was to stay and teach with me next year. I'd support her (our needs were simple, expenses few, and between my salary and Mamia's generous monthly contribution, we'd be fine). But I'd have to put it to Viv such that it didn't sound like charity so she didn't feel trapped and beholden.

When we returned to Trove, Mamia stayed at my house with us for a couple of weeks to help Viv settle in. Between them trust grew, easing the clamped ground of Viv's anxiety. Her desire for a mother swirled around Mamia, testing for fissures and fumaroles. When she saw the steadfast love that dwelled within my mother, she came to rest in gentle arms, as others had, sought and was granted her share. Still fragile, she trod cautiously around Mamia and me, and we made sure every step she took was met with simple kindness. Evenings we three wove a tapestry of stories from our pasts, old griefs dissolving in the sharing. At one point Mamia asked whether Viv would like to see a therapist, but she assured us that our friendship provided the healing she needed. She was extravagantly thankful to have landed in our terrain, and we likewise surged with the gratification of offering a distressed spirit the refuge of our family.

In a molten stratum beneath my concern for Viv roiled a selfish, awkward new pleasure. I was coming to love having her around. Hadn't realized to that point how much I missed waking up to amiable companionship, sharing the day's work, the evening meal. On the night before Mamia's departure, I formally invited Viv to live and teach with me for the coming year as if doing so were a great service to me (true) and one of many choices she might be deliberating (not). She responded likewise with gracious humility that it would be an honor. We toasted our new partnership.

After she had recovered enough to feel comfortable, I took Viv into town to meet my friends and neighbors, who treated this gorgeous young woman like a movie star. She was an extraordinary specimen of human loveliness but so unassuming that I'd forgotten how striking a first glimpse might be. Admiration tinted with envy smiled from the young men: How did Scarface pull this one off? More than any of them, Rio was arrow-struck. He believed me capable of astonishing intellectual feats but not a miracle like Viv. Much as he lionized me, he was determined to best me in any contest for Viv's love, which he soon learned was not a prize to be won nor a title conferred but a gift of the heavens like rain.

The summer ripened into an idyllic garden of friendship. As Viv and I went over my plans for the coming year, I discovered in her a tremendous affinity for collaboration. She persuaded me to teach *One Hundred Years of Solitude*, which she had studied the previous year and I had as a junior at UNM, a challenging text but well worth the effort. We deliberated whether to approach the novel through characters or events since it was pointless to do so chronologically. We made course outlines together, figuring out ways to connect texts thematically, created essay topics and discussion questions. Her enthusiasm fed mine, and more than I thought I ever would, I longed to start the year.

Rio, meanwhile, found that the demands of the college application process required him to be at my house nigh daily, where Viv and I groomed his essays to a high gloss. Every word was open to challenge; he produced multiple drafts of Stanford's short-answer questions; even his articulation of extracurricular activities was worth dissecting. Utterly at the mercy of a smile from Viv, blithered to mush by her praise, he rewrote each sentence not for Grand's "Hats off, gentlemen," but to catch the lilt of Vivienne's heart.

Unannounced visits from other neighbors were also becoming fairly common since I had emerged from seclusion. Jess stopped by, always with a treat for the cats, whom he had deputized to keep an eye on the territory. Good scouts if you were on the hunt for rogue cottontails. When Floyd Jr.'s son Skip heard that Rio was getting extra help on his college apps from Viv, he, likewise smitten with her, began churning out drafts for her review. Skip was popular among his classmates, who sometimes accompanied him to my place. A couple of them, Quade and Clancy, asked about building a treehouse in the aspen grove, an idea that won May and Viv's support, which brought it to fruition, Orlando supervising. In this casual way the former Hermitage of mine gained status as a summer hangout, and I regained my former status as a friend to the good folks of Trove.

With Viv at my side, I began accepting the Strangers' invitations to come over in the evenings, and they reciprocated, stopping by fairly often after dinner. Rio, a fixture at my house for thin-disguised reasons, connected with Joaquin over a love of the land and literature, and surprisingly, music. That Rio's sonorous bass could be lifted in song, and that he could set words he adored to melodies, were talents he discovered through Joaquin's tutelage. May, her brother's shadow, usually came with him. Viv and Lori were like sisters, passing Miranda between laps, talking hopes and memories. Orlando, Chloe, and Mamia occasionally added their charms to the circle. I beamed at the center, joining whichever conversation attracted me, reveling in the merry band I had fortuitously drawn. The after-dinner songfests took on new life, me still mouth-harping, Lori and Miranda clapping. You see why I called it idyllic? I wouldn't have let myself invent this scene.

As good as it gets. Almost. I needed a beloved to snuggle with. Had to keep believing I'd find her, or she me. Late twenties, just coming into my prime. Main thing, when she appeared, I had to be worthy. Kind. Honest. Her-centric. That's a promise. The fates are merciful. I won't have to spend the rest of my life alone.

School started in late August. When the students learned that Viv would be teaching with me, I became their hero. It was a dream we had all privately shared. Dynamic, bold, infused with the excitement of doing "real work" rather than being pampered in the ivory tower of her elite school, she elevated our class discussions, pushing Rio and the seven other seniors (to say nothing of me) to unexpected heights, sometimes perilous but other times breathtaking in the new overlooks they provided. Despite her success, Viv unfailingly deferred to me, and the students followed her lead. I'd had no trouble with them before, but now they were so eager to secure my respect that I had to be careful not to breed disciples.

Rio's brilliance was intensified by Viv's presence. He transcended goals he set for himself, matching Viv stride for stride. While she and I foresaw all of our students leading productive, thoughtful lives, we had no doubt that Rio was meant for greatness. It would be a privilege to have known him: no, it already was. His classmates likewise gave him all the latitude he deserved, treated him as a scholar-in-residence. He was the North Star by whom we all navigated, and Vivienne was the moon who rocked our tides. To her the students turned with problems, fears, intimate questions, as well as guidance on setting the course of their voyage. They reserved me for literary and philosophic conversations on deck. A harmonious trio, we pulled together, exuberant.

Thus September sailed by, *One Hundred Years of Solitude* transmuted into four weeks of bliss. The juniors and freshmen, too, were well content, assured by the seniors of our skill and judgment. To be a teacher, Viv and I agreed, was the greatest good, a life that fulfilled itself in the living of it. My writing languished, as it had all summer, and I didn't care. Better, perhaps, to write in later years when I had something of real import to say.

In the fifth week, an unexpected offer catapulted Viv into a new orbit. An influx of Central American kids from refugee families had filled the primary grades, especially first. Why these families had fled their home became brutally clear over time; why they picked Trove as a destination at the onset of winter was an enigma. Longtime residents were pressed for income during these months, and newcomers found that for them, very few possibilities existed. Still, as small towns can and do, especially those accustomed to strangers, Trove made room for them where there was none. That included providing schooling for their children, nearly all of whom were monolingual Spanish speakers. Viv, fluent in their language, was offered a position as Educational Assistant in the first grade. The salary was dismal, but she reveled in the chance to earn it working with these displaced little ones.

"I don't like being entirely dependent on your and Shelley's generosity," she explained. "There are things I need that I hate to ask you for. Personal things," she added when I opened my mouth to protest. "Plus it's wonderful to have a chance to help children who so thoroughly deserve it. I think I can really become a catalyst for change in their lives."

No arguing with that. But all of my students, I foremost among them, felt bereft without her in class. Had to remind myself that I'd planned to be on my own and that I could fly without my magic feather, even if I didn't like or want to. The seniors found comfort in knowing that each week was punctuated with an "end," during which they could be at my house ostensibly getting help on their college essays. Some, I noticed, added three or four new schools requiring different essays to their list of applications.

"Okay, my friends, buck up and let's muster on," I told the seniors as we began discussion of Vonnegut's *Slaughterhouse Five*, the next novel on our syllabus. "Viv chose this book, so do her proud. I'll give her a full account of class over dinner tonight."

"Mr. Mann, are you sure Viv isn't your girlfriend?" From Quade, expressing a doubt many of the kids at the school harbored.

I regarded him with eyebrow arched. "Can you picture me not being sure about that, Q?"

Rio grabbed the helm and steered the class toward *Slaughterhouse Five*. "Listen. Why does Vonnegut keep telling us to listen, as if we weren't paying attention? Like here, at the start of Chapter 2, 'Listen: Billy Pilgrim has come unstuck in time.'" Rio's notebook had an impressive queue of issues for us to address.

We were chugging through the bombed-out countryside of WWII Germany on the moribund train carrying Billy and other starving POWs when Vonnegut rocketed us to

Tralfamadore, billions of miles away from Earth. While we had met the aliens, earlier, here a full picture of their world emerged. I went for the jugular.

"Why do you think Billy invented these little green toilet-plunger-shaped creatures with eyes on their hands who breathe cyanide and communicate telepathically and see all time at once?"

Opal grazed me with a skeptical look. "Invented?"

Pause. "Opal, you don't seriously think Tralfamadore is real?"

"Don't you?"

I closed my eyes, the way the little green aliens did when they found something Billy said ridiculous. "Opal, they're a literary device, an incredible one in the midst of this antiwar novel."

"You sound like Billy's horrible daughter when she says he's crazy."

"Do you believe there's life on the other planets, Mr. Mann?" Isaiah, throwing us completely out of orbit.

"There could be, but that's not the point here. Billy creates this imaginary geodesic-domed-shaped zoo on an invented planet where he and Montana Wildhack, a porn star, are the central attractions and everyone loves him. Why?"

"We have no way of knowing what life on other planets is like. Billy could be the first time-traveler to experience this place, and he's trying to share what he knows with a bunch of doubting earthlings."

"Maybe that's why he keeps saying 'Listen.' Because he's sure we won't." Skip, gloating: nailed it.

I turned a pleading eye on Rio, but he seemed to be enjoying this conversation too much to intervene. Or he wanted to watch me go it alone, sans Viv.

"You think Billy is a reliable narrator?" I pinned Astrid with that familiar question.

"I think Billy is the most honest person in this book."

"Character."

"Whatever. He is wise and good, even when other people are horrible to him, like his dad and Roland Weary."

"Billy's kind of like the love-child of Jesus and Cinderella."

"Listen, if Billy says he was abducted by aliens and taken to Tralfamadore, then that's what happened."

"They teach him so much stuff he'd never know otherwise, like about death and how many sexes it takes to make a baby." Quade grinned. "Seven. Five of them are in the fourth dimension, invisible to us."

"Does that sound credible to you?"

"Why would he make it up?"

"*Why* is exactly the right question to ask!" I exalted, briefly.

"'There is no *why*,' Mr. Mann, according to the Tralfamadorians. See page 97."

"Vote!" Isaiah, exacerbating the lunacy. "Who believes in Tralfamadore?" Every hand but Rio's zinged up, fingers pointed beyond the ceiling at the interstellar space where Billy and Montana were copulating to the delight of a thousand toilet plungers.

A vision of Justine fighting to dematerialize Kafka's bug skittered by, and to the students' amazement, I burst out laughing. "Okay, okay, you Billy loyalists, god love you." My voice burbled as I fought for control. "What about Kilgore Trout, the mad novelist whose books Billy worships? On page 138, Trout's *Gospel from Outer Space* features a visitor shaped very much like a Tralfamadorian. Isn't Vonnegut giving us a clue here about where Billy's fantasies originate?"

Clancy shook her head in gentle disbelief, speaking slowly as though I were not very bright. "Billy's already been to Tralfamadore. Otherwise he wouldn't know who the visitor looked like."

"Or maybe," Bug-Mann said, choking on suppressed laughter, "The whole sci-fi element is a metaphor."

My eyes, leaking hysteria, pleaded with Rio's. As long as it was me versus the class, we'd never get back to earth. Obligingly, he hauled himself off the sidelines to walk six-gunned down Sane Street, where the others, blinded by his sun, would be vanquished.

"Listen," Rio said, very deliberately, "it doesn't matter whether Tralfamadore is real to you or me or Mr. Mann. It is real to Billy." Hey, I thought, still reliving the Kafka debacle from my youth, that's my line. "In the midst of a dismal life he's unenthusiastic about living, in the midst of the annihilation of an unarmed fairytale city, in the midst of a world wherein nothing makes sense, Tralfamadore is no less likely a creation than Earth.

"Really, I mean think about it: war, if we weren't used to its atrocities, is absurd, an utterly ridiculous squandering of all that we hold dearest. We spend centuries creating works of astonishing beauty that we then obliterate in an hour. And yet we continue to engage in warfare time and again. Vonnegut holds up the mirror to this mental illness of ours by creating a parallel universe in Tralfamadore. Why should we believe the possibility of one more than the other? Or another way to think about it is that after seeing such pointless cataclysmic destruction, what can't we believe?

"Billy isn't able to articulate his horror, but he desperately needs not only an escape from earth, but also a destination where he is loved and revered as classically handsome. Maybe we all do; maybe that's one reason we want to believe in Tralfamadore. Another is simply that the little toilet-plungers are so cute and obliging. Like Zen Yodas: so wise, so appreciative, totally unfazed by everything. And, like, who doesn't want a Barcalounger?" With a grin, returned by his whooping classmates.

Yes, back in the country of literature. I'd make Rio a special dessert for his genius. I was preparing to move on to the associations that triggered Billy's time travel from earth to Tralfamadore when Opal broke in.

"I've got to ask: What the hell is a Barcalounger?"

And we were off on another expedition, one that led to Quade promising to bring to class an authentic Barcalounger his folks had stored in the attic and never used. "Just a thought, yo, but maybe whoever sits in it will be magically transported to Tral-world."

At least, I thought, they'll never forget this novel.

That night when I entertained Viv with a description of the seniors' conversation, she laughed but wistfully. "Yes," I nodded, assuming I knew her thoughts, "I wish you'd been there, too."

"It's not that, Alex. I was thinking, I wish you'd been like that with our senior class. What changed?"

"I don't know for sure. Good kids, maybe—no offense."

"Seems to me they have to be hooked first, then instead of reeling them in and letting them flop around on the bank, you play the line out and let them take the lead."

We'd been creating strategies for teaching the 9th graders *The Old Man and The Sea.*

"Sharing the power. Giving their learning precedence over my teaching."

"That's it!" Viv concurred. "Your faith in them inspires their faith in you. It's symbiotic."

It's doing what you know is right, I said to myself. Makes them good, and you.

Meanwhile, in the overcrowded first grade, Viv had already won the devotion of the refugee children. An opening strategy she proposed to Betty, the teacher she was assisting, was that each of the new kids be paired with a hometown child, every pair having specific goals, like learning words from each other's language. The hidden goal was that the new kids would be integrated naturally. Her program was off to a splendid launch, its unsought blessing being that while the kids were happily engaged, Viv and Betty had time to plan their curriculum.

Thus October, a month of uncommon grandeur I'd always regarded with melancholy, its hues chiming farewell, blossomed with an unseasonable profusion of successes. Among them was a new friend for me, Aria Fitzgerald, whose son Darcy was in Viv's class. Aria taught math to most of the same kids I taught, so we regularly shared stories and insights about them. By predilection Aria was an actress, but some bad years had made her cautious about indulging this yen. She performed summers at the Trove Classic Theater and lived with their technical director, Boone, who also worked off-season at the liquor store, not ideal given his habit of depleting the stock on gray afternoons. Of Darcy's father Aria said little, only once referring to him as a scoundrel.

Boone was not alone in his craving for a drink to fend off the winter doldrums, and the liquor store was thriving. A couple of the Central American refugee men had found part-time work expanding the storeroom, which is where I ran face-on into them one Saturday. We stopped short on first encountering one another; I had glimpsed the newcomers around town but no more than that, as they had a way of making themselves invisible. I'd catch sight of them across the street and in the next instant they vanished. Others had remarked on their ability to melt away, as if the past had taught them that to remain unnoticed was essential to avoiding harm. Which, I soon saw, this duo had not managed to do.

"Hola," I ventured, drawing on the paltry remnants of my Spanish. "Me llamo Alejandro."

Enrique returned my greeting, introducing himself and his companion, Domingo, who nodded hello. We stood in silence then, exchanged stares of recognition, all three of us riven by scars. Enrique bore slash-welts, like cuts by a knife, one sloping from ear to chin and another across his throat, manly scars that could have originated from a fight. But Domingo's face was a ruin searingly worse than mine: the larger half of it rough-laid over scar-skin. Dark gouges and knots averred a gruesome mauling. The eye on that side was a slit through which little could be seen. Burned or scalped, the flay of some torture I cringed to imagine. Instead my first thought was a flash of relief: X-Mann was no longer an anomaly. Encouraged by our common disfigurement, I thought to use it as a way of making friends with them.

"Soy como ustedes," I grinned, pointing at my face. "Fuego." (*I'm like you. Fire.*)

"Yes, we hear of your accident, Alejandro." A courteous but unsmiling reply from Enrique. "Maria help with first grade. Estrella in class." After a pause added, "I am content you get out of the fire."

"And I am glad you both survived your…misfortunes." Cowed by Enrique's advantage in knowledge and language, I retreated from my assumption that we were comrades in scars.

"No accident for Domingo and me." Quiet, his expression opaque. "Torture. Him and me, we lucky ones escape, others no."

I lowered my eyes, which snagged then on Domingo's hands. Fingers missing or crookedly healed, the skin there, too, puckered in crude jags. My stomach curdled. How much of him was similarly mutilated? How did it feel to dwell inside that bulk of pain? Was there any escape from it but death, which had surely been the intended outcome?

I thought about my weeks in bed after the fire, the bandages changed daily, the antibiotics and salves, my mother's tending. When my scarred face and chest emerged, I had mourned myself as the most unfortunate young man conceivable. Wrecked past hope, damaged beyond repair, too ugly to love: a tragic figure exiled to a lifetime of guilt and grief.

The measure of suffering is experience, which is ultimately individual and incomparable, though we constantly weigh our own against others to hearten or pity ourselves. The greater suffering of others reassures us that our lives are blessed and dwarfs whatever adversity they may hold. We assess our wellbeing by that of others despite the futility of doing so. It doesn't assuage our hunger to know that people elsewhere are starving nor comfort us to realize that others are comfortless. All it does is add an element of shame that amplifies our misery. And shame leads as often to defiance as to redress.

Still, it was clear that these men had suffered more than I had. Their devastation hurtled past complaint into a silence that granted them an aura of virtue otherwise unattainable. Not that those who withstood this kind of catastrophe were morally superior, but that from within the abyss, they had preserved their humanity.

Bowed by the horror of their past and their apparently inexhaustible powers of self-restoration, I was at a loss for words equal to conveying my respect and sympathy for their travail. *Lo siento mucho* (*I'm so sorry*) was pathetically inadequate, but thoughts more eloquent had fled to some withered synapse of my brain. It was left to Domingo to break the silence, his speech impaired by the damage to his mouth, which I saw now also lacked several teeth.

"Puedo trabajar todavía, con mi amigo." (*I can still work, with my friend.*)

I nodded to indicate I had understood. "Domingo work good," added Enrique. "In our old town, he best building man. Strong. Muy inteligente."

It took some effort to construct Domingo in my mind as he must have been. Is that why the torturers went after him, because he was the best, the leader?

"Y un hombre muy…brave," I tried to say.

"Valiente," Enrique translated for Domingo.

We fell silent once again, shifting awkwardly at the maw of a cavern too dark to breach. They were so patient, but the cold was piling in, and they needed to get to work.

"Bueno." Enrique extended his hand to me, Domingo following suit. I clasped both their hands with mine, thankful for this universal symbol of good will. As they turned away and headed off, I noted Domingo's uneven gait. A man scourged head to foot. Both of them ill-clad for the weather. Near the entrance, they veered off and headed around back toward the traditional workers' access. I watched them disappear, confounded by the revelation of their immense suffering—we call it *true*, as though lesser pain were not, but mean absolute: a fathomless torment of which we can only imagine the surface contours. A *true* that renders us mute.

28

Go Forth and Prosper

At the onset of winter, a harsh one though late this year, the seniors' first applications to college were in and a kind of stupor overtook them, bred by fatigue, augmented by the restless anxiety of waiting for the outcome. Their malaise infected me; classes became a struggle. Though I did not yield to the temptation to slacken our pace, discussions were plodding. We were reading upbeat pieces, Siddhartha and selected Sedaris short stories, which they appreciated but wanly. Frustrated, I turned for motivation to the juniors and the ninth graders, who were still lively and engaging. This was my second year with the nines, so we had developed a strong, playful rapport. We were traveling with Odysseus on his wayward journey home from the Trojan War, and they had written an extra adventure for him, ranging from hilarious to perilous, all of which were push-pinned to the walls. I was confident these students were faring well and were safely in hand until the flood-tide day our ship crashed into a rock of misperception.

A storm brooded on the horizon, raising wind and darkening the morning. If it stayed on course, it might deliver a whopping snow. We could feel the pressure in our marrow, inciting an agitated energy that drove the conversation into odd whorls. The kids spoke in nonsequiturs that I somehow grasped. We leapt from masks to pets run over in the street to adoption to earthquakes. Later, as I mused that the discussion had been a prime example of the Absurd, it came to me that the underlying theme was fear, which may have been provoked by the advent of winter, a time that challenges the strength of our resistance to death.

I was about to let the students go out for a break when I heard Ed call Jaime a "greaser." An old slur whose origins, and possibly meaning, he surely didn't realize: no excuse, of course. Only two of the boys in this section were Hispanic, and it was imperative I address any prejudice toward them. I stopped everyone in mid-rise.

There followed an impassioned lecture about pejorative language, whether it was ethnic or racial slurs or described other features, such as "lame." Yes, I did cite Ed's put-down of Jaime as the reason for this talk. My blood was up, and I gave full vent to the danger of using hurtful language to imply a position of supremacy. Explained that it was a form of bullying. That the group in power bore the greatest responsibility for speaking with care and civility—and then I went off on power, recognizing who has it and why. Some faces rigidified to stone as I continued, some were alertly narrow-eyed, others confused. My sense was that this might be the most significant teaching I had done and would come to be transformative knowledge for them.

Finished at last, pulsing with zeal and emotionally thinned by the exertion, I looked directly at each of them. "Questions? Thoughts?" My standard inquiry at the end of a presentation. No one spoke. But teaching in the Ville I'd learned patience through asking myself what I would have said were I they and then holding the pause long enough to arrive at an answer. This time I waited beyond that span, allowing discomfort to grow till Jaime found the courage to interrupt it.

"I know what you heard Ed say is bad, Mr. Mann. He knows, too. We're best friends, all our lives. Neighbors. I'm just two weeks older than him. So we call each other stuff, because we can. Like I call him 'gringo' or 'whitey' or paleface' and he calls me 'greaser,' like you heard, or 'wetback,' usually after we go swimming." Nervous chuckles. "We're best friends," Jaime repeated. "So it's okay. We mostly never let anyone hear us because we know they'll get mad. Ed kind of let it slip; he should have waited till we were outside." Jaime and Ed exchanged intimate grins.

Start with the students. A moment aside with Ed and Jaime. Since I hadn't done that, I stood egg-faced surrounded by glares. No way out that didn't involve my conceding the boys' right to a personal code of friendship that defied the governing orthodoxy. In private they could call each other whatever they liked. No power issues intruded on their bond. It was a consensual plunge into forbidden territory, none of my concern. I backed out with all the musterable authority and grace I could and let everyone go for an overdue and extra-long break. Mine was a chance to recover, alone at the table, where I considered how to reenter the prevailing current to soothe their violated stream. I should have been out there in its midst, letting them have their say to me instead of one another.

Paced absently over to the window seat, my eyes, though looking out, focused inward. How and where would we go from here? Just move on or dwell further, try to regain equilibrium? What would I have preferred as a student, and what did I, as a teacher? Move on, revisit later, from a new perspective. Better ask them, let them talk about it among themselves before deciding. They were running, circling, it looked like, chasing someone, or playing some game. Jean stood outside the ring, hands hipped, head shaking. I watched the odd configuration more closely now but knew I'd have to go out to see what they were doing.

Halfway to them I heard a little scream, a "No!" and laughter from the circle. Jean, noticing my approach, yelled, "Stop it, you guys!" but they didn't get the message. I broke into the circle, which fell back, revealing crouched Herminio at its center, surrounded by little stones, the other students poking him with sticks. A five-second tableau before I rushed in and shielded Herminio with my arms.

"Break's over."

I strode back to the schoolroom ahead of them, Herminio and I, both of us shaking. Straight to the bathroom, where I checked him carefully. No injuries except to the vital organs of trust and pride. I washed his face anyway, combed his hair free of twigs and leaves, dusted off his jacket and pants. Only then did I ask him to tell me what happened, as calmly as I could over the rage churning in my gut.

"It started as a game, but not a really good one. We were kind of having fun. But people were mad about stuff." He was searching for a way to tell me that wouldn't make things worse. "Gary—someone started saying 'Sticks and stones will break my bones but words will never hurt me' and someone else said, 'It's the other way around, remember?' He said it angry. And then…someone pushed me and they made a circle and I couldn't get out and they were throwing things at me and laughing and kind of singing 'sticks and stones will never hurt me.' They were little stones, but I was scared. And then you came."

"They were poking you with sticks."

"Not too hard."

"You're a brave lad. Hang in there with me while I have a talk with the class."

"They're going to hate me."

"They're going to apologize to you. And be extra nice from here on."

I cooled myself to a simmer as we walked into the room. This time I began with the students, asking them what I'd just asked Herminio. "Tell me what happened." And they did, honestly ashamed, everyone adding a piece to the confession. Without prompting, they apologized to Herminio, assuring him that he was a great kid and they'd never be mean to him again.

"Why?" I asked. "What prompted you to gang up and bully him? You're all good people. Why did you do it?" As I spoke, I knew the answer: they were angry with me. But I refrained from saying it because I wanted them to—or perhaps I didn't. Shrugs, headshakes were all I got, and for the time decided to leave it at that, though clearly everyone was still unsettled. "Salad bowl," I announced, which meant we all traded places, Herminio and I, too. It was an exercise in changing perspective, I'd explained early on, and also served as a mini-break.

We meditated in silence for a minute before trying to restart the conversation with responses to a question I'd asked two days ago that now seemed presciently apt: Describe the role of the crew in *The Odyssey*. I was on the verge of giving them a few minutes to gather their thoughts and check their notes when Felina countered with her own question, "Do we have to make up our answer or can we just google it?" My gorge rose and the impending eruption spat lava over her derisive words. "Instead, handwrite an essay on the subject. Due at the end of class. Computers closed."

Nothing was resolved and we parted for the weekend bleakly at the edge of the crackling storm.

My classroom calendar had daily aphorisms on it, today's sorely discerning: "Experience is a hard teacher because she gives the test first, the lesson afterward. –Vernon Law"

So humiliated I could not tell Viv about the incident, I spent a racked night amid tormented nightmares of other mishaps that awaited. Sleep opened its arms to me and then in its demented way, snatched them back, not once but repeatedly. Whenever I was on the verge of collapsing into its embrace, a sudden itch, an illusory need to pee, a twitch or frack, some discomfort jarred me awake. I yielded to insomnia, promising myself to sleep late, and was tortured into reliving the day, the underlying cause of my restlessness, my mind looping the grief I'd caused and endured, backwards from the end, over and over. Felina's scathing rejoinder—"Do we have to make up our answer or can we google it?"—chicken-boned my craw. Just when I thought maybe we were over the worst of it, she'd exposed the dark strata of fury still roiling.

The roil sank me at last into a thin slumber, which ended in another chthonic scene: I was lecturing the class after they'd bullied Herminio. Flipped around and lunged at the bookshelf where in my dream I had foresightedly stashed a dozen copies of *Lord of the Flies*. Coasted them across the table with a sharp order to have this book read by Monday, when we'd talk about the resonance between the action of the novel and their own behavior. Herminio opened his, and right away I saw my blunder. How would he feel hearing the account of Simon's death? Or even Roger's harassment of Percy and the other littluns? No, no, all wrong. They needed to read about kids who were brave and empathetic, heroes who risked their lives for one another. I pitched around the table grabbing for the copies to take them back, but the kids held onto them, glaring at me as they chanted, "Kill the pig. Cut his throat! Bash him in!" The nightmare riveted me from sleep, but I was thankful for its warning, which had saved me from going awry again.

Other dreams of folly pierced the night, too jumbled to unravel. And then, near dawn, one that offered a path to reconciliation.

"What happens," I said to the class the following Monday morning, "when Odysseus forgets about his crew because he falls under Circe's spell?" As though we were just moving on.

"They turn into pigs." Louisa, my perennial first responder.

"Is that Odysseus fault?"

"Kind of. It's more Circe's. And he does make her turn them into men again, but they want to go home and Odysseus has blown off the voyage completely."

"Right. So the crew has to get him back on track. What's their role in this story?"

They sighed, opening their notebooks. "No, don't worry about what you wrote. Just think for a minute." Silence. Then from Gary:

"They are like the conscience, reminding him of what he has to do. Because he hasn't been paying attention to what they need."

"Without them, he'd never get home." Marjorie pointed out.

"He thought he knew what he was doing, but he was way off-course," I smiled at them and let the parallel sink in. "I'm sorry, crew, for letting you down. Thought I was doing the right thing, but I forgot to check in with you before making that assumption. Here's something to remember when you all become teachers, parents, or sea captains: start with the crew. Find out what they know and need and think and want. Then you're more likely to get where you're going, not so likely to go off-course."

They were quiet, but the iron bands squeezing the air in the room sprang open and released us to breathe in sync again. Next time you'll know what to do, I reminded myself, but there won't be one, will there, Captain?

In early December Mamia wrote that Frank was back, staying in my old room over the garage. A man who traveled light, but only in terms of stuff. "He's fought another round with drinking, looks washed-out, old. I'm giving him shelter from the proverbial storm as long as he stays dry, which the illness is forcing him to be anyway. He's in bad shape, sweetheart, used up his dreams, and I don't expect him to be with us much longer on this earth. How would it be if I brought him down the next time I come so he can meet his granddaughter? See you again? He should depart with a sense that some good he has done will remain."

It was a moving entreaty, but I hesitated to interrupt my teaching. However long ago, I had written Joaquin to tell him of my experience with Frank and gotten a bitter reply. To bring up his father again now that he and I had replenished our friendship irked me. Especially since Frank had succumbed to the bottle once more. Finally, I went to Lori for advice. And here's how trusting our relationship had become: When I showed her the letter, asked her what to do, she curled her arm around my twig-thin waist as naturally as Mamia would have.

"Poor Alex," she consoled me, "you're stuck in the middle again. Let me take this burden from you. I don't think Frank should come down; Joaquin won't forgive him, won't want him near his place or us. But I'm going to tell him what Shelley wrote, and if I can get Frank to promise he'll stay away from Trove, Miranda and I will go up to Summerville to meet him in the safety of your mother's house. Just for a couple of days."

"I should go with you." Which was true. Frank had absolved me of guilt, inspired courage in me at a point when I didn't know how to go on. He had given Mamia the only pleasure in a brace of years of unrelieved suffering after the fire. To us he'd been a good man. I owed him a farewell visit, however awkward it might be to show up with Lori and Miranda, more or less in place of Joaquin. And how would *he* take my going? As treason. A hard-liner on mercy, Joaquin was, rarely expected or offered it.

"Why don't you go at winter break?" she suggested. "Meeting me and his granddaughter seems like plenty for one visit." Right, as she always was. I hugged her as easily as I would have Mamia. No weird vibes left between us, another miracle Lori had wrought.

Her trip up with Miranda was an arduous ten-hour haul because the bus broke down outside Gunther and they had to wait hours for another in the cold at a tiny convenience store whose bathroom proclaimed itself out of order (but thanks to the baby, she gained private access). They didn't get into the Ville till close to midnight, yet Shelley and Frank were there to meet them, dear souls. Thus, Frank's first sighting of his granddaughter was behind the bus station, a wretched area, in the buggy yellow light grudgingly illuminating it. Both Miranda and Lori were exhausted, half-frozen. Barely able to summon a civil greeting. Home to shower and sleep. The visit didn't begin till the following morning when Frank and Shelley rustled up an enormous pancake-egg-bacon-fruit-and-fresh-oj breakfast. A grand two days followed, sad in the loom of Frank's jaundiced skin, his lack of appetite, nosebleeds. Lori recognized the signs of cirrhosis, as did they all, realizing, too, that this brief visit was hello and goodbye. They told stories and took turns holding Miranda, made occasions for laughter, but the tinge of their fleet hours together was regret. Miranda would not remember her grandfather, and he would not see her grown into a splendid woman. To foreknow his absence hurt.

After the ordeal of her trip up to the Ville, Shelley and Frank were insistent about driving the two back, despite Lori's protests: That kind of fluke muddle wouldn't happen again. No, no, was their firm reply: they'd be in Arroyo in four hours, where Joaquin would meet them. Just once Frank ventured the idea of seeing his son again. Lori didn't say so but thought it was clear he should have that chance, they both should, to reconcile, yet when she talked it over with Joaquin, he was defiantly opposed. Even to a hand-off in Arroyo. To a restraining-order-distance wave. Joaquin would come to Willow Springs to pick up Lori and Miranda at a cafe where Shelley and Frank would leave her. He had no contact, as he'd sworn he wouldn't, with his father, who died less than a month after the visit. To Lori's amazement, even then he felt no pang of conscience, instead relief, as if an excruciating curse had been lifted from him.

Not so I, who had planned to write a letter to Frank that Lori could take along, in advance of my Christmas visit. I defended myself against my guilt by claiming there hadn't been time. The days before she left were long and strenuous: seniors' college essays to revise, recommendations to write. My plate was overflowing. I couldn't gather my thoughts to write a dying friend. Pathetic excuse in retrospect, and if I'd imagined how near his death lay, I would have summoned the presence of mind to do it. Now my failure was another knot in the whip of contrition I scourged myself with late at night.

In January, storm after storm heaved through the countryside. A foot of snow, then twenty inches, another foot, eighteen inches, immense winds reeling like dervishes across the hills. Clouds blustered grim, trees succumbed to merciless snow loads. So far, this winter was the coldest on record. School was open erratically, all of us straining to keep ahead of the weather. Getting wood in became urgent and fraught. On the upside, the long drought had been temporarily vanquished.

Third quarter senior year is a slog under the best circumstances, as I well knew, and while some teachers allow classes to drift through like flakes, I had assigned the biggest novel of the year, Ralph Ellison's *Invisible Man*. The kids joked that given all the snow days, it was more like invisible class. Those who read the book loved it, but building a coherent analysis and discussion of its themes was a challenge. I praised the kids amply for hanging in there. The 9th graders were studying short stories, and the juniors' poetry, with a particular emphasis on metaphors; both were units well suited to intermittent class sessions.

Since Viv and I were stuck at home, our captivity gave Rio freedom to visit as often and stay as long as he liked. Neither of us minded his becoming a de facto member of our odd household. He read as much as we did, initiated stimulating conversations, and did the dishes. His boundless patience with cat-scratching won him a place at our hearth as well as in our hearts. While he was attached to the cats and devoted to me, all of us knew the primary reason he was here.

Our little clan was sitting before the fire reading (they) or drowsing (the cats and I) one afternoon when Rio stretched violently and cast his history book aside.

"Here's the thing, Alex," he contended, as though we'd been talking, "Ellison's novel is terrific and I could write a twenty-page paper for you easily, twice that much, on the theme of unmerited suffering. But what I really want to do is write a naturalist's view of Trove. I have so many ideas that flit past and are gone while I'm doing some elementary experiment in physics to prove gravity. I read about US relations with Japan and think about pine trees. I know the value of being a well-rounded person, and I expect to be one all my life, like my father, but right now, right now, I want to pursue ecology as far and deeply as I can."

"I get it," I assured him. "It sometimes feels like you're waiting for your life to begin, but believe me, it already has. Don't wait to start living." Bland blather, but I couldn't summon a decent response just then.

From the pocket of his jacket hung a book on *The Hidden Life Of Trees*. He caught me reading the title. "Beautiful little treatise. By a German forester. This is what I read for myself." The ardor in his voice roused my conscience. Why should this young man, who had produced numerous outstanding essays on literature, be denied his heart's desire? It was his education, not mine, I was here to support.

"All right, skip the Ellison paper and write the one you want to." An impulsive decision that surprised all three of us and one that, we were to learn, also fomented a rebellion in the senior class and ultimately set me on the road to my life's work.

When the grueling storms of January and February were relieved by a bright spell of thawing in early March, the seniors gathered their teachers and Principal Santistevan to deliver their manifesto on a new curriculum. As ramparts of snow dissolved into mud and foolhardy crocuses greened, the North Star with his entourage of compatriots laid out their plan for the fourth quarter to us. While the younger kids tromped the hills and woodlands, reveling in a chance to shed their layers and open their pores to the sun that washed my classroom with the scent of fresh earth, we were respectfully informed that from here on, every senior would be following a self-designed curriculum based on individual interests. Each handed us a copy of the course of study they would be following. Rio, clearly the mastermind, thanked me for the inspiration to undertake this program, more credit than I deserved. The rebels faced us, determined to bend us to their will.

It was a bloodless revolution. Bloodless? It was glorious! Fourth quarter of senior year is the like the last lap of a race no one is going to win. Students and teachers despairing over how to get through April and May, harkening to the siren song of the world beyond the windows, they loudly griping about why they had to be here when they were already into college, a complaint we echoed among ourselves. Now here, before us, a group of fourth-quarter seniors who wanted to study, had designed their own curricula that were far more demanding than ours would have dared be. It was a Rio-wrought miracle. All of us teachers, decorously rejoicing, agreed that yes, gladly we would collaborate with the seniors whenever we weren't teaching the youngers. Only the principal, Gloria Santistevan, remained unpersuaded.

"I value you students taking the initiative on this program," she began. "The ideas are exciting, but they may be harder to realize than you think. We should have been planning this program over the last many months. Then we would have faced potential obstacles, dealt with them, and be ready now to begin—or not, having recognized that it isn't a workable concept. At this point, I foresee that a large part of this program will be discovering its pitfalls, attempting workarounds: less learning in the core areas you have identified and more learning about how to implement the program." She offered the students a thin smile. "Your intentions are admirable, but I can't simply let you out of school early."

Rio stepped forward, energized by her opposition. "Two of the most vital attributes we need to take with us as we head out into the world are independence and courage. This program gives us the opportunity to further develop both. If, when, we make mistakes, we will use them as tools for learning. And should we fail to meet our goals, we will not have failed you but ourselves." He paused. "The original meaning of school is a place of instruction. A place is not limited to a building with classrooms, but anywhere and everywhere that we may be. Thus we are simply widening our sphere, allowing the people of this town, their knowledge and enterprises, the river grand, the hills and skies of this magnificent place to be our school." He raised an eloquent arm. "Please, Mrs. Santistevan, take down these walls!"

She had to laugh, as did we. "Oh, Rio. What will we do without you? All right, then. I will take a look at these self-designed curricula, talk with your teachers, and think further about this possibility. Mind you, I am not approving the program, simply considering it."

As she did, with all and each of us, an intense exploration of its advantages and drawbacks. We teachers made an earnest attempt to discuss the program objectively though we were already sold and found it difficult to suppress our enthusiasm. Rio hovered persistently at Mrs. Santistevan's elbow, elaborating on his arguments, until, with a suddenness that surprised all, she yielded. "Go forth and prosper," were her words, delivered beneficently at the end of a long day.

We swooped into mapping out a schedule around the sun-struck late afternoon table in my classroom, which had become the seniors' rebel headquarters. Because I'd been credited with inspiring this program, I was charged with its oversight, a job I intended to be generous about sharing. I will confess to some qualms when the initial high subsided. Gloria's questions gnawed at me; her well-grounded concerns became mine. Would the seniors actually do the work they'd set for themselves and what would we do if they didn't? After a difficult night's worrying, I talked with Aria about my doubts, who, to my relief, shucked them off. "What can we do when they don't complete the work we assign them? Not much—so really, not much to lose by giving their program a try. This way, they're answerable to themselves, own their failure or success. At the end they'll be writing self-evaluations, and I'm betting they are less forgiving of a shoddy performance than we would be. But if not, Alex, that's what we'll learn from this noble experiment. I think it's a great learning opportunity, for all of us."

More doubts and questions arose, but having cleared the Santistevan hurdle, we were determined to bring the program to happy fruition. Finding mentors for each of the seniors was our most pressing task. The scope of interests they wanted to pursue was wider than our expertise. They would need guidance to direct their reading and thinking, professionals who could lead them further in, launching them on trajectories they did not yet know existed. None of us had the medical training to help Skip, who wanted to be a veterinarian, nor the knowledge of engineering Opal needed for advancing her studies, though Aria could certainly get her started. I could teach Isaiah the fundamentals of journalism, our history teacher could work with Astrid on international relations, and Aria could prepare Quade for the theater, but for Judith who would wanted to be a river guide and Clancy who was determined to be a chef, our collective abilities fell short. Rio, of course, would thrive on his own, but he had Viv and me to fall back on.

"Trove is a resourceful place," Aria said, unperturbed by my worries. "Let's each and all talk to everyone we know about the mentors we need. We'll find them." And again, right she was.

"Lori," Viv fired at me on the drive home. "With a degree in nursing, can't she give Skip the direction he needs for eight weeks?"

And extraordinary veterinary skill, I added to myself, mentally running my fingers over the cavity formed by Tiger's missing ribs. Lori of course. She was the one who nudged me back into teaching, so she could hardly refuse to help out, not that she would anyway. But thinking of her, I realized we should offer the mentors a stipend of some kind. I'd have to relinquish a portion of my fourth-quarter salary, which fortunately I could do.

Rio called when we got home. "My dad says Oscar's not too busy yet, this time of year, and he'll ask him about teaching Judith the river. She already knows a lot, just not about guiding."

As it turned out, Quade's uncle Jonas was an engineer. My shoulder muscles were softening like the hills after our toothy winter.

"Gregorio!" Viv exclaimed, and I was abashed I hadn't thought of my good friend at once. He could use Clancy in the kitchen, and she could learn on the job. If she did well, maybe he'd hire her for the summer. Greg loved talking about cooking, and though he might be reluctant to part with his secrets, Clancy's enthusiasm would overcome his reserve.

Viv laughed. "Isn't it great to discover we're not the only teachers in this community?"

Indeed. So much positive, supportive energy emanated from so many. The mentors learned how and what to teach through the students' needs and direction, which grew from what they were being taught. The rhythm of our days became the swell of breath, the course of the sun. Tucked away in a folder in my bottom desk drawer were the schedules we'd originally made. Relics now, for every week we made a new one, together, that flowed organically from the week before. My oversight role became a study in minimalism.

Most astonishing to me were the overlaps in the seniors' courses of study. Isaiah rode along with Judith and Oscar, then wrote an article that the tourist information center excerpted, and that became a promotion for Oscar's River Tours. Other businesses quickly sought him out, but they wanted visuals, so Quade was enlisted to become the video and photo documentarian. He loved the role, shifted his theatrical ambitions in that direction. Aria taught him how to conduct a good interview and found him far better suited to doing so than to delivering Henry V's St. Crispin's Day speech. When he interviewed Gregorio and Clancy, the seeds of a cooking show sprouted. Lori plunged enthusiastically into her mentorship of Skip, loaning him her medical books, reviewing what he learned, and even driving him to Calhoun once a week, where he shadowed Dr. Roman. "This is definitely the life for me," he told her after his days at the clinic, and Dr. Roman concurred, offering him a summer internship. Astrid laid out a global adventure for herself, studying the history and culture of the places she would visit. It was a route she would one day follow, well prepared. Opal found the principles of engineering as natural to her as if she had been born knowing them. "Every page I read I feel like I've read before," she told Jonas. "It's like I've always known this stuff." He was astounded by her hunger and aptitude.

Viv, keen proponent of this undertaking, integrated herself into our midst, trailing garlands of beneficent praise that she wreathed us with, giving her time to the seniors as though she had an infinite store. Rio glowed in the caress of her responsive admiration; while I was the first reader of his work, she was the most prized one. Writing essays on the land rather than on literature, his resonant voice evoked a profound love of place that bespoke a spiritual ardor. Like a classical scholar or poet, his explorations ranged into the metaphysical, for he found in nature a transcendent grace that could merely be hinted at, seen peripherally, "heard, half-heard in the stillness between two waves," quoting T. S. Eliot, to whom I had introduced him.

Mentally composing a long letter to Rose and Justine as the weeks spun by, I wove a path among the sundry endeavors, each night making notes that would in the end become the backbone of each senior's evaluation. As I wrote, my thoughts began to stray from their success to what could become a personal triumph: I envisioned this program growing to be the leading edge of a new movement that would establish me as an innovative educator and launch my career. Swelled by the thought as we neared the finish line, I wandered onto the veranda one star-flecked evening to marvel at the unlikely road that brought me here, both to this hillside and to this moment. Sturdily as I believed in free will and chance directing my life, for good and ill, viewing again, anew, the tortuous route of my arrival to the present point, I was overwhelmed by a sense of destiny. Unimaginable, the confluence of events that had transpired, and that I should claim responsibility for their unfolding or dismiss them as chance. But perhaps it only feels destined because it feels right, I argued with myself. Did your actions during the fire feel destined? Just let me have my epiphany, I silenced the doubter within. I'm forever reading about characters in literature having them; let me just once have one.

A brief interlude of feeling chosen it turned out to be. Friday afternoon in mid-May, two weeks before graduation, Gloria stopped me in the midst of my rounds, invited me to sit with her at the schoolyard's faculty lunch table under a leafing willow.

"Alex, forgive my initial skepticism," she began. "This program has been a tremendous success. I was wrong to doubt you, the seniors' dedication, the whole thing. You should write it up for *Transforming Education*, which public school administrators receive monthly. It's a well-respected journal. I can help you get the article published."

I leaned forward to effuse my thanks, but she held up a hand to forestall me.

"You should know that I am very happy and grateful to have had you on staff this year. You are an excellent teacher who has produced strong results. Test scores, attendance, quality of student work, all up. Again, despite my reservations, you have prevailed." She paused, smiled warmly, and at that instant a bass note of warning sounded in my head. "I want you to know how highly I think of you so that you will understand my regret at having to deliver this next piece of news."

We both shifted position as if a tremor had shaken the earth underfoot. "Alfredo was thinking of taking a job at a school in Denver, as you know. But as it turned out, the offer was conditional on his teaching a mix of English, history, and PE, which did not appeal to him. So he told me today he's staying. And Leona will be returning." Her eyes held mine captive. "Which means I don't have a position for you next year, Alex. I'm very sorry, believe me, to let you go. And I hope," she added, "you'll be willing to sub for us again."

The strategy I mastered when the bandages first came off my face and chest once again saved me from an emotional response: Show no horror. Stay at a great remove from yourself. I'd had less preparation than the last time but more experience with disappointment.

"I'm very sorry, too." I spoke evenly, betraying nothing but comradely agreement. "It's been a fantastic year for me, and I appreciate all your support." Racheted my face into a smile that answered hers. "You were kind to let me know right away. Unfortunately, you caught me en route to watch Judith navigate the river, and I have to keep moving. Like the river," offering her a grin that soured at the edges.

"Of course. I won't keep you. Just didn't want you to get the word by way of rumor. Again, thanks for all you've done and, and—and we'll miss you." For how long? But it was nice of her to say so.

The river within me was more turbulent than the Rio Sol with its spring runoff. Gloria's words beat against the rocks of disbelief, sucked under by grimy currents and spewed up the gullet, depositing bile on a dry tongue. I'd lost my job, been let go, dismissed, fired. The thing that had almost happened in the Ville but been averted by my nimble comeback. No moves to make this time that would save me. In a town the size of Trove, there were two positions teaching high school English: only two, both filled, period. Life was so unfair. If I wanted to teach again, I'd have to leave the town I'd chosen to be my home. Play that guy with a summer cabin "hoping to come back after I retired" waiting game, which had always saddened me when the elderly folk of Vista Grande told of working elsewhere for decades to get back there. Trove people didn't do that because it was much too tough a place for those who hadn't spent their lives acclimating to the environment. I was supposed to be one of them, wool and granite, unassailable, a man of few words and many stories.

Given a choice, the mind absorbs shock slowly, and I gave it that option. Tonight I'd say nothing to Viv or Mamia, who was here visiting. By Sunday I'd have found the right tone in which to tell them, one that indicated the job wasn't a great loss, I'd more or less expected it, anyway, and now I could get back to my writing, so rudely interrupted by this teaching gig. Envisioning myself saying those words flung me back onto the rocks, tear-jammed.

Viv had been offered a half-time job teaching second grade on a provisional license, leading her immigrant kids further into English proficiency. With her teaching only in the mornings, she could come into my classes in the afternoons, a pleasure I'd missed this past semester. She would be teaching on a waiver, as I had been, and both of us were planning to get our licenses through online courses. We'd been looking forward to doing it together, though I was further along because of the classes I'd taken in Summerville and we were on different tracks, elementary and secondary, plus hers required finishing college along with doing the coursework for licensure. We would continue as we had been, talking about our students and curricula as we prepared dinner and ate. It was a great plan, but now, I would have nothing to contribute to the conversation. What did you do today? Wrote. About what? Yeah, about what I couldn't fathom. I was done with the "Rosie and Bug" story. The best writing I'd managed so far was drawn from the classroom. Without the students, what line of thought would I pursue?

Above all, without Rio. He'd been accepted to Stanford, no surprise to any of us, and tuition was fully covered due to his family income. Maybe he would hate the ivied cloister, as Viv had her school, and return home. He and I could do something together, start our own school or write a book or go off on an expedition.

I could go back to work in Joaquin's greenhouse. Not that he had money to pay me, but I loved the plants and was good at deliveries. I could pretend that that was what I'd wanted to do all along, which at one time was true.

Gloria might have been lying about how much she admired my teaching. Avenging her frustration with my insistence on introducing a rogue curriculum, thus undermining the set order of her school. Maybe she had been privately outraged by the seniors' fourth-quarter rebellion, which I had seemingly encouraged, a move that could be construed as a challenge to her authority, although I'd simply been acquiescing to the students' wishes, mostly Rio's. Maybe she hated me, had offered Alfredo a raise to stay here and unwittingly force me out. He who had two job offers while I had none. So unjust. All Gloria's sweet talk a clever guise to distract me.

Shut up, you pathetic first-worlder! I used Mamia's forbidden phrase for the second time ever to still the inner whine. Check this out: You're young and in good health with enough money to live comfortably, the fates willing, for the rest of your days, in the most beautiful place on earth. You have a wonderful circle of friends, including an incredible housemate and two extraordinary cats, the best mother ever, and time to do as you please. It's only that last bit you need to figure out, and if you can't do that, Mann, shame on you. Pretty much anyone would trade places. Remember Enrique and Domingo.

Turning into my driveway, I eased my head onto my shoulders and relaxed. It was a temporary setback, no more, and new opportunities abounded for the year ahead. I'd take a full load of courses for my teaching license and finish by spring, cross that off the list. With Viv here to take care of the place, Mamia and I could make serious plans for our long-postponed trip abroad: Scotland, France, Spain, Germany, and beyond. My thoughts had climbed onto a cheerier plateau when I mounted the steps to the veranda and Viv came running out, full tilt, to greet me with a wild hug.

"Alex, oh Alex, I have amazing news! Mrs. Santistevan offered me a fulltime job teaching second grade! Fulltime! Just like you!"

One's fortune rises while the other's falls. The scales measure a collective justice, weighted over centuries: this time, mine, solidly balanced by hers.

29

Wellsprings

Newborn, the fawn at meadow's edge rose, swayed, reeled sideways, fell back on its haunches, spindle legs disarrayed, threw its weight forward, lurched headfirst into its mother, ricocheted, and dropped to its knees, rested a minute before it stood again, wobbling. A pattern that closely mirrored the advent of spring this year, welling and crashing, making another foray and drifting into an unstable stance. Early promises had been readily broken as the seasons fought for dominance. One day I dressed for summer, the next for winter. These same opposing tides clashed in me as I struggled to hold my balance in a new identity. TeacherMann to Nobody Yet. The latter was not a state new to me, but having been cast out of the role I believed was my destiny just when I was beginning to be the person I genuinely thought I was, made it feel unfamiliar. The mantle of teacher I'd desired was fused to me, blood and bone. Want had grown to need.

This May morning was typically capricious, wind scudding moody clouds that nipped at the sun. I sat in a vista dell among the aspen, watching the fawn, contemplating a secret project I'd conceived and replaying its far-reaching consequences. I would ask Orlando to build me summer quarters here in this glade, where I would sleep from last frost to first. I'd begun designing its simple contours: a small raised frame on blocks, screened in, whose roof and walls could be covered with canvas that rolled up and down. Double bed, nightstand with candled lamp, rugs laid on wood flooring. It would be a retreat from my sanctuary, a bit redundant, but the craving to be immersed in trees outweighed the foolishness of building a separate bedroom so near my home.

In this fantasy I slept by myself but not alone. Children squirreled high up in their treehouses among the aspen. I called them my pupils, they who transformed light into vision and allowed me to learn through them. They would become the source and reflection of my teaching. Our conversations would often flow deep into the evening, when, like Heraclitus and his friends, we "tired the sun with talking and sent him down the sky." To fall asleep thereafter amid the murmur of children hidden in the trees, to the incantation of trees hidden in the night, to an extravagance of stars, *that* I envisaged as descent into paradise. To wake to their laughter, the purest rapture.

Why would they come, these imagined children? The first would follow May, Ed, Jaime, and other friends. And I'd feed them, body as well as mind. They could play games and take hikes, fish, pan for gold, build birdhouses. Most important, I would tantalize them with the big philosophical questions most people thought them too young to contemplate. I would be brother, mentor, teacher, companion. The Hermitage would rise to mythical status from the tales they carried away.

And from our conversations I would carry away the heart of a book to be written in winter: a series of provocative essays, entitled *The Philosophers' Grove*, based on the questions I raised and our subsequent exploration of them. I would listen faithfully and commit their wise innocence to memory overnight, then record it from the distance of slept-on recall to make it more natural. I would provide impetus in the essays for the readers to join the conversations, perhaps create an online site where they could add their responses, start a wider, ongoing conversation in which my pupils would be the foundational voices. Every winter I would add another volume with further questions to draw insights from new pupils. In this manner I would weave my writing and teaching into one. Brilliant.

My mind had burrowed on through the jeweled caverns of this fantasy, the vision of becoming a renowned teacher morphing to fit my newly unemployed status. Illumined now as Master of the Grove, I was at the heart of a sweeping educational resurgence wherein critical thinking turned the key that unlocked students' dormant engagement with learning, revealed their perspicacity, and unleashed the deep vein of ethical, generous behavior that I trusted lay within everyone. A new golden age would be born of these philosopher-citizens, one I would not live to know, though, like Moses, I could foresee the promised land they would create.

The aspects of this fond vision I did not explore were what these phenomenally fruitful questions would be nor who the astonishing pupils that generated such enlightening discourse were. In my imaginings they were all super-Rio's, children of indefatigable curiosity, piercing intelligence, gifted reasoning, spacious minds, flawless characters. Among whom silly teen chatter might erupt briefly but interest them far less than the nature of reality.

I'd soothed myself with this reverie spun in the days since I'd been let go from the school, which had been tumultuous, difficult. A marked Mann, withstanding condolences from students and colleagues, forcing myself to reassure them I'd be fine, to continue working with alacrity dredged from a sour pit, to hide interior chaos beneath good cheer. I had to make them believe that all was well so they would stop keening and leave me alone to nurse my pain. My two best sources of comfort were Mamia and Viv, who followed my lead, concealing their devastation behind masks of encouragement. Time to write, to read, get licensed, and travel. How wonderful!

Rio was not dissuaded. His fury, loosed first on me for allowing myself to be dismissed, then redirected itself at Gloria, whom he confronted with wild admonitions for firing her best teacher. When he overstepped the limits of her patience and almost lost the right to speak at graduation, he hurled his frustration back on me till I, too, snapped.

"You're making things worse, Rio. There's nothing to be done."

"Nothing to be done?" he roared back.

"Why do you care anyway? You're headed to Stanford. None of this affects you."

"So you're just going to go on subbing and hole up with your novel that you won't let anybody read?"

"Maybe. Lots of possibilities I might explore."

"What about the senior program? Weren't you planning to grow that into a full year?"

We had talked about that, he and I, then expanding it to juniors and year by year down through the grades. An idealistic notion that I had not developed or proposed.

"Could you at least talk to Santistevan about that idea?" he persisted.

Which I did, briefly, and predictably to no avail. What about running it for the seniors' second semester instead of just fourth quarter? I compromised. Not that she had agreed to run it again at all. Rearranging teachers' schedules and rooms and so on, especially with more students, would be impossible, she responded, and it wasn't my place to argue the point, though I could have. She relented a bit, seeing me so defeated, and invited me to talk to her in February about the possibility of instituting the program fourth quarter once more, perhaps with just a few students particularly well suited to it. Of course, she couldn't pay me for any work I might do on the program, floating the implication that another teacher might be directing it in my stead.

My news met a scathing retort from Rio. "Well bargained, maestro. You're a hell of a negotiator. I should have been with you." He threw a stone hard into the river, on whose bank we were standing. It ricocheted off a protruding rock and landed at my feet. I squatted, picked it up, a chip of basalt from a volcano eons extinct. Long view, X. Don't let him hurt you too much.

One week left, during which the seniors would give presentations of their projects, bound to be excellent, and then graduation. Before my firing I had planned a big party for afterwards, which now I dreaded but could not cancel if I were to maintain the pretense of light-heartedness. Moreover, the purpose of this gathering had been twofold, for the date of graduation coincided with Viv's twentieth birthday. To give her the celebration she deserved, I'd invited the whole crew to a potluck at my house: seniors, mentors, teachers, Santistevan, and the families of all, which included my Mamia, a large mutigenerational party in the lea of the erstwhile Hermitage. The jewel in Viv's crown would be a magnificent cake Gregorio and Clancy were creating that no one was allowed to see before its official unveiling.

The immediacy of work that had to be done to prepare for the party relieved me of the burden of thinking about my future. Mamia, Viv, and I cooked and baked, cleaned and rearranged the house, washed windows, trimmed vines, assembled, borrowed, and bought the necessary dishes and cutlery. A tight fit given the schoolday schedule, but the work was fulfilling and completed with a tenderness that made me feel a bit fatherly, as if Mamia and I were planning the event for our daughter. Soon I would turn thirty, which was not old but seemed so when I reflected on where I had been a decade ago: at the end of my sophomore year at UNM, my English major declared, a bold, swank dude unscarred, already fielding congratulations for a cascade of stupendous reviews the novel I was bound to write would garner. Mann of no doubts or regrets cracking open the world. What a simplistic view of life I'd had. I wasn't nostalgic but glad that once I'd been given the chance to dwell in it. Viv had not known such freedom to believe in herself until Trove, and she was only now testing its durability.

The night before the celebration we were up into the wee, exhausted, dawdling over finishing touches to achieve needless perfection, when Mamia turned abruptly into me, her head on my chest. "I wish Harvey were here with us. I miss him so much." I jerked, unmoored by her confession, and stepped away.

Viv curved in from behind to hold her. "I wish it as much as you." She who'd never met him said the words that should have been mine. Too late I leaned in to add my embrace to Viv's, Mamia sandwiched between our bodies. The missing a familiar air surrounding us.

That moment of yearn stirred musings I had long not visited. I lay abed thinking of Mamia's outcry, the loneliness she so seldom expressed. Did she miss my father continuously or just when the wind of an hour carried his memory to her? Her many friends, dearly treasured, her son beloved, her life full of good, could not bridge the gap Harvey had left. She'd mentioned once that she still slept on her side of the bed, unable to claim the center. My mind stumbled over her office niche in our former house: on her desk stood a 5×7 of the three of us at my high school graduation. In it she, smiling at her son, looked confidently blissful. Mamia, too, had harbored grand dreams for me.

Both of us had had to overcome despair over the lost harvest of those dreams, nurture ourselves on the gleanings of faltered hope, and reconstitute our lands from barren hearts. It was not a recovery we made jointly, thanks to my deliberate isolation, which, at the time my only way forth, made hers more difficult. In my youth it had often been that way, my caring less about her survival than my own. She now sixty, a number far older than I could conceive her being except in terms of twice my years, which she was in wisdom and love. At the near edge of old age and (putting myself in her place) of terror at the approach of decrepitude, which signals proximity to the unbecoming of self so arduously created. For as youth is a passage into life, old age is a passage out. Not a phase we grow beyond, not a seasoning that prepares for the next one, but a waning shouldered with profound reluctance and vigilance, loomed by dread that at the end we may no longer know enough to know that we know nothing. Mamia, of course, never spoke of such fears, which had absolved me of worry but now, being aware that they must exist, impelled me to talk with her about them. And about my own, personal and wider ones, for knowing what likely lay ahead for my generation might be more gruesome than not remembering what lay behind. Living through it more horrific than not having to. But I would leave that unsaid, a foolish justification for the implied luck of being old.

Rebounding off my interior unease, the echo of her words flung me into a sphere of preternatural light. I braced myself for an assault, shielded my eyes and scanned the territory. Unrecognizable at first in the glare, the hallway to my classroom slowly came into focus, and I relaxed my stance. The hallway, of course: where else would I be? But it was not as I knew it. Stretching beyond my line of sight, a hall without end, the doors on either side closed, and throughout, silence. Paused to take stock. A holiday I'd forgotten? A disaster? Arrived too early? I tried the first door to my left, its knob stiff, shoved in my key, which didn't fit the lock, wiggled the knob forth and back till unexpectedly it yielded.

Inside, a candled scene, windowless, the masked, black-robed figures seated high above me, laughing among themselves, which stopped upon my entrance.

"Excuse me," I said, backing away. The door was gone.

"We will not," thundered a mask. My eyes, centered on it, now revealed terrible disfigurement.

"You're late. It does your case no good to keep us waiting."

Wounds, some bleeding fresh, others scabby crusted. All of the masks, I saw by the flit of candlelight, were mutilated, hideously gashed by cuts and scars. My face throbbed.

"The verdict has already been delivered," another hissed. "Guilty."

"Guilty!" a chorus of bellows. Impossible to count the wavering forms that were both one and many.

"I don't remember the trial."

"Add perjury to the charges!"

"I'm sorry."

"No excuse."

"What have I done?"

"What have I done?" Spat back in a perfect mock rendition of my voice. "Add feigned ignorance, too."

"Who are you?"

"Who are you?" They jeered, again in my voice. "Add contempt."

With dizzying effort I puffed myself up. "You have the wrong man. I can prove it." Though how would I, not knowing the charges.

"Falsifying his identity: add that, too."

Tried to move nearer the lambent judges but I had been immobilized, except for my head, which swung loose on my shoulders, bone and sinew having come unhinged.

Yielding then as if to the ache of a feverish illness, I wailed, "Haven't I suffered enough?"

"Evidently not."

It came to me as clear as spoken, though it was not: I could expect no mercy.

"What is my sentence?" Viscous words, slow to emerge.

"What is my sentence?" Laughter rocked them, jarring me. Where was the humor in my condemnation? "You are already serving it, fool." Voices indistinguishable from mine.

"What court is this? What right do you have pass judgment on me?" Shrieking from the gallows.

"Released on his own recognizance!" boomed one and all, still agasp with dissolving hilarity.

"It's never worked before." A whispered emanation, absolved by shrugs and sighs. "But what choice do we have? Imprison him for loitering?" Another outburst of mirth.

"He's already been fired."

Their derision roused a wind that blew a spark down onto me. "Fired!"

"It's not my fault!" I screamed at them and trying to back away, stumbled, fell as their derision rose. More sparks flew, catching.

"Guilty as charged! Sentenced to life."

Twisting spineless, I exerted the muscle of my will to snail toward where the door once was.

In unison, they trumpeted, "Crippled by guilt, guilt, guilt."

Writhing, my voice distorted: "I'm over all that."

Caustic titters.

"Guilt your pretext to hobble from one failure to the next, to justify inaction, indecision, incapacity, or indolence. A stone in your gut whose weight has crushed your ambition."

The room was singeing, brittle voices gone to smoke. Defeated, I lay slack, unable to save myself through escape or retort. Convicted by their knowledge of my case. They had named my faults and immolated me for the shameful denial of my pusillanimity.

Blazing, a sear of air but without heat. From incalculable depths my interlocutors' voices faded to ash. The room caved.

"Let me out!" I shrieked aloud, awakening myself with these words as early shafts of morning grazed my windows. The crystal hummingbird prismed, stippling the wall with rainbow hues. Heaving, I bound my eyes to the dots to regain a foothold in this tranquil land. But the gravity of the inquisition, and the truths that emerged from it, would not be shaken. Like light through glass, the voices, fire-tongued, refracted my own. Threw back the covers in disgust: I will not let my dreams speak for me.

This putrid one had, however, tarnished my mood, and lest it undermine the gaiety of the final preparations, I volunteered to tie balloons to the mailbox by the road. Unnecessary, since everyone knew where my house was, but it would give me some time alone to restore myself. Mamia and Viv interpreted my anxiety as resulting from the job loss, and to some degree they were right.

As it so often did, the beauty of the land dispelled my gloominess. This was a spangling day, early green velveting the hills, infant leaves unfurling on the aspen, new growth emerging from pine and spruce boughs, hummingbirds at my feeders, wild iris blooming along lowland streams. The kind of day that, as we often said, reminded us of why we lived in Trove despite the harrowing winters.

Overlooking the landscape from the veranda as the guests began to arrive, excitement at the prospect of my first real party at the Hermitage swept apprehension aside. Aria and Belle danced toward me, arms laden with casserole dishes. I grinned and raised my fists in a victory salute. They cheered. Viv, in a brilliant floral dress, ran past me down the steps to hug them, and Mamia encircled me with her arm. Five trucks caravaned up the driveway behind them. Dr. Roman had come, to Skip's delight, and Floyd's family surrounded him with gratitude. Rio with his clan were among the most spirited partygoers, generous in their praise of the celebration we'd prepared. Rio hung on Viv as she flitted from guest to guest. An hour into the merriment, Gloria Santistevan walked up the slope from her car. I thought she'd chosen not to come, for my sake, but of course since she'd promoted Viv, she had every reason to be here. We exchanged a courteous hello before she quickly moved on.

As if by agreement, no one mentioned my dismissal, although I sensed a subdued undercurrent tempering their greetings to me. Mamia and I focused utmost attention on Viv, who reveled in it. Her sole happy memories of childhood birthdays had been that each brought her one year closer to leaving home. Here, among friends, safe and beloved, she glistened in the festive, traditional role of the birthday girl: blushing when we sang to her and when she blew out the candles in one breath, for which we clapped and shouted. Though she kept her wish secret, she confessed that we were essential to its fulfillment.

The merriment and rounds of congratulations lasted till sunset's chill propelled an urge toward home. Parents lured their youngsters out of the treehouses and other nooks, students walked mentors to their cars. Still, after bringing in food and cleaning up the party site, a goodly number of folks remained, settling into the rambling center of my house. Joaquin started a fire when the temperature went down with the sun. The talk quieted, laughter mellowed, as we took on evening's drowsier pace. A profound sense of comfort entered me, sitting among friends. I wouldn't mind Athena slowing the moon tonight, I smiled, for a wide span of hours. The poignance of this being perhaps the only evening of its kind tinged it with gentle melancholy.

Rio's bass tones stirred me from my trancelike ease, overriding the murmur of smaller conversations.

"Do you know how envious the younger kids are of us?" he was saying to Gregorio. "They've seen how excited we are, how captivated by all we're learning. It's awakened them to what school could be. Should be. For everyone."

"It's going to become the standard for the end of senior year, don't you think?" Chloe swept a fond eye over her surrogate son. May was curled up between her and Orlando.

"What I'm talking about is making it the standard, period," Rio insisted. "For all of us, at any age. Whoever wants to learn through the lens of their most passionate interest. To me the difference is that within the vast world of knowledge and understanding, we pause at a given arrangement to say, learn this. It's all right to do that because the world can be grasped in myriad ways. What's not all right is that everyone only gets to learn one set arrangement. I say keep the kaleidoscope of possibilities turning, instead of making students captive to a random pattern fixed by a rigid hand."

Oscar was not buying it despite Rio's eloquence. "So you're talking about kids doing nothing but what you all did for two months? That'll kill whatever passion they might have had. I mean, I'm a certified river rat, but if I'd had to study the river day in and out in school, I'd probably have moved to the Arabian desert."

A few chuckles did not deter Rio. "You've got to use a wide-angle lens. Then there's plenty to see, a lifetime's worth."

"What about reading and writing and 'rithmetic? Still got to learn the basics even if your passion is skydiving."

"Of course." His retort carried an edge. "And if the child is very young, you'll be developing and refining their interests. They'll grow with the child. The point is," he emphasized, "school should be committed to stoking the fire within us rather than tamping it down, which is currently what happens too often."

"None of you guys strike me as real repressed." Playing it for humor, Oscar was, a hard approach to defeat when folks are basking in success. But help arose from a dusky corner.

"I'll sign you up to be a sub for my classes, Oscar, see how you like jumpstarting kids at eight on a winter morning." Alfredo, my counterpart in English, a friend and ally, came to Rio's defense. "I can see the advantages of Rio's idea for a new kind of school."

"I'd enroll Darcy," Aria said. "And I'd teach at a school like that gladly."

"Count Miranda in," Lori affirmed. Joaquin thumb-upping, nodded.

"Alex, Alex." Rio moaned as if he'd been wounded. "That's your cue, Mann."

"To—"

"To say, I'll start a school like that and hire you!"

"Oh, yeah." I eye-rolled Rio. "Wise veteran teacher with flawless track record and a couple of mil from winning the lottery opens unorthodox school in Trove. How can I miss?"

"Don't be so dismissive," Aria frowned. "It's an intriguing idea. School is a human invention, and as such, always open to reform and revision. If you started small, it might be well worth a try."

Viv, Aria, Lori, and Rio. This was too sweet an evening to argue the impossibility of this enterprise. "Okay," I grinned. "Make it so, starship commanders," saluting them as though we were still chatting playfully about the school.

Aria returned my grin but hers was sharp. "Some dreams bear pursuit."

Orlando took up the cause. "As Mark Twain said, 'The secret of getting ahead is getting started.'"

"Speaking of which, I've been meaning to ask you about a building project." I froze: bad timing. My summer quarters were not something I wanted to talk about it just then. "A bookshelf along this wall," sweeping my hand toward it.

"I'll be glad to, Alex, as well as take charge of the interior woodwork and furniture for your school."

Abort diversion. Head straight in and let the starship go where it will. "That's a solid offer, thank you, Orlando. Thank you all."

The "all," I felt certain, did not include Gloria Santistevan, observing this scene calmly by the fire. My eyes anchored on hers, and in them I found the insurmountable hurdle I'd anticipated.

"How do you feel about having a competing school in town, Gloria?"

"Good of you to ask," she began, genuinely appreciative of my concern. "It's an interesting idea that might serve the town if your program serves the people who need it most." Leaning in, she caught all of us by the ears. "As you know, we had an influx of Central American immigrants this year, and I expect more to come. They travel here in families, a term that has a wide embrace. It's something the Anglo culture with its emphasis on the individual doesn't grasp. If the older sister's family came last year, this year she will bring her younger siblings' families and possibly cousins' families as well."

Gloria paused, and although I knew where her speech was heading, I was amazed to discover how much she knew about these immigrants. My face must have registered surprise.

"This is something I only talk about with long-time friends, Alex, but I am the daughter of first-generation immigrants from El Salvador. Our early years in southern New Mexico were hard and frightening. We fled our home with nothing and found here no work, no welcome. So we just kept going north till we landed in Calhoun, where I grew up. My parents, who were illiterate, valued schooling above all else, and they were determined that I get a strong education; every extra penny went toward college for me. The day I graduated, I became, in their view, truly an adult—one who was already successful by virtue of her degree. It may not seem like much to you all, but the fact that I was immediately hired to teach American history in Trove and later promoted to principal has contented and fulfilled all three of us."

She shook off her tale and drove full-throttle to the point. "If, along with a few of your gifted chosen students"—she read an objection on my face—"gifted with a passion, although I understand that may be more an outcome than a qualification: If along with those students you are willing to serve a group of these new young émigrés who need individualized attention and curricula, who deserve the utmost opportunity they can be given, whose lives can be transformed by a truly bilingual education, then I can see how you might be an important asset to the community and my school."

Viv opened her arms as if the niñitos were rushing toward her. "Absolutely, yes, por supuesto!"

Others assented with amens and applause.

Second graders in a program designed for independently mentored project-based learning? Not a good fit, I thought. But no need to worry with so many other obstacles to overcome. Just enjoy the revelation of everyone's faith in me. Especially Gloria's, an unexpected gift.

"A fantastic idea," I said warmly. "Let's talk further about it in the weeks ahead."

Spearheader Rio charging full tilt: "Why not now?"

Gloria's headshake overrode him. "Monday. I'll be happy to talk with those of you who are interested Monday morning in my office. This evening, let's simply relax and rest for a bit on our laurels. We just finished an excellent school year."

As the moon rose toward Orion's belt, Viv, Mamia, and I cleaned up the place well enough to let it go till tomorrow. Exhausted by her first big party, Viv bade us goodnight and slipped away to bed. Mamia and I, though equally tired, were still pumping adrenalin. With a final glass of wine in hand, we sat on the veranda, rocking and talking, as she liked to say. Went over the afternoon's events, dissecting interactions and behaviors. Each filled in moments the other had missed. In due course, we got around to the idea of the new school.

"Is this something you really want?" my seismomother asked, she who could detect the slightest tremor of unrest in me.

"I don't know."

"Because you don't have to do it. You were looking forward to having time off to write."

"I lost my job."

"Do you believe in your program?"

"It was an incredible success," I said too fiercely, irritated at having to mount a defense. "Best way I've seen to engage students' intellect and imagination."

"And teaching: you love it?"

"Why are you asking when you already know?"

"Because what I don't know is why you aren't leaping at this opportunity. Which I thought you wanted more than anything."

"It's never going to happen."

"Not unless you plunge in after it."

Beat and still in the grip of the nightmare, I'd needed a trigger warning before she spoke those words, and without one, it was she whom I dove into. "Oh, yeah, that's what I do best, plunge in after something I want."

She reared back, stunned by my harsh tone, then swung toward me. "My God, you're still in the burning house." Laid her hand on my arm, which stiffened. "Alex, please, it's time to let go of—"

"Papito? Did him a solid. Hersch, too. Cabin, bought on impulse—how'd that work out? Lori, got her to take the plunge and lost my—lost Yeats. Rotten at making impulsive moves, throwing myself headlong into anything. No more. Not screwing things up again. I've got no place left to run." My pitch had risen to hysteria.

Mamia looked shorn. See? I thought. What did I tell you about plunging in? Her bulls-eye interrogation had spun me back into the masked accusers. Trapped in dread of further exposure, I coiled against my rocker, prepared to strike. She waited till I seemed to have quieted down, though I was still vibrating inwardly.

"Your beloved Vonnegut says we have to keep jumping off cliffs and developing wings on the way down."

"Nothing good has come of my hurtling. Better to hold back, recede into abstention, tread the safe path, accrue no more guilt, which would crush me. Better to do nothing than to do more harm."

Mamia's expression contorted into incredulity. The candles flared. A spark from one of them arced down and took fiery hold of the varnished wood floor. I rushed over and stamped it out. Another, then more. Put out the candles! The voice from last night yelled, mine and theirs. If this place burns, it's not my fault! Moron! We know that. I tripped and nearly fell to my death in the blazing room dimensionless. Struggled to keep my footing as I kicked at the door, already open, and rolled clear. Into a storm-drenched wildness, signifying lost desire.

However it may have appeared to her, Mamia watched me wrestle my way out of the conflict silently. When I emerged, she exhaled deep and slow, then laid her face in her hands, and the mask came off. Restored to Mamia, her mien comforting once more.

"Don't let guilt and fear continue to imprison you, my beloved son. They are ruthless jailors, and your confinement will only grow worse in their hands."

"I can't afford to fail again, let others down. Ruin them."

She nodded but did not yield to my qualms. "Taking risks is the nature of our lives, Alex, from one end to the other. Petrifying, of course it is, but you can't stop living to stave off dying."

I was listening to her and to the call of memory at the same time. "When I was a kid, my motto used to be, 'Don't do anything you regret and don't regret anything you do.' I got away with that for quite a few years. Although looking back, there might have been things I should have regretted doing."

Mamia smiled. She knew well the young man I was talking about. "It's an idyllic harbor to dream in, trusting that you can live without making a mistake, but it means you'd have to give up learning." She cast her gaze onto the moonlit slope where we'd partied. "Worse than having too much to regret is having nothing to regret."

"Since the fire," she went on quietly, "whenever you can't face life or figure out how to pursue your hopes, you flee. Give up. You wear your guilt like a scar, much deeper than the ones you bear." Her voice, trembling, rose. "It's time to stand and fight for what you love, Alex, regardless of the cost. Stop surrendering before the battle out of fear you'll lose. Stop using mea culpa as a motto and let it instead pave the way to forgiveness, for yourself and others." Speaking, urgently: "Make this school work if it's something you really want. Make your life count, make it be about something you believe in."

I followed her eyes down the hill, and we rocked in a brimming silence. Times peopled by losses mortared by regret welled my thoughts. Entombed in the past, a weight equalized by compassion. You have to call a truce with your self-imposed wrack of guilt and shame, Frank had said; you have to be the one to commute your sentence, to forgive and free yourself to go on. Not in the hope that you'll never do others wrong again but in the faith that you can do right by them. And will, whatever it demands of you. The illusion that I had done as he counseled was engendered by a fundamental misconception: I had not realized that there was a distinction between guilt and fear of failure. That the former is the progenitor of the latter. That while I may have, to a point, absolved myself of guilt for past failures, I had no intention of incurring more in the future by failing once again.

Or of admitting failure that might have implicated me. When the idea of my heading up a new school arose, my first response was to bury it under a welter of objections. Why? It involved risking defeat, a chance I no longer took. From this moonlit perspective, I could see that I had reverted to my boyhood wish to live regretless. Backing up, away, down, out had become my modus operandi when the possibility of guilt-inducing failure arose.

But I was almost thirty, too old to be playing the "get out of life free" card. It was time to redefine defeat as a failure to take a risk on behalf of something I believed in doing. If the reasons to act were constructed on a sturdy moral, ethical, and humane foundation, then I should try, heedless of the odds against prevailing. That resolve, like a deep breath,

 Memory's Fire

loosed the constriction in my frame: I would grant myself the right to do what I most profoundly desired. Foremost at the moment, to open my heart to Mamia.

"The questions you asked me earlier about what I wanted, which I think you already knew the answers to: Yes, I want to teach, more than anything. Yes, I do want to try running a school based on this new program, though after just a fourth-quarter trial with seniors, I'm not sure it's the best approach for long-term learning. It will have to be revised and I don't know how we'll bring the little ones into it. I'm confused and apprehensive and overwhelmed by the prospect of creating a topnotch innovative school, but I believe, with trepidation, it's possible, and if I can manage it, yes, there's nothing I'd rather do with my life." It was my turn to smile. "Writing was Plan B, Mamia. On reserve for someday."

"Tell them, tell everyone that. It's what they've been waiting to hear."

The wheels on the prospective school-within-a-school kept turning, its momentum growing. Where I had seen insurmountable obstacles (funding, a building, staff, materials), others saw enticing challenges. At our Monday meeting, Gloria suggested exploring the possibility of using the abandoned miners' lodge up the street from the school. Colorado had robust funding from a variety of sources for historical preservation, and she was confident this building would qualify for one or more grants. Rio volunteered to do the research and help Viv and me write the applications, to which Gloria said she would append a strong letter of support. It would be billed as an extension of the Trove school, which was necessary because of the influx of new students. Aria pointed out that we could easily gather a labor force for the work, given the scarcity of jobs and the skills the new families brought.

Sharing faculty and staff was a tricky issue. Gloria proposed I start with six immigrant children and six older ones who were keen to try the mentorship program. Viv mentioned that one of the mothers of her little ones had been a schoolteacher in Honduras before she was forced to flee. Maria's English was basic but improving, Viv said, so we might consider having her teach in the bilingual program for the immigrant children—if we had the money to pay her, which Gloria would request from the state based on student numbers. Current teachers and students would have to move between facilities when possible, or deal with a large class when necessary. While building a schedule had always been easy, Gloria was willing to tackle a complicated one. Paying mentors and me: that problem remained unsettled.

"Yes" became the byword of the next several weeks. Rarely had I experienced so much positive, supportive energy from so many. It was as though the community had been waiting for this idea to break through the rocky ground of doubt into their eager hands. The prospect of work was a great incentive. For writing the grant application we'd inspected the lodge and drawn up initial plans for how to proceed, yet despite our explanation of the brevity of good weather for construction, the funding was not approved till August. Then the crew dug in with alacrity, but we had to concede the building would not be even partially ready for us till second semester. "So it goes," I told the chagrined Rio, quoting Vonnegut's philosophical Tralfamadorians. It wouldn't hurt to have a bit more time to plan and prepare. He could be an online member of the team from Stanford.

Creating a curriculum for this unorthodox school was particularly tantalizing to him, as it was to Viv and me. Viv had the clearest head when we discussed how to proceed with the young immigrants; she and Maria were staunchly in favor of giving them a secure bilingual foundation by teaching basic content in both languages for the first three years. In the process, Viv explained, she and Maria would discover the field of study that drew each student's interests and begin to nurture them.

Meanwhile, I contemplated ways of easing the six older students, self-selected, into the mentor program. With Rio brandishing his spear of determination, a host of ideas were explored, pieced together, revised, and in many cases discarded. I favored Howard Gardner's "multiple intelligences" approach from the late twentieth century: teaching standard courses in the morning, working independently and with mentors in the afternoon. It seemed likely, Gloria had intimated, that I would end up serving in both phases of the program as well arranging the mentorships and overseeing this mini-school.

We continued to lay our plans without discussing salary. I reconciled myself to a first year without one. Because, to my delight, I would be teaching again, among other responsibilities far more complex than I had conceived myself managing. But as Rilke had advised me years ago in college, "We must hold to the difficult…that something is difficult is a reason the more for us to do it." Then, I had thought *him* difficult, but his letters and poems had remarkable staying power. I spurred myself forward on the strength of his wisdom.

Mamia offered to research sources of funding to pay the mentors and me, but her efforts faltered. The salaries of public school teachers were meant to come from the state, and though we had enough new students to hire Maria, I did not have an officially titled role and the mentors were supposed to be volunteers. However, if we applied for a charter and ran it ourselves, Mamia proposed, then we could create a structure that would include all of us. She was an aficionado of charters, which is why I was a graduate of the one in Vista Grande and likewise a fan. It could take up to three years to be granted a charter, and we had to convince Gloria of the value of the Trove school becoming one, but the idea offered a tuft of hope on the wide plains my mind was roaming.

In deliberation on that barren headland, I should have seen her coming from a good ways off. Charged toward me with her typical aplomb, intuiting that I needed her before I knew I did. Rose. Trove a way station on her travels through the Southwest. Katherine had died (unawares), and Rose was dealing with the vast (her word) estate she'd inherited. After touring the house and settling into her room, lunching in town at Gregorio's, and inspecting the work on the lodge while hearing a jumbled, multivoiced account of progress on the new school she already knew about, at the crepuscule of day Rose sprawled on the veranda, a glass of wine in one hand, Tiger on her lap, and commenced to tell Mamia, Viv, and me one of her meandering tales about the journey to her mother's various properties, all of which she'd sold for vast sums.

"Here's the thrilling part." She sat upright, still animatedly lucid three wines later. "I am starting a foundation with the money! Justine and I are going to dispense grants to causes we deem worthy, primarily those connected to education and the environment.

Maybe also cat rescue," she smiled at me, caressing Tiger. "I'm sure there'll be other causes I haven't thought of yet. It's going to be so much fun giving other people Katherine's money! We're calling it The Best Foundation."

Amid our applause, Mamia held up her hand. "When are you taking applications?"

"No," I frowned at her.

The thought of being further indebted to Rose, whose house I was renting for a song, embarrassed me deeply. But Mamia's question was juggernauting toward a foreseeable response. Yes, of course, what better cause? You can help me create a draft of the application form. By October, my request for modest funding for the mentors had been doubled, the generous amount paying them a good wage and me a salary as program director, with an additional allotment for equipment and materials we would need.

Rose de Medici, I called her in my awkward thank you note. We patrons have a price, she responded. I desire a full narrative review of the year from you in a beautifully crafted letter. Victories and disappointments, discoveries and inquiries. Submit it together with your application for renewal of the grant. And, X, stop with the servile apologies. I'm giving away the money to lots of wonderfully enterprising folks; why shouldn't you be one of them? In gratitude, I planted a Tess of the d'Urbervilles climbing red rose by the veranda to honor The Best Foundation.

The traditional start of school at summer's end panged me. I had to avoid walking by, voyeuring at the windows. Soon, X, soon enough, you'll be in full swing, running hither and yon, in charge of a hundred unforeseens, but above all, you'll be teaching. I was already doing so on a loop in sleepless hours, introducing books, leading discussions, responding to anticipated questions. My inner Freud diagnosed me with an obsession caused by deprivation.

Of a crisp fall morning, seated at my traditional corner table with my fork poised over Gregorio's wake-up, head-clearing, red chile burrito, I looked up to see Maria standing at the window, studying the cafe with muted longing. Waved to her to come in and join me. She hesitated, as if resisting temptation, then surrendered to desire. And hunger, as became clear when I treated her to a matching breakfast.

Maria would be working with me in the new school, but I had not yet made an effort to get to know her, as I now resolved to do. Both of us were free and experiencing a like impatience to get underway. Her English was passable, my Spanish pathetic, so although we began to meet regularly at Gregorio's, our work together snailed. To arrive at a shared vision of the run of our days challenged both our linguistic capabilities and our approach to education. She favored old-school techniques, which I recognized might be essential for dual-language learning, but I feared too much rote work would dull the youngsters' spirits. Though Viv would have been a great help in communicating and reconciling our views, we were determined to succeed on our own. That we came to like each other in the interstices of our struggles made it possible.

The unspoken between us was the personal and the past. I had a plethora of unasked questions about her journey here and why Trove, her kinship to the other immigrants, how all of them were being treated by the homeowners, what drew her to teaching, what her life had been like before, and more. She undoubtedly had many questions for me as well, but neither of us knew how to open such a conversation. This bridge across our substantial differences, still under construction, would, I believed, take years to complete. We stood each on the other side of the river speaking over its currents, whose depths held our own. Until, unexpectedly, a chance remark of mine led Maria to step boldly forth, making the bridge by walking it.

"Even though your students won't be participating in the mentors' program, I hope we can persuade the parents to play an active role in the classroom," I said. "From my own experience, what I learned from my mother and father is the cornerstone" (I pointed to one on the lodge, where we had paused on our morning walk) "of my education. And not just *what* I learned, but the idea that learning is important and that it would make me wise someday and…happy."

She nodded, staring at the cornerstone. Deciphering my meaning. Searching for the words to reply. Following the trail of another thought, which led to a story.

"For me, it was my grandmother," she said at last, and we resumed our stroll in silence down Main Street to a park bench that we often came to rest on. I waited, sensing her on the bridge.

"She our teacher, my grandmother, magnificent teacher. She drives proud with us in her wagon to one-room school to teach all farm children and ones who live in village. I am the youngest, two years only, but I grow up in the school. We have very little books and other material; all things shared. The old students, they help teach young ones. Enrique learned me to read." She smiled. "Domingo rides in the wagon with us. I know him all my life.

"It is not so good and easy as you think, Alejandro." Maria must have seen dreaminess in my expression. "Our village, high in mountains, it's too cold in winter, and we must bring firewood for stove to keep schoolroom warm. We are many days hungry and sick; sometimes old children are need to work on farms. When I am four, my bigger sister, my favorite, dies. And others die, too. With all such hardness, it may seem foolish to learn reading, writing, adding, subtracting, all the basics you think too much boring. But it is not, and that is thank you to my grandmother, the magnificent teacher. She make us feel like kings and queens for what we learn. She never miss a day to show how important is school."

Maria paused to catch her breath, clearly strained by the effort to find words whose eloquence conveyed the passion her tone held. I was on the verge of offering a supportive remark when she laid a hand on my arm, signaling me to let her continue uninterrupted.

"The eyes of my grandmother, they are like natural water coming up from under the ground—how to say that?"

"Springs. Wellsprings."

"Wellsprings. In Spanish, *ojos*, the same word for eyes and wellsprings. Like fresh water, my grandmother eyes, pure full of joy, of new ideas, of hope and faith. They flow and flow over. She believe we are good to learn, she believe to learn make us grow up, like you say, wise and happy. To learn, yes, but most important, the magnificent teacher make us happy and wise. My grandmother, she teach until she blind, but still, her eyes not seeing nothing, are wellsprings. Still flowing over with her joy and faith in us. She give us these gifts. She is a teacher all her life."

And I, even at this great remove, felt inspired by her. By Maria's eulogy as well. She radiated the dynamism imbued by her grandmother. Her story had provoked a further multitude of questions but more vital, an assurance that the young immigrant students would be in the hands of a compelling teacher and thus would thrive no matter her approach.

Maria turned toward me for her pivotal declaration.

"I become village teacher when my grandmother blind. She tell me this, Alejandro: she say teaching is like loving. Can be in many kinds, can be a wildcat love or a feather love, what is best needed to teach. But must be some kind, because without love nobody learns."

Hadn't I, when I applied for a full-time position, come to the same understanding? And hadn't Justine said likewise? We were, it seemed, kindred spirits who all recognized that teaching is an act of love. The wellspring's confirmation of the truth of that idea swelled through me. What was referred to as a *calling* was the voice of love, summoning our embrace.

"My grandmother, she keep notes of her teachings. On the pages of a book of open paper, her great treasure. She give it to me, and I have it always to read when I teach." She hesitated. "I will borrow it to you."

"Lend," I said automatically. "Oh, sorry. Thank you. I would very much appreciate that."

"Lend? That is good. I like to know more English."

"And I would like to learn more Spanish," occurring to me as I spoke how much I did want to.

"Vivienne can read my grandmother's notes to you and translate to help learn."

I nodded, but from that suggestion a far better one arose. "Or you can read them to me, Maria, and I can tell you what I understand as we go along. I will learn the ideas as well as the language. Then maybe I can try speaking with you in Spanish, and you can correct me when I make mistakes."

The smile she had earlier reserved for memories of her childhood she focused now on me. "Bueno. But you must do the same for me. Give me something of you to read."

I stepped onto the bridge, returned her smile with a grin. My unfinished writings might come to some good use. "Yes," I said, "it's a deal." Paused. "That means I agree with great pleasure."

In bed that night, in the silver hour provoked by unexpected illumination, the words of Maria's grandmother pealed. She had spoken of love as having many guises, a wildcat love, which suggested that she didn't mean coddling, but a love that could be fierce and merciless, though never deliberately cruel. Or a feather love, so light its touch was nearly imperceptible. Moreover, I mused, it's an act of love that creates itself in being given. And its fulfillment lies in…

I began to weave my thoughts together as a way of elucidating them further to myself, Composed, rewrote them on the loom, inventing the pattern of words as I went along, memorizing them until I was satisfied enough to get up and transcribe them to the computer. No chance of recalling them in the morning and little chance of falling asleep until I could.

The next day, after a bit more revision, I decided to try them out on Viv, whom I had told about Maria's extraordinary grandmother and our shared beliefs about the art we practiced.

"Teaching is an act of love," I began with a nod, "that creates itself in being given, transcends the understanding it endows, and is made manifest in the reverence for truth and virtue it bestows. It is a love that seeks the learners' fruition by revealing the promise of their gifts to them. It is a love that calls us from the haven of ourselves to make a life among other learners who are also called to discover that which can only be gleaned through the communal art of teaching."

I exhaled. "Suggestions?"

Viv shone affirmation. "It's beautiful. As is. I'll help you translate it into Spanish as a gift for Maria." A worthy challenge, to read it to her. "Really, Gloria and all of your teachers should have a copy." I started to protest. "As a working document they can revise or add to. A place to start."

It was only that. As Maria and I made our slow way through her grandmother's notes, I discovered a treasure of anecdotes recounted by a woman who possessed inspiring empathy and insights into children. Oralia Morales discerned potential in their restless meanders, found ways to ignite their imaginations in the wasteland of cold and hunger. And as she had done with the children, her creative powers and her fortitude spellbound me. Emboldened, humbled by her wit, her tenacity, her faith in education, the yearning to begin teaching swelled to an ache that sang through my dreams.

30

Many Roads to the Mountain

When Rosie and I were at Hunter Elementary and tight friends, on blustery days we used to stand together at the edge of the playground during recess, arms wide, leaning into the wind. Silent and apart yet as one, we billowed, reveling in the sensation of weightlessness, pressing forward against the wind that bore us back: the ecstatic freedom of being held suspended in air.

As Maria and I got to know each other through her grandmother's notes, I flashed on that feeling of letting myself go: leaning into a wind of equilibrium. Even while our friendship retained an element of formality, it grew from collegial to close. She spoke with me as if honesty had no inverse and our words were a tangible force with enduring consequences. Silence, too, furthered communication, our thoughts rolling unbroken from its midst into speech. Captivated by Oralia Morales's notes, Maria and I each attained enough fluency to be at ease in the other's language.

The notes! I was not only stunned by Señora Morales' ingenuity as a teacher and her sagacity as a thinker, but also by her eloquence as a writer. This woman from a remote village could have, under different circumstances, been a star in the education galaxy. Instead she had shone unobserved, enlightening her fortunate students and now, by extension, me. In one note of particular significance to my development as a teacher, she set down an aspect of her philosophy of learning:

"Children do not travel a single path to learning. They move like creatures of the wild, foraging, seeking comfort and safety. They wander where their needs take them. At times they meet to drink from the same river, then go off on their own again."

I am translating loosely, but that is the insight one of her notes conveyed. It brought to my mind a Zen story I'd heard from Mamia's friend Ariadne years ago. Ari was encouraging me to worry less about what my teachers expected of me and more about what I expected of myself, suggesting that I might have to head out on my own to achieve a true understanding. As the initiate in this tale discovers:

An old Zen Buddhist monk has a novice who serves and studies with him. The young monk is stunned by his mentor's visionary wisdom and asks him one day how he gained such breadth of knowledge. The elder points to a peak beyond the monastery and tells the novice that deep in the mountain dwells a master whose acumen surpasses all others, and it was this sage who taught him all that he knows. So, with gratitude, the novice leaves to go in search of the master.

After many, many years he returns, no longer a young man, and finding the ancient monk on his deathbed, kneels to whisper in his ear. "Sensei, I have traveled all through the mountain, following the direction you pointed me in, and yet I have not found the master whose acumen surpasses all others."

The ancient one turns his face toward him. "Ah, my son," he says, "there are many roads to the mountain. Your road and my road are not the same."

Though they had traveled very different roads, they were drinking from the same river, Oralia Morales and the Zen master. I wondered whether there was a metaphorical book of wisdom that all gifted teachers had read, a common understanding they all shared and if so, whether it had to be rediscovered by every neophyte who sought to excel. "Lost and found and lost again and again," T. S. Eliot murmured. It ought to be passed along genetically, like an instinct, I snapped back at him. Fight, flight, teach. Superbly.

Building on her grandmother's notes, Maria and I constructed a framework for the school I was coming to think of as ours. She convinced me of the importance of the foundation and a common central ladder; I persuaded her of the inspiration of the spire and the individualized periphery. We clambered about on our scaffold, separately and together, helping each other to join the pieces into a supportive whole.

Gaps in understanding remained, but with attentive respect we overleapt them. Given the difference in our status in the school, community, and culture, I believed it was primarily my responsibility to do the jumping. When to my chagrin I was unaware of a rift in our perceptions, Maria helped me to realize it. As happened on the morning that talk turned from the one-room school to my ill-fated Trove cabin aerie, which grabbed her interest and led us in due course to slog the mountainous terrain to my place. She wanted to see the cabin, claiming it might serve as a home for her family despite my disparaging account of its stark condition and inaccessibility. Unthinkable to me that a family could live there, but therein lay the rift I had failed to see.

The approach to the cabin was a steep haul in summer, precipitous now in winter, snowdrifts obscuring rocks and sheered edges. The day was brilliantly cold, a high wind lilting the trees. We trudged single-file, each step laid down with caution. Maria's jacket was thin, her boots rubber; a small woman, she was bound to be freezing. But undeterred, she trekked behind me, her sure-footed vigor driving us on. When we crested the last slope and arrived at the cabin, she was not even breathing hard.

No one had lived here since the night of the storm, and I had only been back once with Mamia to assuage her curiosity about the desolate cabin where I'd nearly perished. Wanted to be rid of it but hadn't bothered, my current plan being to let the cabin return to the earth through benign neglect, perhaps thereby freeing its ghosts. Inaction: the default mode—mine, not Maria's.

"Ay, que vistas hermosas!" she exclaimed. "Alejandro, this is where God comes to take joy in His creation."

"It's also where ghosts come. As I found out and the previous owner did, too. Drove us both away."

Maria eagle-eyed me. "We all have our ghosts. It is our duty to honor them, give them place at the table. Unhappy, homesick, lost souls are haunting ghosts. Tranquil ones, a blessing. But they are all ours to live with and to love."

She was right, as my own waning companions in the aspen grove had illumined for me.

Inside, the place looked just as it had when I bought it except for mouse turds in the corners, though only a few as there was nothing to eat but the walls. Maria inspected the interior with great care, tapping beams, rocking the floor, squinting at the roof, examining the window and woodstove. Measuring it in her head. At the door, she nodded.

"The house is built strong. Good boards, no holes or bendings. Can you help me see the roof?"

I stirruped my hands for her foot, and gripping a porch column, she propelled herself up. Her upper body flattened against the roof, she tested the shingles within reach.

"Pretty good, I think." And slid down.

We stood for a moment surveying the landscape. The view really was dazzling. Backdropped by the Rocky Mountains, pine, aspen, and spruce undulated over hills down to the Rio Sol, an intermittent gleam. A pair of hawks sailed the blue. Definitely a panorama postcard. I'd not bothered to look around when I was negotiating deliveries to Chewie.

"How much you sell for?"

I thought a hundred, to break even, but luckily forsook that idea before opening my mouth. "For nothing."

"You will not sell?" Astonished, misunderstanding my intentions.

"For no money. Nothing. It is yours, Maria. I will sign over the deed. Hard to imagine how you will live here in winter, but if you want to—" at which point I was almost swept down the torrential chasm. "Where are you living now?"

She shrugged. "Nowhere good. Seven in two rooms. And we have to pay."

Seven people in two rooms. Christ. I tried to think through what that would be like, for sleeping, for meals, using the bathroom. How could Maria be so composed and stalwart coming daily from those conditions? How could she even function? Obviously Trove had not been as hospitable as I thought. And what about you, Mann? My house, its spacious rooms, inhabited only by Viv and me: the living/dining downstairs area could easily sleep five, maybe more. Never occurred to me to offer refuge. If Maria saw it—the idea flushed me inward with embarrassment. Seven people in two rooms.

Maria packed her body into a resolute stance. "Here, for our own place, Domingo and Enrique build more rooms. They are very skilled, you know that."

I did, from their work on the lodge.

"Estrella be happy here, too. *Will* be happy," she corrected herself. "We can make the road better. Bring wood." A narrow smile. "I tell you once, remember, we grow up with no water or electric or heat. Here we *will* do more; here we *will* live well."

No doubt. And I would help insure that. Contribute building materials. Road equipment. Whatever they needed.

"It's great that you are including Domingo in your family."

A quick frown of incomprehension. "Domingo is my husband." Head cocked, dawning. "You think Enrique is?"

I nodded, ignorance once again flustering me. It had never occurred to me that those two could be a pair. "I've seen you and Enrique together a lot. And him with Estrella."

"Enrique is my brother. He and Domingo are best friends. We are all." Maria's face turned to pain. "Domingo was in our youth a beautiful man, so handsome and good. We love each other very much." Breathed deeply to regain her calm. "Enrique lives with us. His wife and little boy, they were killed in the massacre."

How had I gone the last many weeks without learning these crucial facets of her history? Assuming I knew more than I did, making up my own stories that fit my sense of who she was. I shook my head internally. Thought I'd overcome the impulse to create others in my image of them.

"I'm sorry I didn't know, Maria." My head bowed, asking her pardon, then lifted to catch her gaze, which was fixed in the distance. "It's a blessing the four of you were able to stay together." The journey to Trove abruptly came into focus, struck me as impossible. Maria hauling her husband near death, her brother badly wounded, her little daughter for thousands of miles.

"Not us only. All who are alive after the massacre travel together. Save each other."

She brought her eyes back to mine, checking me out again, to be sure. "You give us the cabin, Alejandro?"

"I do. And you live happily ever after in it."

Stretched out her hand to me. "It's a deal!"

The cabin exhaled in relief.

I clambered out of the rift. The sun of new truths lit my heart. Still and all, it would be a massive undertaking to make this place habitable for the four of them.

Refugees are birds on forced migration who carry within them the map of their homeward flight. Perching temporarily where they can, they keep watch equally for danger and opportunity. My cabin, hers, staking the high ground, was a defensible spot from which threats could be seen at a great distance. Perhaps that was one reason the place appealed to Maria. Her more vital aim being to root in a new land. Albeit in this case, one less fertile than the home they were driven from.

They have to forget so much, these refugees who had winged desolately north. So much of what they knew is useless here. Which wild plants are edible, when to plant a garden, how to cook what grows, what to wear and how to make such clothing, how to converse in the tongue they did not arrive knowing. One thing they will not forget is that they can always lose their home wherever it is, that no home is more secure than life, which is at every moment eradicable. We would like the place we've lived to outlast us, but that is the wish of innocence or arrogance. I, too, remember how easy it is to lose your home.

To find a new one required Maria's tenacity and vision—or my dumb luck. And for both of us, a friend.

On a Sunday afternoon in November I wandered into what had been the lobby of the old miners' lodge, which now had insulation, new wiring, plumbing, dry wall, and subfloor. This and the bathroom off of it is where we would start. The one window framed a craggy ridge that overlooked Trove, offering a spectacular vista, though just a slice of what lay beyond the pane. Looking at the burly clouds tumbling by dizzied me, and my mind pulled apart, strands of it alighting on moments as yet unlived that might be. In that unfettered state, I saw the schoolroom completed, radiant with morning, the window open in spring to admit a slender breeze, and under it the deep ledge Orlando had built as a place for kids to rest and ruminate. "You can learn plenty from daydreaming," a claim he made with firm authority. I settled myself crosswise on that ledge and wandered farther into the future. Saw the embrace of trees between outcroppings ascending the ridge, and in the classroom, their wood hewn into table and chairs, floor, sill, ceiling, benches, doors. The light streaming in stirred an enchantment that suffused all that transpired here. Education made magic, revealing the wizards and sages beneath ordinary demeanors. The fables they spun between these walls elevating them to erudite, virtuous, benevolent souls. I smiled, returning to the present. The ledge worked. In a flash it had conjured lofty musings from this vibrant winter afternoon.

A meadowlark trilled on a fencepost, and I leaned over to catch a glimpse of it. As often as I'd heard the song, it never failed to induce sweet melancholy. The lark called again, from somewhere beyond the periphery of the window—which, I realized with a jolt, could be a symbol of last spring's senior program: a window that was meant to open into an ever broader view in years to come. But the students entering my extended mentor program would need the full landscape of possibilities to explore from the outset and onward. More than a window: the whole sphere, origins and related influences, known worlds and those waiting to be born. A vision unimpeded by walls, a sense of expansiveness that would grow yearslong with them. Rio's kaleidoscopic wide-angle lens came into focus as I deciphered its translation into curriculum. "There's plenty to see," he'd said. "A lifetime's worth." My breath caught. Some great new beast of an idea was emerging from its lair. The weight of it propelled me to my feet and home to Viv.

She sat bundled on the veranda, watching the crimsoning sky. I slowed my approach, hesitant to disturb her peace, and aware, for the first time acutely aware, of the heartsore whose gnaw I'd been disregarding. Viv.

Though this year was set, I knew she would not, could not, stay on and on to teach with me. Someday college lay ahead for her, a life bigger than Trove. I had come to cherish her as a housemate with benefits, meaning someone to talk with honestly about my days in the classroom and beyond. She had collaborated on the planning of my first year teaching here, had reviewed the success of our strategies after and revised them when needed. She was integral to every aspect of this new school, a gifted teacher and planner, so young but so instinctively right, immensely creative and engaging. Viv's devotion gave our work significance. It would hurt to live here and teach without her.

"Alex," she yawned, pushing herself onto her feet. "Dinner's ready." Over her shoulder, leading me in. "There's something I need to talk to you about."

"Same here." Thinking this could be a natural lead-in to her plans.

Viv's culinary expertise was another housemate benefit I'd enjoyed. It had put some beef on my emaciated frame, which pleased me but not nearly as much as it did Mamia. The carne adovada casserole, crisp and aromatic, sizzled as she drew it from the oven. I was quiet after initial words of praise, trying to hold on to my beast and find an opener for asking about her.

"You go first." Viv's usual directive. She liked to build on my foundation.

"You know T. S. Eliot, my source and solace and inspiration?"

"T. S. practically lives with us. 'In my beginning is my end. In my end is my beginning.'"

"Exactly!"

"Exactly what?"

"'The end is where we start from.' In the program for the mentored students. It can lead us back to the beginning. Where we've come from as the opening focus rather than where we're going. Just for instance, what are the origins of rocket science? You know Ed's interested in that." Despite, or more accurately because of the "greaser" incident, Ed and Jaime and I had gotten close. Both of them would be students in the new mini-school, along with four others, self-selected.

I answered my own question. "Stars, planets, nebulae—an insatiable craving to fly among them, to explore them. So, yes, for Ed: astronomy. Learn more about where he might go, not simply how to get there. And," my thoughts roving now among heretofore unaddressed possibilities, "for Ruth the genesis of theater, which will take her into distant rituals and ceremonies. And further, into archaeology.

"Carina, the budding novelist, can go back into the history and the art of bookmaking. I remember seeing an old letterpress in the museum storeroom. Maybe it can be resurrected, she become a printer."

Viv jumped aboard. "And learn bookbinding." Minds aligned, spirits synced: conceptual convergence. Happens more often than you might guess in a setting of pastoral quietude.

"And write stories from different eras. Study movements in literature, which will lead her into social and cultural ones. Write in the styles of the times, of prominent authors. She'll find her voice through coming to know theirs. I'll create an extensive reading list." Which I was inspired to do right then, my thoughts flooded with possibilities.

Fork halfway to the plate, Viv had stopped eating. Her eyes, illumined by the last rays, flickered green-gold. Staring intently at the tines as though they emanated wisdom, she tongue-wiped her lips, sat forward.

"Darcy, remember how he read about panning for gold and wanted to try it himself? He ended up being much more interested in the organisms populating the water he was sluicing than the gold. He could go back in history, too, to the formation of the earth, how it evolved and the multiple roles water played. Get to know watersheds, environmental politics, the interplay of human and natural forces. That will carry him into the oceans. Currents worldwide, the life and health of rivers and seas. Their animals and plants." She shook her head. "It's a lot more than he can learn in ten years."

"I know, but he'll learn what and how to learn more as he goes on." I was an unassailable force on the charge.

Viv nodded. "The fair Ms. Mayflower, as you call her, will need less guidance than freedom. Like her brother, perhaps even more of a prodigy. Structure, yes, to build her days on, but little else."

"Agreed." I walked to the stove and heated some water for cocoa. The cats wandered in.

"Jaime wants to become a doctor, which means he'll have to have some serious equipment, like a high-powered microscope," Viv reflected. "A skeleton. Creatures to dissect. We can ask for donations. Lori will do a great job of teaching him biology and the fundamentals of medicine, but, like Skip, he needs to see the skills applied, practice them, do an internship, maybe with Doctor Darrell. Although I know how you feel about him, Alex." Purple jumpsuit, goat meat, muzak. Yeah, no.

"We might want to look a little further. And then why shouldn't Jaime also study the history of medicine from a variety of cultural perspectives? That's a rich and controversial field. Also the roles different belief systems played in healing. Plants and other sources of cures. That should be enough to keep him busy—and all of them and us and other mentors. Lots of research into finding valid source materials, which we'll be teaching them how to do as we learn. But I'm pumped. This feels like the right way to go." I was on my feet, roughing the floorboards like an anxious pony. Scooped up Tiger, who, in preparation for another massacre after a long day's nap into night, had been winding himself between the chair legs in quest of any leftover crumbs. At moments of exhilaration, I liked to squeeze him like a stress ball.

"There's lots of crossover," I went on, "so the kids will have common ground for discussion and collaboration, interdisciplinary but focused at the same time. New and yet such a natural progression. It strikes me we'll be steering them toward the kinds of thing people of earlier eras, living close to the land, would have sought to know. The essential wellsprings of civilization."

"I love it!" Viv cut in. "Such an amazing spectrum of journeys." She paused, closed her eyes. "In my mind I see them as crepuscular rays, lighting possible routes into and beyond their imagining. Wider and wider the farther they go." A fluttery smile, pleased with her evocative metaphor.

"You are a remarkable teacher, Mr. Alex Mann. I feel so lucky to be here, right now, at the inception of this idea. It's like standing at the threshold of terra incognita. But—"

"You won't be around for long to see where it leads." I sat down, hanging onto Tiger. "No worries. I knew this would happen. It's incredibly great to have you with me, Viv. But I know you have your own future to consider. You've been—"

"That's not what I was going to say." She picked up La Negra, who had come looking for Tiger and stood by Viv's chair, switching her tail in aggravation. I took a quick mental snapshot of our symmetry, the two of us facing each other, cat to cat.

"What I was going to say is remember to go slow. Start with the students, as you often remind me. You've made all these astonishing leaps between concepts, which we should write down, but the students need to make their own, over time, according to their personal inclinations. Like, for instance, Carina may not be interested in bookmaking but language, the etymology of words she uses, or languages, learning several, translating, who knows what. We can suggest the existence of these pathways, but setting off on them is their choice. And it will be their call as to whether the journey is compelling or dead ends."

Ah, Vivienne. At twenty she had the intelligence and wisdom of an elder. Perhaps she was what Mamia's neighbor Tularosa called an old soul, someone who, in the Hindu belief, had been reincarnated this time as a mature woman, born with several lifetimes' experience in her compass.

I affirmed Viv's insight with a vigorous nod before returning to her inevitable departure. Preferred to rip the bandage than peel it. "In any case, I know I can't count on you staying beyond next year." Tiger slipped to the floor and headed out. I reached over and draped my hand on hers. "Seriously, I'm so thankful to have you with me at the new school's inception. And as a housemate. You are at the heart of everything good that happens, in the classroom and here at home, and—"

"And here's what you do need to know." She smiled, eyes on mine. "I have loved being a part of your life, working with you, with the students, the genesis of the mentor program and the new school, living on this magnificent land. I feel at home here as I never have elsewhere. If you'll keep me, I'll gladly stay."

She waved off my trout-in-the-air mouth. "Oh, yeah, don't worry, I'll finish college at some point, but I'm learning much more here than I would there. So many ways to get a degree now without leaving home. Like, I've looked at an online program in Cultural Studies that sounds right for me."

Viv forked her last bite and leaned back, sated from stomach to brain.

The evening star had long since been eclipsed by a galaxy-studded sky, and no Tinkerbell glimmered in the rafters, but an undreamed wish had been fulfilled. Viv staying. Our lives together going on. Friends. Partners. Colleagues. Who knew but I would someday add Spouse to that line-up, I thought before laughing at that preposterous notion. Beauty and the Beast. Disney-doodle-dandy, Bug: snap out of it, Hersch would have said. Be glad of what you have. And truly I was. Am.

Talking, we crossed the dateline; late arced into early. Neither of us was tired. Viv had been recording all our ideas, apprehending that we had entered a magical zone of inspiration that would be hard to reconstruct. One idea built on the next as concentric waves of thought lapped outward toward a receding shore. How to introduce this program to the students and their mentors (of whom we would need more or others), procure resources, invent trajectories and consider the challenges to their fruitful outcome. Her stack of notes grew daunting, but some intoxicating stream of energy pulsed us obsessively onward. Shortly before first light I made coffee and defrosted cinnamon rolls. Not for over a year had I pulled an all-nighter, and I exulted afresh in the state of heightened clarity it induced. Or at least the perception of that state.

"We must provide opportunities for each of our students to teach, Viv. Really teach. More than making presentations and putting on exhibits. As an essential part of their schooling, a contemporary version of what Maria's grandmother did in her one-room schoolhouse. For instance…"

On and on we went until the sky was radiant with dawn and I began to mix up words, said "relevation" for revelation without noticing, threw extra syllables into adverbs, like "looseley" speaking, and substituted gibberish for English, as in "forelocken asperance," which might have meant "For instance" or "forgotten experience." Viv stretched and wavered to her feet. "Time for bed," she announced. Right again, as I stiff-backed myself up from the chair.

"What an incredible night!" She rounded the table, took me in her arms and held on, an unprecedented gesture of intimacy. If you stay very still, my lone waking brain cell murmured, she'll keep hugging you. Which I did, and she. Her burnished hair against my cheek, head cradled in my neck, breast to rib, groin in the crook of my legs, which enclosed hers. Our nerves vibrating in unison as they conveyed the pleasure message to our recharged brains. Yes, *our*, because when she spoke again, it was about a hug outlasting our embrace.

"Alex," her voice smothered in my shirt, "if ten years from now neither of us has a life partner, would you marry me? It can be a friend-marriage, you know. You don't have to sleep with me or anything, though I would kind of like to have a child. But not if you don't want to."

I held her more tightly to signal concurrence.

"I will. Yes to everything, yes to whatever you want. But, Viv, I think it's very likely that you'll find a terrific young man your age and fall in love with him before you're thirty. Already Rio would give up everything for you. Your charisma and intelligence have inflamed him. And, believe me, there will be a slew of others. Once the men around here discover you're available, I'll have to put a deadbolt on the door."

"I'm as torn with scars as you are, Mann, but mine are not as visible." Here she disentangled herself from my arms, encountering some resistance as these limbs sought of their own volition to hang onto her. Face to mine, lips less than a kiss breadth apart.

"You'll go slow, Alex. You'll be gentle. Patient. You understand about scars. I won't have to explain or apologize."

"You won't ever have to do anything you don't want to," my voice fervent, "with me." I stepped back. Her proposal was the kind of gift you put in a treasure chest not for use but for the secret joy of knowing that it was given you with love and is yours.

Viv swayed unsteadily, her arms loose, eyes fuzzy. "Bed. I'm so tired." She smiled into the light, "Need a few hours rest."

Me, too, so weary, I thought after her, rebuking the stairs for having to be climbed. Sleep cloaked my shoulders. But not yet. Sludging toward the door when Tiger intercepted me with a meow and a nigh trip-fall. I growled at his audacity; he laser-looked me back. Sunrise may be bedtime for you, bub, but for me it's breakfast. For her, too, the dame in black, his face added as Montenegra rippled up behind him. Double scoops and a can of tuna.

I reached down to stroke him, and he spooled infinity between my legs, purring, his cheek rubbing my foot. It was an obsequious gesture made with the sole intent of procuring a meal. Tiger, my beloved overlord who has seen me through a rugged twelve years. A lot more trouble than you signed up for, but you've handled it magnanimously. Heroically, in truth. Big paws, big heart, as no one says but I. Long tail, longevity. You better stick around to see how it all turns out.

La Negra joined Tiger's parade, and cat-manacled, I scuffed to the cupboard where their food was stored. Dished and spooned the allotted amount of dry and wet, the latter a redundancy as they had surely dined on live wet during their nocturnal foray. It's good that I expect no thanks, I telepathed to them, since you give me none. See you in bed.

Tomorrow had indeed become today. Fatigue wracked my mind, but my excitement had not abated. I lay down vibrating wakefulness, my bones throbbing. If only a ten-minute nap would rest me so I could go forward as though today were tomorrow. If only sleep were a choice we made, like what to eat or where to hike. A thing we could postpone till we were ready. Simply one of many ways to restore ourselves, some less elusive. A tall glass of spring water and done. A back scratch and you're good to go. A tender thought and like new. A kiss. A splash of wind, a wind of light. A waft of lilacs. River's purl. Soughing of memory. The ancient cadence of trees lofting into dawn.

The End that Was in the Beginning

I drowse, a state of liminal consciousness in which the sense of being awake is not in measure with measured time, sleep is self-aware, and bobbing between them, like flickers of sun in a brook, dreams are memories and ruminations, the past and the possible. After the long night's journey into day, I arrive where I started, at the end that was in the beginning. Weary, elated, I bask in the first-light avian choirings, a crescendo of surround-sound in my summer woodland quarters. Leisure is the unconstrained gift of this spell, a quieting of the spirit that no longer exists apart from the flow of the whole. I am and am not, I know and do not, I can and cannot, but liberated from wants and desires, the difference between them is immaterial.

This is the hour when my thoughts snag on downstream filigree, purl through a lattice of images, and released, drift on.

Mamia ripples past, my stronghold, mother-saint, beloved by all who enter her sphere, she to whom I and others turn with absolute assurance her heart is always open. Here she is with my boyhood hand in hers, kissing my father good-morning, laughing with Hersch, feeding Caleb, Tiger. Giving Rose the warmth she sought, Lori refuge, Frank care and a place to die. And here she is with his ashes, which she offers Clarice, who declines. Mamia then considers scattering them in Trove but hesitates, keeps them in a closet in the guest room until finally she releases them, all alone, across a mountain vale where she and Frank once picnicked, west of Summerville, home of his final gig. Ashes. A leaf catches at my throat before skittering on. Some, pray very distant, day it will be my turn. Mamia has bought a place in Trove, where, welcomed by the natives and courted by several, she has made herself a home. Dave, one particularly ardent suitor who would have been on his knees to her if (in Floyd's words) "his bald head hadn't been over his heels in love," would marry her tomorrow. Dave cautions her, "Don't wait till you lose your good looks, Shel," like she wasn't getting more radiant with the years, like she was ever short of dinner and dance partners: not my mother. She and Chloe have formed a close friendship and are exploring the idea of opening a bookstore together. Meantime, she helps at the school, elevating Miranda Michelle to an advanced pupil who at seven is reading Greek mythology. Mamia, universally adored, the rising sign I was born under.

Rose, bonnie lass of Scotland, my first love and dear friend, dwells contented with Justine in scholarly pursuits, writes and visits occasionally, she who granted me a home and helped fund the school, nexus and purpose. The Tess of the d'Urbervilles rosebush I planted in her honor, the one I was trimming only yesterday, thrives by the veranda, its full-scented blossoms drawing bees and hummingbirds. Rose, close as a sister, a path that forked from mine, stemmed from a common source. Ancient eddies subtext our talks and letters.

Joaquin, friend for eleven years, rival for just part of one, alter-father and fellow writer. The two of us running the rapids together. My point of entry into Trove. He has become a man of peace, which is a kind of happiness more reverent than euphoric. His anger diluted, though it still falls short of clear-water. Mornings in the greenhouse, where he has developed a rapport with the plants akin to what I had, afternoons with Lori and Miranda and poetry, evenings with songs and neighbors. He's farmed out deliveries, and his business is growing. Not likely nor seeking to be stock-market rich in this lifetime.

Lori and I, our lives twined daily at the school and still in undercurrents of which we speak privately, a blessing of overwintered youth. Now when we come upon each other at Yeats' grave, where we each go to commemorate and beg forgiveness repeatedly of our son, which, merciful babe, he always confers, and of one another, it is a gift we, too, mutually bestow. I caused her fall, in every sense, and his. She left his fate to the gods, and they, justly outraged by her coldness, took him from her. We retrace our shared sorrow in code. Humility long ago cleared the dark air between us, gave us a truer secret than Yeats' fatherhood. Razed the palisade we once constructed against empathy. Her betrayal does not cancel mine but mirrors it, each reflecting the other. We can look upon one another unflinchingly and with gratitude for our durable friendship, for Miranda and Tiger, for the profound fulfillment of teaching together.

So much to hold on to, so much to let go.

The marry-me maid of red-gold hair and brimming heart swirls by, she who lives now in Florence with Anton, whose name's origin bespeaks his character: "Highly praiseworthy." Anton, roommate to Rio sophomore year who came to visit, lured by tales of Trove, Viv, the school. Anton, brilliant young man of exceeding wealth, ambition, talent, with chiseled features and an Italian villa, who in turn lured Viv away from us—though she stays in touch. Rio, distraught, foundered, the landscape of his heart in ruins. But he is a man of extraordinary resilience and will prevail, being, as I assure him, still destined for greatness though bereft of Viv. As am I, the perpetual second best man, who sleeps solo in his bower.

But I haven't been, as Trudel used to say, squatting on my pity pot: a bit of Texas color she'd picked up that suited her remorseless nature. The Trove School, now a charter that encompasses the original institution, continues to be a wellspring of joy from which we all drink avidly, new ideas burbling forth, carving tributaries that flow together and apart but all streaming into a broad reservoir that nourishes us. Gloria remains at the helm of the school, but Maria and I are program co-directors, exactly as we want to be. She and I continue to teach and learn a great deal from each other, not simply about ideas and methods but about the rewards of working collaboratively. Five years in, our program has revealed the capacity of young children to become creative partners in their education, to build their own vessels for learning and sail them on rich voyages into unexpected harbors. We are onboard with them, to guide, advise, and navigate as needed, help them anchor their studies in requisite skills. Happily, the serious excitement bred by this approach among even the younger students is infectious; it is becoming a rooted behavior and outlook.

Secure on the crest of a ridge, Maria and her family have made of Chewie's dubious cabin a comfortable abode. Three bedrooms, a live-in kitchen, and a bathroom, the last a gift from Mamia and me that included the well and plumbing. Not surprisingly, four more casitas have sprung up along the mountainside, bermed into what looked like an impossibly steep slope where they snug the land. At first I wondered whether this little colony would segregate the refugees, but not so in Trove. The communal labor that the town's needs dictate keeps us mingled, all skills on deck. The colony's members are the remnant band of massacre survivors from the same village, and living here in close proximity evokes their homeworld. Maria is as near as they have to a leader, matriarch and magistrate, mentor and mother. Her position at the school garners her unconditional respect in every role.

An added boon is that the school has contributed substantially to the economic wellbeing of Trove, including these newcomers, and thereby strengthened the sense of community. Better still, the school has fortified the townspeople's incomes through fulfilling work. Our mentors bring a wide range of talents to the students, from academic to artistic to practical. Education as we define it is not limited to traditional expectations nor directed to a single end. We were granted that freedom through our charter and have evidenced its worth through our students' accomplishments, which have been made known. My last year's annual narrative for Rose grew into an article that has been published to some acclaim, through which more grants have been procured, our resources now bountiful, mentors well paid, classes and coffers full. It's a highly enviable situation these days, some of which is attributable purely to luck, but the small size of The Trove School is also of crucial import. And while ours is clearly not a model that works for the mass-market public education system, its success is being replicated elsewhere.

Among the most beloved mentors is Aria. She runs an innovative math program built on principles and patterns that, in her words "begins with wonder and ends with awe" and has drawn national attention. She also heads a vibrant drama project, teaching acting, directing, writing, and tech, as well as the literature and history of the theater, its social and political impact, and a wide range of interactive life skills. Summers she works with the Classic Theater in Trove in various capacities on stage and off. The two students who are apprenticed to her there are enamored of the theater but also intrigued by the many avenues open to them through it. I am likewise enamored: of Aria. Since Boone's eviction for drunk-and-disorderly conduct, she has no attachments other than Darcy. And Mamia is very fond of Aria, the breadth of their camaraderie greater than mentoring at the school. I see their friendship as laying the groundwork for our becoming a family. That Aria hasn't yet shown any romantic interest in me would be disheartening to a less seasoned swain.

With each love that ascends on the horizon I notice myself becoming less desperate, which seems illogical since I'm not getting any prettier with age. Nor am I less lonely though I'm rarely alone. I fantasize with the same erotic ardor as in my younger days, and more explicitly now. Introduced to a new woman, I inquire about her with an eye to finding a possible mate. I yearn and in the restive hours between midnight and morning, occasionally despair. Bachelorhood is not a state I can conceive of settling into or for. Yet whoever comes next, whatever love grows fruitful, I will not be the impetuous, demanding man I was. No pitching myself at her, no burying myself in her, no being transported into another realm. No illusion that love requires not less than everything. It will be a giving of what can be and an acceptance of what cannot be. A gentle union at the border of two souls. And I bear in mind Viv's caution to go slow.

Learning to go slower than your inner compulsion takes time, which might sound ironic but is absolutely, rivetingly obvious, since time itself is the measure of pace. And though it is, we use it to mean far more, treat it as a palpable commodity rather than a space and a span we inhabit.

Driving the urge to speed up is the misconception that the more we accomplish, the more we have stuffed into an hour, a day, a week, the more time we have somehow found, engendered, made. Yet when we fill every minute with achievement, the universal cry is, "I have no time!" In truth, time is widened by frugality: Use less, have more.

Above all we elegize the timelessness of childhood. Sigh together in nostalgic recall of the elasticity of our days when we frolicked unawares of using or losing time. Time was as we were, and that, I have come to think, is the uncomplicated key to setting a pace we can live by. To immerse ourselves in what we are doing, in who we are being, alone and among others of every species, is the inestimable measure of our passage. We live by our own dictates, and time courses around us, adhering to our strides, its tempo set by us.

For me going slow has become a song of praise. I say "Hats off" to Camus' Grand, writing and revising one sentence to perfection. I think of Rilke, whose ten *Duino Elegies* emerged year by year for a decade. Or Sophocles' *Oedipus Cycle*, a lifetime's unfolding in three dramas that reflect the wisdom of age, finished when he had the perspective of eighty-some years and saw the world over the shoulder of death. Writing is no longer about how far I get in an hour or a month, when I'll be done with this project or that or how old I will be when I do. Writing is what I am at home doing when I am, a ritual I've created to sustain myself. Sophocles' eighty years, even Rilke's ten, no longer seem astounding or repelling. It is the arc that their pieces drew them through: arriving at the end that lay in the beginning, they grasp, for the first time, the sprung heart of what they've written.

Which reminds me of a story I heard about a woman in the north country who was swallowed by an avalanche. She was not found by the rescuers yet emerged on her own from the snow and staggered off across the mountains. Ended up at some indeterminate point in a small settlement of twelve families, a mountain hamlet where she had seemingly never been, but on her arrival she knew everybody, though no one knew her, a kind of reverse amnesia. Or maybe, they thought, she'd come from a different time, one long past, one yet to come. She was familiar with all their stories, the ancestral lore of many generations, their customs and beliefs, familial interweave. Shunned at first as a witch, she was at last taken in by an old couple who chose to see her as an emissary of the divine, an angel come to take the place of their long-dead child, whom she remembered. It's a story that to my mind suggests that perhaps on some inaccessible plane we all know one another, simply no longer recognize each the other.

Much as you who've come all this way with me know that you've made a new friend, one you can depend on. You can pull into my driveway and find a welcome any day. If you're willing to pitch in, it doesn't matter why you're here. Maybe you've had a thought about shifting from wind to tree, rooting somewhere, whether you're a pioneer species or incline toward settled ground. Yearning perhaps to call forth a lover from the expanse of anonymous bodies you graze on your journey to an uncertain destination. I can't help you much there yet except to say, forge the home in yourself that others seek. And go slow.

If you come just now, there'll be no one at the house, but leave your stuff on the veranda and walk up to the grove, where I'll be dozing in my summer bed. You'll hear the avian choir and the wakening sibilance of children hidden in the trees, their voices like waves lapping a harbor. Stretch out for a bit; I'll join you when the sun crests Indigo Peak.

A foresighted visitor, you'll have lined your pockets with cat treats so Tiger and La Negra, back from the night's safari, will cuddle up beside you. There's nothing more relaxing than the feline duo purring, in sync. And no better endorsement than theirs.

The cats may be your port of entry, but thenceforward it's your move. That you can greet everyone here by name, jump right into the conversation like the woman in that story, renders you the stranger in familiar territory whose power is unveiling common ground by showing us who you are, who we are. We all bear scars, and most have tight-roped over death at least once, a shock that still fracks the memory. Yet beyond these strata dwell intimations of unrealized kinship quarried from our yen to be known and embraced whole. That's where you come in.

About the Author

E. A. GRAY has published work in a number of genres and venues, under this and her common name, Lisa Gray Fisher. Her poetry has appeared in diverse journals, ranging from the Parisian zine *Breakfast All Day* to *The Christian Science Monitor, Mediphors, and War, Literature, and the Arts.*

In 2015 she published a comedic novel entitled Full Body Wag (see fullbodywagbook. com for a fuller description). Two characters from that tale cross over into this one in far more serious and complex roles. Gray's most recent endeavor is a play script, still in development.

By summers (and now full-time) a writer, during the school-year season Gray has been an English teacher at Santa Fe Community College and for most of her career, at Santa Fe Preparatory School, where she headed the English department for twenty years. Earlier, she worked as an editor at the trade division of Houghton Mifflin in Boston and as a drama teacher, both of which experiences proved invaluable in the English classroom. Gray's inventive electives became a hallmark of her multifaceted work at Santa Fe Prep, courses such as Rebels, Outcasts, and Imposters, The Darkness Within, The Soul of Wit, Awakened Voices, On the Road, and Hinges of Light. The thinking she did with so many brilliant students in her classes, and all that she learned from and with them, serve as the foundation for *Memory's Fire.*

Gray's love of the Southwest is endemic. Raised in Colorado, she and her husband Rick, in turn, raised their children in New Mexico, across a state borderline that does not interrupt the flow of rivers or run of mountains. The immense land- and sky-scapes of this region are embedded in Memory's Fire, beloved by her characters as they are by her. At present, the fragility of the Southwest under the onslaught of climate crisis is a constant source of anguish that triggers an advance nostalgia for what may well be lost.

Acknowledgments

I lit *Memory's Fire* with the love of teaching, writing, family. The story does not parallel lived experience, but the ideas are an expression of my views of this triad known and revered. Where the story came from, in its many iterations, remains a mystery to me. Each chapter told itself, surprising me with a story I did not know and that led unexpectedly into the heart of another, revealing new aspects of the characters and their worlds. The excitement and awe of discovery were a gift that unfurled as I wrote.

The earliest incarnation of what became *Memory's Fire* appeared more than ten years ago, during a semester's leave from Santa Fe Preparatory School. In the midst of a horrific fire summer, resulting from a severe drought and heatwave, the concept for the first part of the novel emerged, and much of Chapter 4 was written.

After I retired from Santa Fe Preparatory School, the fire within was unleashed: I wrote daily, on no particular schedule, burning through chapters of this novel with unquenchable ardor. While much of that first draft has been revised many times over in the ensuing years, its surging energy remains the force infusing the story of the novel.

The Fisher family owned a cat named Tiger for fifteen years. He would not have minded lending his name to the cat in *Memory's Fire*, who is in nearly every other respect a fictional creation. The only trait they share is unencumbered audacity and hence, bone-crushing peril in the jaws of a coyote.

Teaching is a way of living for me. I have walked its labyrinthine, arduous, startling, euphoric, perplexing, tormenting, compelling, enlightening, addictive path for most of my life. Teaching is my birthright: my paternal grandmother helmed a one-room schoolhouse and both of my parents taught at Colorado College. As a child I was taught to revere teaching as a noble art. At eight, I gave neighborhood kids horse-drawing lessons, and I expected them all to adhere to my school of equine portrayal. At ten, I recruited them to act in plays I'd written, teaching them how to take direction and emote. As an adult, I taught English literature in a remote village in the northern New Mexico mountains; I began those courses without books or a curriculum, inventing each class session as we went along.

As a teacher at Santa Fe Prep, mine was a tale of the discovery of gifts my students possessed that were formerly unrealized, of possibilities that lay unsuspected within them, of passions that were suddenly aroused by literature, writing, and discussion. I loved most of all that stunning, luminous moment when I saw a student suddenly galvanized, transformed into a thinker. What before was difficult and tedious became a welcome opportunity for self-expression. As profoundly stirring as such a metamorphosis was to me, my greatest excitement arose from trying to imagine how it must feel from the students' end, at their age and in those rooms on the Prep campus. I remember well the sense I had of finally awakening during an English class when I was in college—and it is absolutely grounded in the image of a place and time. Being, in turn, an alert witness to the miracle in my students, recognizing, lauding, and nourishing it, was glorious.

That moment is only the first of many more it initiates throughout our intellectual lives.

Memory's Fire owes its heart to my years in the classroom. Alex's destiny guided my intentions from the start, though what the final outcome would look like and how he would reach his destination were a mystery that unraveled as I wrote. Alex is not, however, a replica of any given student I have known. Like sedimentary rock, he is built of layers of students I taught, as all the other characters contain schists of everyone, including myself and you, my family. We're all in here, and more as well, but not as the people we are or seem to be.

My family, to whom this novel is dedicated, includes both my immediate one and the wider ring of friends. I am grateful to have been able to open these pages to several of them in manuscript form and to get invaluable assistance from their responses.

My first reader of the initial draft and final version of *Memory's Fire* was my husband Rick—a teacher himself and a brilliant artist. He is a close and supportive reader who caught many errors and incongruities in the text. My daughter Kristina always offers me encouragement and inspiration. She and her husband Phil are dedicated felinists. My sister Sherry Martin (also a teacher), who read a final draft, provided thoughtful suggestions for changes, along with a warm commendation.

My son Eliot has been far more than a reader: rather, a partner in launching *Memory's Fire* into the public arena. The plan for its release was his: weekly serialization of the story on its website, which he designed. He also designed the print and electronic editions. Further, he created the audio version, narrating and editing it and disseminating it as a podcast for ease of access, and later as a full audiobook. The main character, Alex Mann, whose story is the central one, would be honored to hear his words on Eliot's tongue. To Eliot I owe an immensity of gratitude and praise. His extraordinary work on my behalf is a gift my mother called "love made visible." I also thank his spouse Erica for lending Eliot to me periodically over the past months.

Another highly influential and wise reader of the first and final drafts was my dear friend and former colleague, Stephanie Schlanger. Her superb insights led me to revise the final third of the novel. Steph awakened me to critical flaws in its direction and pacing and outcome. It was such a tremendous help to me to have a perceptive, writerly friend whose guidance made the novel far stronger and more credible.

Loren Bienvenu, an exceptional student from years past who went on to become an Honors English major at Harvard and is himself a superb writer, read the manuscript with stunning care, noting phrases and passages that struck him, catching yet more errors, and identifying one key relationship that needed critical development to make sense. I treasure his inspiring notes, his insights, and his astute recognition of a problematic assumption I had made and then revised. It is a great joy to have Loren as a friend and now a neighbor.

Nancy Buechley, a very close and trusted friend who has journeyed with me through many decades, read an early version of the manuscript and pointed out a number of disjunctures in the story, as well as effective confluences of event and turns of phrase she found compelling. She read with a loving, critical eye that helped to focus mine and led to a number of revisions. I am very grateful for her astute suggestions and comments.

Jackson Buckley, a marvelous former student who co-taught with me for a semester at Santa Fe Prep, offered me an inspiriting and thorough response to the manuscript at a middle stage of its development. His deep reading of the story encouraged me see particular moments and ideas with fresh excitement, knowing how much they had touched him as true and meaningful. Jackson has been a great ally in my quest for a publishing route, strongly affirming the path I have chosen. He himself has recently published a book on reading literature through an enlightening process he has developed. Jackson remains a stalwart and cherished friend on this journey. He and I have exchanged handwritten letters for the past several years, a pleasurable communion in the age of email.

Gayle Kuldell, a splendid friend of many years, read an earlier version of the manuscript with care and enthusiasm, and she has been wonderfully supportive of the novel's progress toward publication.

Jacqueline Laing, a wonderful friend of several decades, read the final version, parceling out chapters to herself, she told me, as a reward for the intense work she was doing—and offering words of praise to me from her keen eye and generous heart.

George Davis, former colleague and enduring friend, who is himself a writer, responded warmly to a nigh-final version of the manuscript, calling it "fascinating and beautiful and timely." I very much appreciate and value his endorsement.

9 780099 653833 6